THE GRILLING SEASON

The Grilling Season

Diane Mott Davidson

BANTAM BOOKS

New York Toronto London Sydney Auckland

THE GRILLING SEASON

A Bantam Book/October 1997

Interior illustrations by Aher/Donnell.
Book design by Ellen Cipriano.

Library of Congress Cataloging-in-Publication Data

Davidson, Diane Mott.
    The grilling season / Diane Mott Davidson.
        p.   cm.
    ISBN 0-553-10000-9
    1. Bear, Goldy (Fictitious character)—Fiction.
2. Caterers and catering—Fiction.   3. Colorado—
Fiction.   I. Title.
PS3554.A925G7   1997
813'.54—dc21   97-20037
                                                   CIP

Published simultaneously in the United States and Canada

Bantam Books are published by Bantam Books, a division of
Bantam Doubleday Dell Publishing Group, Inc. Its trade-
mark, consisting of the words "Bantam Books" and the por-
trayal of a rooster, is Registered in U.S. Patent and
Trademark Office and in other countries. Marca Registrada.
Bantam Books, 1540 Broadway, New York, New York 10036.

PRINTED IN THE UNITED STATES OF AMERICA

BVG 10 9 8 7 6 5 4 3 2 1

To Sergeant Richard Millsapps
Investigator, teacher, friend

The author wishes to acknowledge the assistance of the following people: Jim, Jeff, J.Z., and Joe Davidson; Kate Burke Miciak, a superb, brilliant editor; Sandra Dijkstra, a wonderfully encouraging agent; Susan Corcoran, an unflagging publicist; Lee Karr and the group that assembles at her home; Connie Leonard, an extraordinary pastry chef, and John William Schenk, an inspired and inspiring chef and caterer; J. William's Café, Bergen Park, Colorado; Katherine Goodwin Saideman, for multiple careful readings of the manuscript; Mark D. Wittry, M.D., Assistant Professor of Internal Medicine, St. Louis University Health Sciences Center; Richard L. Staller, D.O., Elk Ridge Family Physicians; Meg Kendal and Alan Rapaport, M.D., Denver-Evergreen Ob-Gyn; Dana Held, Cigna Healthcare of Colorado; Mary Frazee, an unparalleled herbalist of Health-Wealth, Pine, Colorado; the Reverend Constance Delzell; Julie Wallin Kaewert; Dorsey Moore; Carol Devine Rusley; Triena Harper, assistant deputy coroner, Jefferson County; Thorenia West; Sergeant Jerry Warren, and as ever, for patience and insights, Sergeant Richard Millsapps of the Jefferson County Sheriff's Department, Golden, Colorado.

Revenge is a dish best eaten cold.

—PROVERB

THE GRILLING SEASON

STANLEY CUP
VICTORY CELEBRATION

Saturday, August 2

Featuring

SOUTH OF THE BORDER APPETIZERS

Layered Dip of guacamole, refried bean purée,
sour cream, cubed fresh tomatoes, and Cheddar cheese
Tortilla Chips
Crudités: cauliflower, carrot, celery,
cucumber, cherry tomatoes
Mexican Eggrolls

◆

ENTRÉE

Goalies' Grilled Tuna
Grilled Slapshot Salad
Mediterranean Orzo Salad
Vietnamese Slaw
Hockey Puck Biscuits, Potato Rolls

◆

DESSERT

Stanley Cupcakes surrounding Rink Cake
Mexican Beers, Chablis, Coffee

Chapter 1

Getting revenge can kill you. If you want real revenge, you have to be willing to pay. Life is not like the movies.

Unfortunately.

With these happy thoughts, I measured out fudge cake batter into cupcake liners and slid the pan into the oven. I set the timer and reminded myself for the thousandth time that I'd let go of the need for revenge. I wasn't a hot-blooded teenager. I was a thirty-three-year-old caterer with a business to run and work to do. Half-past six on a cool August morning? What *I* needed was *coffee*.

You never let go of the thirst for revenge.

Yeah, well. Maybe hearing other people's sad stories sparked thoughts of my own. Or in this case I'd heard one unhappy story, one story needing justice. But what could I do for a client in emotional pain? I'd agreed to cater her hockey party. A nurse had told my client Patricia McCracken that hosting this sports celebration would distract her from her problems. But whenever we discussed the menu, Patricia didn't want to talk about *vittles;* she wanted to talk about *vindication.* And I was as unenthusiastic about jumping into her revenge fantasy as I was about washing dishes after a banquet.

For five years, I'd run the only food-service business in the small mountain town of Aspen Meadow, Colorado. My son, Arch, was fourteen years old. Just over a year ago, I'd married for the second time. Add to this the fact that I'd already sought punishment for the scoundrel who'd recently wronged Patricia McCracken. I'd barely escaped with my life.

I retrieved unsalted butter and extrathick whipping cream from my walk-in refrigerator, then reached up to my cabinet shelves for aromatic Mexican vanilla and confectioner's sugar. *Stay busy*, I had advised Patricia. *It'll help. Make your guest list. Plan your decorations.* Some people despise slates of tasks and errands. But I revel in work. Work keeps my mind off weighty matters. Usually.

Take this morning, for example. After finishing the cupcakes I needed to check my other bookings, make sure our sick boarder was sleeping peacefully, then rush to pick up Arch from an overnight party. Before zipping back to my commercial-size kitchen in our small home, I was going to deliver Arch to the country-club residence of his can't-be-bothered father. My ex-husband, ob-gyn Dr. John Richard Korman, was the father—and scoundrel—in question. He was the man my client Patricia McCracken obsessively hated; he was the man I had escaped from. He was known to his other ex-wife and me as the Jerk. Small example of Jerk behavior: Dr. John Richard Korman would no more pick up his son from an overnight than he would beat some eggs for breakfast. And careful of that word *beat.*

I stared at the menu on my computer screen and struggled to refocus on the task at hand. After much hesitation, Patricia had finally decided that her party would be a two-month-late celebration of the Colorado Avalanche winning the Stanley Cup. But making the plans with her hadn't been easy. One week she didn't care about the menu; the next she obsessed about details, such as how long to grill fish. After many discussions, Patricia had finally ordered Mexican appetizers, grilled fish from Florida (the Avs had beaten the Florida Panthers in the Cup finals and I'd dubbed the entrée Goalies' Grilled Tuna), three kinds of salads, puck-shaped biscuits, and homemade potato rolls. Plus a dessert Patricia's husband had christened Stanley Cupcakes. I sighed. After dropping off Arch this morning, I still faced a truckload of food prep. Not only that, but this evening's event promised to be raucous, perhaps even dangerous. I mean, hockey fans? Now *there* are folks who take revenge *seriously*.

I turned away from the computer. Our security system was off, so I opened the kitchen window and took a deep breath of summery mountain air. The postdawn Colorado sky glowed as it lightened from indigo to periwinkle. From the back of my brain came the echo of Patricia's furious voice.

"I'm telling you, Goldy. I need to see someone *punished*."

I slapped open the other window and tried to block out the memory of her anger by inhaling more crisp air skimming down from the snow-dusted mountains. August in the high country brings warm, breezy days and nights cool enough for a log fire. Heaven.

Unless you have to deal with John Richard Korman, my own inner voice reminded me. *Then it can be hell.*

Perhaps I should have told Patricia, an old friend who until now had loved cooking, to prepare herself for a descent into the underworld. I took a bag of coffee beans from the freezer, then sliced a thick piece of homemade oatmeal bread and dropped it into the toaster. The interior wires glowed red; the delicious scent of hot toast filled the kitchen.

Poor Patricia. After years of infertility and after adopting a son just before her first marriage had gone sour, she had remarried, endured a year of fertility drugs, and become pregnant. But she lost the baby. Unexpectedly, horribly, and *avoidably*, according to her. John Richard was her obstetrician. And she blamed him for the baby's death.

Now she wanted my help. I had been married to Dr. John

Richard Korman, she reminded me; I'd suffered through an acrimonious divorce. How could she deal with her rage against him? she wanted to know. How could she get through this?

I'd told her I'd cooked with much imagination when I was furious with the Jerk. But no matter what I'd said two weeks ago while booking the event, it hadn't been enough. Patricia, short and pear-shaped, with bitten-down nails and eyeliner applied with a shaky hand, had fumed like a pressure cooker. She'd shaken her mahogany-with-platinum hair and complained that I wasn't helping. She wanted revenge on the Jerk, and she wanted it *now*.

I took a bite of the crunchy toast and looked out my window at a dozen elk plodding through our neighbors' property. We live just off Main Street in Aspen Meadow, but the elk pay no attention to houses, fences, or any other sort of human presence, as long as the humans don't carry guns. In July and August the herds move down from the highest elevations in anticipation of hunting season, when hunters march into the hills in search of the huge dusty-brown creatures. When darkness engulfs the mountains, the elk's bugling, along with their hooves cracking through underbrush, are the only heralds of their arrival. Other times, you don't know the elk have been through until every last one of the leaves on your Montmorency cherry trees has been stripped. Deep, telltale hoof-prints in nearby mud usually betray the culprits.

A dog barked at the elk and the herd trundled off, leaping over a three-foot-high fence as if it were nothing. I glanced back at my computer screen, but again couldn't rid myself of the image of Patricia McCracken tapping the fleshy nub of her index finger on her bone-white Corian counter.

"Everyone hates him, Goldy," she'd declared. "John Richard Korman *and* that damn HMO that you have to belong to if you want him for your doctor. I can't believe we signed up. I can't believe I ever wanted John Richard as my doctor. But I'm telling you. He's going down."

And so then I'd heard the whole story. Patricia had been diagnosed with placenta previa, a precarious condition that jeopardizes the stability of the unborn child. Total bed rest is usually recommended; Patricia had begged John Richard to prescribe a hospital stay. She'd been denied it.

Seven months into the pregnancy, Patricia had hemorrhaged and the baby was asphyxiated. Devastated, she'd sued John Richard for malpractice and AstuteCare, her HMO—otherwise known as ACHMO—for negligence. She said her lawyers were certain she would win. But Patricia, understandably, was depressed. She wanted more, and she didn't like the idea of waiting for vindication. She wanted . . . . Well, what? Money? To drive John Richard out of his practice? To force him into a public confession?

"Will he admit he made a mistake?" she'd demanded of me two weeks ago. "Will he apologize? Will he confess he ruined my life?"

Next question. Naturally, I'd felt too sick to tell her the truth.

I spread a thick layer of tart chokecherry jelly on what remained of the toast. As the menu was set, the contract signed, and the first installment check written, I'd tried to warn Patricia gently. John Richard Korman was the most powerful, best-known ob-gyn doctor in town. The Jerk would not go down lightly. He *never* acknowledged making a mistake. And he'd certainly die before doing so publicly. But Patricia, whose fine-boned facial features and small, quivering nose above her plump body always put me in mind of a rabbit, had stiffened. She was having none of it. She had filed her suits. And she was out for blood.

I brushed crumbs off my hands. I hadn't wanted to argue with her. I'd told her to sue away, we needed to talk about setting up her party. Sheesh. A headache loomed. I really needed coffee.

I greedily inhaled the luscious scent of Italian-roast beans as they spilled between my fingers into the grinder. Tap water gushed into the well of my espresso machine. I had thought I wouldn't talk to Patricia again until tonight, but she had called yesterday. The woman was so obsessed that she'd been frantic to share news. She'd informed me that John Richard wouldn't be engaging in a prolonged legal battle with her. It seemed the Jerk was having severe financial problems.

Now I must confess, *that* news made my ears perk up. Being desperate for justice is a psychologically dangerous place to be. You hope that some lie, some transgression, some publicly witnessed crime will trip up your personal enemy. Nothing happens. Meanwhile, the desire for revenge can eat you up, give you insomnia, and—horrors—take away your appetite. You have to let go or die. So you need at least to *say* you're starting over and getting on with your life. All of this I had done. But now: Was this really happening? Could I watch the sun rise, sip some espresso, and rejoice in my ex-husband finally facing the music?

The coffee grinder pulverized the beans with a satisfying growl. I didn't want to be premature. I couldn't imagine that there would finally be punishment for the man who had broken my left thumb in three places with a hammer. I reached for the coffee doser and touched my hand. The thumb still wouldn't bend properly even now, seven years after the orthopedic surgeon who'd set it insisted I'd be throwing pizza dough in no time.

"He's got to pay," Patricia had insisted shrilly when she'd called yesterday. "I don't understand why you could never get him to pay, Goldy."

It hadn't worked like that. I tamped the grounds into the doser and remembered how stupefied I'd been when John Richard had gone unscathed. This in spite of the fact that he'd repeatedly beaten me. Time after time I'd had to escape from the house clutching Arch tightly, trying to get to a safe house. But after he'd smashed up my body and our marriage, John Richard had gone on with his life, his practice, his girlfriends, and his lifestyle. He'd remarried, divorced again, and taken up right where he'd left off. Until now, it seemed as if the man had been able to get away with anything. The odds looked good that he'd survive Patricia's legal threats, too.

I ran scalding water into a Limoges demitasse to heat it, then fitted the doser into place. I dumped the water out of the warmed cup, delicately placed it under the doser, and pressed the button. In the face of unrelenting curiosity from the town about the progress of her lawsuits, Patricia had spent most of the last two months at her condo in Keystone, a ski resort just over an hour away from Aspen Meadow. After booking the hockey party, she'd gone back to Keystone for two final weeks of peace, punctuated only by calls to me about her party. She'd discovered what I knew well: that it was nearly impossible to avoid the nosiness and gossip of Aspen Meadow.

Steaming twin strands of espresso spurted into my cup and I frowned. When John Richard and I were married and stories had come to *me*, of his flings with patients, nurses, and anyone else who fell under his gorgeous-guy spell, I'd confronted him, cried, yelled, threatened. And I'd paid for my protests with the usual pattern of black-and-blue marks: bruises on my upper arms from being grabbed and shaken, a black right eye. Sometimes worse.

"You must have tried to do something," Patricia had protested. "Why couldn't you do anything?"

I pushed the doser to stop the flow of coffee. Excuse me, Patricia, but I *had* done something. I'd stopped listening to the gossip. I'd planned a divorce as I taught myself to make golden-brown loaves of brioche, delicate poached Dover sole, creamy dark chocolate truffles. I'd fantasized about opening a restaurant or becoming a caterer. I'd dutifully kept close to a hundred of my newly developed recipes on our family computer. In one of the Jerk's last acts before I kicked him out, he'd reformatted the computer's hard drive. I'd lost every recipe.

I sipped the rich, dark espresso, blinked with caffeine-induced delight, and scowled at the next cupcake pan. Maybe Patricia couldn't understand why I hadn't done *more*. Let's see: I'd sought help from the church. Our priest hadn't wanted to hear about John Richard beating me up. Donations from the rich doctor might fall off. And then I'd tried to file criminal charges. But when divorce proceedings began, John Richard's high-powered lawyer had assured me that pressing criminal charges against his client would threaten his ability to pay child support. Worse—it might even bring on a custody battle.

Faced with such consequences and the fear of losing Arch, I'd given up seeking punishment for John Richard Korman. But the law had changed, and now a bruise-covered spouse didn't have to press charges. Back then, however, the legal system had failed me. Still, at age twenty-seven, I'd been glad enough to get out of the marriage with my life and my child.

"I can't believe you couldn't convince people how bad he was," Patricia had contended. "I mean, between you and Marla? Come on."

During the eight years of our marriage, and even in the six years since the divorce, the Jerk's behavior was unknown to many, dismissed or disbelieved by others. And yes, he'd dished out disdain and disloyalty to his second ex-wife, Marla Korman, who'd since become my best friend. I grinned, thinking of good old Marla. She'd kill the Jerk if she had the chance, but she'd had a heart attack last year and was trying to be careful.

I should have told Patricia I *had* tried to have the Jerk penalized in some way, any way. But I'd been determined *not* to go crazy. Patricia, though, was on the edge. A very dangerous edge. I set down my coffee and stirred another bowl of cake batter. The scent of chocolate cake perfumed the kitchen. Her malpractice suit would put him out of business, Patricia insisted. She apologized that this could mean a loss of child support for Arch. I told her not to worry about us. I'd manage, I always had. Patricia claimed that no matter what, she was going to make John Richard pay, and she was going to bring down ACHMO at the same time. *Good for you*, I thought now, with an involuntary shiver.

I began to scoop silky dollops of cake batter into the next pan. I put down the spatula, sipped more coffee, and smiled. There was another reason why I'd given up the need for revenge. Just over a year ago, happiness had come into my life like an unexpected houseguest determined to stay. I'd married a homicide investigator who worked for the sheriff's department. Tom Schulz's bearlike, handsome presence, his kindness and intelligence, his affection for Arch and me, still felt like a miracle. I glanced up at one of his recent presents to me: a blond doll dressed the way you might imagine a Tyrolean caterer would be, with a snowy lace apron over a royal blue vest and skirt. Actually, the doll's official name was Icelandic Babsie, and Tom had bought it for me to celebrate an upcoming booking to cater a doll show. He'd told me I could sell the doll in a year and retire on the profits. In addition to his other virtues, the man has a sense of humor.

Tom was like a slice of capital-*G* Grace, a concept I sometimes discussed with my Sunday school class. Plus, being married to a cop finally made me feel safe. And through all this—divorce, building a business, raising a child, remarrying—I'd held my own. I'd kept my friendships, made new ones, even stayed the course in our local church, where we now had a new priest and I still took my turn teaching Sunday school and making muffins for the after-service coffee. Which brought us to the present moment.

Rejoicing in the suffering of others is a sin. Well, then. Call me a big-time sinner.

The timer beeped and I remembered the hockey fans. I checked the cupcakes—not quite done—reset the timer, and again studied the menu for the party. I took a deep breath and ordered myself to let go of all the negative thoughts that Patricia's vengeful tale had provoked.

"He's going to run out of money," Patricia's voice echoed.

I still did not know how, in addition to the legal mess, the Jerk had gotten himself into a deep financial pickle. I'd promised Patricia I'd listen to the details of *that* news when I catered her party.

I grimaced at the list of dishes to be prepared and tried to picture the setup at the McCrackens' Aspen Meadow Country Club home. The McCrackens were adding *playing* hockey to *celebrating* hockey. So I would start with beer and a vegetable-and-chip tray with layered Mexican dip served at the end of the driveway during the in-line skating, provide more drinks and Mexican eggrolls upstairs in the living room, do the grilling and barbecue buffet on the large deck, then finish in the living room with cupcakes and coffee. Actually, the McCrackens did not live too far from the Jerk's year-old million-dollar house. The million-dollar house he might have to sell. *Oh, too bad.*

Think about hockey, I scolded myself. Fix the frosting for the Stanley Cupcakes. I'd told Patricia the NHL wouldn't approve of her husband's name for the dessert. She'd retorted that she didn't care. I fitted the electric mixer with a flat beater and recalled how breathless Patricia had been with her news yesterday about John Richard's impending financial demise.

"We were *right there* when they auctioned off his Keystone condo," she'd squealed. "It went for sixty thousand below market. This must be the juiciest revenge you've *ever* envisioned," she'd added with glee.

Not quite. John Richard still had the Aspen Meadow house, a condo in Hawaii, white and silver Jeeps with personalized license plates—the white one said OB and the silver said GYN, just in case anyone wondered what kind of doctor he was—and a wealthy, beautiful, smart, new girlfriend whom I grudgingly admired.

The beater began its slow circuit through the pale, unsalted butter. John Richard's girlfriend, Suz Craig, was the executive vice-president of the AstuteCare Health Maintenance Organization. I didn't know if Suz's feelings for John Richard were being affected by Patricia's suit against ACHMO. I *did* know that as of four weeks ago, John Richard and Suz were nuts about each other. To celebrate going together for six whole months, he had given her a full-length mink coat, bought on sale at the beginning of the summer, Arch had informed me. Suz had even modeled the coat when I'd catered a corporate lunch at her home in July. And why shouldn't I have catered for her? Suz had unabashedly informed me that she was a great businesswoman. Well, so was I.

Suz was young, thin, blond, a whiz at her job—by her own accounting—and eager, I thought, to show me that she wasn't going to make the same relationship mistakes that I had. What that meant, I didn't know, and didn't want to ask. Suz had confided that she'd given John Richard a solid gold ID bracelet as a way of showing her six-month-old affection. I'd tried not to roll my eyes. The only stage of relationship John Richard did well was infatuation. But if John Richard and his girlfriend wanted to act like high school sweethearts, I wasn't going to stop them. His relationships never lasted very long.

No, Patricia McCracken hadn't been quite on the money when she'd said John Richard's financial crash was the juiciest revenge I'd ever envisioned. John Richard had not yet lost the malpractice suit. His girlfriend hadn't renounced him. He wasn't in jail; he hadn't even been publicly humiliated. A declaration of personal bankruptcy, which was what I was assuming was about to happen, was not the kind of revenge I'd always hoped for.

But it was close.

Chapter 2

When I opened the oven to take out the cupcakes, the scent of chocolate drenched the kitchen. I drank it in and immediately felt better. Thinking dark thoughts was unappealing; thinking dark *chocolate* thoughts was vastly better. That was the conclusion I'd come to yesterday as I whipped up a batch of fudge. Stirring the sinfully rich pot of candy, I'd decided I really *didn't* want to get a blow-by-blow description from Patricia of John Richard's condo being auctioned off, after all. Listening to sizzling gossip while grilling tuna during the party tonight could lead to frayed nerves, scorched fish, or worse.

Nor could I quite picture hearing about the woes of John Richard Korman while catering to a large group of hockey aficionados. The fans would be hollering with blood-mania at slow-motion videos of battered hockey players slamming other bruised and injured players into the glass—while I celebrated a vengeance I'd tried to put behind me years ago? Something about that didn't quite work.

I straightened and rotated my shoulders. My right shoulder was scarred from the time John Richard had shoved me into a dishwasher and I'd landed on a knife. I'd fallen on my left shoulder when he pushed me down the stairs in a drunken rage. Both shoulders seized up with pain from time to time. Yesterday, when I was making the fudge, the ache in my upper back had been unbearable. Of course I'd suspected it was because my body didn't want to be reminded of John Richard. *Let go of it,* I'd admonished myself. I'd called Patricia in Keystone and said I didn't want to hear any more about the Jerk.

"You don't want to hear before our hockey game about your ex-husband's ruin? Don't you want to hear what he said to my lawyer about the money the suit is costing him?" Patricia had shrieked. When I'd said no, she seemed stunned by my lack of interest. "You're crazy. This whole thing is a *huge* comedown for him." Then she said—I swear she said this—"You must be out of your pucking mind."

Maybe so. But my shoulders felt better today. I swirled thick whipping cream into a mountain of snowy confectioner's sugar for the cupcake frosting. Yes, I could wait to hear the news. *Now* I could wait, that is. Tom Schulz, even if he was my husband, had always felt that justice would eventually triumph. I guess that's why he's in the business he is.

It is going to happen, Tom had frequently assured me. *John Richard Korman will go too far, get caught, and be nailed.* In fact, I had been vaguely aware that John Richard was having financial problems. After all, I hadn't received a child support payment in three months. He was usually late, but not this late. Despite Patricia's dire news about the Keystone condo, I'd actually been hoping that John Richard could talk to me this morning about his money situation, without lawyers, without lying, and without loudness. Fat chance.

But, as they say, I was going to be in that neck of the woods, so I might as well try to chat with him. With Arch as a buffer, and before John Richard had had a drink or two, we could occasionally communicate. Besides, if I thought we could get something settled, it would make the chauffeuring job this morning less irksome. The

house where Arch was staying was only two miles from John Richard's neo-Tudor monstrosity, while it was close to ten miles from our
place.

I was doing the pickup because Arch had been desperate to
attend the party. The poor kid had not made many friends at the
private school he'd started attending two years ago. Now that he was
going into ninth grade, he relished the idea of someone inviting him
over, even if it was because he was one of the few kids not currently
away on an exotic summer vacation. *An invite is an invite,* Arch had
reminded me seriously as he nudged his tortoiseshell glasses up his
nose and donned a too-large pair of denim shorts to go with a rag-
gedy nut-brown shirt that matched his hair. *And I'm going.*

I slid the bowl of frosting into the walk-in, set the cupcakes on
racks to cool, and scribbled a note to Tom to have one for breakfast if
he craved an early-morning chocolate fix. I would be back soon, I
wrote. Tom had been out past midnight working on a case. In the
hours before dawn he had crept in and tried not to wake me. But
whenever he pulled the Velcro straps off his bulletproof vest, I woke
in a sudden sweat. For over a year, he'd been telling me I'd get used
to it. I never had.

I tiptoed upstairs to check on our boarder. Recovering from
mononucleosis, nineteen-year-old Macguire Perkins was spending
the summer with us until his father came home from teaching a
course in Vermont. A tousle of red hair, a patch of pale skin, and loud
snores indicated that Macguire was sleeping, as usual. Arch's bloodhound, Jake, dozed at Macguire's side, while our cat, an adopted
stray named Scout, kept a watchful emerald eye from his perch on
the dresser.

I finished getting ready and quietly crept out our front door.
Another fresh morning breeze whispered through the aspens. After a
nastily wet spring, we were enjoying what the locals call a one-in-ten
year for wildflowers. This was probably going to be a one-in-ten year
for the elk population, too, but I didn't mind. I revved up Tom's
dark blue Chrysler sedan that he'd left in the driveway behind my

van. Backing out, I tried to avoid blue flax, blush-pink wild roses, and brilliant white daisies, all nodding in the warm wind.

Actually, one of the reasons I'd come to admire John Richard's current girlfriend, Suz Craig, was that she had learned the names of nearly a hundred different kinds of flowers that were being put in as part of an elaborate landscaping project at her country-club home. While I was setting up for the business lunch in July, Suz had taken the time to point out the varieties of campanula and columbines that her landscapers were planting between the quartz boulders and striped chunks of riprap rock. Even businesswomen who were vice-presidents needed a hobby, I supposed. The lunch had been a going-away gig for some AstuteCare people visiting from out of town. As ACHMO's regional veep, it was Suz's job to provide their "day in the mountains," a de rigueur excursion for visiting out-of-staters. The buffet as well as the day had been Colorado picture-postcard perfect: sapphire-blue sky, sweet mountain air redolent of pine, platters of chilled steamed Rocky Mountain trout, and luscious chocolate truffles.

The only mishap of the catered lunch had occurred when Chris Corey, the overweight head of ACHMO's Provider Relations, had taken a spill down an incomplete set of stone steps. Chris had sprained his ankle and Suz had vowed to fire the landscapers. One of the guests had taken a bite of trout, winked at me, and commented that *firing people* was what Suz did best. I'd made a mental note. Maybe she'd dump the Jerk before too long. I wondered how he would react.

The sedan's engine purred as I passed Aspen Meadow Lake, where the early-morning sun and whiff of breeze had whipped the placid water into jagged sparkles. At the Lakeview Shopping Center across the road from the lake, a tattered banner, ruffling slightly, announced that Aspen Meadow Health Foods was under new management. Beneath the banner a beautifully painted sign advertised the upcoming doll show at the LakeCenter. BABSIE BASH! the curlicued script screamed. GO BERSERK!

I pressed the accelerator and hummed along with the engine. When I thought about Babsie dolls these days, I didn't think *berserk*, I thought *bread and butter*. Starting Tuesday, I'd be catering to the doll folks for two days. The bash organizers had warned me that they didn't want any food to get on the display tables, the Babsie costume boxes, the eensy-weensy furniture, the tiny high heels, the fanciful costumes, or, God forbid, the dolls. I'd assured them I could do all their meals, including a final barbecue, outside—complete with finger bowls, if they wanted. They'd said I should find a Chef Babsie outfit to wear. I'd been afraid to ask them if they were kidding.

Once I'd rounded the lake, the sedan started uphill toward the country-club area. Actually, Suz Craig had always reminded me of Babsie. Beyond her looks, though, I had to admit that Suz had a phenomenal mind and a charismatic personality to go with her statuesque, size-six body. I never had been able to understand how the Jerk could attract women like her.

I glanced in the rearview mirror at my slightly chubby face, brown eyes, and Shirley Temple–blond-brown curls. "He got you, didn't he?" I said to my puzzled reflection, then laughed.

The stone entryway into the country-club area had been graffiti-sprayed by vandals. The vandals' defacement of property was one of this summer's ongoing problems in our little town. Still, I knew my way to Arch's friend's house without having to decipher the spray-painted street signs. The developer for the old part of the club had been an indiscriminate Anglophile. He'd given the streets names like Beowulf, Chaucer, Elizabethan, Cromwell, Tudor, and Brinsley. As long as you knew a bit about English history, you were in good shape. I approached the turn to Jacobean Drive, where Suz Craig lived, and hesitated. I pulled over and the sedan tires crunched on the gravel. Despite my best intentions, I was suffering a typical Jerk-inspired dilemma. Would he be home yet?

Tom's cellular was close at hand. I could call John Richard first to make sure he was awake and ready for Arch's arrival. On the other hand, I didn't want to wake him up and risk one of his infamous tantrums. If I drove past Suz's and saw one of his cars in the drive-way, I would know to stall on picking up Arch. But stall how? I tapped the dashboard in frustration.

Okay—I remembered that the woebegone landscapers had been planning three patios, along with a series of steps, on Suz's sloping property. The vandalism had been so bad in the country club that Suz had confessed to being afraid to have the flagstones deliv-ered and left outside, where they ran the risk of being spray-painted with cuss words. So Suz's garage was full of flagstones, and if John Richard had spent the night with his girlfriend, one of his Jeeps would be sitting in her driveway. This, in spite of the fact that his house was close by. But John Richard never walked for exercise; he played tennis.

I revved the engine, turned up Jacobean, and immediately knew something was wrong. I rolled down the window and tried to figure out what didn't fit. The rhythmic, slushy beat of automated sprinklers buzzed across manicured green lawns. On both sides of the road bunches of trim aspens, conical blue spruces, and butter-cup-flowered potentilla bushes were all picture-perfect. Picture-per-fect except for one thing. In the ditch running beside Suz's driveway, one of the landscape people had inconsiderately dumped one of the quartz boulders.

One of the quartz boulders? No.

I slowed the sedan, carefully set the parking brake, and got out of the car. Then, feeling faintly dizzy, I walked toward the ditch. Suz's cheerily painted mailbox had been knocked or driven over and lay in the middle of the street. The block letters of the name *Craig* gleamed in white paint on the shiny black metal. I looked back at the ditch.

It was not a quartz boulder that lay in the dirt.

It was Suz.

Oh God, I prayed, *no*.

I moved haltingly toward the ditch. Loosely clad in a terry-cloth bathrobe, the exposed parts of Suz's slender body were blue and white. Her shapely legs were improbably skewed, as if she were running a race. Her blond hair, normally tied back in a pert ponytail, was soaked with mud. It clung to her face like seaweed. Her bruised arms hugged her torso, while her blue lips were set in a silent scream. She did not appear to be breathing.

What to do? Call somebody? Tom? No, no, no, there might be hope, if an ambulance could get here quickly. Plus, some logical voice whispered, I needed to call for help as if I didn't have any idea as to what had happened. Which I didn't. *Which I did.*

Get into the car. Dial 911. A whirring noise in my ears made thinking difficult as I ran to the sedan. Too late, too late. Emergency Medical Services wouldn't be able to do anything. I knew it even as my shaking fingers punched 911 and Send on the cell phone. The connection was not immediate, as frequently happens in the mountains. One second, two endless, endless seconds. There was no movement from the ditch. Very faintly, from a distant part of my brain, I could hear Tom's voice.

He will go too far. Get caught. Be nailed.

C h a p t e r   3

I told the 911 operator who I was, where I was, and why I was calling. "She doesn't seem to be alive," I added. Did I know CPR? the operator wanted to know. No, no, I replied, sorry.

"Just stay where you are," the operator commanded.

For some reason I looked at my watch. Five to seven. I had to call Tom. Although I knew it would irritate the 911 operator, I disconnected and punched the digits for the personal line into our house.

"Schulz," Tom barked into the phone.

"Listen, something's happened . . ." This was a mistake. Even with the worst-case scenario, which I did not want to contemplate, I surely knew they would never assign this—what would he call it?—this *matter*, this *incident*, this *case*, to my husband.

"It seems . . . I didn't . . ."

"Goldy," Tom commanded, "tell me what's going on. Slowly."

"I . . . I was driving up Jacobean in the country-club area," I began, and then told him bluntly exactly what I was looking at through the windshield—a young woman. Looked like Suz Craig, John Richard's girlfriend. Lying half-dressed in a ditch. Not moving. Not breathing.

"Sit tight," he ordered. "If you see John Richard, or anyone, say nothing. If someone comes, get out of the car. Don't let anybody near that ditch. I'll be there before the ambulance. Fifteen minutes, maybe twenty. Goldy? I'll be there."

I closed the phone and felt relief. I scanned the quiet landscape and had a sudden memory of the time a live power line had snapped during a blizzard and landed on our street. Touching the wire meant sure electrocution. The most important job, the fire department had warned, was to keep people, especially children, away from the dark wire that had curved onto the street like a monstrous snake. And how similar was this situation? I couldn't think. I only knew I had to keep prying eyes and intrusive, questioning people away from what lay in that ditch.

And speaking of children, I had to call Arch. Of course I couldn't remember the number of the house where he was. People named Rodine. I called Information, got the number, and phoned. Gail Rodine didn't sound too happy, but I told her tersely that there would be a delay before I arrived.

"I'm leaving to start setting up the doll show at ten," Gail petulantly announced.

"I'll be there long before that," I said, and disconnected before she could whine any more.

I peered out through the windshield of Tom's car and wondered how long it would be before someone came along. Tom was right: *Sit tight*, he'd said. If someone saw me, a stranger, standing in the road looking out of place, that would excite curiosity. My heart quickened as the front door to one of the houses swung open. A chunky man in a dark bathrobe came out, bent to retrieve his newspaper without looking up the street, then waddled back through his columned entryway. I let out a breath of relief that I quickly gasped right back in as John Richard's white Jeep roared into view from the opposite side of Jacobean.

What should I do?

Don't let anybody near that ditch.

John Richard catapulted the Jeep up into Suz's driveway. Apparently he'd taken no notice of Tom's car or of me sitting in it. Springing from his own vehicle, John Richard turned and scanned the road. Did he hesitate and narrow his eyes when he saw the toppled mailbox, then my sedan? I couldn't be sure. The soil between the house and the ditch had been churned up and heaped into a small hillock by the landscapers. The body in the ditch could not be seen from the house. At least I hoped it couldn't. John Richard turned back to his Jeep, reached into the passenger-side seat, and pulled out a bunch of roses.

I'm going to be sick.

I knew without knowing what had happened. They'd fought.

You left, angry, thinking she was going to be just fine. You wanted her to recover; take aspirin; cry a little. You'd call later. But she stumbled out the door, looking for help. She fell into the ditch and died. And yet here you are with roses. You bought them at the grocery store this morning. The store is open all night and always helps you with your morning-after remorse. So here you are, figuring you can just patch everything up.

Not this time.

I forced my leaden hand to open the sedan door. Fear pulsed through every nerve. But I'd told Tom I would keep people away from the ditch, and I had to do that. Even if that meant undergoing this most dreaded of confrontations.

John Richard had already bounded up to Suz's door and was impatiently ringing the bell. He didn't take any notice of me until I was almost by his side. Then he turned and faced me, and I prayed for strength: mental, spiritual, and physical. Especially physical.

By any panel of judges, John Richard would be declared one of the handsomest men to walk the earth. His wide, dark blue eyes regarded me as his angular face instantly assumed its familiar what-the-hell-do-you-want expression. The bunch of roses wobbled in his large, strong hand.

"Why are *you* here?" he demanded. "What's your *problem?*" Of course, I couldn't find my voice. When I didn't respond immediately, he smirked. "Suz said you seemed real interested in her place. Smells a little bit like *obsession* to me."

Don't get into an argument.

"Well . . . I . . . uh," I faltered. I looked at him warily. Was he going to lose his temper? Turn all that rage on me? In front of this upscale neighborhood with its watching windows? "I . . . was actually driving by . . . looking for you. I . . . didn't want Arch to arrive at your place and have it be empty." My voice sounded absurdly high.

He surveyed the street for my van. "Really."

I held my breath. *Please let the body not be visible from the house.*

"Where is Arch?" asked John Richard, the man I had once loved. The man I now loathed beyond measure, the man I did my best to ignore, despite his constant bad behavior, which always demanded attention. "Where is your *van?* Look at me, dammit." His blue eyes drilled into mine. His icy, threatening tone was all too familiar. "Why won't you *tell* me why you're *here?* No Arch? No van? This certainly smacks of the ex-wife *spying* on the ex-husband's girlfriend."

"I just—"

At that moment the familiar wheeze of my van sounded its way up Jacobean. Tom parked behind his own sedan and within three seconds was striding across Suz's lawn from the acute angle of the neighbor's yard. Smart man. Any visual diversion from the ditch would buy time. With one of his large, pawlike hands, Tom motioned for me to move away from John Richard. I inched backward until my feet bumped the edge of the porch. Tom's green eyes never wavered from John Richard as he approached the porch where we stood.

"What the—?" John Richard was furious. "Is this some kind of family incident? You'd better tell me what's going on, Goldy," he commanded.

Take a wild guess. But I was going to say nothing to that arrogant voice.

Bordering the expansive front step was a fat clay pot brimming with vivid red geraniums and dusty-blue ageratum. I had backed up beside it and now stared down at the tall red flowers, unable to meet John Richard's enraged gaze. "I don't really know very much," I murmured.

"Hey there," said Tom, as if we were all meeting on the golf course.

John Richard wasn't fooled for a moment. "You want to tell me what the *hell* you're doing here at seven o'clock in the morning, cop? Or why Goldy just happened to be passing by?"

Tom's wide face stayed flat, passive, totally unreadable. He blinked and took a deep, measuring breath that pulled up his expansive chest. He regarded John Richard's handsome face and athletic frame.

Finally Tom said, "We seem to have a situation here."

"What?" cried John Richard, incredulous. *Or acting incredulous,* my skeptical inner voice immediately supplied. John Richard's face tightened with fury—and something else. "What kind of situation?" His voice was stone-hard, but there was a crack in that stone, something rarely heard when he spoke: *fear.* "What's the matter with you two?" He turned his wrath on me. "What, did Suz call you early this morning, Goldy? Trying to get a little girlie sympathy? Strength in numbers, right? Just like you and Marla, a whimpering duo going for the gold medal in pettiness." He swept his scathing glance over Tom and me. "So you just rushed right out early in the morning, then called your personal police squad to back you up, right? What did Suz tell you, that we mixed it up last night?"

"You mixed it up last night," Tom quietly repeated.

John Richard flung the roses down. The paper made a crinkly sound as the bouquet landed on the grass, and a bloodred petal shook free. "Well, let me tell you, both of you, this is none of your damn business, do you understand me? Suz has lots of problems you don't even know about. It really wasn't as bad as—"

He was silenced by the wail of a siren. The ambulance screamed from the club entryway. I knew from all Tom had told me that unless a victim's body has mold on it, the paramedics feel duty-bound to try to revive that victim. Still, as the ambulance shrieked to a halt, I wanted them to do their damnedest. I prayed they would be able to bring Suz back while knowing in my heart that it was no longer within the realm of possibility.

Tom strode off the porch in the direction of the ambulance. When the paramedics were out of their vehicle, Tom pointed. The medics vaulted toward the ditch.

"Jesus Christ," muttered John Richard as he shoved past me. Caught off balance by the power of his push, I fell backward onto the flowerpot. I tripped off the edge of the porch and landed facedown in the dirt. When I scraped the soil off my elbows, I thought I heard a forlorn meow. I looked around but only saw John Richard. He was a preppy vision in khaki pants and burgundy shirt as he swiftly approached the area where the emergency medical folks were establishing their territory. "Hey! I'm a doctor!" he called. "What's going on?"

The medics were already working and paid him no heed. From beside the ditch Tom issued instructions. When John Richard arrived at the side of the ditch and yelped at the sight there, Tom shook his head grimly.

I pulled myself up, brushed the dirt off my clothes, and walked down the driveway. Neighbors were clustering on their porches. Three men walked purposefully toward the activity, as if they'd been appointed by the homeowners' association to find out what was going on and therefore were above nosiness. Tom pointed to me, then swept his arm toward the approaching men. *Keep those guys away.* I picked up the pace.

"Okay, folks," I said to the men, "just stay back. Please . . . That man's my husband and this is a medical emergency."

One of them, a bald, pinch-faced fellow whom I recognized as a minor dignitary from the Bank of Aspen Meadow, narrowed his eyes at the ditch. "That's not your husband, that's your ex—"

"The ex and the current," I replied sharply. "The current's a cop and he has *asked* me to keep you all—"

"What happened?" rasped another man. He was short and pudgy and sported a goatee that matched his gray sweatsuit. "Aren't you . . . haven't I seen you . . . aren't you the town caterer?" He inhaled angrily. "I demand to know why that ambulance is here. Was there a break-in? I have children. Tell me what's going on." The third man, tan, white-mustached, wearing gardening clothes and a billed cap, nodded mutely.

"You'll find out soon enough," I said, just a decibel higher than necessary.

From the ditch John Richard squawked. I couldn't help it: I turned around. I couldn't see Suz, but I saw the medics working to hook her up to some equipment. I knew the drill: Check for vital signs. In those horrible few moments they'd already sought her pulse. They'd looked into her eyes to see if the irises were fixed and dilated. The only problem I was having was in accepting the next step. A dull thump reverberated through the air. *Dammit.* They were trying to get her heart to beat. Once more the thump echoed through the morning stillness.

Even though my view was partially blocked, I knew the next stage was for the paramedics to send telemetry down to a Denver hospital. An emergency-room doctor would make the declaration to stop trying to resuscitate.

John Richard shrieked: "What the hell is that thing doing there?" He torqued his head around and stared at Suz's house.

One of the paramedics was holding something. The medic held it out to Tom, affording me a sideways view of it. He held a piece of jewelry, a thick, heavy gold bracelet.

I stared, uncomprehending, at the bracelet, then felt my eyes being drawn to the naked spot on John Richard's left wrist. My worries about personal bankruptcy seemed a century old. The street felt as if it were moving under my feet. *Steady, girl.*

"I don't believe this!" John Richard yelled. "This is entrapment! This is a setup! Why won't you talk to me?"

The three bystanders I was trying to keep away from the ditch nudged urgently past me.

"Hey!" I yelped. "You can't go—"

But by the time I caught up with them, they stood beside the ditch. Damn them. Tom could not stop the men from gaping at the medics and poor, wretched Suz; he was talking into his mobile phone. And what was I now hearing? No. Yes. Tom was reciting the Miranda rights to John Richard Korman.

"Stop this," John Richard protested loudly as Tom's caution continued. "You have no idea what you're doing! Suz had . . . She . . . AstuteCare had more . . . enemies . . . than I have patients. She was into more—"

I could not believe my ears. This was so fast . . . too fast. What had John Richard said or done? He and Suz had "mixed it up." And the ID bracelet—where had the medics found it? Were John Richard's admission of a fight and a piece of his jewelry enough to warrant an arrest? Apparently so. But John Richard had brought flowers, he must have *thought* Suz was alive, or must have wanted to *believe* she was alive, or wanted to *appear* to believe she was alive.

Tom said quietly, "You're under arrest. I've just arranged for transport." He reached in his back pocket for his handcuffs. He must have brought them, I thought, stupefied. Tom must have brought the cuffs and his badge and his weapon, when I told him where I was and what I'd seen.

John Richard leaped forward and swung at Tom; the three

neighborhood ambassadors jumped back. John Richard's fist shot upward again. But Tom was ready for him. He grabbed John Richard's
right arm and swung it forcefully around. Cursing, John Richard fell
to his knees. Tom put his other hand into John Richard's back and
brought him easily to the ground. John Richard yelled, threatened,
cursed, and reminded Tom of what he would do to him the minute
he got free.

Tom leaned over and said, *"Shut. Up."*

Chapter 4

With practiced quickness, the paramedics transferred their energy from trying to revive Suz to pulling back. They authoritatively called out orders and pushed aside the bystanders. No matter: The group of people, which had now grown to five, had turned their attention from Suz and could not stop staring, fascinated, at John Richard. Handcuffed, he knelt in the street. Tom kept him there. Tom's muscular body leaned toward John Richard. My husband spoke into my ex-husband's ear. I could not make out what he was saying over the voices of the medics. But if the twisted look of fury on John Richard's face was any indication, it wasn't good news.

Tom turned and made an announcement to the mesmerized bystanders. "Okay, you five, here's the deal. Go stand in different driveways until we've stabilized this situation. Police officers will come talk to you when they arrive. Do *not* discuss this among yourselves." He paused to make sure they understood. Two nodded; the others just stared. "All right, thank you. Go ahead, please, move away. Now."

As the men promptly defied Tom's orders by departing in a whispering cluster, John Richard raised his angry voice, demanding to be let out of the handcuffs. The medics ignored him, as did Tom, who once again pulled the mobile unit off his belt and made a call. I heard him say the words "captain," "video," and "team."

Tom spoke again to John Richard, then helped him to his feet. The Jerk, cuffed, shook loose of Tom's arm, then stalked angrily to the base of Suz Craig's tar-streaked driveway. Tall and elegant even with his arms bound at an improbable angle behind him, Dr. John Richard Korman stood shifting his weight from one khaki-clad leg to the other. I thought absurdly that he looked as if he were considering poses for an art class. Above his gorgeous, chiseled face, which occasionally spasmed with rage, his blond hair was only slightly tousled from his exchange with Tom.

I turned away, disbelieving. Was this really happening? There was a buzzing in my ears. My eyes burned. I sat down on the curb and focused on Tom.

Tom knew what he was doing. He could switch into his take-charge mode without a hitch. He nimbly moved his beefy body around the periphery of the ditch. He gave a few more instructions to the paramedics, who plopped down listlessly on the dirt-strewn incline. He had probably told them to do nothing until the coroner arrived. Then, his face set in that intimidating expression I knew so well, Tom walked in the direction of the driveway and John Richard. I tried to remember a time when I had seen these significant men from my life standing next to each other. I failed. And this certainly wasn't the circumstance where I wanted to make the comparison of how the two appeared and how they acted. I looked away, up the street.

If I was right about what Tom had told the paramedics, the coroner would be arriving soon in his van. As my eyes skimmed the row of big, beautifully maintained houses, I wondered helplessly about Arch. I still had to go get him. I needed to stand up and put one foot in front of the other and tell Tom I was leaving. But exactly how would I say that? *I've got to go tell my son that his father has been arrested for murder?* I stayed put.

Tom, meanwhile, gently took a stiff John Richard by the elbow and guided him up the driveway toward the house. Reluctantly, I stood and followed. The buzzing in my ears was not from the sprinklers. *Get Arch, get out of the club, and get back home.* But who would take care of my son at home, comfort him and talk to him? I had a party tonight. Could Macguire help, even though he was bedridden with mono? Not likely. I would think of something. For now, I had to get away from here. The bystanders, perched like friendly watchdogs on this street full of posh houses and lush green lawns, watched my journey up the driveway with undisguised interest.

"I need to leave," I announced to Tom. I darted a sideways glance at John Richard. Tom had directed him to the far end of Suz's porch, where he perched stiffly on the edge of a white wicker couch. I flinched at the sight of his scathing stare and his silent, enraged face. I cleared my throat. "I need to get Arch."

"You do that!" John Richard exploded, but not, I noticed, loudly enough for the nosy neighbors to hear. I looked at him curiously. His outburst contained no sadness. No grief. "Go get Arch!" he yelled, his face shaking. "Tell him *why* we can't go hiking! And be sure to let him know what you and your buddy have cooked up here! Arch is bound to just love it!"

My temper snapped. "Listen!" I yelled back, "I was just driving up—"

"Save it!" John Richard hissed. The cords in his neck strained. "No more child support if I'm in jail! Think about it!"

"Look, you." I tried to stop the angry shaking of my voice but could not. "I haven't gotten any child support since—"

"Goldy." Tom's passionless tone mercifully stilled the exchange. He waited until he had my complete attention. "Don't get

Arch yet. You need to stay here, make a statement." His face was calm. "And you should see a victim advocate."

"Victim advocate?" John Richard bellowed. "What does she need an advocate for? *I'm* the damn victim here!"

I gaped at Tom, dumbfounded. Of course. I had discovered the body. The police had to question me. And the psychologists' recommendation for a person discovering a body was that that person was traumatized and needed comfort. But this wasn't the first murder victim I'd found. I'd managed before without an advocate. Still, what was the psychologists' recommendation if your *ex-husband* was charged with the murder you'd stumbled upon? I couldn't think. I swayed as I stood between the overturned geranium pot and the wicker furniture. What had I been doing just a moment ago? Oh, yes. I'd been having an argument with my ex-husband about money. Now I was having a conversation with my current husband about an advocate.

You must get Arch, my inner voice urged. *You must tell him what's happened before someone else does.* Trauma? You bet. Undreamed-of trauma. But like most women, I couldn't take time out from the other crises of my life to be taken care of. "I don't want an advocate," I told Tom. "I'm okay."

Even as I spoke Tom was pulling the phone off his belt. "What's Marla's number?"

"Oh, right!" John Richard raged. "Let's get old *Marla* over here. One big happy family. Hey! I have an idea! Ask that fat dumb broad how she planted my ID bracelet in that ditch."

Tom ignored him as I recited Marla's number. Should Marla really come, though? I didn't want this situation to aggravate her cardiac condition. She should not come here, I muttered. When Tom asked, I gave him the address of Arch's friend, Sam Rodine. It was near enough to Marla's house that she could meet me there. While Tom murmured into the phone, the coroner's black van pulled up beside the curb. A warm breeze swished through the aspens. The babble of voices on the street increased in volume.

"I don't believe this," muttered John Richard.

"No, Marla . . . Goldy's fine, just upset," Tom was saying. "But I need you to take care of her for a while. Meet her over at the Rodines' house and bring some iced coffee or something. Just be with her, okay?" While he was talking, his eyes never left the two men from the coroner's staff who were going about their grim work in the ditch. I noticed John Richard's eyes never strayed toward that spot.

"Look, Marla, Goldy will tell you what's going on when she meets you, okay? I need to go," Tom said in his conversation-ending voice. "She'll be tied up here for about fifteen minutes, so . . . Sure you can get dressed that fast. Yes, Goldy is with me now. No, we're not at home. Marla, please . . . Okay, look, Goldy and I are over on Jacobean, here in the country-club area."

Marla's squawk through the receiver was audible across the porch. Of course Marla didn't need to ask *where* on Jacobean we were. She was the one who had called me seven months ago and in a tremulous, indignant voice, announced the name, address, and all the vital statistics she'd gleaned on John Richard's latest conquest, Suz Craig.

"No, *don't* come over, we've got enough confusion as it is. Goldy won't be here too much longer. . . ." Tom sighed. "Yes," he said finally, "John Richard Korman is here, too. Marla, remember what I said. Goldy will be on her way to the Rodines' place in a quarter of an hour." Then he muttered, "See you later," and disconnected. Well, that was one way to get out of a conversation.

Tom leaped off the porch without explaining where he was going. He stopped to talk to someone from the coroner's van, then hustled back to us. He held up a hand to me: five minutes.

"Okay, Mr. Talkative," said Tom to John Richard. He sounded almost cheery as he snapped the phone back on his belt. "You've been wanting to talk and now you've got your chance. How about telling us exactly what happened here?"

"That's *Dr.* Talkative to you, schmuck." John Richard tossed his head, suddenly calm. His changes in mood, of course, were well known to me. "And I've been Mirandized. I'm not saying another word until I talk to my lawyer. *Just* the way you told me to." Then John Richard turned. His dark blue eyes spit fire at me even as his voice remained hideously even. "But as for you, I *know* you're behind this. One way or another, I'm going to find out how. And if you tell my son about this in any way that makes me look bad, I'll have you hauled into court so fast you'll think our breakup was a caterers' picnic."

Oh, sure, I thought. But I didn't want to hear his empty threats. I was leaving. Of course, I wanted to ask John Richard what kind of "mixing up" he and Suz had done the night before. *Mixing up.* What a euphemism. How about, "I beat up women when they don't do what I want?" In the near distance, sirens wailed. I shivered and wondered about the ID bracelet that Suz had so proudly given John Richard. And why would John Richard think Suz wanted to call *me* this morning? The sirens shrieked louder and a police car, lights flashing, burst into view. I knew better than to try to have any further conversation with John Richard.

The police car squealed to a stop behind the coroner's van. A uniformed policeman and a tall, dark blond plainclothes woman I didn't recognize came up to the porch and asked if I was Goldy Schulz, the person who'd found the dead woman. Was I ready to make my statement? they wanted to know.

Just then, there was one of those unexplained moments of utter silence. The breeze dropped. The coroner's staff in the ditch was still. The speculative buzz on the street ceased. Even the sprinklers stopped their metronomic splatting. Maybe the quiet was in my head. Maybe I was going to pass out.

"Mrs. Schulz?" inquired the tall female officer, who had said her name was Sergeant Beiner. She leaned in close. "Are you all right?"

"Yes," I whispered. "I need . . . need to go get my son."

"Very soon," she replied, as she straightened. Sergeant Beiner was fiftyish. Her six-foot height was somewhat mitigated by a hump-back, and her narrow face was actually topped with a rooster-style burst of blond and gray curls. "We're making an exception so you can go in just a few minutes. You *should* be coming down to the department," she added, with a wary glance at John Richard. Then her tone turned sympathetic. "But since you have to go pick up your child, Mrs. Schulz, we'll just ask a few questions now. We know where we can reach you if we need to talk to you some more later. Okay?"

I nodded. "Later," I said dully, "I'll be at home."

The sergeant gently led me off the porch, out of earshot of John Richard and Tom. She motioned for the uniformed policeman to stand by her side as she ticked off her questions: How did you get here? What exactly did you see? What did you do? Did you see anybody driving away? Did you see anybody in the area?

While she made notes, I told her everything: I arrived in Tom's sedan between six-thirty and seven, I saw a body in the ditch; I called 911 and Tom. No one drove away. No one showed up except Dr. John Richard Korman, clutching a bouquet. It was a painful recitation. Sergeant Beiner said she or one of the primary investigators would be by to see me later in the day. I walked unsteadily back to the porch.

"I'm leaving," I told Tom. He stepped off the porch and gave me a wordless hug. I murmured, "I'll be okay" into his chest. Then I pulled away.

Behind me, the grating noises of a stretcher being wheeled across the pavement disturbed the quiet of the neighborhood. Another meow directed my attention to the porch steps. A small calico ball of fur dashed out and clawed at the upended geraniums. It was Suz's cat, Tippy. I snagged the small feline and was rewarded with a scratch on the arm. Tippy, shivering and terrified, then scrambled up my arm. When I tried to coax her down, she dug her claws in and remained poised on my shoulder. Her little body trembled next to my head.

Two more police cars wheeled up Jacobean, red and blue lights flashing. I walked to my van with Tippy the cat perched resolutely on my shoulder. I knew the cat was part of the crime scene. But she would be ignored and abandoned if I didn't care for her. So I took her. Three more uniformed Furman County deputies crossed Suz Craig's lawn to Tom. Two more hauled equipment toward the ditch. No one noticed me.

The video team began to record the scene. I averted my eyes and opened the van door. The cat leaped into the back. I stared at the keys in my hand. My ring was just like Tom's: keys to the house, keys to the sedan, keys to the van. I tried hard to remember what it was I was supposed to do with these keys. *It could have been me.* After a moment of fumbling with the ignition, I started my van, and stepped hard on the accelerator. *It could so very easily have been me in that ditch, if I hadn't gotten out all those years ago.*

The dozen people gathered on porches stared with avid interest as my van chugged down the street. One man shook his head at my noisy progress. His red scalp blazed in the warming sun. Along the street, the velvety lawns glowed like chartreuse carpets.

Suz Craig took my place. But it could so very easily have been me.

Chapter 5

The cat howled the two miles to Hadley Court. I pulled up in front of a three-story, white-brick-and-blue-gingerbread-trimmed Victorian-style mansion that was about as far from a mountain contemporary as it was from Mars. Marla's Mercedes squealed around the corner as I eased to the curb. Behind her tinted windshield I could see she was talking excitedly on her car phone, which she quickly hung up when she spotted me. She threw open her door and came bustling toward the van.

Marla's raspberry-colored sequined sweatsuit did not flatter her portly figure. In one hand she held a covered glass and in the other a paper bag. My dear friend always brought something that she thought would make you feel better. Usually the only thing I needed was to see her, and as usual, the sight of her rushing toward me, her rhinestone-studded sunglasses jiggling up and down on her concerned face, brought a wave of relief.

Wealthy by inheritance, talkative by nature, and pretty in an unconventional way, Marla had endured being married to John Richard for six years less than I had. After John Richard's first few rampages, Marla had also shown much more confidence than I had when it came to ridding oneself of a burdensome spouse. She'd shoved an attacking John Richard into a hanging plant and dislocated his shoulder. She'd then managed to cut the marital knot with great expertise. She and I had become fast friends when her divorce was final, proving that even the worst marital experiences can hold some redemption. Last summer she'd survived a heart attack. Earlier *this* summer, she'd survived a disastrous breakup with the one guy she'd been serious about since divorcing the Jerk. We had a history, the two of us. And I loved her dearly.

"Okay, tell me," she began without preamble when I hopped out of the van to greet her, "are you okay? Probably not," she added with an opulent, scarlet-lipsticked frown.

I fought off an unexpected wave of dizziness. "I don't know. No. Probably not."

"Let's get back in your van, so people don't come out and start asking a bunch of questions. Jeez, this town—I've already had two calls on my cellular." Her brown eyes softened with sympathy and she proffered a plastic-wrapped crystal glass. For the first time, I noticed her hair was damp. "Look, Goldy, I brought you an iced latté. Well, actually half espresso and half cream dumped over ice. Very naughty, but oh so good." She held up the brown bag in her other hand. "And here we have a whole bunch of meds that I just dumped out of my medicine cabinet. They're mostly tranquilizers. Which do you want first?"

"Coffee and downers?" I asked incredulously. I sagged against the van door. I wondered if any Furman County victim advocates carried lunch-bags full of prescription tranquilizers. Probably not.

"Come on, back in you go." Marla hustled me into the van, where the air was even warmer than it was outside. But the interior of my vehicle was familiar and smelled faintly, even pleasantly, of cooked food. The cat was uncharacteristically quiet. I rolled down my window; Marla did the same.

"Just drink this," she commanded, thrusting the glass into my hand. "Tom said to bring you—" Abruptly she stopped. She blinked. "One of my friends on Jacobean called. Suz is *dead*? Are they sure? Lynn Tollifer, you know her? She and her nosy teenage son, Luke, live across the street from Suz. Luke told Lynn that Suz's body was in a ditch at the end of her driveway. Who found her? You?" I nodded and took a tiny sip of the chilly liquid. It tasted like melted ice cream. Marla clutched the top of her frizzy brown hair. "Suz dead! I don't believe it, but I do believe it."

"It should have been me. But he got Suz Craig instead." My voice cracked. I sagged against the headrest. "Gosh, I'm feeling—" John Richard's glare, his anger, haunted me. And I'd had such a strong feeling that he'd been acting, playing a part, but why? And what part? Why come over the morning after you'd had a fight with your girlfriend, bearing flowers, if you'd hurt her badly? If you'd killed her? But he hadn't meant to hurt her badly. At least that's what he always said. He probably hadn't meant to kill her, either.

"Do you think he beat her up so badly she died?" Marla asked.

"Yes, I do. Suz had a black right eye. And bruises on her arms—" I choked.

"Mother of God."

"I don't know what to do."

"Drink your coffee," Marla ordered sharply. "We can talk about all this later. If you don't look better in five minutes, I'm calling an ambulance for you and taking Arch home myself."

The air inside the van, despite the open windows, felt stifling. Marla slid toward me smelling of floral soap and powder. She'd obviously just jumped out of the shower when Tom called her, and I felt a fleeting sense of regret to have caused her trouble. Then the weight of the morning's events smacked me like one of those Jersey-shore waves you're not expecting, and I didn't know whether I wanted the espresso or enough tranquilizers to put me out for a few days.

"Okay, Goldy, look at me," Marla commanded sharply. "Keep

drinking that coffee." I took another sip and stared into her large, liquid brown eyes. "Still feeling light-headed?"

"I'm doing a little better," I replied in a voice that didn't even convince me.

"Your first problem is Arch. Think what—"

The sob that nearly choked me turned into another and then a whole barrage that wouldn't quit. Marla hugged me and spoke soft words of no import. Still crying, I glanced up. Gail Rodine was staring out her front window. She probably wasn't expecting to see two women, one with a Mercedes and one with a beat-up van, hugging each other while one sobbed effusively, out in front of her elaborate Victorian cottage. On second thought, Gail Rodine probably was about to call the vice squad.

"I have to get my act together," I croaked.

"Yeah, you do," Marla replied hopefully. "What you need is some medication. Chill you out a little." She thrust the brown bag into my hand and I peered tentatively at bottles of Librium and Valium, foil-encased capsule samples of God-only-knew-what, even a hypodermic. I carefully pulled out the needle, which was labeled Versed. From Med Wives 101, I knew this was a high-potency tranquilizer.

"Where on earth did you get all this?"

"Goldy, with the legion of doctors who are either treating me or going out with me, and an ex-husband who's a doctor, you wonder that? Which one do you want?"

"None. I need to parent, cook, cater, and drive this van without benefit of altered states of consciousness. I won't be able to perform any of those tasks if I'm floating inside a drug-induced cloud somewhere in the stratosphere." And just as uncontrollably as the sobs had begun, they ended, and I giggled. Marla shrugged philosophically, dropped the needle back into the bag, and shoved the bag into my glove compartment. Then she started to laugh herself.

"Look, Goldy, I promised Tom I'd help and that's what I'm going to do. Okay, here's what you tell Arch. You say there's been an

incident and his father might be in trouble. Dear old Dad's gone
down to the sheriff's department to talk to the folks there. Dear old
Dad will be talking to his lawyer over the weekend. With school out,
with no town paper until Wednesday, and with the Denver TV stations covering their own murders, Arch won't hear about the arrest
except from the Jerk himself, maybe tomorrow." Marla exhaled triumphantly.

"It's going to be awful. . . ."

"Yep," she agreed matter-of-factly. Again she ran her bejeweled
fingers through her tangled, damp hair. "But let me clue you in to
something, kiddo. You are not responsible for the Jerk's problems.
He is. A hard lesson that took both of us a lot of years to learn, but
there it is. Right?"

I stared out the window in sullen silence. Hard lesson, indeed.

"Okay now. Next step," Marla breezed on, "who's at home?
Somebody to screen your calls? Be with Arch?"

"Macguire Perkins."

"Oh, great. How's he doing? Is the mono over, or almost over,
or what?"

"He's sleeping, as usual. Not eating. But he could be good for
Arch. You know, be someone to talk to besides me about what's
happening."

"Does Macguire do anything that would get Arch out of the
house? You know, go out to the movies, whatever?"

"I suppose," I murmured. What did Macguire do? Not much.
Virtually nothing at all, to be honest. "He's under doctor's orders to
get mild exercise. And for Macguire 'mild' means 'with as little exertion as possible.' I urge him to take a walk most days. Sometimes
Arch goes along, and they make it as far as John Richard's office."

"Okay, you'll have to get Arch to go out with Macguire for a
stroll today. You want him out of the house for a bit. You know your
phone's going to start ringing."

I sighed. "You know you can't make Arch do anything when he
has his mind set on something else. Which he will have when he

hears this news. Besides, Arch was supposed to go hiking with John Richard and spend the night with him while I worked the McCrackens' Stanley Cup celebration party here in the club."

"Good," said Marla bluntly. I wondered confusedly why everything seemed good to her today. She cast an appraising eye at the Rodines' house. Gail's face was no longer in the window. "I'll call Arch's friend. What's his name, Todd Druckman?" I nodded, and she went on. "I'll ask Todd if Arch can go over and spend the night. That'll get him out of your house. Can Macguire accompany you and help tonight? Is he contagious or anything?"

"No, he's not contagious. But I can assure you he won't have the energy for it." I stared glumly out the window. "How can you talk about all this now?"

"Uh. Let's see. 'Cuz your husband the cop asked me to take care of you?"

I touched her forearm and she tilted her head questioningly. "Is this really happening?" I asked my best friend. "Did John Richard finally kill someone?"

She didn't answer, because at that moment we both heard a very faint voice calling, "Mom?"

Arch had come out onto the Rodines' porch. At fourteen, he was still much shorter than his peers, with tousled brown hair and a generally scruffy appearance. He had changed into khaki cutoffs and a T-shirt printed with the Biocess logo. Biocess was the product of a drug company for which John Richard had been doing endorsements lately. Unfortunately, the only things Arch or I ever got out of John Richard's high-paying endorsements were ugly T-shirts and pens that leaked all over the place. Arch's tortoiseshell glasses winked as he shielded his eyes against the sun and frowned at Marla's and my cars in the street.

"We'll be up to get you in a minute, Arch!" Marla called. "You don't need to come out yet!"

Without replying, Arch turned on his heel and retreated into the house.

"So do you think he did it?" I pressed, not able to let it go. "Do you think John Richard Korman actually, finally, went over the edge and killed someone?"

"Of course I do," Marla replied evenly. "With ten or twelve drinks in him and something to set him off? No question. You said yourself you saw the bruise marks. And the Jerk had something big to set him off, take my word for it."

"What? I mean, besides some money problems."

"He didn't have anything *besides* money problems, Goldy. He and ACHMO are being sued by the McCrackens, and even with malpractice insurance, he's going to have costs. I heard the malpractice people hired an attorney, ACHMO had to hire several attorneys, and John Richard had to hire his own separate attorney. You know how much preparation these trials are going to take. My guess is the financial mess of his lawsuit is eating him alive." She said it smugly. I wasn't the only one who wanted John Richard to suffer. "Look, you haven't had any child support for months, right?"

"Three, to be exact."

Marla raised her eyebrows in mock astonishment. Of course she'd heard me complain about John Richard slacking off in this department numerous times. She went on. "You were so eager to get out of that marriage that you took a one-time financial settlement and minimal child support. Now every time you need something for Arch, like, say, tuition money, you have to go back and negotiate, or should I say *beg*. Right?" I nodded dully and glanced up at the porch. Arch was nowhere in sight. Marla wagged a finger at me to make sure I was paying attention. "My lawyer went for a part of the practice. Ten percent of the gross income per annum. Not that I needed it, but I figured the best way to punish the Jerk was in his pocketbook. If you—"

I interrupted impatiently. "Marla, a woman is dead. Where is this going?"

"To the bank, honey. Back in the good old pre–managed care

days, I got sixty to eighty thou a year, a reliable ten percent of six to eight hundred thousand of the Jerk's gyn and baby-delivery practice. But things began to change. With more and more of his patients signing up with HMOs instead of half of them being insured and half paying out of pocket, his income started to decline. He supplemented it with endorsing that designer antibiotic for pregnant women with infections. What's the name of it?"

"Biocess," I supplied.

"Right. Another fifty thou a year there, of which I got a paltry five. Plus he began to work in the hospitals on the weekends, but you know how he hates to have his social life tied up, even if working a weekend shift brought him in another sixty thou a year. All this was getting exhausting for the poor fellow."

"Marla—"

"Wait. Then he got bought out by the AstuteCare Health Maintenance Organization, aka ACHMO, which sounds like a sneeze more than an HMO, but—" She shrugged. "We don't need to be reminded of *that* little transaction, which also brought into our lives the now-dead-as-a-doorknob Ms. Craig."

Poor Suz. An ache pierced my chest.

"Goldy, these days, if you want to have a baby in Aspen Meadow, or if you want to have the Jerk as your gynecologist, you or your husband or your significant other has to belong to ACHMO, yes? I mean, God only knows why any sane woman would insist on having John Richard as her doctor. But he does have his supporters, I suppose. How strong that support might be depends on your willingness to pony up with the cost of ACHMO membership."

"Marla, I know this. And that ACHMO bought his practice for one point one mil, and he bought the fancy new house in the club over by Suz. So what?"

Marla said patiently, "So *I* got a hundred ten thousand when he sold the practice, but in the two years since then I've only received thirty thousand dollars the first year, twenty this year. Don't you get it? His annual income has dropped by more than half. Enough to get him mightily ticked off, wouldn't you say? First I called that new secretary of his, the sweet young thing? You know who I mean."

"ReeAnn Collins," I said. ReeAnn was a lovely twenty-three-year-old who'd been working for John Richard for the last ten months or so. I'd suspected ReeAnn was half in love with him, of course. I'd thought of warning her off, as I always thought I should. But I never did. I hadn't warned Suz Craig, either. A stone seemed to form in my throat.

"ReeAnn didn't know anything about why my reimbursement was dropping off," Marla went on smoothly, "so I called AstuteCare. I demanded to know how much money John Richard was due to get and when."

"Sheesh, Marla."

"Oh, it was fun. I talked to Suz Craig's secretary and then I talked to some guy named Chris Corey, who handles Provider Relations. Corey used to be a doctor, but now he's making it big in administration," she added with a coarse laugh. "He was so-o-o polite, trying to tell me that how much John Richard made was none of my frigging business."

"Yes, I know him—" In my mind's eye, I saw a heavy man tumbling down a flight of steps. "Chris Corey sprained his ankle over at Suz's."

"Yeah, I've seen him limping around. He lives with his sister, Tina, up here. She's one of the women in charge of the Babsie show at the LakeCenter."

I tried to focus. I didn't care about the Coreys. "Are you telling me," I said, "that John Richard has gone from earning up to eight hundred thousand dollars a year down to making three hundred thousand dollars a year?"

"Sad, ain't it?"

"And he supplemented *that* income by endorsing Biocess and working in the hospital. You're saying you didn't like the way your share dropped and you tried to find out if he was stiffing you." What on earth did any of this have to do with the death of Suz?

"Right!" Marla said firmly. "So *finally* I called my *lawyer* about the drop in income and told him about all the people I'd talked to. My lawyer made some more calls and then let me know that the Biocess endorsement was in some kind of limbo. Plus John Richard hasn't yet received the latest bonus he was supposed to get from ACHMO. A bonus in the big fat neighborhood of two hundred thousand dollars. When the bonus does come through, I should see some more cash. I would love to have my cut of that, Goldy. But mainly I did all this just to annoy John Richard, because I knew it would get back to him that I was nosing around. The guy is up to his ears in debt from the good old days, what with payments to *you*, and payments to *me*, and payments on his *condos*, and payments on his new *house*, and payments on his *cars*, and dealing with the *McCrackens*. So. I wanted the Jerk to know I was on his case. I wanted him to squirm."

"And the connection to Suz Craig is . . ."

Marla raised an eyebrow. "Didn't I tell you? Suz was the one who decided whether or not he got the bonus."

Chapter 6

Marla and I were prevented from further discussion of John Richard's plummeting finances and mounting problems by the sudden reappearance of my son. Arch bounded awkwardly off the Rodines' porch and frowned as he lugged his overnight bag toward us. I had the sinking feeling that the overnight had not gone well. Marla asked if I wanted her to stay and I said no. After giving Arch a quick, wordless hug and me a bright, reassuring smile, she vavoomed off in her Mercedes.

"Why was Marla here?" Arch asked as he clicked his seat belt in place. He had the thickened voice and strong boy smell that always seems to accompany the morning-after of slumber parties.

"Just visiting," I said lightly.

"Do you think Dad's up yet? I haven't had any breakfast."

"You don't seem very happy," I observed, more as a probe to see if anyone had called the Rodines to report the situation on Jacobean Drive.

"Oh, well." His tone was disgusted. "I mean, we were going to have breakfast, we were supposed to, but then something happened." He shook the hair out of his eyes. "You know Clay Horning?"

"Yes." Clay Horning was the resident hooligan of the Elk Park Prep eighth grade. I kept my opinion to myself, however.

"Clay took half a dozen of Mrs. Rodine's Babsie dolls off a chair. He couldn't understand why Mrs. Rodine had them there. I mean, she never plays with them, but they're on the chairs, on the tables, on the sofas, on the beds, on the bureaus, everywhere! You ask me, Mrs. Rodine is a doll junkie! Anyway, Clay wanted to see how the heads from some of the dolls would look on the bodies of others. He pulled off all the heads and was switching them around— I mean, they pop right on—when Mrs. Rodine had a hissy fit. She swung her frying pan at him. Clay jumped out of the way, but all the uncooked bacon slid out on those headless Babsies. Do you believe that something so *stupid* could ruin a slumber party?" He shook his head. "Some people."

I didn't reply. After a few seconds Arch pushed his glasses up his nose and squinched his mouth to one side. "Mom? I don't mean to complain." He waited for me to speak. "Are you upset about Mrs. Rodine and the frying pan? Or are you mad that she didn't give me anything to eat? I'm really not that hungry."

"Mrs. Rodine is not an easy person to deal with," I said softly. "But I don't want to talk about her, Arch. Let's just sit here a minute. I need to think."

He shrugged. "Ohh-kay. What-ever."

I watched my son and felt my heart ache with love, with my inability to communicate, and with foreboding. In the last year Arch had finally adjusted to a new family life. He adored Tom, while maintaining a ferocious devotion to his father. But John Richard did little more than tolerate Arch and use him in arguments with me. When Marla's nephew, our much-loved boarder Julian Teller, left for

Cornell, the resulting hole in Arch's life had been filled by an adopted bloodhound, Jake. Lately, Arch and Macguire Perkins had become friendly. The two boys liked to listen to music and—as they put it—*hang out* at John Richard's office. All of which now seemed charmingly innocent and faraway. It was unlikely that they would still hang out at the office of a doctor who'd been accused of murder.

Before I could phrase what needed to be said, a forlorn feline howl erupted from the back of the van. Another quickly followed. Arch whirled.

"Mom? Is that Scout? What's going on?"

"No." I sighed. Tippy wanted out. "I'll be right back." When I hopped from the van, Gail Rodine, a top-heavy, matronly brunette, stood glaring on her spacious porch. Holding a clipboard to her chest, she scowled at me, as if my presence at her curb was intrusive. At Gail's side was a tall, similarly heavyset woman with long blond braids. The blonde appeared to be wearing a doctor-type jacket. I yanked open the van's rear door and caught sight of the little calico cat lurking behind my spare tire. "Come on, Tippy," I urged. "Out you come."

Suz's cat did not need to be coaxed. She leaped from the van, crouched on the Rodine lawn, then dashed to one of the blooming pink rosebushes encircling the porch. The cat tried frantically to claw her way up a rosebush. Gail Rodine squawked. The woman with the blond braids swiftly descended the porch steps, arms outstretched. Between Gail's angry yelps, the soothing words the blond woman offered the panicked cat were barely audible. The cat, sensing a friend, leaped from the destroyed rosebush into the open arms of the woman. Then she clawed her way up to her shoulder.

"Mom?" said Arch. "What is going on? Whose cat is that? It looks like Ms. Craig's."

"I'm so sorry," I said, approaching the blond woman, whose hand reached up to stroke the cat on her shoulder. "It's not mine, it's . . . somebody else's." Her wide blue jacket had "Dr. Babsie" embroidered in dark blue script over her heart. "I know you, don't I? Do you practice in our town? I'm Goldy Schulz."

The woman let out a strange, eager laugh. She gave me an intense blue-eyed look. "You're the caterer, right? You're doing several meals for us next week. I'm Tina Corey. Head of the Aspen Meadow Babsie Doll Club. How do you know me?"

"From church?" I guessed, without adding that her face was only vaguely familiar. But St. Luke's had three services each weekend and it was possible to go for years without knowing another parishioner's name.

"Mom?" Arch called from the van. "We need to go or Dad's going to be *really* upset."

I signaled to him to wait. "I . . . I've met your brother, Tina. Chris. At ACHMO. Are you a doctor, too? I mean, it says . . . on your jacket . . ."

She chuckled again. "No-o, this is just the adult-size Babsie-as-Veterinarian costume. Do you like it?"

"I . . . uh . . . sure. I need to go. Want to give me the cat? She's not mine." But when I reached out to Tippy, the cat hissed at me.

"Animals always love me," Tina assured me. "Want me to return her to her rightful owner?"

"Actually," I said, desperate, "if you'd just be willing to take care of her for a while until we can get her turned over to the Mountain Animal Protective League—"

Tina opened her eyes wide. "Never! I'll keep her! I have a bunch of cats already. What's her name?"

"I think the owner called her Tippy."

Murmuring, Tina reached up and gently removed the cat from her shoulder. Gail Rodine glared. "Sweet baby!" crooned Tina, "I'll have you fixed up in no time."

"Thanks, Tina," I said, not waiting for the cat's reply. "See you next week. At the doll show." I trotted back to the van, not daring to glance at Gail Rodine. I hopped back into the driver's seat and cleared my throat. There was no easy way to do this, despite what Marla had said. "Listen, Arch," I said. "Dad's in trouble."

He moved impatiently in the seat next to me. "What?" Behind the thick lenses his eyes grew wary. "Is he okay?"

"Not really. I mean physically he's okay, but—"

"What do you mean, then? Dad's in trouble?" Anxiety cracked his voice. I was desperate to comfort him even as my own voice trembled with each revelation. *Dad's down at the department with Tom* and *Looks like he and his girlfriend had an argument* and *Actually, nobody knows exactly what happened, but Suz Craig is dead.* Arch's reaction— dumbfounded denial—was followed by panic.

"She's dead? Suz is dead? Are you sure?"

"Yes. I saw her body lying in a ditch when I drove by her house this morning. And your dad's under arrest." I took a deep breath. "He's been accused of killing her."

Arch looked out the window. Gail and Tina were seated, conversing, on the porch. The cat was in Tina's arms. "But . . . that doesn't make sense."

"Hon, I know."

He was silent, then said: "When will I get to see him?"

"I'm not sure."

"But, why were you driving by Ms. Craig's house in the first place?"

"Arch, please. I just wanted to avoid taking you to an empty house."

He faced me again. His voice rose with confusion. "Whose empty house? Why? What are you talking about?"

"Dad's! I mean, I thought he might have spent the night at Suz's place and not be home yet! I . . . was just trying to see where he was so I could spare you some pain," I gabbled helplessly. "I didn't know what I was going to stumble on to."

"Well, you didn't spare me any pain," my son said harshly, and turned away from me to stare out the window again.

As I drove the van back into Aspen Meadow, I did my best to act loving and patient. It didn't work. Arch had retreated into silence.

Why did John Richard Korman continue to mess up our lives? That was the question to which there was no answer. My knuckles whitened as I gripped the steering wheel.

At home Arch slammed out of the van ahead of me. Macguire had let Jake into our fenced backyard. The hound howled with delight at our arrival. Anticipating my worry about the neighbors' complaints, Arch became intent on getting Jake back into the house. I sat in the van contemplating Arch's short legs and flapping T-shirt and the crisis that confronted us.

My son would talk to me about how he was feeling, I felt sure. Only he would do it in his own time. We always worked things out, I told myself. But I felt a twinge of uncertainty. I slid out of the van and trod carefully across the wooden deck I'd added to the back of the house some years before. Suddenly I stopped and stared at the diagonal slats. *The deck, the doggone deck.* Dizzily, I sank down on a cushioned redwood chair.

The deck had been my idea. My present to John Richard on our fifth anniversary. Oh, Lord, why was I thinking about this now? Because everything was erupting: my life, my family, my mind. The world felt like a pinball machine flashing TILT with no way to turn it off.

I gazed down at the deck. I had saved the money out of what John Richard called my "grocery allowance," what I later referred to, once I learned how much money he was really earning, as my "pittance." Naively, I had thought the deck would be a wonderful place for us to gather as a family. I'd even believed that John Richard and I would enjoy watching the progress of its construction. Ha.

I ran my fingers over the smooth redwood railing that always smelled so wonderful after a rainstorm. When the builders started, John Richard had second-guessed and criticized every aspect of the construction. *Why redwood? It's too expensive. Why do you have to have it so big?* The next day: *Why is it so small? Why don't you add a barbecue?* and despite the fact that he wasn't contributing, he'd yell *This is costing a mint! Do you think I'm made of money?* In the end, he'd declared he was never going to sit out on our lovely redwood deck. So the deck stood empty. To his friends, he'd laughed about my project. He'd called it Goldy's Golden Goof.

After the divorce papers were signed and I had deposited my settlement check, my very first act had been to drive to Howard Lorton Galleries, the most exclusive furniture store in Denver. There I'd impulsively ordered a thousand dollars' worth of deck furniture.

Why rehash old history now? Once again my brain supplied a warning. *Because he's barged into your life again, and it's not just to declare bankruptcy.*

Watch your back, Goldy.

Chapter 7

Inside the house, Arch was on the phone. He looked at me solemnly, then shook his head.

"ReeAnn," he said impatiently into the receiver. Had John Richard's secretary called us? Or had Arch just phoned her? "I don't *know* what you're supposed to tell the patients. Better see who's on call for Dad . . . I don't know! Look, would you please ask him to give me a ring if he phones in?" His voice cracked. "No! How should I know what they're doing to him?" He banged the phone down and regarded me dolefully. After a moment he said, "You look terrible, Mom."

"Thanks."

"Why don't you cook or something?"

I glanced around the kitchen. *Cook or something.* The rows of cupcakes sat waiting to be iced. The remains of my coffee fixings lay in a heap by the sink. Nothing beckoned.

"Mom, please." Arch gave me a quick hug, then pulled back, embarrassed. "It's going to be okay. It's just all a big mistake."

"Oh, honey . . ." But words failed.

"Let me go see if Macguire went back to bed after he let Jake out," Arch announced abruptly. "It's time for him to be up, no matter what, don't you think?"

"Yeah, sure." I shook my head as Arch left to rouse our boarder. To keep from brooding, I made another espresso.

"I'm up, I'm up," Macguire Perkins hollered through the closed door of his room. His muffled voice echoed mournfully down the stairs.

I slugged down the coffee, hauled myself over to our walk-in refrigerator, and stared at the contents. Fixing breakfast for Macguire Perkins—maybe that was a *cook or something* challenge I could handle. Arch was right: I seemed to think more logically when preparing food, anyway. And with Macguire as a buffer, perhaps Arch and I would be able to discuss his father's status as a murder suspect without further fireworks. I heard more banging upstairs.

"I'm up, didn't you hear me?" called Macguire. "Why is everyone tormenting me?"

Good old Macguire, I thought as I got out eggs and butter. With no plans one year after graduating from the same prep school that Arch attended, Macguire had begun the summer working part-time for me. Macguire's father, the headmaster of Elk Park Prep, had agreed to let Macguire live alone in their house on the school grounds for three months. Meanwhile, Perkins senior was off to direct a summer seminar in Burlington, Vermont. When he started as my assistant, Macguire confessed that he was reluctantly trying to decide what to do with his life. What he wanted to do with his life wasn't catering, I discovered after he'd been working in the business a few weeks. Then Macguire made the announcement that he'd decided to become a police detective. Unfortunately, he'd run amok.

Against all advice, Macguire had tried to solve a case on his own. The result was that a criminal had savagely beaten him and—in a raging storm, by the side of the road—left him for dead. Macguire had ended up in the hospital with multiple bruises and lacerations.

Unfortunately, that was just the beginning of his medical troubles. After being discharged from the hospital, he'd gone home to Elk Park, where he immediately developed strep throat that quickly evolved into full-blown infectious mononucleosis.

Headmaster Perkins had flown home and asked for my help. Macguire was unable to swallow anything more than liquids and began to shed weight at an alarming rate. During the first three weeks of July, he lost twenty pounds. His doctor said when Macguire finished his antibiotics, he needed rest, support, nutritious food, and very moderate exercise. But Headmaster Perkins couldn't picture trying to help his son get better while the two of them lived out of suitcases in a Vermont bed-and-breakfast, no matter how quaint the setting. That was when Perkins senior begged me to allow Macguire to live with us for the remainder of the summer.

"Just give the kid three squares a day. Or even three cubes. You know, steaks," he'd told me. A square meal or a cube steak? The headmaster thought he was hilarious. For the most part, Perkins senior was merely ridiculous. "Under your care, Goldy dear," he'd announced airily, "I have no doubt my son should recover nicely in a week or two."

I'd said yes, and as a result Macguire Perkins had been living with us since mid-July. But *recover nicely* was exactly what the teenager hadn't done. Of course, our observation of Macguire was inevitably colored by our experience with the now-absent Julian Teller, whose high energy, intellectual sharpness, and enthusiastic affection for our family had been hallmarks of his time with us. Julian had done everything from loving Arch as if the two were the closest of brothers to cooking wildly inventive vegetarian dishes for our family meals. To Julian's surprise but not to ours, he'd been offered a great summer job working in the kitchen of a chic hotel in upstate New York. We felt his absence deeply.

When Tom and Arch and I had agreed to take Macguire in, I'd secretly hoped that Arch would somehow be the beneficiary, because he would have a new friend Julian's age.

Arch, sensing my motive, had mumbled, "It's like when your dog dies, you can't just go out and buy a new dog."

"Arch, give him a chance," I'd protested.

"Trust me, Mom, it's not the same."

But despite Arch's initial reluctance, he'd grudgingly accepted having Macguire as a boarder. Macguire was slow-moving, honest, and sweet. Furthermore, he presented a much more challenging rehabilitation situation than we'd ever faced with Jake, Arch's beloved bloodhound, who'd been fired from law enforcement for being suspected of being unreliable. Which the dear dog wasn't, as it turned out.

The problem with Macguire, however, was that he would not eat. He said he couldn't—he wasn't hungry. Wouldn't or couldn't, the result was the same. The boy would not take nourishment.

In the breakfast department Macguire shunned bacon and sausage; scrambled, poached, boiled, or fried eggs; toast or English muffins; ready-to-eat cereal, oatmeal, or granola; yogurt shakes; fresh fruit of any kind. I had yet to convince him to swallow anything more than orange juice. He claimed his stomach hurt whenever he ate even the smallest morsels. His doctor had proclaimed, "When he gets hungry, he'll eat." In the three weeks he'd been with us, however, that hadn't happened. But I was ever hopeful. Now I set aside the eggs and butter and went back to our refrigerator. There I retrieved a bowl of homemade chocolate pudding left over from a catering job. I ladled spoonfuls of it into a crystal parfait glass.

Arch clomped back into the kitchen after completing his summoning duty, flopped into a chair, and turned doleful eyes to me.

"When do you suppose I'll be able to talk to Dad? He hasn't called his office and ReeAnn is having a fit."

"I don't know," I answered truthfully.

"But . . . is Dad in jail? When will he get out?" Arch insisted.

"Um, I'm not sure. He's probably being processed."

"Oh, great. Like liverwurst."

I let this pass, set the chocolate pudding on the table, and started to mix up a batch of hockey-puck biscuits. If Macguire wouldn't go for traditional bacon-and-egg-type breakfast-taste sensations, perhaps he'd flip for chocolate and biscuits.

While Arch contemplated the table, wrestling with his confusion, I sifted the flour with the other dry ingredients while my food processor cut through the shortening. I mixed in the buttermilk, patted out the dough, cut it into circles on a sheet, and set the sheet in the oven. Then I cleaned the doser and refilled my espresso machine with water. This would be my fourth quadruple-shot of the morning, but I desperately craved the clearheadedness that caffeine usually offered. Unfortunately, such clarity had eluded me ever since my gruesome discovery on Jacobean Drive.

Nevertheless, the coffee-making process gave me time to think about how to deal with Arch. I wished that I hadn't told Marla it was okay to leave. She'd have been able to help me with this minefield of a dialogue, cowardly as that sounded. Arch's questions were difficult to answer, not only because they were delivered in an alternately pleading and hostile manner, but also because the answers themselves were sure not to please him. When would John Richard be freed? How was I going to tell my son that bail was not supposed to be granted in capital cases? Of course, occasionally something was wrong with the arrest or the evidence, or the judge had a surpassing reason for granting bail. Sometimes the suspect's standing in the community was so impeccable that the judge let him or her out once a huge bail had been set. But John Richard's reputation was far from impeccable.

I took a deep breath and poured Macguire some juice. "Your father's lawyer will go before a judge first thing Monday morning and at least *try* to get him out on bail. I have to tell you, Arch, it would be unusual for the request to be granted. And if bail is set very high, I don't know if your father has that kind of cash or equity in his house."

Arch's face darkened and he turned away from me. On some level he seemed to be aware of his father's financial problems. "What about Tom? Are they going to assign Tom to this case?"

"I doubt that very much," I said carefully. "It would probably be viewed as a conflict of interest."

Arch flashed back around. His forehead was so furrowed with alarm that I felt my heart slam against my chest. *You bet it's a conflict of interest,* I could imagine him saying. But to my surprise his distress went the other way. "They're not going to assign Tom? But I thought you said he was the best the department has! If they don't assign Tom, how will we ever prove Dad's innocent?" I was speechless.

So Arch's question hung unanswered as Macguire Perkins galumphed slowly into the kitchen. His yellowed eyes were difficult to look at, as were his hollow cheeks and emaciated frame. When I first met him, he'd been strong, a basketball player and bodybuilder. Now, thin and lethargic, Macguire seemed to teeter on his long legs like a precariously staked scarecrow.

"Well," he murmured without enthusiasm, "how's everybody?"

"Not so hot," Arch mumbled.

Macguire sat down at the table, ran his fingers through his long, unevenly shorn red hair—going to the barber gave him a headache—and stared forlornly at the pudding and juice. Then he sighed and pushed both away. Undaunted, I poured him a glass of milk. He took one sip. When I pulled the hot, puffed biscuits out of the oven, he said, "I hope you didn't make those for me. Because I can't even look at them. Sorry."

"It's okay," I lied encouragingly, and set the pan on a rack to cool. So much for today's hearty breakfast.

"My dad's been arrested," Arch announced in a tone that said, *Can you believe the injustices of this world?*

"Bummer," replied Macguire. He took another tiny sip of milk, then said, "My dad was arrested once, but he doesn't want anybody to know."

"For what?" asked Arch, who of course wanted to know.

"Drunk and disorderly," Macguire replied matter-of-factly. "It was after my mom left and Daddy-o couldn't handle it."

Arch closed his eyes and shook his head. I turned away and ran hot water and soap into the biscuit-batter bowl.

"I have to cater tonight," I announced. "Stanley Cup celebration party. Marla is calling Todd to see if you can go over there, Arch. Do you feel up to helping me, Macguire?"

"Can I see how I feel later?" His smile was wan. "I want to help. You know folks think that if there's a thin caterer, they won't gain any weight eating the food you serve."

Before I could voice my opinion about this theory, Arch sighed. "I don't want to go to Todd's," he said morosely.

"Man," said Macguire, "you are in one tight mood, big A. Why don't you go for a walk with me? We'll go visit Kids' Vids if you want, see if they have any cool new games."

Arch sighed again. "It's going to rain. Besides, Dad might call."

Macguire strained his neck to look outside, where the sun shone between a few drifts of cloud. "What, you predict the weather? That's pretty cool." By the door, Jake let loose with another of his howls. "Come on, buddy, we'll go by your dad's office and see if there's any news. We'll even take the dog. If it rains, we'll all get wet."

"Oh, you just want to go see ReeAnn," Arch accused.

When Macguire's jaundiced-appearing face blushed the color of a sweet potato, I knew Arch had found a target. I said, "ReeAnn probably won't be in any mood for company."

"Sure she will," Arch countered. "ReeAnn likes to see Macguire. They took driver ed together, and now she has a Porsche. He's had a crush on her forever. And not even because of the Porsche," he glumly added.

"Gee, Arch," Macguire said, "thank you for pointing all this out. You and the hound dog want to walk or not?"

Arch regarded me warily from behind his thick glasses. "So can Dad call me from the jail or what?"

"You can call him and then he'll call you back. But I'd say you might be better off waiting. Besides, as you know, he'll have to call his office at some point."

"All right," said Arch, defeated. He took Jake's leash from its hook on the wall and departed.

"So what's Dr. Korman been arrested for?" Macguire asked as soon as the door closed on Arch.

I said, "Murder." Outside, Jake howled with happiness.

Macguire sipped the milk and didn't miss a beat. "Oh yeah? Who'd he kill?"

"Macguire, if you want to go into police work, you need to learn to say, 'Whom did they *say* he killed?' "

"Okay, who'd they *say* he bumped off?"

"His girlfriend. Suz Craig."

Macguire's rusty eyebrows shot up. "Uh-oh. How'd he do it? Wait. How're they *saying* she bought it?"

"Beaten to death, looked like. The technical term would be multiple blunt-force injuries, I think." I had another flash of Suz's bruised and broken body in the ditch.

"Huh," said Macguire. "Too bad." On the deck, Arch was having a noisy heart-to-heart with Jake about the attachment of the leash. "So this dead broad was your ex-husband's chick? Or . . . one of them, anyway?"

I took a steadying sip of coffee. The only activity Macguire energetically pursued during his convalescence was reading Raymond Chandler. Unfortunately, it sometimes took me a moment to translate the private-dick lingo. "Why do you ask that?"

Macguire frowned. "Uh, ask what?"

I said patiently, "Why did you ask if Suz Craig was *one* of his . . . girlfriends?"

"Well, wasn't she? I thought he had a lot of girlfriends."

"Yes," I said cautiously. "But I thought Suz was his *only* girlfriend. His only current girlfriend."

"Oh." He scowled at the milk he'd scarcely touched. "Well."

"Macguire, I've tried to put as much distance as possible between my ex-husband's love life and myself. I don't ask for any details."

"So, what're you saying? You're feeling bad because his girlfriend croaked, huh?"

"Yes." I exhaled. "A woman is dead, and like it or not, at the moment I'm feeling extremely guilty because I never pressed charges against him and got him sent to jail. If I had, maybe Suz Craig would be alive today."

"Don't feel too bad, Goldy." His face assumed its typically philosophical expression. "Nobody can go back in time. It's a bummer, but there it is." He shrugged.

I took another discreet sip of my coffee and bit into one of the biscuits. It was moist, hot, and comforting. "Macguire, do you know if my ex-husband had *other* current girlfriends besides Suz Craig? Did you hear or see something . . . at his office, say? Why did you say 'one' of his girlfriends?"

Macguire scraped back his chair and avoided my eyes. "Uh," he replied slowly, "maybe I should just talk to Tom about it."

"Probably that would be a good idea. But it's unlikely Tom will be assigned to this case."

"Bummer." He sighed.

"Did Dr. Korman have another girlfriend that you know about?"

"Oh, well, no, not exactly. Maybe I'm just imagining things because I was, like, jealous. I just thought . . . that he had something going with ReeAnn."

"You saw John Richard and ReeAnn together? Away from the office?"

"Well, yeah. He was over at ReeAnn's house once, in the evening, when I dropped by to give her a book about Porsches. I mean, I didn't have to take it over. I was like, taking it instead of mailing it because I just wanted to see her. But Dr. Korman was over there and they were cooking out."

"How long ago was this?"

"Oh . . . end of the school year, I think. You know Arch and I walk over to the office sometimes. But ReeAnn and I never talk about any deep stuff while Arch is visiting his dad. Or seeing if his dad wants to visit." He thought for a moment. "But one time I did ask her if she wanted to go to the CD store with me—"

"Macguire."

"Yeah. Well, when we went to the store, we looked at CDs and talked about this and that and I asked ReeAnn if there were, like, any guys in her life at the moment, and she got all secretive and said, maybe. Then I asked her about her job, and she had all kinds of things to say. She didn't like the secretary who had worked there before her, because that woman was fired to make way for ReeAnn. Or so ReeAnn thought."

"Beatrice Waxman."

"She called her Battleaxe Woman. Battleaxe Woman wouldn't help ReeAnn learn the filing."

"Filing?"

"Filing, filing claims, something. But the person ReeAnn really hated big-time was this Craig lady with the HMO. Suz Craig. Some hotshot veep, right?"

"A vice-president, yes."

Macguire shook his head, remembering. "Well, Tom might want to get somebody from the department to talk to ReeAnn about Ms. Craig. ReeAnn was trying to work on billing with the HMO, and Ms. Craig drove her crazy. I'm telling you, I don't know why, but ReeAnn really hated that Craig woman's guts."

Chapter 8

From our front porch I watched thin, sweatsuit-clad Macguire lope painfully down the sidewalk after Arch, who had changed into too-large green Bermuda shorts and a faded green T-shirt—both garments left behind by Julian. With his short arms outstretched and his glasses slipping down his wrinkled nose, Arch tugged unsuccessfully on Jake's leash. The bloodhound's long tawny legs lunged briskly down the pavement. When the unlikely trio spun past the corner store in the direction of John Richard's office, I wearily turned to go back to my kitchen. *Your dad's under arrest.* Despite Marla's beliefs to the contrary, no amount of walking was going to make that better.

At the front door I was brought up short by the security system panel that had been installed two summers previously. Back then, after almost four years of being on my own, I'd begun to go out again. To go out *occasionally*. To go out occasionally with *men*. And just when I'd thought John Richard had mended his ways, his behavior suddenly became a problem. Why should I have been surprised?

He hadn't liked the idea of me dating. To demonstrate his opposition to my new social life, he'd threatened a reduction in child support—through his lawyer, of course—and then had taken to driving slowly past our house. Well, I'd been a psych major in college; I knew passive-aggressive behavior when I saw it. Amid the Jerk's protests of uninvolvement—*I never went near your place, bitch*—I'd gotten the system, both for deterrent and for actual security. And by and large, the system had done the trick.

This morning John Richard Korman had once again been utterly adamant concerning his innocence. But we weren't talking about cruising past someone's house or making financial threats. Still, he'd almost convinced *me* he hadn't killed Suz Craig. At least for a brief moment, I'd suspended disbelief and accepted his story. Now, of course, I was equally certain he'd been lying. *They'd mixed it up,* he'd said. John Richard Korman always had an explanation ready for losing his temper and beating the living daylights out of whatever woman was offending him. People couldn't change that much in two years. People couldn't change that much in a *lifetime.* I made a mental note to ask Tom if Suz Craig's house had a security system.

I was about to punch the panel buttons when a sheriff's department car pulled up in front of the house. Two women got out—Sergeant Beiner and a uniformed woman I didn't recognize. I nodded and waved. Of course. Sergeant Beiner had said she'd be coming over later. I would have to answer more questions. Well, maybe they could tell *me* a thing or two.

Sergeant Beiner's step was spry as she strode up our sidewalk. Her high, feathered top of blond-gray hair shook when she asked me how I was doing. When I said I was passable, she smiled briefly, showing slender, yellow teeth, and asked if she could run a few more things by me.

"Deputy Irving will take notes."

Deputy Irving, a curly-haired brunette with a plump face and a uniform that pulled tightly around her midsection, nodded. Deputy Irving was under thirty, with no wedding ring.

"I'm sure you know the questions," Sergeant Beiner began in a soothing, apologetic tone. When she smiled, her face wrinkled pleasantly. "Down at the department, we're aware of your record of detection."

"Thanks," I replied. "I want to help."

"We also remember that you managed to break somebody out of jail once. Somebody who was innocent, as it turned out."

"You have nothing to worry about this time," I assured her. "Would you like some coffee? I've had the equivalent of about sixteen cups today, I think. One more can't hurt."

Both women shook their heads. I invited them to be seated on the porch chairs. When the three of us were settled, Deputy Irving dutifully pulled out her notebook and recorded my name and address. Again I told the sergeant about spotting Suz Craig in the ditch by her home around a quarter to seven and about phoning for medical help.

"Did you suspect she was dead?" Sergeant Beiner asked mildly.

I looked away. "Yes. But I know the drill too, Sergeant Beiner. That's why I phoned EMS."

"A woman on the street named Lynn Tollifer saw you through her front window. She didn't know why you went back to Schulz's car after starting up the street. She figured you were calling about vandalism. Mrs. Tollifer said she couldn't see the ditch from her window. See the body, you know."

"My friend Marla Korman got a call from Lynn about Suz, and Lynn said her son told her about Suz . . ." I paused. "You don't think vandals had anything to do with . . ."

Sergeant Beiner shrugged. "You were there for the arrest." It wasn't a question. She regarded me with the same calm manner that infused her voice. "Of course you've got somebody to vouch for your whereabouts during the night." That wasn't a question, either.

"Tom can vouch for me. He came in at midnight. What exactly did Lynn's son see?"

Sergeant Beiner gave me the same wrinkle-faced smile she had when she arrived at the house. "How well did you know Suz Craig?"

I tried not to envision the pale corpse in the ditch when Suz's name was mentioned. Impossible. "I catered for her once," I replied. "And of course she was my ex-husband's girlfriend. His current girlfriend. Or at least one of them," I added. Deputy Irving scribbled away. "I'm not sure if he had other girlfriends, but he might have. His secretary, ReeAnn Collins, might know. She keeps his calendar. Plus, it's possible ReeAnn might have been seeing John Richard herself."

When asked, I spelled ReeAnn's name for them.

Sergeant Beiner rocked back in her chair. "How long ago did you cater this event for Ms. Craig?"

"Little less than a month. July tenth, I think. No, wait, the eleventh. It was a Friday, and the group of people had all been visiting for a week at the Denver office of the AstuteCare HMO. ACHMO."

"What group of people?"

"Human Resources. That's what one of them told me. ACHMO is based in Minneapolis and that's where the team was from."

"Did any of them talk to you?"

I thought back. Steamed trout, vegetable frittata, coleslaw, wild rice salad with porcini mushrooms, fruit cup, chocolate truffles. Everyone had seemed to be in a good mood. "They were happy. Suz seemed pleased, too, with all her landscaping underway. She was pointing out the plants that were being put in as part of a landscaping project. I think it was being done by Aspen Meadow Nursery."

A look passed between the two officers. Sergeant Beiner regarded me with pursed lips, then said, "Suz Craig fired Aspen Meadow Nursery. By all accounts, she was pretty hard to work for."

"Really? Well, I think she fired the nursery because one of her department heads fell down the stone steps. He sprained his ankle, and she mentioned she was going to fire her landscapers." I paused. "Actually, I'm surprised. She seemed so excited about their work."

"Was Suz Craig a demanding client when you catered for her?" Beiner wanted to know.

I thought for a minute. Had Suz been hard to work for? Not even slightly. Although most of my clients were wonderful, I'd had enough horrendous ones to know the type. "I didn't have any problem with her. It was a one-shot deal, though, not a long-term project. If anything, she seemed unusually accommodating." I remembered Suz, her blond ponytail bobbing, her shiny blue silk skirt skimming her knees as she stepped along the newly laid path. "She praised me to the skies for my food, and insisted I go around her property with the guests. She even helped me with the cleanup." When the two policewomen said nothing, I added, "That's unusual, believe me."

"Were these people from Minneapolis still around when she was so magnanimously cleaning up?"

"All five department heads were there. The Provider Relations man left because of his injury. He was the one who fell down the steps. The HR guy asked me for a recipe."

"HR?"

"Human Resources. The head of HR at the Denver office of AstuteCare is Brandon Yuille. Do you know him? His mother died last year, and his father, Mickey Yuille, bought the Aspen Meadow Pastry Shop not long after. Now that Mickey keeps baker's hours, I hardly ever see him. But I'm friends with the Yuilles. We swap recipes and food. I made them some fudge last week and they gave me some Thai peanut sauce." I paused. "So. That's who was there that I can remember."

Beiner raised her eyebrows. "All those people were still around when Ms. Craig was doing the dishes with you?"

"Well, yes."

"Maybe she wanted to impress the Minneapolis people with her versatility. Do you know anything else about her?" Beiner prompted me.

"She was single. Wealthy. Smart. Very pretty."

"Right."

I sighed deeply, because I knew what was coming next.

"Okay, Mrs. Schulz," said Beiner. "You have any idea why someone would want Suz Craig dead?"

If Arch were here, he would say, *"Don't answer, Mom."* And of course, really, I didn't *know* that John Richard would want Suz dead. But he could lose his temper so easily. Especially if the woman with command of the purse strings had pulled those strings shut.

"My ex-husband, Dr. John Richard Korman, is having money problems. Severe money problems. He's a member doctor of the AstuteCare HMO, they pay him a salary. What I heard was—"

"What you heard from whom?"

"His other ex-wife. Marla Korman. You might want to talk to her. Marla told me that John Richard hadn't yet received his bonus. Apparently, Suz was the one who decided whether he got it or not."

Beiner nodded; Irving wrote and flipped a page.

"Know about her relationships with anyone else? Neighbors? Friends?"

"She was fairly new in the community. To be fair, I think she moved up here to be closer to John Richard."

"What did your ex-husband say to you about their relationship?"

What did he ever say to me about a relationship he was having? *The woman I'm with now is so much nicer/smarter/prettier/more together than you.* I shrugged. "The usual. He adored her."

"Mrs. Schulz? Does your ex-husband have any reason to think *you* disliked Suz Craig?"

I couldn't help laughing. "John Richard believed I was jealous of Suz. Which of course I was not. I really didn't know too much about their relationship. He was going out with her last night, I know that. Then this morning he mentioned that they'd 'mixed it up.' That's one of his terms for beating up a woman. Another one is 'getting physical.' " As if his losses of temper were bouts. "You know that my complaints of his violence against me, including photographs of my face and body, are part of police record."

Her voice a tone lower, Beiner said, "You're saying there's not much to like in John Richard Korman."

"I divorced him."

The sergeant made a circular motion with her finger and Deputy Irving closed her notebook. In the same low tone, Beiner asked, "So do you have a theory on this? I'd really like to know."

Unexpectedly, the old rage surged up. The thought of sitting on my porch and calmly saying, *Yes, I think he beat this woman to death*, made me ill. I clenched my teeth, cleared my throat, swallowed hard. "The facts of the case will tell you what happened," I said finally. "Just beware of John Richard Korman. He's the most accomplished liar you'll ever meet." When no more questions were forthcoming, I asked, "Are we done?"

The two women stood. Sergeant Beiner followed Deputy Irving down the steps. Then she turned back.

"Are you sure you're all right, Mrs. Schulz? You look kind of green around the gills. Do you need a victim advocate?"

"I need Tom."

The sergeant nodded. She said, "I'll call him from the car," and strode away.

Back in my kitchen, I decided against calling Marla. It was getting on to late morning. No matter how difficult, I had to put this catastrophe behind me. I had to do the rest of the food prep for the hockey party. Besides, Marla was undoubtedly on the phone at this very moment, chatting up her country-club cronies to glean everything she could about Suz Craig and her relationship with John Richard Korman. Marla would give me an exhaustive report of her findings before long, of that I could bet the contents of my refrigerator.

I tried to stir the chilled frosting with a wooden spoon. Too cold. I stared at my silent phone. Good old Marla. While I'd done everything in my power to distance myself from John Richard, the fact that we had Arch in common meant I had to deal with my ex-husband, at the very least, on a biweekly basis. Marla, on the other hand, had no children in common with the Jerk, had no reason to see him at all, in fact, and yet she took the greatest delight in following, and reporting on, his every escapade. Her way of despising John Richard was to gloat over and widely publicize each of his setbacks, even if they were slight. And when he had some kind of triumph, like being bought out by ACHMO, her compensation for his good fortune was that she got a cut of the deal.

I set aside the icing, booted up my computer, and studied the menu for tonight's party. The last thing I wanted to do was work an event. My thoughts slipped back to poor, sweet, confused Arch, and I suddenly realized I'd been selfish. *He* needed a victim advocate. I put in a quick call to the office of the therapist Arch had worked with several years ago. An answering machine at the shrink's office picked up. Feeling disconsolate, I left a message saying my fourteen-year-old son was going through a crisis and needed help asap.

Work, I told myself. *You'll feel better.* The kitchen clock was closing in on eleven-thirty. My contract time for the party setup was five o'clock, and I had miles to go before packing up and taking off.

I filled my pasta pentola with water and set it on to boil. Three salads for this evening and one of them was . . . One of them was . . .

One of his girlfriends was . . . John Richard had a girlfriend besides Suz Craig? Black-haired, perky, distance-cyclist ReeAnn Collins, of all people? Of course, I'd always been convinced that John Richard had fired his previous secretary, stodgy, reliable Beatrice Waxman, and hired nubile ReeAnn, because of the latter's looks. I doubted ReeAnn—whose father, according to Macguire, had promised her a Porsche if she'd get a job—had any prowess with word processing. Or, heaven only knew, computerized billing.

And how did Macguire fit into all this? He'd gone over to Ree-Ann's townhouse—another gift from Daddy—at dinnertime, with the flimsy excuse of delivering a book. He'd found John Richard there before him, barbecuing with his secretary. Dinner with the secretary did not an affair make, although with John Richard it probably did. Well, I would tell Tom, as I'd promised Macguire. And I would go over to visit ReeAnn, I suddenly decided.

The hockey-party menu indicated that I had promised Mediterranean orzo salad, a vegetable mélange I'd dubbed Grilled Slapshot Salad, and Vietnamese Slaw, all of which needed to be prepared and chilled. While the pasta was cooking, Marla called.

"That didn't take long," I commented as I began to pit Kalamata olives.

"Give me a break, I've been worried about you. How are you doing?" Her voice trembled with concern. I felt the usual pang of gratitude that she was such a long-suffering friend.

"I'm not doing very well at all." I rinsed my hands. "It's like I'm having post-traumatic stress disorder. Every time I look around this house, something reminds me of the Jerk."

"Take a Valium. Go lie down for a while."

"For crying out loud, Marla, I've got a party tonight."

She paused to take a bite of food: *her* tranquilizer. "Oh, right, the McCrackens' hockey party. You're going to have to wear a T-shirt that says 'I don't know anything.' Otherwise, the guests are going to drive you nuts wanting to know what's going on. Plus Patricia's husband is a doctor, isn't he?"

"Her first husband was. Skip. Skip interned with John Richard and Ralph Shelton. Don't you remember?"

"Not really. That was before my time with the Jerk, honey."

"Well, Skip dumped Patricia when she said she wanted to adopt a child. I got to know Patricia when she was going through the divorce. Her new husband is a dentist. Clark."

"Still, their friends all know the Jerk, so you're going to get a slew of questions."

Ah, Aspen Meadow, which alternated between being intimate and incestuous. "I've already had a slew of questions. The cops just left."

"What did they want?"

"Oh, the usual. What did I see. What did I know about her. What did I know about the two of them."

"Hmph. Have you heard anything else? About the two of them, I mean?"

"No." I sliced the olives into delicate black bits. Then, as usual, my curiosity got the better of me. I murmured, "How about you?"

She took another noisy bite of whatever she was chewing and then washed it down with something liquid. "Well, I've been trying, God knows. I've been waiting ages for the Jerk to get his due, although I'm truly sorry Suz Craig had to die for it." She paused. "Okay. For one thing, John Richard and Suz were at the club bar last night, drinking and arguing almost until the place closed at midnight."

"Aspen Meadow Country Club?" I asked. "Says who?"

"Yes, the country club. You know how John Richard loves to see folks and be seen. And the person who said so was Fay Shelton, current wife of Dr. Ralph Shelton, recently fired by ACHMO by none other than Suz Craig herself." She paused. "Or so I heard. Hold on, there's somebody at my door."

I moved the olives aside and began on some fat, ripe tomatoes that smelled so delicately sweet, I was tempted to pop a couple of juicy red chunks right into my mouth. But the health inspector had recently sent out a sign to be posted in all commercial kitchens: NO SMOKING, EATING, OR DRINKING IN THE FOOD AREA! USE PLASTIC GLOVES WHEN HANDLING RAW MEAT! Across the state, chefs had promptly denounced the first admonition. How were they supposed to serve what they were preparing if they couldn't taste it? A subsequent missive from the inspector allowed as how we could taste with a plastic spoon, which was to be immediately tossed out. As Macguire and Arch would say, *Whatever.*

"Can you believe that?" Marla asked when she returned to the phone. "Frances Markasian from the *Mountain Journal* here at my doorstep already, wanting to interview me about what a bloodsucker my husband was. I told her *ex*-husband and suggested she go back to covering the doll show. Then I got this idea: 'Press Babsie—' "

"Frances knows about Suz? She knows about John Richard's arrest?"

"She knows *all* about it. Maybe she's got one of those police-band radios. More likely, somebody who lives on Jacobean called her. Frances insisted she needed to talk to me. Said it was urgent. What would be urgent about talking to me?"

"What in the world did you say?"

"I told her to come back on Monday," Marla replied gleefully. "I know I'll have more to report on the Jerk's bloodsuckiness by then."

"For heaven's sake." I glanced at the clock. Nearly noon. "Exactly when was Ralph Shelton fired?" I tried to remember the last time I'd catered any event where the Sheltons were present, but drew a blank. I'd known Ralph when John Richard was in medical school with him, and Ralph had a different wife and a daughter I adored. But when your marital situation changes, many of the friendships sadly seem to evaporate. "Where do the Sheltons live, exactly? Aren't they over there near John Richard?"

"Yes, of course. On Chaucer, I think. Ralph's a huge hockey fan so you'll probably see him tonight. Listen, though, here's something else I found out from Fay. Her hubbie, Ralph, wasn't the only one who had problems with Suz Craig. There was a nurse with a gambling addiction. ACHMO didn't fancy one of their RNs taking the bus up to Central City and avidly playing the slots, hour after hour."

"Gambling? Do you know the nurse's name? Would Fay?"

"She didn't say, but I could ask her. On second thought, the word is that Ralph Shelton has a temper, which he usually reserves for yelling at referees at Avalanche games. If I act nosy, he might slam me into the glass. Metaphorically speaking, of course. You're more subtle, Goldy. *You* should go talk to him."

"Oh, sure. What am I, the local gal who deals with bad-tempered doctors?" I heard Tom's Chrysler roll into the driveway.

"How's Arch handling his father being arrested?" Marla asked.

"Wretchedly. He and Macguire are out for a walk now."

"Did Arch like Suz?"

I sighed. "Arch never likes or dislikes John Richard's girl-friends. He just tolerates them. It's a survival mechanism."

"You know he's going to want you to help him clear his dad. You've acquired a reputation as a woman who can nose around criminal cases like that godawful bloodhound of his."

I groaned. "Yeah, sure. This is one criminal case I'm going to keep my nose out of, thanks all the same."

"Listen," she insisted, as I heard Tom's footsteps approach on the deck. His slow trudge signaled that things were not going well. "You could drop by the Sheltons' place on your way to the McCrackens', Goldy. Say you got lost, need directions, and"—here she raised her voice to a trill—"oh, *by the way*, Ralph, old buddy, any ideas about what John Richard and Suz Craig were squabbling about last night? Think he got mad enough at the club bar that he went home and beat her to death?"

"Marla—"

"On second thought, Ralph baby," she trilled, undeterred, "were you so mad at her for canning you that *you* went home and killed her? Keep your hockey helmet on now, Ralph, and your stick down—"

"Please, I *have* to go."

"Promise you'll call me if you have any more post-traumatic whatever-it-is flashes."

I hung up.

Tom lumbered into the kitchen and headed straight for the sink to wash his hands. I suspected it was less because of my careful training than it was his desire to rid himself of whatever psychological muck he was bringing home from the sheriff's department. His face seemed haggard and downcast. My heart sank.

"I'm sorry," I blurted out, "it looks as if you've been dealing with John Richard."

"Don't be sorry," he said as he dropped into one of the kitchen chairs. He had pulled on blue jeans and a navy cotton shirt when I'd called him this morning. Despite the casual clothes, he didn't look as if he'd had anything close to a casual day. He rubbed his eyes, then added, "It's not your fault he is the way he is. Never was."

"He's like herpes," I said. "You just never know when he's going to erupt."

Tom offered no reply. I glanced at him expecting a smile, but his handsome face stayed set in deep thought, his lovely liquid green eyes fixed on the table. I turned back to the orzo salad.

The densely fragrant chèvre cheese fell into appetizing bits as my knife sliced through it. I chopped fragrant fresh basil and crisp stalks of celery, then mixed them in with the orzo. Next I whisked seasonings into balsamic vinegar and began to beat in garlic-flavored oil for an emulsion. When the dressing turned thick and creamy, I poured it over the orzo and vegetables, then stirred it carefully. Although I knew the salad should chill, I was ravenous. I delicately mixed in the chèvre, then reached for a plastic spoon to have a taste. When I put the spoonful into my mouth, the pungent Mediterranean flavors of crumbly cheese and garlic-robed pasta almost made me swoon.

I turned to Tom. "Hungry? I'll bet you haven't had anything besides vending-machine coffee and Danish."

"Sure. I'll take whatever you've got going."

I ladled out a large bowl of the warmly fragrant pasta salad. On a whim, even though it was just past noon, I poured him a glass of Chianti. I figured he needed it. Then I poured myself one, figuring I needed it even more.

Mediterranean
Orzo Salad

1 cup (6 ounces) uncooked orzo pasta

3 tablespoons finely chopped red onion

1 cup seeded, chopped fresh tomato
   (about 3 small tomatoes)

1/4 cup chopped celery

2 tablespoons chopped fresh basil (or
   more if desired)

2 tablespoons finely chopped pitted
   Kalamata olives

2 tablespoons capers

1 teaspoon "grained" Dijon mustard

1/4 teaspoon sugar

1 tablespoon balsamic vinegar

2 tablespoons garlic oil (available in
   specialty food shops, such as Williams-
   Sonoma)

Salt and freshly ground black pepper

3 1/2 ounces chèvre, crumbled

Bring a large quantity of water to a boil and
cook the orzo just until tender ("al dente").
Drain and allow to cool. Mix the pasta with the

onion, tomato, celery, basil, olives, and capers. In a small bowl, whisk together the mustard, sugar, and vinegar. Gradually beat in the oil until an emulsion forms. Pour this vinaigrette over the pasta mixture and season with salt and pepper. Chill the salad. When it is cold, mix in the crumbled chèvre, then serve.

Serves 4

"This is absolutely delicious," he murmured appreciatively after the first few bites. "I'm sure the hockey folks will love it." I gave him a kiss, thanked him, tucked the rest of the salad into the walk-in refrigerator to chill, and turned to the mountain of mushrooms, onions, and zucchini I needed to trim for the Grilled Slapshot Salad.

I said, "Want me to keep working, or do you want me to sit with you for a bit?"

He shook his head. "Think I need my hand held?"

"No, I didn't mean—" I blurted out. But he held out his hand and I took it.

"No. Fault's mine, Miss G. I've been put in the background on this case and I'm blaming you, which I shouldn't. Actually, please stop worrying about *me*. You're the one who should be stressed out. My wife the caterer, the one who refuses to see a victim advocate no matter how bad things get."

"Oh, please."

"*Oh, please*, yourself, Miss G. Talk to me."

I sat at the table across from him and took a sip of wine. Its acrid taste burned into my chest. I sighed. "This . . . event. It's horrid. Whenever I stop chopping or cooking, the memories flood in. I'm desperate to know what's going on. At the same time, I want—I *need*—it to be over."

He nodded. "Makes sense. Should we all go up to the cabin for a while?" Tom's lovely, remote log dwelling outside of Aspen Meadow had flooded this spring, and he'd lost his tenants. Tom and I had scrubbed the floors and walls. Over the Jerk's objections that we were spoiling Arch, we'd paid him to wash the windows. But we hadn't yet advertised for new renters. Maybe going to the cabin wasn't such a great notion. I knew Tom, Arch, and Macguire wouldn't relish being away from our home base for an extended time. And if I stayed up there alone, I'd brood and fret even more.

"No, thanks. I just need to work. Be with you all. And . . . although I know it's going to be tough, I'd like to keep informed on what's happening. Arch is going to have questions around the clock."

His fingers stroked my hair. "Okay. Keep cooking, if that's what you need to do. And I'd be happy to tell you what's going on. It'll make me feel as if *I'm* doing something on this case." He sounded glum.

I frowned at the vegetables. "There's one thing I told Beiner that you should know." I related to him Macguire's suspicion that ReeAnn Collins, John Richard's secretary for the past six months, was romantically involved with him. Tom put down his fork, retrieved his spiral notebook from his back pocket, and made a note. While I heated the kitchen stovetop grill for the Slapshot Salad, I shared Marla's news about John Richard and Suz's fight at the club last night, and that Suz had reportedly fired a doctor named Ralph Shelton and a nurse whose name I did not know.

"Yeah"— Tom shook his head—"there was some kind of problem with this Craig woman being able to keep people. We don't know much yet, but we do know that."

I nodded, then felt a pang of guilt. "Are you sure you want to talk to me about the case? I mean, after what happened last time, when Marla got into so much trouble?"

He looked at me intently. "Miss G. I can't believe you'd really want to get any more involved in this than you are already."

"Excuse me, but my first responsibility is to Arch. Whatever that looks like." I felt the edge creep into my voice and despised myself for it. Tom, after all, was not the enemy. "I'm sorry. I . . . just need to know what's going on. No surprises."

"Some cases have surprises. It's the nature of the work."

"Maybe so, but I need to know the surprises in this case before Arch does."

He sighed. I slathered slices of zucchini with a mixture of olive oil and minced garlic. When I laid the glistening wedges on the heated grill, Tom pushed his empty bowl aside.

"All right. Near as they can figure, Suz Craig died between three and five this morning. Rigor hadn't set in when the medics arrived, which is one of the reasons they tried to revive her. There

Grilled
Slapshot Salad

2 tablespoons extra-virgin olive oil
Salt and freshly ground pepper to taste
3 large or 4 small garlic cloves, pressed,
    or 1½ teaspoons finely minced garlic
3 medium-size or 4 small zucchini
8 ounces fresh whole mushrooms
1 sweet onion (sometimes called
    Mexican sweet onion or Peruvian
    sweet onion)
2 ears fresh or frozen corn, defrosted
1 tablespoon (or more) sherry vinaigrette
    (see Exhibition Salad with Meringue-
    Baked Pecans, page 308)
1 to 2 tablespoons chopped fresh basil

Whisk together the oil, salt, pepper, and garlic and divide it between two 9- by 13-inch glass pans. Slice the zucchini on the bias into ¼″ slices, place the slices into one of the pans, and mix carefully with your hands so that all the zucchini slices are lightly coated with the oil-garlic mixture. Trim the stems of the mushrooms. Slice the onion horizontally into ¼″ slices. Place the mushrooms, onion slices, and corn into the other glass pan and again mix carefully by hand so that all the vegetables are lightly coated with the oil-garlic mixture.

Oil and preheat the grill. Preheat the oven to 400°. Place the zucchini slices on the grill and cook briefly—no longer than 30 seconds—on one side only. Place the zucchini slices back into their glass pan, cooked side up, and put them into the oven while you prepare the rest of the salad (no longer than 10 minutes). Briefly grill the mushrooms, onion slices, and corn on all sides, until they have grill marks but are not cooked through. This should only take a few minutes. Remove the onion slices and mushrooms and set them aside to cool. Holding each ear of corn perpendicular to the cutting surface, slice off the kernels. Remove the zucchini from the oven. Combine the zucchini slices, mushrooms, onion slices, and corn kernels. Pour the vinaigrette over the vegetables and carefully stir in the fresh basil. Serve immediately or chill for no more than 1 hour.

Serves 4

are signs of a struggle in her house, pots and pans strewn about in the kitchen. The guys are out doing a neighborhood canvass asking questions, but so far there's very little."

"Two policewomen were over here."

"Beiner and Irving. They're good." His sandy eyebrows rose. "There was more vandalism in the country club sometime during the night. Looks like kids painting street signs and fences again, but who knows? One possibility is that Suz surprised the vandals somehow, and they killed her. On the other hand, only the club's walls and a few street signs were spray-painted last night. We thought we were dealing with late-at-night vandals, but we may be dealing with early-morning ones. Of course, that wouldn't explain why her kitchen pans were on the floor. Or why she died clutching a gold ID bracelet that said '*To JRK: You're the best. Love, SC.*' " He took a deep breath. "Korman, of course, is claiming someone stole his bracelet. He also says he left her house between midnight and one o'clock, after they had that little disagreement you were referring to."

I removed the grilled zucchini slices with their lovely diagonal dark stripes, then placed them in a separate, lightly oiled pan to finish in the oven. "Little disagreement, my Aunt Fanny. John Richard will drink and argue for *hours*. Sometimes he loses his temper right away, sometimes he waits, especially if he's trying to get something out of you. Like a bonus, say." I slipped the pan into the oven. The air was wonderfully fragrant. "I think he just snapped. Beat the daylights out of her, then had no idea she'd walk out of her house and go looking for help. That's my theory, anyway."

Tom shrugged. "He's been unwavering on the leaving-at-one story. But even if he did leave after assaulting her, if she walked out of her house and died from falling into that ditch, he's still our man."

"Tom, if there's something I know well, it's that John Richard lies. He lies so much it's exhausting to try to untangle what he says. This morning, when I saw those roses in his hand, I thought: *This is one of his lies*. It just comes naturally to him. I used to try to figure out why he lied. I thought it was because his mother was an alcoholic or because of the trouble with his father. But that's no excuse. He's still a pathological liar."

Tom actually chuckled. "Yeah, Miss G., they usually are." He pushed his chair out from the table. "How about a hug for a hard-working cop?"

I smiled and dumped the mushrooms on the hot grill, where they made a delicious hissing sound. Then Tom pulled me into his lap for a marvelous, tight embrace.

"Captain called me in for a heart-to-heart," he murmured into my ear. "They're appointing a district attorney's investigator to head the case. But I'm not officially *off* the homicide investigation. I'm just behind the scenes. Can't go anywhere or interrogate anyone or gather any evidence unless I take somebody with me. That's how they avoid conflict of interest."

"I thought you hated that D.A.'s investigator. He's always mooching food. What's his name?"

"Donny Saunders. The laziest guy in a four-state area. And arrogant on top of that." He sighed. "Better go get those mushrooms before they burn."

I jumped up and scooped the mushrooms into a large bowl, then placed golden ears of corn and thick, glistening onion slices on the grill. They hissed and sputtered and filled the kitchen with a divine scent. I flipped the slices and rotated the corn so the kernels browned evenly. When I was removing these, I felt Tom's arms gently circling my waist.

"I'm cooking," I reminded him as I turned off the burners.

He nuzzled my cheek and whispered, "Looks to me like you're almost done. And I'm not hearing Arch, Macguire, and Jake. Can that possibly mean we have the house to ourselves for one brief moment?"

I tried to suppress a smile. I couldn't. "Actually, it does."

He took my hand and we walked wordlessly up the stairs. The

bedsheets were cool and inviting. As we began to make love, a warm, gentle summer breeze filled the lace curtains, like a woman's skirt being lifted.

"I love you," I said afterward.

He turned his handsome, wide face to me and smiled. "I love you, too."

"And in case reading ID bracelets has put any doubt in your mind," I added, "*you're* the best."

Chapter 9

Tom kissed me and said that unless I needed him, he was going to catch up on his sleep. I told him to nap away, I still had tons of work to do. Then I tiptoed down the stairs and took the chilled bag of tuna fillets out of the walk-in refrigerator just as the boys traipsed back into the kitchen with Jake. While Arch diligently ran water and plopped ice cubes into a bowl for his bloodhound, Macguire slouched with a gusty, exhausted sigh into one of the chairs. He put his head in his hands and groaned. I ran the water to rinse the fish. I was waiting for Macguire to say, at long last, that he was hungry. He didn't.

"I should go back to bed," he said after another guttural moan. "I'm so tired. Can you do this bash without me?" When I told him I could, he turned to Arch. "Buddy? Thanks for the walk. Sorry we couldn't get over to your dad's office. I'm trashed now, need to hit the sack."

Arch nodded and poured himself a glass of pink lemonade.

"Macguire," I attempted, "please, can I fix you a little something to eat—"

He waved this away and put his head in his hands again, apparently too weary to climb the stairs to his room. I placed the first tuna fillets in a glass pan. Unfortunately, at that moment Murphy's law of telephones kicked in and my business line rang. I begged Arch to answer it so I wouldn't slime the receiver with fish juice. He gave me a world-weary look that immediately changed to one of concern when he realized who was on the other end of the line.

"Oh! Dad! How are you doing? Can I come see you?"

I swallowed hard. Macguire blinked and then blinked again, his expression turning quickly from fatigue to interest. I patted the fillets dry, then washed my hands, trying to decide what to do. Grab the phone from Arch? Write him a note to let me talk? Did I really want to speak to the Jerk? I viciously ground pepper over the fish. But it was too early to marinate the fillets. I dithered, stamped from foot to foot while trying to catch Arch's eye, then snapped plastic wrap over the fish.

"Oh, Dad, I'm so glad you called me. Wow, I'm sorry you have to . . . Oh, that sounds awful! Gosh, I can't believe . . ."

Saturday, just past noon—less than five hours since the arrest. John Richard had been processed; was he calling me or his son? Had he talked to his lawyer? Why call here? Unfortunately, despite my feelings on the subject, I could not prevent Arch from talking to his father.

"Where's Tom?" Macguire whispered as I forced myself to turn my back on Arch and glare at the menu. I was not going to listen to the conversation. No matter what the Jerk was up to, I still had to finish my next catering task.

I said, "Tom's asleep."

Still the earnest whisper from Macguire. "You should wake him up. He should know—"

"Macguire. If John Richard Korman wants to talk to me, he

Goalies' Grilled Tuna

4 (6 to 8 ounces each) fresh boneless
   tuna steaks
Salt and freshly ground black pepper
¼ cup sherry vinaigrette (see Exhibition
   Salad with Meringue-Baked Pecans,
   page 308)

Rinse the tuna steaks and pat them dry. Place
them in a glass pan, season with salt and pepper, and pour the vinaigrette over them. Cover
with plastic wrap and marinate for 30 minutes
to 1 hour.

Preheat the grill. Grill the steaks for 2 to 3 minutes per side for rare, 5 minutes per side for
well done.

Serves 4

would have demanded to do so. That's the way he is. But he called our son. They have a right to talk. And as a witness, I *can't* talk to him."

Still, when I sneaked a glance at Arch's freckled face, I was shocked. My son's cheeks, previously flushed with color from his walk with Macguire and Jake, were now translucently pale. A scowl set his face in an expression of worry so deep that I hated John Richard more than ever. How *could* the man drag our son into this? Arch held out the phone.

He said eagerly, "Mom, Dad wants to talk to you."

Well, great. I shook my head vigorously at the proffered phone. Arch's eyes flared wide behind the tortoiseshell glasses.

"Yes, yes, you have to!" he whispered fiercely.

I reached for a kitchen towel and grabbed the receiver. "What is it?" I asked in a clipped tone. "I'm not supposed to be talking to you. You must know that. I'm a witness, remember?"

"Witness to what?" His voice grated through the wire. I was sorely tempted to hang up. No matter how hard I tried to put this man out of my life, he always insisted on reappearing, full of menace. At that moment I didn't care what kind of trouble he was in. I didn't want to hear about it. I didn't want to be a part of it.

Arch leaned toward me and whispered earnestly, "You need to help Dad, Mom. Please!" Behind Arch, Macguire opened his eyes wide. He had perked up considerably since the phone call began. If Macguire was thinking about getting involved with criminals again, I'd have the kid thrown into jail myself.

"I'm listening," I said brusquely into the receiver. "But you're jeopardizing your case by talking to me."

"I'll take that chance."

"I have a lot of work to do."

"Well, excuse me for interrupting your cooking schedule," John Richard snarled. "I just need to discuss this mess that *you* got me into. Understand? I'm in a life-threatening situation here. I'm sitting in the jail, I don't know what's going on, and I need you to do something for me. If you hadn't been cruising by Suz's house at that hour—"

"I told you," I said through clenched teeth. Just like the man to make Suz Craig's murder my fault, just because I'd had the bad luck to discover her body. "I didn't want Arch to get to your place with nobody home—"

"Shut up and *listen* for once, Goldy, will you? There's a whole line of thugs waiting to use this phone. I just . . . I can't . . . nobody will *tell* me anything. It's driving me nuts. I need to know what the police have found out about *when* Suz died."

More than ever, his supreme arrogance astonished me. "Even if I knew that"—which of course I did—"I couldn't tell you. Look, I don't think we should be—"

"When she died is important—"

"Why do you think I—"

"Well, I'll find out soon enough," he fumed. "If you want our son to suffer from this escapade, because that's all it is, then just *be difficult.*"

I said nothing. I'd learned this lesson the hard way. You talk, you give him something to criticize. You say nothing, you may eventually get out of the conversation. Without getting hurt.

"Goldy? Are you listening to me? Goldy? Or are you holding the phone away from your ear?"

I smiled at Arch and Macguire, who were both staring at me in consternation. "I'm listening," I replied evenly.

John Richard resumed his fake-earnest tone. "Look. It's just that if I could know the *time* of death right now, instead of having to wait for the damn lawyers to jaw about it, a lot of things could get cleared up. My attorney is hiring his own investigator, and he thinks if we get the right judge there's a chance I'll be able to get out of here on Monday—"

Dream on, I thought. Actually, as I'd told Arch, one in a million chance. I'd heard of it exactly once. So in our state that would make it one in four million point . . . What was our state's population?

"Did you hear what I said?" my ex-husband yelled.

"Monday," I repeated. I glanced at the tuna fillets and the menu with lists of dishes I still had to prepare for this evening. Actually, I was running a bit ahead of schedule. No way I was telling him *that*, though.

"Okay, now listen up," the Jerk continued, undaunted, "I want you to use that morbid curiosity of yours to check on a few things. First, there's this nurse named Amy Bartholomew. Suz fired her. Now she's doing something with the new health-food store, I think. Also, Suz had an unpleasant visit in July from Ralph Shelton. Do you remember him? She fired him, too. Plus, Suz had some kind of delicate material—"

"Hey! Stop!" I interrupted him. Goosebumps ran over my skin. "I can't do any of that. Even *you* must recognize how inappropriate it would be for me to go poking around—"

"No, I *don't* recognize that—"

"It is hard for me to believe that your self-centeredness extends this far," I snapped. "You cannot possibly think that the wife of a police officer, who happens to be your badly treated ex-wife, should go snooping around—"

"Mom!" Arch's eyes blazed. "Stop it!" he hissed. "You *have* to *help* him!"

"My self-centeredness!" John Richard was shrieking. "My *self-centeredness*!"

This time I did hold the phone away from my ear. Arch pressed his fingers against his eyes and shook his head. The tormented expression on his face made my heart ache. With a ragged breath I said: "John Richard, I need to get off the phone."

His icy tone chilled my blood. "I did not kill Suz Craig. I loved her." He paused, then continued very deliberately, "It's time for you to set aside your *own* self-centeredness. For the sake of our son and his mental health, you need to help me prove that I'm being set up for this damn murder. Do you understand?"

I covered the phone with my hand. "Arch?" I asked with as

much calmness as I could muster. My son gave me a defiant look, scowled, and crossed his arms. He was silent. "Would you please go upstairs for a few minutes and let me finish this phone call?" After a fractional hesitation he turned and hurtled out of the kitchen. Macguire made no move to go anywhere except to shuffle toward the walk-in, muttering about needing a Pepsi. "Macguire," I pleaded, "just give me a minute here, okay?"

"I'm not going to bother you," Macguire said innocently. "I just need a pop. Maybe I'll see something in there that will make me hungry. You never know."

"Goldy," John Richard raged, "could you let go of domestic life for a *minute* and listen to me? I did not commit this crime. I left Suz's house at one A.M. When I left, she was fine."

"If you left her house at one and she was fine," I repeated calmly, "then tell that to your investigator. If you have done nothing wrong, then you have nothing to worry about." Then I hung up.

"What's going on?" asked Macguire solicitously. He held a soft-drink can in one hand and the parfait glass of chocolate pudding in the other—the same one he'd turned up his nose at earlier.

I cleared my throat. "Apart from the fact that my ex-husband has been arrested for homicide and my son believes I should try to get him off?" I sighed. My head ached. I sat down, rubbing my temples. "Let's see, the only other things going on are that I've got a big party to cater tonight. Oh, yes, and my son is absolutely furious with me. Apart from that, not much."

"Bummer," said Macguire. He set the pudding aside, untouched, poured the soft drink into a glass, then slurped fizz from the top. "Know what? I don't need a nap, I think. I'll see if Arch wants to talk or listen to music. We'll be quiet, though. We won't bother you, I promise."

I murmured a grateful thanks and stared at the ingredients for a second batch of biscuits. As usual when dealing with John Richard, a sense of unreality closed in. Was I crazy, or was he? He was crazy. No question. A crazy liar, always had been. But then—and this had always puzzled me—how could he be so successful in the rest of his life, the part of his life that did not involve me? He had a fantastic job, lots of money, and a steady stream of girlfriends. People *liked* him. Was it his looks? Well, that was part of it. And he was intelligent. No genius, but he could sound good and fake his way through the situations he knew nothing about. Add to that his great ability to talk and charm his way into people's hearts. And so far he'd been able to lie and cheat his way out of the many, many messes he'd made. And he'd been able to keep the messes quiet.

I did not kill Suz Craig. Yeah, sure. I again measured flour, baking powder, and salt into my food processor, scooped in smooth white vegetable shortening, and let the blade slice the mixture into tiny bits. *Then why were you bringing flowers over this morning? Why did she have a death grasp on your ID bracelet? Why are you trying to find out the time of death? So you can change your story?* I shuddered. I was *not* going to help him. No matter how manipulative he managed to be. No matter how much he dragged Arch into this.

Poor Arch. I pulsed the processor and watched the blade bite through the ingredients. He wanted so much for me to help his father. But I couldn't. The man was evil. I dribbled in buttermilk until the dough clung together in a ball. I wanted to tell Arch that trying to follow one of his father's lies to get to the truth was futile. You get involved with John Richard, you get sucked into a vortex just like old Captain Ahab, and end up at the bottom of the ocean. As I scooped the silky dough out of the processor, my mind reverted to one of its common themes: How come the evil people in your life don't just *die?* How come the evil people in your life are able to kill smart, promising women like Suz Craig?

Well, the rain falls on the just and the unjust.

Then again, *had* Suz been so smart and promising? Had there perhaps been an evil side to Suz Craig, too? I thought of the rumors Marla had gathered about the dead woman. *No, no, no,* I chided myself. *Don't get into this.* So what if she fired Amy Bartholomew, the nurse who supposedly had gambling problems? So what if she fired

Ralph Shelton? I preheated the oven and rolled out the biscuit dough into a soft, rectangular pillow.

Suz, after all, was a boss-type person, and a boss-type person sometimes had to fire people. As sole proprietor of my business, I was thankful I'd never had to perform that particular function myself. I brandished the puck-size biscuit cutter I'd finally found at a baking supply store and cut the dough into circles. Then I arrayed them carefully on a cookie sheet.

I was *not* going to get dragged into this. *Suz had an unpleasant visit in July from Ralph Shelton. Do you remember him?* John Richard's sarcastic voice echoed in my thoughts. Of course I remembered Ralph Shelton the doctor, the hockey fan extraordinaire. We used to be friends. Like John Richard, Ralph had specialized in ob-gyn at the University of Colorado Medical School. Another buddy of theirs had been Patricia McCracken's ex-husband, Skip. Skip had moved to Colorado Springs, and I hadn't seen him in years.

Ralph Shelton. What was his history? I set the timer for the biscuits and thought back. Ralph had divorced his first wife, a petite, very erudite teacher, and over her pained objections, obtained sole custody of their daughter, Jill, who was Arch's age. Problem was, Ralph hadn't been able to take care of Jill when he'd gone on business trips, had late meetings, or had to deliver a baby. So he'd turned to me to take care of his daughter, over and over and over. Meanwhile, Jill's own mother was desperate to have the girl down in her new place in Albuquerque. With mounting problems in my own marriage and young Arch unable to shake a string of ear infections, I'd finally told Ralph I couldn't take care of his daughter three or four times a week. Combined with my separation from John Richard, this had meant the end of the friendship with Ralph Shelton, unfortunately. The worst part was that Ralph had finally sent his daughter to live with her mother in New Mexico. Arch and I had missed Jill terribly. She'd been a fun-loving child with such an infectious laugh that our house had felt empty for weeks after she moved away.

The timer beeped. I slapped the cookie sheet out of the oven with an overenthusiastic bang, then rolled and cut out another batch of biscuits. I stared at the cutter in my hand. I'd been so proud of myself for finding the cutter. When the biscuits were baked, they were the exact dimensions of a hockey puck. Perfect for tonight's party.

Ralph's a big hockey fan, Marla had told me. No kidding. Back in the medical-school days, the only way Ralph Shelton could relieve his academic anxiety was to go to hockey games at McNichols Arena, where he'd bought lifetime season tickets for our ill-fated first NHL team, the Colorado Rockies. I had never understood how Ralph could vent his frustration by cheering for such a poorly performing team. Glumly reporting their losses whenever we got together, Ralph's face had been ruddy and lined. What little hair he had had turned prematurely gray around a widening bald spot. Whether the hair loss resulted from the pain of being a Rockies hockey fan or the prospect of practicing medicine, I knew not. When the franchise had moved on, Ralph had been disconsolate. Whether his enthusiasms had subsequently shifted to baseball, when the new team named the Rockies were swinging bats and setting homerun and attendance records at newly built Coors Field, I knew not. By then, Ralph Shelton had passed out of my orbit. And I'd had my hands too full with the divorce from John Richard to care.

Wait a minute. Sometimes a girlfriend will dye her hair, and become virtually unrecognizable. I watched my oven timer ticking down the seconds until this batch of biscuits would be done. I remembered Ralph Shelton; I'd seen him quite recently. I just hadn't recognized him out of context and with a new look. His bald head had been covered by a billed cap. He'd exchanged his sports-fan garb for gardening clothes. He'd grown a mustache that was prematurely white. I watched my clock. What else? He'd been eager to see what the paramedics were doing. This morning, my old friend Ralph Shelton had been one of the gawking neighbors on Jacobean Drive.

Chapter 10

The food, I scolded myself. *Work!* I perused my recipe for Vietnamese slaw. Napa cabbage, carrots, very lightly steamed snow peas—all these needed to be julienned. When my hand became tired from slicing, I decided to stop and check the phone book. Ralph and Fay Shelton lived on Chaucer Drive, one street over from Suz Craig's street. So what had Ralph been doing up so early this morning? Taking a stroll around the neighborhood? I couldn't wait for Tom to wake up.

The phone rang. Patricia McCracken's voice zinged across the wire. "I can't cancel this party," she wailed.

"You'd better not," I exclaimed as I stared at the mountains of colorful vegetables I'd already cut into uniform thin slices.

"The police have been here, Goldy. I was so nervous about seeing everybody at this party, my first public appearance since I filed the suits, that I took a sleeping pill last night. I don't remember a thing." She took a deep breath and added defiantly, "I didn't kill that HMO lady."

"Oh-kay," I said as I searched my shelves for rice wine vinegar. "Do you think John Richard killed her?"

"I don't know."

"See you at five then." She didn't wait for me to say good-bye.

What an odd call. I whisked sesame oil with the rice wine vinegar and thought back to the wet spring we'd just come through. I had seen Patricia and her son, Tyler, once, at the library. It had been a momentous spring for our town library, but not because the incessant rain had brought any heightened demand for books. The cause for sensation had been the foxes that had made their den in the rocky hillside behind the windowed reading room. When a litter of five cubs was produced, the births became big-time small-town news. Soon the fox cubs were claiming the early-evening hours to cavort, tumble, and prance through the quartz and granite spillway in full view of an audience of excited children of all ages. Never mind that reading in the high-windowed room became impossible. Any visitor to or from the library was greeted with the same query: "Seen the foxes?"

Paying a visit to the reading room, Arch and I had encountered Patricia dragging a recalcitrant, whining Tyler with one hand and balancing an armload of Dr. Seuss books with the other.

"Did you see the foxes, Tyler?" I'd asked her son happily. "Are they out tonight?"

Tyler had given me a grumpy stare and let out a wail. Patricia had snarled, "We're not interested in a family of foxes. Not now. Not ever."

Startled, I'd pulled open the massive door to the library for Arch. When he passed by me, he'd mumbled, "What—does she raise chickens or something?"

Not even close, I realized now as I folded the sweet-sour dressing into the slaw ingredients. Struggling with the recent loss of her baby, Patricia hadn't wanted to see the fox cubs playing. The notion of a big, happy family had been slipping from her grasp. I covered the enormous bowl with plastic wrap and popped it into the walk-in refrigerator.

"If you're making so-good food noises, I want some," Tom announced cheerfully as he strode into the room. "Oh, man." He took in a greedy breath. "More biscuits?"

I nodded and removed the last cookie sheet of the golden, puffed rounds, then silently split one, slathered it with butter and blackberry jam, and handed the plate with it to Tom. When he finished, I'd tell him about seeing Ralph Shelton.

While he sat down and began to eat, I put in another batch of biscuits. I iced the dark chocolate cupcakes, which would surround a centerpiece hockey-rink-shaped cake provided by Aspen Meadow Pastry Shop. I placed the cupcakes in covered plastic containers. I wasn't going to brood anymore. I was in my wonderful kitchen, filled with marvelous scents, and feeding the man I loved most in the world. Then I realized he was watching me.

"Tom? What is it?"

"Final batch of biscuits about to come out?"

"In a little bit."

He paused, then glanced at the clock. "How's your time going? When do you have to leave?"

"In about an hour. Why?"

His face grew wary. "I'm worried about Arch."

"So am I. But what makes you mention it? Did he tell you about the phone call?" Doggone John Richard, anyway.

Tom shook his head. "No, he didn't. He didn't say a word. When I went by his room, he was sitting ramrod stiff in his desk chair, staring at nothing. I asked him if he wanted to talk, and he said 'Not to you, I don't.'"

My spirits, briefly raised by my productive work, fell flat. I guessed Macguire had not been successful trying to entice Arch into listening to music. I grabbed a chair and sat. "Tom. Arch wants me to help John Richard. He's desperate for me to prove his father's innocence."

Tom groaned. "Goldy, you can't. I told you I'd keep you informed. But this isn't like that time you found the body in the woods by Elk Park Prep. This time the prime suspect showed up at the scene, started raising Cain, and was arrested. You can't get involved in this: you're a *witness*. Listen, let's get Arch down here to talk—"

I held up a hand to stop him. "John Richard called here about a half hour ago."

"He called here? Wanting to talk to you? Do you know how illegal that is?"

"I told him. He claimed he called to talk to Arch. But then he told Arch to put me on. Even from jail he was his usual manipulative self, whining to Arch and demanding to know from me what time Suz died so that he could use his medical knowledge of rigor mortis to prove he's not the murderer."

Tom chuckled cynically. "That guy. Maybe he was trying to reconstruct his timetable." He frowned. His sandy eyebrows drew into a furry, uneven line. "You didn't tell him anything, did you?"

I shot him an exasperated look. "Of course not."

"I can just tell," he said resignedly, "that this is going to be one holy mess."

"Listen, Tom, remember when I told you about a doctor Suz had supposedly fired, one named Ralph Shelton? What I didn't tell you was about John Richard's and my history with him." Briefly, I summarized how we'd all known one another years ago, when Arch was small. "Anyway," I said, "Ralph's a tall bald fellow with a white mustache. I know he was one of those guys I shooed away from the ditch this morning. I didn't recognize him because he looked so different with a cap on his head. Plus, his hair used to be gray, not white, and he didn't have a mustache."

Tom narrowed his eyes. "You're kidding."

"I'm not. Ralph was there, trying to see what the paramedics were doing. He was wearing gardening clothes and a baseball cap. Your guys must have talked to him in their neighborhood canvass." I thought back to the fashionable camouflage-print pants, wide suspenders, dark billed cap, and handspun collarless shirt Ralph had been wearing that morning. In retrospect, it was perhaps too studied an outfit to have donned so early in the morning. But something else nagged at my memory. What was it? Something about Ralph hadn't looked quite right. What? But my tired brain refused to yield any details.

"I'll check on Shelton," said Tom curtly. "But I do think you need to go talk to Arch. I'll pack this stuff up."

"The last time you packed my stuff I had to make risotto from scratch for a Fourth of July party. As I recall, you thought it would be funny to substitute ingredients on me, so I wouldn't go snooping around in a suspect's house."

He stood and rinsed his dish. "I thought," he said without missing a beat, "that I would be keeping you out of trouble by making you do extra work that time, Miss G. Besides, I apologized and you forgave me. No fair hassling me about it now." He reached into the pantry for several of the large cardboard boxes I used for carting food.

I walked up the stairs, thinking. Shower, change, call Marla—all these I had to do before leaving. Plus talk to Arch, get him smoothed out on his father being thrown into jail under suspicion of committing a brutal murder. Sure.

My son sat slumped in his desk chair. His lank brown hair was uncombed. His glasses perched halfway down his nose. Julian's cast-off T-shirt hung on his motionless body. I longed to hug him tightly, the way I had when he was small and I'd always been able to comfort him.

"Arch. Hon, please. Let's talk."

"About what?" His voice was toneless.

"May I come in?"

His eyes didn't leave the pile of magazines on his desk. He shrugged. "I thought you had a party to do."

"Arch, please, I'm worried about you."

"Yeah, well, *I'm* worried about *Dad*." He whirled and faced me, his brown eyes ablaze. "You just don't care, do you?"

I sat on the bed. Honesty was the best policy. "You know how when you leave your homework in your room? I don't snatch it up and go running to school to bail you out. It's called being responsible for your actions—"

"Oh, Mom!" he yelled, his tone disgusted. He glared at me. "Don't treat me like a baby! Just don't start, okay?"

"No, then," I said frankly, "I don't care about your father. I only care about you."

"If you cared about me," he shot back fiercely, "you'd be willing to at least *think* about whether he did this murder or not. Dad isn't lying."

"Did he tell you that he hit Suz the way he used to hit me? He admitted that to Tom and me, you know. That was one of the reasons Tom arrested him this morning. I'm just telling you the truth here, Arch. I'm sorry if the facts are so painful. I don't mean to hurt you."

He pushed abruptly out of his chair. "I need to go. I need to go check some things out."

"What things?"

"There's a nurse who runs a health-food store—"

"Don't you even think about doing your father's investigative errands, young man. His lawyer will hire an investigator on Monday."

"So now you're going to say I can't go to the health-food store?"

"What are you planning on doing there?"

"I don't know yet." He stood in front of the mirror and frowned at himself. Apparently going to the health-food store did not warrant clothes changing or hair combing. "Don't worry, Mom." His voice carried a hint of conciliation. "I'll get Macguire to go with me."

"He's asleep," I said, hoping this was true. I hadn't heard a peep out of Macguire since he'd shuffled out of the kitchen carrying his soft drink.

"I'll wake him up! It'll be good for him to walk again, anyway."

"He'll pass out."

"Mom!" Once again I got the angry, indignant stare. "Will you stop bugging me? Why won't you at least *admit* Dad might be down there in jail for no reason? Whatever happened to *innocent until proven guilty?*"

I rose from the bed, walked to the door, and assumed a quiet tone. "I love you, Arch. I just don't want to see you getting involved in your dad's problems."

He pushed past me. It was an unconscious, but more gentle, imitation of his father's shove by me that morning. "Sorry, Mom. I already am involved. I wish you would help him. He really needs you."

Well, great. I quietly made my way to Tom's and my room to get ready for the evening party. My heart ached.

Fifteen minutes later I'd showered, changed, and punched in a call to Marla's answering machine. When I went out the door, luminescent gray clouds billowed just at the edge of the western horizon. Even this early in August, snow would be falling each morning on the highest peaks to the west. When the afternoon sun warmed and wilted that ephemeral white blanket, the mountain towns on the Front Range would get a brief, deliciously cooling rain. But first the moisture would build into luxuriant cumulus towers that resembled fantastic, brilliant mushrooms. Once these clouds completely filled the western sky, they would spill eastward over the hillsides.

Tom had loaded my supplies and announced that he was going to the hardware store, one of his favorite Saturday-afternoon occupations. He seldom came home with more than a dollar's worth of washers, screws, and nails. Sometimes Arch accompanied him. But I found these excursions deadly boring. Guy stuff. Not surprisingly, Arch had declined accompanying Tom, and my husband had rumbled off alone in his dark sedan.

Arch. I revved the van and backed out of the driveway. It was early, a good thing since I needed to drive around a little bit to think. At the end of our street, I turned and headed along the creek. When I passed Aspen Meadow Nursery on the left and Aspen Meadow

Barbecue on the right, I chewed the inside of my cheek. Arch couldn't forsake his father. I didn't really want him to. Despite John Richard's coldly selfish behavior, Arch clung fiercely to the hope of getting love from his other parent. And John Richard spoiled Arch enough with material things—usually when he felt guilty over reneging on a promise—that Arch's longing for a relationship remained like a sharp hunger, seldom fed.

I made a U-turn, drove back through town, and headed up toward the lake. Perched on the edge of the waterfall between the lake and lower Cottonwood Creek, a gaggle of shiny black cormorants arched their backs and eyed the water beneath for fish. Arch used to love to go down to the lake when he was little and feed the waterfowl, now strictly prohibited, as human feeding messed up the birds' willingness to migrate. Arch had known distress back then: the pain of the playground, the agony of his parents' divorce. Then as now, I had tried to soothe and protect him. But his distress this time didn't change the fact that Dr. John Richard Korman, batterer of women, had finally been caught. And then, in front of a street full of nosy neighbors, he'd resisted arrest. I dreaded Arch hearing about *that* scene.

What was painfully inevitable, I knew, was that John Richard would maintain his innocence to his son and anyone else who would listen until the proverbial bovines came home. No matter what he did or what folks he hurt, John Richard would insist to the end that he was not responsible for his actions. Well, we would just see about that.

I passed the lake. In the near distance cars sent up a nimbus of dust as women from the Aspen Meadow Babsie Club drove into the LakeCenter parking lot on their way to set up for the doll show. What Arch couldn't see was that this crime—this *event* with Suz Craig—was going to change everything. The publicity surrounding the arrest, the breadth of the investigation, the preliminary hearing, the trial, the conviction, the sentencing—these would alter his relationship with his father forever. Perhaps it was this coming change that Arch sensed. So he'd plunged into denial. Who wouldn't?

I passed a solitary rower at the edge of the lake and turned the van in the direction of the country club. Since I was still a bit early, did I dare swing by Aspen Meadow Health Foods, to see if Amy Bartholomew, the nurse-without-a-poker-face, was in? No, I'd had enough crime for one day. Besides, Arch and Macguire might be headed over there. If my son thought I was checking up on him, he would have a fit.

Dread made my heart heavy, the way your chest hurts when an election is going to the wrong people and all you can do is watch the numbers mount. I swung through the entryway to the residential part of the country club, where a crew dressed in white overalls and white billed caps was busy at work eradicating the vandals' painted handiwork from the stone walls. I shook my head. I felt helpless watching Arch's dilemma, which was sure to end worse than any election. The best I could hope for was that it would all be over soon.

It was this idea of expediting things that made me turn onto Jacobean and from there chug left on Sheridan, then on to Chaucer, where I eased up in front of the Shelton place. The house was a massive, out-of-proportion two-story neo-Georgian. White-painted brick contrasted with shiny black shutters and window boxes lush with bright red geraniums and artfully dripping variegated cream-and-green ivy.

What exactly was I doing here? Trying to disprove John Richard's theory, whatever it was, about Ralph Shelton? Trying to remember what it was I had seen this morning? I didn't know. I parked behind the Sheltons' van and hopped out of my own. I knew the rules: Anybody who might testify in a case is a witness. Not only had I witnessed all that had transpired between John Richard and Tom, I'd seen, or thought I'd seen, Ralph Shelton this morning. If I ever had to testify, I didn't want to think about how I could be challenged because of the contact I was now making with Ralph. I also tried not to think about how upset Tom would be with me for making this little sleuthing side trip.

Apart from this morning, how long had it been since I'd talked to Ralph? Too long. I'd last seen his daughter as a four-year-old. Now Jill was a teenager, like Arch. I rapped hard on the elaborate, gleaming brass knocker. Of course, Ralph probably wouldn't even be home. Saturday afternoon on a gorgeous Colorado summer day? He was probably out playing golf.

But he was not on the fairway. Even before the doorbell stopped donging "Three Blind Mice," tall, white-mustached Ralph answered the door. He had changed from the gardening clothes to a collarless navy shirt and faded blue jeans—Calvin Klein at Home.

"What is it?" He stared at me with eyes that seemed to be made of yellow glass.

"Ralph!" I exclaimed brightly. "Ralph, don't you remember me? I used to take care of Jill, about ten years ago."

He pulled himself up. "I am Dr. Shelton."

Always. *Is your first name Doctor?* I smiled. "Ralph, it's Goldy Korman. Now Goldy Schulz. Don't you remember me from all those years ago? I'm a caterer now."

He squinted and cleared his throat. "Goldy?"

"We . . . saw each other in front of Suz Craig's house, when the police were there. This morning. Don't you recall? Over on Jacobean. I didn't recognize you, either. And then I remembered. And after all we'd been through together way back when . . ."

But I couldn't come up with a last-minute lie to push myself into a conversation with this man. Instead, I stared mutely at the right side of his face, where there was a square, expertly cut gauze bandage. I saw again what I'd seen this morning. Just at the upper end of the bandage, under the clear tape, were the beginnings, just the very beginnings, of four vertical gash marks. The kind of scratches that could be made by a woman's nails, when she was fighting you off.

Chapter 11

Forgive me, it's been such a trying day." Ralph's unctuous tone made me even more uneasy. "I never would have known . . . and this morning when you were ordering people around, you seemed so distraught. . . ." He tilted his bald head and closed his amber eyes, as if struggling to recall the events. Then he shook his head. "Terrible tragedy. The police even questioned me, since I was out on my walk when . . ." He paused. "But why are you here now? I mean, if you want to catch up on old times, then give me a call and we can set up a lunch or something. . . . I'll bring some pictures of Jill, she's playing soccer down in New Mexico. . . ." His voice trailed off. A country-club doctor choosing to have lunch with a caterer who was married to a cop? Not likely, regardless of our history. But Ralph pressed on, with an eagerness that seemed almost sad. "Actually, I've missed all of my old friends lately, things have been going so badly . . . and now this has happened. Should we set up a lunch right now?" His hand went nervously to the top button of his shirt. "That would be a terrific idea."

"Oh! Well, actually, I can't make any appointments now, I'm looking for the McCrackens' house." It was lame, but it had to do. "Do you know Clark and Patricia McCracken? Remember, Patricia used to be married to Skip all those years ago. . . ." He squinted skeptically and I rushed on. "I'm catering a Stanley Cup celebration there tonight, at the McCrackens', and I just can't remember exactly where they live, and then I remembered you were such a big hockey fan . . ."

But he had already held up a hand for me to wait. I fell silent as his tall form disappeared down a hallway whose walls were bathed in a vertigo-inducing print of floating cabbage roses. Beyond, I glimpsed a country kitchen with frilly curtains and gleaming copper. I wondered if Ralph had found another job after being fired by ACHMO. If he had not, I doubted he'd be able to keep up life in his old income bracket.

"Twenty-two Markham," he said pleasantly as he returned, waving an engraved invitation. Then he regarded me. "I'm going over there in just a little bit myself. We've remained friends, in spite of everything. It's amazing that she . . . Well. The guests are all going to skate, get another dose of Cup fever. Sound good? But how can you cater at a house you haven't visited?"

I was ready for this one. "Do it all the time. Actually, I thought I knew where the McCrackens' place was. But after this morning my life seems to have turned upside down." I stared helplessly into his yellow eyes, so much like those of a cat. "It's just been a night-mare."

He grinned sympathetically. "Yes, well, I'll just see you over at the McCrackens' place—"

I leaned against the doorframe. "Ralph, can you just show me how to get to Markham? Please? I'm feeling extremely disoriented."

With obvious reluctance, he walked outside and gestured at Chaucer, where, as I well knew, I needed to take two rights and then a left to get to the McCrackens' place. He turned and again squinted. My forlorn expression must have finally ignited a spark of curiosity, for before going into his house, he hesitated.

"How did you happen to come upon . . . Suz Craig . . . er, in the ditch?" he asked abruptly. "I mean, did you drive over it or something?"

"I was on my way to the Rodines' place to pick up my son and take him to his father. I just saw her there . . . in front of her house. Uh . . . how about you?"

"Oh, I was out for my walk."

I sighed. "I'm sorry for ordering you around this morning. Did you say the police questioned you? I seem to remember them wanting to talk to everybody, you know?"

"Yes, well." He cleared his throat. "You wouldn't believe what they wanted to know from me." He rubbed his bandaged cheek. I felt my own face heat up. "How had I scratched myself, they asked. So I told them what I'm telling you." I didn't like the tone of his voice. Did it mask hostility, or was I imagining things? "Our cat doesn't like to go to the veterinarian's. She scratched me when I tried to put her into the cage."

I nodded sympathetically and thought that Sergeant Beiner was probably on the phone with the veterinarian right now, finding out if in fact Ralph Shelton had just brought a female cat in for a visit. I thanked him for helping me, then backed away. Time to grill fish for the McCrackens.

"So," Ralph said slowly, "the police suspect my old friend, John Richard Korman?" His fingers brushed the top of his shirt, then went to his bandage again. Suddenly, he didn't seem to want me to leave.

I shrugged as convincingly as possible. "Who knows? I try to keep up with that guy as little as possible." I turned toward my van. "Thanks for your help, Ralph."

"Wait," he called. "I'm sorry. Of course you have as little to do with him as possible. I . . . I remember how he treated you." I turned back and waited for him to speak. Finally he said, "It's just that I've had such a horrible morning." I pressed my lips together. "I knew her, you know," he said bluntly. Was his voice wistful? Hard to tell. "I knew Suz Craig."

"Really?" I asked. "Oh, right, the HMO. And you're a doc. I hardly know anyone in the medical business anymore. Do you practice in Denver?"

"I *did*. Our group was affiliated with ACHMO. Still is, actually, I'm just not a part of it." He heaved a sigh. "I'll see you at the party later. Sure you know where you're going?" Before I could answer, however, he said, "Good-bye." Then he closed the door.

Well, doggone. Ralph was in some kind of pain, no question, and it wasn't just from cat scratches. I gave the brass knocker one last glance and walked back to my vehicle—in case he was watching through a window—and hightailed it over to the McCrackens' place. Within five minutes I'd eased up to the curb in front of a tall wooden house that had been stained a bilious purple, with shutters painted a dull maroon. They should have photographed this place for a National Hockey League advertisement. Avalanche flags hung from the lampposts along the walk. Oversize Avalanche banners were draped from each upstairs window. The place looked like a sporting-goods store.

When I drove into the McCrackens' driveway, though, I was prevented from pulling up to the back entrance. A rope had been put up around a large, rectangular paved area that had been marked with bright white lines to resemble a hockey rink. I couldn't imagine what my tires would do to all those brilliant chalky lines if I drove over them. I dreaded contemplating how I was going to unload, much less serve.

Clark McCracken, a long-legged fellow with a thin, sweating red face and lots of sweat-streaked brown hair, flapped his arms maniacally as he came loping down the drive toward me. He was wearing a maroon Avalanche jersey, shiny maroon shorts, and stiff, bulky kneepads that made his gait resemble the canter of a crippled racehorse. No question—this man was ready for the end-of-the-driveway game. There was also no question that he wasn't ready for my van to ruin all his chalk marks. I sighed. Unloading a hundred pounds of supplies anywhere near the shortest route to the kitchen was going to be impossible. I rolled down the window and resolved to stay pleasant.

"Need you . . . to park . . ." Out of breath, Clark wobbled, stiltlike. I certainly hoped he wasn't participating for more than five minutes in today's face-off or whatever the hockey equivalent of a scrimmage is. "Park behind the line," he blurted out as he pointed to the closest chalk stripe. He pressed his hair against the sides of his head and gasped. "Then . . . you can walk down with the beer and food to where we'll be playing, with a tray or something."

"Clark," I began patiently. "There is no way—"

"Back up then," Clark interrupted, waving dismissively toward the front of his house. "It'll be okay, the cake's going to come in that way, too. Back to the sidewalk. Open your doors and . . ." He took another deep, agonizing breath and squeezed his eyes shut. "I'll help."

Oh, sure, I thought as I gunned the van in reverse. *And within ten minutes of you trying to help me, I'll be trying to remember the CPR course I took right after Marla had her heart attack.* The van sputtered. I braked a little too hard at the beginning of the sidewalk, a herringbone-brick path that led back to the garishly decorated house.

It was not my place to tell Clark McCracken that he should not be tugging two fully loaded dollies up his sidewalk so soon before his party. But Clark seemed determined to be as physically involved with the setup for his hockey celebration as possible. I knew what he would do next—splash ice water on his face, comb back his sopping hair, and leap down the stairs to be the official greeter. Then, with an enormous sense of justification, our host would slug down a speedy half-dozen beers before beginning the roller hockey derby in his driveway, which would be followed by a lot more brewskis, a minimal amount of food, and passing out on a piece of patio furniture before I'd finished serving the entrée. That is, if he didn't hurt himself with all the activity first.

On second thought, maybe I should summon an ambulance. Just in case.

"Okay," he said, still panting heavily. "What goes in first?"

Twenty minutes later I was set up in the kitchen. Clark, wheezing from his exertions, made a martyrlike declaration that he was going to light his gas grill—ever a man's job, even if no actual starting of fires was involved.

"Clark," I cautioned politely, "please be careful. There was just a big article in the *Mountain Journal* about how those grills need to be checked—"

Again I got the dismissive wave. "Don't quote Frances Markasian to me, please. I've never heard of mountain moths building nests in propane grills! What will that woman think of next?" He rolled his eyes. "I don't believe a word that crazy woman writes. She's not a reporter, she's a viper looking for a cause. Explosions from moths, give me a break! But don't worry, I'm going to clean the vents. It's my job."

"Just be careful," I repeated gently.

I unwrapped the appetizers for the party: an enormous oval basket of fresh vegetables meant to resemble, as did the rest of tonight's food, a hockey rink. In the place of the goals were baskets of chips, and in the center of the rink-basket I gently lowered a huge crystal bowl of Mexican dip, my own concoction of thick layers of guacamole, cubed tomatoes, smooth sour cream, shredded crisp lettuce, chili beans mashed with picante sauce, sliced black olives, and an ample blanket of golden grated cheddar cheese.

"Ooh, may I taste?" Patricia McCracken cooed as she tiptoed into the kitchen. Her tousle of streaked curls was held back with a twisted headband printed with tiny Avalanche logos. But her fine-featured face was haggard. She wore an oversize Avalanche jersey that reached almost to her knees. She looked like a coed who'd spent the night in a fraternity house, complete with borrowed pajamas and bags under her eyes.

Despite my best intentions to cater this event, I couldn't help but ask what was on my mind. "Patricia, are you sure you want to go through with this? You look exhausted."

"Yes," she said, "I do. Tyler's already over at somebody's house. Besides, what am I going to do, call everyone and say, 'Sorry! Murder in the neighborhood! Gotta cancel!' Oh, gosh, that reminds me, the centerpiece cake's not here yet. Could you call the bakery and find out if Mickey is going to send somebody over with it?"

"No problem."

Patricia extended an index finger to scoop up a bit of dip. I punched in the buttons for the Aspen Meadow Pastry Shop and handed Patricia a small plastic bowl of dip that I had set aside for sampling. She wrinkled her nose and whined, "Is this the same?"

"Patricia, please. Of course." I removed the plastic wrap from the Grilled Slapshot Salad.

"Well, it doesn't *look* the same." She shoveled a pile of dip onto one chip and popped it into her mouth.

"Aspen Meadow Pastry Shop," announced Mickey Yuille in the sad, gruff voice I recognized so well.

"Mickey, hi, it's Goldy Schulz. I'm over at the McCrackens' place and she's waiting for her cake. Can I tell her it's on the way?"

Mickey sighed. "Brandon always insists on helping out with my Saturday deliveries. But now they've had some kind of crisis down at his office, and my other guy is sick, so all the Saturday-afternoon deliveries have been delayed."

I held my breath. Brandon Yuille, head of Human Resources at ACHMO, was already being questioned? By whom? The police? His Minneapolis head office? "We *really* need somebody to bring the cake over," I implored.

"Yeah, yeah, okay. That's what I was going to tell you. Brandon came in late. He's out on his rounds now and should be there any minute. And say! Great fudge, Goldy. Brandon brought me some made from your recipe. Come by and see me sometime. I want you to try out my new cinnamon rolls. They're bigger than the other guy used to make them."

I thanked him, hung up, and unwrapped the biscuits. To Patricia I said, "The cake's on its way."

Using two chips, Patricia scooped up another precariously balanced load of dip from the plastic bowl. "Mm-mm," she exclaimed as she delicately wiped an errant glop of sour cream from the side of her mouth. My words registered and she gave me a puzzled look. "The cake is on its way? So are my guests! We're starting the hockey game earlier than we'd planned, in case we need overtime!" Her voice was full of panic.

"Patricia! Are you sure you're okay?"

"No, I'm *not* okay, thank you very much. Am I ever going to see John Richard in civil court now, do you think? Unlikely. I sold my car to pay my lawyer's retainer. Your ex-husband is sucking me down a drain." She sounded very bitter.

Captain Ahab, I thought again, and cocked an ear toward the hallway. "I think either the cake or some of your guests might be arriving." I loved catering. Occasionally, though, while placating a nervous hostess, I ended up burning the butter or committing some other *faux pas culinaire.* I wanted her to leave the kitchen, but I didn't want to hurt her feelings.

"Clark can greet the guests," she rejoined excitedly. "I want to talk about what happened this morning. What did you see? Were you in on the—"

Mercifully, she was interrupted by dark-haired, handsome Brandon Yuille. Banging through the kitchen door, Brandon balanced an enormous white box on his outstretched arms. The cake. I motioned to the kitchen island and he expertly slid the box to safety. With his eyes twinkling, Brandon swept his long hair off his forehead. Of medium height and slightly—but appealingly—chubby, he wore a loose yellow oxford-cloth shirt with no tie, khaki pants, and

loosely tied brown leather boat shoes. He was good-looking and single, although somewhat too young for Marla, much to her chagrin.
With a flourish, he opened the top of the cardboard box.

"Oh, Brandon, it's super," I said admiringly. The rink-shaped
cake was actually made of two thick layers of ice cream topped with
a thin layer of yellow cake. Mickey had icing-painted all the right red
and blue lines and the Avalanche logo. He'd even placed tiny plastic
hockey players at various places and miniature goals at each end.
"The cupcakes will look perfect surrounding it. Let's get it into the
freezer."

Patricia was staring at Brandon. "Don't you work for
ACHMO?" she demanded suspiciously.

He reddened. "Yes, I . . . I'm just helping my father. . . ."
His look grew puzzled. "Wait a minute. You're the one who's suing
. . . Oh, I'm sorry, I know you've had a hard time—"

"You all are spying on me," Patricia responded hotly. "Don't
think I don't know about all the records you've been trying to get
your hands on or have destroyed. You can leave my home now."

"I apologize for coming," Brandon mumbled as he slid the cake
into the freezer.

"Patricia, please," I soothed. "Mickey Yuille is the new proprietor of the pastry shop. Brandon works for ACHMO during the week
and helps his father on the weekends. Brandon, I'm sorry about
this—"

But Brandon's leather shoes were already making squeaking
noises as he hastened out of the kitchen. So much for asking him any
questions about ACHMO's response to the recent demise of their
vice-president.

Patricia sniffed. "If I'd known the pastry shop guy was related
to an ACHMO guy, I would have had you make the centerpiece
cake." She made it sound as if that was the last thing on earth she
wanted.

One of the guests, a slender, energetic woman with curly black
hair, crashed into the kitchen. Her blue eyes shone with anticipation

as she hurtled toward us. "Listen, Goldy, what's the real dirt on your husband?" Two more women crowded in behind her, whispering and staring at me avidly.

Oh, brother. Every bone in my jaw ached from being clenched. I leaned against the refrigerator and glanced longingly at the fish fillets. Should I pretend I didn't know what was going on? With my *husband*? *Actually, ladies, my* husband *is a cop who spent the afternoon running errands. That is, after he arrested my* ex-*husband.*

"Out, out, out," Patricia commanded with surprising authority. To my relief, her noisy friends backed out of the kitchen. "And it's her *ex*-husband!"

I could hear a muffled whine: "But we want to hear about . . ." The door closed on them.

"Your poor son," Patricia said, suddenly remorseful. "He must be in agony. And how embarrassing it'll be when his friends start talking about all this. I'm so glad Tyler's not here. I certainly don't want him asking questions. Keep right on with your work, Goldy. I'm staying with you until Clark starts the hockey game. You need protection from those busybodies."

Of course, she was right. So was Marla. I *should* have worn a shirt that said I DON'T KNOW ANYTHING.

"It's ACHMO." Patricia said it dismissively as I steadfastly organized my supplies. She munched another dip-loaded chip reflectively. "You ever try to talk to somebody on the phone there? ACHMO reminds me of a church I went to once. Everybody hates everybody. The institution doesn't function and it's everybody else's fault. The more you try to replace people, the worse it gets. Better to just burn the place down and start over."

"What do you mean?"

"You know what they did to me," she said. Actually, I had never asked for the litany of volleys in Patricia's negligence lawsuit against ACHMO. I knew she had lost her baby. I was not so interested that I had to hear all the details of the legal battle. Nor did I want to. "You heard ACHMO canned Ralph, of course," she continued conspiratorially. "He'll be here tonight, poor thing."

"I did hear he had been fired." I could sound as sympathetic as the next person. "Did Ralph find a new job?"

She nodded. "He was lucky to get something with another HMO, but it's in administration. I'm sure there are many, many people Suz Craig fired," she stated in the same offhand tone. "But two in Aspen Meadow? Please. We should get federal funds." She lifted another chip as she raised an eyebrow.

"The other person she fired is Amy Bartholomew?"

"So you know about Amy. Yes. The woman's a real healer, Goldy. Amy's the one who told me to have this party. Suz lost a gem in her. But Amy sees people at her health-food store now. I don't believe she ever supported six slot machines in Central City, the way they said."

I placed the biscuits on a buttered cookie sheet and covered them with foil to reheat later. "Well," I said hopefully, "the police are bound to sort it out. Maybe you'd like to check on your guests . . . ?"

Unfortunately, Patricia still seemed to be in no hurry to leave. "So are they . . . going to put your husband on the case? The investigator? That would be something, wouldn't it? I can't imagine—"

"No, Patricia." I peered out the window that overlooked the driveway. The male guests had divided themselves into two teams: one wearing T-shirts, the other not. A half-dozen men sat on the wooden retaining wall strapping on in-line skates, while another three—helmeted, padded, barechested—were taking tentative gliding turns around the drive. Their faces were hostile and they appeared to be yelling. Hurling insults at each other already? "Uh, do you have a doctor around? I mean, just in case there's a problem with the hockey game outside?"

Alarmed, Patricia stepped up to the window beside me. "Oh,

for crying out loud, they've started? Uh-oh, there's Drew Herbert. He's got the logo of the Detroit Red Wings tatooed on his chest." She rapped on the glass. No one outside paid the slightest attention. "Who is . . ." One of the skaters took a spill and Patricia yelped. "Oh, Clark's going to get *us* sued!" With this, she rushed out of the room.

Two nets abutted opposite ends of the driveway. One goal stood by the paved edge that gave way to the sloped front lawn and Tyler's swing set, the other had been pushed up against a high retaining wall made of four-by-fours. Transfixed, I watched from the window until all twelve men were skating at a dizzying speed. Wielding lethal-looking hockey sticks, they bunched and raced, bunched and raced, all the time weaving past one another in furious pursuit of a bright purple tennis-size ball.

The score seesawed between the Shirts and the Chests, with the Shirts leading in high-fives and the Chests in sweat-production. About ten spectators, including the three women who had barged in on me, gathered on the driveway sidelines, hollering and laughing and swilling what looked like large gin-and-tonics in what I hoped were plastic—not glass—cups. What had happened to the beer? Had Clark brought it down to the end of the driveway?

When the score was two to one, a fight broke out over whether one of the Chests had skated out-of-bounds. First two, then four, guys started jostling one another. Unfriendly shoulder shoves accompanied open-mouthed braying.

Squawking, Patricia dashed into the fray. We were still twenty minutes from when I was supposed to bring out the first batch of appetizers for two dozen people. But if this squabble heated up much more, I'd have fewer mouths to feed than I'd planned.

The men argued and gestured with their hockey sticks. *Here!* they seemed to be saying. *No, the ball went out over there!* Two more women, apparently mindless of their own physical safety, rushed in from the sidelines to try to break up the conflict. Patricia stabbed a finger accusingly in her husband's face, while another woman decided her husband needed to have his red face sloshed with gin-and-tonic. When Clark pushed Patricia aside, she turned and stomped back up toward the house. The conflict continued unabated.

Two men popped each other on opposite shoulders while skating sideways and trying to keep their balance. Then one of the Shirts unstrapped his helmet and snapped it upward, smacking it into the nose of his opponent in the melee. The man flailed backward, then did a belly flop forward on the blacktop. The battle ceased briefly while the injured man lay flapping his arms and legs. His squeals for help were muted—probably he had landed on his diaphragm.

Patricia McCracken, her face red and her voice shrill, rushed back into the kitchen. "Beer! Dammit, Goldy! What are you standing there for? Beer! Don't wait for halftime! Take them some beer now!"

I mumbled something about a medic being a better idea than a bartender but scrambled obediently around the kitchen, where I quickly filled a Styrofoam cooler with three six-packs and a shower of ice. Beer didn't seem a very good idea to me, especially on top of all those gin-and-tonics. Still, my contract did not include ground cleanup, if it came to that. I marched carefully down the walk to Clark McCracken, who gestured grandly toward his cement-hockey game.

"Take it down to them! Take it down!" he hollered, his face scarlet with exhaustion and what I suspected was pain. "*Throw* the cans at them if you have to!"

Without Clark, the players had resumed their game, which I found incredible. The Shirts and the Chests were skating around one another with even more alacrity and daring than before. One helmeted player thwacked the ball toward the goal and barely missed the net. Instead, the ball bounced off the retaining wall and smacked one of the female spectators in the knee. Her shrill squawk of pain went utterly unheeded as the skaters bent and swerved around one another to pass a newly produced ball.

"Beer break!" I called as the cans chinked against one another with what I hoped was an inviting sound. But the players could not hear me or the cans as they pushed, grunted, and jostled for position. Clark, somehow revived, whooshed past and waved me down to the sideline. I sighed, heaved the Styrofoam chest above my rib cage, and clink-clomped closer to the players, keeping a wary eye on the game.

Clark bellowed enthusiastically to his fellow skaters: "Hey, guys! A beer break would—"

But I never heard him finish. From the chalked line where I stood, I was suddenly aware of a shift in the game. Like a tornado that had changed direction without warning, a gaggle of sweating skaters loomed. Charging out of the crowd came Ralph Shelton, hell-bent in my direction. I dropped the beers. The Styrofoam chest landed on my feet. Spilling ice filled the air as Ralph Shelton slammed into my stationary, unhelmeted, unpadded body. As he hit me, the look on his bandaged face was a determined, angry grimace, as if he had every intention of killing me.

Chapter 12

There was, apparently, a shortage of doctors. In any event, no one stepped up to offer me help. I lay on the pavement one second, two seconds, three. My eyes felt permanently crossed. As far as I could determine, everyone seemed to be clustered around Ralph Shelton.

I gasped but couldn't bring any air in; the wind was gone from my body. Blood dripped from my forehead. Finally some people moved toward me. Their mouths chattered incomprehensibly. *Move,* I told myself. *Get up.* But I didn't. I couldn't.

I groaned and lifted one shoulder. Pain pierced my stomach and shot up my legs. My calves had been gashed by Ralph's in-line skates. Even more agonizing was my head, which throbbed unremittingly.

As I speechlessly eyed the gaggle now gawking down at me, I was convinced that the cement had cracked my skull. Perhaps I had a concussion. Perhaps my brains were leaking out. Well, I had agreed to cater to a group of hockey fans. I probably didn't have any brains left to leak.

"Goldy?" A strange woman's voice accused me from faraway. "Why did you drop the beer?"

I closed my eyes.

When I opened them again, I was sitting in a gleaming blue-and-white bathroom. I had a vague recollection of someone lifting me and then placing me into this space. I studied my surroundings. Thinly striped blue porcelain tiles covered the floor, ran up the walls, surrounded the tub. Someone had wiped off my legs, arms, and face. The room swam. This was a nightmare, and I was dinner on a Staffordshire plate.

"I won't be much longer," came a comforting voice from the vicinity of the sink. Water was running. I risked eyeing the sink area.

The plump woman who stood beside me was of medium height. Her strawberry-blond hair shone. In the mirror I could see she had a kindly face. Actually, *two* kindly faces. I groaned and closed my eyes.

An impatient, distressed voice spoke from the doorway. "Lucky you're coming around, Goldy." My heart sank: Patricia. This *was* a bad dream. "We're starting on that vegetable basket you put out. Are you all right now? My husband can't put the fish on the grill until you're ready."

"Ready for what?" I muttered as the kindly red-haired lady smeared a gold-colored jelly on my forehead. The jelly looked like Vaseline and smelled like something you'd get in a Navajo gift shop. "What are you doing?" I asked uneasily, even as the comforting warmth of the salve magically removed the throbbing in my head. "Do I know you?"

"Shh, shh." The woman smoothed more salve on my right arm. "Now smear some of this on your other arm." I obeyed. More water spurted from the faucet. The red-haired Florence Nightingale handed me a glassful. "Can you drink some of this and then put this under your tongue?" When I nodded mutely, she shook out a speckled beige tablet from a wide brown bottle that hadn't come from any pharmacy.

"I'm not taking any drugs," I said firmly. Or at least I think I did.

Her laugh rippled off the porcelain walls. "This is about as far from drugs as you can get," she assured me.

"Goldy, did you hear me?" pleaded Patricia, my former friend, my former pleasant client. "We're going to start on your appetizers. Clark's putting on a video of one of the Cup games and I want dinner to be served in forty minutes. If you're still going to cater this party, you'd better pull yourself together."

I clasped the tablet. It was still difficult to bring Patricia into focus. "Ah, do all the skates have their guests off?" I managed. Dyslexic sentence. Still couldn't think right. No wonder press conferences after hockey games were so uninformative. "Ah . . ." I tried again. "Guests have their skates off?"

"Of course they do," Patricia retorted. "You've been in here for almost a quarter of an hour. I'm worried that the grill's going to run out of propane. When that last buzzer sounds, I want these guests to have grilled fish on their plates. Please hurry!" Then she turned on her heel and stomped away. I hoped Clark had put on a video of the last game of the 1996 Stanley Cup. Then we would have dinner in five hours, and I would have the last laugh.

"Don't mind her," said the red-haired woman. "And by the way, I'm a nurse. Put that pill under your tongue. It's a homeopathic treatment for shock and pain."

"What . . . ?"

But I was in too much pain to argue. I obediently slipped the pill under my tongue and got a smile as a reward from my new guardian angel. Doggone if this woman didn't have an aura. On the other hand, maybe my head injury was even worse than I feared.

She said softly, "It's called arnica, from a flower of the same name."

"Who're you?" I managed.

"Ralph Shelton called me," she replied in that mellifluous voice that reminded me of stirred custard. "I live close by." She concentrated her warm brown eyes on mine. "Ralph and I used to work together. He was so worried about you. He told me you were an old friend of his." She added gently, "My name's Amy Bartholomew."

I gagged on the second tablet as Amy patted more of the salve on my right shin. "I thought you . . ." What did I think she was going to look like, Kenny Rogers fresh from singing "The Gambler"? "What's that you're putting on me?" There was a taste of grass clippings in my mouth from the pills. "This stuff in my mouth tastes funny."

"The salve contains goldenseal, olive oil, comfrey, yarrow, white oak bark, and all kinds of other healing herbs. Beginning to feel any better?"

I nodded, then waited for the pain in my head to pulse in punishment for my unwise move. To my astonishment, it didn't. I looked down at my legs: my stockings were torn; bloody scratches crisscrossed my knees. I wished I had a change of clothes, but of course I did not. Amy continued to dab salve on the cuts. When she finished, she told me to hold out my hand. I did, and she shook a handful of the tablets into my palm.

"Take two more now, then another four in half an hour. Then four more every hour until you go to bed. Okay?"

"Okay." I was still trying to calm the chaos in my head. "Do you have a card or something? I mean, so I can pay you? I doubt the McCrackens will cough up the money for your time and supplies."

Amy shook her head and chuckled. "Don't worry about it. Patricia is a customer of mine. Come see me, though, on . . . say, Monday or Tuesday. At the store. I want to take a look at your eyes. You know where I am? By the lake?"

I nodded again. Hesitantly I said, "Do you . . . did you hear about Suz Craig?"

Her face darkened. "Don't bring up negativity now. You can't digest it. You need to get better. Focus on healing."

I sighed deeply. *Focus on healing.* I'd discovered the corpse of a murdered woman, my violent ex-husband was screaming threats from his jail cell, my son was furious with me, I'd been hit in a roller hockey derby, the party I was catering was going down the tubes, and my scratched and bloodied body would be covered with bruises for weeks. *Focus on healing?* No problem.

After Amy left, I ordered myself to stand up. Then I checked in the mirror. Not as bad as I would have thought. There were three separate but relatively small cuts on my face and neck. My right eye was already pink and beginning to swell. My right shoulder hurt. The headache still echoed darkly in the back of my skull. I popped in a couple more arnica tablets and tried to concentrate on setting up the salads.

The guests were fully engaged in watching one of the playoff games between the Avalanche and the Chicago Blackhawks. I scanned the room for Ralph Shelton. Apparently he'd gone home. But questions nagged. Had he deliberately run into me? Had he meant to hurt me? Or was it just difficult to stop on in-line skates? I refused to ponder these questions until I was safely at home. First, I had a dinner to serve.

I tiptoed past the noisy living room to the security of the kitchen and spooned the salads into their bowls. My spirits began to revive as I poured the marinade over the tuna and heated the Mexican eggrolls I'd made the day before. The smell of hot south-of-the-border food was marvelous. I sliced one of the eggrolls to make sure it was suitably hot and crispy, then dipped it into an avocado-lime mixture and took a bite. The eggroll skin crackled around the chile-laden stuffing of chicken, black beans, cumin, and melted cheese. Yum. I was feeling so much better it was amazing. Now all I needed was a Dos Equis, a hot shower, and a leap into bed. Fat chance.

I slipped the biscuits and potato rolls into the oven, passed around the eggrolls, and received a gratifying chorus of *oohs* and *ahs* and *I'll have another one of those*. No one commented on my bruised and battered face. I put the fish on the grill and checked on the heating biscuits. Frowning, Patricia devoured half an eggroll. Her face softened. Could she be feeling remorse for scolding me after I'd been slammed nearly senseless by one of her guests? I wondered. Maybe she'd realized I could sue *her*. Maybe she just liked Mexican food. I tested a corner of the grilled fish: flaky and deliciously flavored with the marinade. Apparently I could still do my job correctly.

The guests, some still wearing in-line skating attire, others clad in Avalanche gear, boisterously tumbled out to the buffet line after the buzzer sounded in the Blackhawks game. One or two eyed me curiously, but no one bothered to ask how I was. At this party, they expected injuries. Nor did they ask me what the story was on the Jerk's arrest. Okay by me: the invincible caterer had work to do.

Soon the guests had munched their way through the main course and I put on coffee to brew. Eventually, the guests were drinking their coffee and eating Stanley Cupcakes topped with slices of ice-cream rink, while lamenting that the beginning of the NHL season was over a month away. I glanced at the clock over the kitchen window. Ten to eight. The sun slid slowly behind the mountains. Just above the jagged, deeply shadowed horizon, thin striations of gray cloud lay in perfect, straight lines. *It's a giant comb*, Arch and I would have said, back when he was little. I ran hot water into the sink and put in the first batch of dishes to be rinsed. I couldn't wait to finish this job.

Just after nine o'clock I heaved the first of my heavy boxes across my deck. Tom was waiting. As soon as he saw my face, he shook his head. He opened the back door, came out, and took the box from me. A huge dark green apron swathed his body. He'd been cooking, as usual, because he knew I would not have had time to eat.

"Miss G!" His face furrowed with worry. "What happened to you?"

"Don't ask. It's not that big a deal, anyway."

He sighed. "You get into more scrapes in a day than I do in a year. And I'm the one with the *dangerous* job."

"You've never catered to hockey fans," I muttered glumly.

"True." He set the box on the counter and chuckled as I flopped into a chair. He stooped to give me a kiss, then eyed my cut cheek. Instead he kissed the top of my head.

Later, when we'd brought all the supplies inside, I asked, "Where is the rest of this family?"

He smiled and started the food processor grating potatoes. "Upstairs. Macguire's had quite a day, his most active in the last month. He's had a long shower. But I think he may be running a bit of a fever. Arch took the dog and the cat into his room and the four of them are laughing over doll-collecting magazines."

"*What?*"

Tom deftly beat an egg, dipped in a flour-dusted fish fillet, then rolled it in shreds of potato. I suddenly realized I was starving. "Don't worry," he went on, "I gave Macguire some ibuprofen. He had an incident over at the lake with Arch. Oh, and Arch isn't going to the Druckmans' tonight, he wanted to stay here and make sure Macguire was okay."

"Back up. What incident? Why were the boys at the lake?"

Tom took a deep breath, not a good sign. "Apparently the health-food store was closed. Macguire was too tired to walk any farther, so the two of them went over to the LakeCenter looking for someone to give them a ride home. One lady—what's her name, Rodine?—said she would if the two boys could bring in some tables. Do you believe that? Why wouldn't she just give the kids a ride home?"

I sighed. "Because she's a gold-plated bitch, that's why."

"Of course Macguire was too weak to lift a table, and Arch was too small, so they asked if they could do something else to earn their ride. So Mrs. Rodine had them carry in some cartons full of boxed dolls. They hauled a crate up on one of the stands inside the LakeCenter while Mrs. Rodine and her pals were yelling directions to some other underlings outside. So Arch and Macguire, trying to be helpful, started to take the doll boxes out of the crate. Once they had them all out, Arch got worried about Macguire, so he went to a soft-drink machine to get the two of them some pops. Meanwhile, Macguire started to take the dolls out of the boxes—"

"Oh, no. No, no, no. The collectors don't want the dolls out of the boxes. The collectors want them NRFB. Never Removed From Box. It makes a huge difference—"

Tom held up a hand. "When Arch came in with the drinks, he tried to warn Macguire, but it was too late."

I repeated, "Too late. Oh, God."

Tom seemed resigned to telling this tale of human folly. Yet his green eyes were merry as he drizzled olive oil on the griddle. "Three women screamed and *chased* Arch and Macguire out of the LakeCenter. Then a guy, one of the helper-husbands, called the sheriff's department on his cellular phone—"

I moaned.

Tom slid the potato-crusted fillets on the hot griddle, where their sizzling sound made my mouth water. "Since I was on my way home from the hardware store, I was the closest." Another smile quirked the corners of his mouth. "So I answered the call. I've done a lot of strange duties in my day. But trying to convince a hysterical trio of women that removing a 1994 Holiday Babsie from its original box is not a chargeable offense—now that was perhaps the most challenging job I've had yet." He chuckled.

I moaned again. "These women didn't actually *do* anything to Arch and Macguire, did they? Why does Macguire have a fever?"

Tom pursed his lips and flipped the fish. "The Babsie ladies chased our boys to the end of the old pier, where unfortunately Macguire lost his balance and fell into the water. A woman in a shell rowed over and held on to him until someone from the LakeCenter could throw out a life preserver." Tom carefully scooped the golden-brown fish pieces into a buttered pan and eased the whole thing into the oven.

I rubbed my aching skull. "I . . . know that doll collecting is a bona fide hobby. Sort of like being a hockey fan. But I just don't understand why these *pastimes* become *manias*."

"I asked the same question. I might as well have asked the ladies' Bible study to describe the Rapture. One woman told me very seriously that doll collecting was like the best sex you ever had, times ten."

I let that pass. While the fish was baking, I moved—slowly, painfully—up the stairs to check on Macguire and Arch, who both immediately demanded to know why I looked so *awful*. I stalled and took Macguire's temperature. It was one hundred degrees even, not enough to call his doctor, he maintained. Then I told the boys I'd gotten hit by a hockey fan. The fan had been wearing blades, I explained, and I had not.

"*Dude*, Mrs. Schulz," said Macguire admiringly. "You're brave."

"No, just dumb enough to be in his way."

Apparently being with Macguire had worked the kind of effect on Arch Marla had predicted it would. My son did not seem preoccupied with his father and the events of the morning. He didn't even appear to be angry with me. At least not at the moment.

He pointed to the magazine in his lap. "Check this out, Mom."

I bent to look at the page. After a second I moved in closer. I wanted to make sure my eyes weren't deceiving me. A Never-Re-moved-From-Box Duchess Bride Babsie was selling for twelve hundred dollars. Another one that *had* been taken out of the box sold for six hundred dollars. The dolls had sold for less than twenty dollars originally, and I remembered my little childhood friend in New Jersey who had taken such delight in playing with her Babsies. In the catalog, I saw one that looked familiar from my friend's collection. It was an MIB—Mint-In-Box—Number One Blond Ponytail Babsie. The doll had just gone at auction for six thousand dollars. I felt faint.

"Mom, are you all right?" Arch asked anxiously.

"I'm fine," I assured him. "I've already seen a nurse, and she gave me a homeopathic remedy."

"Homeopathic?" Macguire grumbled. "What is *that*?"

"It means natural," I explained. "Please don't stay up too late. I don't need *both* of you to get sick."

Arch gave me an exasperated look and I closed the door before I could offend him further. Ten minutes later I was scrubbed, robed, and more ravenous than ever. In honor of my service to hockey fans, Tom had named his creation Power Play Potatoes and Fish. He served them with a fine julienne of carrot, steamed baby peas, a small green salad, and southern spoon bread topped with pats of butter. I took a greedy bite of the fish: Tom's pairing of a crunchy potato crust with the delicate texture and rich taste of Chilean seabass was divine, and I told him so. He smiled and told me the recipe was now taped to my computer screen. Then he frowned.

"What was the name of the guy you said hit you?"

"Dr. Ralph Shelton," I mumbled, mouth full of succulent fish. "Remember? I told you about him earlier today. He's an old friend of ours. Used to be with ACHMO, but according to town gossip he was fired by Suz Craig."

"Right. And I was going to check on him, which I did. Which I actually told Donny Saunders to do, more accurately. By the way, did the gossip say *why* this Dr. Shelton was fired?"

I indicated a negative and took a bite of the carrots and peas, celestially fresh, sweet vegetables. The spoon bread was as rich and tender as anything Scarlett O'Hara had ever put into her mouth. I made "mm-mm" noises and Tom nodded in acknowledgment.

"Brandon Yuille, you know him?" he asked, his mind still on work.

"He's the head of Human Resources for ACHMO. He's also

the son of a baker in town. He was at Suz's house when I catered over there. I saw him today, but briefly. Why? Have you talked to him?"

"Yeah, a whole team went out to talk to the ACHMO department heads, but most of them are in San Diego at a conference. Medical Management, Member Services, Health Services, Quality Management—four of the six people who had to deal with Suz Craig on a daily basis are gone for the week, although they're coming back early. The only department heads left in town were Human Resources and Provider Relations." He took a breath. "John Richard Korman is absolutely insistent he's innocent. The cops who're questioning him? They're getting real tired of hearing about Suz Craig doing *this* to make enemies, Suz Craig doing *that*."

"I hope they're ignoring him. John Richard Korman is probably the worst enemy Suz Craig ever made. The most dangerous, certainly."

Tom shrugged. "He's the prime suspect, so the department is concentrating on him. But Donny Saunders has asked me to help him out. I agreed."

"So where does Brandon Yuille come in?"

"Korman insists that Yuille and Suz Craig were having some kind of feud. Yuille claims he was with his father at his bakery from midnight to five last night, so he couldn't have killed Ms. Craig."

"You called Brandon?"

"Caught him unawares. He'll probably never talk to me again without a lawyer present. And he's not the most talkative man in the county," Tom observed. "Anyway, he was awfully vague when I wanted to know why Ralph Shelton left ACHMO."

"You asked him that? Brandon was vague or he didn't know?"

Tom's face was unreadable. "Your ex-husband maintains that Ralph Shelton hated Suz, too. I'm wondering if his firing had anything to do with Patricia McCracken's lawsuit against ACHMO."

"What are you *talking* about? I mean, I know Ralph is an obstetrician, but . . ." I felt muddled. It had been too long a day.

Power Play
Potatoes and Fish

4 (6 to 8 ounces each) fresh Chilean
    seabass fillets
1/2 cup flour
2 eggs
4 large russet potatoes
2 tablespoons olive oil
Salt and freshly ground black pepper

Preheat oven to 400°. Butter a 9- by 13-inch
baking dish.

Rinse off the fillets and pat dry with paper towels. Sprinkle the flour on a plate. Beat the eggs
in a shallow bowl. Peel the potatoes. Grate
them onto a large, clean kitchen towel that can
be stained. Roll the potatoes up in the towel
and wring to remove moisture. (It is best to do
this over the sink.) Divide the potatoes into
four piles.

In a wide skillet, heat the olive oil. Working
quickly, dip each fillet first in the flour, then in
the egg. Pat half of each potato pile on the top

and bottom of each fillet (the equivalent of one grated potato per fillet). Bring the skillet up to medium-high heat. Place the potato-covered fillets in the hot oil, salt and pepper them, and brown quickly on each side. When all the fillets are browned, put them in the buttered pan and bake about 10 minutes, or until they are cooked through. *Do not overcook the fish.*

Serves 4

Tom stood and picked up my whisker-clean plate. He ran water into the sink, then said, "What I did get out of Brandon Yuille was this: Ralph Shelton used to be associated with an ob-gyn practice down in Denver. Shelton was on call at St. Philip's Hospital when Clark McCracken brought his wife, Patricia, in the night she lost their baby. There she is, losing blood and disoriented and Shelton tells her he's with ACHMO. Even though they're old friends, our Patricia McCracken hauls off and slaps the guy across the face. He fell, and it knocked the wind out of him. That woman's unbelievably strong, even when she's sick."

"But," I protested, "we all used to be close. Besides, Ralph Shelton wasn't the problem. John Richard and ACHMO were."

"That night Patricia McCracken sure *saw* Ralph Shelton as the problem. Then the chain of events goes like this. She files one suit against Korman; she files another against ACHMO. Ralph leaves his practice under a cloud. Our investigation is very preliminary at this point, but it looks as if after that Shelton took an administrative job with another HMO. One named MeritMed."

I said reflectively, "But Ralph and the McCrackens seem to have buried the hatchet. I mean, he was invited to their hockey party tonight."

Tom grinned. "Yeah, after their little tussle in the hospital Patricia apologized all over the place to Shelton. Maybe she's trying to be sweet to him these days, so that he'll tell her some inside stuff on ACHMO that she can use against them in her suit. I mean, now that he's persona non grata there."

"Ralph seems to stick together with another persona non grata," I commented as I poured two dessert sherries. I told Tom about being tended to by Amy Bartholomew, nurse lately of ACHMO. "She's involved with natural remedies now." That reminded me. I sought out my last four arnica tablets and washed them down with the glass of cream sherry. It may not have been what the homeopaths would have recommended, but I thought it was wonderful.

Tom pulled me into his lap. "Tell me we're going to have a break from talking about this case tomorrow, Miss G. This guy gets arrested first thing in the morning, and it ends up ruining our entire weekend."

It could ruin a lot more than our weekend, I thought glumly, but didn't say so. "You're always telling me how if a case isn't solved in the first forty-eight hours, it's unlikely it'll be solved at all."

"Wait. One more thing. Suz Craig *did* deny Korman his bonus. Late last week."

I sighed. "That's what Marla was afraid of."

"You still don't think this case is solved?"

"I think this case is far from over. But we won't mention a word of it tomorrow. Besides," I teased, "I want to talk some more about the joys of doll collecting. I'm not sure I believe their claims. I mean, *best sex times ten?*"

"You do have to wonder," he replied, deadpan, then led me upstairs.

Chapter 13

You'd think after all I'd been through, I would have slept without a break for twelve hours. Not me. I slept for two.

I awoke at midnight damp with sweat, wrenched from sleep by a nightmare starring John Richard. I'd been jolted awake believing I was Suz Craig, and I was being beaten to death. Perhaps my muscles had cramped after my collision with Ralph Shelton. Whatever the reason, sleep was impossible.

I tiptoed to the kitchen, where I made myself a hot chocolate and topped it with a fat dollop of marshmallow cream. Nothing like chocolate and marshmallow to soothe the nerves. When I was eleven and had failed a social studies test, I'd headed straight to the drugstore and ordered chocolate ice cream slathered with spoonfuls of creamed marshmallow. Did they even make that kind of sundae anymore? I wondered.

I sipped the chocolate, booted up my computer, and started a new file: *JRK ARREST*. I remembered Arch's words: *He* really *needs you*. Well, I didn't care about what John Richard Korman needed.

But I was interested in the truth. And I needed Arch to believe I cared about *him*.

It had been a tempestuous day. I had promised Tom we wouldn't talk about the case on Sunday. Still, the information about the crime now bubbling up reminded me of the schools of minnows that can occasionally be seen at Aspen Meadow Lake. If you don't get out your net right away, you're going to lose them.

I began by listing everything I knew about the people involved. Suz Craig had run the Denver office of the AstuteCare Health Maintenance Organization. John Richard Korman, one of the ACHMO providers, had been dating Suz for the past seven months. On the home front, Suz had bought a luxurious house in Aspen Meadow, where she'd been doing an expensive landscape project. On the business front, she had reportedly fired employees without remorse, and refused those she didn't fire their bonuses. And she had presumably enforced the rules of the HMO, which could have had some implications for Patricia McCracken's case. Patricia sure thought so. Maybe I had to find out the details of her case, after all.

QUESTION, I typed. *Why exactly is Patricia suing both JRK and ACHMO?*

QUESTION: Did Suz Craig fire Dr. Ralph Shelton? If so, why?

QUESTION: Was gambling really enough of a reason for Suz to fire Amy Bartholomew, R.N.?

QUESTION: What did JRK and Suz Craig argue about at the country club?

I sighed. How would I get the answers to these questions? And why should I? I saved my file, shut down the computer, and sipped the steamy hot chocolate. The marshmallow had melted into a creamy layer on the chocolate surface. I licked it off carefully, the way a child would. Outside my kitchen window, elk bleated. I did not feel the remotest bit tired. I needed to get some sleep. How on earth could I face church in a state of exhaustion? Then inspiration struck.

Cook! That'll relax you. Put all these people and all these questions out of your head for a while and whip something up. I fingered the containers of Dutch-processed cocoa and the jar of marshmallow cream I'd left on the counter. Why couldn't you put these together in a cookie? Surely there could be nothing like chocolate and marshmallow in a *cookie* to soothe the nerves?

I put some hazelnuts in the oven to toast, then melted a jagged brick of unsweetened chocolate in the top of our double boiler. I combined sun-dried cranberries and oversize morsels of semisweet chocolate in a bowl, then scattered the hazelnuts to cool on a plate. I began to feel better. By the time I was beating unsalted butter with sugar and cream cheese, I was humming, and this was a mistake. Jake came bounding into the room on his long bloodhound legs, followed closely by a sleepy-eyed Arch clad in rumpled pajamas. Arch fumbled with his glasses and stared in puzzlement at the bowls, the butter wrappers, and the whirling beater.

"Gosh, Mom! What are you doing? Did you forget something? Do you have to take cookies to church?"

"Sorry, honey, I just couldn't sleep. How about some hot chocolate with marshmallow? That's what I used to have when I was your age and flunked a test. Or when I was your age and couldn't sleep. It always worked, despite what they now say about the caffeine in chocolate."

"Well, I *could* have slept if you hadn't awakened Jake," my son grumbled crossly. He shuffled to the back door and opened it, but the elk had stopped bugling and Jake wasn't the least bit interested in a midnight run. Resigned, Arch closed the door and flopped into a chair. "Sure, I'll have some cocoa, thanks." Immediately he was up, offering Jake one of Tom's homemade dog biscuits. "Yeah, boy, there you go! Don't worry, I'm not going to have a treat unless you do!" The large, tawny dog wagged his tail, licked Arch's face, and whined with canine contentment.

I heated more milk and stirred it into a smooth, thick paste of cocoa, sugar, and cream. In his corner, Jake crunched appreciatively.

Chocolate
Comfort Cookies

1 cup chopped hazelnuts

2 cups (1 11$\frac{1}{2}$-ounce package) extra-large
semisweet chocolate chips (Nestle's
mega-morsels)

$\frac{1}{2}$ cup sun-dried cranberries

1 cup (2 sticks) unsalted butter, softened

1 cup granulated sugar

1 3-ounce package cream cheese,
softened

1 egg

2 tablespoons milk

2 ounces best-quality unsweetened
chocolate, melted

1$\frac{1}{2}$ teaspoons vanilla

2 cups plus 2 tablespoons all-purpose
flour (high altitude: add 2 more
tablespoons, for a total of 2$\frac{1}{4}$ cups)

$\frac{1}{2}$ teaspoon baking powder

$\frac{1}{2}$ teaspoon salt

$\frac{1}{4}$ cup Dutch-processed cocoa

1 cup commercially prepared
marshmallow cream

Preheat oven to 325°. Spread nuts on an ungreased cookie sheet and roast for 7 to 12 minutes, or until they are lightly browned and some skins have loosened. Set aside to cool.

Butter 2 cookie sheets. In a large bowl, combine the chocolate chips, cranberries, and cooled nuts; set aside. In another large bowl, beat together the butter, sugar, cream cheese, and egg until very creamy and smooth. Beat in milk, melted chocolate, and vanilla. Sift together the flour, baking powder, salt, and cocoa, then add to the butter mixture. Blend in the marshmallow cream, stirring until thoroughly combined. Add the chips, cranberries, and nuts. Stir until well mixed. Batter will be thick.

Using a $\frac{1}{4}$-cup measure or a 4-tablespoon ice cream scoop, measure out batter and place 2 inches apart on cookie sheets, putting no more than 6 cookies per sheet. Bake 13 to 17 minutes, until puffed and cooked through. Cool on sheet 1 minute; transfer to wire racks to cool completely.

Makes 2 dozen

His dark eyes favored my son and me with loving glances. Arch gave him two more dog biscuits, then watched while I generously glopped marshmallow cream on top of his drink. When I put the steaming mug in front of him, I expected him to pounce on the rich treat as expectantly as I had. Instead, he blew tentatively on the foamy top, then sipped.

"Mom. There's something I need to talk to you about." He put his mug down. "It's about Dad." When my face fell, he quickly said, "Go ahead, make your cookies, it's not important." He added earnestly, "I really mean it, Mom. I don't want to disturb you. Cook, if it'll help you go back to sleep. I just have a couple of questions. . . ."

He had questions, I had questions, everybody had all kinds of questions. My headache returned with a vengeance. I beat the egg and milk into the batter, then added the melted chocolate and vanilla. Once the oven was preheated and the cookie sheets buttered, I measured out what I thought would be a judicious balance of dry ingredients and began to mix them into the batter. These cookies promised to be terrific. But apprehension had drained the joy from cooking experimentation.

Arch said, "So. When was the last time there was an execution in Colorado?"

"Arch!"

"No, really, just tell me. And . . . was it by lethal injection?"

I sighed and scooped the batter onto the cookie sheets. "No, the last execution used the electric chair. And it was over thirty years ago, I think. Law enforcement in Colorado has switched over to lethal injection. But they've never used it."

"The death penalty"—his voice cracked—"is for first-degree murder, right?"

I slid the cookie sheets into the oven and turned. "Arch—"

"Just tell me."

"Yes, for first-degree murder. But—"

"Are you going to help Dad?" he demanded.

His question stung. I set the timer and tried to think of what to say. Finally I asked, "What would you like me to do?"

"Oh, you know," he replied earnestly, "that stuff you do sometimes, go around asking questions, like that. Try to help with the investigation the way you do with Tom."

"Tom's off this case, and I'm a witness. Which is supposed to mean that I don't go around talking to people connected with the case."

"You did when you found that guy's body out at Elk Park Prep and when that lady was killed in the parking garage."

"Those were different. I didn't see any suspects, and I certainly didn't witness an arrest for homicide. And besides, those things happened when I was pretty ignorant about law enforcement."

His thin body sagged. "So that means no." His tone turned morose. "If Dad does get out of jail on Monday the way he thinks he will, I think I should go live with him. Until the trial. I mean, it might be the last time I would see him."

I couldn't believe we were having this conversation, in the middle of the night, in the warm security of our home, here in our warm kitchen. In the extremely unlikely event that John Richard got out of jail anytime before his preliminary hearing, I couldn't imagine that he would *want* Arch to live with him. Whatever punishment I had envisioned for the Jerk during all these years, it hadn't looked like this. It hadn't looked like losing my son.

"Arch," I said quietly, "are you threatening me with moving out? 'Cause that's what it sounds like."

"Mom! Of course not! I'm just trying to do what's right here. He *is* my father."

I struggled for clear thoughts and the right words. "Okay, look. If I can talk to some people . . . and those conversations would help lead to justice . . . *Justice*, I'm talking, Arch, not 'getting somebody off.' There's a difference."

"Yeah, yeah, truth, justice, and the American way. Courtesy of SuperMom."

"Arch!"

"Okay, okay."

"If I could talk to some people but not jeopardize my position as a witness, would you stay here at home? Your dad's really not . . . set up to take care of you. And I would worry about you."

He nodded, whispered "Okay," and drank his cocoa in silence. Then he sniffed, mumbled, "Be right back," and left the room. Jake, ever faithful, scrambled after him. I took the cookies out of the oven and set them on racks to cool.

When Arch returned, he clutched a wadded-up tissue. I couldn't tell if he'd been crying. "I was just thinking, Mom." He'd changed his tone, a clear indication that he wanted to discuss a new topic. "You said you were having a cup of hot chocolate to drink right now, because you couldn't sleep? But when you can't sleep, you should go out for a drive. Don't you remember? That's what you used to do when I was little. When I couldn't sleep, you took me out for a drive, and you said it made you sleepy, too."

"Oh, hon—"

"You probably don't remember, but you *used* to say that driving me around was like having hot chocolate when you were little. The rhythm of the car put me to sleep the way the hot chocolate did you. Even if it was the middle of the night, if I was fussy, you would take me. I don't remember the drives, I just remember you telling me we used to go."

I nodded and checked the cookies; they were almost cool. I remembered the drives, all right. And I hadn't taken them just because Arch was fussy. Time and again, I'd gripped that steering wheel the way fear had clutched me. Rocking over bumpy mountain roads, I'd been desperately trying to figure out a way to escape from my life, from John Richard Korman's abuse, and a marriage I just couldn't hold together anymore. I had been lost in the worst way, and it had taken years to get my *life* on the right road.

Now I packed up the cookies, stacked all the dirty dishes in the sink, and threw away the ingredient debris.

"A drive sounds like a great idea," I told my son. "But what do you say we get some sleep first?"

Arch agreed. For once, he wasn't in the mood to taste my new cookies, and neither was I.

Chapter 14

I begged the Almighty to help me rest up before church began the next morning. Finally I fell into a restless slumber at dawn. Tom woke me, bearing a cup of steaming espresso.

"If you want to make it to the late service," he advised gently, "we need to get a move on." As I struggled upright and promptly winced, Tom added with concern, "Sure you don't want to just stay in bed this morning?"

I assured him I was just stiff. Plus I'd been up during the night cooking. He shook his head and began to massage my aching shoulders. My lower back was still in spasm, and my right ankle throbbed. After drinking the espresso, I checked the ankle. It was ominously blue-black. I limped into the bathroom to take a hot shower, dabbed bits of makeup over the scratches on my face, and finally felt ready to get spiritual succor. While Arch rummaged through the clean laundry for a pair of pants, I tiptoed into Macguire's room. His forehead felt hot, but he moaned a refusal when I suggested his seeing a doctor. I begged him to take a couple more ibuprofen, which he did.

By the time I closed his door, he was asleep. Damn Gail Rodine for making Macguire fall into the lake over her damn silly dolls.

When Tom, Arch, and I arrived at the massive oak entryway to St. Luke's Episcopal Church, the two men in my life held the doors ajar chivalrously. I hobbled through. When the sea of faces turned to appraise my entrance, I immediately realized we'd have done better asking for communion to be brought to the house. For the infirm, having the sacrament delivered was a common enough practice. But it wasn't a very common practice for a caterer who'd been trampled by an inebriated hockey player the same day her ex-husband was arrested for murder. So I hadn't thought of it.

Still, I should have known what kind of spectacle, and fuel for gossip, my bruised self would present. The ripple of whispers rose to a wave. Marla, wearing a lilac-print designer sundress, bolero jacket, matching purple earrings and high heels, immediately bustled over.

"I don't think they're staring because they want to book a buffet brunch," she confided.

"Gosh, Marla. Thanks for the news flash."

The choir shuffled into the vestibule. I took advantage of their arrival to whisper to Marla, "I told Arch I'd ask around about John Richard."

Her taupe-and-lilac-shadowed eyes widened at my confession. "Bad move, Goldy Schulz."

Tom guided us to a pew at the back and the four of us squeezed in. Marla hugged Arch and palmed him two Cadbury bars, which he stuffed into his pants pocket. If Marla's cardiologist ever X-rayed her Louis Vuitton handbag and discovered the bulges were chocolate bars and cream-filled cupcakes, he'd probably have cardiac arrest himself. She leaned close to me.

"Check out who's visiting. I'm an Episcopalian, so I can't point."

It took me a few seconds of scanning the pews to locate Chris Corey, his sister, the cat-loving Tina, and Brandon Yuille, sitting together on the opposite side of the nave. Tina had already told me she was a parishioner. Brandon attended occasionally. I'd never seen Chris at St. Luke's before.

"Probably here to plan Suz's memorial after coffee hour," Marla whispered. "Anyway. As long as you're poking around, have you heard anything new? And what happened, did you lose a fight with your blender?"

I glanced quickly at Arch. My son always made a good, but not perfect, pretense of not listening to adult conversations.

"No and no," I whispered back to her. She opened her mouth, probably to ask another question. Mercifully, the opening bars of the processional hymn rang out. "I'll tell you all about it later."

As much as I tried to concentrate, my eyes wandered back across the nave where Tina and Chris sat with Brandon. As the Old Testament lesson was read, I tried to recall when I'd seen Tina attending church, if ever.

To my horror, I giggled. *Stress.* I gulped and caught a glimpse of Marla's puzzled face, as well as the sudden confused looks from the two Coreys and Brandon Yuille. Well, great.

As we rose for the reading from Luke, I thought of what Marla had said about why two ACHMO department heads would be in church this morning: all the other department heads were away in San Diego. Chris and Brandon were indeed probably here to make funeral arrangements for Suz Craig. Suz had no relatives to perform this task, and Arch had told me that Suz was a nominal Episcopalian. Arch had also reported that Suz had accompanied John Richard on his rare appearances at St. Luke's. Of course, John Richard did not go to church so much to worship as he did to brag about or show off whatever new possession he had, be it car, condo, or concubine.

Stop. In any event, our priest, now delivering his homily, liked to think of St. Luke's as a happy, if not always harmonious, family. Supposedly only family members could use the church building, even if they were dead. You couldn't be baptized, married, or dispensed to the Hereafter unless both you and the people making the arrangements were churchmembers. So it looked as if Suz belonged to St. Luke's, albeit posthumously.

Man, what was the matter with me? I squeezed my eyes shut and focused on the intercessions. A woman prayed for the repose of the soul of her neighbor, Suz. By the time I opened my eyes, the woman's prayer had ended. I had not seen who it was. Brandon quietly echoed the supplication for Suz, then offered a plea for his father, who spent many hours alone. My mind took off again. Brandon had been at the bakery with his father from midnight to five? Sounded like a weird explanation of your whereabouts, even if your father *was* a lonely widower. The idea of *spending many hours alone* made me think of John Richard, who, I was willing to bet, was not attending chapel this morning in the Furman County Jail.

During the offertory, two visiting bagpipe players sounded the mournful notes of "Amazing Grace." While one of the choir sopranos sang the lyrics, my brain reverted to Ralph Shelton. Why had I had the strong feeling Ralph was hiding something when I went to his house? He'd been so hesitant, as if he wanted to talk to me but was afraid to. At the words, "I once was lost, but now am found," I glanced over at Arch. Tears slipped out of his eyes. My heart twisted in my chest.

Forget hugging him. Forget asking what was wrong. I knew better than to treat a fourteen-year-old boy in a way that would embarrass him. Still, it had been years since I'd seen Arch weep openly. I rummaged through my handbag, found a paper napkin, and wordlessly handed it to him. Without acknowledging me, he snatched the napkin. Tom patted my shoulder. Marla shook her head.

During the final hymn, Arch decamped to the men's room. As soon as he left the pew, Marla leaned over. "We should skedaddle before the horde descends on us during the coffee hour. Let's see if Brandon Yuille or the Coreys will talk to us. As ex-wives of the accused, we can say we have the right to know why he might have killed their boss."

"I don't want to leave Arch. . . ."

Marla said, "Arch'll be better off with Tom than with you right now. Think about it. Tom should take him down to the jail for visiting hours." She addressed Tom: "Can the Jerk see Arch today?"

Tom ignored the perplexed glances we were receiving from the people in the pew in front of us and nodded. "Let me take him down to see his father, Miss G. It'll be okay," he reassured me.

My sore shoulders slumped in defeat. Arch returned. The four of us bowed as the cross went by. Then we waited endlessly for the choir, bagpipe players, and priest to process out. When I finally told Arch that Tom would take him to see his dad while Marla and I ran a few errands, he brightened. I was surprised. I'd have thought he'd have responded with apprehension. It seemed I was past knowing what my son needed.

Marla pinched me and I scooted out of the pew, ignoring my aching body. I was feeling every hour of my age today. Once we were outside, she used her sixth sense—the one that fed on gossip—to locate Brandon Yuille and Chris and Tina Corey, who were standing by a pine tree at the edge of the parking lot.

"Yoohoo!" Marla called. "Need to chat for a sec!"

Brandon waved unenthusiastically while Chris, his ankle still in a cast, shifted the weight of his cumbersome body and forced a smile. Brandon, ever sharp, wore khaki pants and a military-style khaki shirt. Tall and heavy, Chris Corey had an enormous potbelly and pale hair and beard. He looked like a young blond Buddha, or rather a young blond Buddha who wore a white dress shirt and gray slacks, and limped. What I'd liked best about Chris when I first met him was that he didn't insist anyone call him doctor. His rumbly baritone had reminded me of a physician from our family's distant past. But when I'd asked him if he'd ever treated us—a pediatrician who'd treated Arch, maybe?—he'd said no. Maybe Chris reminded me less of Buddha than of Santa Claus. When he smiled, his blue eyes crinkled. Apparently, Tina, a female version of her portly brother, hadn't been able to find a Babsie-goes-to-church outfit. She wore a severe black cotton suit, and her hair was twisted back in a tight bun.

"I know you two probably don't want to talk right now," Marla gasped to the men, out of breath from her brief but determined trek across the gravel-covered lot. "Actually, we don't either." She feigned a sadness as fake as squirt butter. "It's just that we *have* to. . . ."

"It's okay," Chris replied amiably, tugging on his blond beard. "It's a tough situation. But we can't visit for long. We're here to plan the funeral."

"We can't talk very much at all," Brandon added, his voice tight. He flipped his long, dark bangs out of his eyes. "The priest just has to finish talking to the coffee-drinkers."

I nodded. The coffee hour was always the time when our pastor had to field questions that fell under the general rubric of pastoral theology. In actuality, coffee-hour questions rivaled anything Ann Landers had ever had to face. *Is God punishing my neighbor with cancer? My son baptized his anole lizard and then the lizard died. Can you give it a Christian burial?* For our spiritual leader, discussing Suz's memorial service might prove to be something of a relief.

Marla plunged right in. "If our ex-husband goes down for murdering his boss, it's going to be bad for us, you know. Much as we don't mind the Jerk suffering, we'd like to know why he killed Suz Craig."

Chris, Brandon, and Tina stared at Marla, open-mouthed.

"That's not . . ." Chris began. "You can't expect us to discuss—"

"Oh, yes, we can," Marla continued brazenly. "You guys are department heads with a big corporation. You need to be responsive to the public, or at least to the ex-wives of the guy who's been charged with murdering your boss. So what we've heard is . . .

there were problems with firing at that HMO. Were there problems in the Human Resources department, Brandon? Did everybody hate her?" When he gaped blankly at her, she turned to Chris. "Can you answer our questions? Please?"

I was embarrassed. This wasn't asking a few questions. This was grilling, with no hot dogs in sight.

"Ah." I leaned in for a few confidential, lighthearted words with Tina Corey. "That doesn't look like a Babsie outfit that I recognize. Let's see . . . could it be . . . Babsie-as-a-Choir-Director?"

Tina's face became rigid. "I don't know what you're talking about."

"Goldy, please," interjected Chris, "could you not—"

"Babsie-as-Altar-Guild-Director?" I attempted, undeterred.

"Be *quiet*," said Tina.

Startled by her harsh tone, I pulled back. Apparently, Babsie wasn't a churchgoer. "Sorry," I muttered. "Er, how's the cat?"

Tina's face remained stonelike. She said nothing. Maybe the cat had run away, and she blamed me. I wished I'd kept my mouth shut. Some people just can't shoot the breeze when they're about to plan a funeral. I shot Marla a pleading can-we-leave glance.

Chris squinted over Marla's shoulder and waved to the priest, who was heading our way with a worried look on his face.

"We don't want to cause a ruckus," Chris said soothingly.

"Then answer my questions," Marla insisted.

"Yes," Chris said softly. "There were problems at ACHMO. It was not a happy place to work."

"You all look so solemn. People are wondering what the five of you are discussing out here," our priest said, joining us.

"Nothing," Marla said gaily. She always sought gossip but rarely shared it when there was no hope of reciprocal dirt. She tugged me away and I muttered good-byes to the two men and Tina. Marla pulled open the door to her Mercedes. I got in on the passenger side. After the van, sitting in the low-slung four-wheel-drive Mercedes always made me feel like an astronaut en route to Uranus.

"I can ask Brandon Yuille and Chris Corey a few questions if I want," Marla said defiantly as she slammed her door and prepared to blast off.

"Yeah, right. You can see how well it went."

"Tough tacks." She revved the car and zoomed out of the lot, then slowed behind a van crammed with tourists from Kansas. "So who should we be talking to if you're going to help Arch? And what are we supposed to say? Or haven't you figured that out yet? 'Hi, we're the two ex-wives of the doctor who's been busted for murder! Can we come in for tea and a little interrogation?'"

I sighed. "Let's go talk to Frances Markasian. You said she came to visit you, why didn't she come to visit me? I think she lives in the Spruce apartments."

Marla pressed the accelerator. "Now *there's* an upscale address."

The Spruce apartment building was a four-story stucco edifice that had probably been constructed when Aspen Meadow was rapidly expanding in the sixties. *Spruce up* was just what the building owners had not done, unfortunately. The seventies had seen the apartment house, which sat perched on a hill overlooking Main Street, painted a blinding yellow. I was willing to wager there'd been no repainting since. Warped and rotted cedar-shake shingles curled on the roof or lay helter-skelter between the crabgrass and the drooping lodgepole pines that flanked the building. Marla pulled the Mercedes next to a wall of yellow cinder blocks that marked off the front parking area. I didn't see Frances's Subaru, but knew there was another cracked-asphalt blacktop behind the building where the residents kept overflow cars.

"Tell me again why we're here," Marla said doubtfully.

"All this happened to John Richard yesterday," I reminded her. "You know Frances Markasian. She's a fast and efficient snooper. If somebody knows anything, she will."

"All I know is that she's also covering the doll show at the lake," Marla grumbled. "Maybe she's doing a story on Coroner Babsies."

The elevator was out of order. We walked up the stairs to apartment 349, the Markasian residence, and knocked. No one home. An elderly man came out into the third-floor foyer and unabashedly watched us as Marla rapped harder. The elderly man cleared his throat.

"Hey, you girls!" he snarled. His white hair had been brutally shaved in a crewcut, and his deeply lined face looked malevolent. "What do you want? You're not more of them, are you?"

I held my index finger up to Marla: *Let me handle this.* To the elderly gent I said pleasantly, "More of whom?"

He made an impatient gesture. "Parade of people all day. That woman's not a reporter, she's a bureaucracy. Get out of here, you're ruining the place."

I felt my cheeks redden.

But Marla wasn't merely blushing. She was purple with rage. "Cool your jets, fella! If we want to look for somebody, we'll look, you got it? We'll knock on every door in the place if we want to. Ever heard of freedom of the press? Do you know where we can find Frances Markasian?"

"Look, you two!" he cackled. "You want stories on your dolls? Grow up! Dolls for grown women," he spat. "You want Frances Markasian, go down to the lake and find her!"

I was ready to retreat, but Marla insisted on having the last word, as usual. She wagged a lilac-painted nail at the man.

"Watch your mouth, please! Collecting is a venerable hobby. And it's a smart investment! Not only that, but you're rude!"

"I may be rude, but I'm not crazy!" he cackled before disappearing into 350.

Marla shot after him and I had to limp along behind her to catch up. Fortunately, the man's apartment door slammed before Marla could force her way in for a confrontation. Marla rapped hard and repeatedly on his door. Squeals of "Shut up!" and "Go away or I'll call the cops!" issued from other apartments. But our white-haired, unpleasant critic did not reappear.

Chapter 15

In the afternoon sun Aspen Meadow Lake shimmered like sugar on ice. Several dozen cars in the dirt parking area made me wonder if there was a waiting line for skiffs and paddleboats. We got out of the Mercedes and approached the LakeCenter's front door.

The LakeCenter was a jewel of that architectural species known as "mountain contemporary." Constructed of row upon row of massive blond logs, wide, soaring trapezoids of glass, polished plank flooring within, aprons of flagstone without, and topped with a phenomenally expensive all-weather shingle roof, the structure was the glory of the Aspen Meadow Recreation District. The interior consisted of a huge space, fancifully called "the Ballroom," and a more intimate adjoining space known as "the Octagon." Both rooms provided unequaled views of the lake. There was a kitchen, too. I would be working there when I catered to the Babsie people. Alas, the kitchen afforded no scenic vista.

Unfortunately, the LakeCenter was locked up tight. We rounded the building, looking for Frances Markasian and any evidence of the doll show. The cormorants paddled furiously along the lake's edge. When they dove for fish, they would stay underwater for so long it seemed impossible that a land-based animal would not drown. But then, miraculously, the sleek black birds would pop back up, triumphantly clasping tiny, slithering fish in their beaks.

When we came up on the boat-rental shop, we found that it was indeed open. Thirty or so people waited for skiffs.

"A land-office business," Marla commented, "despite the fact that it's on the water."

"But no Frances," I pointed out.

"Think we should go talk to those other people John Richard mentioned, Ralph Shelton and Amy Bartholomew? And how'd you get messed up, anyway?"

"I'd rather not see either of them just yet. Ralph Shelton banged into me yesterday at the McCrackens' party. Literally. Amy Bartholomew patched me up. Before Ralph used me for a landing pad, I tried to ask him some questions about Suz. He didn't have much to say. Ditto with Amy, except I got some New Age gobbledygook about Suz Craig's negative karma. I don't want to ask them any more questions until we know better what we're looking for."

"What exactly are we looking for?" Marla said as she va-voomed the Mercedes.

"I wish I knew."

"Speak for yourself," she shot back. "We know the Jerk did it. I'm looking for lunch."

"Hold on a minute," I replied. "Frances hates to cook. She's a cheapskate, but every now and then she shows up at the Aspen Meadow Café, especially if she's doing an interview and the paper is springing for the meal. With any luck, we could run into her there."

We trekked over to the café, but Frances Markasian was again nowhere in evidence. So Marla insisted on treating me. With the Jerk finally in jail where he belonged, she claimed, we should have every manner of salads to celebrate. Using her best queenly manner, she waved at the waitress and announced: "Bring 'em all." Soon platter after platter arrived: roast beef salad, pasta salad, corn and pepper salad, fruit salad, and an arugula salad with toasted walnuts that I went wild for. I knew from experience that I'd never get the recipe from the café chef, so I made a mental note to reinvent it in my own kitchen, using some meringue-baked pecans I had frozen. Not one to neglect balance, Marla ordered a bottle of champagne and hot popovers to go with our salads.

I laughed at her indulgence. Really, I'm extremely fortunate that I have both Marla and Tom to be sure that I'm regularly fed as well as loved and fussed over. For someone in the food business, such care is a rare treat.

Marla claimed to want none of the leftovers. When our waitress handed me the bulging bags of goodies, I observed, "Our family will have enough here for a week."

"That's the idea," Marla replied happily. "Besides, dealing with the Jerk, you're going to need all the help you can get."

When she was signing her credit-card slip, a newly arrived group of diners caught my eye. I grabbed Marla's arm. "Hey, check it out."

She followed my gaze. We watched Frances Markasian trying to decide which of the outside patio tables would suit. With her were Chris Corey and his sister, Tina. Tina had changed into some kind of costume. This time, I was *sure* it was a Babsie outfit.

"Do you know why Tina changed into that getup?" I asked Marla, who made it her business to know as much as possible about the lives of Aspen Meadow residents.

"The costume? Who knows. Tina is an aide at Aspen Meadow Preschool. She's the head Babsie-club organizer, too, so it might have something to do with the show starting. Maybe Frances is interviewing her."

Tina now sported the same long blond pigtails she had at Gail Rodine's house yesterday. She wore a frilly lace blouse and a royal-blue vest with matching skirt, both covered with a lace-edged, snow-white apron.

I said, "For the doll show I've mainly been dealing with Gail Rodine. She's in charge of hospitality and security." Marla made a face. I pushed my chair back. "I promised Arch I would help him. Let's go crash their lunch."

"Mah-velous," she said. "I love crashing anything."

Frances was peering into the café for a waitress. As she did so, she impatiently tapped one foot. The foot was encased in a duct-tape-wrapped sneaker. Her black trench coat was, of course, unnecessary in the August heat. But Frances was (or fancied herself) a high-powered investigative reporter temporarily trapped in Aspen Meadow, Colorado. With long, wildly frizzy black hair, skin of an unhealthy pallor, thrift-shop clothes, and a chain-smoking habit that would undoubtedly blacken her lungs within a decade, she at least knew how to *dress* the part.

Frances's ambition in the county was legendary. She went after every crime and disaster story like a starving wildcat pouncing on its prey. Her headlines were certainly creative. In May we'd had I-70 DRIVER SHOOTS ROADSIDE BUFFALO IN COLD BLOOD! June had seen EXPLOSION IN MOTH-INFESTED PROPANE GRILL SAILS PRESIDENT OF KIWANIS INTO CREEK! Readership of our town paper had tripled since Frances had come on staff two years ago.

"Hey, Goldy," she said amiably as we neared her table. She pushed the black frizz from her forehead. "I've already been by to see you today, but you weren't home. Do you know the Coreys? Chris is head of Provider Relations with ACHMO—the AstuteCare Health Maintenance Organization in Denver. And this is his sister, Tina. She works at Aspen Meadow Preschool and presides over the local Babsie doll club."

"Good to see you, Frances. And I know both Coreys," I replied. "In fact, we've already chatted this morning."

Chris brought his unwieldy bulk to a standing position, balancing awkwardly on his cast. His pale beard bobbed as he greeted us.

"We're sorry to disturb you," Marla lied in a breathy gush.

Frances rumbled a laugh and lit a cigarette. "No, you're not sorry. Anyway, this is great. I'm absolutely *desperate* to talk to Goldy. Sit."

Tina nodded at us. Her cold manner had changed completely from her behavior at church. She blushed. If I'd been wearing her outfit, I'd have blushed, too.

Gaping at Tina, Marla said, "Well, Heidi, where'd you leave your sheep?"

Chris smiled indulgently, but the color deepened painfully on Tina's neck and cheeks. She lowered her head and smoothed the frilly apron. I knew better than to ask about the cat again. Frances scowled in the awkward silence. This was not a good way to start a lunch-crashing, no doubt about it.

"Wait a minute," I said enthusiastically. "I know that outfit, Tina! It's the Icelandic Babsie!" Tina raised her head, grasped a blond pigtail, and gave me a shy smile. "I'm catering the doll show," I reminded her, since she seemed not to have remembered me at church. "Do you remember me from the Rodines' place yesterday?" I shook Tina's limp, fleshy hand. "Do you remember me?"

Tina regained her composure. "Of course. You gave me my new kitty."

Finally, we were on solid ground. Maybe she just didn't discuss dolls or cats at church. "That cat sure took to you," I said warmly. Tina beamed.

Under her breath Marla muttered, "Gosh, Goldy, run for office, why don't you?"

Our waitress reappeared, and Chris announced that he was treating everyone, what would we like? Chris, his sister, and Frances ordered sandwiches. Marla, suddenly the picture of charm, said she'd love some fudge meringue pie. I went for Linzertorte and iced coffee, trying to think of how to ask Frances my questions about John Richard. *What have you dug up? Are you on to something? Exactly why did you want to see me this morning?* Lucky for me, Frances pried so blatantly that we were spared subtle inquisition. Instead, she plunged right in.

"Hey, ladies, think your mutual ex-husband will grant me an interview from behind bars?" Her slightly yellow teeth flashed in a wide, crooked smile.

"I don't know," I answered sincerely.

Marla said, "I'll pay for you to do the interview, if you get a photo of him in an orange suit that you publish in the paper."

"Has it been hard, or are you two just *loving* this?" Frances wanted to know, with her usual sensitivity.

Marla shrugged.

"I wouldn't say I'm loving it," I told Frances tartly. "A woman is dead. Plus my son's suffering pretty badly, especially after his father called from jail yesterday. Arch is down there visiting him right now."

Too late, I realized I should have kept my mouth shut. Frances and I were friends, but nothing came before a scoop. She dug frantically in her voluminous black handbag, yanked out a pen and a grimy pad of paper, and began to scribble. "What did Korman say in this phone call that upset Arch?"

"Nothing! Please, stop taking notes. For crying out loud, Frances, this is *personal*."

Chris mumbled, "Maybe we should talk about something else, Frances. I don't think—"

She gestured imperiously. "It's always personal for somebody, Goldy."

"Don't give me that low-brow journalistic jive. Please. If you want me to stay here and visit, promise not to print anything about my son."

She kept on scribbling, pursed her lips, and pushed her hair out of her eyes. "Okay, I won't if you'll let me run some stuff by you. Besides, I'm sure you'll want to hear all I've learned about this Craig business. Chris here"—she flapped a casual hand in his direction—

"is an insider. There's all kinds of scuttlebutt. You know this town. Once something happens, it's like a . . ." She closed her eyes and sought the perfect simile. "Like a . . . volcanic energy erupts around the desire to know what's going on."

Chris took a deep breath and shifted his weight uncomfortably. Tina sipped some water. Marla, of course, was all ears. But Mount Saint Frances calmly lit a cigarette. My attempt to ask Frances a few delicate questions was going awry pretty quickly.

"Run some stuff by me?" I echoed. "Such as?"

"Okay, this is top secret. If somebody comes up to the table here and wants to know what we're talking about, we say I'm interviewing Tina for the doll show."

"So what are you running by me?"

"ACHMO is planning a raid," she informed me blithely, her tone a shade lower. "On John Richard Korman's office. Tomorrow morning."

Marla shrieked with glee. I said, "A raid? Frances, what on earth are you talking about?"

Our food arrived and I was thankful for the momentary distraction. A raid? What were they looking for? And why would ACHMO raid anyone's office? This could not be true. I assumed an expression of polite interest and, because the waitress hovered over us, attempted to change the subject.

"How's your ankle coming along?" I asked Chris. "I should have asked after church."

He smiled shyly. "I'll be kicking field goals in no time."

Frances took three bites of her sandwich, pushed it away, and relit the half-finished cigarette she had carefully squashed out when the food arrived. "So. You want to hear about the raid or not?"

"Yes, yes, yes," urged Marla, eyes sparkling.

"Why don't you just tell the police about it?" I asked. The Linzertorte was delicious, a crunchy crust covered with jewel-colored raspberry jam. "A raid by the HMO has *got* to be illegal, Frances."

"But it isn't." Chris's surprisingly powerful baritone commanded attention. "We do it all the time. Usually we call first, which is what we'll do tomorrow. We come in to check information in the files."

"*What?*" Marla exclaimed. "What about patient confidentiality?"

Chris readjusted his ankle and went on. "Marla. Goldy. May I call you by your first names?" Frances nodded, I noticed, before we had the chance. "It's in our contract," he continued. "We can visit any practice we own. A nurse, a doctor, someone with medical training who's working for the HMO, comes in. It's not really a *raid*." He grinned indulgently at Frances, who was lighting her second cigarette. "We just want to check how certain procedures get billed, and we do it by going through individual files. The provider's office has to let us have what we want."

Well, my curiosity was piqued, no question. John Richard in jail and ACHMO was going to crash into his office to go through his *files*. Small wonder that Frances was interested, too.

"What are you going to be looking for tomorrow morning? Something related to Suz Craig?" I asked mildly.

"And may I come?" demanded Marla.

Chris's reply was matter-of-fact. "No, oh, no. And actually, Suz is—was—the one who ordered this visit. It's been planned for a while, but we were waiting until Korman was called out on a delivery. Now we've got a perfect opportunity to go in. And it's not what the Medical Management person will *say* she wants that matters. Or what I say, as head of Provider Relations. Since she's a nurse and I'm a doctor, that's how ACHMO gets around the patient confidentiality issue. But in this case what we *say* we want and what we'll *actually* be after are two entirely different things."

"What is it you'll actually be after?" I inquired innocently. "And why are you telling us this?"

Chris tugged on his beard. "What we'll be looking for are personal notes from Korman about the McCrackens' suit. At least, that's what Suz, and now the chief honchos at ACHMO, want us to be looking for. And those *would* be illegal for ACHMO to lift. The corporation is trying to cover itself, and it's taking the opportunity of Korman being out of the way to be thorough. Frances will tell you about it. She's going to write an article exposing the whole thing."

"Frances is going to write an *exposé*?" I said, wide-eyed.

"Imagine that," commented Marla. "And will this exposé help or hurt the no-good doctor in jail for murder?"

Frances scowled as she crushed out her cigarette and lit another. She muttered, "The timing could be a little better. The angle I'm going to be looking for is: Did Korman have a clue that Suz Craig had this raid on his records planned?"

"What do you get out of this, Chris?" I asked. "Don't you still work for ACHMO? Won't this article get you into trouble with them?"

"I want people to know what the HMO is up to," he answered darkly. "You shouldn't be able to just go through people's files whenever you want. And Frances is going to keep my identity a secret. I can't afford to lose my job."

"But ACHMO wouldn't have killed one of their own, would they?"

A pained expression wrinkled the heavy folds of his face at my question. "I don't think so. Neither does anyone I've talked to. You can imagine, Goldy, all of our phones have been ringing off their hooks ever since the captain down at the Furman County Sheriff's Department called ACHMO's chief honcho in Minneapolis yesterday. One of my higher-ups at corporate called and said now was the time to go through Korman's records, the way Suz planned. So that's why they're sending me in tomorrow—to find any personal notes Korman might have left in his office." He paused and blinked at me. His eyelashes were so pale, they were invisible. "Everyone at ACHMO is convinced your husband beat Suz to death."

"He's my *ex*-husband," I said quietly. Why did no one seem to remember this?

"My ex-husband, too," said Marla defiantly. "So get your facts straight before you go off insulting us."

Frances leaned affectionately toward Chris and whispered something in his ear. Tina fluffed the lace on her Icelandic Babsie blouse. And I sat back and thought that now I had one more thing for the sheriff's department to ask John Richard: *Know anything about Suz's dirty little scheme to betray you?*

"Look, Goldy," Frances said, "there are two things we want to talk to you about. First of all, Patricia McCracken. Seen her lately?"

"As a matter of fact, I catered a party for her last night."

"Is that where you got banged up?"

I nodded and pretended not to notice the way the two Coreys stared at my face. I concentrated instead on the sky, where layers of pink cloud were again gathering in the west.

Frances persisted. "Now we all know Patricia got dumped by a doctor, then married a dentist. She doesn't have the kind of money she used to, since there are at least fifty dentists in Aspen Meadow. Back in the old days she had a way of displaying the three things she bought with her divorce-from-the-doc settlement: a too-large diamond ring, a sapphire bracelet removed and perpetually left behind in exercise class, and an always-filthy white Triumph whose leather seats her son, Tyler, had smeared with fingerpaints when he was a toddler."

"She just sold the Triumph to pay her lawyer's retainer," Marla interjected. "Everybody in town knows that."

"Have you met Tyler?" Frances asked, unfazed. "He's a five-year-old monster."

"I know him," Marla said. "He's a brat."

"Oh, no," said Tina. They were her first words in a while. "He's extremely creative. He used to help me with the hamsters. He just has a lot of energy, that's all."

Frances raised an eyebrow at me.

"Yes, I've met Tyler," I replied. "Arch baby-sat him a couple of times when Tyler was younger. But the kid was so hyper that Arch said he'd never go again, no matter how broke he was. Last night the McCrackens took Tyler over to a friend's house rather than risk him wrecking their party, which got wrecked anyway," I muttered, thinking of the hockey free-for-all and my aching bones.

"Uh-huh," replied Frances, bored. She fished in her purse again, pulled out a can of Jolt cola, and popped the top. She was never without several cans, and given its triple-caffeine hit, I doubted she ever slept at all. Now she took a long swig, then dragged on the cig. I wondered if her doing an article on HMOs would have any influence on her unhealthful habits. Somehow, I doubted it. The cigarette dangled from her mouth as she handed Chris the Jolt and pawed again through her purse for another notebook. She retrieved it, flipped a few torn and curled pages, and announced: "Okay, here it is. Our Patricia begged Dr. John Richard Korman to stick her in the hospital when the placenta previa was causing problems in the pregnancy. But ACHMO wouldn't cover it. ACHMO said Patricia should rest right in her own snug little bed until she was ready to deliver. With all of the McCrackens' money tied up in their heavily mortgaged house and Clark's mostly off-again dentistry practice, the prospect of an open-ended hospital stay was enough to conjure up bankruptcy. So Patricia peddled her jewelry," Frances added with relish. "The diamond ring and sapphire bracelet paid for a one-month hospital stay that ACHMO wouldn't spring for plus babysitting for Tyler. She couldn't sell the Triumph because she would have had to buy a new car when she had the baby, and the Triumph had depreciated too much even to give her a down payment. And little Tyler's fingerpainting on the white seats didn't exactly add to its value."

Frances looked at me as if expecting praise. I looked back at her in silence. Marla rolled her eyes.

Frances sighed. "So she sold the jewelry and stayed in the

hospital until she ran out of money. Then she checked into a low-cost suite near the hospital, you know about those? She put that on her credit card." Frances raised her eyebrows, pressed her lips into a grim line, and flipped another page of her notes. "But it wasn't enough. She lost the baby at seven months. Talk about bitter—that woman's saliva could pickle a turkey."

"Frances," I chided. "You don't have children. You can't imagine the loss—"

"Yeah, yeah, yeah. So Patricia McCracken went nova. She sued Korman. She sued ACHMO. Her lawyers accepted the cases on contingency. Patricia took out a second mortgage on their Keystone condo and sold the Triumph after all, to pay the other legal fees. She didn't care what she spent, as long as she brought John Richard Korman and ACHMO to their knees. You can't sue an HMO for malpractice. So she's trying to sock them with negligence, for even having Korman as a provider. What Patricia *didn't* tell me, but I was able to find out from another source, is that our very same Mrs. P. McCracken was arrested last week for smashing flagstones in Suz Craig's driveway."

I sat up straight. *"What?"*

Marla murmured, "For heaven's sake, Goldy, what good is it to have you married to a cop if he doesn't even keep us supplied with news of local crimes?"

"Ah," said Frances. "Marla and Goldy are finally interested. You know how angry that woman was? I'll tell you. She was screaming about how if she couldn't have her baby, 'some conniving coldhearted childless bitch' "—she glanced at her notes, "and I quote, 'isn't going to entertain with a big patio paid for with blood. With BLOOD!' "

"But Patricia McCracken was in Keystone last week," I pointed out.

"Not the whole week she wasn't. Anyway, after the arrest, Suz Craig didn't press charges. But Ms. Craig did get a restraining order against Patricia, who agreed to undergo psychological evaluation. She also agreed to enter grief therapy for people who've lost their babies before delivery, as soon as she returned from a planned trip to Keystone." Frances slapped her notebook shut with a triumphant *thwack*.

"Except for the flagstone story, did you get all this from Patricia?" I asked.

"Of course I did," Frances responded hotly. "What the hell kind of reporter do you think I am? And I had to give Tyler all the candy corn I usually keep in my purse to keep him from crawling all over me."

Marla said, "Candy corn? Is that the best you could do?"

Tina Corey *tsk*ed.

To Tina's brother I said, "How come ACHMO doesn't recommend hospitalization for placenta previa?"

"I don't make the rules, Goldy. Some MBA does. What ACHMO did wasn't illegal, unfortunately."

I turned back to Frances. "But if Patricia is suing, isn't there some kind of gag order on her talking to you?"

"Gag order? Are you kidding?" Frances pulled out another cigarette and lit it with the end of the one she was finishing. "That woman is dying to have her story published in the most incendiary manner possible. The only reason she talked to me was that the *Denver Post* and *Rocky Mountain News* weren't interested. And coupled with what I know about ACHMO swooping into the Jerk's office to search for notes on the case . . . well." She inhaled in a satisfied manner. "ACHMO is going *down*." She smirked at me.

I had the sudden feeling I needed to get home and check that Arch had survived his jail visit. "Well, we'll see. Marla, are you ready?" Without waiting for a reply I said, "We need to fly, Frances."

"Hold on, you haven't told me anything yet about Suz's murder. I don't want to talk to you just about Patricia McCracken." Frances began to rummage in her purse again while Marla popped a last bite of pie in her mouth. "Look, I've got a few things to show you."

"Frances, I can't *tell* you anything. You must be able to under-stand that—"

Her nicotine-stained fingers held out three newspaper clip-pings. Reluctantly, I took them. Marla peered over my shoulder. Frances swiped the hair out of her left eye and demanded curtly, "Tell me if either of you know either of these guys in the first one."

Two smiling men held up glasses of wine to the camera. MER-ITMED HMO CELEBRATES NEBRASKA SUCCESS. Well, bully for them, and I hoped they were quaffing an Omaha vintage. But there was no doubt that I knew one of the two men. In fact, I had seen him yesterday, up close and personal. The caption read: "Ralph Shelton, M.D., and Mark McCreary, Chief Executive Of-ficer, MeritMed, observed the company's success in the Cornhusker State." I checked the date: May 14.

I tapped the blurry images. "Ralph Shelton used to work for ACHMO, now he works for MeritMed. So what?"

Frances blew smoke in a steady stream off the patio. "Mer-itMed has an office in Denver." She squinted at me; I shook my head. "In March Ralph Shelton was fired from AstuteCare by Suz Craig."

I looked at Chris. "You want to tell us a little more about those problems with firings?"

He shrugged. Marla demanded, "Do either of you know *why* Ralph was fired?"

Chris shook his head. "Not yet."

While Marla read the first article, I perused the second piece. It was much shorter, with no accompanying photograph. It was an an-nouncement from a paper in Vail.

Dr. John R. Korman will address the Colorado Association of Obstetricians tonight at 8 P.M. on "Postpartum Use of Anti-biotics." Summit Stag Hotel, across from Vail Valley Medical Center.

The article was older than the first, dated in early January.

"Frances," I asked, perplexed, "why are you showing us this? I don't know John Richard's schedule. He goes to these conventions if it means he can ski and whoop it up. The only times I know what he's up to is when we have to change our visitation arrangements with Arch."

Airily, Frances waved this off. "Do you know your ex-husband's relationship with a drug company named Bailey Products?"

"Yes," interjected Marla, her voice sour. "John Richard travels around, or he used to travel around, touting their product. Something called Biocess. How do you know about it?" When Frances glanced at Chris, Marla pressed, "Do you know what happened to the Biocess endorsement money?"

Frances nodded. "Yeah, I found out from Ralph Shelton, who also used the stuff in his practice. Ralph's old buddy John Richard Korman pushed Biocess from Portland, Oregon, to Portland, Maine. At least until recently. Check this out."

I took the article Frances now proffered, and again Marla read over my shoulder. This was from a newspaper in Omaha, and like the first clipping, was also dated May 14. The headline ran: MEDICAL CONFERENCE ATTENDEES WARNED OF ANTIBIOTIC'S POSSIBLY LETHAL SIDE EFFECTS. I skimmed this one, too, which basically said that an HMO executive was warning his colleagues in other HMOs that in the course of their standard audits, his organization had found that Biocess had been linked to one death from liver failure, and several cases of negative side effects, plus higher costs postpartum. I skipped to the end of the article, where a Bailey Products spokesperson said that an Adverse Event Form had been filed with the FDA and that Bailey had put the use of Biocess on hold until they could do more studies of the antibiotic.

"Hmm," I said noncommittally, and handed the article back to Frances.

She took it and said, "So Biocess, Korman's much-loved designer antibiotic, was discovered to cause liver damage. And the cornucopia of goodies from Bailey Products available to John Richard Korman was suddenly empty."

"There's your answer to what caused that blip in income," I told Marla.

Frances went on. "Now you two, of all people, should know Korman's financial situation had become really, really bad. In fact, everything was about to come crashing down on his head. And think how much worse it would become if Suz Craig denied him a big fat bonus. Which she did."

I said to Chris, "Why did Suz deny the bonus? Why would she?"

"Legitimately?" he asked with a frown. "We send out questionnaires to a sampling of a doctor's patients. If we get even one serious complaint, the bonus is automatically denied. Or if a doctor refers patients to specialists too much, or if he refers too little, the bonus is denied. If he hasn't seen enough patients or cut costs over the past year, the bonus is denied."

"Now that's what I call both a carrot and a stick," Marla murmured.

I said, "Look, Frances, we both knew he was having money problems." But truly, neither Marla nor I had known the full extent of the problems.

"Yeah, yeah," Frances was saying. "And now ACHMO is going to raid him. And you know they'll make him the fall guy for the McCracken mess if they find one scrap of paper they can use to blame him for the whole thing."

I asked Chris, "You mentioned that you'd be looking for what you called 'personal notes' that John Richard might have made when you go in tomorrow. What kind of notes?"

Frances eagerly interjected: "They're looking for anything John Richard might have written to cover himself, like 'I told Patricia that my recommendation was for her to go into the hospital. But then I had to tell her that the HMO vetoed it.' Or like 'Told P.

McCracken today that HMO had denied her hospital stay because they're penny-pinchers. Cheap sons of bitches!' " she finished with a flourish.

I addressed Chris Corey. "Do you think there were such notes? And exactly who is going in looking besides you and the Medical Management lady? Somebody who represents Suz's interests in protecting ACHMO?"

Chris leaned forward. "Korman and ACHMO are not exactly on the same side on these suits, you know. If Korman kept notes to try to cover himself, ACHMO wants those notes very, very badly. If Korman criticized the HMO to a patient, he violated the terms of his contract with us. Worse for AstuteCare, if the HMO recommended bedrest at home while Dr. Korman claims *he* recommended a hospital stay or she'd lose that baby . . . Well, you can see what would happen to the malpractice suit, and how bad ACHMO would look. ACHMO needs to know what he's thinking, what he's done." He shook his head glumly.

"Something else," Frances said. "Chris tells me ACHMO was considering putting Korman on probation as a provider, just for being sued for malpractice."

Marla erupted in a gale of laughter. As Frances lit yet another cigarette, I wondered how ACHMO was reacting to the Jerk being accused of murder.

Frances exhaled and went on. "Plus, if Korman was saying one thing to Patricia McCracken and another to ACHMO, then ACHMO claims they can put him out the door. And, believe me, if Korman got kicked off the ACHMO provider list, he'd have *nothing*, since he sold his practice to them. And the person deciding about his probation is Suz Craig. Or should I say *was* Suz Craig?" she concluded gleefully.

"Why don't you talk to the police?" I asked with a glance at Chris. He shook his head sadly. "Why tell me?"

Frances quirked her bushy black eyebrows and, true to form, ignored my questions. Of course I already knew the answer: Because she wanted a story. "Listen," she demanded, "did Korman give either you or Marla anything to keep? Like any files or packages or notes on the McCracken case? I won't be able to nab ACHMO without something concrete."

Again Marla burst out laughing. "He gives me any files, he knows I'm going to shred them. Goldy might smoke them in her barbecue."

"Are you kidding?" I protested. "I'd put them through the vegetable shredder."

Frances shook her head. "Okay, okay, it was worth a try. But think. You probably heard the story about Suz and John Richard arguing at the club Friday night. After what I just told you, wouldn't it make sense that they argued about *money*? He says he needs his bonus, she says he'll be lucky not to be cut off by ACHMO completely. Goldy, does Tom know yet what they were fighting about?"

"I'd like to stay married, thanks, Frances." I'd had enough. "Okay, Marla, I really need to get home. I'm worried about Arch."

"I'm with you," she said heartily, and took a last sip of coffee. We shook hands with Chris and Tina, thanked them for treating us to dessert, and started to leave.

"Hey! Hold on!" Frances cried as she nipped along behind us. "I need to know what Korman called about from jail!"

I finally managed to get Frances to let go of the Mercedes door handle by promising to call her if there were any momentous developments in the case of John Richard. "Momentous developments" to me meant anything the Furman County Sheriff's Department public information officer was about to announce to all the newspapers, but I did not make this clarification to her.

Frances's black coat billowed out behind her and the smoke from her cigarette whipped away as she strode back to the café for another Jolt cola. I would call her if *I* wanted to know something. But next time I'd be careful not even to mention Arch.

Chapter 16

At home Macguire announced he was having trouble swallowing. His fever had abated somewhat, but he still would not eat a morsel. I made him some soft-serve strawberry Jell-O. After three bites he announced he needed to go back to sleep. Well, great.

I perused the contracts for the doll-show meals that Gail Rodine and I had worked out. Babsie-doll collectors were apparently as paranoid about getting mayonnaise on those itsy-bitsy plastic high heels as they were about having their dolls taken out of their original boxes. So the Babsie-bash organizers, despite the fact that they were expecting over two hundred people per day at the show, had only sold tickets for forty box lunches on Tuesday. Then on Wednesday a sit-down breakfast for the executive committee and helpers—twenty people—would be followed that evening by a concluding barbecue, for which the show organizers had sold sixty tickets. All the meals would be served on the LakeCenter patio picnic tables. A guard would be stationed at the back door so that not a smear of barbecue sauce could touch a single doll's ponytail. Best of all was that Gail

Rodine's down payment would provide the first installment of Arch's fall tuition at Elk Park Prep, an expense John Richard was supposed to cover. The likelihood of *that* happening was now as slender as spaghettini.

Arch, Tom, and I had takeout Chinese food that Tom had insisted on bringing home. I was both curious and apprehensive to hear the details of their afternoon. *How did your father look in an orange suit? Was he handcuffed?* And most important: *Did he say he did it?* But Arch mumbled that he didn't want to talk about it. I was bothered that he was so very subdued. While we were doing the dishes, I brought Tom up to date on all I had learned from Frances and Chris Corey. He placed the last serving spoon in the dishwasher, washed his hands, and took some notes that he said he'd pass on to the D.A.'s investigator. Then he set his notebook aside and told me that Arch hadn't uttered a word all the way home.

"Did you see John Richard, too?" I asked him.

Tom shook his head. "Miss Goldy, you'd better prepare yourself. This is a classic lose-lose situation. Tomorrow John Richard may get out on bail. It's a long shot, but . . . The county judge who's coming up on rotation? Name's Scott Taryton. Taryton's stated publicly that he's tired of all the mollycoddling women are getting these days. For mollycoddling, read *rights*."

"Oh, don't—"

Tom held up a fleshy palm. "Listen. A female judge down in Denver let a first-degree murder suspect out on thirty thousand dollars' bond last summer. The woman had shot her husband, alleging abuse. Taryton blew a gasket when that judge granted bond. We've been waiting for some kind of retaliation from him. Setting bond for a man implicated in a murder—especially one stemming from a domestic dispute—would be just his cup of tea. John Richard could be it."

"But isn't there a law about not letting murder suspects out?"

Tom scowled. "Oh, sure. Murder suspects, according to state law, need to be held without bond until a hearing on the evidence.

But after bail was granted last summer for that other suspect, the upholding of that particular state law has become fuzzy. Fuzzy enough for Taryton to do exactly what he wants."

"God help us."

"Taryton's no friend to women," Tom concluded grimly.

It was no wonder that I once again had trouble sleeping. The insomnia came despite an expert shoulder massage from Tom and a late-night phone check from Marla—did I want help from her for any of the doll-club events? I thanked her and said I would be fine; I needed the work to keep my mind occupied.

I fell asleep dreaming of dolls bearing trays of grilled burgers. At two I awoke with my heart hammering. *Bam, bam, bam,* John Richard used to hit me. He'd shake me and then strike my face with his fist. I'd try to get away or fight back. No use. *Bam.* One leg, the other leg, my back. He was a great believer in symmetry.

I shuddered and crept out of bed. Then I took a shower to relieve my cramping muscles. I toweled off and listened for noise in the house. Had I awakened anyone this time? Apparently not. I dressed silently—sleep was now impossible—and suddenly remembered Arch's advice: *You should go out for a drive. That's what you used to do when I was little. When I couldn't sleep. . . .*

Should I? Well, why not. I found my keys and purse and tiptoed out onto the back deck. Overhead, shreds of cloud drifted across a river of stars. The air was warm. A sudden *bleat! bleat!* accompanied a rustling of leaves. A wave of panic swept over me. Then I saw a dozen elk moving slowly under the pine trees. It *was* a one-in-ten year for the big animals.

I sat in the van and wondered how long a drive I needed to make to get tired enough to go back to sleep. I didn't have anyplace to go. But even as I turned the key in the ignition I knew where I was headed.

My van engine sounded loud on Main Street. All the stores, of course, were dark, from Darlene's Antiques & Collectibles to the Doughnut Shop. A breeze washed through the aspen trees lining the street. Cottonwood Creek splashed and rumbled, while a cloth sign advertising Aspen Meadow Barbecue flapped like a forgotten flag. Gone were the rows of motorcycles ordinarily parked at acute angles in front of the Grizzly Bear Saloon on summer evenings. They had roared off into the night hours earlier, and the saloon was engulfed in darkness.

The van chugged past the spotlight trained on the waterfall emptying out of Aspen Meadow Lake. The cormorants had abandoned their perch, and I wondered fleetingly where the birds spent their nights. The LakeCenter roof twinkled with a string of Christmas lights that our recreation district board had insisted would give the place a festive look year-round. They'd been right.

The small shopping center housing one of our two grocery stores was also dark, except for the Aspen Meadow Pastry Shop, where, I was sure, the ever-industrious Mickey Yuille was making cinnamon rolls for his Monday-morning customers. Perhaps Brandon was there keeping him company.

At the entrance to the country club, a dark car sat under the streetlight. Its door read MOUNTAIN SECURITY, but no one was inside. Perhaps the fellow had succumbed to sleep and was lying across the front seat. I was tempted to find out how ticked off he would be if I blasted him with my horn.

I turned onto Jacobean and glanced at the clock on my dashboard. Eleven minutes from our house to Suz's, no traffic. The streetlights cast a neon glow on the asphalt and all the mown lawns. The yards were perfect except for Suz's. There, mounds of topsoil lay untouched, and yellow police ribbons were pulled taut around the crime scene and the house.

Even though it was only one day after the murder, the sheriff's department could not afford to put deputies in front of the house. I pulled up slowly by the ditch and glanced again at my dashboard clock. Thirty-two minutes after two. John Richard's place onto Kells Way was three blocks in one direction, then another two around a curvy road that cut a circle through the club's residential area, then two more blocks in the direction of the golf course. His house was on the downhill side of the road leading to the course. I wondered if there were police ribbons around it, too.

When my van accelerated noisily down Jacobean, I saw a curtain being drawn back in the Tollifers' front room. A yellow trapezoid of light framed a figure peering out. Apparently, I wasn't the only one with insomnia tonight.

A scant six minutes later I turned onto Kells Way. Here the streetlights were tucked into the tops of lodgepole pines. The light that fell on the asphalt shifted and swayed with the movement of the trees. Six minutes to the street sign—but how long to his driveway? I let the van drift down to the curb in front of the mammoth mock-Tudor residence that John Richard occupied all by himself. It took only a few seconds. I cut the engine and rolled down the window. Was I feeling tired? Not even remotely. So much for Arch's prescription for insomnia.

The wind picked up. Wind chimes on a nearby deck swirled and tinkled. The sound filtered through the rush of clicking aspen leaves. I breathed in the sweet summer air and wondered if John Richard had a window in his cell.

Okay, now, *think*. If John Richard had left Suz's house around one A.M., as he claimed, then he could have been back at his place before one-ten. Say he went inside. Had a few more drinks. Decided to go back and finish their argument. This was a possible reconstruction of events, but not a likely one, given his violent way of finishing things once he'd started them.

My neck stiffened and I tried to get comfortable. The pain in my shoulders had subsided to a mild ache. I reached for a tablecloth I kept stored in a plastic bag behind the passenger seat. I shoved aside the earphones and wires of Macguire's Walkman and pulled out the damask cloth. Tucking it around me, I tried to envision another way of timing Friday night's events.

No matter how much other people may not have liked Suz, John Richard was the one who'd been with her, arguing with her at the club, possibly about his terrible financial situation. Say he'd fought with Suz at her home, left her dead or near dead, then had gone back to his house around three or three-thirty A.M. This, I thought, was a more likely scenario. It fit the way he acted. Once he was enraged, it could have taken him several hours to work his way through it. What had Tom said? *Near as they can figure, Suz Craig died between three and five . . . Rigor hadn't set in when the medics arrived.* If John Richard left Suz sometime after three A.M., then everything fell into place.

The breeze died; the rustle of leaves and pine needles stopped. In the distance a car rumbled around the club's circle. A wide swath of light swept the end of Kells Way. Then there was sudden quiet.

Say John Richard's fight with Suz had gone on and on. She screamed and contradicted him. The argument became violent, with pots and pans being used for weapons. Then Suz finally got the usual *bam bam bam.* Then more arguing and maybe another horrible whack. Then he left in a huff, with her hurt and screaming. She would have cried for him not to leave her in such a state. Then she stumbled outside for help, fell into the ditch, and died. All this would explain why rigor hadn't set in until just after seven A.M.

There was a noise on the street that was not from a tree, a car, a herd of elk, a sprinkler system, or a set of wind chimes. My heart stopped. Someone whispered with loud insistence.

"Hey, man! Aren't you *done* yet?"

My spinal column turned to ice. The voice was about fifty feet away, on the same side of the street where I sat in my van. Whoever this was, he or she or they must have come along after I'd parked my vehicle, during that ten minutes when I'd been sitting deep in thought.

I cut my eyes both ways, without moving, but could make out

nothing. Kids sneaking home after hours? Car thieves? Burglars? If a couple of guys were going to rob a private residence, I didn't care. I just didn't want them to add *assault of caterer* to their list of crimes.

"No, man, I'm not *done*!" came the urgent whispered reply. "This fluorescent stuff is dripping all over the damn place! Plus, I'm almost out! So hand me another can and shut up!"

There was grunting and clinking. "I'm tired of doing a good deed, man!" was the bitter response. "That security guy comes this way right on the hour!"

"I told you to shut your mouth, or the neighbors will get him here even earlier!"

"But it's almost three!" his partner insisted. "He's going to be here any second! We need to split! Just *leave* it!"

My dashboard clock said 2:52. Eight minutes until the security guy showed up . . . if he did. Ever so slowly, inch by inch, I leaned forward to look out the windshield. If I could see them, I could figure out how to drive off without incident. Kells Way was a dead end. If these two guys—whoever they were, whatever their intentions—were in front of me, I could rev the ignition, throw the van into reverse, and zip backward up the street. If they were *behind* me on Kells, I could make a U-turn and accelerate across someone's driveway to get past them.

Spotlights shone down on the homes, driveways, and lawns on each side of the street. John Richard's house boasted spotlights above the garage that did not quite illuminate the two darkened stories of the rambling, beamed structure. Nothing out of place appeared on his blacktop. Then I noticed several cans that looked as if they'd been discarded to one side of the driveway. Farther over, almost to the stone entryway that was topped by an expansive burgundy awning, I could see the bottom of a ladder. Why would John Richard have left a ladder out? He hated doing home repairs.

Inching forward slowly in my seat, I strained my eyes to see more. A figure was moving through the trees. Then I made out someone on the ladder. A car door slammed, and the movement under the trees abruptly stopped.

"Hurry *up*, man! What're you doing, getting high on fumes?"

This whisper came from high on the ladder. From the same direction as the car door, a motor started up. Someone was going somewhere. The guy under the trees scrambled up the ladder rungs, and I heard the unmistakable *hiss-s-s* of a spray-paint can.

It was the country-club vandals.

The car that had started around the circle above Kells revved and moved. Was it the security man? I couldn't tell. Headlights coursed along the left side of the street, the dead end, then John Richard's house.

One of the vandals was at the bottom of the ladder. The other was at the top. Young men, lean and tall, dressed in dark colors. In the approaching headlights a dripping, crooked word painted in brilliant yellow appeared above them.

KILLER

Chapter 17

I shivered again. Perspiration sprouted on my forehead and palms. The vandals who had caused so much property damage in the club area were spray-painting their verdict on John Richard's house. Or maybe it was something they'd seen. Well, I'd forgotten the cellular phone and couldn't call the cops. So these guys would have to make their point to law enforcement on their own. I was getting out of here.

I pumped the accelerator, turned the car key. The motor strained, didn't turn over, died. I'd flooded the engine. I turned the key again, didn't pump the gas. This time the engine whined and died again. Footsteps thudded across John Richard's lawn. Dammit all, anyway.

Frantically, I rolled up my window. But I couldn't reach across in time to close the one on the passenger side. A lanky figure in a black ski mask pulled up the lock, wrenched open the door, and scrambled in. I could smell the sweat on his body. *They're kids*, I told myself. *Don't panic.* Behind the black mask the vandal's eyes glared menacingly at me. He grabbed my upper right arm.

"Get out of the car," he hissed angrily. "And shut *up.*"

"Let *go,*" I said evenly, tugging away from him. "I was just sitting here because I went out for a drive—"

His fingers bit into my arm. "Shut up and *get out.*"

"Stop pulling on me and I will," I replied in a quiet, non-threatening voice that I hoped didn't betray how furiously my heart was hammering. To my astonishment, the figure in black loosened his grip slightly. I shed the tablecloth and hopped awkwardly onto the street.

"Watch her," Vandal One ordered Vandal Two. In the street-light I could see Vandal Two was brandishing a tire iron. "I gotta check her van," the first guy said. "See if she's got some kind a weapon or night-vision camera in there."

"That's ridiculous, of course I don't," I snapped. "I'm just a caterer." I strained to see up the street. The passing car had disappeared without turning down Kells Way. Where was the security man?

"Oh, yeah?" said Vandal Two, a smirk in his voice. He twirled the tire iron inexpertly. "Kinda early for fixin' breakfast, wouldn't you say?"

"Listen, guys. The man who lives here, the guy who was arrested? He's my ex-husband."

"Really," said Vandal One. He spat. "What, this guy's in jail, you've got an old key, you figure you'll go in and pick up a few things while he's not around?"

"No. That's not why I'm here."

Vandal One leered ominously. "Then why *are* you here?"

When in doubt, tell the truth. "I couldn't sleep. I went out for a drive."

Vandal Two's eyes sparked behind the mask. He raised the tire iron. "You'll sleep if I knock you over the head."

The words were out of my mouth before I could pull them back. "Hey, tough guy! I thought you were so worried about the security man driving up!" This warning earned me a rude shove on the shoulder. I stepped back and said, "Why're *you* here?"

Vandal Two stabbed a finger at the house. "Can't you read? We know he did it."

In the darkness it was almost impossible to see the ugly yellow word. "Ah. Killer. How do you know that?"

"Wouldn't you like to know. We see lots of things."

I shrugged. But if these two knew anything about the attack on Suz . . . "How—"

"Wait a minute," exclaimed Vandal One, "you said you're a caterer? I read about you."

I said mildly, "And you are . . . ?" When he didn't answer, I went on. "So why are you so certain my ex-husband killed her?"

"You think we have time to tell you anything?" erupted Vandal Two. To his compatriot he urged, "Come on, let's get out of here."

"I'm married to a cop," I announced hastily. "If he catches you, he'll ream both of you out so bad you'll get a life sentence for shoplifting when this is over. Both of you," I added, stalling for time. Where in the world was that security guy, anyway? "But if you'll talk to me about why you think my ex-husband is guilty—"

The guy with the tire iron waggled it in my face. "I know why you're here. Insomnia, my ass. That doc goes down, I'll bet you inherit this house. You're too shy to gloat over your loot in the daylight, but you just couldn't sleep until you got a good look at your new place."

I was tempted to ask: Just how much of that paint did you inhale, anyway? But there was no telling these two anything. No telling them that, come those circumstances, Arch would inherit. Not that my son would want this enormous place. Not that my son would want anything besides having his parents alive and well and out of jail. But I needed to know if they had seen something Friday night.

And where was the security man? Why did no neighbors seem to hear me out here arguing with vandals?

I made a decision. The vandals probably wouldn't hurt me, despite the pop Vandal Two had given my shoulder. These two were cowards, which was why they defaced other people's property at night. Still, they were angry young cowards, so I would have to be careful.

I took a tentative step toward my van. "I want to go home. Are you going to tell me why you think my ex-husband murdered that woman? Or do you want the cops swarming all over here tomorrow with their fingerprint equipment? Actually," I said offhandedly, "they'll probably do that, anyway. A murder investigation is a whole different ball game from cleaning up graffiti, guys."

Vandal Two lifted his chin mockingly. "You're just dying to know, aren't you?"

"Yeah. I am."

Vandal One pressed forward. "We saw him," he said, his mouth so suddenly close to mine, I trembled in spite of myself. His breath smelled of potato chips. "The Korman guy left that night in a white Jeep. He's gone two minutes and then comes back in the Jeep, only slower this time."

"What time did he do this leaving and returning? Where were you when you saw all this?"

"Oh, bitch, what do you think I am—Rodney King with a videocamera?"

"Rodney King didn't videotape—"

"Shut up," growled Vandal One. "The doc leaves in his Jeep. About ten minutes later he drives up again, but the lights are off."

"What do you mean, the lights are off? And was it two minutes or ten minutes? Are you sure it was Korman? Was it a white Jeep or a silver one? He has one of each."

"Look, it was a white Jeep. And it happened. He drove away fast and came back slowly, with no lights. He knocked on the side door and what's-her-name yelled at him a little bit. Then she let him in."

Vandal Two hissed, "Suck it up, man, somebody's coming! We gotta split!"

The tire iron clanged to the pavement. The boys bolted. I peered up Kells Way into the glare of headlights. The approaching car was not the security car. The driver stopped, opened a mailbox, and stuffed in a newspaper. This person didn't bring security; he brought the news. He would be no help. Spooked by some ambushes in Denver, the newspaper delivery folks now wouldn't stop if you were bleeding your guts out in six feet of snow. But I didn't need this person's assistance.

I whirled and peered into the shifting light of the yards. The vandals had vanished. They had found a magical way of disappearing through people's property. From what vantage point had they watched Suz Craig's house the night she died? The two guys hadn't seen me drive down Kells Way. Perhaps they'd been vandalizing the club road signs on an adjoining block when I'd parked.

The metallic slap of mailboxes being opened and closed punctuated the night air. There was no sign of the security man and no sound of a pickup truck or some other vehicle being driven away. Where had the vandals gone? I had no idea.

It was time to boogie.

By the time I drove past the security car with its still-dozing watchman and arrived home, the dashboard clock read three-forty-five. Time flies when you're avoiding insomnia. I shivered my way into pajamas, eased into bed, and slid my arms around Tom's warm body. No use waking him. A reasonable morning hour would be a better time to tell him all that had happened.

But I'd awakened him anyway. He turned over and mumbled, "Where in the *world* have you been, Miss G.?" I shushed him gently and curled in closer. But he took my cold hands in his warm ones. "I went downstairs looking for you . . . then I saw the van was gone. Honestly, I've been a wreck."

I wove my cold legs through his deliciously warm ones. "I couldn't sleep, so I went for a drive. I wanted to . . . to *time* the driving distances over by Suz Craig's. How long from Suz's house to John Richard's, you know. But"—I hugged him tight—"I ended up interrupting a pair of vandals spray-painting John Richard's house. You're not going to believe it, but these guys were painting the word 'Killer.' So I talked to them—"

"*What?*" Tom extricated himself from my embrace, threw off the sheets, and turned on the lamp. Soon he was dressed in a terry robe and had one of our zillion leaky Biocess pens poised over his trusty spiral notebook. He said, "Would you care to make a quick statement, Mrs. Schulz?"

I sighed, then told him all about the vandals on Kells Way. I included their rude shove and their nonvideotaped account of how they'd seen John Richard drive away from Suz's house in his Jeep that night and then return very slowly, lights out. "They thought I was in front of John Richard's tonight so that I could steal something from inside the house. Or to gloat over inheriting the place."

Tom tapped his notebook. "You didn't hear them drive away? But yet you say they were afraid of the country-club security man. Who never showed up."

"Maybe they hid in their car or their truck," I offered.

He scowled. "Maybe. More likely, they're teenagers who live right there somewhere. They probably took off on foot or on bike, figuring they could come back later for their paint and ladder." After a moment of pondering, he turned off the light and pulled me close.

I murmured, "I'm sorry I worried you."

His breath brushed my ear. "Please don't do any more middle-of-the-night neighborhood prowling, okay? Can we get you a pre-scription for sleeping pills? It'd be safer."

"No, thanks." I hesitated. "Tom. It takes almost ten minutes to get back to John Richard's house. These guys couldn't tell me if it was ten minutes or two minutes between when he roared off and when he returned. And why would he drive back so soon? He never recovers from a fit of temper that fast."

"Haven't a clue. I'm going back to sleep. But I want a promise from you. A couple of promises, actually."

"Name them."

"Miss G. You seem determined to poke your nose into this. Maybe you doubt Korman killed the woman. Maybe you're trying to help Arch. But you're snooping around. Don't disagree." When I nodded, he went on. "Okay, promise me: You won't go down to that ACHMO office. You won't break into John Richard's office and go through his files. You won't break into Suz Craig's house or John Richard's house. We—official law enforcement—will go to the offices and interview the people. We will go through the files, search the houses, all that. Okay?"

"What *can* I do?"

"Do what you always do. Talk to people. Feed them your great food. And *try* to stay out of trouble. Promise?"

I sighed. "You drive a hard bargain, cop."

He sighed too. "Let's just say I love my wife. And I want to keep her alive."

The next morning, Monday, I was sleeping so deeply when Tom left that he didn't bring me coffee. I didn't even hear Arch go out, although he left me a note taped to the computer saying he'd be back from his friend Todd's house by dinnertime. I banged around the kitchen making espresso and toasting homemade bread. I started a sponge for the brioche I would use for the doll people's box-lunch sandwiches. No other catering assignments loomed, so I checked that I had the right smoked meats and cheeses, plus some almonds, lemons, and seedless raspberry jam. I wanted to start experimentation to make my own Linzer tarts. I reread the last line in Arch's note: *You* promised *to help Dad, Mom.*

Right. Help him without visiting the ACHMO office, without

breaking into Suz's or the Jerk's house, without sneaking into the Jerk's office to go through files. How about this: I could visit John Richard's office and *not* poke into files. Couldn't I?

I put in a call to Tom's phone and got his machine. Any leads on the vandals? I wanted to know. Or on anything else? Call me back. After I finished breakfast—crunchy toasted Anadama bread thickly slathered with butter and apple butter—I checked on Macguire. He was sleeping. I felt his forehead. The fever seemed to have broken.

His yellow-flecked brown eyes opened wide when I withdrew my hand and he groaned. "What's up?"

"Not much. I just wanted to check on you. Any chance you'd want to walk over to John Richard's office with me in a little bit? ReeAnn will probably be there."

It's amazing how energizing infatuation can be. With much groaning, Macguire roused himself, showered, shaved, and dressed. When he shuffled into the kitchen, his white cotton T-shirt and dark jeans hung so limply on his emaciated frame that I found myself begging. After all, it's my profession to *feed* people.

"Please, Macguire. *Please* eat something. Let me fix you some juice and toast. People love my homemade bread and—"

"No. Thanks." He surveyed the kitchen dispiritedly, then looked at my anxious face and relented. "Okay. I'll have a little glass of juice and a piece of bread. Don't toast it, though. Toast is too crusty. Hurts my throat."

He swallowed less than a quarter-cup of juice and nibbled a third of a slice of crustless homemade bread. At least it was something.

When we walked through the door of John Richard's spacious, all-beige office fifteen minutes later, ReeAnn Collins was in a state, and it wasn't a good one. Holding the lengthy phone cord in front of the marble counter, she paced across the deep-pile carpet, complained into the receiver, and gestured furiously with her free hand. Her buxom figure was shown off to splendid advantage by a size-too-small white T-shirt and clinging black biking shorts. Her curly black ponytail and long, pouffed bangs bobbed as she bent from time to time to whack at magazines that spilled from the beige-painted tables.

"First Judy calls in sick. She's a nurse, but she can't tell me what kind of sickness she has. So here I am, left to do everything, and then the sheriff's department calls and says don't touch anything. They're on their way." She nodded us distractedly toward the waiting-area chairs. "Then *ACHMO* calls," she continued into the phone, "and says don't give anything to the *sheriff's department.*" I sat down and wondered, as I always did, how hugely pregnant women could ever extract themselves from these deep, soft couches once their appointment time arrived. ReeAnn stormed on. "ACHMO says the files belong to them, and if I give the sheriff's department anything, I'm in deep yogurt. So then they say they're on *their* way." She set her heart-shape, usually quite pretty face into a pout as she listened to the advice from the other end of the line. She examined her black-and-purple-painted nails and sighed. "Okay. Bring your bike rack. Noon." She slammed the phone down and examined us bitterly. "What do *you* want?"

Macguire tucked his chin into his neck and gabbled something unintelligible. Poor kid. Aside from ReeAnn's plentiful figure and pretty face, I couldn't figure the attraction. Maybe it was the black-and-purple nails.

"ReeAnn," I reassured her, "we're here to help you. You see, I talked to somebody from ACHMO after church yesterday, and after what happened to Ms. Craig—"

She stabbed a dark fingernail at Macguire. "Are you the one who told the cops I didn't like Ms. Craig? Because they came to my place yesterday, you know."

"Er, I, no—" Maguire stammered. "I guess I—"

Before he could continue his feeble protests, ReeAnn pointed the fingernail at me. "Uh-huh. And you, Mrs. Ex-Korman Number One, exactly how're you going to help me? My boss is behind bars and the cops think I hated his girlfriend? What're you going to do, hire a temporary nurse to come in and help out? Call all the expectant women and recommend other doctors to them? You going to loan me some money from your catering biz when I don't get paid this week?"

"ReeAnn, you're upset. Please call me Mrs. Schulz. Or Goldy."

"*I* know," she said spitefully. "You're here about money. That's what Mrs. Ex-Korman Number Two is always calling about."

I replied calmly, "I'm not interested in money, or at least only marginally. Listen, do you know *why* the ACHMO people are coming today?"

She sighed dramatically and looked away. "I never know. One week it's 'Let's see how you're billing ultrasounds.' Then they pull out ten records of women who've had ultrasounds. If one of the patients happened to say, 'Oh, my, I'd like to have an ultrasound because I'm worried about the baby,' and the doc writes that in the woman's file, you can kiss your reimbursement good-bye."

I said, "Hmm." Chris Corey had explained that the HMO came in to the doctors' offices to check billing, but I still didn't know the reason. "Why does what the patient says about the ultrasound matter?"

"Be-cause," she supplied impatiently, "if you want to be sure ACHMO is going to pay for the ultrasound, there has to be a *medical* reason for the test. And the ultrasound has to be the *doctor's* idea, understand? Even if it's the patient's idea, we have to dress it up like the doctor figured her life was in danger if she didn't have an ultrasound. Otherwise, ACHMO doesn't fork over the money for the ultrasound. Understand? Welcome to the world of managed care, Mrs. Ex-Korman Number One."

This was going to be fun, I could tell. The phone rang. ReeAnn dealt with the problem—a woman seeking an appointment—by referring her to another doctor. Then she turned back to us.

"So what do you two want, anyway? To talk about ACHMO coming? I don't have time."

I said bluntly, "Do you think my ex-husband killed Ms. Craig?"

My question seemed to surprise her. She pursed her lips and opened her eyes wide. Macguire watched her in enamored awe. Then she reached back to twirl her ponytail while she considered. "He could have," she replied noncommittally.

When she didn't say more, I prodded, "How about Patricia McCracken? Do you think she could have lost her temper with Suz Craig?"

ReeAnn snorted. "That's just as likely." The phone rang again. "Listen, I'm sorry, I really don't have time to chat—" I waved to her to answer the phone. ReeAnn disposed of this caller by advising her to give the pharmacy a ring.

"Where's Patricia McCracken's file?" I asked as soon as the secretary was not-so-ready to chat again.

Her laugh was derisive. "You gotta be kidding if you think I'm going to show you a patient file."

"I don't want you to *show* me anything," I replied patiently. "What you might want to do is try to find something. It's what the ACHMO people are going to be here looking for. It could be a letter, a note, something about the McCracken suit. If John Richard wrote a few lines to himself about Patricia McCracken's care and the ACHMO people take them, it *will* adversely affect me and my son. John Richard could be found at fault in the malpractice suit and we'll lose financial support. Actually, what I really wanted was for Patricia to win her suit."

ReeAnn shook her head vigorously; the ponytail bobbed. "You've *already* lost financial support," she said scathingly. "He was thinking you were making so much money from your food business, he didn't have to pay anymore. And then when Bailey Products dumped Biocess . . . It's been awful. And he works so *hard*," she whined. "And what'll happen to *me* if they try him for killing her?"

I took a deep breath. I'd always suspected that ReeAnn and John Richard were cut from the same self-centered cloth. Now I was sure of it. But had ReeAnn and the Jerk been romantically involved in the few months she had been working for him? Could ReeAnn have been jealous of Suz Craig? Jealous enough to kill?

"My son," I said with a smile, "is extremely upset about his dad being in jail. So I promised him I'd ask around to see if there was anything to clear him, okay?"

"Uh, ReeAnn, remember?" Macguire interjected feebly. "Remember when you mentioned you were involved in a project with the HMO? Something to do with Ms. Craig? Remember, you called her Ms. Crank? That's probably why the police came to visit you."

"That woman was a first-class bitch," ReeAnn spat. "And that's exactly what I told those cops. I did call her Ms. Crank. And you know what Ms. Crank's favorite saying was, don't you?" Macguire and I looked at her expectantly. She raised her voice and trilled, " 'I don't *do*—I *delegate*.' "

"Oh, yes," I mumbled, remembering that that was precisely what Suz had said to me regarding the preparation of food for her business lunch. "I guess I did know that. But she did help me with the dishes when I worked for her, and she could have delegated that—"

"Cheap!" ReeAnn fumed. "I finally told her, 'Don't tell me to *do* another thing, okay? *Delegate somewhere else!* I don't work for you!' "

"What exactly did she want you to—"

I was interrupted by a knock at the door, followed by the entrance of Brandon Yuille. Today he wore a loose blue oxford-cloth shirt with no tie, navy pants, and Top-Siders.

"Hey-ho, we're here!" Brandon's cheery greeting was more along the lines of *How soon will Christmas dinner be ready* than *This is Eliot Ness, get up against the wall.* "Hey, Goldy! What're you doing here? I forgot to ask you yesterday, did you try that Thai sauce I gave you?" His whole attitude was much brighter than when I'd seen him after church. Behind him, however, Chris Corey appeared even glummer than he had the day before.

"Ah, no," I replied, "not yet."

"Well, then, why're you here?" Brandon asked again, still smiling.

"I'm just looking for some of Arch's, er, homework papers."

"In August? Isn't school out?"

"They've been missing for a long time."

ReeAnn slapped a pile of files down on the counter and shot me a knowing look of exasperation.

"Well, boys, here's a batch of D & Cs for you to look through. Did I guess right?"

"Nah, we need C-sections," Brandon announced brightly. "They've been missing even longer than homework papers." His laugh was infectious, and I found myself smiling in spite of myself. To ReeAnn he said, "Should we start in there?" He motioned down the hall to the filing office.

"That sounds just great." ReeAnn didn't do sarcasm well. "As if I had some choice, right? I've got to stay here and do the phones."

"Here's the list of the files we'll be looking for," Chris said meekly as he squeezed his pudgy body behind the counter and consulted a clipboard. He waited a moment until Brandon was out of earshot. I nipped over to the counter. "Did you do a dummy duplicate of Patricia McCracken's file?" Chris asked ReeAnn urgently.

"Yes," she whispered back. "Just the way you told me. I've got the original up here." She pointed to a shelf. The phone rang; she snatched it.

"What?" she squawked. "It's *your* turn to bring lunch! You think I can handle one more thing today? Forget it! Tuna sandwiches!" Then she slammed down the phone. It didn't sound as if she got along very well with whoever it was.

I said, "Chris! I thought you wanted ACHMO to be caught trying to take the file!"

He harumphed and readjusted his capacious belt. "If Brandon takes the dummy with McCracken's name on it before the police get here," he whispered impatiently, "then they'll still be committing an illegal act. And with ReeAnn keeping the real file, your husband's lawyer can still have the information he needs."

"He's my *ex*-husband, okay?" I hissed fiercely. "And I thought you said it would be a Medical Management lady coming here today. What has Human Resources got to do with checking billing? Does Brandon ever do that?"

Chris shrugged grandly. "They're scared." And then, balanced precariously on his cast, he lumbered off after Brandon.

"Don't remove anything, fellas!" I called after them. "My husband's a cop and I'll tell on you!" To ReeAnn I said softly, "The sheriff's department is on its way?"

"Supposedly." She eyed the telephone on the marble counter, as if debating which friend she should complain to next.

"Uh, I guess we'll be going," Macguire announced. His face was as sallow as I'd seen it since he'd been living with us. Despite his words, however, he didn't seem to have the energy or the will to move.

"ReeAnn," I whispered as I scooped up the back copies of *Architectural Digest* she'd spewed on the floor during her first manic phone call. "Can we please talk for a few minutes? It's for Arch."

"I don't know where his homework is."

"Please."

"I have to answer the phone."

"I know you were romantically involved with my ex-husband," I improvised. When I said this, ReeAnn shot Macguire a withering look. "It's okay," I added.

"I'm involved with somebody else right now, not an old geezer. And I was with *him* all Friday night. My new boyfriend can vouch for me, and I told the cops that, too."

"Fine." I tried to think. "Just tell me— What was Suz Craig working on that she was trying to delegate? Delegate to you, I mean? It seems odd she'd ask you to do work for her, when she had a whole army of secretaries to choose from at ACHMO."

ReeAnn snorted again, her trademark. "I'm not a secretary, I'm an *assistant*. And the stuff Ms. Crank had me do was penny-ante. 'Make our dinner reservations.' 'Call Aspen Meadow Nursery. Get them to come out and fix my steps.' "

When she seemed reluctant to go on, I prompted, "That's it?"

"Well. Not exactly." She bit the inside of her cheek, then confided, "It's what John Richard told me she tried to delegate to him that was really weird, if you want to know the truth."

"The truth would be great."

She leaned close. "She wanted him to put some stuff—I guess it was papers or something—in a safe place, somewhere the ACHMO people couldn't find them."

"What stuff? How do you know it was papers? The kind of papers they're trying to find now?" Suddenly I remembered what John Richard had said to me on the phone: *Suz had some kind of delicate material.* . . . What material? I'd thought it related to Ralph Shelton, but was that wrong? "Are you sure it was papers?"

She shrugged indifferently. "Who knows?" The phone rang. RecAnn answered it and started to redirect another patient. To my surprise Brandon Yuille suddenly appeared at my side. He flashed me his movie-star smile.

"Goldy? May I talk to you for a minute?"

"More Thai sauce?" I said brightly.

"Please. Just right outside the front door. Just for a sec, if you don't mind."

I walked outside with him. I'd tell him what he wanted to know—maybe—if he'd answer a couple of questions, too. I made my voice pleasant. "Brandon, I was wondering . . . Was Suz Craig as hard to work for as some people say?"

His fine-featured face bloomed pink. "Some people thought she was . . . difficult." His tone grew guarded.

"So, what people are we talking about?"

He brushed my question away. "Goldy, there's something important I need to ask you, but it's . . . delicate." Man, they all loved that word, like they had to rinse out some lingerie. "You know how folks going through a divorce will sometimes hide assets from each other? Like money?"

I laughed. "Of course I do. Who's getting the divorce?"

He squirmed. "I . . . can't say. But you know about hiding assets?"

"Sure. One person in a marriage hides assets, the other gets to hire a forensic accountant, as I had to do, to go through the books of the person doing the hiding. Sometimes you find the stash and sometimes you don't. Lucky for me, I did."

Brandon's eyes, ordinarily deep brown, turned almost black. His voice became painfully earnest. "I promise, Goldy, if John Richard has given you anything to hide . . . we . . . I . . . need to know."

I almost laughed again. I imagined a list of intimate—make that *delicate*—questions: Have you had cosmetic surgery? Do you dye your hair? How much do you weigh? which could develop into How much money do you make? Now, apparently, to that invasive list I could add: Has your abusive ex-husband given you anything incriminating to hide?

"Brandon," I said with equal earnestness as the phone pealed again inside, "if my ex-husband had given me a bald eagle that he had shot and stuffed, I wouldn't tell the ACHMO honchos."

Brandon Yuille, my foodie buddy, turned on his heel and strode away. I immediately felt bad. I liked Brandon; I didn't want to alienate him. From inside the office ReeAnn said, "What? Who? Yeah, she's here. Goldy!"

When I went back into the office, Chris Corey had not reappeared and Macguire was still slumped in one of the chairs looking catatonic. As soon as Brandon found out the call wasn't for him, he brushed past ReeAnn on his way back into the file rooms.

"Man!" ReeAnn exclaimed, gesturing with the phone. "What is *his* problem? Anyway, the phone's for you."

I sighed and walked back to the counter. "Yes?" I said tentatively into the receiver.

"Miss G." Tom's warm, calm, reassuring voice. "I had a feeling you'd be over there. Bad news, I'm afraid."

"Go ahead."

"I warned you. The judge did it. John Richard made bail. He'll be out in two hours, probably back up in Aspen Meadow by noon."

"No."

"Yes. Now listen, you're a witness in this matter. He's been warned not to talk to any witnesses, but you know how poorly this guy follows directions. If he shows up at the house, or does anything to try to contact you, you ignore him, understand? Call us. We don't want this case ruined before it even starts."

"Okay." My voice was on novocaine.

"Goldy? Don't want to press a point here, but you're in danger. You found the body. You saw him drive up with the flowers. You're the main person who can testify about his physical abusiveness. He's in some kind of mental state, and he may just want to rid himself of you altogether. Is Macguire there? I thought we agreed you weren't going to go poking around through files."

"I'm just here at the office for a few minutes. And I'm not doing any poking through files. The people poking are the ACHMO folks. Are your people on their way? ReeAnn said they were."

"They should be there in five minutes. Be sure you're in your kitchen in two hours, okay? I'm warning you, Goldy. I don't want you hurt. Okay, please put me on with that secretary so I can get her to kick those ACHMO guys out until our people get there."

I handed ReeAnn the phone, then told her that Macguire and I had to go. She tossed her ponytail in a suit-yourself gesture. But Macguire and I were not going straight home. We had someone else to warn.

Chapter 18

As we drove away from the office, I waited for a barrage of questions from Macguire. Ordinarily, the teenager took great interest in criminal cases. But he regarded me dully when I said we had one further stop to make.

"You don't want to go right home?" he asked. "You're always talking about how dangerous the Jerk is."

"I promised Arch I'd ask a few questions."

He shrugged and was silent. When we rounded the lake, spumes of dust were rising from the LakeCenter parking lot. The doll-show organizers had arrived. Without enthusiasm, I realized I needed to talk to them, too, before I went home, so that made *two* stops. I pulled into the lot of the sleek wood-paneled Lakeview Shopping Center, a two-story, L-shaped constellation of boutiques and offices that had recently been constructed on the old site of a gaudy saloon. Before the saloon went bankrupt, it had boasted a Vegas-style light display arranged in the shape of a covered wagon that appeared to roll from one end of the building toward the lake.

But drunk wannabe cowboys exiting the saloon frequently thought the neon wagon was going to roll over them. Numerous car accidents had ensued. The sheriff's department had ordered the light display turned off, and that had been curtains for the saloon.

I parked in front of Sam's Soups, which had a For Lease sign in its darkened window. Food service in Aspen Meadow is always a touchy business, and Sam's alternately gluey and thin soups had not been a local hit. Next door to Sam's, Aspen Meadow Health Foods had held on, but only by going through a number of permutations. Up until a few months ago, my friend Elizabeth Miller had offered everything from twenty-pound bags of millet to gallon jugs of soy milk. Elizabeth had sold the store to Amy Bartholomew, R.N., late of the AstuteCare HMO and new purveyor of homeopathic remedies.

Only she wasn't purveying at the moment. Amy's paper clock sign indicated that she opened at eleven. It was barely ten. Not only that but Amy had scribbled "Most Days" on the clock's center. Great. I glanced across the road at the LakeCenter.

"Mind if we drop by over there?" I asked Macguire, pointing at the LakeCenter. "I just want to see how they need me to set up for the breakfast Wednesday."

"Sure." He gave me a weary smile. "I'm not ready to go back to bed yet. I feel as if I spend my life between the sheets." His face was cadaverous. Poor guy. I felt terrible that ReeAnn Collins had treated him so offhandedly. It's difficult to take cruel treatment from a member of the opposite sex, especially from someone you care about. At nineteen, I'd been some kind of basket case myself when it came to relationships, and I hadn't been struggling with mononucleosis and a flaky, egotistical father in the bargain.

"We'll come back over here when the proprietor opens," I promised. "You want to rest for a minute before we go talk to the Babsie Bash ladies?"

"Whatever," Macguire repeated, apparently too tired to think of anything new to say. He stared glumly at the lake, a meadow of sparkles broken up by paddle- and sailboats. I wondered how Tom thought I'd be protected from the Jerk with poor, listless Macguire accompanying me. *He's out.* I shivered. But I shook this off, the same way I always tried to rid myself of thoughts that included the Jerk.

Soon we were back in the van, rocking over dirt potholes, past the boundary of the municipal golf course, and into the wildflower-rimmed lot of the LakeCenter. After I parked, the two of us walked toward the large log building, where men and women with plastic-coated badges that said DEALER were carting boxes of wares inside.

"Gail?" I said when we approached.

Gail Rodine, in conversation with a uniformed man, lifted her chin in acknowledgment. Actually, her chin was about all I could see of Gail's face. She sported a floppy-brimmed hat that sprouted feathers in every direction and might, I reflected, serve well as a center-piece for the annual Audubon banquet. Her mid-thigh-length dress was a glittering black-and-white-striped affair. Where did this woman get the money for her hobby? The LakeCenter was not a cheap space to rent, and I was not a cheap caterer to hire. The local Babsie club must get a cut of the profit made from the sale of dolls, and that percentage must be considerable.

"I'll be with you in a moment," she announced, and continued her low murmur with an older man in a gray security uniform that hugged his belly like a sausage casing. The man's complexion was splotched, his nose was bright red, and his silver-gray hair lay in flat, greasy curls against his head. He punctuated every few sentences of Mrs. Rodine's with a hiccup. He was not the sort of security guard to inspire confidence. Still, I stopped a respectful distance away from their conversation. Despite the fact that Arch had spent the night at the Rodines' house, Gail and I did not move in the same social circles, as we both well knew. Wealthy folks are very conscious of service-sector people who are intrusive. Macguire held back another ten feet behind me. I think the memory of the women chasing him to the end of the dock two days before made him less anxious to be sociable.

Gail Rodine motioned me forward as she announced crisply to

the guard: "And this is our caterer. She'll be here to set up the box lunches tomorrow, and our breakfast on Wednesday just before nine o'clock." She cocked an eyebrow at me, as if daring me to contradict her agenda. Actually, I needed to get in closer to eight on Wednesday. But before I could utter a word, Gail noticed Macguire. Her face stiffened with anger.

I tried to sound reassuring. "Gail, we're just here today to check that the ovens are working and to see where you want the buffet to be. Plus, day after tomorrow, I need to get in closer to eight or eight-fifteen. Would that be okay?"

She lifted her chin, and I had a glimpse of a hooked nose and an auburn-lipsticked mouth with a cruel slant. "Eight will be fine. You said 'we.' Is this . . . person . . . your assistant? If so, you may come in now, he may not," she proclaimed imperiously. "That boy has already made our lives quite difficult here. And we're preparing to take our morning tea break. The break will be held in the same place as the brunch."

"Okay," I managed to choke.

"Well, then." She bristled impatiently. "Come and see what I'm talking about."

Gail marched ahead of me down the path. Ordinarily, I adore my clients. They're happy to book me. They enjoy planning the menu. They rave about the food I lovingly prepare. Ordinarily, things end happily, with future bookings in sight. But sometimes you can sense when things are going to go badly. Gail had been cruel to the kids at Arch's slumber party; she'd been mean to Macguire when he'd merely tried to help. I'd just seen her give the security guy hell and I could feel that I was next in line, right before the tea break. I tried to wipe from my mind a sudden vision of Gail Rodine bobbing in a lake of Orange Pekoe, with her Babsie dolls tied around her neck. I suppressed a groan. Behind me, Macguire turned and shuffled back to the van.

I followed Gail past the bored-looking, slightly ripe-smelling guard—after all, what kind of drinking stories could he get from protecting dolls?—and into the kitchen. The large and serviceable space was as I remembered it: two ovens set against one wall, a sink overlooking the parking lot. Two lengthy counters separated the kitchen from the ballroom. These counters doubled as a snack bar in the winter months, during skating season, but would serve for me as a prep area. I checked that the ovens worked and looked briefly into the ballroom, where dealers were cracking open long tables and setting up tiers of empty shelves for their displays.

"In the morning," Gail explained grandly over the bustle of dealers, "I want all the food out back. Nothing can touch the doll displays, remember. You can wheel the food trays out through here."

She swished toward the wall beside the kitchen, then expertly opened a door in what looked like a solid block of logs. The door—actually a rectangle of sawed logs that snugged into the wall—gave out on the flagstone patio on the side of the structure. Gail moved outside. She briskly pointed out the grill for Wednesday's final meal, the picnic tables on the deck overlooking the lake where dining would take place, and the tall doors between the ballroom and the deck.

"No dolls beyond this point, unless they have been purchased," she said firmly. I smiled, nodded, and wondered how Macguire was doing. After promising Gail that I'd be back the next day with the box lunches, I zipped back to my van.

Macguire, chin in the air, mouth open, had fallen asleep with his head cocked against the neck rest. There was no way he could have been comfortable.

When the van jolted out of the dirt lot, he was startled awake. He blinked, then muttered, "Uh, I'm ready to go home."

"Just one more quick stop. I promised this nurse I'd be in to see her today. Plus I want to warn her about my ex-husband being released from custody. He mentioned her on the phone from jail. I should let her know he might show up."

"Then I'd better go in with you," Macguire said wearily. "If your ex has already gotten up here, you'll need backup."

We bumped back over the potholes, pulled into the Lakeview lot, and parked in front of the health-food store next to a Harley-Davidson. An Indian cowbell attached to the door gonged as we entered. Inside, ruffled green gingham curtains framed the windows. The pinewood-paneled walls were hung with pictures of the Maharishi Mahesh Yogi and other dignitaries of the vegetarian world. The distinctive smell of exotic herbs and incense that permeates most health-food stores enveloped us.

Even though the store had only been open ten minutes, two people had preceded us. One was Patricia McCracken, whose pear-shaped body was stuffed into a white tennis dress that contrasted with the more exotic surroundings. She sat at a table with Amy Bartholomew. Amy sported a green-flowered Indian dress embedded with spangles. The other person in the store, a black-leather-clad burly man with shoulder-length, curly black hair, studied two shelves stacked with brown bottles. An array of silver rings spilling down his left ear flashed in the sunlight whenever he leaned forward to study a label.

"Even in disguise," Macguire whispered, "I don't think Korman could look like that."

"You're right," I whispered back.

At their table Patricia and Amy were in intimate communication. Patricia's voice cracked with pain; Amy's voice exuded its liquid warmth. After nodding briefly to acknowledge our arrival, Amy directed Patricia to hold a bottle to her heart with her left hand. With her right hand Patricia was told to press her forefinger and thumb together in an okay sign. Then Amy asked a question and gently pried apart the fingers of Patricia's right hand. "Six a day?" Amy murmured, and pulled. The okay sign opened. "Eight a day?" It opened again. At twelve a day Patricia's fingers wouldn't budge. Amy wrote on a yellow pad while Patricia wrote a check. A novel approach to prescription, this.

Patricia gave me an apologetic glance as she exited. "Do you still hurt from Saturday?"

"I'm fine," I told her, not quite truthfully. "But listen. John Richard's out on bail. I don't think he'd come after you, but when he loses his temper with women . . . Well. Be careful."

Patricia's face tightened and she swore under her breath. Then she shook her head and moved away from me without asking another question.

Amy was already eyeing Macguire by the time the cowbell rang behind Patricia. After an appraising squint, she moved to Macguire's side. The thin teenager towered over her.

"You're not well," she murmured.

"Yeah, lady. Really."

"I'll be with you in a sec."

Macguire nodded without interest. He stopped in front of a rack of magazines. Amy slipped over to the shelves, where she seemed to know exactly what the Earring King wanted. I watched her hand him a large cellophane bag filled with lots of small cellophane bags, each of which was crammed with multicolored capsules. I could imagine Frances Markasian's loud headline: COP'S WIFE ARRESTED IN HEALTH STORE DRUG BUST.

The Earring King glared at me. "What're you staring at, woman?" he demanded.

"I'm sorry," I stammered. My mouth had gone dry.

"Edgar, you need to transform that anger," Amy gently reprimanded the man. "It's blocking you."

Emanating hostility that showed no sign of being transformed, Edgar slapped down some dollar bills for his cellophane bags, mumbled that he didn't want the change, and clanged through the door. A moment later a motorcycle engine split the silence. Amy shook her head of red hair.

"Cancer," she said sadly. I didn't know if she meant the disease or the astrological sign, and wasn't about to ask. She looked at me and said, "How's that shoulder?"

"Fair."

"Let me treat your friend and then you. How's that?"

"Well . . ." How was I supposed to say this? *My ex-husband called from jail. He suspects you of killing his girlfriend. Or he wants to pin the murder on you. Now he's on the loose and may come looking for you, Amy. Better pack up your alfalfa sprouts and hit the trail.* "I need to talk to you without interruption," I said somewhat lamely.

"No problem," Amy replied brightly, and blithely turned the the door's paper clock to CLOSED.

Amy beckoned to Macguire. He shuffled behind us as she led the way to the back of the shop, where small tables were sandwiched between two refrigerated cases that held plastic bottles of chlorophyll and other substances I wouldn't want to ingest. Next to the bottles were plastic bags of adzuki, black, and pinto beans, a few tired-looking carrots, and a small selection of packaged grains. Macguire flopped into a chair and I sat next to him. Amy clasped one of Macguire's hands in hers; he immediately withdrew it. I had the same discomfiting sense I'd had in the McCrackens' bathroom—that Amy was way ahead of me, and I wasn't sure I wanted to catch up.

"Perhaps you should just treat me," I told her. "I don't really have any authority to—"

But Amy was absorbed with Macguire's eyes. He turned his face away from her and rubbed his temples. She said, "What do the M.D.s say?"

"The . . . Oh," I faltered, "well, Macguire has mononucleosis, and he . . . what worries me is that he doesn't have any appetite. The doctor has said he should be getting better, but . . . Anyway, he's staying with me until his father gets home later in the month, and I'm not sure his father would approve of—" I was yakking away. Why did this woman always make me yak?

"Macguire?" Amy asked in her kind, melted-milk-chocolate voice. "Do you want to be healed?"

Macguire tilted his head skeptically, glanced swiftly at Amy, then stared at the floor. "I guess."

"Okay. Just relax." She had him remove his watch. Then he touched his head with first one hand, then the other.

"What are you doing?" I blurted out.

She replied without looking at me. "I'm reading his aura."

Oh, *that*! I reflected. *Of course.* Marla and I would have to offer it in Med Wives 101.

Amy took a small flashlight from her pocket, then opened and smoothed out what looked like a paper diagram or chart of some kind. "Look at me." This Macguire did, and for the next five minutes Amy shone the flashlight in his eyes and consulted her chart. When she'd made a few notes, she rose and briskly began to gather supplies. A bottle of chlorophyll. Five brown bottles of pills. Cellophane bags similar to the ones the Earring King had purchased. Then she commenced the same drill she had with Patricia: Macguire held the medicines to his heart, and Amy asked questions and tested the response by pulling apart his fingers pressed in the okay sign. I kept an eye on the door, in the remote case the Jerk showed up.

Finally Amy seemed happy with a combination of three bottles of pills, two cellophane bags, and the chlorophyll. She asked Macguire if he wanted her to run through putting together his twice-a-day regimen. As usual, he replied dully in the affirmative.

"You'd better watch this, too," she told me, and then showed us the sheet. He was to take ten capsules twice a day, plus a teaspoon of chlorophyll dissolved in a cup of cold water. Yum-*my*!

I pointed at the capsules. "What's in these?"

"Shark cartilage," she replied, "pau d'arco bark, essiac tea, rosehips—"

A vision of Macbeth's witches rose before me. "Okey-doke," I interrupted her, before we could get to eye of newt.

"Are you ready for me to take a look at you?" she asked.

"Sure," I said enthusiastically. What did I have to lose?

While Macguire dutifully swallowed his capsules with a glass of springwater spiked with chlorophyll, I got the same flashlight-in-the-eye treatment he'd received. Again Amy consulted her chart.

"Hmm," she said. Then the beautiful brown eyes and faded-freckled face regarded me sadly. She bit the inside of her lip and then made her pronouncement: "You're depressed."

Great, I thought, *got herbs for it? Prozac bark?* Instead I said, "Since it's truth-telling time, Amy, there's something I really need to talk to you about."

"Your ex-husband. Dr. Korman."

"How did you know?"

She smiled. "I may run a health-food store, but I don't live in the next galaxy. Suz Craig and I didn't get along, as you said you knew, when I helped you out at the McCrackens' house. What, you think Dr. Korman is going to come gunning for me? I was a victim of Suz's nastiness, so now I'm a suspect in her murder? Is Dr. Korman trying to say I killed her?"

Without warning, I felt infinitely dejected. Maybe it was Amy's suggestion that I was depressed; maybe it was my acknowledgment of the truth. A woman was dead. If my ex-husband had killed her, he would pay. But so would my teenage son, who would pay a long-lasting price in emotional pain. If John Richard had not killed Suz, then finding out who did would be left to the D.A.'s investigator, Donny Saunders. Saunders, who, last time we'd met, had informed me radicchio was the name of a mobster. No wonder my spirits were low.

"Let's get you some herbs for that depression," Amy said decisively. She moved to the same area of the same shelf where she'd pulled down the bottle for Patricia McCracken. Hmm.

And then I, too, went through the drill of holding the herbs to my heart and having my fingers pried open. Within five minutes I, too, was swallowing mammoth capsules whose ingredient list included only three things I recognized: bamboo sap, ginger rhizome, and licorice root. It didn't sound like a mixture I'd use in a cookie.

"So is Patricia McCracken depressed, too?" I asked Amy. "About losing her baby?"

Amy lifted her eyebrows. "Wouldn't you be?"

"Depressed enough to get really angry with Suz Craig?"

"Who knows? Suz distressed a lot of people."

"Including you." When she gave a single nod, I swallowed, then said, "Why'd she fire you?"

Amy smiled placidly. "Is that what Suz said, that she fired me? No. That's what she always said when people couldn't get along with her . . . that she fired them, as if they were the incompetent ones." She shook her head gently. "I quit ACHMO. My payout from the pension plan helped buy this shop."

"Why'd you quit?"

"Why'd you divorce Dr. Korman?"

"Because he abused me."

"Aha! Same here. Only Suz Craig didn't abuse people physically. She beat them up *mentally*." Amy said it as if it were a disease. "When I left, I thought, now why did that take me so long?"

"Meaning . . . ?"

She frowned and pondered my question. For a long minute she was silent. Then she answered, "AstuteCare has been in Colorado for eight years. I was with them from the beginning, moved up to Medical Management. There was a group of department heads, including Brandon Yuille and Chris Corey, who also lived in Aspen Meadow. We worked as a team. Suz joined ACHMO two years ago. It was the beginning of hell."

Hell. Interesting. "Why? What did she do to change things?"

"We used to have a weekly meeting to discuss problems we were having. What we needed in the new Provider Relations Manual, that kind of thing. Suz would scream and yell. 'What's the matter with you people?' was her favorite. And then she'd viciously attack every person in the room for being stupid, lazy, incompetent. Or, in the case of Chris, fat. 'How's a tub of lard supposed to set a model for health?' Suz used to yell at him. You get the idea. Brandon Yuille's father, who'd just lost his wife, was remodeling and reopening the pastry shop. Suz was on Brandon's case constantly about being there on the weekends instead of working overtime for her.

She claimed Brandon came in too tired to be of any use, because he was up all night baby-sitting his father, on and on. It was none of her business that Brandon's father was a widower and alone and desperately needed his company. But she *made* it her business. She made his life miserable."

Aha, more hell. "Wasn't there anybody you could complain to?"

She shrugged. "It was coming to that. A group of them was trying to go over her head."

"And did they? And to whom?"

"They talked about it. But I'd had enough. Her cruelty was unbearable. I couldn't stand it anymore. The last—no, let's see, the *next-to-last*—straw for me came about five months ago when I was negotiating to buy this store. I saw the store as a long-term project for my retirement. Originally I was planning just to have it open on the weekends, until I could build up the clientele over about a ten- or fifteen-year period, when I retired from ACHMO. But Suz never wanted you to be in charge of your own destiny. *She* wanted to be in charge of your destiny."

"She knew you wanted to open this store?"

Amy smiled sadly. "Suz made it her business to know personal details about the people who worked for her." She shook her head. "Anyway. One of the ACHMO doctors had a gambling problem. Suz asked me—privately, mind you—to follow the guy to the casinos in Central City, see what he was up to, and try to talk to him. See if he'd go into some kind of self-help group, therapy, whatever. If I did, she said, she promised to co-sign one of my loan applications. I didn't feel good about it"—she shrugged—"but if one of our providers had an addiction that would negatively affect the care he gave, I believed I should help find that out. So, I agreed to follow him."

"So you don't gamble?"

She laughed softly. "No. I followed this provider of ours to Central City and found him playing slots. I watched him for two hours, then confronted him. He convinced me to dance with the one-armed bandit for a while so I could see how much fun it was. I dropped eighteen dollars in quarters into two slot machines and never made more than a dollar. Then I convinced this guy—a pediatrician, if you can believe it—to have some coffee, to talk to me. Over coffee he said he wasn't going to quit gambling. I was wasting my time. Suz got rid of that doctor and now he's in Utah, leading rock-climbing expeditions. Different kind of gamble, I guess. Then Suz spread it around that *I* had the gambling problem. At that time people were bidding for this store space and I was working feverishly on loan applications. Because I hadn't succeeded in rehabilitating the pediatrician, Suz refused to co-sign for me, and I didn't get my loan. When I confronted her about trying to destroy all my plans for the future—to destroy *me*—she claimed I was paranoid."

"And so you quit."

Amy looked away for a moment. Then she said, "Well, not just then. You know how it is with institutions you're involved with. Institution of marriage, institution of the job, institution of the church. At first you're doing work you love and everybody's nice. Then maybe the work gets boring but you like the people so much you don't want to leave. Then some of the good people leave and you think, well, it's not as good as it used to be but it's better than going out there looking for something new."

I looked over at Macguire, who was perusing a magazine on nudist colonies.

"Pretty soon," Amy went on, "there are only a handful of people you like, or a handful of *things* you like, about the institution. Then bad things begin to happen. In our case at ACHMO, we got Suz Craig, a female vice-president we didn't like. She came in and made us all miserable. And although we got a great deal of camaraderie out of talking about her behind her back, it was scant comfort."

"I still don't understand why someone didn't complain."

She sighed. "There was talk of it, but you know, who was going to bell the cat? Human Resources? Brandon Yuille is so terrified of losing his job that he wouldn't even join in on our gossip. Poor guy, he had enough to deal with with his mother dying."

"Was she covered by ACHMO?"

"Don't know," Amy replied. "Brandon talks a blue streak about food and always brought us goodies, but about his personal life he was extremely closemouthed."

"How about Chris Corey? Did he hate Suz Craig, too?"

"We all hated her, Goldy. She tormented Chris for being over-weight and for being late on his deadlines. She used to say that this wasn't a waiting room where he could be an hour late for all his appointments. And so on and so on. She was cruel and spiteful and manipulative. Plus she was ruining the HMO with the way she was handling cases like Patricia's. She wanted us to find dirt on the people suing, without realizing how that kind of activity could backfire. An HMO can't survive bad publicity. People just won't sign on."

"So if you didn't leave when she refused to co-sign your loan, why did you finally leave?"

"You know, I never could figure out if Suz wanted me to leave or wanted me to stay. If she wanted me to leave, why didn't she just let me buy my store? If she wanted me to stay, why did she threaten to use the gambling issue in a way that would hurt me? I'm telling you, the woman was just *mean*." She sighed. "The *very* last straw for me was when we had a team meeting and in front of all my colleagues, Suz told me I was over the hill, didn't know the first thing about healing people. She even said I didn't dress like a profes-sional."

I couldn't help it. I eyed Amy's shapeless, spangled dress-that-could-double-as-a-nightgown. She laughed.

"Don't worry, Goldy, I didn't wear this kind of thing to work. But I wasn't going to wear short wool suits that came up to my behind and didn't even keep my legs warm in a Colorado winter."

"So you . . ."

"I went home after the public dressing-down Suz gave me and I looked in the mirror, hard. I asked myself, 'Are you happy?' And the answer was such a resounding 'No' that I went in the next day and quit. Then she threw a fit about my quitting. She swore she'd tell anyplace I applied that I had gambling problems and couldn't hold down a steady job. 'Who am I going to hire in your place?' she wanted to know, after screaming at us for weeks that we were expendable. I just listened and kept telling myself, 'In eight hours, Amy, you will never have to listen to this tyrant again.' Because that's what Suz was—a tyrant."

"And so you just walked out."

"Yup. Cleaned out my desk, took my two weeks of vacation as my notice, and that was it. I never looked back. I had some savings to tide me over, used my pension payout to buy the store instead of getting a loan, and now I'm doing what I love." She smiled. "By next year I may even be showing a profit. I'll start some new pension savings."

I looked at the brightly decorated store, the sparsely filled shelves of herb capsules and poorly stocked freezer, the "health" magazines that included the soft-porn rag Macguire was finding so entrancing. But the place, like Amy, had . . . well . . . the place had an aura. And the aura was one of happiness. Aura! Yikes! Listen to me!

"You know what I'm talking about," she insisted. There was a slightly accusatory tone in her voice. "You opened your catering business after being married to Dr. Gorgeous. You must be ecstatic to be free of him."

"It's . . . well . . ." From the wall, the Maharishi beamed down at me. "It's *nirvana*," I admitted.

"Then you know what I'm talking about."

"I do. But now Dr. Gorge—John Richard has been charged with Suz Craig's murder and my son is suffering like you wouldn't believe. For my son's sake, I need to find out if his father really killed her."

Amy considered the green gingham curtains at the front of the store for a long time without replying. Then she said softly, "I believe in the forces of the universe, Goldy. He who has sinned will sin again. The truth will all come out. You need to trust."

"I do trust, Amy. But to everyone's astonishment, John Richard Korman is out on bail. He may come looking for you, want to ask questions, and then lose his temper. It's the control freak in him. Very predictable. Anyway, I'd feel better if you weren't alone. Can you get somebody to work in the store with you? At the very least, keep the phone handy in case you have to dial 911." I reached out for her hand. "John Richard called me from jail. He wanted *me* to come over and investigate you."

Amy pulled her hand away from mine. Her voice grew chill. "Is that why you're here?"

"Amy, please. I know this man. I'm here to warn you. He was involved with ACHMO, you were involved with ACHMO, and most certainly you didn't get along with Suz." I paused. "John Richard thinks you might have killed her, and that you've set him up to take the fall for you. Believe me, he's not a person you want to have gunning for you."

She shook her head as she ran her fingers through her shiny red hair. "These people," she muttered sadly. "I swear."

Chapter 19

Jake's earsplitting howls greeted Macguire and me before the van turned into our driveway. The cause for this canine distress was the arrival of Donny Saunders. The investigator for the Furman County district attorney sat on the top step of our front porch. Well, well, it was about time.

Donny boasted slicked brown hair, a prominent nose and fore-head, and an arrogant, horse-toothed smile he displayed whenever he stole the credit for a major bust. The closest Donny Saunders usually came to an arrest was sending seized material to a lab. Most recently, a uniformed officer had discovered twenty-five kilos of co-caine during a speeding stop. Donny Saunders had filed the report and then brayed endlessly afterward about making the biggest drug seizure in the history of the county.

At the sight of him, I took a deep breath. A good investigator would have been at my door no later than Saturday afternoon, right after I'd discovered the body of Suz Craig and been questioned by Sergeant Beiner and her assistant. Two days had now gone by. The fact that Donny was finally paying me a call was not a good sign that the crime was being efficiently investigated.

"Hey, Goldy, how you doing!" he greeted me. "Got anything to eat? I'm starving! And you better do something 'bout that dog!"

I struggled to appear friendly even as I gagged at Donny's Vegas-style suit of shiny blue fabric that shimmered and glinted as he swaggered toward us. I introduced Macguire, identifying him only as a houseguest.

"I'll need to talk to you alone," said Donny with his usual smug self-importance as I opened the front door. What a hospitable statement.

"Gosh," murmured Macguire in a hurt tone, "that's the third time today people haven't wanted me around when Goldy Schulz talks to them. Do I have b.o. or something? Guess I'll just go sit by myself. Wait till it's time to take ten more herb capsules." Before I could soothe his feelings, however, he plodded to the backyard to reassure Jake. After a moment the howls ceased. Unfortunately, *my* torment was just beginning.

"I've got a lot of cooking to do," I warned Donny. "I'm doing a big event tomorrow."

The enormous shoulder pads inside Donny's sapphire suit rose ominously when he shrugged. "Not to worry! How would I bother you? Cook away, little lady! A woman's place is in the kitchen! Ha! Ha!" His good-ole-boy tone made me grit my teeth. "But say," he bulldozed on, "you got anything good to eat that's, you know, ready?"

I closed my eyes, tried to count to ten but only got to four. I remembered my promises to Arch on the one hand and to Tom on the other. Maybe I could actually learn something from Donny. But I doubted it.

I suggested a cheese sandwich and Donny eagerly accepted. He quickly added that bread kind of stuck in his craw and he'd need three or four beers to wash the crumbs down. My hopes for our conversation sank to a subterranean level unavailable to geologists.

But since the brioche had completed its first rising, I removed it from the refrigerator along with a six-pack of Dos Equis. I punched down the cold, silky mass of dough, set it aside for its second rising, and proceeded to make Donny a sandwich of thickly sliced homemade bread, pesto, fresh tomato, and chèvre. He asked for his second beer when I placed the sandwich in front of him. I handed him the cold bottle with the hope that it might loosen his tongue to share information I hadn't heard yet. I dreaded to think, though, what my husband would say about my plying an investigator with brewskis in the middle of the day.

"Say, this is pretty good!" Donny mumbled, mouth full. He took another enormous bite and munched thoughtfully. "Whaddaya call this white cheesy stuff?"

"Chèvre."

His horsey teeth pulled into a wide grin. "Nah, Goldy, that's a *truck*."

I forced a smile. "What do you want to talk about, Donny?"

"Okay," he said seriously, wiping his mouth and then using his napkin to blow his nose. "Few things." He swigged the beer. "Suz Craig. You found her."

"Yep." I decided I'd better cook. Otherwise the temptation to lose my temper might be too great. "I sure did find her." I took out a cutting board and a zester and ran the tool down the side of a lemon. Zest strands curled outward, sending a fine, pungent mist of lemon oil onto the board. "I saw her in a ditch as I was driving down the road just before seven last Saturday."

"And she was your ex-husband's girlfriend."

"She was, indeed." I minced the zest, then retrieved a coffee grinder that I used exclusively for pulverizing fruit zest and nuts. "Haven't you read my statement?"

He gestured with the now-empty beer bottle and unsuccessfully repressed a belch. "I took a look at it. Now, what we need to establish here is John Richard Korman's prior patterns. You know, his similar activity. How he used to beat you up. How he almost killed you. That's the way I'll build my case." He eyed the Dos Equis carton longingly, but I ignored him. "Goldy," he continued, gushing with sincerity, "I've seen *lots* of criminals like this before. Once they do it, they get a taste for it. They keep doing it. Until they kill somebody."

"Wait, Donny. What about the autopsy results?"

"Coroner's office should have 'em at the sheriff's department by the time I get back to the office. But don't you worry your pretty little head about that. So, when was the last time John Richard Korman clobbered you?"

I took a shaky breath, remembering. "Seven years ago. He broke this thumb"—I gestured—"in three places not too long before we divorced."

"Okay, I'll have to check what the pathologist says about Suz Craig's hand, if there're any contusions there. If we're lucky, maybe he broke her finger, too. How would Korman attack you? You don't mind me asking?"

"He'd grab my arms, shake me very hard. He liked to punch me in the face, even though most high-income abusers are devious enough to avoid the face. I usually ended up with a black eye."

"Which eye?" He was not writing.

"The right. Which was the black eye on her, too, I noticed."

"You're correct there, little woman. Okay, now when he clobbered you, would he knock you out right away? Or would the fight go on for hours?"

I gripped the knife. Recalling these events never became less painful. "It depended on how angry he was," I said softly. "But, Donny," I couldn't help interjecting, "what about the facts of *this* case? Since I never pressed charges, a judge may not allow all this. Have you talked to anyone down at Suz Craig's office? At ACHMO?"

"Oh, yeah. I was down in Denver talkin' to some execs at the HMO this morning—"

"Which execs?" The only ACHMO executives in town had

been busy raiding John Richard's office in Aspen Meadow. Had the rest of the department heads returned from the San Diego conference?

"Well . . . talking to Suz Craig's secretary, actually, 'cuz most of the rest of the guys are off on some trip. But you can learn more that way. Those gals really know what's cooking, if you know what I mean." He winked.

"Ah." I put down the knife and zapped the lemon zest in the grinder. Then I pulverized the blanched slivered almonds and piled them into a pale mound. "So. What did Suz's secretary have to say?"

"Well . . ." He reached for another beer, pried off the top, and took a long swig. "I really shouldn't say."

"Why not? Maybe I could help you. Fill in the blanks."

He harumphed, popped the last of the sandwich into a corner of his mouth, chewed, and licked his fingers. Sometimes I wondered if the only decent food Donny ever got was when Goldilocks' Catering got mired in one of his investigations. "I'm telling you, Goldy, nobody likes Korman. But nobody liked that Craig woman, either. I mean, *nobody*. You know, you'd think people wouldn't speak ill of the dead. But get right down to it, I'm surprised nobody did her right there in the office. Course, they didn't have the pattern, like our Doc Korman."

I beat unsalted butter with sugar, egg yolks, vanilla, and lemon zest; measured out flour and the other dry ingredients, and then mixed them with the creamed mixture to make a nutty, buttery, heavenly-smelling dough. "Have you been looking at any other facts of the *case*, Donny?"

"Tha-a-a-at's why I'm here, right?"

I wondered briefly if I could nip out for one of the tranquilizers Marla had given me. Maybe Amy's herb capsules had sedative powers. But no—there was a chance Donny's boastfulness would win out and he'd tell me what Suz's secretary had had to say. If I didn't appear too eager, that is. So I concentrated on the question of how to provide a high ratio of tart raspberry jam to cookie dough. Scooping

Babsie's Tarts

1 cup (2 sticks) unsalted butter, softened

¾ cup sugar

2 egg yolks

1 teaspoon vanilla extract

2 teaspoons finely grated lemon zest (see
Note)

1½ cups bleached all-purpose flour (add
one tablespoon in high altitudes)

1 teaspoon ground cinnamon

¼ teaspoon ground cloves

¼ teaspoon salt

1 teaspoon baking powder

1¼ cups blanched slivered almonds,
ground (see Note)

1 to 1¼ cups best-quality *seedless* red
raspberry jam

Beat butter until creamy. Add sugar and beat
until thoroughly incorporated. Beat egg yolks
slightly with vanilla and lemon zest. Add to
creamed mixture, stirring thoroughly. Sift dry
ingredients together, then stir into creamed
mixture. Stir in almonds.

Preheat oven to 350°. Spray two nonstick cupcake pans with vegetable oil spray. Using a 2-tablespoon scoop (or measuring out in 2 tablespoon increments), place one scoop of batter into each cupcake pan. Pat the batter gently to cover the bottom of each cup. Do not indent the dough or the jam that is to be cooked in the center will leak through. Place 2 teaspoons of jam in the center of each tart.

Bake for about 15 minutes, until the batter has risen and turned golden brown around the jam. After the pans have been removed from the oven, use a sharp knife to loosen the edges of each tart. Allow the tarts to cool in the pan until cool to the touch, at least 1 hour. Using a kitchen knife, gently lever the tarts out onto cookie racks and allow to cool completely. You may serve them plain, or sprinkle with powdered sugar and serve with a scoop of best-quality vanilla ice cream.

Makes 2 dozen

Note: Citrus zests and nuts are easily ground in a *clean* coffee grinder.

the dough into cupcake pans and then topping them with spoonfuls of jam would work. I ignored Donny and set about buttering a pan.

He continued eagerly. "You listening? You wouldn't have believed how much that secretary, name of Luella Downing, hated Ms. Craig. Luella was in some kind of state this morning."

I *tsked*, but continued assiduously spraying a pan.

"See," he persisted, "this Luella resented Ms. Craig 'cuz Ms. Craig had made it her business to know some money details of Luella's divorce." I looked up from the pan and raised my eyebrows. Donny smirked triumphantly. "I told Luella I wouldn't prosecute or nothing." I hid my exasperation and nodded knowingly. He went on. "Come to find out that Ms. *Craig* knew *Luella* had liquidated her IRA and put the money into her *parents'* account so's Luella's *ex* wouldn't find it. Our Ms. Craig used that info to get Luella to shut up about the taping."

I dropped the pan on the counter. "Taping of what?"

He held up a hand. "I'm getting there. And don't worry, I checked to see where Ms. Luella was over the weekend, just in case she'd gotten it into her head to off her boss over the IRA stuff. Luella was organizing a rummage sale for her parents' church in Aurora. The story checks out—Beiner went to the church and interviewed the parents."

A minute amount of admiration for Donny wormed its way into my brain. "So . . . what was Luella taping?"

"Luella wasn't taping. Suz Craig was. Any meeting in her office." He lowered his voice. "Like the frigging White House, you asked me. See, nobody but Ms. Craig and Luella knew. Luella says if she'd dropped the dime on her boss, she would have lost her job and possibly her IRA bucks."

"Does Luella know what was on the tapes? Did she transcribe them?"

"No, oh, no. Luella just happened to discover Ms. Craig loading a fresh tape into the machine built into her desk. See, one time Luella walked in on Ms. Craig without knocking, checking on some correspondence or something, and saw her fiddling with this machine. Luella says, 'What in the world are you doing?' That's when Ms. Craig says, 'You tell anybody about this and I'll fire you and tell your ex where your IRA dough is.' The one thing Ms. Craig told Luella was never to touch the machine. The boss lady told Luella she taped the meetings to cover herself. She also labeled the tapes and put them in a locked cabinet."

"Good Lord. So what happened? How were they discovered?"

"When Ms. Craig turned up blue in a ditch, somebody called Luella. Turns out Luella was already home from the rummage sale. Soon as Luella heard her boss was dead, she called corporate HQ. Somebody was there even though it was Saturday. Luella hollered, 'You guys need to know about these tapes and go get 'em before the press gets hold of 'em. Old Suz Craig was such a bitch, there's no telling what's on those tapes.' Corporate HQ has a cow and sends two guys to Denver Saturday night. They're scrambling like mad to break open her locked cabinets when somebody tips off the sheriff's department. They show up with a search warrant and seize the tapes they've found, plus use Ms. Craig's keys from her house to search all the office cabinets for more."

"You learned all this from Sergeant Beiner? Or from Luella Downing?" I asked suspiciously.

"Little of both. My job, you gotta put everything together."

"And why do you suppose Luella is spilling her guts to you?"

His eyebrows lifted. "Hey, Goldy! Ace caterer amateur detective! Wake up! Luella shouldn't have called Minneapolis first, she should have told the *cops* about the tapes first. This morning Luella's suddenly got a big case of remorse, ooh, ooh, she meant to tell us, but she didn't want to lose her job, see, is what she's saying. Meanwhile, our department takes an inventory. Looks like *one* day's tapes are missing, and the people at ACHMO swear they don't have a clue where they are. So, bit later in the morning, the sheriff sends a team back up to Suz's house. They turn up nothing."

"Sheesh."

"So I'm thinking about your ex-husband, see. I'm thinking, why did he and Suz Craig have that catfight on Friday night? And then I think, the missing tapes, of course! John Richard probably has them."

What? I pressed my lips together and turned away. I had to think. *Delicate material,* John Richard had said. I nudged soft scoops of dough into each cup. And what had ReeAnn said? *She wanted him to put some stuff . . . in a safe place, somewhere the AstuteCare people couldn't find them.* I ladled tart, inky jam on top of each dough disc. At John Richard's office this morning, Brandon Yuille had asked me the same question: *If John Richard has given you anything to hide . . .* I popped the cupcake pan into the hot oven.

"What could be on the tapes?" I asked, perplexed. "And who could have them?"

"Well, now, those *are* the questions, aren't they? The execs are scrambling like crazy. Where're the tapes, these powers-that-be want to know. And, believe me, this morning? *All* the ACHMO secretaries were pulling up the wall-to-wall trying to find the damn things. Meanwhile, back at the ranch, since Suz Craig's house has turned up nothing, the duty judge gives our guys a search warrant for *Korman's* house. No tapes, but somebody messed up his house *bad* with paint—"

"One day's tapes . . . What day? What folks met with Suz Craig that day?" I interrupted.

"Luella's trying to reconstruct that." He shook his head and burped. "Korman doesn't have anyplace he hides things, does he?"

"He's compulsively neat. And he's just sold his place in Keystone." I chewed the inside of my lip. "He hasn't been to his condo in Hawaii since June. I guess he could have stashed the tapes there. But if they're in Hawaii, what would happen if Suz wanted them back?"

"Man, would I love it if the department sprang for a trip to the islands! Damn! You got another beer?"

"Donny. Are you driving?"

He pulled his chin into his neck. "Well, yeah, but you don't need to worry about a coupla beers, Goldy, I can handle it. And don't worry, I'll call out to Hawaii for a search warrant. Now, how 'bout—"

"Let me fix you some coffee. You know my husband's a cop. I wouldn't want you having an accident after drinking beer at our house. It'd look bad."

"Okay," he said reluctantly, eyeing the espresso machine on my counter. "Only don't give me any of that cappuccino crap or I'll barf."

I fixed Donny plain black coffee, which he slurped noisily. The nut-scented Linzer tarts resembled circular stained-glass windows when I removed them from the oven. Since they would go in the doll-show box lunches, I decided to call them Babsie's Tarts. While I was placing them on a rack to cool, I asked Donny if there were any suspects besides John Richard. He said not since Luella's alibi had checked out. I asked him if they'd caught the vandals who'd defaced John Richard's house, and he said, "Oh, do they think it was vandals?" Finally I asked him if he knew about the bonus John Richard was supposed to get, but didn't.

"Yeah, yeah. That's part of my theory. The Craig lady didn't approve the usual bonus for Korman, so he didn't have any money, and so he wouldn't give her the tapes he'd hidden, and so they argued and he killed her." He turned the corners of his lips down, shook his head. "It was his pattern," he concluded smugly. "Say, those smell awful good."

I put a warm, crumbly Babsie's Tart on a small plate and handed it to him. "Ah . . . did you find out why exactly Suz didn't give him his bonus? Did Luella clue you in on that?"

He placed the small tart in his mouth, lounged back in the chair, and held up one finger as he chewed. "Billing," he said finally. "He didn't bill right. I'm going to *really* grill Korman's secretary about that. You know, about whether Korman and Ms. Craig ever argued about bills. Plus there's a malpractice suit outstanding against him. The HMO didn't like that, or the fact that they were being sued by the same patient. So our doc was in hot, hot water. Boiling. More reason to kill Ms. Craig." He glanced at his watch. "Talk about billing! I need to see a couple more people today or the department will have a fit over the hours I submit."

"How come?"

"Well, usually I bill by the hour, but they've been saying I'm too thorough with each person and spend *too* much time investigating. Whoo-ie! Now I bill by the people I talk to. Plus, even though I have a photographic memory, I have to write up a report on each interview. And believe me, those reports can be a bear, you're typing 'em up the middle of the night."

"I'm sure you can manage it," I said reassuringly as I escorted him to the door.

"I wouldn't mind the typing so much," he said disconsolately, "if only I didn't get so hungry."

So I gave him another tart. Donny Saunders may be a pig, but I can never resist a hungry soul.

To my surprise, Arch called and asked if Todd could spend the night. I said yes, and was further pleased when Arch asked for his favorite dinner, baked potatoes with a variety of toppings. I was hopeful that fixing the potatoes would help me reflect on Donny Saunders's visit. Tapes? What tapes? And where were the missing ones? I'd learned just enough to be frustrated. If Frances Markasian ever did a story on the waste of taxpayer money, I'd point her in the direction of old Donny.

I filled a wide frying pan with extrathick bacon slices, and for some reason thought of the composer Schoenberg. Schoenberg had been quoted as saying that his music contained all his secrets. His compositions held the key to unlocking the inner workings of his soul. You just had to know how to listen. Somehow, all the information before me might contain enough data to unlock the secret of what had happened in the early hours of Saturday morning. I just didn't know how to decipher it.

The phone rang. It was the therapist's office calling to say I'd be getting a call later in the day about scheduling Arch. Apparently there was no way the temporary secretary could do anything now. I sighed and said I'd be waiting for her call.

I trimmed crisp green broccoli for one of the potato-toppings and thought of Arch. He and Todd were planning an extended "jam" tonight. Jamming, I'd learned, was not about food, but about music. Fine with me. I wanted Arch to have a regular social life instead of fretting about his father. Truth to tell, though, it pained me that I couldn't relate to the music that today's fourteen-year-olds liked. I'd faulted my parents for finding the Rolling Stones execrable. But the Rolling Stones made *music*. What Arch and Todd listened to was just *noise*. Well, I thought with a sigh, *Schoenberg's* mother probably had trouble with her son's music. Come to think of it, I thought as I retrieved a dozen fat Idaho potatoes from my pantry, Schoenberg's music pretty much sounded like noise to me, too.

As I washed and pricked the potatoes, I remembered to call the town veterinarian. I was still wondering about the scratches on Ralph Shelton's face and if they'd truly come from his feline. The veterinarian's receptionist said that under no circumstances could she tell me anything about the care of Ralph Shelton's animals. Patient confidentiality seemed alive and well these days, if you were a cat. Well, maybe Tom would know.

I placed the potatoes in the oven, then kneaded the brioche dough gently, divided it, and set it into loaf pans for its third and final rising. By the time Arch, Todd, and Tom arrived home, I'd put the loaves in the oven and finished making the dinner. Todd Druckman, who was baby-faced and slightly pudgy, and had hair that was even browner and straighter than Arch's, pronounced ours the best-smelling kitchen he'd ever visited. A pile of baked potatoes invited slashing and filling. I pointed to where the boys could choose from a vat of creamy cheese sauce bubbling on the stove, broccoli florets heaped in a steaming pile, and a mountain of hot, crispy bacon that beckoned with its mouthwatering scent. The real surprise occurred, however, when Arch, Todd, Tom, and I were bustling around setting the table. We didn't even notice Macguire entering the kitchen.

"Hey!" he said. "What smells so great?"

For a moment we were all speechless. Macguire, hungry? Then Tom winked at me. "What is it Cinderella's godmother says? Sometimes miracles take some time?"

I looked at my watch. "Yeah. Six hours. That's when we left the health-food store. Amazing." Macguire still shuffled and his body was achingly thin. But healthy color infused his cheeks for the first time in a month, *and he wanted something to eat*! Both were momentous developments. I offered a silent prayer of thanks.

The potatoes were indeed out of this world: each flaky bite was robed in golden cheese sauce and melded stupendously with the tender broccoli and crunchy bacon. Macguire, to my amazement, slowly ate two potatoes slathered with toppings, then laughingly pronounced himself so full his stomach ached. Tom, Todd, and Arch cleaned every last bite from their plates. Our meal was full of companionship, good food, and laughter. I never once thought of the corpse I'd found in the ditch.

Arch broke the spell of family life. He said suddenly, "I wonder what they're having at the jail tonight."

"Hon," I replied gently, "your dad's out on bail. This morning we—"

"You found out this morning that he got out? And you didn't call me at Todd's?"

"I thought . . . if your dad wanted to call, he would—"

"And you probably wouldn't let me talk to him!" He looked accusingly from me to Tom. "And I'll bet you haven't done anything today to help him, either!"

"Excuse me, young man, but I *have too done something*—"

But before I could finish my sentence, Arch threw down his fork and ran out of the room.

Tom shook his head. Todd looked bewildered. I silently put

a half-dozen Babsie's Tarts on a plate, handed Todd a six-pack of soft drinks, and told him to go on up and see what he could do. Todd took the plate along with the pop cans and gratefully excused himself.

"Maybe I should go, too," Macguire announced in a guilty tone, and left. Minutes later I saw the light on the phone flash red, indicating that Arch was making an outgoing call from upstairs. The call did not last long. Probably Arch had called John Richard's number and left a message on his machine. My mind immediately leaped to a fresh question: If the Jerk wasn't home to answer his phone, where was he?

Tom said, "Let me do the dishes, Miss G."

"You do everything," I said, disconsolate. "Bring home take-out. Do the dishes. Put up with us. Put up with *me*."

"You make a great dinner," he countered as he started hot water running in the sink. "And you're the one who tries to do everything. You can't make everything go smoothly."

"At least I'd be a better investigator than Donny Saunders."

Tom chuckled. "Sorry, Miss G., but that's not saying much."

While he was doing the dishes, I asked him about the tapes from Suz Craig's office. He said the department was listening to the tapes they had found and making an inventory of them. I told him about the discussions I'd had with Amy Bartholomew and ReeAnn Collins. He nodded and didn't take notes, indicating he'd already heard similar information at his office. Then he punched buttons on the espresso machine. A few moments later he placed a demitasse of crema-laden espresso in front of me and sat down across the table.

I sighed. "If I drink this, I'm going to be up all night."

"Aw, drink it. You're going to be up all night anyway. You're going to be up every night until this is over. And trust me, Goldy, these things *always* come to an end. One way or another."

I closed my eyes and sipped the rich, satisfying espresso. When

Tom placed the last dish in the dishwasher, I slid the golden-brown brioche loaves out of the oven and placed them on racks to cool. Their rich, homey scent bathed the kitchen.

Tom said, "Let's take some cookies out on the deck. I want to talk to you about the autopsy, but I want to be somewhere the boys won't hear us."

"Chocolate, coffee, and death. Dark topics all."

We stretched out on one of my fancy deck-furniture couches that had been in disuse for so long. The night air was sweet, mellow, and filled with the buzz of unseen insects. Just above the mountains' dark silhouette, Venus glowed like an ice crystal.

We savored the Chocolate Comfort Cookies in silence, curled together in each other's arms. The cookies were chock-full of fat chocolate chips and crunchy toasted hazelnuts. The sun-dried cranberries gave a delicious, tart chewiness to each bite.

I asked Tom if the cops had called Shelton's veterinarian and he said yes. The scratches on Ralph Shelton's face had been inflicted by his cat but were minor. Then Tom sighed. He asked, "Did you also know Suz Craig had a cat?"

"Yes, a shy calico one named Tippy. Saturday morning, right after you went to talk to the deputies, that cat jumped into my arms. I know Tippy was part of the crime scene, but I was afraid she'd get trampled if I abandoned her. I left her with Tina Corey. Why?"

He didn't answer right away. I snuggled in close and just enjoyed his warmth.

"Here's what we found out today," Tom said at length as he massaged my back. "Suz Craig's security system was turned off. Also, Suz Craig didn't die from falling into the ditch. She died of a subdural hematoma. No blood, because she was hit with her cat's scratching post. It's a solid metal cylinder covered with carpeting. You know what a subdural—"

"Yes. A blow causes bleeding into the brain. The bleeding brings on death."

"Right. It takes eight hours for lividity to fix, and she'd only been in the ditch two, maybe three hours before you found her. It's very unlikely she could have gotten the fatal blow there. So somebody put her outside. Why, we don't know. We're still waiting for the drug screen to come back; that'll take a few days."

"Yes, I remember."

Tom continued thoughtfully. "Here's the odd thing. She definitely has the same pattern of bruises that you used to have when John Richard attacked you. If he'd beaten her up and killed her immediately, the bruises wouldn't have shown up on the corpse. Bruises take about three or four hours, minimum, to develop, unless the victim's one of those rare people who show a bruise within an hour. So what happened between the time Suz Craig got beaten up and the time she died of a blow from the cat's scratching post? And how did she get into that ditch?"

"The vandals say John Richard left that night and then came back. Or somebody in a Jeep just like one of his, no lights, came there."

"Yeah." Tom sighed wearily. "I know what they said. We're checking to see if any white Jeeps were rented anywhere in the Denver area. And we've got the drug screen to wait for. Plus the skin under her nails has been sent to a crime lab. So we'll know more by the end of the week. If it's Korman's skin, at least we'll have him for assault."

But not necessarily for murder. Would he walk? I didn't want to think about it.

As Tom had predicted, I did not sleep well. At one point I crept down to the kitchen and typed into the computer my own notes on what ReeAnn Collins, Amy Bartholomew, Donny Saunders, and Tom had told me. I didn't have a photographic memory. But then, after what I'd been through when I lived with the Jerk, I'd prayed *never* to have a photographic memory.

Chapter 20

Despite the fact that Tuesday morning dawned with a bright sun and jewel-bright hummingbirds whirring past my downstairs windows, I did not feel the least bit cheered. Tom had left early. I went through my yoga routine trying to empty my mind—not easy. Today, among all the other crises, I was set to begin catering to the doll people. I'd read recently about the necessity of going into a zone of enjoyment when doing your work, especially if you expected to derive pleasure from your career over the course of a lifetime. I tried to see the zone and imagine Gail Rodine not in it.

I sliced the cooled brioche loaves and then began making the box lunches. Each lunch would contain four sandwich triangles: cucumber, smoked salmon, Swiss cheese, and the pesto-tomato-chèvre combination that Donny Saunders had gobbled up so ravenously. I shuddered and fixed myself an iced latté. Something Donny had said kept swimming up just below my consciousness as I smoothed cool mayonnaise over the bread slices and laid out the sandwich fillings.

When I finished wrapping the sandwiches, I tucked a miniature bottle of white wine, wrapped cheese straws, a cup of plum, orange, and banana fruit salad, and a plastic bag with a Babsie's Tart and a chocolate cookie in each box. As I closed the last cardboard box, my eye fell on the computer. Computer, disks, tapes. Tapes. *If Luella had told anyone about the taping, she would have lost her job.* How significant were these meetings that Suz had taped? I didn't know, and I'd promised Tom I wouldn't go nosing around at ACHMO. I put in a call to Brandon Yuille's office. I would apologize for snapping at him at John Richard's office, then pump him for info. When his assistant asked suspiciously who was calling and I told her, I had to wait two minutes for her cold response that Mr. Yuille was unavailable. I asked if I could call back at a more convenient time. She responded icily that there just was no convenient time. Fine. I hung up and called Chris Corey's office.

His secretary put me right through. "Goldy!" His deep, rumbly voice sounded surprised. "What's going on? Korman hasn't come over to bother you, has he?"

"He wouldn't dare. Listen, Chris, something one of the investigators said has been bothering me." I hesitated, remembering I'd promised not to mention that Luella was the one who had spilled the beans to Donny. "It relates to what we were talking to Frances about Sunday at the café. You said ACHMO was going into John Richard's office looking for notes about the McCrackens' suit."

"Well . . . yes."

"It's just that I heard there were some missing tapes, too."

Chris grunted. "Don't remind me."

I persisted innocently, "What's going on? Why would Suz keep tapes of meetings in her office?"

He lowered his voice. "Look, Goldy, it's a huge crisis. Everybody's upset about it. Nobody seems to know *why* she was taping in her office. *Secretly* taping. Makes it much worse."

"You say that as if there were other taping systems."

"Yeah, sure. The microphones in our *main* meeting room are sound-activated, and everybody knows that everything *there* gets taped, then transcribed so we have accurate minutes for each meeting. It could have been Suz was afraid of industrial spying, and that's why she did some kind of backup taping in her office. Maybe she kept the tapes locked up there and took them from her office to her home or wherever because some threat had appeared."

"Did she know about your work with Frances?"

"Not unless Frances told her, and that's unlikely."

"Who could be doing spying that would make Suz worried?"

"Look. Our meetings are confidential, Goldy, and if another HMO like MeritMed is trying to find out the details of our expansion plans, there could be hell to pay. And with legal action outstanding against us, the thought of having tapes of other in-house meetings floating around where anybody might get their hands on them is causing mass paranoia in corporate headquarters, believe me."

"Are you sure Suz had them?"

"No! What sends shivers up the bowels of HQ is that somebody Suz *fired* might have them. If anyone besides Luella knew Suz was taping, there could have been motivation to get in and steal them, especially if they might prove something against ACHMO. Plus," he added darkly, "they're panicked that Patricia McCracken might have them somehow. That woman's gone a little bonkers. It wouldn't surprise anybody here if she'd managed to steal the key to that cabinet, break into the office, and swipe the tapes from one of the days when Suz met with our lawyers about the McCracken case."

"So you don't even know what day's meetings are missing?"

He groaned with frustration. "We're trying to reconstruct, but it's a huge mess. We should know today. We're supposed to have security, but you know how that goes. Anyway, Goldy, speaking of meetings, I've got to go to one now. Damage control. Good luck with whatever it is you're working on."

"I'm not really working on anything, Chris. It's just that my son is very upset. I promised him I'd try to help his dad, much as I dislike the man."

I hung up and packed the lunches between freezer bags guaranteed to keep food cold. When I was almost done, Macguire came down to breakfast. His transformation was remarkable. His cheeks were genuinely pink. There was a spring to his only slightly wobbly step, and he had a broad smile on his face that made me laugh.

"Let me fix you some toast," I offered. "And some eggs, maybe?"

"Sounds great." While the frying eggs sizzled in the pan, Macguire dutifully washed down his ten herb capsules with water turned a science-fiction green by the chlorophyll. "Todd and Arch are still asleep," he announced. "I'll wake them up at ten. They listened to music until three A.M. I'll fix 'em breakfast, too. Toast, probably." His grin warmed my heart.

I thanked him for tending to Arch and Todd, declined his offer to help load my supplies, and hauled the first cardboard box out to my van. When I came back into the kitchen, my phone was ringing.

"Goldy, my God, I'm so glad I got you." Ralph Shelton's voice sounded exhausted and strained. "Look, I'm terribly sorry about running into you at the McCrackens' party. I just got out of control on those blades. Are you all right?"

"Sure, Ralph." No use troubling him with a litany of my lingering aches. "Thanks for calling."

He hesitated. "I just need to talk to you for a minute. Remember when you were over here asking how to get to the McCrackens' place?"

"Yes. What's the matter?"

"Well. I was supposed to drive to Omaha this morning, but they got word that . . . Oh, God, I need to know if you know anything about these tapes that Suz Craig was making. Please tell me, Goldy, I'm leveling with you. As an old friend."

I took a deep breath. "Why do you care about them?"

His voice wavered, as if he were about to cry. "Because I went in to see her last month, on the fourteenth to be exact, and . . . I just can't let anyone know what we talked about. Please, Goldy, help me. Suz was trying to destroy me. Do you have the tapes? Does John Richard? Are they at his office? Or his house? I've already driven past Suz's house and there's that damn yellow tape all around it—"

"Ralph, calm down. First tell me—exactly why were you fired from ACHMO?"

For a moment I thought he wouldn't answer. But then he sighed. "Patient complaints. No sexual misconduct or anything like that. It's just that I have a terrible bedside manner. I always have. You can imagine how that can kill you in ob-gyn. So. I was offered an administrative job with MeritMed. I took it."

I recalled Suz's secretary, whom Suz had kept in line with threats. "Was Suz threatening you in any way?"

He hesitated. "You've learned a lot, haven't you? She did threaten people. Yes, I was one of them. But it was all . . . exaggeration. I left before she could ruin me," he concluded darkly. "But if someone gets hold of those tapes . . . Oh, God," he moaned.

"Did you . . . were you . . . did you do something to Suz Craig?"

"Of course not, what the hell do you think I am?"

Well, that was what we didn't know, wasn't it? "I honestly don't know where the tapes are, Ralph. And John Richard's out on bail. You could give him or his office a call. But his secretary is frantic with the mess, and there's no telling what kind of emotional state John Richard is in. If I were you, I'd stay away from both of them."

"Yeah, well, you're not me."

At the LakeCenter the Babsie-doll show was in full swing. The security guard, even more hung over today than before, grunted a question about whether my assistant would be helping me, because he had strict orders not to let "that young fellow" near the dolls. I kept my patience and told him my assistant would not be accompanying me today. The armed guard escorted me past the display tables, where shiny arrays of statuesque, ultraslender, elaborately coiffed Babsies in lacy, sequined gowns elicited choruses of oohs and aahs from the crush of excited visitors. Even I was impressed, especially when I saw the price tags.

At the appointed time, I passed out box lunches on the patio to women clutching blue lunch tickets. While they ate, I indulged in a more detailed tour of the show. One table was dedicated solely to Holiday Babsies from 1990 to the present. All the dolls belonged to Gail Rodine. All were marked "Not for Sale." The costumes were festive and fantastic: tiny rhinestones glistened above shimmery red and green taffeta gowns; white furs set off dark velvet evening dresses. Another table featured Babsie as astronaut, Babsie as veterinarian, Babsie as a prima ballerina, Babsie horseback riding, Babsie walking her poodle on the Champs-Elysées, even Babsie as President. All that was missing was Babsie as Elvis. A long aisle was devoted to Babsie accessories. I looked with awe at teensy-weensy toreador pants; high heels; sequined leotards; compartmentalized Babsie suitcases; flip-curled wigs in blond, black, brunette, and red hair; and sexy lingerie that befit the Babsie Massage Parlor. As Donny Saunders would say, *Whoo-ie!*

The few attendees not indulging in box lunches were cooing over a table on the far side of the ballroom. When I joined them, I realized their drooling wasn't from craving my cucumber-brioche sandwiches. Their eyes were greedily fixed on a display of a single Babsie. I stared at the display: Babsie in a "Japanese exclusive" gown. I didn't know if that meant the gown was made or sold in Japan or both. No matter. I was transfixed by the miniature image of a fashion plate.

Babsie's blue eyes, rosy cheeks, and bow-shaped mouth were demure, and her long, perfect blond coif did not reveal a single flyaway strand. The bodice and skirt of the tiny full-length gown were made of snowy white satin, and the toes of itsy-bitsy pink high heels peeked out at the hem. A hot-pink embroidered chiffon over-skirt pouffed and swirled above the white satin. A minuature stole of the same pink fabric hugged the doll's shoulders, while a choker of minuscule pink pearls decorated her neck. *Very nice,* I thought appreciatively, *the sort of thing you'd wear to an inaugural ball or a royal wedding.* Then I looked at this Babsie's price tag: three thousand dollars. When the woman next to me asked if I didn't think it was just unbelievable, I said, "Yes, incredible beyond words." Never let it be said that I was a caterer who couldn't appreciate her clients' hobbies.

The first woman said, "The dealer said to me, 'How can you refuse this adorable doll?' Now I feel as if this poor doll is a refugee who will starve if I don't buy her!" A tear slid down one of her cheeks.

A second woman whispered, "I've got a spy in France. You should see my phone bills. But when the French Babsies come out—you know, the ones we can't get?—I have my spy get it. She airmails it in a plain brown wrapper. For security. It costs me, but it's worth it."

John le Carré, eat your heart out. I tore myself away from the dolls and returned to the patio. In a large plastic garbage bag I collected dirty cups, wrappers, used plastic spoons, and empty miniature wine bottles. Suddenly the cormorants near the shore rose in a frenzied flutter, and I was dimly aware of a distant *wap wap wap wap wap.*

I sat on one of the patio benches and squinted at the sky. *Wap wap wap,* louder and louder. In the summer, this was the most dreaded sound in Aspen Meadow. It was the Flight-for-Life helicopter. Usually the only time you heard it was when someone, frequently a child, had drowned, fallen while rock climbing, or been lost for hours after straying from a wilderness hike.

I trotted to the Dumpster near the lake and lofted in the trash bag. The helicopter circled near Main Street. That was odd. The copter appeared to be hovering over Cottonwood Creek, not too far from our house. I reached into my apron pocket for the portable cellular phone I took to events and shakily punched in our number, reminding myself that not all disasters in Aspen Meadow had to involve me.

One second, two seconds, three . . . then the phone connected and Arch answered on the first ring. "I'm okay, Mom."

"How did you—?"

"Are you kidding? All you do is worry about me. I heard the helicopter a minute ago and called Marla to make sure she wasn't having another heart attack. She'd already found out what was going on. Somebody was in an explosion. A grill at the park blew up. They think some mountain moths built a nest in the vent. Then when the person lit the propane, the grill exploded, just like Frances Markasian wrote about in the paper. Oh, wait, there's the other line. Maybe it's Marla again."

I watched the slow sweep of the second hand on my watch while I waited for Arch to come back on the line. As usual, I tried to reconstruct where Tom was—

"Oh, Mom," Arch said, his voice subdued. "Marla says that, you know, she survived the explosion, but she's burned and bloody—"

"Who survived, Arch?" I was frantic. "Marla?"

"Oh, no, Mom. The person trying to light the grill . . . the person who got hurt . . . It was ReeAnn."

Chapter 21

I asked Arch how Macguire was doing. He was asleep. I asked if Arch had heard from his father. He said no. I told him to make sure that all the windows were closed and that the security system was armed. And stay inside, I said. It wasn't a logical order, it was an emotional one, a fact my son hotly pointed out. I told him I'd be home in less than an hour. Then I disconnected and called Tom.

He wasn't at his office. I checked my watch: two o'clock. Rather than leave a message, I redialed the department and asked to speak with Sergeant Beiner. When she answered, I identified myself and told her what had happened.

"Hold on," she said. In the background she rustled paper. "This ReeAnn? Korman's secretary, right?" I insisted that this accident involving ReeAnn had to be related somehow to Suz Craig's murder.

Calmly, Sergeant Beiner said, "How?"

I bit the inside of my cheek and watched the cormorants land back on the lake. A hummingbird soared and then dipped to sip the nectar from a nearby poppy.

"How," I repeated not so patiently to Sergeant Beiner, "could an accident involving ReeAnn Collins relate to Suz Craig? John Richard might have thought she killed Suz and decided to punish her. Aah . . . maybe somebody thinks ReeAnn has possession of something incriminating."

"Hmm," said Sergeant Beiner, clearly unconvinced.

I told her I knew about Suz secretly taping meetings. I added that Donny Saunders and Chris Corey had reported that some tapes were missing. Maybe somebody thought ReeAnn had them. Maybe Patricia McCracken or Ralph Shelton or *somebody* was so desperate for the missing tapes that they had tried to blow ReeAnn up. Sergeant Beiner said that these people had all known ReeAnn for some time, why do something to her *now*?

"I don't know," I replied persistently. "Maybe because of the tapes. But there is a connection, I'm certain of it."

"Goldy," advised Sergeant Beiner, "take a breather."

"Please help me," I begged her. "I know you usually keep the families of those affected apprised of the progress of an investigation . . . Can't you please help us, just so we'll stay informed and my son won't have so much anxiety?"

For a moment she was silent. Then she said tersely, "Patricia McCracken I don't know about. She called this morning to get an update on the criminal investigation so she can decide what to do about her civil suits. I just called her back an hour ago. Now"—there was a rustle of pages and I knew she was consulting her notes— "Amy Bartholomew was interviewed by Donny Saunders this morning. Ms. Bartholomew told him she was leaving to go camping alone for a few days in the Aspen Meadow Wildlife Preserve, and that *you* were the one who told her to get away for a while. Maybe she didn't go, but I don't think that she had any grudge against ReeAnn Collins that was life-threatening. Do you?"

"I guess not."

"As for Dr. Korman, he's out on bail, as you no doubt are aware. You might want to put your efforts into recalling that judge in the next election." She paused. "I don't know about Ralph Shelton. We'll have somebody go up and talk to him. But I have to tell you, it's going to be a while."

"Okay." I felt defeated, not because I wanted Amy or Patricia or Ralph or somebody at ACHMO or even John Richard to have hurt ReeAnn, but because I was completely confused. I mumbled an apology to Sergeant Beiner for bothering her and hung up.

I raced back to the LakeCenter and finished cleaning up the box lunches. Occasionally, I reflected as I stooped to pick up the last of the trash the visitors had left, I have a great culinary idea that fails. But before I know things aren't going to work out, the inspiration stokes my energy and makes my brain fire on all cylinders. Blue cheese pizza was the product of such thinking. Coffeecake swirled with frozen pitted Bing cherries was another, as was sausages baked with apples and hominy. They were all failures. I'd gagged on the too-salty pizza. The coffeecake turned first inky, then mushy, then inedible. And when Arch had had two bites of the sausage concoction, he'd asked if we could go to Burger King for breakfast.

Most of my food ideas and experiments succeed. But it's hard to bear that in mind when the failures occur. And instead of responding to these setbacks with an optimistic, Thomas Edison–style, now-I-know-what-doesn't-work attitude, I usually feel frustrated and angry that I spent time and money on ingredients yielding such disasters. Worse, the anguish accompanying the failures always plunges me into a psychological well of uncertitude. Questions like Are you really in the right line of work? and Who do you think you are, anyway? taunt me. Eventually, of course, I always pull myself together, toss the messes in the garbage, and go on to the next concoction.

It was that pulling-together time that I now longed for. Poor ReeAnn.

When I pressed the buttons on our security system and entered our home, the warmth inside brought a small lift in my spirits. It's not so bad, I told myself. ReeAnn was alive, if injured. I was upholding my promise to Arch. I was trying to find out what really had happened to Suz Craig. I didn't want to clear the Jerk, I didn't even care if anything *ever* exonerated him. But I did want to know what had happened, and why, so that when they hauled John Richard off for an extended prison stay, I could tell Arch with a clear conscience that I had done my darnedest.

I called Lutheran Hospital and asked to check on the condition of ReeAnn Collins. Since I was not family, I was told, the information could not be divulged. Upstairs, Arch and Macguire were listening to what could advisedly be called music. Macguire showed me a huge box of imported chocolates that Marla had brought over. She'd told the boys she was going down to Lutheran Hospital to check on ReeAnn personally, and she'd call me later. I knew she'd get the info. When Marla told people she was a family member, they rarely argued.

The boys offered me a wrapped Mozartkügel and I took it. It was somewhat ironic that the only way these two would acknowledge the classical masters of music was through candy. Within moments more chocolate bulged in their cheeks and noise blared down our street. I thought again of Schoenberg's mother and retreated hastily to my kitchen.

I booted up my computer and went through the file I'd opened on the circumstances surrounding Suz Craig's death. What significance could ReeAnn have to the murder of Suz Craig? What was the link? I couldn't see any, apart from the fact that ReeAnn had known all about the Jerk's affairs, and probably a great deal about Suz's as well.

I scrolled back through my computer file and reread an early entry, where I summarized the catering job I'd done at Suz's house in July. It had been a clear, sunlit day, with clouds piling up over the mountains to the west and birds flitting among the blue campanula and columbine. Suz had been nervous about the appearance of her yard with its unfinished landscaping. She'd fretted about the weather, since she hadn't wanted the ACHMO honchos to be soaked by an unexpected mountain shower. She'd shown little interest in the food preparation and presentation. To me this said: Career woman whose postcollege path did not detour through the kitchen. Which was just fine. That kind of client uncritically appreciates my work, even thinks of it as a kind of magic. Suz had appeared cheerful, but she had not really enjoyed the food. And when Chris Corey had fallen down the steps, she'd been distraught.

All of this begged the question I'd never thought to ask in the first place: Why had the Minneapolis people been visiting in July? The people at the party had certainly made no mention of an annual review, audit, or meeting. In retrospect, that seemed strange. When I'd asked one visiting staff member what had brought him out to Denver, I'd received a noncommittal response along the lines of "Fighting fires." Exactly what kind of fire? Suz's guests had all been from Human Resources at ACHMO headquarters, that much I knew. I did have a foodie buddy in the Denver ACHMO HR office. But the last time I'd seen Brandon Yuille, at John Richard's office, he had been upset with me for not telling him where the Jerk would hide something. Now I realized he'd probably been referring to the missing meeting tapes, as well as notes about the malpractice and negligence suits. I felt guilty all over again for snapping at him, and resolved to be reconciled before asking him more about Suz.

To keep my promise to Tom, I knew I couldn't pay Brandon a visit at the ACHMO office itself. Not that they'd let the ex-wife of the man accused of murdering their vice-president through the doors. So instead I phoned Brandon's office and again identified myself: Goldy Schulz, the caterer, the *friend of Brandon's*. Once more Brandon's secretary was either well-trained or just her usual wary self. She asked the nature of my call.

"I need to apologize to him for a misunderstanding we had. Also, I'd like to talk to him about a lunch I catered a while ago," I replied. I avoided mentioning the name of Suz Craig. "We talked about Thai food and fudge, remind him of that. I have a couple of questions about the event itself."

There was a pause. "Aah," the secretary said finally, with mock regretfulness, "it looks as if Mr. Yuille will be in a meeting for the next three days."

"Don't they ever take breaks?" I asked good-naturedly. "This won't take long."

She didn't respond immediately. I had the feeling she was looking straight at Brandon, who was vigorously shaking his head. At length she stiffly announced, "I can connect you with Mr. Yuille's voice mail, if you'd like."

I assented and briefly told the recorded voice that I was trying to help my son deal with his father being arrested by keeping him informed about the murder investigation. Could Brandon forgive me for being short with him at Korman's office? And could he satisfy my curiosity, tell me why the Minneapolis HR team at Suz's house had come to Denver in the first place? Finally, did he happen to know if anyone had it in for John Richard's secretary, ReeAnn Collins, who'd just been badly injured in a barbecue incident?

Well, I thought as I hung up, *that ought to either ruin our friendship or take it to a whole new level.* I had the disconcerting feeling that I'd been too pushy. Moreover, whether any useful information would come out of my requests was, it seemed at this point, extremely questionable.

I wanted to cook. But my growling stomach announced I was too hungry to concentrate. I'd had nothing to eat in the last eight hours except a piece of toast, coffee, and a Mozartkügel. Looking around, I dove into the container of Chocolate Comfort Cookies like a madwoman. Although I've read accounts of how addicts heighten their drug experiences, in my opinion nothing beats a large mouthful of dark, velvety chocolate on an empty stomach. I closed my eyes, bit into the cookie, and waited for the rush. An ecstasy of shivers began in the small of my back. I sighed with chocoholic contentment. Now I was ready to face whatever the rest of the day cared to deliver.

According to my catering calendar, the following morning—Wednesday—Gail Rodine's doll-club board of directors wanted a fancy breakfast by the lake. I'd promised her baked scrambled eggs with cream cheese and shrimp, fruit kebabs, honey-cured ham, and an assortment of breads. My supplier had delivered the meat last Friday. I heaved the plump, bone-in ham onto the counter to check if it had been spiral-cut as I'd ordered. It was, and would only need heating in the morning. The eggs and shrimp I would assemble at the LakeCenter, but the breads needed to be organized today.

I had two large loaves of the brioche left over from the box lunches, plus several dozen dark pumpernickel rolls that I'd made and frozen particularly for this event. But one more bread was needed to round things out. Experimenting to put together a delectable new bread for an upscale breakfast? *Please don't throw me in the briar patch.* Thomas Edison, here I come. I knew I could do it. I scanned the walk-in pensively.

In the use-up-stray-ingredients economy that good caterers invariably subscribe to, I noted egg whites left over from making the Babsie Tarts, a couple of oranges that I'd ordered along with the lemons, and several unopened jars of poppy seeds. I pounced on these ingredients. I'd assemble a cakelike orange poppy-seed bread. Or die in the attempt.

As always, cooking lifted me from the doldrums. While the egg whites were whipped into a froth, I measured the dry ingredients and then delighted in the fine spray of citrus oil that slicked my fingers when I scraped the zest from the oranges. Outside, the sun shone brilliantly in a deep blue sky and a warm breeze swished through the aspens. I opened the window over the sink. The boys' music reverberated along the street. Out back Jake howled an accompaniment. I smiled. If the music made the boys happy, I wasn't going to say a thing.

I was folding the poppy seeds into the batter when John Richard Korman jumped in front of the window. I screamed and dropped the bowl in the sink. The bowl shattered. Jake howled. Locked out back, the dog couldn't help me. I'd disarmed the security system. I hadn't turned it back on. Oh, God.

Unthinking, I wheeled around wildly for the phone. But by then John Richard had pulled off the screen, reached through the window, and grabbed my wrist.

"Let go!" I cried as I wrenched my hand back. "Go away!" I screamed. He lurched up through the window, with my wrist still in a death grip. His free hand slapped my face. He smelled like whiskey.

"Shut up!" he growled. "I'm telling you, Goldy," he said in a menacing voice as I opened my mouth to scream again, "shut the hell up. I want to talk to you. I want to talk to Arch. Let me in."

Instead I pushed hard to try to get him out. Mercilessly, he twisted my wrist. I cried out in pain. Again he told me to *shut the hell up*. Then he yanked my hand over the window frame. Blood spurted from my forearm where the skin scraped against the metal. Poor Jake howled to no avail. My abdomen pressed painfully against the sink. My feet barely touched the floor.

"Who wrote that shit on my house?" He twisted harder on my wrist. "The neighbors say you know. Who was it?"

"Vandals." I put my free hand on my face, trying to protect it from another slap. "Vandals. The sheriff's department doesn't know who they were. They can't find them. This isn't a good idea," I warned him. "Just go away. I promise I won't tell Tom."

"Why didn't you open your door when I knocked?"

"I didn't hear you."

"I *said*, 'Why didn't you open your door when I knocked?'"

"I told you . . . agh . . ." Pain shot through my wrist again. "I didn't *hear* you."

"Bullshit. Listen. I didn't kill her, Goldy." With his other hand he seized my chin and forced me to look in his eyes. "I did not kill Suz Craig. She'd been *rep*rimanded"—another tug on my arm made me squeal—"by the Minneapolis people and faced being *fired*. We had a *fight*, but I didn't *kill* her. *They* killed her." His fingers bit into my wrist so savagely that I whimpered.

"Tell the cops," I gasped. "Tell . . . your lawyer."

"I did! I just wanted to tell *you*!"

His handsome face twisted in rage. I knew he would hit me again. I was panicked about the two boys upstairs. I couldn't let Arch see us like this again. I wouldn't let the Jerk *hurt* me like this again. Stunned with pain, I frantically searched for something—anything—to rescue me. There was no knife in sight.

Through gritted teeth he said, "I want to talk to that kid you have living here. Perkins. I think *he* painted my house."

Pain shot through my arm. I squirmed to get some leverage against the sink.

"For-*get* it!" I screamed. With my left hand I seized the heavy piece of ham on the counter. I swung the meat up, then down on top of John Richard's head. The meat glanced off his forehead and his eyes rolled up in his head. Releasing my wrist, he stumbled backward.

I lurched for the phone, dropped it, retrieved it, pressed 911. I shouted that I had an intruder, my ex-husband, John Richard Korman.

I screamed, "He hurt me! I'm bleeding!"

"Is he there now?" The 911 operator spoke calmly.

I scrambled for the window in time to see John Richard, one hand clutching his temple, limping toward the street. "Yes, yes, but he's leaving! Hurry!" I yelled. "Quickly! Come and get him and take him *away*!"

But I already knew it was too late. The Jeep roared and he was gone.

Chapter 22

I closed and locked the window. Outside, Jake had not stopped his incessant howling. I let him in through the back door. He bounded over to me immediately, whining, putting his muzzle up to my face, trying to lick it. I floundered into the bathroom to wash the blood off my arm. Unfortunately, the sound of sirens brought Arch and Macguire rushing down the stairs.

The bloody fingers of my left hand pressed the lock on the bathroom door. I couldn't talk to anyone just yet. When the boys called, I responded by saying I'd be there in a minute. I looked dreadful. My face was blotchy; my right cheek bore the scarlet imprint of John Richard's hand. I turned the cold water all the way up and splashed and resplashed my face. It had been a long time since the Jerk had treated me like this. Our house boasted a security system, a bloodhound, and a live-in policeman. None of these had helped.

Would we ever be safe?

.   .   .

The next hour passed in a daze. At my insistence, Arch and Macguire went back upstairs. The two policemen who came to the door, both deputies I did not know, asked if I could tell them where John Richard had gone. I gave them his address in the country club and begged not to have to go down to the department to make my statement. The deputies instructed me to write down exactly what had happened. As I was scribbling, one of the cops called Tom, who was not at his desk. The other took the ham into evidence. I almost laughed, but I couldn't stop trembling enough to do so.

By contacting and attacking a witness in the homicide investigation in which he'd been charged, John Richard had gotten himself into deep trouble. When the sheriff's department located him, they would arrest him again. Somehow knowing this did not make me feel much better. All I could think of was Arch.

I took a shower, changed into fresh clothes, and searched for my son. I found him on a portable phone in his room. Judging from his confidential tone, he was talking to his buddy Todd. When I knocked on the door, he quickly disconnected.

"May I come in?"

I could tell he felt horrible. His voice cracked when he whispered, "Mom, are you okay?"

"No, hon, I'm really not."

"I didn't even have a chance to see him."

"I know."

Arch slumped morosely on his bed, his lips pressed together. Finally he said, "I just feel as if it's so hopeless. You promised you'd help him and—"

"I *have* tried to help him," I interrupted, careful to keep my tone soothing. "Not because of anything good he's done, but because I promised you that I would—"

"Excuse me, Mom, but you have *not* helped him. He says he didn't kill Ms. Craig. I believe him."

"Arch, please. I have spent the last three days on the telephone asking questions, going around talking to people, and—"

Behind the glasses, his eyes burned ferociously. "And what have you found out? Nothing!" Guiltily, he softened his tone. "I know you want him to go to prison. In your heart."

Poor, miserable Arch. It didn't help that he was probably right. I did want John Richard in prison, where he couldn't hurt another woman. I said patiently, "I am waiting for people to call me back. I can't make people talk to me."

He got up and slid halfway under his bed. When he inched back out, he was clutching his backpack. "Sorry, Mom, but I'm going to live with the Druckmans for a while. At least until Dad's hearing. Todd's mother said it was okay." He opened a drawer and began pulling out shorts and shirts. "If I hadn't been here, Dad never would have come around and started hitting you. He was probably looking for me."

"Honey, please, please don't go."

"This way," my son continued, avoiding my eyes, "we won't have another big mess with the police coming over. Please leave my room now, Mom."

He'd ordered me from his room. He wouldn't speak to me. He refused to even *listen*. I retreated to my kitchen, where I sat in silent shock for ten minutes. Then I called the Druckmans to apologize for my son being a freeloader and to see if I could at least bring over some food. Kathleen Druckman assured me that she was happy to have Arch for as long as he wanted to stay. I didn't need to deliver any meals, either, she said with a laugh, she'd be insulted. She and her husband would even take Arch down to the jail to see his father. And was it true that John Richard had knocked me unconscious with a whole poached salmon? I said no, thanked her again, and hung up.

Macguire had left a note taped to my computer: *Going out for a walk, hope you're okay. See you at dinner. Can we have pizza?*

Not even Macguire's renewed appetite cut through my misery.

When Arch slammed out the front door, I almost burst into tears. Instead, I dialed Tom's number.

It was four o'clock. He wasn't there, so I left a very brief voice-mail message. John Richard had been here. Both Arch and I were okay. If he wanted more information, he could talk to the officers who, I hoped, would have arrested John Richard by the time he got this message.

The memory of the Jerk's slap rushed back into my conscious-ness. But what had he shrieked about Suz Craig? *She'd been repri-manded.* For what? I put in another call to Brandon Yuille. He was the Human Resources person, after all. Unfortunately, he again refused to speak to me except through his secretary. I told her to ask Bran-don if the ACHMO bigwigs were about to fire Suz Craig and if so, why. And remind him, I said, that I was sorry we'd had a misunder-standing. Also that I had a close personal relationship with the inves-tigative journalist of the *Mountain Journal* and she'd just love to start bothering him for an interview. I hung up with a bang that did nothing to improve my mood.

I cleaned up the mess in the kitchen left from my fracas with the Jerk. To fulfill Macguire's request, I mixed up some pizza dough and set it aside to rise. I called my supplier to see about replacing the ham and got her machine. Then, because I couldn't think of anything else to do, I started over on the orange poppy-seed bread.

This time, just as I was again at the fateful point of folding in the poppy seeds, the phone rang. I thought it might be Marla or Tom or even Brandon Yuille getting back to me, but I was wrong. To my surprise, it was Patricia McCracken.

"Well," she demanded breathlessly, as if none of the sorry events of the last three days had ever transpired and we were still happy confidantes, "what have you found out?"

"About *what?*" I gently scraped a poppy seed–speckled pillow of the light, moist batter into a buttered and floured loaf pan.

"About John Richard, silly! Has he gotten himself into any more trouble?"

"Like what?" I really did not want to discuss this. Any info I gave Patricia would be all over Aspen Meadow in an hour, given her feud with the Jerk. At least she hadn't heard the crazy story about him hitting me with a salmon.

"My neighbor's son was driving by the park when the helicopter came down. I heard ReeAnn was burned over three-fourths of her body," she continued. "Was she with John Richard? You don't know what happened with that, do you?"

This was the woman who had complained so bitterly to me about our community's obsession-with-disaster? Incredible. Some people just can't see themselves as fostering the very problem they're griping about.

"I can't talk, Patricia," I responded. "I need to finish making some bread."

Bitterly, she said, "You're not much help," and hung up.

Not much help. Well, wasn't that what everyone was saying about me these days? I slid the bread into the oven, then rebooted my computer and added *According to the Jerk, Suz was reprimanded by ACHMO HQ honchos* to my list of what I knew about her. A brief time later, I took the golden-brown bread out and placed it on a rack. It perfumed the kitchen with its rich, orangey scent. Macguire arrived home as I was feeding the dog and the cat. I assured him I was just fine and told him I'd be kneading cloverleaf rolls in no time. He looked skeptically at the slap marks on my face and the thick bandage I'd placed over my forearm. But unlike Patricia McCracken, he was too polite to say anything.

Tom arrived shortly after six, bearing vegetarian calzones and a deep-dish sausage pizza. He unloaded the food, gently examined my face and arm, and cursed John Richard. He carefully punched down the mass of pizza dough I'd already made, zipped it into a heavy-duty plastic bag, and popped it into the freezer. When he finished unwrapping the Italian feast, I felt tears prick hard.

"Please, Goldy, don't, don't," he crooned as he gathered me up in his arms. "What you've been through . . . I'm so sorry I wasn't here. I feel like I failed you."

"You didn't."

"I did."

"Oh, Tom. Arch has gone to live with the Druckmans until John Richard's hearing."

"He'll be back," he said confidently.

I let him hold me. "All this food," I muttered finally, "it's going to get cold."

He held me out at arm's length. His warm green eyes gave me a skeptical look. "That's what I brought my convection oven into this house for, remember? You like pizza, don't you? Even if it's pizza made by somebody else?"

You like pizza? "Sure," I said uncertainly, and sat down at the table while Tom preheated the oven and opened a bottle of Chianti. I shivered. *Even if it's pizza made by somebody else?* Tom had gently asked.

My afternoon encounter with John Richard had brought another assault of memories I thought I'd repressed. One time, I *had* tried to serve pizza made by somebody else. Arch had been three months old and sick with a painful ear infection. Exhausted from being up with him all night and then all day, I'd ordered a pizza for dinner. John Richard had thrown a fit, of course. He'd torn the pizza into bits and dumped them in the garbage disposal. If he'd wanted take-out pizza, he'd shouted, he would have stayed single.

Without being asked, Macguire set the kitchen table. Not one of us mentioned my son. Arch must have told Macguire his plans to live with the Druckmans. Again, Macguire was too polite to mention it.

The strange thing about going through a difficult time is that eventually, you get hungry. The Italian sausage on the pizza Tom had brought home provided a sharp, juicy complement to the crunchy crust. The calzones were so stuffed with steaming tomatoes, onions, peppers, and cheese that it was hard to take a bite without making a mess. By the time we finished eating, my mood had lifted somewhat.

"Something I need to discuss with you all," Tom said in the gentle voice he used whenever he needed to drop a bombshell.

I said, "Uh-oh."

"The deputies couldn't find John Richard," he announced matter-of-factly. "He wasn't at his house. There's an APB out on him, but you need to know he's at large."

"That sucks," Macguire said.

"It's probably just as well Arch is at the Druckmans'," Tom continued. "Here at home, we need to keep the windows shut all the time. Turn on the attic fan if you need ventilation. But the security system stays *armed*. I mean it."

I rubbed my temples and tried to give myself a silent pep talk. No uplifting thoughts came. When Macguire offered to do the dishes, Tom and I consented gratefully. Upstairs, the Chianti and relaxing meal finally took effect. No matter how bad the news is, not only do you have to eat, you eventually have to sleep. I hadn't slept well since I'd discovered Suz Craig's body. I yawned.

"Put on your pajamas," Tom ordered with a loving smile, "and let me rub your back."

"It's not even eight o'clock."

"Miss G., let me take care of you. No fussing."

I winced as I pulled the pajama sleeve over my bruised arm, then remembered the arnica and antidepression herbs from Amy Bartholomew and slid the tablets and capsules onto the table next to the bed. Before I could take any, though, I had to ask my husband a few questions.

"Tom," I said as I lay carefully on my stomach, "where could John Richard be?"

"Aw, he's someplace he thinks is safe. With friends, probably. I don't think he'd dare come after you. Not after today."

"Beg to differ." After a moment I said, "Arch doesn't think I'm looking into the charges against his father. After all I've done, that almost hurts more than anything."

Tom's large hands pressed and massaged my aching body. "He's a kid, Goldy. He just doesn't understand. Cut him some slack."

"I've cut him tons of slack. He just hasn't cut any for me."

Tom chose not to respond to this. Under his hands my weary muscles began to relax. I felt my eyes closing.

"I've got something else to ask you," I said weakly.

"I wish you wouldn't talk."

"Has anybody at ACHMO told you Suz was about to be fired? Or why?"

He chuckled. "Korman sure claimed that in his interview. But he was the only one who mentioned it, and he can't prove a thing. Everyone else swears her job was secure."

"Ah," I said. I downed the herb capsules and slipped the arnica under my tongue. A few minutes later, I did not resist when sleep claimed me.

I awoke at two A.M. in such a state of alertness that I felt sure Arch had come home, the security alarm had gone off, or either Scout or Jake was scratching to go out. None of these was the case. I looked out the window: the night was still. No breeze or rush of creekwater was audible, of course, as every single window in the house was locked up tight. I turned on the dresser light and saw a note from Tom.

Miss G., Arch called before he went to bed. You were sleeping so soundly I didn't want to wake you. He wanted to tell you good night and that he loved you. Also, Marla phoned. ReeAnn C. is banged up pretty good but they think she's going to pull through. T.

Peachy. But it was not worries about Arch or even ReeAnn that had awakened me. It was something else.

If Suz Craig was about to be fired, or was even in danger of being fired, how could that relate to her being murdered? And why had Brandon Yuille, my buddy-in-Thai-food, refused to answer any of my calls? Was he still annoyed about our conversation at the Jerk's office, despite my apologies? John Richard was on the loose, but I doubted he was watching our house. I slipped on jeans, sneakers, and a sweatshirt. During the day, Brandon could refuse to return my calls all he wanted. But at this hour, I knew exactly where to find him.

Chapter 23

The Aspen Meadow Pastry Shop had undergone a sea change since Mickey Yuille, my old master baker friend, had bought it, refurbished it, and hired an energetic cleaning service. Lacy, pristinely white European-style curtains now hung in the windows. The glass display cases, formerly messy with weeks of fingerprints, gleamed spotlessly in the dimmed light of the cozy dining room. The former owner had offered a hodgepodge of almost-stale cookies and partially baked pastry shells. These had been replaced by appetizing rows of truffles, chocolate-dipped macaroons, and French cream cookies so buttery, they gave new meaning to melt-in-your-mouth.

Since it was a quarter past two in the morning, I stopped lusting over the offerings in the dark shop-front and looked for movement in the kitchen. An oblong of yellow light illuminated Mickey hustling back and forth. As I sidled across the front window to get a better view, I caught sight of Brandon. He sat at a long table, gesturing as he spoke earnestly to his father. The back door had been left partially open, probably to bring cool night air into the oven-heated space.

I nipped past the comics shop, the insurance agent's office, and the Christian Science Reading Room. I rounded the back of the building and came noiselessly up to the back entrance with its open door. Mickey *had* suggested I come by for some fresh, hot cinnamon rolls. Now the unmistakable scent of that most prized of spices, Indonesian cinnamon, came wafting out into the darkness. I pushed the door open and stepped inside.

"Howdy all," I said brightly, as if I customarily popped into closed bakeries at two A.M. "I had insomnia, so I just thought I'd drop in."

Mickey, balding, shrunken, but with a smile so endearing he always reminded me of a stuffed troll, looked up from the thick layer of golden dough he was rolling out. "Goldy! So glad to see you!" He set aside his marble rolling pin and bustled forward to embrace me. He smelled marvelous, sweat mixed with spice and flour. His long white apron dusted my outfit. I grinned and returned his hug, then looked over at Brandon. His handsome face was no longer set in its usual impish expression. He looked as if a monsoon had arrived at his doorstep.

"Morning, Brandon," I said pleasantly. "So glad I could run into you here. I've been trying to call you to apologize for our misunderstanding at my ex-husband's office."

His shiny dark hair fell in his face and he immediately brushed it back. "Sure, okay, no hard feelings," he mumbled without visible enthusiasm. "Glad to see you."

"Coffee, coffee, let's have some fresh," said Mickey, obviously glad of my company, even if his son was not.

"Why didn't you answer my calls?" I asked Brandon as I sat in one of the chairs at his father's worktable. Out of earshot, Mickey ran water and measured out ground coffee.

"I can't call you back," Brandon rejoined. "They are watching me every second. I'm afraid every call of mine is monitored. . . ."

"Who's 'they'? Who would monitor your calls?"

Brandon's handsome face screwed up in dismay. "The same guys who were here before, from the headquarters office of Human Resources. They've come back in from Minneapolis until the preliminary hearing with your ex is over. I'm telling you, Goldy, it's a bad scene."

"You think that's a bad scene? My fourteen-year-old son has *moved out* until the preliminary hearing. That's how ticked off with me he is over this case. I want to find out what the *hell* is going on with my son's father a whole lot more than your corporate bigwigs do." He said nothing. "Please, Brandon. Please help us."

Brandon exhaled unhappily. "Whatever I tell you, you've got to say you didn't hear it from me."

"Brandon, for heaven's sake! You didn't participate in any illegal activity, did you?"

His smile was a younger, less wrinkled version of his father's. "Of course not. No illegal activity. I didn't even kill Suz Craig, as is believed in some circles."

"What circles?"

His face turned pink. "Oh, you know. The gossip mill."

"Was she about to be fired by ACHMO when she was killed?"

His father reappeared with the coffee. It was marvelous, dark and hearty. We took grateful sips and showered praise and thanks on Mickey.

"You all go ahead and visit," Mickey told us. He eyed the rectangle of dough. "I gotta work."

"Can't we help you?" I offered. Cloth towels shrouded the domed top of another enormous bowl of risen dough.

"Naw, naw," Mickey replied, waving a floured paw. "The priest is doing grief work with me. Says I gotta work. Stay busy. Best antidote. I like having you here, though."

I looked back at Brandon, who shrugged. He murmured, "Just let him. He knows what he needs. I'm here for company. When I help him, it's usually on the weekends."

"Was Suz about to be fired?" I asked Brandon again. "Or had she been submitted to some kind of disciplinary action?"

Brandon sipped his coffee and was silent. For a moment I feared he'd decided not to answer. "Not exactly reprimanded. She was . . . being observed. In her dealings with people." I waited for him to go on. He shifted in the wooden chair. "Headquarters had had a lot of complaints." He seemed to go into a trance as he watched his father spread butter on the rolled dough.

"Complaints from whom?" I prompted.

Brandon blinked and shrugged. "Everybody who'd ever had to work with Suz Craig."

When he seemed in danger of going into another trance, I said, "Amy Bartholomew said the same thing. She said Suz set a trap for her. Amy wanted to control her own destiny, as she put it, and Suz had other ideas. Suz accused Amy of compulsively feeding the slots up at Central City. Then Suz tried to make it impossible for Amy to buy the health-food store."

Brandon's eyes were on his father as he sprinkled dark cinnamon sugar over the golden dough. "Yeah, I know. I'm the very young, very unsuccessful head of Human Resources, remember?"

"Amy said Suz criticized you for spending too much time here with your father and for coming into the office too tired to do good work. She criticized Chris Corey, too."

"Oh, boy, don't remind me." He looked at the ceiling. "Chris was putting together a new Provider Relations Manual. He's very thorough, and Suz kept changing the language of certain guidelines. It was her fault he missed the deadline. But she threw a fit anyway, in front of everybody."

"Did she criticize Ralph Shelton?"

"Of course," he said simply. "She told us she was putting together a file of patient complaints, plus a critical letter from her, into a packet to go to MeritMed."

"Why would she do that? He already told me that was why he was fired."

"Who knows? Plus, Goldy, I'm not convinced she should have fired him. Every doctor gets unhappy patients. Last year, the state board of medical examiners received over seven hundred and fifty complaints. Eighty-five percent were dismissed." He sighed. "And then Shelton was so pathetic, calling each of us after she fired him, to see if we could stop her from sending the packet of complaints on. We all suspected Shelton was trying to renew his old friendship with Korman to get *him* to prevent her from sending the packet to Shelton's new employers at MeritMed. But apparently Korman repeatedly gave Shelton the brush-off through that cute secretary of his."

"Sort of the way you gave me the brush-off today."

"Sorry. I really *was* in a meeting."

"Did Suz criticize and threaten John Richard, too?"

Brandon's large brown eyes and narrow face suddenly seemed overcome with sadness. "She could be the warmest, most loving person you could ever imagine." He paused and looked away. "She could also be vicious. Every day when I drove into that parking lot, my stomach would clench. What kind of mood was she going to be in today? What would she try to do to me? How could I fend her off?"

"Did she want to have control over John Richard?" I persisted.

He frowned, then shook his head. "Who knew? He didn't share much with us, you know, the administrators. Suz's control of *information* was what concerned her, and she was good at it." His forehead wrinkled. "I did hear that Korman's billing was problematic, and that he didn't automatically qualify for a bonus he was expecting."

"Who told you those tidbits?" When he shrugged, I went on. "Where do the ACHMO honchos come in? Why were they here last month? One of them told me they were fighting fires."

He sighed again. "I might as well tell you. *We're* the ones who complained about Suz to headquarters. Naughty us. Amy didn't tell you about that?"

"She said something was planned."

"The department heads did an end run. We called Human Resources at headquarters. 'This woman is killing us,' we said. 'You have to get rid of her.' "

"Wow."

He jabbed the air with his finger. "But listen! HQ is always telling us: 'Our vision is to build a cooperation-based organization! We want to have open lines of communication! Call on us *anytime* for help!' " His scowl deepened. "Did that ever backfire."

"How?"

"They came, they listened, they left. You catered a nice lunch for them their last day, after we'd been meeting with them all week telling them how horrid our boss was. That next-to-last day, guess what? They met with *her.*"

"Uh-oh."

" 'Uh-oh' is right! Open communication? Sounds more like *betrayal*, don't you think? They told Suz, 'Brandon Yuille says you criticize him too much. He can't get his work done hiring new people if he has to listen to complaints about you all day.' And to this Suz said, 'You know, Brandon's just lost his mother. I'll take him out to lunch this month.' "

"Oh, no."

"Oh, yes. The very last day, those HR people had the nerve to tell us about their conversation with her, and all she'd promised. They said they'd solved our little *personnel* problem. So you can see why our lunch showed a few cracks of tension."

His father slid a baking sheet from one of the large black ovens along the wall. Inside I could see flames. I had a fleeting vision of Hansel and Gretel.

Brandon went on. "And then the following week Suz called each of us in. To me she said, 'You ever complain about me again, I'll fire your ass so fast you won't know what hit you. I'll make sure you never get another job in Human Resources anywhere in Denver, or anywhere in the country, in an HMO.' " His laugh was empty.

"Then you won't believe what else she said. 'Brandon, I swear I'll have your medical records altered so it says you've got cancer just like your mother.' "

"Oh, come on. Surely—"

"Come on yourself. You don't think she had access to our medical records? How naive are you?"

"I just can't believe it."

"Goldy, believe it."

At this point Mickey interrupted us by setting blue plates of hot pastries in front of each of us. He beamed like a magician.

"Oh, my gosh," said Brandon, "bear claws."

I did not know if this Danish-style pastry shaped like a giant claw was indigenous to the Rocky Mountains. I'd never heard of it before moving out here. I bit off one finger of the almond-paste-filled delicacy. Butter oozed between the flaky layers. A light, sugary glaze and crunchy sliced almonds complemented the rich filling. Another luscious reason to live in Colorado.

"Thank you so very much," I told Mickey. "You can't imagine how much I appreciate this."

He poured me more hot coffee. "Of course I do. Food-service people are the last ones to sit down and actually enjoy *eating* anything. Besides, I love the company, as Brandon can tell you. I'm about to make some sour-cream cakes now. . . . You two need anything else?"

"Thanks, Dad. No," said Brandon warmly as he squeezed his father's hand. For the first time I noticed the bags under Brandon's eyes. His schedule must be brutal, I thought. He'd told the cops he went to bed at eight P.M. every night so that he could be here by two A.M. It wasn't a regimen I would want to follow on any long-term basis, especially since I'd tried it for the last few nights and now felt like a walking zombie.

"I'm going to leave in a few minutes," I told Brandon. "I think I understand better now why everyone, especially my ex, had trouble with this woman. It's hard to believe that Suz would threaten you with changing your medical records, though. Couldn't anybody call her on trying to intimidate people? It sounds so much like black-mail."

Brandon chewed the last of his bear claw. "Great idea, Goldy. Now we know those meetings she had with us in her office were taped. When I called headquarters the week after HR left, they said to me, 'You get proof she's threatening you and we'll fire her.' Not that I would trust them. But I checked the labels on the tapes Luella Downing found. None were from the Monday after the HR people left, when Suz went on her threatening rampage."

"That's it?" I said, astonished. "Monday—what would it have been, July 14? The tapes from that day are missing?"

"Why? You know where they are?"

"No," I said with a sudden yawn I couldn't suppress. "I don't have a clue."

When I crawled back into bed at four, Tom rolled over and said, "I'm beginning to think there's someone else."

I started to laugh and couldn't stop. They were the kind of giggles you get when you're very young, at camp or a slumber party, and can't contain, no matter how valiantly you try.

"Uh-huh," he said. "You got another statement to make? Some wrongdoing you encountered out on your prowls?"

"I can't . . ." I said between giggles, "help it . . . if I can't . . . sleep."

"Soothe me, then. Tell me where you went."

"To the pastry shop. Had a bear claw. Sorry, I didn't bring you any."

He put his arms around me and growled. "Promise me the next time you go on one of these excursions, you take me with you. I feel like a kid who always gets left behind."

I snuggled into his arms. "Okay. Whither I go, thou goest. Or words to that effect."

"So did you find out anything about Korman at the pastry shop?"

"Sort of. The missing day's tapes are for July 14, when Suz Craig called in all the employees who'd complained about her to HQ and threatened to fire them. She must have met with other people that day, too, like Ralph Shelton. So . . . if you had tapes of your-self blackmailing people, where would you hide them?"

"I'd destroy them."

"Oh, cop, you're a lot of help."

Chapter 24

My yoga regimen that morning was made more difficult by the phone ringing insistently at six o'clock. I pulled myself out of a contorted asana with the hope that this was the sheriff's department calling to tell us they'd captured the Jerk. No such luck: over the wire came the commanding voice of the much-dreaded dollmeister, Gail Rodine.

"The board doesn't want you to use the grill tonight for our final dinner," she announced without a hint of apology for calling so early. "I mean, after what happened to ReeAnn Collins, we just . . . feel it's too dangerous."

Thinking of the mountains of hamburgers I had made and frozen, and the bags of chicken breasts I had been planning to marinate, my heart plummeted. I could never get them *all* grilled at home and reheated at the LakeCenter, without ruining them. "What would you like, then?" I asked carefully. "It'll be impossible to order in more food supplies before tonight."

"Well . . . what do you already have on hand? Anything that you could grill, say, at home and then heat up?"

"Some I could do," I said confidently. "The last thing I want is for a client to be worried about preparation. But what I have on hand . . ." I mentally weighed the chicken. "If I grill the chicken I have, it will only feed half your folks. I'll have to make . . ." I mentally scanned my refrigerator. "I'll prepare a Camembert pie to fill things out. It'll contain shrimp and vegetables, too." From under the rumpled covers Tom's sleep-worn face appeared. I held my hand over the receiver and mouthed, "Client needs whole new dish for tonight."

"Macguire said he wanted to help you," Tom replied as he rolled back under the sheet. "Give him some chopping to do. He's worried about how depressed you are about Arch. He really wants to go back to being your assistant."

"Goldy?" Gail Rodine. "Goldy, are you listening to me? How much extra is this going to cost?"

"I do want you, the board, and the guests to be comfortable, Gail—"

"Don't worry," she said, clearing her throat, "I've already called a Denver caterer, and he said no one could meet our needs for a fancy dinner by five o'clock tonight without an exorbitant surcharge."

"Gail, please—"

"That's ridiculous!" she shrieked into my ear. "I told them, 'You don't want us to get blown up by a propane grill, do you?' "

"The Camembert pie retails for approximately forty dollars. You're already getting grilled Chicken à l'Orange and rice. I can add a tossed salad of field greens and perhaps a molded fruit salad, if I have time. Plus vanilla frozen yogurt with those chocolate cookies you had in your box lunches. There's only a five percent surcharge for changing the menu at this late date."

"Fine, fine, put it on our bill." She rang off.

"I'm afraid to ask what that was about." Tom's voice rumbled as he headed for the bathroom.

"Woman doesn't want to stage her last barbecue tonight," I said as I groaned before starting a final stretch. "Doesn't want to end up like ReeAnn."

"Figures. Hey, let me see that." He walked over to me, a manly vision in T-shirt and cotton undershorts. He touched my arm. "My God, Goldy! Look at that bruise! I *swear* I'm going to kill Korman myself, one of these days."

I twisted and frowned at the black-and-blue mark that had formed on my lower arm from being banged around by John Richard. I hadn't noticed it until now. "Oh, well. Say, do you want to go back to bed?"

He smiled at me but touched the bruise gently. "Does it hurt?"

I gave a doctor-style shrug. "I'll live, if we have a roll in the hay first."

He obliged, and we had a wonderful, warm, intimate time. Sometimes the best thing you can do in the morning is go right back to bed.

After a while Tom said, "I'm going to help you with this breakfast, and go in late. By the way, I bought you another spiral-cut honey-cured ham. It's in the walk-in."

I grinned and kissed him. "You're marvelous beyond words. And thank you—I'd love the company this morning."

I fixed myself an espresso while Tom took his shower. Because the hospital had rebuffed me, and because it was too early to call Marla, I made a quick call to the sheriff's department: ReeAnn Collins was out of danger and recovering from third- and second-degree burns. John Richard Korman, unfortunately, was still at large. And no, the duty officer informed me, Korman had not shown up at the Druckmans' house.

I sipped the espresso and wondered how Arch was doing. He'd only been gone one night, but it felt like an eternity because it was so open-ended. *I'm going to live with the Druckmans for a while. At least until Dad's hearing.* I got out leeks, tomatoes, and cream cheese, then retrieved two large bags of shrimp from the freezer. When Tom appeared in the kitchen, with his hair freshly washed and a tiny glob of shaving cream stuck under his ear, I was doubly glad he had decided to stay. Nothing like loneliness and a violent ex-husband on the lam to make one brood.

"Give me a job, Captain Cook," Tom demanded merrily after he'd chugged down the espresso I'd given him and heard the news about ReeAnn and the Jerk. "The less savory the job, sir, the better."

That was easy: I despise poaching and shelling shrimp. Now I not only needed the shellfish for the doll-club board breakfast, I needed them for the dinner, too. "If you could cook and shell all that shrimp, I'd be eternally grateful."

He eyed the bulging bags and chuckled. "Aye-aye, sir."

I started on a brioche-style dough that would form a delectable top crust for the dish I'd decided to call Collectors' Camembert Pie. While we were both working, Macguire made a sudden appearance in the kitchen. I glanced at the clock: not even seven. "This is unexpected," I remarked. "What's up?"

"Give me something to do," he said bravely, his voice still thick with sleep. "I want to help."

I cut a glance at Tom, who resolutely bent over the shrimp. These two had conspired to cheer me up, no question about it. Fine. To Macguire, I pointed out the plump tomatoes to be seeded and chopped, artichoke bottoms to be trimmed, asparagus to be steamed and sliced, Camembert to be thickly cut, and Parmesan to be grated.

"I'll worry about putting it all together when I get home," I said with a smile.

"Uh," said Macguire, "that's a lot of food for breakfast, isn't it?"

"It's for dinner, Macguire."

"Oh." He rubbed his eyes. "Well, can I go back to bed until about ten and start chopping then?"

I laughed. "Of course." When he had hauled himself back upstairs, I beat the eggs for the main course. "Tom," I said thoughtfully as I chopped tomatoes and leeks, "what's the time frame for John Richard's trial?"

"Preliminary hearing should be in about another three weeks. The county's prosecuting attorney needs to see if there's enough evidence to go to trial. As soon as the drug screen's done and the skin and hair under Suz Craig's fingernails are analyzed, they'll know more than they do now. But as you know, there's already a lot of evidence against him."

"What about the vandals?"

"No sign of them. They could be anybody. They could have been hired by somebody sympathetic to Suz Craig."

"Hmm, I don't think so." I melted butter, put in the chopped leeks, and stirred the gold-and-green mixture. The aroma was deliciously sharp and fresh. "I guess it's conceivable that someone rented a white Jeep. Someone who knew what kind of car John Richard drove. The person would have to live close by."

Tom expertly drained the shrimp and ran cold water over them. "The only people connected to the case who live *very* close by are Patricia McCracken and Ralph Shelton. Patricia says she was asleep and her husband backs her up. Ralph Shelton says that after he and his wife got home from the country club, they went to bed. The wife says he was next to her in bed the whole night. But she admits she's a sound sleeper."

"Lucky her." I stirred the bright red tomatoes into the bubbling mass of butter and leeks, then gently stirred in the eggs. "I wish I knew why I can't find out what's going on inside ACHMO."

His voice quivered with anger. "I wish *I* knew why I can't seem to protect you from that violent ex-husband of yours."

"Not to make any excuses for him, but the man can't deal with

Doll Show
Shrimp and Eggs

1 teaspoon Old Bay Seasoning

8 large frozen easy-peel shrimp

3 tablespoons butter

¼ cup chopped leek, white part only

⅓ cup chopped fresh tomato, seeds and
  pulp removed

6 eggs, slightly beaten

Salt and freshly ground black pepper

3 ounces cream cheese, cut into
  ¼ inch cubes

Preheat oven to 400°.

Bring a pint of water to boil and add the Old Bay Seasoning and the shrimp. Cook the shrimp until they are *just* pink. *Do not overcook the shrimp.* Drain and peel the shrimp, then cut each one in half. Melt the butter in an oven-proof skillet, then add the leek and tomato. Sauté gently for about 5 minutes, until the leek is softened.

Pour the eggs into the leek-tomato mixture, season with salt and freshly ground pepper, and cook over medium-low heat, stirring occasion-ally to prevent browning, until eggs have almost congealed but still have some liquid left. Stir in the shrimp and the cream cheese. Bake in the oven for about 10 minutes, or until cream cheese is melted and eggs are completely con-gealed.

Serves 2 to 3

Collectors' Camembert Pie

Crust:

 ⅓ cup milk
 2 tablespoons butter
 2 teaspoons sugar
 2½ teaspoons (1 package) dry yeast
 ¾ teaspoon salt
 1 egg, slightly beaten
 1½ teaspoons oil
 1¼ cups flour (or more)

Heat the milk, butter, and sugar until the butter is melted. Remove from the heat and set aside to cool slightly (to 105° to 115°). Stir the yeast into the milk mixture and let it stand for 10 minutes. Stir in the salt, egg, and oil. Add the flour ¼ cup at a time, stirring well, until each addition is thoroughly incorporated and dough holds together well. Turn out onto a lightly floured board and knead for 10 minutes, adding small amounts of flour if necessary, until dough is smooth and satiny.

(Or use a dough hook and knead in a mixer for the same amount of time.) Place the dough in an oiled bowl and turn it once to oil the top. Cover the bowl and set aside to rise at room temperature until tripled in bulk (about 2 hours). Punch the dough down, roll it into a rectangle approximately 9 by 13 inches, and place it in a jumbo-size zippered plastic bag. Refrigerate for up to 6 hours. When you begin to prepare the pie, remove the bag from the refrigerator to allow the dough to come to room temperature.

Filling:

 1 tablespoon Old Bay Seasoning
 36 large (1½ pounds) easy-peel shrimp
 8 ounces fresh asparagus, trimmed
 1 pound fresh tomatoes, cored and
  seeded
 1 pound canned artichoke bottoms (5 or
  6 per can)
 2 12-ounce wheels (1½ pounds)
  Camembert
 1 cup mayonnaise
 ⅔ cup freshly grated Parmesan
 2 teaspoons pressed garlic (4 to 6
  pressed cloves)

¾ teaspoon dried thyme, crumbled

¾ teaspoon dried rosemary, crumbled

¾ teaspoon dried oregano, crumbled

In a wide skillet, bring a quart of water to boil and add the Old Bay Seasoning. Add the shrimp and cook until *just* pink. *Do not overcook the shrimp.* Drain the shrimp and discard the cooking water. Peel the shrimp and set it aside until you are ready to assemble the pie.

Slice the asparagus spears into thirds. Slice the cored and seeded tomatoes into eighths. Drain the artichoke bottoms, trim them of any rough edges, and slice each artichoke bottom into sixths. Scrape most of the rind off the Camembert and slice each wheel into sixteenths. (You will have thirty-two pie-shaped pieces of cheese.) In a small bowl, thoroughly combine the mayonnaise, Parmesan, garlic, and herbs.

Preheat the oven to 350°. Butter a 9- by 13-inch glass pan. Assemble the pie by placing half of the shrimp in the bottom of the pan (three rows of 6 shrimp each), then evenly layer half of the

asparagus, half of the tomatoes, half of the artichoke bottoms, and half of the Camembert over the shrimp. Using a small spoon, dab half of the mayonnaise mixture over the Camembert layer. Repeat the layers in the same order, ending with the last layer of shrimp. Carefully place the brioche dough over the top and cut several vents to allow steam to escape.

Bake for 45 minutes, or until dough is golden brown and filling is hot and bubbly. Allow to cool slightly before serving, about 5 or 10 minutes.

Serves 6 to 8

frustration. Especially when he's had a few drinks. Maybe he knocked on the front door the way he said he did. But just because I didn't answer right away is no reason to lose his temper."

Tom shook his head, then measured out the shelled shrimp I needed for the breakfast dish: Doll Show Shrimp and Eggs. I stirred in the shrimp, then removed the pan from the heat. At the LakeCenter this morning I would add the cream cheese chunks to the eggs, vegetables, and shrimp, then bake the dish for a short time, just until the cheese melted and the ingredients had all melded into an irresistible mélange.

"Why don't you just bake it now?" Tom, ever the efficient cook, wanted to know.

"You can't put the dish in too early or it won't come out right."

"Ah. Well. If I leave now I'll be exactly an hour late. Think you can handle the rest of the morning?"

"With you for a helpmate, my dear sir, I can handle anything."

He sighed skeptically. "Just be careful, Miss G., please?"

"Yessir. Now, please, go serve and protect and don't worry about me, okay? Stop crime. Make America safe for the consumption of apple pie. *My* apple pie."

After he left, I brushed my fingers thoughtfully over the ugly bruise on my arm. Something I had seen and something I had said were working their way into my consciousness. It takes at least three hours for an injured area to turn black and blue, I knew that from Med Wives 101. As well, alas, from personal experience.

But black-and-blue marks didn't form on a corpse, as Tom had pointed out. Suz had had a nasty blowout with John Richard, and she'd had the exact pattern of bruises he usually inflicted. He'd even *admitted* they'd had a fight. Yet he was equally adamant that he'd left her alive after their argument and gone home. And really, the way he'd acted at my window yesterday was more typical of him: He got frustrated and he blew up. Then he either beat you until you submitted, or until something else stopped him, like the hanging plant

Marla had whacked him with once, or the ill-fated ham I'd cracked over his head yesterday.

And Suz hadn't accidentally fallen into the ditch. She'd been beaten to death with a metal scratching post and then her body had been dumped into the ditch. It didn't make sense.

Even if someone else had killed her and wanted to put the blame on John Richard, *how could he or she even know Suz and the Jerk would be together that night? How could he or she know he'd lose his temper?* And even if the Jerk had beaten Suz up, a killer wanting to pin the murder on John Richard would have had to wait *until the bruises formed* so that it looked as if John Richard had not only beaten her but finished her off. Like the timing on the egg dish I was preparing, the killer's timing would have to be perfect.

And then I remembered what I'd said to Tom: *You can't put the dish in too early or it won't come out right.* If John Richard had not murdered Suz Craig, then whoever had had taken great pains to plan it.

I glanced at my watch: seven-forty-five. I quickly packed up the ham, the eggs, and the breads for the breakfast, which was scheduled to start at nine. This last day of the doll show would begin at eleven. The doors would close at four so that the ballroom could be cleaned. Then the show would reopen at five and close at seven. The final dinner for the board and their guests was set for eight o'clock, to take full advantage of the magical evening light on the lake.

I slipped my cellular phone into my pocket, but not before I'd taken note of three numbers: Patricia McCracken, Frances Markasian, and Lutheran Hospital, in case ReeAnn Collins was well enough to talk. Regardless of the fact that I had catering to do today, I had a crime to try to solve. My heart ached. I wanted Arch home. I wanted to know, once and for all, what had happened in Saturday's early-morning hours. And I was going to find out. For Arch, and for me.

Carefully, I scanned our garage and my van's interior. No Jerk.

Where could he be? Twice during the short drive to the LakeCenter I had the discomfiting feeling that someone was following me. But my rearview mirror yielded nothing unusual, and even when I pulled onto the shoulder of the lake's frontage road, no one else stopped. I put it down to nerves.

At the LakeCenter the portly, disheveled security guard again looked and smelled like the "before" picture in an advertisement for Alcoholics Anonymous. His disheveled gray hair was a mass of greasy curls; his red-veined eyes resembled a back-roads map of Utah. In the trash can next to him three empty whiskey pint bottles looked incriminating. As before, I felt sorry for him. And like any kind-hearted caterer, I asked if he wanted some coffee and toast once I got the board's breakfast under way.

"Wha . . . ?" he slurred. "Break . . . fast? Oh, yeah. Sure, coffee. Put some brandy in, you got any. 'Kay?"

So much for good deeds. I sighed and asked if there was any way he could open the side door for me.

"Yeah, sure. Pull your van 'round the far wall. It's 'kay. I can't leave the front for more than a minute to help ya, though. Gotta protect the damn toys. I'll open the door from inside, it's 'kay, I can trust ya. Right?" He burped and disappeared to open the side door.

While the oven was preheating for the eggs and ham, I sallied back and forth to put down an extension cord for the large coffee urn and set out the silverware and plates. The morning was quite cool, and the warming promise of the large coffeepot gurgling on one of the picnic tables seemed especially welcome. The pussy willows beside the lake path shifted and whispered in the breeze. A red-wing blackbird warned its compatriots of my presence by squawking and raising one wing. I smiled, sliced and arranged the bread, then poured the juice. When I'd given the guard a large mug of coffee and put the eggs and ham in the oven, I dialed Lutheran Hospital and asked to be put through to ReeAnn Collins. If she was not well enough to talk, I would not press her.

A man, sounding too old and serious to be ReeAnn's unreliable boyfriend, gruffly answered the phone. I identified myself and asked to speak to Ms. Collins. The phone was handed across.

"Helloo-oo!" a woman cooed merrily.

"R-ReeAnn!" I stuttered. "It's Goldy Schulz. You sound so— good! I was sorry to hear about the accident."

"Yes," she said with unusual pleasantness, as if she were enjoying the attention. "Right now I've got bandages on my body from the burns. I can't do much moving yet."

"I'm so sorry this happened to you."

"Well, you know, I got thrown into the creek by the explosion. The doctor told me it was a good thing, getting cold water on the burns right away. Anyway, I'm in excellent physical shape. Even though I was numb, I managed to paddle over to the creekbank. Everybody was pretty impressed. Plus now I'm on painkillers," she added with a giggle. "Beats working, that's for sure. Gotta roomful of flowers from my boyfriend. Plus, I've met a couple of cute interns, if the b.f. doesn't work out."

"ReeAnn," I whispered with relief.

"Plus," she continued gaily, "there's a cop at the door and one here to answer the phone, 'cuz the sheriff's department figured out there was explosive in the grill."

"*What?*"

"Oh, I forget what kind it was. The boyfriend feels guilty." She sighed. "Somebody *supposedly* from his bike shop called and said 'Forget the sandwiches.' Then whoever it was set up our lunch for twelve-thirty. I was going to get there at noon, dump charcoal on the grill, get it started. I got to the park, dumped on the charcoal, and the grill went ka-boom. Total bummer. So," she said in a hungry-for-news voice, "how's John Richard? Have you gotten any money? Think he's going to be able to give me my last paycheck?"

I swallowed. "You haven't heard from him?"

"Are you kidding?" she scoffed. "The only people I've heard from are my boyfriend, my mother, and the damn ACHMO people. They still seem to think I've hidden some tapes of theirs. I told them what I've always told them: Go to hell. Now the sheriff's department screens my calls. So have you gotten your money or not?''

"No, I haven't gotten it." I thought again about my speculation concerning timing. What had John Richard and Suz been arguing about Friday night at the club? "Ah, ReeAnn, if it's not too much trouble, do you remember if there was something that happened on Friday, some negative thing that could have set off a fight between John Richard and Suz Craig?''

"How could I forget? It was the last day I worked with him. That Friday, a FedEx came. When I opened it, I thought, Uh-oh, the doc's going to be ticked off now! First the condo in Keystone, now he's gonna lose the one in Hawaii!''

"And the FedEx was . . .''

"A letter from Suz Craig's office at ACHMO. Saying no bonus this year. He went ballistic.''

No kidding. But this was interesting, since I was thinking about timing. The no-bonus notice hadn't come by postal service—too unpredictable as to arrival time. Nor had the denial of bonus come as a phone call—too easily argued with. Whoever had sent the letter had sent it FedEx, so he or she could be absolutely certain the message would arrive on a certain day, and virtually guarantee a conflict.

"What did the letter say?''

She sighed impatiently. "Something about how we hadn't done the billing properly or consistently or within their guidelines or something. And he wasn't going to get his bonus. That's it. At the bottom, it said, 'signed for and on behalf of Suz Craig.' I told him it was because she was afraid to sign it!''

"Who signed it for her?''

"Didn't say. I couldn't tell, anyway, because John Richard snatched that letter away and started to have one of his fits.''

I gritted my teeth. I checked the timer for the eggs: one minute to go. The doll collectors had gathered outside and were drinking their juice and pulling large cups of coffee for themselves from the silver urn. "ReeAnn, look, I just have one more question for you, and it has to do with Suz Craig." She groaned. "I'm just trying to figure out about that night, Friday. Was there any reason they were going out? Did they have a standing date for Friday night?"

"Oh, now that I *do* remember, because Ms. Crank was always wanting them to celebrate their little anniversaries. First month of going out, they exchange balloons; second month, they buy each other workout clothes; on and on until they've been going together six whole months, then she gets a fur coat and he gets an ID bracelet, for God's sake. Pullleeze."

"And Friday night was . . ."

"August first? The Month Seven anniversary, where have you been? I think she wanted tickets to Bermuda, but instead she got herself killed. What can I say? She should have given him the bonus. Oh, man, listen to me. I need another painkiller." Chortling, ReeAnn hung up.

The timer beeped. I took out the casserole and had a taste with a small plastic spoon. The silken texture of the eggs, combined with the tomatoes, leeks, hot, barely melted chunks of cream cheese, and seasoned poached shrimp, was divine. I carried the pan out and placed it next to the warm ham and baskets of bread. The doll board members included Tina Corey dressed as Sea Queen Babsie and Gail Rodine in a formidable wide-brimmed hat covered with netting. They all piled up their plates with food and talked excitedly about what a smash their opening day had been. I was surprised to see Frances Markasian, her wild black hair and ratty trench coat at odds with the perfect coiffures, stylish clothes, and occasional doll costumes of the board members, at the end of one of the picnic tables. She whispered to me that she was covering the show for the paper.

"I'm telling you, Goldy," Frances said as she shoveled up a heaping forkful of eggs, "I'm going to have to do a bikers' convention next, to recover from this."

"I need to talk to you," I whispered back. "I'm just about done serving here, and I was going to call you today, anyway. I have some information and some . . . lingering questions about Suz Craig's murder."

She brightened. "You promised you'd share stuff with me and you're actually going to do it? Wonders never cease. These eggs are yummy."

"Thanks. I'll give you the recipe. Want to talk?" I asked conspiratorially.

She dropped her fork, eased off the picnic bench, and shouldered her huge purse. "I need to take notes while we talk. Let me meet you in the kitchen, before I die of ecstasy."

Chapter 2 5

"I've been thinking about you a lot lately, Goldy," Frances announced when she'd heaved herself up on one of the counters, armed with her notebook, a newly popped Jolt cola, and a cigarette strictly forbidden by the signs posted everywhere in the LakeCenter. She blew the smoke in a rolling stream out the kitchen's open window. "With all that John Richard's up to, it's almost as if you're being punished, too. I heard he beat you up and then skipped. Any idea where he is?"

"No. And if those women catch you smoking around their precious dolls, you'll be punished so badly you'll never be able to say the words 'Bail-Jumping Babsie' again."

She shrugged. "Aw, you're breaking my heart." The cigarette dangled from her thin lips. "Spill it. Tell me everything you've got. I've got a police band radio, remember. How badly did John Richard hurt you yesterday?"

"I'm okay," I said briefly. "You remember who Ralph Shelton is?"

"Course I remember. I may have been covering the doll show, but I haven't been covering it from Peoria. He's the guy, the ob-gyn doctor, who got canned by Suz Craig. I went over to his house. Asked him about the scratches on *his* face and he said it was from a cat, then slammed the door in *my* face. The vet wouldn't talk to me about Shelton's cat."

"Yeah, I know. Have you discovered anything about what was going on between Ralph Shelton and Suz Craig?"

"I thought you got me out here to tell *me* stuff."

I took a deep breath. Brandon Yuille hadn't told me I couldn't share what he'd divulged; I just couldn't say he was the one who'd given me the info. "Apparently, there were patient complaints outstanding against Shelton. Not only did Suz fire him, she was trying to use the complaints to poison his future at MeritMed. Or so I heard."

Frances made a quick note. "Very good, Goldy. Who'd you hear that from?"

"Can't say."

"Was it Chris Corey?" I shook my head. She smiled. "Well, I *had* heard about the patient-complaint action, and how Suz planned to use it, from Chris Corey." Another stream of cigarette smoke swirled out the window. "What else have you been able to get?"

"That's it." Which, of course, was not true.

She inhaled reflectively. "Chris also told me Ralph Shelton had an appointment with Suz Craig in her office on Monday morning, July 14. What were the two of them going to talk about, do you know? This patient-complaint packet?"

Monday morning, July 14. The missing day in Suz's secret tapes. On that Monday morning, *what* had Ralph Shelton talked to Suz about? Had Ralph received some of Suz's wrath that day, too? I had no idea. *Could* the Jerk have Suz's tapes from July 14? Had whoever tried to blow up ReeAnn thought the Jerk had given *ReeAnn* those tapes? Didn't know that either, and I certainly wasn't going to start speculating with Frances. We were friends, but there are some things you just don't share with a journalist.

"I still think Korman did it." Frances stopped scribbling but held her pen poised. "I'm just looking at ACHMO for my other story. But you're really into this."

I slumped against the counter. "It's awful."

Frances energetically stubbed out her cigarette in the sink, then slapped her notebook closed. "Two things, Goldy. You seem very stressed. It's your involvement in this case."

"Oh, gee, Frances, how would you like it if your violent ex-husband was accused of murder? How would it feel if he came over and tried to beat you up before escaping to God-knows-where? Relaxing? Besides, I'm asking questions to soothe Arch, I told you."

Frances swept a dark mass of frizzy hair off her forehead. "Know what, Goldy? You need a hobby."

I said glumly, "Cooking used to be my hobby."

"Naw, you need something else. It *is* like you're being punished, you're so obsessed with this case. You need to get some distance."

I grabbed a box for the dirty breakfast dishes. "What would you suggest, Frances, doll collecting?"

She burst out laughing and jumped off the counter. "Now *you're* punishing *me*."

It took a solid hour to clean up after the breakfast. By the time I finished, I felt as drained as the empty silver coffee urn. But the breakfast had been a success. When the doors opened for the hordes waiting to get into the doll show, I was glad I could slip out the side exit and avoid the stampede. I hustled to my van. A phone call to the McCrackens wouldn't do. I stepped on the gas and headed toward the country club. I wanted to see Patricia in person.

She was pushing Tyler the Terrible on their swing set constructed on the sloping backyard beyond the driveway, scene of the infamous roller hockey game. For a moment I stood watching them, unobserved. It had been a long time since I'd seen Patricia look happy. Her face was relaxed, her arm movements enthusiastic and graceful. She and Tyler were wearing matching navy sweatsuits.

With each tug on the ropes she cooed to her son, a blond little fellow whose round face and squeals of laughter showed he was loving every minute. I almost hated interrupting them. On the other hand, unlike Patricia, my son was estranged from me, and I had information to gather before Arch and I could be reconciled.

"Howdy!" I called, and stepped carefully down the embankment. "I was in the neighborhood! Thought I'd stop by!"

Patricia smiled unenthusiastically and allowed the swing rope to go slack, which caused Tyler no end of grief.

"Keep swinging," I told her, once I was beside her. "Don't disappoint him."

Obediently, she started pushing again, but less energetically, so that Tyler again squawked.

"Do you want me to do it?" I suggested. "I felt bad about not being able to talk to you yesterday when you called. So I just thought I'd come by. Sort of for an update."

She brightened and moved aside so that I could push Tyler, who gave me only one command: "*Really* hard, okay? *Really* hard."

"Okey-doke," I agreed, and gave him a good push as Patricia flopped onto the grass, watching us. Tyler squealed with delight. "Hey, buddy!" I called to him as he lofted up over the hill. "I'm a swing pusher from way back! I'm the queen of the swing pushers!" I gave him another vigorous shove and he yelped happily.

"Be careful," Patricia cautioned.

"One of the reasons I'm here is that I want *you* to be careful," I said in a normal voice so as not to frighten Tyler. "John Richard is out on bail. And now he's disappeared."

She lifted her pale eyebrows. "I took tae kwon do before I got pregnant and after I got out of the hospital. Have a red belt, black stripe, now. I can take care of myself. What's the other reason you're here?"

"Well, I was just thinking about John Richard's finances."

She wrinkled her rabbitlike nose. "He had to auction the condo just . . . what? In the last ten days."

"But why auction it at all? See, he hadn't gotten news about his bonus yet—"

Patricia perked up. "Bonus? Did he not get a bonus from ACHMO?"

"Apparently not."

Patricia's grin was wide. "I may be able to use that in my suit."

"Anyway, I'm just wondering . . ." I gasped from the exertion, but Tyler crowed with delight. "You said you'd give me the details at the hockey party, but everything got so crazy . . ."

She smiled wickedly. "Oh, I *do* know why he had to auction the condo, Goldy. My husband said it was almost as if I'd planned it, so I could make Korman miserable."

I inadvertently stopped pushing and the swing knocked me in the abdomen. I recovered, but Tyler howled. I pushed again, a tad more moderately. "Why did he have to auction off his condo?"

She squinted at me. Keeping track of Tyler's trajectory so I wouldn't get whacked again, I couldn't return her look. "Because of his legal bills. Have you ever been sued?" When I shook my head, she said, "You're looking at ten thousand just to get started. At least fifty thou to keep your lawyer going. Sure, he had malpractice insurance, but it didn't cover everything, not by a long shot. He just didn't have the cash he needed." She plucked a piece of grass from her skirt. "I was so happy when they auctioned off that condo, you can't imagine." She chuckled, then stood and brushed the rest of the grass from her skirt. She walked over to spell me with the swing pushing. "Goldy, listen. I may *wish* I were God," she said very deliberately. "Unfortunately, I'm not. But let me tell you. John Richard Korman hasn't begun to suffer for what he did to me. And he won't be able to escape, no matter how hard he tries."

As if in agreement, Tyler emitted an earsplitting yowl. I fled.

I called Macguire from the cellular once I'd roared out of Patricia's driveway. To my astonishment, he answered on the first ring.

"Goldilocks' Catering!" He brightly launched into my official greeting. "Where Everything Is Just Right! Whaddayawant?"

"Macguire! Please don't say 'whaddayawant?' to potential clients. It sounds unprofessional."

"Oh, *Goldy*! Sorry! No problem. Listen, I'm chopping all these vegetables. They look good, too! Think you should slip a little chlorophyll into the filling?"

"No," I said firmly. "Listen, did Arch call?"

"No, but that therapist's office called you back and said everyone's on vacation. You want a therapist for Arch, you're going to have to use a referral to someone in Denver."

Great, I thought. First, of course, I'd have to convince Arch to come home.

"Also," Macguire went on, "Mrs. Druckman called. She's taking Todd and Arch down to the Natural History Museum. Oh, and Marla called, too. She was on her way to Denver to see ReeAnn, wanted you to come have lunch with her, just so you could relax! But it's too late now, she's gone."

"That's okay, I'll come home."

"No, don't! Let me finish what I've got going here. If you come home, you'll just mope around about Arch. You should go out for lunch! How about Aspen Meadow Barbecue? My buddies and I think it's great. Plus, you've got that dinner tonight, you might as well get some food now! Have a bowl of chili and a beer! Relax and leave the chopping to me!"

"Macguire—"

"Oh, oh, *scrrk, scrrk*"—he started making fake squishing noises—"you're breaking up, you know, it's those *scrrk scrrk* cellular phones *scrrk*!" And he disconnected.

"Macguire," I said to the dead phone, "I've seen you do this trick before." But I smiled anyway and dutifully headed the van in the direction of Aspen Meadow Barbecue, famed creekside hangout of construction workers, truck drivers, wannabe cowboys, and assorted tough guys, all of whom had the single-minded intention of

getting completely smashed at lunch. An outdoor dining area separated the hard-drinking crowd inside from tourists and the occasional
brave group of ladies coming for a luncheon get-together on the
water. The last time Marla and I had eaten there, she'd told me that
the de rigueur item for the crowd inside was extra hot chili con-
sumed with shots of tequila.

But Marla wasn't with me today, I remembered. I sighed. Did I
really want to have lunch out alone? Macguire was doing the prep for
the dinner tonight, and I could use a break. Across the street from
Aspen Meadow Barbecue was a banner draped across the wooden
sign of Aspen Meadow Nursery. It advertised a perennial-and-bush
sale. I thought of Frances's admonition: *You need a hobby.* Well,
maybe I'd go scope out the shrubs before braving the rough lunch
crowd at Aspen Meadow Barbecue.

I wandered through sparsely stocked aisles and finally decided
on some Fairy roses. The bushes featured lovely pink blossoms and
were guaranteed hardy at our altitude, a key asset. As I loaded them
into the van, I pictured Tom getting a huge kick out of my sudden
interest in things horticultural.

Wait a minute. I stopped dead and looked again at the carved
sign: ASPEN MEADOW NURSERY. In the list of questions I'd entered into
my computer about Suz Craig's murder, had I even thought to look
into these people, *also fired by Suz Craig?* No. Well. No time like the
present.

I hustled back inside and told the cashier that on second
thought I'd like to have my yard landscaped. And I wanted to have
the same person who'd done Suz Craig's in the Aspen Meadow
Country Club. Suz had raved to me about the great work he'd done.

The cashier's face fell. "Uh, you sure?"

"Absolutely."

"Well, Duke's out in the yard. Big blond fellow. Better go catch
him, he does an early shift, then goes out with the guys for lunch on
Wednesdays, then he goes home and sleeps. I have to tell you, Duke
didn't like that Craig woman. You might want to find somebody else,

if she was your friend. He had a big grudge against her. Still does, even if she's dead."

Yes, yes, I thought, *take a number and get in line.* The cashier pointed me in the direction of the nursery's yard, which was on the same side of the street as Aspen Meadow Barbecue. The man at the yard gate pointed to a Paul Bunyanesque, platinum-haired giant who wore ear protection and drove a Cat loaded with mulch. The gate guard waited until the Cat had turned in our direction, then waved to the giant, whom I assumed was Duke. Duke dumped the mulch in the waiting bed of a truck, then chugged over to us. He flipped a switch and the engine died. He hopped out of the Cat and loomed over us—he was at least six foot six—and asked the gate guard what he wanted, for crying out loud. The guard jerked his thumb in my direction.

Duke turned his attention down to me. His dark blue eyes were not friendly. The bus-yellow ear-protection device dangled from one of his meaty hands, and I had the feeling that if he didn't like what I had to say, he'd pop it right back on. I looked way, way up at him.

"Ah, I understand that," I began sincerely, "you did some landscaping for Suz Craig. I thought it looked great."

"Yah, what about it? You a friend of hers?"

"Well, sort of—"

"Okay, see ya later," he said abruptly, and snapped the ear protection back on.

"Wait!" I yelled. Duke scowled, opened his eyes wide, and tugged off the metal ear muffs.

"I gotta go, lady. I'm going out to lunch in a few minutes and I need to finish this load. You want a landscaper, ask the people at the nursery to give you a referral someplace else. I don't want to work for nobody who liked that woman. Got it? See ya later, okay?"

"Well, hold on," I said, desperate now. "Just talk to me. I don't really want landscaping. I catered for Suz Craig and I'm having some problems—"

Duke smirked knowingly. "Ah, she stiffed you, too, huh?"

"What?" Then I understood. Suz Craig had refused to pay him for his work. I assumed a sad expression. "We had terrible problems," I confided.

Duke looked at the sky and shook his blond head. "Honestly, people like that—"

"You heard she was killed."

"Yah. No wonder."

"So you thought she was hard to deal with, too. I'm just wondering if your story is similar to mine."

"I'll tell ya, I'd have to be half plastered to tell my story about that woman. But then you wouldn't be able to shut me up."

Inspiration struck. I asked, "How quickly can you finish your load?" He grunted something unintelligible. Undaunted, I went on. "How does tequila and chili sound? My treat."

Duke grunted again, something that I decided to take as a yes. I said, "Let's do lunch."

Chapter 26

Inside Aspen Meadow Barbecue, there was only one free table. I quickly nabbed it for Duke and me while scoping out the restaurant's interior. All I needed now was someone I knew informing my new drinking buddy, Duke, that my husband was a cop. That could put a chilling effect on our lunchtime chat. But of the two dozen men ranging from scruffy to burly at the bar and tables, no one looked familiar.

Once Duke had seated himself and called greetings to a few of his pals, I slipped over to the bartender. "Two tequila doubles for my friend, but just give me water, because I'm driving us home. When I signal, bring us the bottles. Put water in mine. I can't drink, but I don't want him to feel as if he's drinking alone."

The bartender, who sported a stiff handlebar mustache, squinted at me appraisingly. "You trying to keep him away from the wheel, or you trying to get him into bed?"

I pulled a twenty-dollar bill out of my pocket. "Just please do what I ask."

He palmed the bill in a way that suggested he'd been bribed before. "I'll give you something besides water, to look more realistic. Tell you the truth, I'm glad somebody's driving Duke home. Every Wednesday I gotta call somebody from the nursery to take him."

Soon Duke and I were crying "Skol" and clinking our first glasses. I took a tentative sip of what turned out to be flat Mountain Dew.

"Whatcha drinking?" Duke wanted to know, his tone already mellowing from defensive to chummy.

"Different kind of tequila. Lime-flavored." We chugged our second shots companionably and I sneaked a peek at my watch. Just past noon. I needed to be home to put together the doll club's dinner no later than three. Subtracting time to get Duke back to his place, that gave us about two hours. I signaled to the bartender to bring us the bottles. The man was so inventive, I had no doubt he could provide a suitable container for my Mountain Dew.

Duke smacked his lips. "Ah. Well. So. What happened to you with that woman? You trying to get money out of the will? That's what I'm doing. Lawyer says it'll take at least a year 'cuz a the criminal investigation. My plants'll croak by then." He shook his head unhappily.

"No! Actually, see, I have a different kind of problem. My ex-husband's the one who's been accused of killing her—"

Duke grinned broadly. "Oh, boy. Mind if I smoke? It's not tobacco, it's a clove cigarette. Heard of 'em?"

"No, but go ahead." In a minute the spicy smoke rose in a cloud. I gagged but plunged onward. "I catered for Suz Craig, even though she was my ex-husband's young, blond girlfriend. No grudges, you understand. But now her death has made a real mess for my family. You know, everybody blaming everybody. So my problem is that I keep looking back at what happened and thinking, How could I have prevented this?"

The bartender arrived and winked at me. He set a tequila bottle in front of Duke and a black ceramic decanter in the shape of an

Aztec goddess in front of me. Cute. Then the waitress arrived and Duke informed her that we wanted two bowls of their hottest chili. I thought longingly of a crisp, cold arugula salad and how well it would go with iced coffee.

"What could you have done to *prevent* it?" Duke now repeated incredulously, shaking his big head. "Nothing. Not a damn thing. Some people are just that way. Bossy, impossible to please. Nothing you do is right for them. I always want to ask new clients, Are you an asshole? 'Cuz if you are, I'd like to know up front. Save us both a lot of time. But, a'course, the nursery owner won't let me." He shook his head again.

"How was Suz Craig bossy to you? She seemed to like the landscape work you were doing when she showed it to me."

Duke raised his bushy blond eyebrows, then tilted the tequila bottle toward his glass. "Oh, sure, she lied. You think everything's fine, when all the time she's getting ready to axe ya. But plain and simple? The woman was a bitch. Too damn smart. Never had to learn how to deal with regular people. Tolerance, you know? She didn't have none. Patience neither." He quaffed another double shot. "For example. She trips on her in-grade steps made outa four-by-fours, the ones she ordered, and all of a sudden she wants new steps. Only she wants flagstone this time."

"Flagstone," I repeated. "Like the patios?"

"Yah. So we order more flagstones and put 'em in the garage with the stuff we've hidden from the vandals. We build the steps. She doesn't like the way they look. Fifteen thousand dollars and two weeks' work time from my crew, and she says, Take out the flagstone, I want granite. Where'm I supposed to get granite steps? I say, Ya want an escalator? I know a guy."

"Someone did fall down the steps and sprain his ankle," I pointed out.

The tequila bottle was rapidly emptying. "Oh, I know, believe me. Big fat guy, shoulda watched where he was going. But it isn't just them steps. She wants white tea roses alternating with pink musk mallow. This is a harsh, dry climate, I keep telling her. Ya want tea roses, ya need Florida. Even if ya put in rugosas, ya need irrigation. Fine, she says, just do it. So we put in a water tank and a drip system. But then she doesn't want to *see* the water tank, right? So we have to wait to put in the rugosas and mallow until a picket fence goes up. And then she says, Ooh, ooh, I need stepping-stones around the picket fence. I say, How 'bout marble? And she gets all huffy."

Our chili arrived. One bite of the fiery concoction almost sent me running for the creek with my flame-spewing mouth wide open. Instead, I drank deeply of the Mountain Dew, right out of the Aztec goddess decanter.

"Damn," said Duke admiringly.

I ripped into several packages of saltines, dumped them over the chili, and ate cracker crumbs as I unabashedly wiped tears from my eyes. When I could finally clear my throat, I asked, "So what finally happened?"

He stopped shoveling chili into his mouth, chewed, and considered. "After all her complainin' and moanin' and us tryin' to accommodate her? One day we show up as usual, though I'm thinkin' I'm going to have to give my crew a year's worth of free beer to keep 'em on this job, and she comes out and says we're fired. The fat guy's fallen down the steps and she doesn't want to get sued. I say, Fine, lady, we just need our tools, and she says, Make it snappy."

He ate more chili. I filled his two double-shot glasses. He drank, then sighed. If the chili was scorching his throat, he gave no sign of it.

"Down by the picket fence there are the rugosas and musk mallow that we just planted. But doggone if she hasn't put in a friggin' half-dozen *marble* stepping-stones, next to the plants, around the fence. Did she do it herself or hire somebody else? I say, Hey lady, who did this? I was only kidding about the marble, I say, and she says for us to get out pronto and send her a bill." His face turned morose. "So the nursery, you know, it takes them about a month to itemize the bill. She hasn't even gotten our bill and she's dead." He ate more chili without a wince, then slugged down another double shot.

"What a mess," I said comfortingly.

Duke shrugged. His eyes had taken on a wet, bleary look. "I asked the cops . . . I said, Could we at least have our plants back? Because I figure we earned them." He drained another shot glass. "They said . . . You know what they said to me?"

"Probate."

"Yah, they said I'd have to wait until probate was over. Until the investigation was done. I said the plants would be dead by then. We never put a pump in the irrigation system." He scraped the last spoonful of chili from the bowl, poured another double shot of tequila, and downed it. How many had he had? I'd lost count at ten. "Some night when I'm trashed? I'm going to go back over there. Dig up those plants we put in. Nobody'll miss them. Pee on her patios, too, while I'm at it. Matter of fact, I should go right now." He regarded me sadly. "Wanna come?"

I said no thanks and paid the bill. By the time I'd deposited Duke at his apartment—he lived in the same complex as Frances—I'd come up with some more questions. But Duke was no help. He stumbled to his door and declared he was ready to dive into bed. At least he didn't ask if I wanted to join him for that, too.

It wasn't too surprising, I thought as I turned the van in the direction of home, that Suz had been so demanding about the landscaping. In the case of the catered lunch I'd done for her, I realized in retrospect, she'd been eager to make nice and accommodate the ACHMO people from headquarters. She'd wanted to seem calm and flexible in front of her own department heads. But landscaping was something you had to live with and look at every day, sort of like your bathroom or bedroom. Still, why fire the nursery just because Chris had fallen down? Had Suz found somebody else to do the work for her? Somebody she liked better?

I pulled over on Main Street. It was only one-fifteen; Duke had gotten drunk a lot more quickly than I'd hoped. Cooking could come later. At that moment Macguire was right: I couldn't quite face going through our door knowing my son wasn't there. I called Tom on the cellular phone, fully expecting to get his machine.

"Schulz," he answered gruffly.

"Hi. Remember Suz Craig's tiff with the landscape people? Did she hire somebody else after that?"

"Well, hey, Miss G., how's it going? Did you hear we found C-Four in that grill? We put two uniforms on guard at ReeAnn Collins's room." I said I knew, but that my urgent question at the moment was about Suz's landscaping. Tom repeated, "The landscape people. Aspen Meadow Nursery?"

"Somebody new."

"Not that we know of. I mean, nobody's come forward saying they need to be paid except for Aspen Meadow Nursery."

"No bills at all? No mail from, say, a construction company, an independent builder? Somebody in the marble business?"

He laughed. "What in the world are you up to?"

"Nothing. Just trying to fill the time between catered events."

After I hung up, I sat in my van and brooded. Suz Craig had squabbled endlessly and bitterly with Duke and his crew. Then she'd fired them, but only after Chris Corey had fallen. Why? Why hadn't she fired them when the first problems erupted? And then Suz had put in some marble stepping-stones that Duke had suggested in jest? Why?

Oh, Lord. Why, indeed.

Why would Ms. "I don't do, I delegate" Craig fire her landscapers and put in some stones herself? Because she'd needed to. I made a careful U-turn on Main Street and headed back to Aspen Meadow Nursery.

When I got there, I knew exactly what I wanted. Did they have a cap, a workshirt, work gloves, and a gardening apron emblazoned with the words ASPEN MEADOW NURSERY and their plant logo? The cashier gave me another one of her quizzical looks but said the owner had always told her that if customers wanted something, even if it was the funny-looking rock bordering the parking lot, sell it to them.

"The shirt might not be clean," she said apologetically.

"The dirtier the better. And I'd like a shovel and a spade, too."

I put it all on my credit card and raced home. In the kitchen Macguire stood back triumphantly from the mountain range of neatly chopped tomatoes, artichoke hearts, and steamed asparagus. Platters were heaped with sliced Camembert and grated Parmesan. I thanked him. Again I was aware of how much better he looked: healthy skin color, shiny-clean red hair, straight posture, a frame that looked as if it had gained at least five pounds in the last two days, bright eyes, and, best of all, a huge, happy smile. No question about it, I was an herb-treatment convert.

"Great job," I told him.

"Need any more help?" he asked energetically.

I surveyed all the work he had done. "Absolutely not. Thank you many times over."

"Two more things," he said secretively, then opened the walk-in. He retrieved a pan of grilled chicken. "I followed your recipe for marinating and grilling this chicken. Just a few minutes in the oven and it'll be ready. I already tasted it. Juicy, succulent, tangy sauce, all that great stuff you always say. I'm a success! I can cook!"

"Macguire, I don't know what to say—"

"Hold on, look at this." He pulled out an enormous Bundt cake pan and held it out carefully for my inspection. Suspended sections of grapefruit glistened inside clear gelatin. "It's from the *Fanny Farmer Cookbook*," he said proudly. "Grapefruit molded salad. No mix. I made it myself."

"You're wonderful. And you really *can* cook."

"Oh, and Arch called just when the Druckmans were getting ready to go to the museum. He was, like, whispering into the phone that the food's not so good over at the Druckmans' place. They should be back by now, so I'm taking him some of the burgers you made for the barbecue-that-isn't-happening tonight. Is that okay?"

Grilled Chicken
à l'Orange

Marinade:

Zest of 1 medium orange
Juice of 1 medium orange
    (approximately ⅓ cup)
1 teaspoon dry mustard
Tiny pinch of cumin (optional)
2 tablespoons red wine vinegar
⅓ cup olive oil

4 boneless, skinless chicken breast
    halves

Sauce:

2 tablespoons butter
2 tablespoons flour
1½ tablespoons sugar
¼ teaspoon cinnamon
¼ teaspoon dry mustard
2 tablespoons red wine vinegar
1½ cups orange juice

In a 9- by 13-inch glass pan, make the marinade
by combining the zest, juice, mustard, cumin, if
using, and vinegar. Whisk in olive oil. Spread
out a sheet of plastic wrap approximately 2 feet

long and place the chicken breasts on it. Spread another sheet of plastic wrap over the chicken breasts. Using the flat side of a mallet, pound the chicken breasts between the plastic to an even ½-inch thickness. Remove the plastic wrap and place the chicken breasts in the marinade. Cover and allow to marinate for 30 minutes to 1 hour.

When you are ready to cook the chicken, preheat the grill. Then prepare the sauce. In a wide skillet, melt the butter over low heat and stir in the flour. Cook this roux over low heat for a minute or two, until it bubbles. Add the sugar, cinnamon, mustard, and vinegar and stir until well combined. Whisk in the orange juice, bring the heat up to medium, and stir until thickened. Lower the heat and cover the pan to keep the sauce hot while you grill the chicken.

Grill the chicken just until cooked through, 3 to 5 minutes per side. *Do not overcook the chicken.* When serving, place the grilled chicken on a heated platter, pour some of the sauce over it, and pass the rest of the sauce.

Serves 4

When I nodded, he added, "Maybe Arch'll come home sooner than you think."

"Maybe."

Together, we packed the food for the doll people's dinner into my van. When Macguire had left with the bag of burgers, I made sure the security system was armed. Then I hightailed it to Suz Craig's house. I had half an hour before I needed to set up at the LakeCenter.

In the van I fumbled with the buttons on the Aspen Meadow Nursery shirt, then tied the apron around my waist and stuffed what I could of my curly hair under the cap. It was too bad the van said GOLDILOCKS' CATERING on the side, but I hadn't thought the Aspen Meadow Nursery cashier would want to loan me one of the nursery trucks.

I assumed a confident, businesslike expression, then hopped out of the van, carrying my shovel and spade. Walking quickly across the lawn, I rounded the house, which still had yellow police ribbons taped across each door. Lucky for me, I knew where the picket fence was. And just as Duke had indicated, next to the roses and musk mallow, gleaming white marble stepping-stones were set around three sides of the fence.

I dug under the first stone and upended it, then dug into the loosely packed soil underneath. Nothing. I set to work on the second and again encountered only dark, loamy dirt underneath the heavy stone. The third and fourth stones were the same.

Exhausted, I leaned back on my heels and wiped my brow. A cool mountain breeze ruffled the tree branches. Without warning, I saw a furtive movement by the next-door neighbor's garage. I held stock-still and waited, but nothing appeared.

I gazed back at the mess I'd made of the path around Suz's small picket fence enclosing her water tank. Two more stones to go. The fifth stone yielded nothing. Under the sixth and final stone I hit the real pay dirt. Under a loose inch of soil was a heavy-duty zippered bag. Inside were four audiocassettes.

Chapter 27

Using my teeth, I wrenched off the work gloves. I shakily unzipped the bag and removed the tapes from their plastic boxes. To my surprise, they were labeled: Corey, Yuille, McCracken, Shelton. And every one was dated Monday, July 14. I shoved the tapes back into the plastic bag, folded the bag under my right arm, picked up the shovel and the spade, and scampered back to the van. I threw the bag of tapes onto the passenger seat, dumped the tools into the back, and jumped into the front seat.

As I was ripping off the nursery apron and shirt, I wondered how I was going to listen to the tapes. I wanted to hear them immediately, but I *had* to cook if I was going to get my job done. Sitting in my van attending to my tape player wouldn't get the Babsie-doll people's final meal prepared. Then I remembered what I'd first grabbed when I was looking for my tablecloth the night I encountered the vandals. I pawed wildly behind the driver's seat and pulled out Macguire's Walkman.

I shivered as I faced forward. I glanced in my rearview mirror.

Why had I sensed another movement close by? Had someone sprinted across the street behind my vehicle? I set the earphones on my head, put in the McCracken tape, revved up the van, and accelerated down the street.

Voices crackled at a slight distance from the recording device. The first audible words were from Suz Craig. It was startling to hear her voice. *"Minneapolis says we're going to have to settle, but I wasn't ready to give in. . . . Chris? Didn't she have an abortion a few years back? Anything we could do with that?"*

Chris Corey's rumbly voice was unmistakable: *"Not an abortion. Her primary-care physician gave her a referral to a psychiatrist. Anxiety. Don't know if we can use it. Or how."*

Suz snapped, *"Put in a call to that Markasian woman, see if she can run something. God knows, I live in that town now, I have to read that local rag. Markasian's gone on and on about McCracken's damn suits. Now she can run an anonymous-source article about McCracken having emotional problems. That'll balance things out. Make her do it, or we'll pull our tasteful little ACHMO ad from that damn paper."*

The meeting was interrupted by a woman buzzing Suz to say that Ralph Shelton had arrived. The tape ended. A car behind me honked impatiently. I'd have to wait until I arrived at the LakeCenter before putting in another tape.

At the waterfall between the lake and Cottonwood Creek, the cormorants perched and preened and regally surveyed their domain. I would miss them when summer was over. Similarly, I would miss the red-winged blackbirds, noisy heralds of my arrival at precisely four o'clock at the side door of the LakeCenter. The guard, sitting in desultory fashion on a trash can, waved me over. I was willing to bet there was nothing about his guarding sojourn in Aspen Meadow that *he* would miss.

I pressed the rewind button on the Walkman, took the headphones off, put on my catering apron, and made my first trip through the side door. A cleaning crew of four—two men and two women— were buffing the highly polished wood floor and gently dusting the tables and displays. At my van, I slipped the Walkman and bag of tapes into my apron pockets. Then I hauled in my second box of supplies. When one of the cleaning women happened to glance up at me, I quickly turned away. I would listen as I worked. After schlepping my boxes into the empty kitchen, I laid out all the ingredients. I slipped in the next tape, marked "Shelton," and began to layer vegetables over the shrimp.

Ralph and Suz exchanged a cold greeting before getting down to business. *"You can't hurt me like this, Suz."* Ralph Shelton's frightened voice shook.

"Excuse me, Ralph, but I can. Know what a group of people from a California church congregation did? Drove two hundred miles to tell another congregation not to hire the priest they were firing. These folks didn't trust the bishop to tell the church considering their old priest that this was a cleric with a credit-card problem. Thirty thousand in debt, to be exact."

There was a pause, then Ralph spoke. *"If you . . . if you . . . go to MeritMed with these complaints about me, which are totally frivolous, I'll tell everybody about your unauthorized use of patient files. Confidential files, mind you."* He tried to sound more confident. *"And that's* not *a frivolous complaint."*

"You helped me get some of those files. You wouldn't dare go public. If I go under for using files, you're coming."

"I don't care." His voice was on the brink of tears. *"You have no reason to be so cruel."*

This was followed by the sound of a door slamming.

Wow. I put in the tape marked "Corey."

Suz's voice began. *". . . you know I've told you how being so fat is unprofessional. And being ungrateful to me isn't going to get you anywhere, either."*

Chris Corey's voice rumbled, *"I'm a physician. I don't appreciate being humiliated in meetings. I'm tired of it."*

"Really?" said Suz. *"You think complaining behind my back is going to do any good?"*

"That wasn't my idea," intoned Chris.

"Don't bring Brandon into this. What do you think, that if this job doesn't work out, you'll go back to being an orthopedic surgeon? You can't just waltz back into being a doc, Chris, you're as rusty as an old knife. Face it, you're finished as an M.D."

"I am so unbelievably tired of listening to you—"

"Something else. You don't think I know all about your sister? Multiple-personality disorder, goes into trances when she's stressed? Tell me, is she Tina when she's taking care of stray animals and dressed up like a doll? Or is that Mary Louise, so prim and proper, who goes to church and doesn't know a thing about dolls? You know I have access to her files. I know everything. Think the school where she works wouldn't like to know about her long history of emotional instability? Think about leaving this job, or criticizing me again to Minneapolis, and your sister's secret is all over the place."

Chris's voice quickly pleaded, *"Don't do that. Tina has only shown two personalities. She's not violent. She's no danger to anyone. She's suffered so much . . . and now her personality's fragmented . . . I take care of her. Please don't hurt her."*

"I just want a fair shake," Suz said firmly. *"You've got a problem, come to me, got it? Those are the rules."*

End of tape. Multiple-personality disorder, good Lord. Actually, I should have suspected something at church. There, I'd asked Tina about a doll outfit and the cat. She'd acted as if she hadn't known what in the world I was talking about. I'd put it down to stress over planning Suz's funeral. But I hadn't been talking to Tina; I'd been talking to Mary Louise. I shuddered to imagine the humiliation that Tina Corey would undergo if the administration at Aspen Meadow Preschool, much less the rest of people in town, found out about a history of psychological problems. For starters, she'd lose her job. Then she would be shunned. Whatever Tina's problems were, if she was functional and her brother was taking care of her, they were certainly none of Suz Craig's business. I placed the Camembert slices over the vegetables, slipped in the fourth tape, and began on the last layers of the pie.

"You called them." Suz Craig. *"You set up the appointments. You got people to betray me. How do you think I'm supposed to feel?"*

Brandon Yuille's voice was the clearest yet. *"Suz, I had to, I had people coming to me day and night complaining about working with you. I couldn't just ignore them."*

"Brandon, you could have talked to me—"

"I tried to talk to you. Before and after—"

"Before and after we broke up?" Suz's laugh was sour. *"Maybe I didn't notice, what with all that passion."* Brandon said nothing. *"Look, I know you're hurt that I started going out with Korman, but he and I are right for each other. You're too young."* Suz made *young* sound like a dirty word.

No wonder Brandon had blushed when he'd told me how caring Suz could be. I suddenly realized why Brandon wasn't talking on the tape. He was crying.

"Brandon! Why did you call Minneapolis in? To punish me? Because it worked."

I heard a sob. *"I was trying to do my job."*

"Well, don't do your job so well, okay?"

"I am going to do my job," he said defiantly. *"I'm in charge of Human Resources. Don't tell me not to do my job."*

"Your job? Your job? You drag your sorry ass into this office late, day after day, looking more tired than a nomad lost six weeks in the desert. You're not doing your job! And you don't find me complaining about you, do you?"

"You're the only one . . . who seems to mind that I don't look good." I heard him blow his nose. He cleared his throat. *"And I thought you didn't care about how I looked anymore."*

Her voice was cruel. *"Listen. If you call the Minneapolis people again, you'll be very sorry. I'll fire your ass and have your records altered so they say you have cancer. You'll never get another HR job in Denver. You won't be able to stay near your father. Something else. You don't think I know your father supported a blond nurse down in Denver while your mother was sick? You think people in Aspen Meadow would want to know their beloved pastry-shop owner two-timed his wife who was terminal with cancer?"*

Even on the tape I could tell Brandon was startled. I could imagine his sparkling dark brown eyes and enthusiastic smile dimmed with pain. *"My mother . . ."*—his anguished voice was just above a whisper—*"was barely conscious for the last three months of her life. That other woman was her nurse."*

"An ACHMO nurse. Your father slept with her."

"You're insane."

"He's lonely, Brandon. During the day I'll bet he's lonely all the time."

And that was the end of *that* tape. Sheesh! Again I was stunned that Suz Craig had had the audacity to make these tapes. And to threaten people like that? Incredible. I could certainly see why she'd felt she had to hide the tapes from July 14. These cassettes were much more incriminating of *her* than they were of the people she was attempting to blackmail. Although someone hadn't thought so. Were there any tapes of the Jerk visiting her office?

I nudged the brioche dough over the pies and slid them into the ovens. They were the kind of concoction you could serve at room temperature or reheated. The final job was to prepare the promised salad. Macguire had filled several large zippered bags with freshly washed bunches of arugula and other delicate field greens. Before leaving home I'd snagged a jar of homemade sherry vinaigrette and packed up a batch of crusty, meringue-coated pecans.

By the time I had the salad assembled, the pie crusts were golden and puffed. The melted Camembert filling, with its garlic-and-herb seasoning, smelled heavenly. I carefully removed the pies and placed them on the counters to cool. I'd reheat them, along with the chicken, just before the closing supper.

I stared at the four tapes on the counter. I needed to do something with them. If Suz Craig had felt they were so incriminating that they should be buried, then I certainly didn't want to keep them. ReeAnn had gotten herself blown up, I was willing to bet, by

Exhibition Salad
with Meringue-Baked Pecans

Pecans:

1 egg white
1/4 teaspoon cinnamon
1/4 teaspoon salt
1/3 cup sugar
4 tablespoons melted butter
2 cups (1/2 pound) pecan halves

Preheat the oven to 325°. Butter a shallow 10-by 15-inch jelly-roll pan.

Beat the egg white until stiff. Mix the cinnamon and salt into the sugar. Keeping the beater running, add the sugar mixture, 1 tablespoon at a time. Fold in the melted butter and the pecans. Spread the pecan mixture in the prepared pan and bake for 15 minutes.

Remove the pan from the oven. Using a spatula, carefully flip the pecan mixture one small section at a time. When all the pecans have been turned over, return the pan to the oven. Bake an additional 15 minutes. Watch them carefully—do not allow them to burn. Cool the pecans on paper towels.

(Only 1 cup of pecans is used in the preparation of the salad. The other cup can be eaten as a snack or frozen in a zippered plastic bag. These pecans also make a wonderful holiday gift.)

Sherry Vinaigrette:

> 1 teaspoon Dijon mustard
> ¼ teaspoon sugar
> 1 tablespoon best-quality sherry vinegar
> 2 tablespoons best-quality olive oil
> Salt and freshly ground black pepper

Whisk together the mustard, sugar, and vinegar. Whisking constantly, dribble in the olive oil. Add salt and pepper to taste. Makes ¼ cup.

Salad:

2 cups (2 ounces) fresh arugula
6 cups (6 ounces) of a mixture of fresh
    radicchio, endive, and escarole

¼ cup sherry vinaigrette
1 cup sugared pecans

Wash, dry, and trim the arugula and the other greens. Tear them into large bite-size pieces. Just before serving, toss with the vinaigrette. Sprinkle the pecans over the top and toss again. Serve immediately.

Serves 4

someone who thought she had these very tapes. I didn't want to have them in the LakeCenter kitchen, in my van, or even in my home. I wanted them to be in a safe place until Tom could get them. But where?

As I scanned the ballroom, I couldn't get the nasty, threatening voice of Suz Craig out of my head. What would she have been able to find out about me? I wondered. If she'd married John Richard, she could have gotten hold of Arch's records from when he was in therapy after the divorce. Maybe she would have used them to gain a reduction in child support, or for some other, more sinister intent. I shuddered. I needed to call Tom. In my haste, I'd forgotten the cellular in the van.

While I was trotting back to my vehicle, I realized I now had to turn this whole thing over to Tom. I'd tried to sustain my relationship with Arch by fulfilling a promise to look into the case of the murder of Suz Craig. John Richard had been accused and appeared, for the most part, guilty. But the case had been more than a can of worms. It had been a tankful. With the tapes I'd discovered, and the physical evidence that would soon come back from the crime lab, Tom would help Donny Saunders figure out what had really happened to Suz.

Still, I couldn't help wondering how someone could have known, or could have taken the time to find out, what he or she had to know to plan out the murder of Suz Craig. *You can't put the dish in too early or it won't come out right.* Timing was everything. Not only would the killer have to know all about Suz, he or she would have to know all about John Richard's financial situation, what kind of car he drove, the ID bracelet, everything. And, most obscurely, the killer would also have to know under what circumstances John Richard used to beat me, what triggered his abusive rages. He or she would have to know about Suz and John Richard's monthly anniversary celebrations and that getting the Jerk totally frustrated would set him off—like lighting a fuse. The killer could get him frustrated by sending him notice of a failure to receive a bonus, when he was already deep in financial hot water.

But it all seemed like a terribly long shot. There was still a slim chance that John Richard wouldn't lose his temper, no matter how provoked.

In my van the cellular phone was bleating insistently. I grabbed it and flipped it open, but whoever it was had hung up. Arch? I called Tom but got his machine. I told him about the tapes and that he should send somebody up to the LakeCenter to retrieve them. Then I picked up the large plastic container of cookies.

The cleaning crew had left by the time I reentered the LakeCenter. The floor gleamed like a mirror and the thousands of little Babsie faces smiled beatifically at me. My cellular squawked again. I thumped the container of cookies down on the counter and reached for it.

"Goldy? Where've you been?" It was Frances Markasian. "I've been trying to reach you for hours! What'd you give me this number for if—"

"Spare me, Frances."

"What happened?" she cried. "Where are you?"

"I'm at the LakeCenter doing a catering job for the doll show. What do you want?"

"One of my sources told me a woman with a van was snooping around at Suz Craig's house, digging around outside. Was it you? What did you find?"

"Nothing. And who's your source?"

"Suz's neighbor, Lynn Tollifer. She saw your van and called me. Did you find those tapes?"

"Frances, you're too much."

"Well, I didn't, I mean . . . I'm coming over. I want those tapes!"

"Forget it! The cops get them—"

"So help me, Goldy, I'll strip that van of yours and pull every pot out of that LakeCenter kitchen, I'll—"

"Cool it, Frances, I don't have the tapes," I lied.

"You're lying, I swear. I'm in a meeting, and my editor won't let me leave. But I'll be over there in half an hour, so help me—"

I disconnected.

Oh, brother. Wait a minute. This place had a live security guard. This place also had vigilante collectors if the guard couldn't do his job. Again, I scanned the LakeCenter ballroom. Where could I put the tapes, in a place that would take Frances forever to find them? The table full of Holiday Babsies looked the most promising. They all belonged to Gail Rodine, and she wasn't selling. I'd stash them in the doll boxes, call Tom again, and have the cops figure it all out.

It was unlikely that I'd have the place to myself for long, so I raced across the ballroom to the right display and slipped one tape each under the skirts of Holiday Babsies from 1991, 1992, 1993, and 1994. There were at least thirty dolls there. Gail Rodine lived in Aspen Meadow, and when she took the dolls back home, Tom could get the tapes without much trouble. He wouldn't be happy about it, though.

When I tucked the flap of the last box into place, I heard a loud thump at the front of the LakeCenter. My skin turned cold. The Jerk. Had I locked the side door? I couldn't remember. I trotted toward it. Unfortunately, the slickly polished floor was as slippery as a skating rink. I skidded sideways, desperately twisted to regain my balance, and finally managed to land with a crash on both of my hands. I yelped with pain. By the time this case was over, I'd be covered in bruises from head to toe.

I tried to roll over and was only partially successful. My back seemed to have regained its flexibility, but the only thing really paining me now was my left hand, in particular, my left thumb. Broken in three places by the Jerk, and destined forever to give me trouble.

I looked at my aching thumb. I looked at it and looked at it, and I had a dawning sense of horror. *You'll be throwing pizza in no time*, the orthopedic surgeon had told me after a particularly savage beating had brought me to the hospital along with the broken thumb. He knew the pattern of bruises inflicted by the Jerk because he'd seen them before. *I'll be kicking field goals in no time,* he'd promised, much later. *What do you think . . . you'll go back to being an orthopedic surgeon?* Suz had said. *Your voice sounds so familiar,* I'd said. *Did you treat Arch?*

No. He'd treated *me.* A long time ago. He could plan the murder because he knew exactly what to do and how to make it look as if John Richard Korman had done it.

At that moment the side door of the LakeCenter swung open and Chris Corey appeared, a heavy, bearded study in fury. He saw me on the floor, holding my aching thumb. He snarled: "I see you're still good at getting yourself injured! How's the thumb? And while you're telling me, give me those tapes!"

Chapter 28

I scrambled to my feet. Pain shot through my body, but I had to think. The front door to the LakeCenter was locked; the back door was locked—for security. Somehow I had to get out through the entrance where Chris Corey stood.

"I don't have them," I replied shakily.

"I know you do! I paid that kid, Luke Tollifer, to watch Suz's house. Where are they?"

"In the car, in the car! My van!"

"Show me!"

I made my way to the door, thinking I might be able to slip past him and run. Before I could squeak by, however, he grabbed my left hand, and then my thumb. Cruelly, he twisted it behind my back. I yelped. At the same time, I noticed the cast on his ankle had mysteriously vanished.

"Where's your phone?"

"In . . . in my apron pocket."

He felt inside my pocket with his free hand, tugged my phone out, and sent it skittering across the shiny floor. "I want the tapes, then I'll leave. Walk to your van, get those tapes, then I'm gone. Scream, and I swear to God I'll hit you harder than I did her."

Oh, God. Fear washed through my body. My feet slid out from under me. He wrenched me up off the slippery floor.

"Please, Chris, don't," I gasped. "Think about what this is going to do to you. To Tina."

"Yeah, yeah. 'Think about Tina' is what I should have done before, huh? Move."

"Okay, okay," I gasped. My thumb throbbed in agony. I feared I'd pass out. Chris pushed me forward through the threshold of the side door. I looked back at him, insanely confused that his limp had also disappeared. As he fiercely nudged me along the log wall, a gaggle of red-wing blackbirds erupted from the wetlands bordering the LakeCenter.

I looked around wildly for help. The parking lot was empty except for my van. Where had Chris parked? I thought about screaming. But who would hear me? We were hundreds of yards from the road, even farther from the Lakeview Shopping Center.

As we rounded the building, Chris pushed me along the sidewalk toward the parking lot. I caught a glimpse of a car on the far side of the building—the side opposite the kitchen. Of course. He'd driven up quietly and parked away from the kitchen. And naturally he knew how to be quiet; hadn't he approached Suz's house in the darkness and quiet, in a Jeep just like John Richard's?

The guard was no help. Chris had clobbered him—the crash I'd heard at the front—and he lay sprawled next to the trash can.

"Where are the tapes?" Chris asked as we neared my van.

"Aah . . . aah . . ."

He wrenched my thumb brutally. "Where?"

"I can't . . . think . . . if you're hurting me," I protested in a low voice. I was using negotiating skills I had learned long ago, to keep John Richard from hurting me. When he relented a bit, I said,

"Aah . . . under the . . . passenger seat. It's a tight squeeze, you'll never be able to reach. Better let me . . . get them."

The first cars of the doll people appeared at the far end of the dirt-road entryway to the LakeCenter. *Stall, stall,* I thought desperately. Chris wrenched open the passenger-side door and pushed me inside, still gripping my thumb.

"You have to let go of me," I gasped. "Or I can't get them." I tried to think. Where was my tire iron? Did I have any spare kitchen utensils anywhere, something I could use on him? He shoved me into the van on my stomach. But at least he relinquished his death-grip on my thumb. I reached under the seat with my numb left hand. Nothing, of course. "Hold on," I called. "Just a sec."

He yanked back on my legs so violently that I thought I would break in two. I landed half in, half out, and on my side.

"Help!" I screamed. I had no idea if the doll people were even within earshot. "Somebody! *Help!*"

Chris picked me up by the waist and threw me on my back on the passenger-side seat. Then he flung his whole, heavy body on top of me. His fleshy hand clamped over my mouth. I kicked wildly. But with him on top of me and outweighing me by a good one hundred and fifty pounds, I had zero leverage.

"Shut up!" he breathed. His hand tightened on my throat. Panic shot through me. He was going to strangle me. I'd never see Arch again. Or Tom. I thrashed wildly. Chris's hand slipped off my throat. The glove compartment banged open.

Marla's bag of drugs fell onto the van floor.

Oh God, help me, I prayed as I strained under Chris's weight. I groped desperately. *Keep calm, keep calm, keep calm.* I reached into the bag, found nothing, scrabbled around frantically. Then my fingers closed over what I sought. I popped off the needle cover.

Chris had grabbed my throat again. He squeezed. With every ounce of strength I had left, I stabbed him with Marla's hypodermic of Versed. I pushed down on the plunger, hard.

Stunned, Chris squealed with pain. His hold on me relaxed momentarily. He screamed again and hauled back to tear the needle from his body. I scrambled through the open door. By the time I was outside, Chris was stumbling dazedly down the parking lot, toward the LakeCenter and his car.

I watched him, open-mouthed, gasping for breath. Was he going to just . . . take off? Was he so big that a dose of a superpotent tranquilizer had no effect on him? He faltered, appeared to trip, and then staggered forward.

"The Babsies!" I screamed at the large group of beautifully dressed women who were sashaying across the lot toward the LakeCenter door. "That big blond man! He's stolen them!" I pointed at Chris. He turned to stare open-mouthed at me, not comprehending. He was slowing down, no question. But he was only twenty feet from his car. "The Babsies!" I shrieked again at the women, gesticulating wildly. "That man knocked out the guard! He's going to take the dolls!"

The women started to trot. Chris gaped at them. Then he turned and floundered toward his vehicle. The women picked up speed.

"No, no!" he cried as the first doll collector attacked him. "No!" I heard him shout when two more women jumped on him. Bellowing in astonishment, he staggered forward. Then, under the onslaught of furious Babsie protectors, he fell to his knees.

I walked shakily back to the LakeCenter to call the sheriff's department. Chris Corey wasn't going anywhere.

Chapter 29

Tom, as it turned out, had been up at his cabin. Empty since high creekwaters had flooded the first floor with two inches of water, unrented since Arch, Tom, and I had spent several weekends scraping off dried mud, the cabin now awaited a professional interior paint job. When Tom drove up and parked half a mile away, then used a little-known path through the woods to approach the place from the back, he had a hunch that the cabin held a squatter—one of the very few people who knew about the flood damage and the time we'd spent cleaning the place up. Unfortunately, John Richard hadn't figured that Tom would be able to take him so easily. By the time Tom arrested the Jerk again, Sergeant Beiner had appeared at the LakeCenter and arrested Chris Corey.

That night, Chris confessed to the murder. He had wanted to end the torment of working for Suz Craig. He remembered how John Richard had attacked me; he had waited for the right time—the silly monthly anniversary. He had stolen the ID bracelet when John Richard was helping a woman with an induced delivery that had been scheduled—and approved—by ACHMO. Finally, he had written the bonus-denial letter. The drug screen on Suz's body fluids indicated that she, too, had been the recipient of a high-potency tranquilizer: morphine. Once Chris had primed John Richard to beat Suz, all Chris had to do was go to Suz's door pretending to be distraught and wanting to talk things out. He'd offered to treat her contusions, then he'd given her a shot much like the one I'd given him. He'd waited until the bruises from John Richard appeared. Then he'd killed her by whacking her with the carpet-covered, solid-metal scratching post. Finally, he'd laid her in the ditch, with the bracelet as the nail in John Richard's coffin. And then he'd gone back to pretending to be a helpful, sympathetic guy, complete with a fake cast.

He just hadn't figured on the tapes. Luella Downing had called him, as well as Brandon, on Saturday to tell him about the existence of Suz's secret taping. He'd used the visit to John Richard's office to look for them. ReeAnn—his ally—had told him she'd didn't have them. In desperation, he'd tried to blow up ReeAnn—he'd learned she was meeting her boyfriend for an outdoor lunch—because he had a feeling she'd stolen the tapes from John Richard. But just in case she hadn't, he'd paid Suz's nosy teenage neighbor, Luke Tollifer, to watch Suz's house, which is how he found out about my digging effort.

That evening the results came back from the crime lab: the skin and hair under Suz Craig's fingernails belonged to John Richard Korman. John Richard was charged with first-degree assault and tampering with a witness. They're talking about a plea bargain, but it looks as if he'll face at least two years in prison.

After the police hauled Chris Corey away from the LakeCenter, Sergeant Beiner took the briefest of statements from me and seized the tapes I pulled from their hiding places in the doll boxes. Gail Rodine, looking on, glared. I'd never get a Babsie booking again as long as I lived. I somehow managed to finish the dinner for the doll people. Happily, the preparation was easy; I couldn't have handled any additional grilling.

On Thursday morning, the day after Chris Corey was arrested, I saw Frances Markasian at Suz's memorial service. Afterward, we talked. I wanted her to leave Arch out of any article she wrote about the case and Chris's arrest. She felt terrible about being duped by Chris, and apologized for yelling at me about the tapes. Of course, I forgave her. Frances said she'd already talked to Brandon Yuille about an exposé on Suz's use of confidential medical files. Brandon had told Frances to tell me Ralph Shelton had agreed to cooperate; he would try to get Amy Bartholomew to help, too. I accepted Frances's promise to keep Arch out of her wrap-up article on the case.

Unfortunately, Tina Corey's mental illness did get leaked, and not just to the *Mountain Journal.* Both the *Denver Post* and *Rocky Mountain News* reported on her history of multiple-personality disorder. She went into a stress trance and ended up in the psychiatric ward of St. Joseph's Hospital. No visitors allowed.

On Friday afternoon, Arch came home. Tom had called him and they'd talked for over two hours. My son was having a hard time, as was to be expected. Macguire picked Arch up at the Druckmans', then drove him to the Coreys' house, where they helped the Mountain Animal Protective League load up Tippy the cat and Tina's other pets into a van, so the animals could be delivered to foster caretakers. But back at home, Arch was dejected. Even when Julian Teller called, saying he was coming for a visit, Arch did not appear cheered. Macguire offered to talk to him up in his room. After the two boys went up, Marla phoned and told us all to sit tight, she was bringing us take-out Vietnamese food for dinner.

Tom and I sat together on the couch. He pulled me close, and I felt the tension that had knotted my body for the last week begin to ebb. He said, "The only thing I can't understand is why you just wouldn't let Korman take the fall for this. I'm glad we've got the right guy, don't get me wrong. But you've wanted revenge for so long. Don't deny it now, I can read you better than you think, Miss G. Plus, this seemed like a perfect opportunity to get Korman sent down. And not just for a year or two."

I sat for a long time, thinking, enfolded in his arms. "I couldn't sacrifice Arch. Just to get my revenge, I mean. Chris Corey wanted his revenge on Suz, and his sister got trampled in the process."

"God," he said, "I love you."

"Mom?" Arch's call came from the bottom of the stairs. "Mom?"

I stood up. "Yes, hon."

He wore a crumpled khaki shirt and baggy black shorts. I wondered if he'd had a shower in the time he'd been at the Druckmans' house. Even his glasses were smeared.

"I'm sorry."

"It's okay," I said.

His chin trembled. "Will you . . . will you take me to see Dad?"

"Oh, please, honey." I beckoned, and he ran toward me. I held him tight, as I always had, from when he was very small. I said, "Of course."

Index to the Recipes

4 Plays by

William Inge

4 Plays BY
William Inge

Come Back, Little Sheba

Picnic

Bus Stop

The Dark at the Top of the Stairs

Grove Press, Inc.   New York

First Black Cat Edition 1979
First Printing 1979
ISBN: 0-394-17075-X
Grove Press ISBN: 0-8021-4237-0
Library of Congress Catalog Card Number: 78-73032

Library of Congress Cataloging in Publication Data

Inge, William Motter.
    4 plays.

    Reprint of the ed. published by Random House, New York.
    CONTENTS: Come back, Little Sheba. — Picnic. — Bus stop. — The dark
at the top of the stairs.
PS3517.N265F6 1979   812'.5'4   78-73032

Manufactured in the United States of America

Distributed by Random House, Inc.

GROVE PRESS INC., 196 West Houston Street, New York, N.Y. 10014

Title IV B

FOREWORD

The experience of my first production on Broadway was frantic and bewildering. The play was *Come Back, Little Sheba,* and it was a modest success. I had always hoped for an overwhelming success, but I felt myself very satisfied at the time that *Sheba* had come off as well as it did. Anticipating success (of any degree), I had always expected to feel hilarious, but I didn't. Other people kept coming to me saying, "Aren't you thrilled?" Even my oldest friends, who had known me during the years when I gave myself no peace for lack of success, were baffled by me. There was absolutely no one to understand how I felt, for I didn't feel anything at all. I was in a funk. Where was the joy I had always imagined? Where were the gloating satisfactions I had always anticipated? I looked everywhere to find them. None were there.

A few weeks after *Sheba* opened, a newspaper woman from the Midwest came dancing into my apartment to interview me, bringing with her a party spirit that could not counter with my persisting solemnity. "Where's the celebration?" she wanted to know, looking about the room as though for confetti. "Where's the champagne?" I knew I was not meeting success in the expected way but I was too tired to fake it. I endured her disappointment in me. I could tell by her twitching features that she was wondering what in the world she would tell her readers. Obviously, she couldn't tell them the truth, that the man who had written a (modestly) successful play was one of the saddest-looking creatures she had ever seen. But she didn't let the facts bother her. She returned home and wrote of the play's success and my reaction to it in a fitting way that wouldn't let her readers down. At the time I was too depressed to care.

Other people, friends and acquaintances, couldn't imagine why I had started being psychoanalyzed at this time. "But you're a success now," they would assure me. "What do you want to get analyzed for?" As though successful people automatically became happy, and psychoanalysis were only a remedy for professional failure. But if the personal rewards of my success were a disillusionment to others, they also were to me. My plays since *Sheba* have been more successful, but none of them has brought me the kind of joy, the hilarity, I had craved as a boy, as a young man, living in Kansas and Missouri back in the thirties and forties. Strange and ironic. Once we find the fruits of success, the taste is nothing like what we had anticipated.

Maybe the sleight of hand is performed during the brief interval of rehearsals, out-of-town tryouts, and opening night. A period of six or more weeks that pack a lifetime of growing up. During that period, the playwright comes to realize, maybe with considerable shock, that the play contains something very vital to him, something of the very essence of his own life. If it is rejected, he can only feel that he is rejected, too. Some part of him has been turned down, cast aside, even laughed at or scorned. If it is accepted, all that becomes him to feel is a deep gratefulness, like a man barely escaping a fatal accident, that he has survived.

All my plays have survived on Broadway. All have met with success in varying degrees. And I feel a fitting gratefulness, because they all represent something of me, some view of life that is peculiarly mine that no one else could offer in quite the same style and form. Success, it seems to me, would be somewhat meaningless if the play were not a personal contribution. The author who creates only for audience consumption is only engaged in a financial enterprise. There must always be room for both kinds of theatre, but it is regrettable that they must always compete together in our commercial theatre. For commercial theatre only builds on what has already been created, contributing only theatre back into the theatre. Creative theatre brings something of life itself, which gives the theatre something new to grow on. But when new life comes to us, we don't always recognize it. New life doesn't always survive on Broadway. It's considered risky.

People still come to me sometimes to tell me how much they admired *Come Back, Little Sheba,* referring to the play as though it had been "a smash hit" (a term which we are too eager to apply to shows). Actually, *Sheba* made out well with about half of the reviewers, its total run being something less than six months. Some of the reviews showed an almost violent repugnance to the play. We did good business for only a few weeks and then houses began to dwindle to the size of tea parties. At one time, the actors all took salary cuts, and I took a cut in my royalties. The show was cheap to run, and so, with a struggle, we survived. We always held a small audience of people who were most devoted to the play and came to see it many times. It is remembered now as "a smash hit" or "a hit," probably because the far greater success of the movie shed more glorious reflections on the play.

Now, I don't see how it could have been otherwise with *Sheba*. It is probably a bad omen if any author's first play is "a smash hit." It takes the slow-moving theatre audience one or two plays by a new author, who brings them something new from life outside the theatre, before they can feel sufficiently comfortable with him to consider fairly what he has to say. A good author insists on being accepted on his own terms, and audiences must bicker awhile before they're willing to give in. One learns not to be resentful about this condition but to credit it to human nature.

I have a tendency, after a play of mine is produced, to look back on it disparagingly, seeing only its faults (before production, I see only its virtues). But after the hiatus of opening night, after enough time passes for me to regard each play seriously, as something finally distinct from myself, I have felt that each one gave me some feeling of personal success, that each one contributed something to the theatre out of my life's experience.

I have never sought to write plays that primarily tell a story; nor have I sought deliberately to create new forms. I have been most concerned with dramatizing something of the dynamism I myself find in human motivations and behavior. I regard a play as a composition rather than a story, as a distillation of life rather than a narration of it. It is only in this way that I feel myself a real contemporary. *Sheba* is the closest thing to a story play that I have written, and it is the only play of mine that could be said to have two central characters. But even this play was a fabric of life, in which the two characters (Doc and Lola) were species of the environment. After *Sheba*, I sought deliberately to fill a larger canvas, to write plays of an over-all texture that made fuller use of the stage as a medium. I strive to keep the stage bubbling with a restless kind of action that seeks first one outlet and then another before finally resolving itself. I like to keep several stories going at once, and to keep as much of the playing area on stage as alive as possible. I use one piece of action to comment on another, not to distract from it. I don't suppose that in any of my later plays I found the single dramatic intensity of action that I found in the drunk scene in *Sheba*, in which Doc threatens Lola's life. I have deliberately sought breadth instead of depth in my plays since *Sheba*, and have sought a more forthright humor than *Sheba* could afford.

In an article I once wrote on *Picnic*, I compared a play to a journey, in which every moment should be as interesting as the destination. I despair of a play that requires its audience to sit through two hours of plot construction, having no reference outside the immediate setting, just to be rewarded by a big emotional pay-off in the last act. This, I regard as a kind of false stimulation. I think every line and every situation in a play should "pay off," too, and have its extensions of meaning beyond the immediate setting, into life. I strive to bring meaning to every moment, every action.

I doubt if my plays "pay off" for an audience unless they are watched rather closely. Writing for a big audience, I deal with surfaces in my plays, and let whatever depths there are in my material emerge unexpectedly so that they bring something of the suddenness and shock which accompany the discovery of truths in actuality. I suppose none of my plays means anything much unless seen as a composite, for I seek dramatic values in a relative way. That is, one character in a play of mine might seem quite pointless unless seen in comparison with another character. For instance, in *Bus Stop*, the cowboy's eagerness, awkwardness, and naïveté in seeking love were interesting only when seen by comparison, in the same setting, with the amorality of Cherie, the depravity of the professor, the casual earthiness of Grace and Carl, the innocence of the schoolgirl Elma, and the defeat of his buddy Virgil. In themselves, the characters may have been entertaining, but not very meaningful.

Bus Stop, I suppose, has less real story than any play that ever survived on Broadway. I meant it only as a composite picture of varying kinds of love, ranging from the innocent to the depraved. With the play's success, I felt quite proud of the fact that I had held the audience's interest long after what would normally be considered the final "pay-off" (when the cowboy and his girl are reunited and go off together). I guess maybe I was trying to prove that a play's merits can exist, not in the dramatization of one soul-satisfying event, but in the over-all pattern and texture of the play. I insisted that the audience be just as interested in what happened to all the characters as they were in Bo and Cherie.

I was sure enough of my craft by the time I started writing *The Dark at the Top of the Stairs* to be able to take my craftsmanship more easily for granted. This play was developed out of the first play I ever wrote, called *Farther Off From Heaven*. Margo Jones produced it in her Dallas Theatre in June, 1947, and I didn't know what to do with it at the time but felt it contained too much good material to keep on the shelf. I had been working on the play off and on for over six years, then in the winter of 1957, settled down on it for serious. It is formed from pretty nostalgic memories of childhood, without being very autobiographical. I suppose it represents my belated attempt to come to terms with the past, to rearrange its parts and make them balance, to bring a mature understanding to everyday phenomena that mystified me as a boy. Again, the story is very slight. I deliberately divert the audience from the main story in order to bring them back to it at the end of the play with a fresher viewpoint. In the play, I try to explore some of man's hidden fear in facing life and to show something of the hidden fears that motivate us all. There is a suicide in the play, of a young, homeless, part Jewish boy who has no sure connection with anyone in the world. Some people felt upon reading the play, and others upon first seeing it, that the announcement of the suicide came as too much of a shock; but every suicide I ever heard of came to me in the same way, with no preparation. I have never heard of a suicide that I expected. We always find the reasons for such events after they happen, in re-exploring the character to find motivations we had previously overlooked. It was this kind of dynamism I wanted most to achieve. And I felt also that maybe I was drawing a little on Christian theology to show something of the uniting effect human suffering can bring into our lives.

The success of these four plays, I must share in each case with my director. This is not just a pleasant compliment. I have come to learn how important good direction is to a play, and to realize that good directors are as scarce as good playwrights. I was most fortunate in finding Daniel Mann, unknown at the time, to do *Sheba*. He sensed all the play's implied values and projected them superbly. Joshua Logan, with *Picnic*, was my second director. We had our ups and downs with that play, which I attribute mainly to my second-play nervousness and indecision. An unstable author, who isn't sure what he wants, is a great liability to a director; so if *Picnic* did not come off entirely to please me (as rumor had it), it was my own fault. Josh only sensed my indecision and tried to compensate for it. Still, I feel *Picnic* was a good show. Josh gave it lovely picturesqueness (he is perhaps the most visual of all directors) and feeling of size. I worked on the play with him for a year and a half, during which time he gave of himself very spontaneously. I can never cease being grateful for all that I learned from him.

Harold Clurman is the only real intellectual I know in the theatre. He seems to me a man who has channeled very powerful emotions into a vitally rational life. I was a little dubious about taking *Bus Stop* to him. I didn't see how he, the most metropolitan man I know, could bring understanding to the play's rural types. But he understood them perfectly, I felt, as though by contrast with himself. And he gave me a beautifully felt production.

Working with Elia Kazan sometimes borders on the supernatural, he intuitively senses so quickly all the dim feelings about a play that lie in an author's subconscious. During production, he is the gentlest, humblest man I've ever known. He talks with actors like a ministering angel, infusing them with courage and insight. His range of understanding is from the most delicately sensitive to the most cataclysmically violent. He is a great creative talent.

I also feel very indebted to the superb actors who have taken part in my plays. I would like to list them here, but I truly would not know where to stop in compiling the list. Anyway, I am deeply grateful for the many talented people who have given of their own freshness and vitality to the parts I have written. If there have been poor performances in my plays, I don't recall them now.

"Success is counted sweetest by those who ne'er succeed," according to Emily Dickinson, and I realize what she meant when I compare the success I once anticipated with the success I found. They are not the same things, at all. But the four plays in this volume represent almost a decade in my life, a decade that was very intensely lived. Publishing the plays now is like tying those years together to file away, years in which I managed to find some expression for my life and experience, and to find response. Maybe this is all that success means.

WILLIAM INGE

Contents

☆

Come Back, Little Sheba

★

Come Back, Little Sheba *was first presented by The Theatre Guild at the Booth Theatre, New York City, on February 15, 1950, with the following cast:*

(IN ORDER OF APPEARANCE)

DOC	Sidney Blackmer
MARIE	Joan Lorring
LOLA	Shirley Booth
TURK	Lonny Chapman
POSTMAN	Daniel Reed
MRS. COFFMAN	Olga Fabian
MILKMAN	John Randolph
MESSENGER	Arnold Schulman
BRUCE	Robert Cunningham
ED ANDERSON	Wilson Brooks
ELMO HUSTON	Paul Krauss

DIRECTED BY Daniel Mann
SETTING AND LIGHTING DESIGNED BY Howard Bay
COSTUMES BY Lucille Little
PRODUCTION UNDER THE SUPERVISION OF Lawrence Langner and
    Theresa Helburn
ASSOCIATE PRODUCER, Phyllis Anderson

Scenes

An old house in a run-down neighborhood of a Midwestern city.

| ACT ONE | SCENE I. | Morning in late spring. |
| | SCENE II. | The same evening, after supper. |

ACT TWO	SCENE I.	The following morning.
	SCENE II.	Late afternoon the same day.
	SCENE III.	5:30 the next morning.
	SCENE IV.	Morning, a week later.

ACT ONE | Scene One

SCENE: *The stage is empty.*

It is the downstairs of an old house in one of those semi-respectable neighborhoods in a Midwestern city. The stage is divided into two rooms, the living room at right and the kitchen at left, with a stairway and a door between. At the foot of the stairway is a small table with a telephone on it. The time is about 8:00 A.M., a morning in the late spring.

At rise of curtain the sun hasn't come out in full force and outside the atmosphere is a little gray. The house is extremely cluttered and even dirty. The living room somehow manages to convey the atmosphere of the twenties, decorated with cheap pretense at niceness and respectability. The general effect is one of fussy awkwardness. The furniture. is all heavy and rounded-looking, the chairs and davenport being covered with a shiny mohair. The davenport is littered and there are lace antimacassars on all the chairs. In such areas, houses are so close together, they hide each other from the sunlight. What sun could come through the window, at right, is dimmed by the smoky glass curtains. In the kitchen there is a table, center. On it are piled dirty dishes from supper the night before. Woodwork in the kitchen is dark and grimy. No industry whatsoever has been spent in making it one of those white, cheerful rooms that we commonly think kitchens should be. There is no action on stage for several seconds.

DOC *comes downstairs to kitchen. His coat is on back of chair, center. He straightens chair, takes roll from bag on drainboard, folds bag and tucks it behind sink. He lights stove and goes to table, fills dishpan there and takes it to sink. Turns on water, tucks towel in vest for apron. He goes to chair and says prayer. Then he crosses to stove, takes frying pan to sink and turns on water.*

MARIE, *a young girl of eighteen or nineteen who rooms in the house, comes out of her bedroom (next to the living room), skipping airily into the kitchen. Her hair is piled in curls on top of her head and she wears a sheer dainty negligee and smart, feathery mules on her feet. She has the cheerfulness only youth can feel in the morning.*

5

MARIE (*Goes to chair, opens pocketbook there*)   Hi!

DOC   Well, well, how is our star boarder this morning?

MARIE   Fine.

DOC   Want your breakfast now?

MARIE   Just my fruit juice. I'll drink it while I dress and have my breakfast later.

DOC (*Places two glasses on table*)   Up a little early, aren't you?

MARIE   I have to get to the library and check out some books before anyone else gets them.

DOC   Yes, you want to study hard, Marie, learn to be a fine artist some day. Paint lots of beautiful pictures. I remember a picture my mother had over the mantelpiece at home, a picture of a cathedral in a sunset, one of those big cathedrals in Europe somewhere. Made you feel religious just to look at it.

MARIE   These books aren't for art, they're for biology. I have an exam.

DOC   Biology? Why do they make you take biology?

MARIE (*Laughs*)   It's required. Didn't you have to take biology when you were in college?

DOC   Well . . . yes, but I was preparing to study medicine, so of course I *had* to take biology and things like that. You see—I was going to be a real doctor then—only I left college my third year.

MARIE   What's the matter? Didn't you like the pre-med course?

DOC   Yes, of course . . . I had to give it up.

MARIE   Why?

DOC (*Goes to stove with roll on plate—evasive*)   I'll put your sweet roll in now, Marie, so it will be nice and warm for you when you want it.

MARIE   Dr. Delaney, you're so nice to your wife, and you're so nice to me, as a matter of fact, you're so nice to everyone. I hope my husband is as nice as you are. Most husbands would never think of getting their own breakfast.

DOC (*Very pleased with this*)   . . . Uh . . . you might as well sit down now and . . . yes, sit here and I'll serve you your breakfast now, Marie, and we can eat it together, the two of us.

MARIE (*A light little laugh as she starts dancing away from him*) No, I like to bathe first and feel that I'm all fresh and clean to start the day. I'm going to hop into the tub now. See you later.
(*She goes upstairs*)

DOC (*The words appeal to him*) Yes, fresh and clean—
(DOC *shows disappointment but goes on in businesslike way setting his breakfast on the table*)

MARIE (*Offstage*) Mrs. Delaney.

LOLA (*Offstage*) 'Mornin', honey.
(*Then* LOLA *comes downstairs. She is a contrast to* DOC'S *neat cleanliness, and* MARIE'S. *Over a nightdress she wears a lumpy kimono. Her eyes are dim with a morning expression of disillusionment, as though she had had a beautiful dream during the night and found on waking none of it was true. On her feet are worn dirty comfies*)

LOLA (*With some self-pity*) I can't sleep late like I used to. It used to be I could sleep till noon if I wanted to, but I can't any more. I don't know why.

DOC Habits change. Here's your fruit juice.

LOLA (*Taking it*) I oughta be gettin' your breakfast, Doc, instead of you gettin' mine.

DOC I have to get up anyway, Baby.

LOLA (*Sadly*) I had another dream last night.

DOC (*Pours coffee*) About Little Sheba?

LOLA (*With sudden animation*) It was just as real. I dreamt I put her on a leash and we walked downtown—to do some shopping. All the people on the street turned around to admire her, and I felt so proud. Then we started to walk, and the blocks started going by so fast that Little Sheba couldn't keep up with me. Suddenly, I looked around and Little Sheba was gone. Isn't that funny? I looked everywhere for her but I couldn't find her. And I stood there feeling sort of afraid. (*Pause*) Do you suppose that means anything?

DOC Dreams are funny.

LOLA Do you suppose it means Little Sheba is going to come back?

DOC   I don't know, Baby.

LOLA   (*Petulant*)   I miss her so, Doc. She was such a cute little puppy. Wasn't she cute?

DOC   (*Smiles with the reminiscence*)   Yes, she was cute.

LOLA   Remember how white and fluffy she used to be after I gave her a bath? And how her little hind-end wagged from side to side when she walked?

DOC   (*An appealing memory*)   I remember.

LOLA   She was such a cute little puppy. I hated to see her grow old, didn't you, Doc?

DOC   Yah. Little Sheba should have stayed young forever. Some things should never grow old. That's what it amounts to, I guess.

LOLA   She's been gone for such a long time. What do you suppose ever happened to her?

DOC   You can't ever tell.

LOLA   (*With anxiety*)   Do you suppose she got run over by a car? Or do you think that old Mrs. Coffman next door poisoned her? I wouldn't be a bit surprised.

DOC   No, Baby. She just disappeared. That's all we know.

LOLA   (*Redundantly*)   Just vanished one day . . . vanished into thin air.
(*As though in a dream*)

DOC   I told you I'd find you another one, Baby.

LOLA   (*Pessimistically*)   You couldn't ever find another puppy as cute as Little Sheba.

DOC   (*Back to reality*)   Want an egg?

LOLA   No. Just this coffee. (*He pours coffee and sits down to breakfast.* LOLA, *suddenly*) Have you said your prayer, Doc?

DOC   Yes, Baby.

LOLA   And did you ask God to be with you—all through the day, and keep you strong?

DOC   Yes, Baby.

LOLA   Then God will be with you, Docky. He's been with you almost a year now and I'm so proud of you.

DOC   (*Preening a little*)   Sometimes I feel sorta proud of myself.

LOLA   Say your prayer, Doc. I like to hear it.

DOC   (*Matter-of-factly*)   God grant me the serenity to accept the things I cannot change, courage to change the things I can, and wisdom always to tell the difference.

LOLA   That's nice. That's so pretty. When I think of the way you used to drink, always getting into fights, we had so much trouble. I was so scared! I never knew what was going to happen.

DOC   That was a long time ago, Baby.

LOLA   I know it, Daddy. I know how you're going to be when you come home now.
(*She kisses him lightly*)

DOC   *I* don't know what I would have done without you.

LOLA   And now you've been sober almost a year.

DOC   Yep. A year next month.
(*He rises and goes to the sink with coffee cup and two glasses, rinsing them*)

LOLA   Do you have to go to the meeting tonight?

DOC   No. I can skip the meetings now for a while.

LOLA   Oh, good! Then you can take me to a movie.

DOC   Sorry, Baby. I'm going out on some Twelfth Step work with Ed Anderson.

LOLA   What's that?

DOC   (*Drying the glasses*)   I showed you that list of twelve steps the Alcoholics Anonymous have to follow. This is the final one. After you learn to stay dry yourself, then you go out and help other guys that need it.

LOLA   Oh!

DOC   (*Goes to sink*)   When we help others, we help ourselves.

LOLA   I know what you mean. Whenever I help Marie in some way, it makes me feel good.

DOC   Yah. (LOLA *takes her cup to* DOC *and he washes it*) Yes, but this is a lot different, Baby. When I go out to help some poor drunk, I have to give him courage—to stay sober like I've stayed sober. Most alcoholics are disappointed men. . . . They need courage . . .

LOLA   You weren't ever disappointed, were you, Daddy?

DOC (*After another evasive pause*)   The important thing is to forget the past and live for the present. And stay sober doing it.

LOLA   Who do you have to help tonight?

DOC   Some guy they picked up on Skid Row last night. (*Gets his coat from back of chair*) They got him at the City Hospital. I kinda dread it.

LOLA   I thought you said it helped you.

DOC (*Puts on coat*)   It does, if you can stand it. I did some Twelfth Step work down there once before. They put alcoholics right in with the crazy people. It's horrible—these men all twisted and shaking—eyes all foggy and full of pain. Some guy there with his fists clamped together, so he couldn't kill anyone. There was a young man, just a *young* man, had scratched his eyes out.

LOLA (*Cringing*)   Don't, Daddy. Seems a shame to take a man there just 'cause he got drunk.

DOC   Well, they'll sober a man up. That's the important thing. Let's not talk about it any more.

LOLA (*With relief*)   Rita Hayworth's on tonight, out at the Plaza. Don't you want to see it?

DOC   Maybe Marie will go with you.

LOLA   Oh, no. She's probably going out with Turk tonight.

DOC   She's too nice a girl to be going out with a guy like Turk.

LOLA   I don't know why, Daddy. Turk's nice.
(*Cuts coffee cake*)

DOC   A guy like that doesn't have any respect for *nice* young girls. You can tell that by looking at him.

LOLA   I never saw Marie object to any of the love-making.

DOC   A big brawny bozo like Turk, he probably forces her to kiss him.

LOLA   Daddy, that's not so at all. I came in the back way once when they were in the living room, and she was kissing him like he was Rudolph Valentino.

DOC (*An angry denial*)   Marie is a nice girl.

LOLA   I know she's nice. I just said she and Turk were doing some tall spooning. It wouldn't surprise me any if . . .

DOC   Honey, I don't want to hear any more about it.

LOLA   You try to make out like every young girl is Jennifer Jones in the *Song of Bernadette*.

DOC   I do not. I just like to believe that young people like her are clean and decent. . . .
(MARIE *comes downstairs*)

MARIE   Hi!
(*Gets cup and saucer from drainboard*)

LOLA (*At stove*)   There's an extra sweet roll for you this morning, honey. I didn't want mine.

MARIE   One's plenty, thank you.

DOC   How soon do you leave this morning?
(LOLA *brings coffee*)

MARIE (*Eating*)   As soon as I finish my breakfast.

DOC   Well, I'll wait and we can walk to the corner together.

MARIE   Oh, I'm sorry, Doc. Turk's coming by. He has to go to the library, too.

DOC   Oh, well, I'm not going to be competition with a football player. (*To* LOLA) It's a nice spring morning. Wanta walk to the office with me?

LOLA   I look too terrible, Daddy. I ain't even dressed.

DOC   Kiss Daddy good-bye.

LOLA (*Gets up and kisses him softly*)   'Bye, 'bye, Daddy. If you get hungry, come home and I'll have something for you.

MARIE (*Joking*)   Aren't you going to kiss *me*, Dr. Delaney?
(LOLA *eggs* DOC *to go ahead*)

DOC (*Startled, hesitates, forces himself to realize she is only joking and manages to answer*)   Can't spend my time kissing *all* the girls.
(MARIE *laughs.* DOC *goes into living room while* LOLA *and* MARIE *continue talking.* MARIE'S *scarf is tossed over his hat on chair, so he picks it up, then looks at it fondly, holding it in the air inspecting its delicate gracefulness. He drops it back on chair and goes out*)

MARIE   I think Dr. Delaney is so nice.

LOLA (*She is by the closet now, where she keeps a few personal articles. She is getting into a more becoming smock*) When did you say Turk was coming by?

MARIE Said he'd be here about nine-thirty. (DOC *exits, hearing the line about* TURK) That's a pretty smock.

LOLA (*Goes to table, sits in chair and changes shoes*) It'll be better to work around the house in.

MARIE (*Not sounding exactly cheerful*) Mrs. Delaney, I'm expecting a telegram this morning. Would you leave it on my dresser for me when it comes?

LOLA Sure, honey. No bad news, I hope.

MARIE Oh, no! It's from Bruce.

LOLA (MARIE'S *boy friends are one of her liveliest interests*) Oh, your boy friend in Cincinnati. Is he coming to see you?

MARIE I guess so.

LOLA I'm just dying to meet him.

MARIE (*Changing the subject*) Really, Mrs. Delaney, you and Doc have been so nice to me. I just want you to know I appreciate it.

LOLA Thanks, honey.

MARIE You've been like a father and mother to me. I appreciate it.

LOLA Thanks, honey.

MARIE Turk was saying just the other night what good sports you both are.

LOLA (*Brushing hair*) That so?

MARIE Honest. He said it was just as much fun being with you as with kids our own age.

LOLA (*Couldn't be more flattered*) Oh, I like that Turk. He reminds me of a boy I used to know in high school, Dutch McCoy. Where did you ever meet him?

MARIE In art class.

LOLA Turk take art?

MARIE (*Laughs*) No. It was in a life class. He was modeling. Lots of the athletes do that. It pays them a dollar an hour.

LOLA That's nice.

MARIE Mrs. Delaney? I've got some corrections to make in some of my drawings. Is it all right if I bring Turk home this morning to pose for me? It'll just take a few minutes.

LOLA Sure, honey.

MARIE   There's a contest on now. They're giving a prize for the best drawing to use for advertising the Spring Relays.

LOLA   And you're going to do a picture of Turk? That's nice. (*A sudden thought*) Doc's gonna be gone tonight. You and Turk can have the living room if you want to. (*A little secretively*)

MARIE   (*This is a temptation*)   O.K. Thanks.
(*Exits to bedroom*)

LOLA   Tell me more about Bruce.
(*Follows her to bedroom door*)

MARIE   (*Offstage in bedroom. Remembering her affinity*) Well, he comes from one of the best families in Cincinnati. And they have a great big house. And they have a maid, too. And he's got a wonderful personality. He makes three hundred dollars a month.

LOLA   That so?

MARIE   And he stays at the best hotels. His company insists on it.
(*Enters*)

LOLA   Do you like him as well as Turk?
(*Buttoning up back of* MARIE's *blouse*)

MARIE   (*Evasive*)   Bruce is so dependable, and . . . he's a gentleman, too.

LOLA   Are you goin' to marry him, honey?

MARIE   Maybe, after I graduate from college and he feels he can support a wife and children. I'm going to have lots and lots of children.

LOLA   I wanted children, too. When I lost my baby and found out I couldn't have any more, I didn't know what to do with myself. I wanted to get a job, but Doc wouldn't hear of it.

MARIE   Bruce is going to come into a lot of money some day. His uncle made a fortune in men's garters.
(*Exits into her room*)

LOLA   (*Leaning on door frame*)   Doc was a rich boy when I married him. His mother left him twenty-five thousand when she died. (*Disillusioned*) It took him a lot to get his office started and everything . . . then, he got sick. (*She makes a futile gesture; then on the bright side*) But Doc's always good to me . . . *now*.

MARIE ʼ(*Re-enters*)   Oh, Doc's a peach.

LOLA   I used to be pretty, something like you. (*She gets her picture from table*) I was Beauty Queen of the senior class in high school. My dad was awful strict, though. Once he caught me holding hands with that good-looking Dutch McCoy. Dad sent Dutch home, and wouldn't let me go out after supper for a whole month. Daddy would never let me go out with boys much. Just because I was pretty. He was afraid all the boys would get the wrong idea—*you* know. I never had any fun at all until I met Doc.

MARIE   Sometimes I'm glad I didn't know my father. Mom always let me do pretty much as I please.

LOLA   Doc was the first boy my dad ever let me go out with. We got married that spring.
(*Replaces picture.* MARIE *sits on couch, puts on shoes and socks*)

MARIE   What did your father think of that?

LOLA   We came right to the city then. And, well, Doc gave up his pre-med course and went to chiropractor school instead.

MARIE   You must have been married awful young.

LOLA   Oh, yes. Eighteen.

MARIE   That must have made your father really mad. .

LOLA   Yes, it did. I never went home after that, but my mother comes down here from Green Valley to visit me sometimes.

TURK   (*Bursts into the front room from outside. He is a young, big, husky, good-looking boy, nineteen or twenty. He has the openness, the generosity, vigor and health of youth. He's had a little time in the service, but he is not what one would call disciplined. He wears faded dungarees and a T-shirt. He always enters unannounced. He hollers for* MARIE) Hey, Marie! Ready?

MARIE   (*Calling. Runs and exits into bedroom, closing door*) Just a minute, Turk.

LOLA   (*Confidentially*)   I'll entertain him until you're ready. (*She is by nature coy and kittenish with any attractive man. Picks up papers—stuffs them under table*) The house is such a mess, Turk! I bet you think I'm an awful housekeeper.

Some day I'll surprise you. But you're like one of the family now. (*Pause*) My, you're an early caller.

TURK   Gotta get to the library. Haven't cracked a book for a biology exam and Marie's gotta help me.

LOLA (*Unconsciously admiring his stature and physique and looking him over*)   My, I'd think you'd be chilly running around in just that thin little shirt.

TURK   Me? I go like this in the middle of winter.

LOLA   Well, you're a big husky man.

TURK (*Laughs*)   Oh, I'm a brute, *I* am.

LOLA   You should be out in Hollywood making those Tarzan movies.

TURK   I had enough of that place when I was in the Navy.

LOLA   That so?

TURK (*Calling*)   Hey, Marie, hurry up.

MARIE   Oh, be patient, Turk.

TURK (*To* LOLA)   She doesn't realize how busy I am. I'll only have a half hour to study at most. I gotta report to the coach at ten-thirty.

LOLA   What are you in training for now?

TURK   Spring track. They got me throwing the javelin.

LOLA   The javelin? What's that?

TURK (*Laughs at her ignorance*)   It's a big, long lance. (*Assumes the magnificent position*) You hold it like this, erect—then you let go and it goes singing through the air, and lands yards away, if you're any good at it, and sticks in the ground, quivering like an arrow. I won the state championship last year.

LOLA (*She has watched as though fascinated*)   My!

TURK (*Very generous*)   Get Marie to take you to the track field some afternoon, and you can watch me.

LOLA   That would be thrilling.

MARIE (*Comes dancing in*)   Hi, Turk.

TURK   Hi, juicy.

LOLA (*As the young couple move to the doorway*)   Remember, Marie, you and Turk can have the front room tonight.

All to yourselves. You can play the radio and dance and make a plate of fudge, or anything you want.

MARIE (*To* TURK) O.K.?

TURK (*With eagerness*) Sure.

MARIE Let's go.
(*Exits*)

LOLA 'Bye, kids.

TURK 'Bye, Mrs. Delaney. (*Gives her a chuck under the chin*) You're a swell skirt.
(LOLA *couldn't be more flattered. For a moment she is breathless. They speed out the door and* LOLA *stands, sadly watching them depart. Then a sad, vacant look comes over her face. Her arms drop in a gesture of futility. Slowly she walks out on the front porch and calls*)

LOLA Little Sheba! Come, Little She-ba. Come back . . . come back, Little Sheba! (*She waits for a few moments, then comes wearily back into the house, closing the door behind her. Now the morning has caught up with her. She goes to the kitchen, kicks off her pumps and gets back into comfies. The sight of the dishes on the drainboard depresses her. Clearly she is bored to death. Then the telephone rings with the promise of relieving her. She answers it*) Hello— Oh, no, you've got the wrong number— Oh, that's all right. (*Again it looks hopeless. She hears the* POSTMAN. *Now her spirits are lifted. She runs to the door, opens it and awaits him. When he's within distance, she lets loose a barrage of welcome*) 'Morning, Mr. Postman.

POSTMAN 'Morning, ma'am.

LOLA You better have something for me today. Sometimes I think you don't even know I live here. You haven't left me anything for two whole weeks. If you can't do better than that, I'll just have to get a new postman.

POSTMAN (*On the porch*) You'll have to get someone to write you some letters, lady. Nope, nothing for you.

LOLA Well, I was only joking. You knew I was joking, didn't you? I bet you're thirsty. You come right in here and I'll bring you a glass of cold water. Come in and sit down for a few minutes and rest your feet awhile.

POSTMAN I'll take you up on that, lady. I've worked up quite a thirst.
(*Coming in*)

LOLA   You sit down. I'll be back in just a minute.
(*Goes to kitchen, gets pitcher out of refrigerator and brings it back*)

POSTMAN   Spring is turnin' into summer awful soon.

LOLA   You feel free to stop here and ask me for a drink of water any time you want to. (*Pouring drink*) That's what we're all here for, isn't it? To make each other comfortable?

POSTMAN   Thank you, ma'am.

LOLA   (*Clinging, not wanting to be left alone so soon; she hurries her conversation to hold him*)   You haven't been our postman very long, have you?

POSTMAN   (*She gives him the glass of water, stands holding pitcher as he drinks*)   No.

LOLA   You postmen have things pretty nice, don't you? I hear you get nice pensions after you been working for the government twenty years. I think that's dandy. It's a *good* job, too. (*Pours him a second glass*) You may get tired but I think it's good for a man to be outside and get a lot of exercise. Keeps him strong and healthy. My husband, he's a doctor, a *chiro*practor; he has to stay inside his office all day long. The only exercise he gets is rubbin' people's backbones. (*They laugh.* LOLA *goes to table, leaves pitcher*) It makes his hands strong. He's got the strongest hands you ever did see. But he's got a poor digestion. I keep tellin' him he oughta get some fresh air once in a while and some exercise. (POSTMAN *rises as if to go, and this hurries her into a more absorbing monologue*) You know what? My husband is an Alcoholics Anonymous. He doesn't care if I tell you that 'cause he's proud of it. He hasn't touched a drop in almost a year. All that time we've had a quart of whiskey in the pantry for company and he hasn't even gone near it. Doesn't even want to. You know, alcoholics can't drink like ordinary people; they're *allergic* to it. It affects them different. They get started drinking and can't stop. Liquor transforms them. Sometimes they get mean and violent and wanta fight, but if they let liquor alone, they're perfectly all right, just like you and me. (POSTMAN *tries to leave*) You should have seen Doc before he gave it up. He lost all his patients, wouldn't even go to the office; just wanted to stay drunk all day long and he'd come home at night and . . . You just wouldn't believe it if you saw him now. He's got his patients all back, and he's just doing fine.

POSTMAN Sure, I know Dr. Delaney. I deliver his office mail.
He's a fine man.

LOLA Oh, thanks. You don't ever drink, do you?

POSTMAN Oh, a few beers once in a while.
(*He is ready to go*)

LOLA Well, I guess that stuff doesn't do any of us any good.

POSTMAN No. (*Crosses down for mail on floor center*) Well,
good day, ma'am.

LOLA Say, you got any kids?

POSTMAN Three grandchildren.

LOLA (*Getting it from console table*) We don't have any
kids, and we got this toy in a box of breakfast food. Why
don't you take it home to them?

POSTMAN Why, that's very kind of you, ma'am.
(*He takes it, and goes*)

LOLA Good-bye, Mr. Postman.

POSTMAN (*On porch*) I'll see that you get a letter, if I have
to write it myself.

LOLA Thanks. Good-bye. (*Left alone, she turns on radio.
Then she goes to kitchen to start dishes, showing her bore-
dom in the half-hearted way she washes them. Takes water
back to icebox. Then she spies* MRS. COFFMAN *hanging baby
clothes on lines just outside kitchen door. Goes to door*)
My, you're a busy woman this morning, Mrs. Coffman.

MRS. COFFMAN (*German accent. She is outside, but sticks her
head in for some of the following*) Being busy is being
happy.

LOLA I guess so.

MRS. COFFMAN I don't have it as easy as you. When you got
seven kids to look after, you got no time to sit around the
house, Mrs. Delaney.

LOLA I s'pose not.

MRS. COFFMAN But you don't hear me complain.

LOLA Oh, no. You never complain. (*Pause*) I guess my little
doggie's gone for good, Mrs. Coffman. I sure miss her.

MRS. COFFMAN The only way to keep from missing one dog
is to get another.

LOLA (*Goes to sink, turns off water*) Oh, I never could find another doggie as cute as Little Sheba.

MRS. COFFMAN Did you put an ad in the paper?

LOLA For two whole weeks. No one answered it. It's just like she vanished—into thin air. (*She likes this metaphor*) Every day, though, I go out on the porch and call her. You can't tell; she might be around. Don't you think?

MRS. COFFMAN You should get busy and forget her. You should get busy, Mrs. Delaney.

LOLA Yes, I'm going to. I'm going to start my spring house-cleaning one of these days real soon. Why don't you come in and have a cup of coffee with me, Mrs. Coffman, and we can chat awhile?

MRS. COFFMAN I got work to do, Mrs. Delaney. I got work. (LOLA *turns from the window, annoyed at her rejection. Is about to start in on the dishes when the* MILKMAN *arrives. She opens the back door and detains him*)

MILKMAN 'Morning, Mrs. Coffman.

MRS. COFFMAN 'Morning.

LOLA Hello there, Mr. Milkman. How are you today?

MILKMAN 'Morning, lady.

LOLA I think I'm going to want a few specials today. Can you come in a minute?
(*Goes to icebox*)

MILKMAN (*Coming in*) What'll it be?
(*He probably is used to her. He is not a handsome man, but is husky and attractive in his uniform*)

LOLA (*At icebox*) Well, now, let's see. You got any cottage cheese?

MILKMAN We always got cottage cheese, lady. (*Showing her card*) All you gotta do is check the items on the card and we leave 'em. Now I gotta go back to the truck.

LOLA Now, don't scold me. I always mean to do that but you're always here before I think of it. Now, I guess I'll need some coffee cream, too—half a pint.

MILKMAN Coffee cream. O.K.

LOLA Now let me see . . . Oh, yes, I want a quart of butter-milk. My husband has liked buttermilk ever since he

stopped drinking. My husband's an alcoholic. Had to give
it up. Did I ever tell you?
(*Starts out. Stops at sink*)

MILKMAN   Yes, lady.
(*Starts to go. She follows*)

LOLA   Now he can't get enough to eat. Eats six times a day.
He comes home in the middle of the morning, and I fix him
a snack. In the middle of the afternoon he has a malted
milk with an egg in it. And then another snack before he
goes to bed.

MILKMAN   What'd ya know?

LOLA   Keeps his energy up.

MILKMAN   I'll bet. Anything else, lady?

LOLA   No, I guess not.

MILKMAN   (*Going out*)   Be back in a jiffy.
(*Gives her a slip of paper*)

LOLA   I'm just so sorry I put you to so much extra work. (*He
goes. Returns shortly with dairy products*) After this I'm
going to do my best to remember to check the card. I don't
think it's right to put people to extra work.
(*Goes to icebox, puts things away*)

MILKMAN   (*Smiles, is willing to forget*)   That's all right, lady.

LOLA   Maybe you'd like a piece of cake or a sandwich. Got
some awfully good cold cuts in the icebox.

MILKMAN   No, thanks, lady.

LOLA   Or maybe you'd like a cup of coffee.

MILKMAN   No, thanks.
(*He's checking the items, putting them on the bill*)

LOLA   You're just a young man. You oughta be going to college. I think everyone should have an education. Do you
like your job?

MILKMAN   It's O.K.
(*Looks at* LOLA)

LOLA   You're a husky young man. You oughta be out in
Hollywood making those Tarzan movies.

MILKMAN   (*Steps back. Feels a little flattered*)   When I first
began on this job I didn't get enough exercise, so I started
working out on the bar-bell.

LOLA Bar-bells?

MILKMAN Keeps you in trim.

LOLA (*Fascinated*) Yes, I imagine.

MILKMAN I sent my picture in to *Strength and Health* last month. (*Proudly*) It's a physique study! If they print it, I'll bring you a copy.

LOLA Oh, will you? I think we should all take better care of ourselves, don't you?

MILKMAN If you ask me, lady, that's what's wrong with the world today. We're not taking care of ourselves.

LOLA I wouldn't be surprised.

MILKMAN Every morning, I do forty push-ups before I eat my breakfast.

LOLA Push-ups?

MILKMAN Like this. (*He spreads himself on the floor and demonstrates, doing three rapid push-ups.* LOLA *couldn't be more fascinated. Then he springs to his feet*) That's good for shoulder development. Wanta feel my shoulders?

LOLA Why . . . why, yes. (*He makes one arm tense and puts her hand on his shoulder*) Why, it's just like a rock.

MILKMAN I can do seventy-nine without stopping.

LOLA Seventy-nine!

MILKMAN Now feel my arm.

LOLA (*Does so*) Goodness!

MILKMAN You wouldn't believe what a puny kid I was. Sickly, no appetite.

LOLA Is that a fact? And, my! Look at you now.

MILKMAN (*Very proud*) Shucks, any man could do the same . . . if he just takes care of himself.

LOLA Oh, sure, sure.
(*A horn is heard offstage*)

MILKMAN There's my buddy. I gotta beat it. (*Picks up his things, shakes hands, leaves hurriedly*) See you tomorrow, lady.

LOLA 'Bye.
(*She watches him from kitchen window until he gets out of sight. There is a look of some wonder on her face, an*

emptiness, as though she were unable to understand any-
thing that ever happened to her. She looks at clock, runs
into living room, turns on radio. A pulsating tom-tom is
heard as a theme introduction. Then the ANNOUNCER)

ANNOUNCER (*In dramatic voice*)   TA-BOOoooo! (*Now in a*
very soft, highly personalized voice. LOLA *sits on couch, eats*
candy) It's Ta-boo, radio listeners, your fifteen minutes of
temptation. (*An alluring voice*) Won't you join me? (LOLA
swings feet up) Won't you leave behind your routine, the
dull cares that make up your day-to-day existence, the little
worries, the uncertainties, the confusions of the work-a-day
world and follow me where pagan spirits hold sway, where
lithe natives dance on a moon-enchanted isle, where palm
trees sway with the restless ocean tide, restless surging on
the white shore? Won't you come along? (*More tom-tom.*
Now, in an oily voice) But remember, it's TA-BOOOOOO-
OOOOOOO! (*Now the tom-tom again, going into a sensual,*
primitive rhythm melody. LOLA *has been transfixed from the*
beginning of the program. She lies down on the davenport,
listening, then slowly, growing more and more comfortable)

WESTERN UNION BOY (*At door*)   Telegram for Miss Marie
Buckholder.

LOLA (*Going to door*)   She's not here.

WESTERN UNION BOY   Sign here.
(LOLA *does, then she closes the door and brings the en-*
velope into the house, looking at it wonderingly. This is a
major temptation for her. She puts the envelope on the
table but can't resist looking at it. Finally she gives in and
takes it to the kitchen to steam it open. Then MARIE *and*
TURK *burst into the room.* LOLA, *confused, wonders what to*
do with the telegram, then decides, just in the nick of time,
to jam it in her apron pocket)

MARIE   Mrs. Delaney! (*Turns off radio. At the sound of*
MARIE'S *voice,* LOLA *embarrassedly slips the message into*
her pocket and runs in to greet them) Mind if we turn your
parlor into an art studio?

LOLA   Sure, go right ahead. Hi, Turk.
(TURK *gives a wave of his arm*)

MARIE (*To* TURK, *indicating her bedroom*)   You can change
in there, Turk.
(*Exit to bedroom*)

LOLA (*Puzzled*)   Change?

MARIE   He's gotta take off his clothes.

LOLA   Huh?
(*Closes door*)

MARIE   These drawings are for my life class.

LOLA   (*Consoled but still mystified*)   Oh.

MARIE   (*Sits on couch*)   Turk's the best male model we've
had all year. Lotsa athletes pose for us 'cause they've all
got muscles. They're easier to draw.

LOLA   You mean . . . he's gonna pose *naked*?

MARIE   (*Laughs*)   No. The women do, but the men are always more proper. Turk's going to pose in his track suit.

LOLA   Oh. (*Almost to herself*) The women pose naked but
the men don't. (*This strikes her as a startling inconsistency*)
If it's all right for a woman, it oughta be for a man.

MARIE   (*Businesslike*)   The man always keeps covered. (*Calling to* TURK) Hurry up, Turk.

TURK   (*With all his muscles in place, he comes out. He is not
at all self-conscious about his semi-nudity. His body is
something he takes very much for granted.* LOLA *is a little
dazed by the spectacle of flesh*)   How do you want this
lovely body? Same pose I took in art class?

MARIE   Yah. Over there where I can get more light on you.

TURK   (*Opens door. Starts pose*)   Anything in the house I can
use for a javelin?

MARIE   Is there, Mrs. Delaney?

LOLA   How about the broom?

TURK   O.K.
(LOLA *runs out to get it.* TURK *goes to her in kitchen, takes
it, returns to living room and resumes pose*)

MARIE   (*From her sofa, studying* TURK *in relation to her
sketch pad, moves his leg*)   Your left foot a little more this
way. (*Studying it*) O.K., hold it.
(*Starts sketching rapidly and industriously.* LOLA *looks on,
lingeringly*)

LOLA   (*Starts unwillingly into kitchen, changes her mind and
returns to the scene of action.* MARIE *and* TURK *are too busy
to comment.* LOLA *looks at sketch, inspecting it*)   Well
. . . that's real pretty, Marie. (MARIE *is intent.* LOLA *moves*

closer to look at the drawing) It . . . it's real artistic.
(*Pause*) I wish *I* was artistic.

TURK   Baby, I can't hold this pose very long at a time.

MARIE   Rest whenever you feel like it.

TURK   O.K.

MARIE (*To* LOLA) If I make a good drawing, they'll use it
for the posters for the Spring Relays.

LOLA   Ya. You told me.

MARIE (*To* TURK)   After I'm finished with these sketches I
won't have to bother you any more.

TURK   No bother. (*Rubs his shoulder—he poses*) Hard pose,
though. Gets me in the shoulder.
  (MARIE *pays no attention.* LOLA *peers at him so closely,
he becomes a little self-conscious and breaks pose. This
also breaks* LOLA'S *concentration*)

LOLA   I'll heat you up some coffee.
  (*Goes to kitchen*)

TURK (*Softly to* MARIE)   Hey, can't you keep her out of
here? She makes me feel naked.

MARIE (*Laughs*)   I can't keep her out of her own house, can
I?

TURK   Didn't she ever see a man before?

MARIE   Not a big beautiful man like you, Turky.
  (TURK *smiles, is flattered by any recognition of his physical
worth, takes it as an immediate invitation to lovemaking.
Pulling her up, he kisses her as* DOC *comes up on porch.*
MARIE *pushes* TURK *away*) Turk, get back in your corner.
  (DOC *comes in from outside*)

DOC (*Cheerily*)   Hi, everyone.

MARIE   Hi.

TURK   Hi, Doc. (DOC *then sees* TURK, *feels immediate resentment. Goes into kitchen to* LOLA) What's goin' on here?

LOLA (*Getting cups*)   Oh, hello, Daddy. Marie's doin' a
drawin'.

DOC (*Trying to size up the situation.* MARIE *and* TURK *are too
busy to speak*)   Oh.

LOLA   I've just heated up the coffee, want some?

DOC Yeah. What happened to Turk's clothes?

LOLA Marie's doing some drawings for her *life* class, Doc.

DOC Can't she draw him with his clothes on?

LOLA (*With coffee. Very professional now*) No, Doc, it's not the same. See, it's a *life* class. They draw bodies. They all do it, right in the classroom.

DOC Why, Marie's just a young girl; she shouldn't be drawing things like that. I don't care if they do teach it at college. It's not right.

LOLA (*Disclaiming responsibility*) I don't know, Doc.

TURK (*Turns*) I'm tired.

MARIE (*Squats at his feet*) Just let me finish the foot.

DOC Why doesn't she draw something else, a bowl of flowers or a cathedral . . . or a sunset?

LOLA All she told me, Doc, was if she made a good drawing of Turk, they'd use it for the posters for the Spring Relays. (*Pause*) So I guess they don't want sunsets.

DOC What if someone walked into the house now? What would they think?

LOLA Daddy, Marie just asked me if it was all right if Turk came and posed for her. Now that's all she said, and I said O.K. But if you think it's wrong I won't let them do it again.

DOC I just don't like it.

MARIE Hold it a minute more.

TURK O.K.

LOLA Well, then you speak to Marie about it if . . .

DOC (*He'd never mention anything disapprovingly to* MARIE) No, Baby. I couldn't do that.

LOLA Well, then . . .

DOC Besides, it's not her fault. If those college people make her do drawings like that, I suppose she has to do them. I just don't think it's right she should have to, that's all.

LOLA Well, if you think it's wrong . . .

DOC (*Ready to dismiss it*) Never mind.

LOLA I don't see any harm in it, Daddy.

DOC Forget it.

LOLA (*Goes to icebox*)   Would you like some buttermilk?

DOC   Thanks.
   (MARIE *finishes sketch*)

MARIE   O.K. That's all I can do for today.

TURK   Is there anything I can do for *you?*

MARIE   Yes—get your clothes on.

TURK   O.K., coach.
   (TURK *exits*)

LOLA   You know what Marie said, Doc? She said that the women pose naked, but the men don't.

DOC   Why, of course, honey.

LOLA   Why is that?

DOC (*Stumped*)   Well . . .

LOLA   If it's all right for a woman it oughta be for a man. But the man always keeps covered. That's what she said.

DOC   Well, that's the way it should be, honey. A man, after all, is a man, and he . . . well, he has to protect himself.

LOLA   And a woman doesn't?

DOC   It's different, honey.

LOLA   Is it? I've got a secret, Doc. Bruce is comin'.

DOC   Is that so?

LOLA (*After a glum silence*)   You know Marie's boy friend from Cincinnati. I promised Marie a long time ago, when her fiancé came to town, dinner was on me. So I'm getting out the best china and cooking the best meal you ever sat down to.

DOC   When did she get the news?

LOLA   The telegram came this morning.

DOC   That's fine. That Bruce sounds to me like just the fellow for her. I think I'll go in and congratulate her.

LOLA (*Nervous*)   Not now, Doc.

DOC   Why not?

LOLA   Well, Turk's there. It might make him feel embarrassed.

DOC   Well, why doesn't Turk clear out now that Bruce is

coming? What's he hanging around for? She's engaged to marry Bruce, isn't she?

(TURK *enters from bedroom and goes to* MARIE, *starting to make advances*)

LOLA   Marie's just doing a picture of him, Doc.

DOC   You always stick up for him. You encourage him.

LOLA   Shhh, Daddy. Don't get upset.

DOC   (*Very angrily*)   All right, but if anything happens to the girl I'll never forgive you.

(DOC *goes upstairs.* TURK *then grabs* MARIE, *kisses her passionately*)

CURTAIN

SCENE: *The same evening, after supper. Outside it is dark. There has been an almost miraculous transformation of the entire house.* LOLA, *apparently, has been working hard and fast all day. The rooms are spotlessly clean and there are such additions as new lampshades, fresh curtains, etc. In the kitchen all the enamel surfaces glisten, and piles of junk that have lain around for months have been disposed of.* LOLA *and* DOC *are in the kitchen, he washing up the dishes and she puttering around putting the finishing touches on her house-cleaning.*

LOLA (*At stove*) There's still some beans left. Do you want them, Doc?

DOC I had enough.

LOLA I hope you got enough to eat tonight, Daddy. I been so busy cleaning I didn't have time to fix you much.

DOC I wasn't very hungry.

LOLA (*At table, cleaning up*) You know what? Mrs. Coffman said I could come over and pick all the lilacs I wanted for my centerpiece tomorrow. Isn't that nice? I don't think she poisoned Little Sheba, do you?

DOC I never did think so, Baby. Where'd you get the new curtains?

LOLA I went out and bought them this afternoon. Aren't they pretty? Be careful of the woodwork, it's been varnished.

DOC How come, honey?

LOLA (*Gets broom and dustpan from closet*) Bruce is comin'. I figured I had to do my spring house-cleaning some time.

DOC You got all this done in one day? The house hasn't looked like this in years.

LOLA I can be a good housekeeper when I want to be, can't I, Doc?

DOC (*Holding dustpan for* LOLA)   I never had any complaints. Where's Marie now?

LOLA   I don't know, Doc. I haven't seen her since she left here this morning with Turk.

DOC (*With a look of disapproval*)   Marie's too nice to be wasting her time with him.

LOLA   Daddy, Marie can take care of herself. Don't worry. (*Returns broom to closet*)

DOC (*Goes into living room*)   'Bout time for Fibber McGee and Molly.

LOLA (*Untying apron. Goes to closet and then back door*) Daddy, I'm gonna run over to Mrs. Coffman's and see if she's got any silver polish. I'll be right back. (DOC *goes to radio.* LOLA *exits. At the radio* DOC *starts twisting the dial. He rejects one noisy program after another, then very unexpectedly he comes across a rendition of Schubert's famous "Ave Maria," sung in a high soprano voice. Probably he has encountered the piece before somewhere, but it is now making its first impression on him. Gradually he is transported into a world of ethereal beauty which he never knew existed. He listens intently. The music has expressed some ideal of beauty he never fully realized and he is even a little mystified. Then* LOLA *comes in the back door, letting it slam, breaking the spell, and announcing in a loud, energetic voice*) Isn't it funny? I'm not a bit tired tonight. You'd think after working so hard all day I'd be pooped.

DOC (*In the living room; he cringes*)   Baby, don't use that word.

LOLA (*To* DOC *on couch. Sets silver polish down and joins* DOC)   I'm sorry, Doc. I hear Marie and Turk say it all the time, and I thought it was kinda cute.

DOC   It . . . it sounds vulgar.

LOLA (*Kisses* DOC)   I won't say it again, Daddy. Where's Fibber McGee?

DOC   Not quite time yet.

LOLA   Let's get some peppy music.

DOC (*Tuning in a sentimental dance band*)   That what you want?

LOLA   That's O.K. (DOC *takes a pack of cards off radio and starts shuffling them, very deftly*)   I love to watch you shuffle cards, Daddy. You use your hands so gracefully. (*She watches closely*) Do me one of your card tricks.

DOC   Baby, you've seen them all.

LOLA   But I never get tired of them.

DOC   O.K. Take a card. (LOLA *does*) Keep it now. Don't tell me what it is.

LOLA   I won't.

DOC   (*Shuffling cards again*)   Now put it back in the deck. I won't look. (*He closes his eyes*)

LOLA   (*With childish delight*)   All right.

DOC   Put it back.

LOLA   Uh-huh.

DOC   O.K. (*Shuffles cards again, cutting them, taking top half off, exposing* LOLA'S *card, to her astonishment*) That your card?

LOLA   (*Unbelievingly*)   Daddy, how did you do it?

DOC   Baby, I've pulled that trick on you dozens of times.

LOLA   But I never understand how you do it.

DOC   Very simple.

LOLA   Docky, show me how you do that.

DOC   (*You can forgive him a harmless feeling of superiority*) Try it for yourself.

LOLA   Doc, you're clever. I never could do it.

DOC   Nothing to it.

LOLA   There is *too*. Show me how you do it, Doc.

DOC   And give away all my secrets? It's a gift, honey. A magic gift.

LOLA   Can't you give it to me?

DOC   (*Picks up newspaper*)   A man has to keep some things to himself.

LOLA   It's not a gift at all, it's just some trick you *learned*.

DOC   O.K., Baby, any way you want to look at it.

LOLA   Let's have some music. How soon do you have to meet Ed Anderson?
       (DOC *turns on radio*)

DOC   I still got a little time.
(*Pleased*)

LOLA   Marie's going to be awfully happy when she sees the house all fixed up. She can entertain Bruce here when he comes, and maybe we could have a little party here and you can do your card tricks.

DOC   O.K.

LOLA   I think a young girl should be able to bring her friends home.

DOC   Sure.

LOLA   We never liked to sit around the house 'cause the folks always stayed there with us. (*Rises—starts dancing alone*) Remember the dances we used to go to, Daddy?

DOC   Sure.

LOLA   We had awful good times—for a while, didn't we?

DOC   Yes, Baby.

LOLA   Remember the homecoming dance, when Charlie Kettlekamp and I won the Charleston contest?

DOC   Please, honey, I'm trying to read.

LOLA   And you got mad at him 'cause he thought he should take me home afterwards.

DOC   I did not.

LOLA   Yes, you did— Charlie was all right, Doc, really he was. You were just jealous.

DOC   I *wasn't* jealous.

LOLA   (*She has become very coy and flirtatious now, an old dog playing old tricks*) You got jealous every time we went out any place and I even looked at another boy. There was never anything between Charlie and me; there never was.

DOC   That was a long time ago . . .

LOLA   Lots of other boys called me up for dates . . . Sammy Knight . . . Hand Biderman . . . Dutch McCoy.

DOC   Sure, Baby. You were the "it" girl.

LOLA   (*Pleading for his attention now*) But I saved all my dates for *you*, didn't I, Doc?

DOC   (*Trying to joke*) As far as *I* know, Baby.

LOLA (*Hurt*) Daddy, I did. You *got* to believe that. I never took a date with any other boy but you.

DOC (*A little weary and impatient*) That's all forgotten now. (*Turns off radio*)

LOLA How can you talk that way, Doc? That was the happiest time of our lives. I'll never forget it.

DOC (*Disapprovingly*) Honey!

LOLA (*At the window*) That was a nice spring. The trees were so heavy and green and the air smelled so sweet. Remember the walks we used to take, down to the old chapel, where it was so quiet and still?
(*Sits on couch*)

DOC In the spring a young man's fancy turns . . . pretty fancy.

LOLA (*In the same tone of reverie*) I was pretty then, wasn't I, Doc? Remember the first time you kissed me? You were scared as a young girl, I believe, Doc; you trembled so. (*She is being very soft and delicate. Caught in the reverie, he chokes a little and cannot answer*) We'd been going together all year and you were always so shy. Then for the first time you grabbed me and kissed me. Tears came to your eyes, Doc, and you said you'd love me forever and ever. Remember? You said . . . if I didn't marry you, you wanted to die . . . I remember 'cause it scared me for anyone to say a thing like that.

DOC (*In a repressed tone*) Yes, Baby.

LOLA And when the evening came on, we stretched out on the cool grass and you kissed me all night long.

DOC (*Opens doors*) Baby, you've got to forget those things. That was twenty years ago.

LOLA I'll soon be forty. Those years have just vanished— vanished into thin air.

DOC Yes.

LOLA Just disappeared—like Little Sheba. (*Pause*) Maybe you're sorry you married me now. You didn't know I was going to get old and fat and sloppy . . .

DOC Oh, Baby!

LOLA It's the truth. That's what I am. But I didn't know it, either. Are you sorry you married me, Doc?

DOC   Of course not.

LOLA   I mean, are you sorry you *had* to marry me?

DOC   (*Goes to porch*)   We were never going to talk about that, Baby.

LOLA   (*Following* DOC *out*)   You *were* the first one, Daddy, the *only* one. I'd just die if you didn't believe that.

DOC   (*Tenderly*)   I know, Baby.

LOLA   You were so nice and so proper, Doc; I thought nothing we could do together could ever be wrong—or make us unhappy. Do you think we did wrong, Doc?

DOC   (*Consoling*)   No, Baby, of course I don't.

LOLA   I don't think anyone knows about it except my folks, do you?

DOC   Of course not, Baby.

LOLA   (*Follows him in*)   I wish the baby had lived, Doc. I don't think that woman knew her business, do you, Doc?

DOC   I guess not.

LOLA   If we'd gone to a doctor, she would have lived, don't you think?

DOC   Perhaps.

LOLA   A doctor wouldn't have known we'd just got married, would he? Why were we so afraid?

DOC   (*Sits on couch*)   We were just kids. Kids don't know how to look after things.

LOLA   (*Sits on couch*)   If we'd had the baby she'd be a young girl now; then maybe you'd have *saved* your money, Doc, and she could be going to college—like Marie.

DOC   Baby, what's done is done.

LOLA   It must make you feel bad at times to think you had to give up being a doctor and to think you don't have any money like you used to.

DOC   No . . . no, Baby. We should never feel bad about what's past. What's in the past can't be helped. You . . . you've got to forget it and live for the present. If you can't forget the past, you stay in it and never get out. I might be a big M.D. today, instead of a chiropractor; we might have had a family to raise and be with us now; I might still have a lot of money if I'd used my head and invested it carefully, instead of gettin' drunk every night. We might have a nice house, and comforts, and friends. But we don't have any of those things. So what! We gotta keep on living, don't we? I can't stop just 'cause I made a few mistakes. I gotta keep goin' . . . somehow.

LOLA   Sure, Daddy.

DOC (*Sighs and wipes brow*) I . . . I wish you wouldn't ask me questions like that, Baby. Let's not talk about it any more. I gotta keep goin', and not let things upset me, or . . . or . . . *I* saw enough at the City Hospital to keep me sober for a long time.

LOLA   I'm sorry, Doc. I didn't mean to upset you.

DOC   I'm not upset.

LOLA   What time'll you be home tonight?

DOC   'Bout eleven o'clock.

LOLA   I wish you didn't have to go tonight. I feel kinda lonesome.

DOC   Ya, so am I, Baby, but some time soon, we'll go *out* together. I kinda hate to go to those night clubs and places since I stopped drinking, but some night I'll take you out to dinner.

LOLA   Oh, will you, Daddy?

DOC   We'll get dressed up and go to the Windermere and have a fine dinner and dance between courses.

LOLA (*Eagerly*) Let's do, Daddy. I got a little money saved up. I got about forty dollars out in the kitchen. We can take that if you need it.

DOC   I'll have plenty of money the first of the month.

LOLA (*She has made a quick response to the change of mood, seeing a future evening of carefree fun*) What are we sitting round here so serious for? (*Turns to radio*) Let's have some music. (LOLA *gets a lively fox trot on the radio, dances with* DOC. *They begin dancing vigorously as though to dispense with the sadness of the preceding dialogue, but slowly it winds them and leaves* LOLA *panting*) We oughta go dancing . . . all the time, Docky . . . It'd be good for us. Maybe if I danced more often, I'd lose . . . some of . . . this fat. I remember . . . I used to be able to dance like this . . . all night . . . and not even

notice . . . it. (LOLA *breaks into a Charleston routine as
of yore*) Remember the Charleston, Daddy?
(DOC *is clapping his hands in rhythm. Then* MARIE *bursts in
through the front door, the personification of the youth that
LOLA is trying to recapture*)

DOC   Hi, Marie.

MARIE   What are you trying to do, a jig, Mrs. Delaney?
(MARIE *doesn't intend her remark to be cruel, but it wounds
LOLA. LOLA stops abruptly in her dancing, losing all the fun
she has been able to create for herself. She feels she might
cry; so to hide her feelings she hurries quietly out to kitchen,
but DOC and MARIE do not notice. MARIE notices the change
in atmosphere*) Hey, what's been happening around here?

DOC   Lola got to feeling industrious. You oughta see the
kitchen.

MARIE   (*Running to kitchen, where she is too observant of the
changes to notice LOLA weeping in corner. LOLA, of course,
straightens up as soon as MARIE enters*) What got into you,
Mrs. Delaney? You've done wonders with the house. It
looks marvelous.

LOLA   (*Quietly*)   Thanks, Marie.

MARIE   (*Darting back into living room*)   I can hardly believe
I'm in the same place.

DOC   Think your boy friend'll like it? (*Meaning* BRUCE)

MARIE   (*Thinking of* TURK)   You know how men are. Turk
never notices things like that.
(*Starts into her room blowing a kiss to DOC on her way.
LOLA comes back in, dabbing at her eyes*)

DOC   Turk? (*Marie is gone; he turns to LOLA*) What's the
matter, honey?

LOLA   I don't know.

DOC   Feel bad about something?

LOLA   I didn't want her to see me dancing that way. Makes
me feel sorta silly.

DOC   Why, you're a fine dancer.

LOLA   I feel kinda silly.

MARIE   (*Jumps back into the room with her telegram*)   My
telegram's here. When did it come?

LOLA   It came about an hour ago, honey.

(LOLA *looks nervously at* DOC. DOC *looks puzzled and a little sore*)

MARIE   Bruce is coming! "Arriving tomorrow five P.M. CST, Flight twenty-two, Love, Bruce." When did the telegram come?

DOC   (*Looking hopelessly at* LOLA)   So it came an hour ago.

LOLA   (*Nervously*)   Isn't it nice I got the house all cleaned? Marie, you bring Bruce to dinner with us tomorrow night. It'll be a sort of wedding present.

MARIE   That would be wonderful, Mrs. Delaney, but I don't want you to go to any trouble.

LOLA   No trouble at all. Now I insist. (*Front doorbell rings*) That must be Turk.

MARIE   (*Whisper*)   Don't tell *him*. (*Goes to door.* LOLA *scampers to kitchen,* DOC *after her*) Hi, Turk. Come on in.

TURK   (*Entering. Stalks her*)   Hi.
(*Looks around to see if anyone is present, then takes her in his arms and starts to kiss her*)

LOLA   I'm sorry, Doc. I'm sorry about the telegram.

DOC   Baby, people don't do things like that. Don't you understand? *Nice* people don't.

MARIE   Stop it!

TURK   What's the matter?

MARIE   They're in the kitchen.
(TURK *sits with book*)

DOC   Why didn't you give it to her when it came?

LOLA   Turk was posing for Marie this morning and I couldn't give it to her while he was here.
(TURK *listens at door*)

DOC   Well, it just isn't nice to open other people's mail.
(TURK *goes to* MARIE'S *door*)

LOLA   I guess I'm not nice then. That what you mean?

MARIE   Turk, will you get away from that door?

DOC   No, Baby, but . . .

LOLA   I don't see any harm in it, Doc. I steamed it open and sealed it back. (TURK *at switch in living room*) She'll never know the difference. I don't see any harm in that, Doc.

DOC (*Gives up*)   O.K., Baby, if you don't see any harm in it, I guess I can't explain it.
(*Starts getting ready to go*)

LOLA   I'm sorry, Doc. Honest, I'll never do it again. Will you forgive me?

DOC (*Giving her a peck of a kiss*)   I forgive you.

MARIE (*Comes back with book*)   Let's look like we're studying.

TURK   Biology? Hot dog!

LOLA (*After* MARIE *leaves her room*)   Now I feel better. Do you have to go now?
(TURK *sits by* MARIE *on the couch*)

DOC   Yah.

LOLA   Before you go, why don't you show your tricks to Marie?

DOC (*Reluctantly*)   Not now.

LOLA   Oh, please do. They'd be crazy about them.

DOC (*With pride*)   O.K. (*Preens himself a little*) If you think they'd enjoy them . . . (LOLA, *starting to living room, stops suddenly upon seeing* MARIE *and* TURK *spooning behind a book. A broad, pleased smile breaks on her face and she stands silently watching.* DOC *is at sink*) Well . . . what's the matter, Baby?

LOLA (*In a soft voice*)   Oh . . . nothing . . . nothing . . . Doc.

DOC   Well, do you want me to show 'em my tricks or don't you?

LOLA (*Coming back to center kitchen; in a secretive voice with a little giggle*)   I guess they wouldn't be interested now.

DOC (*With injured pride. A little sore*)   Oh, very well.

LOLA   Come and look, Daddy.

DOC (*Shocked and angry*)   No!

LOLA   Just one little look. They're just kids, Daddy. It's sweet.
(*Drags him by arm*)

DOC (*Jerking loose*)   Stop it, Baby. I won't do it. It's not decent to snoop around spying on people like that. It's cheap and mischievous and mean.

LOLA (*This had never occurred to her*)   Is it?

DOC   Of course it is.

LOLA   I don't spy on Marie and Turk to be mischievous and mean.

DOC   Then why *do* you do it?

LOLA   You watch young people make love in the movies, don't you, Doc? There's nothing wrong with that. And I *know* Marie and I like her, and Turk's nice, too. They're both so young and pretty. Why shouldn't I watch them?

DOC   I give up.

LOLA   Well, why shouldn't I?

DOC   I don't know, Baby, but it's not nice.
(TURK *kisses* MARIE'S *ear*)

LOLA (*Plaintive*)   I think it's one of the nicest things I know.

MARIE   Let's go out on the porch.
(*They steal out*)

DOC   It's not right for Marie to do that, particularly since Bruce is coming. We shouldn't allow it.

LOLA   Oh, they don't do any harm, Doc. I think it's all right.
(TURK *and* MARIE *go to porch*)

DOC   It's not all right. I don't know why you encourage that sort of thing.

LOLA   I don't encourage it.

DOC   You do, too. You like that fellow Turk. You said so. And I say he's no good. Marie's sweet and innocent; she doesn't understand guys like him. I think I oughta run him outa the house.

LOLA   Daddy, you wouldn't do that.

DOC (*Very heated*)   Then you talk to her and tell her how we feel.

LOLA   Hush, Daddy. They'll hear you.

DOC   I don't care if they do hear me.

LOLA (*To* DOC *at stove*)   Don't get upset, Daddy. Bruce is coming and Turk won't be around any longer. I promise you.

DOC   All right. I better go.

LOLA   I'll go with you, Doc. Just let me run up and get a sweater. Now wait for me.

DOC   Hurry, Baby.
(LOLA *goes upstairs.* DOC *is at platform when he hears* TURK *laugh on the porch.* DOC *sees whiskey bottle. Reaches for it and hears* MARIE *giggle. Turns away as* TURK *laughs again. Turns back to the bottle and hears* LOLA'S *voice from upstairs*)

LOLA   I'll be there in a minute, Doc. (*Enters downstairs*) I'm all ready. (DOC *turns out kitchen lights and they go into living room*) I'm walking Doc down to the bus. (DOC *sees* TURK *with* LOLA'S *picture. Takes it out of his hand, puts it on shelf as* LOLA *leads him out.* DOC *is offstage*) Then I'll go for a long walk in the moonlight. Have a good time. (*She exits*)

MARIE   'Bye, Mrs. Delaney.
(*Exits*)

TURK   He hates my guts.
(*Goes to front door*)

MARIE   Oh, he does not.
(*Follows* TURK, *blocks his exit in door*)

TURK   Yes, he does. If you ask me, he's jealous.

MARIE   Jealous?

TURK   I've always thought he had a crush on you.

MARIE   Now, Turk, don't be silly. Doc is nice to me. It's just in a few little things he does, like fixing my breakfast, but he's nice to everyone.

TURK   He ever make a pass?

MARIE   No. He'd never get fresh.

TURK   He better not.

MARIE   Turk, don't be ridiculous. Doc's such a nice, quiet man; if he gets any fun out of being nice to me, why not?

TURK   He's got a wife of his own, hasn't he? Why doesn't he make a few passes at her?

MARIE   Things like that are none of our business.

TURK   O.K. How about a snuggle, lovely?

MARIE   (*A little prim and businesslike*)   No more for to-night, Turk.

TURK   Why's tonight different from any other night?

MARIE   I think we should make it a rule, every once in a while, just to sit and talk.
(*Starts to sit on couch, but goes to chair*)

TURK   (*Restless, sits on couch*)   O.K. What'll we talk about?

MARIE   Well . . . there's lotsa things.

TURK   O.K. Start in.

MARIE   A person doesn't start a conversation that way.

TURK   Start it any way you want to.

MARIE   Two people should have something to talk about, like politics or psychology or religion.

TURK   How 'bout sex?

MARIE   Turk!

TURK   (*Chases her around couch*)   Have you read the Kinsey Report, Miss Buckholder?

MARIE   I should say not.

TURK   How old were you when you had your first affair, Miss Buckholder? And did you ever have relations with your grandfather?

MARIE   Turk, stop it.

TURK   You wanted to talk about something; I was only trying to please. Let's have a kiss.

MARIE   Not tonight.

TURK   Who you savin' it up for?

MARIE   Don't talk that way.

TURK   (*Gets up, yawns*)   Well, thanks, Miss Buckholder, for a nice evening. It's been a most enjoyable talk.

MARIE   (*Anxious*)   Turk, where are you going?

TURK   I guess I'm a man of action, Baby.

MARIE   Turk, don't go.

TURK   Why not? I'm not doin' any good here.

MARIE   Don't go.

TURK   (*Returns and she touches him. They sit on couch*) Now why didn't you think of this before? C'mon, let's get to work.

MARIE   Oh, Turk, this is all we ever do.

TURK   Are you complaining?

MARIE   (*Weakly*)   No.

TURK   Then what do you want to put on such a front for?

MARIE   It's not a front.

TURK   What else is it? (*Mimicking*) Oh, no, Turk. Not tonight, Turk. I want to talk about philosophy, Turk. (*Himself again*) When all the time you know that if I went outa
here without givin' you a good lovin' up you'd be sore as
hell . . . Wouldn't you?

MARIE   (*She has to admit to herself it's true; she chuckles*)
Oh . . . Turk . . .

TURK   It's true, isn't it?

MARIE   Maybe.

TURK   How about tonight, lovely; going to be lonesome?

MARIE   Turk, you're in training.

TURK   What of it? I can throw that old javelin any old time,
any old time. C'mon, Baby, we've got by with it before,
haven't we?

MARIE   I'm not so sure.

TURK   What do you mean?

MARIE   Sometimes I think Mrs. Delaney knows.

TURK   Well, bring her along. I'll take care of her, too, if it'll
keep her quiet.

MARIE   (*A pretense of being shocked*)   Turk!

TURK   What makes you think so?

MARIE   Women just sense those things. She asks so many
questions.

TURK   She ever *say* anything?

MARIE   No.

TURK   Now *you're* imagining things.

MARIE   Maybe.

TURK   Well, stop it.

MARIE   O.K.

TURK   (*Follows* MARIE)   Honey, I know I talk awful rough

around you at times; I never was a very gentlemanly bastard, but you really don't mind it . . . do you? (*She only smiles mischievously*) Anyway, you know I'm nuts about you.

MARIE (*Smug*)   Are you?

(*Now they engage in a little rough-house, he cuffing her like an affectionate bear, she responding with "Stop it," "Turk, that hurt," etc. And she slaps him playfully. Then they laugh together at their own pretense. Now* LOLA *enters the back way very quietly, tiptoeing through the dark kitchen, standing by the doorway where she can peek at them. There is a quiet, satisfied smile on her face. She watches every move they make, alertly*)

TURK   Now, Miss Buckholder, what is your opinion of the psychodynamic pressure of living in the atomic age?

MARIE (*Playfully*)   Turk, don't make fun of me.

TURK   Tonight?

MARIE (*Her eyes dance as she puts him off just a little longer*) Well.

TURK   Tonight will never come again. (*This is true. She smiles*) O.K.?

MARIE   Tonight will never come again. . . . (*They embrace and start to dance*) Let's go out somewhere first and have a few beers. We can't come back till they're asleep.

TURK   O.K.

(*They dance slowly out the door. Then* LOLA *moves quietly into the living room and out onto the porch. There she can be heard calling plaintively in a lost voice*)

LOLA   Little Sheba . . . Come back . . . Come back, Little Sheba. Come back.

CURTAIN

ACT TWO | Scene One

SCENE: *The next morning.* LOLA *and* DOC *are at breakfast again.* LOLA *is rambling on while* DOC *sits meditatively, his head down, his face in his hands.*

LOLA (*In a light, humorous way, as though the faults of youth were as blameless as the uncontrollable actions of a puppy. Chuckles*) Then they danced for a while and went out together, arm in arm. . . .

DOC (*Sitting at table, very nervous and tense*) I don't wanta hear any more about it, Baby.

LOLA What's the matter, Docky?

DOC Nothing.

LOLA You look like you didn't feel very good.

DOC I didn't sleep well last night.

LOLA You didn't take any of those sleeping pills, did you?

DOC No.

LOLA Well, don't. The doctors say they're terrible for you.

DOC I'll feel better after a while.

LOLA Of course you will.

DOC What time did Marie come in last night?

LOLA I don't know, Doc. I went to bed early and went right to sleep. Why?

DOC Oh . . . nothing.

LOLA You musta slept if you didn't hear her.

DOC I heard her; it was after midnight.

LOLA Then what did you ask me for?

DOC I wasn't sure it was her.

LOLA What do you mean?

DOC I thought I heard a man's voice.

LOLA Turk probably brought her inside the door.

43

DOC (*Troubled*) I thought I heard someone laughing. A man's laugh . . . I guess I was just hearing things.

LOLA Say your prayer?

DOC (*Gets up*) Yes.

LOLA Kiss me 'bye. (*He leans over and kisses her, then puts on his coat and starts to leave*) Do you think you could get home a little early? I want you to help me entertain Bruce. Marie said he'd be here about five-thirty. I'm going to have a lovely dinner: stuffed pork chops, twice-baked potatoes, and asparagus, and for dessert a big chocolate cake and maybe ice cream . . .

DOC Sounds fine.

LOLA So you get home and help me.

DOC O.K.
(DOC *leaves kitchen and goes into living room. Again on the chair is* MARIE'S *scarf. He picks it up as before and fondles it. Then there is the sound of* TURK'S *laughter, soft and barely audible. It sounds like the laugh of a sated Bacchus.* DOC'S *body stiffens. It is a sickening fact he must face and it has been revealed to him in its ugliest light. The lyrical grace, the spiritual ideal of Ave Maria is shattered. He has been fighting the truth, maybe suspecting all along that he was deceiving himself. Now he looks as though he might vomit. All his blind confusion is inside him. With an immobile expression of blankness on his face, he stumbles into the table above the sofa*)

LOLA (*Still in kitchen*) Haven't you gone yet, Docky?

DOC (*Dazed*) No . . . no, Baby.

LOLA (*In doorway*) Anything the matter?

DOC No . . . no. I'm all right now.
(*Drops scarf, takes hat, exits. He has managed to sound perfectly natural. He braces himself and goes out.* LOLA *stands a moment, looking after him with a little curiosity. Then* MRS. COFFMAN *enters, sticks her head in back door*)

MRS. COFFMAN Anybody home?

LOLA (*On platform*) 'Morning, Mrs. Coffman.

MRS. COFFMAN (*Inspecting the kitchen's new look*) So this is what you've been up to, Mrs. Delaney.

LOLA (*Proud*) Yes, I been busy.

(MARIE'S *door opens and closes.* MARIE *sticks her head out of her bedroom door to see if the coast is clear, then sticks her head back in again to whisper to* TURK *that he can leave without being observed*)

MRS. COFFMAN   Busy? Good Lord, I never seen such activity. What got into you, lady?

LOLA   Company tonight. I thought I'd fix things up a little.

MRS. COFFMAN   You mean you done all this in one day?

LOLA   (*With simple pride*)   I said I been busy.

MRS. COFFMAN   Dear God, you done your spring house-cleaning all in one day.
   (TURK *appears in living room*)

LOLA   (*Appreciating this*)   I fixed up the living room a little, too.

MRS. COFFMAN   I must see it. (*Goes into living room.* TURK *overhears her and ducks back into* MARIE'S *room, shutting the door behind himself and* MARIE) I declare! Overnight you turn the place into something really swanky.

LOLA   Yes, and I bought a few new things, too.

MRS. COFFMAN   Neat as a pin, and so warm and cozy. I take my hat off to you, Mrs. Delaney. I didn't know you had it in you. All these years, now, I been sayin' to myself, "That Mrs. Delaney is a good for nothing, sits around the house all day, and never so much as shakes a dust mop." I guess it just shows, we never really know what people are like.

LOLA   I still got some coffee.

MRS. COFFMAN   Not now, Mrs. Delaney. Seeing your house so clean makes me feel ashamed. I gotta get home and get to work.
   (*Goes to kitchen*)

LOLA   (*Follows*)   I hafta get busy, too. I got to get out all the silver and china. I like to set the table early, so I can spend the rest of the day looking at it.
   (*Both laugh*)

MRS. COFFMAN   Good day, Mrs. Delaney.
   (*Exits. Hearing the screen door slam,* MARIE *guards the kitchen door and* TURK *slips out the front. But neither has counted on* DOC'S *reappearance. After seeing that* TURK *is safe,* MARIE *blows a good-bye kiss to him and joins* LOLA *in*

the kitchen. But DOC *is coming in the front door just as* TURK *starts to go out. There is a moment of blind embarrass-ment, during which* DOC *only looks stupefied and* TURK, *after mumbling an unintelligible apology, runs out. First* DOC *is mystified, trying to figure it all out. His face looks more and more troubled. Meanwhile,* MARIE *and* LOLA *are talking in the kitchen)*

MARIE   Boo!
(*Sneaking up behind* LOLA *at back porch)*

LOLA (*Jumping around)*   Heavens! You scared me, Marie. You up already?

MARIE   Yah.

LOLA   This is Saturday. You could sleep as late as you wanted.

MARIE (*Pouring a cup of coffee)*   I thought I'd get up early and help you.

LOLA   Honey, I'd sure appreciate it. You can put up the table in the living room, after you've had your breakfast. That's where we'll eat. Then you can help me set it.
(DOC *closes door)*

MARIE   O.K.

LOLA   Want a sweet roll?

MARIE   I don't think so. Turk and I had so much beer last night. He got kinda tight.

LOLA   He shouldn't do that, Marie.

MARIE (*Starts for living room)*   Just keep the coffee hot for me. I'll want another cup in a minute. (*Stops on seeing* DOC) Why, Dr. Delaney! I thought you'd gone.

DOC (*Trying to sustain his usual manner)*   Good morning, Marie.
(*But not looking at her)*

MARIE (*She immediately wonders)*   Why . . . why . . . how long have you been here, Doc?

DOC   Just got here, just this minute.

LOLA (*Comes in)*   That you, Daddy?

DOC   It's me.

LOLA   What are you doing back?

DOC I . . . I just thought maybe I'd feel better . . . if I took a glass of soda water . . . .

LOLA I'm afraid you're not well, Daddy.

DOC I'm all right.
(*Starts for kitchen*)

LOLA (*Helping* MARIE *with table*) The soda's on the drainboard. (DOC *goes to kitchen, fixes some soda, and stands a moment, just thinking. Then he sits sipping the soda, as though he were trying to make up his mind about something*) Marie, would you help me move the table? It'd be nice now if we had a dining room, wouldn't it? But if we had a dining room, I guess we wouldn't have you, Marie. It was my idea to turn the dining room into a bedroom and rent it. I thought of lots of things to do for extra money . . . a few years ago . . . when Doc was so . . . so sick. (*They set up table*—LOLA *gets cloth from cabinet*)

MARIE This is a lovely tablecloth.

LOLA Irish linen. Doc's mother gave it to us when we got married. She gave us all our silver and china, too. The china's Havelin. I'm so proud of it. It's the most valuable possession we own. I just washed it. . . . Will you help me bring it in? (*Getting china from kitchen*) Doc was sortuva Mama's boy. He was an only child and his mother thought the sun rose and set in him. Didn't she, Docky? She brought Doc up like a real gentleman.

MARIE Where are the napkins?

LOLA Oh, I forgot them. They're so nice I keep them in my bureau drawer with my handkerchiefs. Come upstairs and we'll get them.
(LOLA *and* MARIE *go upstairs. Then* DOC *listens to be sure* LOLA *and* MARIE *are upstairs, looks cautiously at the whiskey bottle on pantry shelf but manages to resist several times. Finally he gives in to temptation, grabs bottle off shelf, then starts wondering how to get past* LOLA *with it. Finally, it occurs to him to wrap it inside his trench coat which he gets from pantry and carries over his arm.* LOLA *and* MARIE *are heard upstairs. They return to the living room and continue setting table as* DOC *enters from kitchen on his way out*)

LOLA (*Coming downstairs*) Did you ever notice how nice he keeps his fingernails? Not many men think of things like that. And he used to take his mother to church every Sunday.

MARIE (*At table*)   Oh, Doc's a real gentleman.

LOLA   Treats women like they were all beautiful angels. We went together a whole year before he even kissed me. (DOC *comes through the living room with coat and bottle, going to front door*) On your way back to the office now, Docky?

DOC (*His back to them*)   Yes.

LOLA   Aren't you going to kiss me good-bye before you go, Daddy? (*She goes to him and kisses him.* MARIE *catches* DOC's *eye and smiles. Then she exits to her room, leaving door open*) Get home early as you can. I'll need you. We gotta give Bruce a royal welcome.

DOC   Yes, Baby.

LOLA   Feeling all right?

DOC   Yes.

LOLA (*In doorway,* DOC *is on porch*)   Take care of yourself.

DOC (*In a toneless voice*)   Good-bye.
    (*He goes*)

LOLA (*Coming back to table with pleased expression, which changes to a puzzled look, calls to* MARIE)   Now that's funny. Why did Doc take his raincoat? It's a beautiful day. There isn't a cloud in sight.

                                                    CURTAIN

ACT TWO | Scene Two

SCENE: *It is now 5:30. The scene is the same as the preceding except that more finishing touches have been added and the two women, still primping the table, lighting the tapers, are dressed in their best.* LOLA *is arranging the centerpiece.*

LOLA (*Above table, fixing flowers*) I just love lilacs, don't you, Marie? (*Takes one and studies it*) Mrs. Coffman was nice; she let me have all I wanted. (*Looks at it very closely*) Aren't they pretty? And they smell so sweet. I think they're the nicest flower there is.

MARIE They don't last long.

LOLA (*Respectfully*) No. Just a few days. Mrs. Coffman's started blooming just day before yesterday.

MARIE By the first of the week they'll all be gone.

LOLA Vanish . . . they'll vanish into thin air. (*Gayer now*) Here, honey, we have them to spare *now*. Put this in your hair. There. (MARIE *does*) Mrs. Coffman's been so nice lately. I didn't use to like her. Now where could Doc be? He promised he'd get here early. He didn't even come home for lunch.

MARIE (*Gets two chairs from bedroom*) Mrs. Delaney, you're a peach to go to all this trouble.

LOLA (*Gets salt and pepper*) Shoot, I'm gettin' more fun out of it than you are. Do you think Bruce is going to like us?

MARIE If he doesn't, I'll never speak to him again.

LOLA (*Eagerly*) I'm just dying to meet him. But I feel sorta bad I never got to do anything nice for Turk.

MARIE (*Carefully prying*) Did . . . Doc ever say anything to you about Turk . . . and me?

LOLA About Turk and you? No, honey. Why?

MARIE I just wondered.

LOLA What if Bruce finds out that you've been going with someone else?

49

MARIE   Bruce and I had a very businesslike understanding before I left for school that we weren't going to sit around lonely just because we were separated.

LOLA   Aren't you being kind of mean to Turk?

MARIE   I don't think so.

LOLA   How's he going to feel when Bruce comes?

MARIE   He may be sore for a little while, but he'll get over it.

LOLA   Won't he feel bad?

MARIE   He's had his eye on a pretty little Spanish girl in his history class for a long time. I like Turk, but he's not the marrying kind.

LOLA   No! Really?
(LOLA, *with a look of sad wonder on her face, sits on arm of couch. It's been a serious disillusionment*)

MARIE   What's the matter?

LOLA   I . . . I just felt kinda tired.
(*Sharp buzzing of doorbell.* MARIE *runs to answer it*)

MARIE   That must be Bruce. (*She skips to the mirror again, then to door*) Bruce!

BRUCE   How are you, sweetheart?

MARIE   Wonderful.

BRUCE   Did you get my wire?

MARIE   Sure.

BRUCE   You're looking swell.

MARIE   Thanks. What took you so long to get here?

BRUCE   Well, honey, I had to go to my hotel and take a bath.

MARIE   Bruce, this is Mrs. Delaney.

BRUCE   (*Now he gets the cozy quality out of his voice*)   How do you do, ma'am?

LOLA   How d'ya do?

BRUCE   Marie has said some very nice things about you in her letters.

MARIE   Mrs. Delaney has fixed the grandest dinner for us.

BRUCE   Now that was to be my treat. I have a big expense account now, honey. I thought we could all go down to the hotel and have dinner there, and celebrate first with a few cocktails.

LOLA   Oh, we can have cocktails, too. Excuse me, just a minute.
(*She hurries to the kitchen and starts looking for the whiskey.* BRUCE *kisses* MARIE)

MARIE (*Whispers*)   Now, Bruce, she's been working on this dinner all day. She even cleaned the house for you.

BRUCE (*With a surveying look*)   Did she?

MARIE   And Doc's joining us. You'll like Doc.

BRUCE   Honey, are we going to have to stay here the whole evening?

MARIE   We just can't eat and run. We'll get away as soon as we can.

BRUCE   I hope so. I got the raise, sweetheart. They're giving me new territory.
(LOLA *is frantic in the kitchen, having found the bottle missing. She hurries back into the living room*)

LOLA   You kids are going to have to entertain yourselves awhile 'cause I'm going to be busy in the kitchen. Why don't you turn on the radio, Marie? Get some dance music. I'll shut the door so . . . so I won't disturb you.
(LOLA *does so, then goes to the telephone*)

MARIE   Come and see my room, Bruce. I've fixed it up just darling. And I've got your picture in the prettiest frame right on my dresser.
(*They exit and their voices are heard from the bedroom while* LOLA *is phoning*)

LOLA (*At the phone*)   This is Mrs. Delaney. Is . . . Doc there? Well, then, is Ed Anderson there? Well, would you give me Ed Anderson's telephone number? You see, he sponsored Doc into the club and helped him . . . you know . . . and . . . and I was a little worried tonight. . . . Oh, thanks. Yes, I've got it. (*She writes down number*) Could you have Ed Anderson call me if he comes in? Thank you. (*She hangs up. On her face is a dismal expression of fear, anxiety and doubt. She searches flour bin, icebox, closet. Then she goes into the living room, calling to* MARIE *and* BRUCE *as she comes*) I . . . I guess we'll go ahead without Doc, Marie.

MARIE (*Enters from her room*) What's the matter with Doc, Mrs. Delaney?

LOLA Well . . . he got held up at the office . . . just one of those things, you know. It's too bad. It would have to happen when I needed him most.

MARIE Sure you don't need any help?

LOLA Huh? Oh, no. I'll make out. Everything's ready. I tell you what I'm going to do. Three's a crowd, so I'm going to be the butler and serve the dinner to you two young love-birds . . . (*The telephone rings*) Pardon me . . . pardon me just a minute. (*She rushes to phone, closing the door behind her*) Hello? Ed? Have you seen Doc? He went out this morning and hasn't come back. We're having company for dinner and he was supposed to be home early. . . . That's not all. This time we've had a quart of whiskey in the kitchen and Doc's never gone near it. I went to get it tonight. I was going to serve some cocktails. It was *gone*. Yes, I saw it there yesterday. No, I don't think so. . . . He said this morning he had an upset stomach but . . . Oh, would you? . . . Thank you, Mr. Anderson. Thank you a million times. And you let me know when you find out any-thing. Yes, I'll be here . . . yes. (*Hangs up and crosses back to living room*) Well, I guess we're all ready.

BRUCE Aren't you going to look at your present?

MARIE Oh, sure, let's get some scissors.
(*Their voices continue in bedroom*)

MARIE (*Enters with* BRUCE) Mrs. Delaney, we think you should eat with us.

LOLA Oh, no, honey, I'm not very hungry. Besides, this is the first time you've been together in months and I think you should be alone. Marie, why don't you light the candles? Then we'll have just the right atmosphere.
(*She goes into kitchen, gets tomato-juice glasses from ice-box while* BRUCE *lights the candles*)

BRUCE Do we have to eat by candlelight? I won't be able to see.
(LOLA *returns*)

LOLA Now, Bruce, you sit here. (*He and* MARIE *sit*) Isn't that going to be cozy? Dinner for two. Sorry we won't have time for cocktails. Let's have a little music.

(*She turns on the radio and a Viennese waltz swells up as the curtain falls with* LOLA *looking at the young people eating*)

CURTAIN

ACT TWO | Scene Three

SCENE: *Funereal atmosphere. It is about 5:30 the next morn-ing. The sky is just beginning to get light outside, while inside the room the shadows still cling heavily to the cor-ners. The remains of last night's dinner clutter the table in the living room. The candles have guttered down to stubs amid the dirty dinner plates, and the lilacs in the center-piece have wilted.* LOLA *is sprawled on the davenport, sleep-ing. Slowly she awakens and regards the morning light. She gets up and looks about strangely, beginning to show despair for the situation she is in. She wears the same spiffy dress she had on the night before but it is wrinkled now, and her marcelled coiffure is awry. One silk stocking has twisted loose and falls around her ankle. When she is sufficiently awake to realize her situation, she rushes to the telephone and dials a number.*

LOLA (*At telephone. She sounds frantic*) Mr. Anderson? Mr. Anderson, this is Mrs. Delaney again. I'm sorry to call you so early, but I just *had* to. . . . Did you find Doc? . . . No, he's not home yet. I don't suppose he'll come home till he's drunk all he can hold and wants to sleep. . . . I don't know what else to think, Mr. Anderson. I'm scared, Mr. Anderson. I'm awful scared. Will you come right over? . . . Thanks, Mr. Anderson. (*She hangs up and goes to kitchen to make coffee. She finds some left from the night before, so turns on the fire to warm it up. She wanders around vaguely, trying to get her thoughts in order, jumping at every sound. Pours herself a cup of coffee, then takes it to living room, sits and sips it. Very quietly* DOC *enters through the back way into the kitchen. He carries a big bottle of whiskey which he care-fully places back in the pantry, not making a sound, hangs up overcoat, then puts suitcoat on back of chair. Starts to go upstairs. But* LOLA *speaks*) Doc? That you, Doc? (*Then* DOC *quietly walks in from kitchen. He is staggering drunk, but he is managing for a few minutes to appear as though he were perfectly sober and nothing had happened. His steps, however, are not too sure and his eyes are like blurred ink pots.* LOLA *is too frightened to talk. Her mouth is gaping and she is breathless with fear*)

54

DOC   Good morning, honey.

LOLA   Doc! You all right?

DOC   The morning paper here? I wanta see the morning paper.

LOLA   Doc, we don't get a morning paper. *You* know that.

DOC   Oh, then I suppose I'm drunk or something. That what you're trying to say?

LOLA   No, Doc . . .

DOC   Then give me the morning paper.

LOLA   (*Scampering to get last night's paper from console table*)   Sure, Doc. Here it is. Now you just sit there and be quiet.

DOC   (*Resistance rising*)   Why shouldn't I be quiet?

LOLA   Nothin', Doc . . .

DOC   (*Has trouble unfolding paper. He places it before his face in order not to be seen. But he is too blind even to see; he speaks mockingly*)   Nothing, Doc.

LOLA   (*Cautiously, after a few minutes' silence*)   Doc, are you all right?

DOC   Of course, I'm all right. Why shouldn't I be all right?

LOLA   Where you been?

DOC   What's it your business where I been? I been to London to see the Queen. What do you think of that? (*Apparently she doesn't know what to think of it*) Just let me alone. That's all I ask. I'm all right.

LOLA   (*Whimpering*)   Doc, what made you do it? You said you'd be home last night . . . 'cause we were having company. Bruce was here and I had a big dinner fixed . . . and you never came. What was the matter, Doc?

DOC   (*Mockingly*)   We had a big dinner for *Bruce*.

LOLA   Doc, it was for you, too.

DOC   Well . . . I don't want it.

LOLA   Don't get mad, Doc.

DOC   (*Threateningly*)   Where's Marie?

LOLA   I don't know, Doc. She didn't come in last night. She was out with Bruce.

DOC (*Back to audience*) I suppose you tucked them in bed together and peeked through the keyhole and applauded.

LOLA (*Sickened*) Doc, don't talk that way. Bruce is a nice boy. They're gonna get married.

DOC He probably *has* to marry her, the poor bastard. Just 'cause she's pretty and he got amorous one day . . . Just like I had to marry *you*.

LOLA Oh, Doc!

DOC You and Marie are both a couple of sluts.

LOLA Doc, please don't talk like that.

DOC What are you good for? You can't even get up in the morning and cook my breakfast.

LOLA (*Mumbling*) I will, Doc. I will after this.

DOC You won't even sweep the floors, till some bozo comes along to make love to Marie, and then you fix things up like Buckingham Palace or a Chinese whorehouse with perfume on the lampbulbs, and flowers, and the gold-trimmed china *my mother* gave us. We're not going to use these any more. My mother didn't buy those dishes for whores to eat off of.
(*He jerks the cloth off the table, sending the dishes rattling to the floor*)

LOLA Doc! Look what you done.

DOC Look what I *did,* not *done.* I'm going to get me a drink. (*Goes to kitchen*)

LOLA (*Follows to platform*) Oh, no, Doc! You know what it does to you!

DOC You're damn right I know what it does to me. It makes me willing to come home here and look at you, you two-ton old heifer. (*Takes a long swallow*) There! And pretty soon I'm going to have another, then another.

LOLA (*With dread*) Oh, Doc! (LOLA *takes phone.* DOC *sees this, rushes for the butcher-knife from kitchen-cabinet drawer. Not finding it, he gets a hatchet from the back porch*) Mr. Anderson? Come quick, Mr. Anderson. He's back. He's *back!* He's got a hatchet!

DOC God damn you! Get away from that telephone. (*He chases her into living room where she gets the couch between them*) That's right, phone! Tell the world I'm drunk. Tell the whole damn world. Scream your head off, you fat slut. Holler till all the neighbors think I'm beatin' hell outuv you. Where's Bruce now—under Marie's bed? You got all fresh and pretty for him, didn't you? Combed your hair for once—you even washed the back of your neck and put on a girdle. You were willing to harness all that fat into one bundle.

LOLA (*About to faint under the weight of the crushing accusations*) Doc, don't say any more . . . I'd rather you hit me with an ax, Doc. . . . Honest I would. But I can't stand to hear you talk like that.

DOC I oughta hack off all that fat, and then wait for Marie and chop off those pretty ankles she's always dancing around on . . . then start lookin' for Turk and fix him too.

LOLA Daddy, you're talking crazy!

DOC I'm making sense for the first time in my life. You didn't know I knew about it, did you? But I saw him coming outa there, I saw him. You knew about it all the time and thought you were hidin' something . . .

LOLA Daddy, I didn't know anything about it at all. Honest, Daddy.

DOC Then *you're* the one that's crazy, if you think I didn't know. You were running a regular house, weren't you? It's probably been going on for years, ever since we were married.
(*He lunges for her. She breaks for kitchen. They struggle in front of sink*)

LOLA Doc, it's not so; it's not so. You gotta believe me, Doc.

DOC You're lyin'. But none a that's gonna happen any more. I'm gonna fix you now, once and for all. . . .

LOLA Doc . . . don't do that to me. (LOLA, *in a frenzy of fear, clutches him around the neck holding arm with ax by his side*) Remember, Doc. It's *me*, Lola! You said I was the prettiest girl you ever saw. Remember, Doc! It's me! Lola!

DOC (*The memory has overpowered him. He collapses, slowly mumbling*) Lola . . . my pretty Lola.
(*He passes out on the floor.* LOLA *stands now, as though in a trance. Quietly* MRS. COFFMAN *comes creeping in through the back way*)

MRS. COFFMAN (*Calling softly*) Mrs. Delaney! (LOLA

doesn't even hear. MRS. COFFMAN *comes in*) Mrs. Delaney! Here you are, lady. I heard screaming and I was frightened for you.

LOLA   I . . . I'll be all right . . . some men are comin' pretty soon; everything'll be all right.

MRS. COFFMAN   I'll stay until they get here.

LOLA (*Feeling a sudden need*)   Would you . . . would you *please*, Mrs. Coffman?
(*Breaks into sobs*)

MRS. COFFMAN   Of course, lady. (*Regarding* DOC) The doctor got "sick" again?

LOLA (*Mumbling*)   Some men . . . 'll be here pretty soon . . .

MRS. COFFMAN   I'll try to straighten things up before they get here. . . .
(*She rights chair, hangs up telephone and picks up the ax, which she is holding when* ED ANDERSON *and* ELMO HUSTON *enter unannounced. They are experienced AA's. Neatly dressed businessmen approaching middle age*)

ED   Pardon us for walking right in, Mrs. Delaney, but I didn't want to waste a second. (*Kneels by* DOC)

LOLA (*Weakly*)   It's all right. . . .
(*Both men observe* DOC *on the floor, and their expressions hold understanding mixed with a feeling of irony. There is even a slight smile of irony on* ED'S *face. They have developed the surgeon's objectivity*)

ED   Where is the hatchet? (*To* ELMO, *as though appraising* DOC's *condition*) What do you think, Elmo?

ELMO   We can't leave him here if he's gonna play around with hatchets.

ED   Give me a hand, Elmo. We'll get him to sit up and then try to talk some sense into him. (*They struggle with the lumpy body,* DOC *grunting his resistance*) Come on, Doc, old boy. It's Ed and Elmo. We're going to take care of you. (*They seat him at table*)

DOC (*Through a thick fog*)   Lemme alone.

ED   Wake up. We're taking you away from here.

DOC   Lemme 'lone, God damn it.
(*Falls forward, head on table*)

ELMO (*To* MRS. COFFMAN)   Is there any coffee?

MRS. COFFMAN   I think so, I'll see.
(*Goes to stove with cup from drainboard. Lights fire under coffee and waits for it to get heated*)

ED   He's way beyond coffee.

ELMO   It'll help some. Get something hot into his stomach.

ED   If we could get him to eat. How 'bout some hot food, Doc?
(DOC *gestures and they don't push the matter*)

ELMO   City Hospital, Ed?

ED   I guess that's what it will have to be.

LOLA   Where you going to take him?
(ELMO *goes to phone; speaks quietly to City Hospital*)

ED   Don't know. Wanta talk to him first.

MRS. COFFMAN (*Coming in with the coffee*)   Here's the coffee.

ED (*Taking cup*)   Hold him, Elmo, while I make him swallow this.

ELMO   Come on, Doc, drink your coffee.
(DOC *only blubbers*)

DOC (*After the coffee is down*)   Uh . . . what . . . what's goin' on here?

ED   It's me, Doc. Your old friend Ed. I got Elmo with me.

DOC (*Twisting his face painfully*)   Get out, both of you. Lemme 'lone.

ED (*With certainty*)   We're takin' you with us, Doc.

DOC   Hell you are. I'm all right. I just had a little slip. We all have slips. . . .

ED   Sometimes, Doc, but we gotta get over 'em.

DOC   I'll be O.K. Just gimme a day to sober up. I'll be as good as new.

ED   Remember the last time, Doc? You said you'd be all right in the morning and we found you with a broken collarbone. Come on.

DOC   Boys, I'll be all right. Now lemme alone.

ED   How much has he had, Mrs. Delaney?

LOLA I don't know. He had a quart when he left here yesterday and he didn't get home till now.

ED He's probably been through a *couple* of quarts. He's been dry for a long time. It's going to hit him pretty hard. Yah, he'll be a pretty sick man for a few days. (*Louder to* DOC, *as though he were talking to a deaf man*) Wanta go to the City Hospital, Doc?

DOC (*This has a sobering effect on him. He looks about him furtively for possible escape*) No . . . no, boys. Don't take me there. That's a torture chamber. No, Ed. You wouldn't do that to me.

ED They'll sober you up.

DOC Ed, I been there; I've seen the place. That's where they take the crazy people. You can't do that to me, Ed.

ED Well, *you're* crazy, aren't you? Goin' after your wife with a hatchet.
(*They lift* DOC *to his feet.* DOC *looks with dismal pleading in his eyes at* LOLA, *who has her face in her hands*)

DOC (*So plaintive, a sob in his voice*) Honey! Honey! (LOLA *can't look at him. Now* DOC *tries to make a getaway, bolting blindly into the living room before the two men catch him and hold him in front of living-room table*) Honey, don't let 'em take me there. They'll believe *you*. Tell 'em you won't *let* me take a drink.

LOLA Isn't there any place else you could take him?

ED Private sanitariums cost a lotta dough.

LOLA I got forty dollars in the kitchen.

ED That won't be near enough.

DOC · I'll be at the meeting tomorrow night sober as you are now.

ED (*To* LOLA) All the king's horses couldn't keep him from takin' another drink now, Mrs. Delaney. He got himself into this; he's gotta sweat it out.

DOC I won't go to the City Hospital. That's where they take the crazy people.
(*Stumbles into chair*)

ED (*Using all his patience now*) Look, Doc. Elmo and I are your friends. You know that. Now if you don't come along peacefully, we're going to call the cops and you'll have to wear off this jag in the cooler. How'd you like that? (DOC *is as though stunned*) The important thing is for you to get sober.

DOC   I don't wanta go.

ED   The City Hospital or the City Jail. Take your choice. We're not going to leave you here. Come on, Elmo. (*They grab hold of him*)

DOC   (*Has collected himself and now given in*)   O.K., boys. Gimme another drink and I'll go.

LOLA   Oh, no, Doc.

ED   Might as well humor him, ma'am. Another few drinks couldn't make much difference now.
(MRS. COFFMAN *runs for bottle and glass in pantry and comes right back with them. She hands them to* LOLA) O.K., Doc, we're goin' to give you a drink. Take a good one; it's gonna be your last for a long, long time to come. (ED *takes the bottle, removes the cork and gives* DOC *a glass of whiskey.* DOC *takes his fill, straight, coming up once or twice for air. Then* ED *takes the glass from him and hands it to* LOLA. *To* LOLA) They'll keep him three or four days, Mrs. Delaney; then he'll be home again, good as new. (*Modestly*) I . . . I don't want to pry into personal affairs, ma'am . . . but he'll need you then, pretty bad . . . Come on, Doc. Let's go.
(ED *has a hold of* DOC'S *coat sleeve trying to maneuver him. A faraway look is in* DOC'S *eyes, a dazed look containing panic and fear. He gets to his feet*)

DOC   (*Struggling to sound reasonable*)   Just a minute, boys . . .

ED   What's the matter?

DOC   I . . . I wanta glass of water.

ED   You'll get a glass of water later. Come on.

DOC   (*Beginning to twist a little in* ED'S *grasp*)   . . . a glass of water . . . that's all . . .
(*One furious, quick twist of his body and he eludes* ED)

ED   Quick, Elmo.
(ELMO *acts fast and they get* DOC *before he gets away. Then* DOC *struggles with all his might, kicking and screaming like a pampered child,* ED *and* ELMO *holding him tightly to usher him out*)

DOC (*As he is led out*)   Don't let 'em take me there. Don't take me there. Stop them, somebody. Stop them. That's where they take the crazy people. Oh, God, stop them, somebody. Stop them.
(LOLA *looks on blankly while* ED *and* ELMO *depart with* DOC. *Now there are several moments of deep silence*)

MRS. COFFMAN (*Clears up. Very softly*)   Is there anything more I can do for you now, Mrs. Delaney?

LOLA   I guess not.

MRS. COFFMAN (*Puts a hand on* LOLA'S *shoulder*)   Get busy, lady. Get busy and forget it.

LOLA   Yes . . . I'll get busy right away. Thanks, Mrs. Coffman.

MRS. COFFMAN   I better go. I've got to make breakfast for the children. If you want me for anything, let me know.

LOLA   Yes . . . yes . . . good-bye, Mrs. Coffman.
(MRS. COFFMAN *exits.* LOLA *is too exhausted to move from the big chair. At first she can't even cry; then the tears come slowly, softly. In a few moments* BRUCE *and* MARIE *enter, bright and merry.* LOLA *turns her head slightly to regard them as creatures from another planet*)

MARIE (*Springing into room.* BRUCE *follows*)   Congratulate me, Mrs. Delaney.

LOLA   Huh?

MARIE   We're going to be married.

LOLA   Married? (*It barely registers*)

MARIE (*Showing ring*)   Here it is. My engagement ring.
(MARIE *and* BRUCE *are too engrossed in their own happiness to notice* LOLA'S *stupor*)

LOLA   That's lovely . . . lovely.

MARIE   We've had the most wonderful time. We danced all night and then drove out to the lake and saw the sun rise.

LOLA   That's nice.

MARIE   We've made all our plans. I'm quitting school and flying back to Cincinnati with Bruce this afternoon. His mother has invited me to visit them before I go home. Isn't that wonderful?

LOLA   Yes . . . yes, indeed.

MARIE   Going to miss me?

LOLA   Yes, of course, Marie. We'll miss you very much . . .
uh . . . congratulations.

MARIE   Thanks, Mrs. Delaney. (*Goes to bedroom door*)
Come on, Bruce, help me get my stuff. (*To* LOLA) Mrs.
Delaney, would you throw everything into a big box and
send it to me at home? We haven't had breakfast yet. We're
going down to the hotel and celebrate.

BRUCE   I'm sorry we're in such a hurry, but we've got a taxi
waiting.
(*They go into room*)

LOLA   (*Goes to telephone, dials*)   Long-distance? I want to
talk to Green Valley two-two-three. Yes. This is Delmar
one-eight-eight-seven.
(*She hangs up.* MARIE *comes from bedroom, followed by*
BRUCE, *who carries suitcase*)

MARIE   Mrs. Delaney, I sure hate to say good-bye to you.
You've been so wonderful to me. But Bruce says I can
come and visit you once in a while, didn't you, Bruce?

BRUCE   Sure thing.

LOLA   You're going?

MARIE   We're going downtown and have our breakfast, then
do a little shopping and catch our plane. And thanks for
everything, Mrs. Delaney.

BRUCE   It was very nice of you to have us to dinner.

LOLA   Dinner? Oh, don't mention it.

MARIE   (*To* LOLA)   There isn't much time for good-bye now,
but I just want you to know Bruce and I wish you the best
of everything. You and Doc both. Tell Doc good-bye for
me, will you, and remember I think you're both a coupla
peaches.

BRUCE   Hurry, honey.

MARIE   'Bye, Mrs. Delaney! (*She goes out*)

BRUCE   'Bye, Mrs. Delaney. Thanks for being nice to my
girl.
(*He goes out and off porch with* MARIE)

LOLA   (*Waves. The phone rings. She goes to it quickly*)
Hello. Hello, Mom. It's Lola, Mom. How are you? Mom,
Doc's sick again. Do you think Dad would let me come

home for a while? I'm awfully unhappy, Mom. Do you
think . . . just till I made up my mind? . . . All right.
No, I guess it wouldn't do any good for you to come here
. . . I . . . I'll let you know what I decide to do. That's
all, Mom. Thanks. Tell Daddy hello.
(*She hangs up*)

CURTAIN

ACT TWO | Scene Four

SCENE: *It is morning, a week later. The house is neat again.* LOLA *is dusting in the living room as* MRS. COFFMAN *enters.*

MRS. COFFMAN   Mrs. Delaney! Good morning, Mrs. Delaney.

LOLA   Come in, Mrs. Coffman.

MRS. COFFMAN   (*Coming in*)   It's a fine day for the games. I've got a box lunch ready, and I'm taking all the kids to the Stadium. My boy's got a ticket for you, too. You better get dressed and come with us.

LOLA   Thanks, Mrs. Coffman, but I've got work to do.

MRS. COFFMAN   But it's a big day. The Spring Relays . . . All the athletes from the colleges are supposed to be there.

LOLA   Oh, yes. You know that boy, Turk, who used to come here to see Marie—he's one of the big stars.

MRS. COFFMAN   Is that so? Come on . . . do. We've got a ticket for you. . . .

LOLA   Oh, no, I have to stay here and clean up the house. Doc may be coming home today. I talked to him on the phone. He wasn't sure what time they'd let him out, but I wanta have the place all nice for him.

MRS. COFFMAN   Well, I'll tell you all about it when I come home. Everybody and his brother will be there.

LOLA   Have a good time.

MRS. COFFMAN   'Bye, Mrs. Delaney.

LOLA   'Bye.
(MRS. COFFMAN *leaves, and* LOLA *goes into kitchen. The* MAILMAN *comes onto porch and leaves a letter, but* LOLA *doesn't even know he's there. Then the* MILKMAN *knocks on the kitchen door*)

LOLA   Come in.

MILKMAN   (*Entering with armful of bottles, etc.*)   I see you checked the list, lady. You've got a lot of extras.

LOLA   Ya— I think my husband's coming home.
65

MILKMAN (*He puts the supplies on table, then pulls out magazine*) Remember, I told you my picture was going to appear in *Strength and Health*. (*Showing her magazine*) Well, see that pile of muscles? That's me.

LOLA My goodness. You got your picture in a magazine.

MILKMAN Yes, ma'am. See what it says about my chest development? For the greatest self-improvement in a three months' period.

LOLA Goodness sakes. You'll be famous, won't you?

MILKMAN If I keep busy on these bar-bells. I'm working now for "muscular separation."

LOLA That's nice.

MILKMAN (*Cheerily*) Well, good day, ma'am.

LOLA You forgot your magazine.

MILKMAN That's for you.
(*Exits.* LOLA *puts away the supplies in the icebox. Then* DOC *comes in the front door, carrying the little suitcase she previously packed for him. His quiet manner and his serious demeanor are the same as before.* LOLA *is shocked by his sudden appearance. She jumps and can't help showing her fright*)

LOLA Docky!
(*Without thinking, she assumes an attitude of fear.* DOC *observes this and it obviously pains him*)

DOC Good morning, honey.
(*Pause*)

LOLA (*On platform*) Are . . . are you all right, Doc?

DOC Yes, I'm all right. (*An awkward pause. Then* DOC *tries to reassure her*) Honest, I'm all right, honey. Please don't stand there like that . . . like I was gonna . . . gonna . . .

LOLA (*Tries to relax*) I'm sorry, Doc.

DOC How you been?

LOLA Oh, I been all right, Doc. Fine.

DOC Any news?

LOLA I told you about Marie—over the phone.

DOC Yah.

LOLA   He was a very nice boy, Doc. Very nice.

DOC   That's good. I hope they'll be happy.

LOLA   (*Trying to sound bright*)   She said . . . maybe she'd come back and visit us some time. That's what she *said*.

DOC   (*Pause*)   It . . . it's good to be home.

LOLA   Is it, Daddy?

DOC   Yah.
(*Beginning to choke up, just a little*)

LOLA   Did everything go all right . . . I mean . . . did they treat you well and . . .

DOC   (*Now loses control of his feelings. Tears in his eyes, he all but lunges at her, gripping her arms, drilling his head into her bosom*)   Honey, don't ever leave me. *Please* don't ever leave me. If you do, they'd have to keep me down at that place all the time. I don't know what I said to you or what I did, I can't remember hardly anything. But please forgive me . . . please . . . please . . . And I'll try to make everything up.

LOLA   (*There is surprise on her face and new contentment. She becomes almost angelic in demeanor. Tenderly she places a soft hand on his head*)   Daddy! Why, of course I'll never leave you. (*A smile of satisfaction*) You're all I've got. You're all I ever had.
(*Very tenderly he kisses her*)

DOC   (*Collecting himself now.* LOLA *sits beside* DOC)   I . . . I feel better . . . already.

LOLA   (*Almost gay*)   So do I. Have you had your breakfast?

DOC   No. The food there was terrible. When they told me I could go this morning, I decided to wait and fix myself breakfast here.

LOLA   (*Happily*)   Come on out in the kitchen and I'll get you a nice big breakfast. I'll scramble some eggs and . . . You see I've got the place all cleaned up just the way you like it. (DOC *goes to kitchen*) Now you sit down here and I'll get your fruit juice. (*He sits and she gets fruit juice from refrigerator*) I've got bacon this morning, too. My, it's expensive now. And I'll light the oven and make you some toast, and here's some orange marmalade, and . . .

DOC   (*With a new feeling of control*)   Fruit juice. I'll need lots of fruit juice for a while. The doctor said it would restore the vitamins. You see, that damn whiskey kills all the vitamins in your system, eats up all the sugar in your kidneys. They came around every morning and shot vitamins in my arm. Oh, it didn't hurt. And the doctor told me to drink a quart of fruit juice every day. And you better get some candy bars for me at the grocery this morning. Doctor said to eat lots of candy, try to replace the sugar.

LOLA I'll do that, Doc. Here's another glass of this pineapple juice now. I'll get some candy bars first thing.

DOC The doctor said I should have a hobby. Said I should go out more. That's all that's wrong with me. I thought maybe I'd go hunting once in a while.

LOLA Yes, Doc. And bring home lots of good things to eat.

DOC I'll get a big bird dog, too. Would you like a sad-looking old bird dog around the house?

LOLA Of course, I would. (*All her life and energy have been restored*) You know what, Doc? I had another dream last night.

DOC About Little Sheba?

LOLA Oh, it was about everyone and everything. (*In a raptured tone. She gets bacon from icebox and starts to cook it*) Marie and I were going to the Olympics back in our old high school stadium. There were thousands of people there. There was Turk out in the center of the field throwing the javelin. Every time he threw it, the crowd would roar . . . and you know who the man in charge was? It was my father. Isn't that funny? . . . But Turk kept changing into someone else all the time. And then my father disqualified him. So he had to sit on the sidelines . . . and guess who took his place, Daddy? You! You came trotting out there on the field just as big as you please . . .

DOC (*Smilingly*) How did I do, Baby?

LOLA Fine. You picked the javelin up real careful, like it was awful heavy. But you threw it, Daddy, clear, *clear* up into the sky. And it never came down again. (DOC *looks very pleased with himself*. LOLA *goes on*) Then it started to rain. And I couldn't find Little Sheba. I almost went crazy looking for her and there were so many people, I didn't even know where to look. And you were waiting to take me home. And we walked and walked through the slush and mud, and people were hurrying all around us and . . .

and . . . (*Leaves stove and sits. Sentimental tears come to her eyes*) But this part is sad, Daddy. All of a sudden I saw Little Sheba . . . she was lying in the middle of the field . . . dead. . . . It made me cry, Doc. No one paid any attention . . . I cried and cried. It made me feel so bad, Doc. That sweet little puppy . . . her curly white fur all smeared with mud, and no one to stop and take care of her . . .

DOC   Why couldn't *you?*

LOLA   I wanted to, but you wouldn't let me. You kept saying, "We can't stay here, honey; we gotta go on. We gotta go on." (*Pause*) Now, isn't that strange?

DOC   Dreams are funny.

LOLA   I don't think Little Sheba's ever coming back, Doc. I'm not going to call her any more.

DOC   Not much point in it, Baby. I guess she's gone for good.

LOLA   I'll fix your eggs.
(*She gets up, embraces* DOC, *and goes to stove.* DOC *remains at table sipping his fruit juice*)

THE CURTAIN COMES SLOWLY DOWN

☆

Picnic

★

Picnic *was produced by The Theatre Guild and Joshua Logan, at the Music Box Theatre, New York City, on February 19, 1953, with the following cast:*

HELEN POTTS	Ruth McDevitt
HAL CARTER	Ralph Meeker
MILLIE OWENS	Kim Stanley
BOMBER	Morris Miller
MADGE OWENS	Janice Rule
FLO OWENS	Peggy Concklin
ROSEMARY SYDNEY	Eileen Heckart
ALAN SEYMOUR	Paul Newman
IRMA KRONKITE	Reta Shaw
CHRISTINE SCHOENWALDER	Elizabeth Wilson
HOWARD BEVANS	Arthur O'Connell

DIRECTED BY Joshua Logan
SCENERY AND LIGHTING BY Jo Mielziner

Scenes

The action of the play takes place in a small Kansas town in the yard shared by Flo Owens and Helen Potts.

ACT ONE

SCENE: *The action of the play is laid on the porches and in the yards of two small houses that sit close beside each other in a small Kansas town. The house at the right belongs to* MRS. FLORA OWENS, *a widow lady of about forty who lives there with her two young daughters,* MADGE *and* MILLIE. *The audience sees only a section of the house, from the doorstep and the front door extending to the back door, a porch lining all of the house that we see.*

The house at the left is inhabited by MRS. HELEN POTTS, *another but older widow lady who lives with her aged and invalid mother. Just the back of her house is visible, with steps leading up to the back door. Down farther is a woodshed, attached to the house by the roof. The space between woodshed and house forms a narrow passageway leading to the rest of* MRS. POTTS' *property. The yard between the houses is used interchangeably by members of both houses for visiting and relaxation.*

Both houses are humble dwellings built with no other pretension than to provide comfortable shelter for their occupants. The ladies cannot always afford to keep their houses painted, but they work hard to maintain a tidy appearance, keeping the yards clean, watching the flower beds, supplying colorful slip covers for the porch furniture.

Behind the houses is a stretch of picket fence with a gateway leading from the sidewalk into the yard between the houses. Beyond the fence, in the distance, is the panorama of a typical small Midwestern town, including a grain elevator, a railway station, a great silo and a church steeple, all blessed from above by a high sky of innocent blue.

The curtain rises on an empty, sunlit stage. It is early morning in late summer, Labor Day, and autumn has just begun to edge the green landscape with a rim of brown. Dew is still on the landscape and mist rises from the earth in the distance. MRS. POTTS *appears on her back porch, at left. She is a merry, dumpy little woman close to sixty. She comes down the steps and stands before the woodshed, waiting for* HAL CARTER *to follow.* HAL *comes out carrying a basket of trash on his shoulder, an exceedingly handsome, husky youth dressed in T-shirt, dungarees and cowboy boots. In a*

75

past era he would have been called a vagabond, but HAL *to-day is usually referred to as a bum.* MRS. POTTS *speaks to him.*

MRS. POTTS   You just had a big breakfast. Wouldn't you like to rest a while before you go to work?

HAL (*Managing to sound cheerful*)   Work's good for my digestion, ma'am.

MRS. POTTS   Now, stop being embarrassed because you asked for breakfast.

HAL   I never did it before.

MRS. POTTS   What's the difference? We all have misfortune part of the time.

HAL   Seems to me, ma'am, like I have it *lots* of the time.
(*Then they laugh together.* MRS. POTTS *leads him off through the passageway. In a moment,* MILLIE OWENS *bursts out of the kitchen door of the house, right. She is a wiry kid of sixteen, boisterous and assertive, but likable when one begins to understand that she is trying to disguise her basic shyness. Her secret habit is to come outside after breakfast and enjoy her morning cigarette where her mother will not see her. She is just lighting up when* BOMBER, *the newsboy, appears at the back gate and slings a paper noisily against the house. This gives* MILLIE *a chance to assail him*)

MILLIE   Hey, crazy, wanta knock the house down?

BOMBER (*A tough kid about* MILLIE'S *age*)   I don't hear you.

MILLIE   If you ever break a window, you'll hear me.

BOMBER   Go back to bed.

MILLIE   Go blow your nose.

BOMBER (*With a look at the upper window of the house which presumably marks* MADGE'S *room*)   Go back to bed and tell your pretty sister to come out. It's no fun lookin' at you. (MILLIE *ignores him.* BOMBER *doesn't intend to let her*) I'm talkin' to *you*, goonface!

MILLIE (*Jumping to her feet and tearing into* BOMBER *with flying fists*)   You take that back, you ornery bastard. You take that back.

BOMBER (*Laughing, easily warding off her blows*)   Listen to goonface! She cusses just like a man.

MILLIE (*Goes after him with doubled fists*)   I'll kill you, you ornery bastard! I'll *kill* you!

BOMBER (*Dodging her fists*)   Lookit Mrs. Tar-zan! Lookit Mrs. Tar-zan!

MADGE (MADGE *comes out of the back door. She is an unusually beautiful girl of eighteen, who seems to take her beauty very much for granted. She wears sandals and a simple wash dress. She has just shampooed her hair and is now scrubbing her head with a towel*)   Who's making so much noise?

BOMBER (*With a shy grin*)   Hi, Madge!

MADGE   Hi, Bomber.

BOMBER   I hope I didn't wake you, Madge, or bother you or anything.

MADGE   Nothing bothers me.

BOMBER (*Warming up*)   Hey, Madge, a bunch of us guys are chippin' in on a hot rod—radio and everything. I get it every Friday night.

MADGE   I'm not one of those girls that jump in a hot rod every time you boys turn a corner and honk. If a boy wants a date with me, he can come to the door like a gentleman and ask if I'm in.

MILLIE   Alan Seymour sends her flowers every time they go out.

BOMBER (*To* MADGE)   I can't send you flowers, baby—but I can *send* you!

MILLIE   Listen to him braggin'.

BOMBER (*Persisting*)   Lemme pick you up some night after Seymour brings you home.

MADGE (*A trifle haughty*)   That wouldn't be fair to Alan. We go steady.

MILLIE   Don't you know what "steady" means, stupid?

BOMBER   I seen you riding around in his Cadillac like you was a duchess. Why do good-looking girls have to be so stuck on themselves?

MADGE (*Jumps up, furious*)   I'm not stuck on myself! You take that back, Bomber Gutzel!

BOMBER (*Still persisting*)   Lemme pick you up some night!

Please! (MADGE *walks away to evade him but* BOMBER *is close behind her*) We'll get some cans of beer and go down to the river road and listen to music on the radio.

(HAL CARTER *has come on from right and put a rake in the woodshed. He observes the scene between* MADGE *and* BOMBER)

MILLIE (*Laughing at* BOMBER)   Wouldn't that be romantic!

BOMBER (*Grabbing* MADGE'S *arm*)   C'mon, Madge, give a guy a break!

HAL (*To* BOMBER)   On your way, lover boy!

BOMBER (*Turning*)   Who're *you*?

HAL   What's that matter? I'm bigger'n you are.

(BOMBER *looks at* HAL, *feels a little inadequate, and starts off*)

MILLIE (*Calling after* BOMBER)   Go peddle your papers!

(*Gives* BOMBER *a raspberry as he disappears with papers*)

HAL (*To* MILLIE)   Got a smoke, kid? (MILLIE *gives* HAL *a cigarette, wondering who he is*) Thanks, kid.

MILLIE   You workin' for Mrs. Potts?

HAL   Doin' a few jobs in the yard.

MILLIE   She give you breakfast?

HAL (*Embarrassed about it*)   Yah.

MADGE   Millie! Mind your business.

HAL (*Turning to* MADGE, *his face lighting*)   Hi.

MADGE   Hi.

(MADGE *and* HAL *stand looking at each other, awkward and self-conscious.* FLO, *the mother, comes out almost immediately, as though she had sensed* HAL'S *presence.* FLO *carries a sewing basket in one arm and a party dress over the other. She is a rather impatient little woman who has worked hard for ten years or more to serve as both father and mother to her girls. One must feel that underneath a certain hardness in her character there is a deep love and concern for the girls. She regards* HAL *suspiciously*)

FLO   Young man, this is *my* house. Is there something you want?

HAL   Just loafin', ma'am.

FLO   This is a busy day for us. We have no time to loaf.

(*There is a quick glance between* HAL *and* FLO, *as though each sized up the other as a potential threat*)

HAL   You the mother?

FLO   Yes. You better run along now.

HAL   Like you say, lady. It's your house.
(*With a shrug of the shoulders, he saunters off stage*)

FLO   Has Helen Potts taken in another tramp?

MADGE   I don't see why he's a tramp just because Mrs. Potts gave him breakfast.

FLO   I'm going to speak to her about the way she takes in every Tom, Dick and Harry!

MADGE   He wasn't doing any harm.

FLO   I bet he'd like to. (*Sits on the porch and begins sewing on party dress. To* MADGE) Have you called Alan this morning?

MADGE   I haven't had time.

MILLIE   He's coming by pretty soon to take us swimming.

FLO   (*To* MADGE)   Tell him they're expecting a big crowd at the park this evening, so he'd better use his father's influence at the City Hall to reserve a table. Oh, and tell him to get one down by the river, close to a Dutch oven.

MADGE   He'll think I'm being bossy.

FLO   Alan is the kind of man who doesn't mind if a woman's bossy.
(*A train whistle in the distance.* MADGE *listens*)

MADGE   Whenever I hear that train coming to town, I always get a little feeling of excitement—in here.
(*Hugging her stomach*)

MILLIE   Whenever I hear it, I tell myself I'm going to get on it some day and go to New York.

FLO   That train just goes as far as Tulsa.

MILLIE   In Tulsa I could catch another train.

MADGE   I always wonder, maybe some wonderful person is getting off here, just by accident, and he'll come into the dime store for something and see me behind the counter, and he'll study me very strangely and then decide I'm just the person they're looking for in Washington for an important job in the Espionage Department. (*She is carried away*) Or maybe he wants me for some great medical experiment that'll save the whole human race.

FLO   Things like that don't happen in dime stores. (*Changing the subject*) Millie, would you take the milk inside?

MILLIE   (*As she exits into kitchen with milk*)   Awwww.

FLO   (*After a moment*)   Did you and Alan have a good time on your date last night?

MADGE   Uh-huh.

FLO   What'd you do?

MADGE   We went over to his house and he played some of his classical records.

FLO   (*After a pause*)   Then what'd you do?

MADGE   Drove over to Cherryvale and had some barbecue.

FLO   (*A hard question to ask*)   Madge, does Alan ever—make love?

MADGE   When we drive over to Cherryvale we always park the car by the river and get real romantic.

FLO   Do you let him kiss you? After all, you've been going together all summer.

MADGE   Of course I let him.

FLO   Does he ever want to go beyond kissing?

MADGE   (*Embarrassed*)   Mom!

FLO   I'm your mother, for heaven's sake! These things have to be talked about. Does he?

MADGE   Well—yes.

FLO   Does Alan get mad if you—won't?

MADGE   No.

FLO   (*To herself, puzzled*)   He doesn't . . .

MADGE   Alan's not like *most* boys. He doesn't wanta do anything he'd be sorry for.

FLO   Do *you* like it when he kisses you?

MADGE   Yes.

FLO   You don't sound very enthusiastic.

MADGE   What do you expect me to do—pass out every time Alan puts his arm around me?

FLO   No, you don't have to pass out. (*Gives* MADGE *the dress she has been sewing on*) Here. Hold this dress up in front of you. (*She continues*) It'd be awfully nice to be married to Alan. You'd live in comfort the rest of your life, with charge accounts at all the stores, automobiles and trips. You'd be invited by all his friends to parties in their homes and at the country club.

MADGE   (*A confession*)   Mom, I don't feel right with those people.

FLO   Why not? You're as good as they are.

MADGE   I know, Mom, but all of Alan's friends talk about college and trips to Europe. I feel left out.

FLO   You'll get over those feelings in time. Alan will be going back to school in a few weeks. You better get busy.

MADGE   Busy what?

FLO   A pretty girl doesn't have long—just a few years. Then she's the equal of kings and she can walk out of a shanty like this and live in a palace with a doting husband who'll spend his life making her happy.

MADGE   (*To herself*)   I know.

FLO   Because once, *once* she was young and pretty. If she loses her chance then, she might as well throw all her prettiness away.
(*Giving* MADGE *the dress*)

MADGE   (*Holding the dress before her as* FLO *checks length*) I'm only eighteen.

FLO   And next summer you'll be nineteen, and then twenty, and then twenty-one, and then the years'll start going by so fast you'll lose count of them. First thing you know, you'll be forty, still selling candy at the dime store.

MADGE   You don't have to get morbid.

MILLIE   (*Comes out with sketch book, see* MADGE *holding dress before her*)   Everyone around here gets to dress up and go places except me.

MADGE   Alan said he'd try to find you a date for the picnic tonight.

MILLIE   I don't want Alan asking any of these crazy boys in town to take me anywhere.

MADGE   Beggars can't be choosers!

MILLIE   You shut up.

FLO   Madge, that was mean. There'll be dancing at the pavilion tonight. Millie should have a date, too.

MADGE   If she wants a date, why doesn't she dress up and act decent?

MILLIE   'Cause I'm gonna dress and act the way I want to, and if you don't like it you know what you can do!

MADGE   Always complaining because she doesn't have any friends, but she smells so bad people don't want to be near her!

FLO   Girls, don't fight.

MILLIE   (*Ignoring* FLO)   La-de-da! Madge is the pretty one— but she's so dumb they almost had to burn the schoolhouse down to get *her* out of it!
(*She mimics* MADGE)

MADGE   That's not so!

MILLIE   Oh, isn't it? You never would have graduated if it hadn't been for Jumpin' Jeeter.

FLO   (*Trying at least to keep up with the scrap*)   Who's Jumpin' Jeeter?

MILLIE   Teaches history. Kids call him Jumpin' Jeeter 'cause he's so *jumpy* with all the pretty girls in his classes. He was flunking Madge till she went in his room and cried, and said . . . (*Resorting again to mimicry*) "I just don't know what I'll do if I don't pass history!"

MADGE   Mom, she's making that up.

MILLIE   Like fun I am! You couldn't even pass Miss Sydney's course in shorthand and you have to work in the dime store!

MADGE   (*The girls know each other's most sensitive spots*)   You *are* a goon!

FLO   (*Giving up*)   Oh, girls!

MILLIE   (*Furious*)   Madge, you slut! You take that back or I'll kill you!

(*She goes after* MADGE, *who screams and runs onto the porch*)

FLO   Girls! What will the neighbors say!
(MILLIE *gets hold of* MADGE'S *hair and yanks.* FLO *has to intercede*)

MILLIE   No one can call me goon and get by with it!

FLO   You called her worse names!

MILLIE   It doesn't hurt what names I call her! She's pretty, so names don't bother her at all! She's pretty, so nothing else matters.
(*She storms inside*)

FLO   Poor Millie!

MADGE   (*Raging at the injustice*)   All I ever hear is "poor Millie," and poor Millie won herself a scholarship for four whole years of college!

FLO   A girl like Millie can need confidence in other ways.
(*This quiets* MADGE. *There is a silence*)

MADGE   (*Subdued*)   Mom, do you love Millie more than me?

FLO   Of course not!

MADGE   Sometimes you act like you did.

FLO   (*With warmth, trying to effect an understanding*)   You were the first born. Your father thought the sun rose and set in you. He used to carry you on his shoulder for all the neighborhood to see. But things were different when Millie came.

MADGE   How?

FLO   (*With misgivings*)   They were just—different. Your father wasn't home much. The night Millie was born he was with a bunch of his wild friends at the roadhouse.

MADGE   I loved Dad.

FLO   (*A little bitterly*)   Oh, everyone loved your father.

MADGE   Did you?

FLO   (*After a long pause of summing up*)   Some women are humiliated to love a man.

MADGE   Why?

FLO   (*Thinking as she speaks*)   Because—a woman is weak to begin with, I suppose, and sometimes—her love for him

makes her feel—almost helpless. And maybe she fights him
—'cause her love makes her seem so dependent.
(*There is another pause.* MADGE *ruminates*)

MADGE   Mom, what good is it to be pretty?

FLO   What a question!

MADGE   I mean it.

FLO   Well—pretty things are rare in this life.

MADGE   But what good are they?

FLO   Well—pretty things—like flowers and sunsets and rubies
—and pretty girls, too—they're like billboards telling us life
is good.

MADGE   But where do *I* come in?

FLO   What do you mean?

MADGE   Maybe I get tired being looked at.

FLO   Madge!

MADGE   Well, maybe I do!

FLO   Don't talk so selfish!

MADGE   I don't care if I *am* selfish. It's no good just being
pretty. It's no good!

HAL   (*Comes running on from passageway*)   Ma'am, is it all
right if I start a fire?

FLO   (*Jumps to see* HAL)   What?

HAL   The nice lady, she said it's a hot enough day already and
maybe you'd object.

FLO   (*Matter-of-factly*)   I guess we can stand it.

HAL   Thank you, ma'am.
(HAL *runs off*)

FLO   (*Looking after him*)   He just moves right in whether
you want him to or not!

MADGE   I knew you wouldn't like him when I first saw him.

FLO   Do *you?*

MADGE   I don't like him or dislike him. I just wonder what
he's like.
(ROSEMARY SYDNEY *makes a sudden, somewhat cavalier entrance out of the front door. She is a roomer, probably as*

old as FLO *but would never admit it. Her hair is plastered to her head with wave-set and she wears a flowered kimono*)

ROSEMARY   Anyone mind if an old-maid schoolteacher joins their company?

FLO   Sit down, Rosemary.

ROSEMARY   Mail come yet?

FLO   No mail today. It's Labor Day.

ROSEMARY   I forgot. I thought I might be gettin' a letter from that man I met at the high-school picnic last spring. (*A bawdy laugh*) Been wantin' to marry me ever since. A nice fellow and a peck of fun, but I don't have time for any of 'em when they start gettin' serious on me.

FLO   You schoolteachers are mighty independent!
(MILLIE *wanders out of kitchen, reading a book*)

ROSEMARY   Shoot! I lived this long without a man. I don't see what's to keep me from getting *on* without one.

FLO   What about Howard?

ROSEMARY   Howard's just a friend-boy—not a boy friend.
(MADGE *and* MILLIE *giggle at this.* ROSEMARY *sniffs the air*)
I smell smoke.

FLO   Helen Potts is having her leaves burned. Smells kind of good, doesn't it?

ROSEMARY   (*Seeing* HAL *offstage*)   Who's the young man?

FLO   Just another no-good Helen Potts took in.

ROSEMARY   (*Very concerned*)   Mrs. Owens, he's working over there with his shirt off. I don't think that's right in the presence of ladies.

FLO   (*As* MILLIE *runs to look*)   Get away from there, Millie!

MILLIE   (*Returning to doorstep*)   Gee whiz! I go swimming every day and the boys don't have on half as much as he does now.

FLO   Swimming's different!

MILLIE   Madge, can I use your manicure set, just for kicks?

MADGE   If you promise not to get it messy.
(MILLIE *picks up the set and begins to experiment*)

FLO   (*Looking off at* HAL)   Look at him showing off!

ROSEMARY (*Turning away with propriety*) Who does he think is interested?
(*She massages her face*)

FLO (*To* ROSEMARY) What's that you're rubbing in?

ROSEMARY Ponsella Three-Way Tissue Cream. Makes a good base for your make-up.

FLO There was an article in *The Reader's Digest* about some woman who got skin poisoning from using all those face creams.

ROSEMARY Harriett Bristol—she's the American history teacher—she got ahold of some of that beauty clay last winter and it darn near took her skin off. All we girls thought she had leprosy!
(*She manages one more glance back at* HAL)

MILLIE (*Laboring over her manicure*) Madge, how do you do your right hand?

MADGE If you were nicer to people, maybe people would do something nice for *you* some time.

ROSEMARY You got a beau, Millie?

MILLIE No!

ROSEMARY You can't kid me! Girls don't paint their fingernails unless they think some boy is gonna take notice.

FLO Madge, will you try this dress on now, dear?
(MADGE *goes inside with the dress*)

MRS. POTTS (*Appears on her back porch, carrying a bundle of wet laundry*) Flo!

FLO (*Calling back, a noise like an owl*) Hoooo!

MRS. POTTS Are you going to be using the clothesline this morning?

FLO I don't think so.

MRS. POTTS' MOTHER (*An aged and quivering voice that still retains its command, issuing from the upper window of the house, left*) Helen! Helen!

MRS. POTTS (*Calling back*) I'm hanging out the clothes, Mama. I'll be right back.
(*She goes busily off stage through the passageway*)

FLO (*Confidentially to* ROSEMARY) Poor Helen! She told me

sometimes she has to get up *three* times a night to take her
mother to the bathroom.

ROSEMARY   Why doesn't she put her in an old ladies' home?

FLO   None of 'em will take her. She's too mean.

ROSEMARY   She must be mean—if that story is true.

FLO   It *is* true! Helen and the Potts boy *ran off* and got married. Helen's mother caught her that very day and had the
marriage annulled!

ROSEMARY (*With a shaking of her head*)   She's Mrs. Potts in
name only.

FLO   Sometimes I think she keeps the boy's name just to defy
the old lady.
(ALAN'S *car is heard approaching. It stops and the car door
slams*)

MILLIE (*Putting down her book*)   Hi, Alan! (*Jumps up,
starts inside*) Oh, boy! I'm gonna get my suit!

FLO (*Calling after* MILLIE)   See if Madge is decent. (ALAN
comes on downstage, right) Good morning, Alan!

ALAN   Morning, Mrs. Owens . . . Miss Sydney.
(ROSEMARY *doesn't bother to speak, usually affecting in-
difference to men*)

MRS. POTTS (*Coming back on from the passageway*)   Have
you girls seen the handsome young man I've got working
for me?

ROSEMARY   I think it's a disgrace, his parading around, naked
as an Indian.

MRS. POTTS (*Protectingly*)   I *told* him to take his shirt off.

FLO   Helen Potts, I wish you'd stop taking in all sorts of riffraff!

MRS. POTTS   He isn't riffraff. He's been to several colleges.

FLO   College—and he begs for breakfast!

MRS. POTTS   He's working for his breakfast! Alan, he said he
knew you at the university.

ALAN (*With no idea whom she's talking about*)   Who?

MILLIE (*Coming out the front door*)   We going swimming,
Alan?

ALAN   You bet.

FLO   Alan, why don't you go up and see Madge? Just call from the bottom of the stairs.

ALAN   (*Goes inside, calling*)   Hey, Delilah!

FLO   (*Seeing that* MILLIE *is about to follow* ALAN *inside*) Millie!
(MILLIE *gets the idea that* MADGE *and* ALAN *are to be left alone. She sulks*)

ROSEMARY   (*To* FLO, *confidentially*)   Do you think Alan's going to marry Madge?

FLO   (*She's usually a very truthful woman*)   I hadn't thought much about it.

MRS. POTTS   (*After a moment, drying her neck with handkerchief*)   It's so hot and still this time of year. When it gets this way I'd welcome a good strong wind.

FLO   I'd rather wipe my brow than get blown away.

MRS. POTTS   (*Looking off at* HAL, *full of smiling admiration*) Look at him lift that big old washtub like it was so much tissue paper!

MRS. POTTS' MOTHER   (*Offstage, again*)   Helen! Helen!

MRS. POTTS   (*Patient but firm*)   I'm visiting Flo, Mama. You're all right. You don't need me.

FLO   What did you feed him?

MRS. POTTS   Biscuits.

FLO   You went to all that trouble?

MRS. POTTS   He was *so* hungry. I gave him ham and eggs and all the hot coffee he could drink. Then he saw a piece of cherry pie in the icebox and he wanted that, too!

ROSEMARY   (*Laughs bawdily*)   Sounds to me like Mrs. Potts had herself a new boy friend!

MRS. POTTS   (*Rising, feeling injured*)   I don't think that's very funny.

FLO   Helen, come on. Sit down.

ROSEMARY   Shoot, Mrs. Potts, I'm just a tease.

FLO   Sit down, Helen.

MRS. POTTS   (*Still touchy*)   I *could* sit on my own porch, but I hate for the neighbors to see me there all alone.
(MADGE *and* ALAN *come out together,* MADGE *in her new*

dress. They march out hand in hand in a mock ceremony as though they were marching down the aisle)

ROSEMARY (*Consolingly*)   Mrs. Potts, if I said anything to offend you . . .

FLO (*Signals* ROSEMARY *to be quiet, points to* MADGE *and* ALAN)   Bride and groom! Look, everybody! Bride and groom! (*To* MADGE) How does it feel, Madge? (*Laughs at her unconscious joke*) I mean the dress.

MADGE (*Crossing to her mother*)   I love it, Mom, except it's a little tight in places.

MRS. POTTS (*All eyes of admiration*)   Isn't Madge the pretty one!

ALAN (*Turning to* MILLIE)   What are you reading, Millie?

MILLIE   *The Ballad of the Sad Café* by Carson McCullers. It's wonderful!

ROSEMARY (*Shocked*)   Good Lord, Mrs. Owens, you let your daughter read filthy books like that?

FLO   Filthy?

ROSEMARY   Everyone in it is some sort of degenerate!

MILLIE   That's not so!

ROSEMARY   The D.A.R.'s had it banned from the public library.

MRS. POTTS (*Eliminating herself from the argument*)   I don't read much.

FLO   Millie, give me that book!

MILLIE (*Tenaciously*)   No!

ALAN   Mrs. Owens, I don't wanta interfere, but that book is on the reading list at college. For the course in the modern novel.

FLO (*Full of confusion*)   Oh, dear! What's a person to believe?
(ALAN'S *word about such matters is apparently final*)

ROSEMARY   Well, those college professors don't have any morals!
(MILLIE *and* ALAN *shake hands*)

FLO   Where Millie comes by her tastes, I'll never know.

MADGE (*As* FLO *inspects her dress*)   Some of the pictures she has over her bed *scare* me.

MILLIE   Those pictures are by Picasso, and he's a great artist.

MADGE   A woman with seven eyes. Very pretty.

MILLIE (*Delivering her ultimatum*)   Pictures don't have to be *pretty!*
(*A sudden explosion from* MRS. POTTS' *backyard. The women are startled*)

FLO   Helen!

MRS. POTTS (*Jumping up, alarmed*)   I'll go see what it is.

FLO   Stay here! He must have had a gun!

VOICE OFF STAGE   Helen! Helen!

FLO (*Grabbing* MRS. POTTS' *arm*)   Don't go over there, Helen! Your mother's old. She has to go soon anyway!

MRS. POTTS (*Running off stage*)   Pshaw! I'm not afraid.

ALAN (*Looking off at* HAL)   Who did that guy say he was?
(*No one hears* ALAN)

MRS. POTTS (*Coming back and facing* FLO)   I was a bad girl.

FLO   What *is* it, Helen?

MRS. POTTS   I threw the *new* bottle of cleaning fluid into the trash.

FLO   You're the limit! Come on, Madge, let's finish that dress.
(FLO *and* MADGE *go into the house.* ROSEMARY *looks at her watch and then goes into the house also*)

MRS. POTTS   Come help me, Millie. The young man ran into the clothesline.
(*She and* MILLIE *hurry off stage.* ALAN *stands alone, trying to identify* HAL, *who comes on from* MRS. POTTS'. HAL *is bare-chested now, wearing his T-shirt wrapped about his neck.* ALAN *finally recognizes him and is overjoyed at seeing him*)

ALAN   Where did *you* come from?

HAL (*Loud and hearty*)   Kid!

ALAN   Hal Carter!

HAL   I was comin' over to see you a little later.

ALAN (*Recalling some intimate roughhouse greeting from their college days*)   How's the old outboard motor?

HAL (*With the eagerness of starting a game*) Want a ride?

ALAN (*Springing to* HAL, *clasping his legs around* HAL'S *waist, hanging by one hand wrapped about* HAL'S *neck, as though riding some sort of imagined machine*) Gassed up? (*With his fingers, he twists* HAL'S *nose as if it were a starter.* HAL *makes the sputtering noise of an outboard motor and swings* ALAN *about the stage,* ALAN *holding on like a bronco-buster. They laugh uproariously together*) Ahoy, brothers! Who's winkin', blinkin', and stinkin'?
(ALAN *drops to the ground, both of them still laughing uproariously with the recall of carefree college days*)

HAL That used to wake the whole damn fraternity!

ALAN The last time I saw you, you were on your way to Hollywood to become a movie hero.

HAL (*With a shrug of his shoulders*) Oh, that!

ALAN What do you mean, "Oh, that"? Isn't that what I loaned you the hundred bucks for?

HAL Sure, Seymour.

ALAN Well, what happened?

HAL (*He'd rather the subject had not been brought up*) Things just didn't work out.

ALAN I tried to warn you, Hal. Every year some talent scout promised screen tests to all the athletes.

HAL Oh, I got the test okay! I was about to have a big career. They were gonna call me Brush Carter. How d'ya like that?

ALAN Yeah?

HAL Yah! They took a lotta pictures of me with my shirt off. Real rugged. Then they dressed me up like the Foreign Legion. Then they put me in a pair of tights—and they gave me a big hat with a plume, and had me makin' with the sword play. (*Pantomimes a duel*) Touché, mug! (*Returning the sword to its scabbard*) It was real crazy!

ALAN (*A little skeptical*) Did they give you any lines to read?

HAL Yah, that part went okay. It was my teeth.

ALAN Your teeth?

HAL Yah! Out there, you gotta have a certain kind of teeth or they can't use you. Don't ask me why. This babe said they'd have to pull all my teeth and give me new ones, so naturally . . .

ALAN   Wait a minute. What babe?

HAL   The babe that got me the test. She wasn't a babe exactly.
She was kinda beat up—but not bad. (*He sees* ALAN's *critical eye*) Jesus, Seymour, a guy's gotta get along somehow.

ALAN   Uh-huh. What are you doing here?

HAL   (*A little hurt*)   Aren't you glad to see me?

ALAN   Sure, but fill me in.

HAL   Well—after I left Hollywood I took a job on a ranch in
Nevada. You'da been proud of me, Seymour. In bed every
night at ten, up every morning at six. No liquor—no babes.
I saved up two hundred bucks!

ALAN   (*Holding out a hand*)   Oh! I'll take half.

HAL   Gee, Seymour, I wish I had it, but I got rolled.

ALAN   Rolled? *You?*

HAL   (*He looks to see that no one can overhear*)   Yeah, I
was gonna hitchhike to Texas to get in a big oil deal. I got
as far as Phoenix when two babes pull up in this big yellow
convertible. And one of these dames slams on the brakes
and hollers, "Get in, stud!" So I got in. Seymour, it was
crazy. They had a shakerful of martinis right there in the
car!

MRS. POTTS   (*Appears on her porch, followed by* MILLIE. MRS.
POTTS *carries a cake*)   Oh, talking over old times? Millie
helped me ice the cake.

HAL   Any more work, ma'am?

MRS. POTTS   No. I feel I've been more than paid for the
breakfast.

HAL   S'pose there's any place I could wash up?

MILLIE   We got a shower in the basement. Come on, I'll show
you.

ALAN   (*Holding* HAL)   He'll be there in a minute. (MRS. POTTS
and MILLIE *exit into the* OWENS' *house*)   O.K., so they had
a shakerful of martinis!

HAL   And one of these babes was smokin' the weed!

ALAN   (*With vicarious excitement*)   Nothing like that ever
happens to me! Go on!

HAL   Seymour, you wouldn't believe it, the things those two
babes started doin' to me.

ALAN   Were they good-looking?

HAL   What do you care?

ALAN   Makes the story more interesting. Tell me what happened.

HAL   Well, you know *me*, Seymour. I'm an agreeable guy.

ALAN   Sure.

HAL   So when they parked in front of this tourist cabin, I said, "Okay, girls, if I gotta pay for the ride, this is the easiest way I know." (*He shrugs*) But, gee, they musta thought I was Superman.

ALAN   You mean—*both* of them?

HAL   Sure.

ALAN   Golly!

HAL   Then I said, "Okay, girls, the party's over—let's get goin'." Then this dame on the weed, she sticks a gun in my back. She says, "This party's goin' on till *we* say it's over, Buck!" You'da thought she was Humphrey Bogart!

ALAN   Then what happened?

HAL   Finally I passed out! And when I woke up, the dames was gone and so was my two hundred bucks! I went to the police and they wouldn't believe me—they said my whole story was wishful thinking! How d'ya like *that!*

ALAN   (*Thinking it over*)   Mmmm.

HAL   Women are gettin' desperate, Seymour.

ALAN   *Are* they?

HAL   Well, that did it. Jesus, Seymour, what's a poor bastard like me ever gonna do?

ALAN   You don't sound like you had such a hard time.

HAL   I got thinking of you, Seymour, at school—how you always had things under control.

ALAN   Me?

HAL   Yah. Never cut classes—understood the lectures—took notes! (ALAN *laughs*) What's so funny?

ALAN   The hero of the campus, and he envied me!

HAL   Yah! Big hero, between the goal posts. You're the only guy in the whole fraternity ever treated me like a human being.

ALAN (*With feeling for* HAL) I know.

HAL Those other snob bastards always watchin' to see which fork I used.

ALAN You've got an inferiority complex. You imagined those things.

HAL In a pig's eye!

ALAN (*Delicately*) What do you hear about your father?

HAL (*Grave*) It finally happened . . . before I left for Hollywood.

ALAN What?

HAL (*With a solemn hurt*) He went on his last bender. The police scraped him up off the sidewalk. He died in jail.

ALAN (*Moved*) Gee, I'm sorry to hear that, Hal.

HAL The old lady wouldn't even come across with the dough for the funeral. They had to bury him in Pauper's Row.

ALAN What happened to the filling station?

HAL He left it to me in his will, but the old lady was gonna have him declared insane so she could take over. I let her have it. Who cares?

ALAN (*Rather depressed by* HAL's *story*) Gee, Hal, I just can't believe people really do things like that.

HAL Don't let *my* stories cloud up your rosy glasses.

ALAN Why didn't you come to see me, when you got to town?

HAL I didn't want to walk into your palatial mansion lookin' like a bum. I wanted to get some breakfast in my belly and pick up a little change.

ALAN That wouldn't have made any difference.

HAL I was hoping maybe you and your old man, between you, might fix me up with a job.

ALAN What kind of a job, Hal?

HAL What kinda jobs you got?

ALAN What kind of job did you have in mind?

HAL (*This is his favorite fantasy*) Oh, something in a nice office where I can wear a tie and have a sweet little secretary and talk over the telephone about enterprises and things. (*As* ALAN *walks away skeptically*) I've always had the feeling, if I just had the chance, I could set the world on fire.

ALAN   Lots of guys have that feeling, Hal.

HAL   (*With some desperation*)   I gotta get some place in this world, Seymour. I *got* to.

ALAN   (*With a hand on* HAL's *shoulder*)   Take it easy.

HAL   This is a free country, and I got just as much rights as the next fellow. Why can't I get along?

ALAN   Don't worry, Hal. I'll help you out as much as I can. (MRS. POTTS *comes out the* OWENS' *back door*) Sinclair is hiring new men, aren't they, Mrs. Potts?

MRS. POTTS   Yes, Alan. Carey Hamilton needs a hundred new men for the pipeline.

HAL   (*Had dared to hope for more*)   Pipeline?

ALAN   If you wanta be president of the company, Hal, I guess you'll just have to work hard and be patient.

HAL   (*Clenching his fists together, so eager is he for patience*) Yah. That's something I gotta learn. Patience!
(*He hurries inside the* OWENS' *back door now*)

MRS. POTTS   I feel sorry for young men today.

ROSEMARY   (*Coming out the front door, very proud of the new outfit she is wearing, a fall suit and an elaborate hat*)   Is this a private party I'm crashin'?

MRS. POTTS   (*With some awe of* ROSEMARY's *finery*)   My, you're dressed up!

ROSEMARY   'S my new fall outfit. Got it in Kansas City. Paid twenty-two-fifty for the hat.

MRS. POTTS   You schoolteachers do have nice things.

ROSEMARY   And don't have to ask anybody when we wanta get 'em, either.

FLO   (*Coming out back door with* MADGE)   Be here for lunch today, Rosemary?

ROSEMARY   No. There's a welcome-home party down at the hotel. Lunch and bridge for the new girls on the faculty.

MADGE   Mom, can't I go swimming, too?

FLO   Who'll fix lunch? I've got a million things to do.

MADGE   It wouldn't kill Millie if she ever did any cooking.

FLO   No, but it might kill the rest of us.
(*Now we hear the voices of* IRMA KRONKITE *and* CHRISTINE
SCHOENWALDER, *who are coming by for* ROSEMARY. *They
think it playful to call from a distance*)

IRMA   Rosemary! Let's get going, girl! (*As they come into
sight,* IRMA *turns to* CHRISTINE) You'll love Rosemary Sydney. She's a peck of fun! Says the craziest things.

ROSEMARY   (*With playful suspiciousness*)   What're you saying
about me, Irma Kronkite?
(*They run to hug each other like eager sisters who had not
met in a decade*)

IRMA   Rosemary Sydney!

ROSEMARY   Irma Kronkite! How was your vacation?

IRMA   I worked like a slave. But I had fun, too. I don't care
if I *never* get that Masters. I'm not going to be a slave *all*
my life.

CHRISTINE   (*Shyly*)   She's been telling me about all the wicked
times she had in New York—and *not* at Teachers College,
if I may add.

IRMA   (*To* ROSEMARY)   Kid, this is Christine Schoenwalder,
taking Mabel Fremont's place in feminine hygiene. (ROSE-
MARY *and* CHRISTINE *shake hands*) Been a hot summer, Mrs.
Owens?

FLO   The worst I can remember.

MRS. POTTS   (*As* ROSEMARY *brings* CHRISTINE *up on porch*)
Delighted to know you, Christine. Welcome back, Irma.

IRMA   Are you working now, Madge?

MADGE   Yes.

FLO   (*Taking over for* MADGE)   Yes, Madge has been working downtown this summer—just to keep busy. (*Now* HAL
and MILLIE *burst out the kitchen door, engaged in a noisy
and furious mock fist-fight.* HAL *is still bare-chested, his T-
shirt still around his neck, and the sight of him is something
of a shock to the ladies*) Why, when did he . . .

ALAN   (*Seizing* HAL *for an introduction*)   Mrs. Owens, this is
my friend, Hal Carter. Hal is a fraternity brother.

MRS. POTTS   (*Nudging* FLO)   What did I tell you, Flo?

FLO   (*Stunned*)   Fraternity brother! Really? (*Making the best
of it*) Any friend of Alan's is a friend of ours.

(*She offers* HAL *her hand*)

HAL   Glad to make your acquaintance, ma'am.

ALAN   (*Embarrassed for him*)   Hal, don't you have a shirt?

HAL   It's all sweaty, Seymour.
(ALAN *nudges him.* HAL *realizes he has said the wrong thing and reluctantly puts on the T-shirt*)

ROSEMARY   (*Collecting* IRMA *and* CHRISTINE)   Girls, we better get a hustle on.

CHRISTINE   (*To* IRMA)   Tell them about what happened in New York, kid.

IRMA   (*The center of attention*)   I went to the Stork Club!

ROSEMARY   How did *you* get to the Stork Club?

IRMA   See, there was this fellow in my educational statistics class . . .

ROSEMARY   (*Continuing the joke*)   I *knew* there was a *man* in it.

IRMA   Now, girl! It was nothing serious. He was just a good sport, that's all. We made a bet that the one who made the lowest grade on the *final* had to take the other to the Stork Club—and *I* lost!
(*The teachers go off noisily laughing, as* FLO *and* MRS. POTTS *watch them*)

ALAN   (*Calling to* HAL, *at back of stage playing with* MILLIE)   Wanta go swimming, Hal? I've got extra trunks in the car.

HAL   Why not?

MRS. POTTS   (*In a private voice*)   Flo, let's ask the young man on the picnic. He'd be a date for Millie.

FLO   That's right, but . . .

MRS. POTTS   (*Taking it upon herself*)   Young man, Flo and I are having a picnic for the young people. You come, too, and be an escort for Millie.

HAL   Picnic?

MRS. POTTS   Yes.

HAL   I don't think it's right, me bargin' in this way.

MRS. POTTS   Nonsense. A picnic's no fun without lots and lots of young people.

ALAN (*Bringing* HAL *down center*)   Hal, I want you to meet Madge.

MADGE   Oh, we've met already. That is, we *saw* each other.

HAL   Yah, we saw each other.

ALAN (*To* MADGE)   Hal sees every pretty girl.

MADGE (*Pretending to protest*)   Alan.

ALAN   Well, you're the prettiest girl in town, aren't you? (*To* HAL)   The Chamber of Commerce voted her Queen of Neewollah last year.

HAL   I don't dig.

MILLIE   She was Queen of Neewollah. Neewollah is Halloween spelled backwards.

MRS. POTTS (*Joining in*)   Every year they have a big coronation ceremony in Memorial Hall, with all kinds of artistic singing and dancing.

MILLIE   Madge had to sit through the whole ceremony till they put a crown on her head.

HAL (*Impressed*)   Yah?

MADGE   I got awfully tired.

MILLIE   The Kansas City *Star* ran color pictures in their Sunday magazine.

MADGE   Everyone expected me to get real conceited, but I didn't.

HAL   You didn't?

MILLIE   It'd be pretty hard to get conceited about *those* pictures.

MADGE (*Humorously*)   The color got blurred and my mouth was printed right in the middle of my forehead.

HAL (*Sympathetic*)   Gee, that's too bad.

MADGE (*Philosophically*)   Things like that are bound to happen.

MILLIE (*To* HAL)   I'll race you to the car.

HAL (*Starting off with* MILLIE)   Isn't your sister goin' with us?

MILLIE   Madge has to cook lunch.

HAL   Do you mean *she cooks?*

MILLIE   Sure! Madge cooks and sews and does all those things that women do.
(*They race off,* MILLIE *getting a head start through the gate and* HAL *scaling the fence to get ahead of her*)

FLO   (*In a concerned voice*)   Alan!

ALAN   Yes?

FLO   How did a boy like him get into college?

ALAN   On a football scholarship. He made a spectacular record in a little high school down in Arkansas.

FLO   But a fraternity! Don't those boys have a little more . . . breeding?

ALAN   I guess they're *supposed* to, but fraternities like to pledge big athletes—for the publicity. And Hal could have been All-American . . .

MRS. POTTS   (*Delighted*)   All-American!

ALAN   . . . if he'd only studied.

FLO   But how did the other boys feel about him?

ALAN   (*Reluctantly*)   They didn't like him, Mrs. Owens. They were pretty rough on him. Every time he came into a room, the other fellows seemed to *bristle*. I didn't like him either, at first. Then we shared a room and I got to know him better. Hal's really a nice guy. About the best friend I ever had.

FLO   (*More to the point*)   Is he wild?

ALAN   Oh—not really. He just . . .

FLO   Does he drink?

ALAN   A little. (*Trying to minimize*) Mrs. Owens, Hal pays attention to me. I'll see he behaves.

FLO   I wouldn't want anything to happen to Millie.

MADGE   Millie can take care of herself. You pamper her.

FLO   Maybe I do. Come on, Helen. (*As she and* MRS. POTTS *go in through the back door*) Oh, dear, why can't things be simple?

ALAN   (*After* FLO *and* MRS. POTTS *leave*)   Madge, I'm sorry I have to go back to school this fall. It's Dad's idea.

MADGE   I thought it was.

ALAN   Really, Madge, Dad likes you very much. I'm sure he
does.
(*But* ALAN *himself doesn't sound convinced*)

MADGE   Well—he's always very polite.

ALAN   I'll miss you, Madge.

MADGE   There'll be lots of pretty girls at college.

ALAN   Honestly, Madge, my entire four years I never found
a girl I liked.

MADGE   I don't believe that.

ALAN   It's true. They're all so affected, if you wanted a date
with them you had to call them a month in advance.

MADGE   Really?

ALAN   Madge, it's hard to say, but I honestly never believed
that a girl like you could care for me.

MADGE   (*Touched*)   Alan . . .

ALAN   I—I hope you do care for me, Madge.
(*He kisses her*)

HAL   (*Comes back on stage somewhat apologetically. He is
worried about something and tries to get* ALAN'S *attention*)
Hey, Seymour . . .

ALAN   (*Annoyed*)   What's the matter, Hal? Can't you stand
to see anyone else kiss a pretty girl?

HAL   What the hell, Seymour!

ALAN   (*An excuse to be angry*)   Hal, will you watch your language!

MADGE   Alan! It's all right.

HAL   I'm sorry.
(*Beckons* ALAN *to him*)

ALAN   (*Crossing to him*)   What's the trouble?
(MADGE *walks away, sensing that* HAL *wants to talk privately*)

HAL   Look, Seymour, I—I never been on a picnic.

ALAN   What're you talking about? Everybody's been on a
picnic.

HAL   Not me. When I was a kid, I was too busy shooting craps
or stealing milk bottles.

ALAN   Well, there's a first time for everything.

HAL   I wasn't brought up proper like *you*. I won't know how to act around all these *women*.

ALAN   Women aren't anything new in *your* life.

HAL   But these are—*nice* women. What if I say the wrong word or maybe my stomach growls? I feel *funny*.

ALAN   You're a psycho!

HAL   O.K., but if I do anything wrong, you gotta try to overlook it.
(*He runs off stage.* ALAN *laughs. Then* ALAN *returns to* MADGE)

ALAN   We'll be by about five, Madge.

MADGE   O.K.

ALAN   (*Beside her, tenderly*)   Madge, after we have supper tonight maybe you and I can get away from the others and take a boat out on the river.

MADGE   All right, Alan.

ALAN   I want to see if you look *real* in the moonlight.

MADGE   Alan! Don't say that!

ALAN   Why? I don't care if you're real or not. You're the prettiest girl I ever saw.

MADGE   Just the same, I'm real.
(*As* ALAN *starts to kiss her, the noise of an automobile horn is heard*)

HAL   (*Hollering lustily from offstage*)   Hey, Seymour—get the lead outa your pants!
(ALAN *goes off, irritated.* MADGE *watches them as they drive away. She waves to them*)

FLO   (*Inside*)   Madge! Come on inside now.

MADGE   All right, Mom.
(*As she starts in, there is a train whistle in the distance.* MADGE *hears it and stands listening*)

CURTAIN

SCENE: *It is late afternoon, the same day. The sun is beginning to set and fills the atmosphere with radiant orange. When the curtain goes up,* MILLIE *is on the porch alone. She has permitted herself to "dress up" and wears a becoming, feminine dress in which she cannot help feeling a little strange. She is quite attractive. Piano music can be heard offstage, somewhere past* MRS. POTTS' *house, and* MILLIE *stands listening to it for a moment. Then she begins to sway to the music and in a moment is dancing a strange, impromptu dance over the porch and yard. The music stops suddenly and* MILLIE'S *mood is broken. She rushes upstage and calls off, left.*

MILLIE   Don't quit now, Ernie! (*She cannot hear* ERNIE'S *reply*) Huh? (MADGE *enters from kitchen.* MILLIE *turns to* MADGE) Ernie's waiting for the rest of the band to practice. They're going to play out at the park tonight.

MADGE   (*Crossing to center and sitting on chair*)   I don't know why you couldn't have helped us in the kitchen.

MILLIE   (*Lightly, giving her version of the sophisticated belle*) I had to dress for the ball.

MADGE   I had to make the potato salad and stuff the eggs and make three dozen bread-and-butter sandwiches.

MILLIE   (*In a very affected accent*)   I had to *bathe*—and dust my limbs with powder—and slip into my frock . . .

MADGE   Did you clean out the bathtub?

MILLIE   Yes, I cleaned out the bathtub. (*She becomes very self-conscious*) Madge, how do I look? Now tell me the truth.

MADGE   You look very pretty.

MILLIE   I feel sorta funny.

MADGE   You can have the dress if you want it.

MILLIE   Thanks. (*A pause*) Madge, how do you talk to boys?

MADGE   Why, you just talk, silly.

MILLIE   How d'ya think of things to say?

102

MADGE   I don't know. You just say whatever comes into your head.

MILLIE   Supposing nothing ever comes into my head?

MADGE   You talked with him all right this morning.

MILLIE   But now I've got a *date* with him, and it's *different!*

MADGE   You're crazy.

MILLIE   I think he's a big show-off. You should have seen him this morning on the high diving board. He did real graceful swan dives, and a two and a half gainer, and a back flip— and kids stood around clapping. He just ate it up.

MADGE   (*Her mind elsewhere*)   I think I'll paint my toenails tonight and wear sandals.

MILLIE   And he was braggin' all afternoon how he used to be a deep-sea diver off Catalina Island.

MADGE   Honest?

MILLIE   And he says he used to make hundreds of dollars doin' parachute jumps out of a balloon. Do you believe it?

MADGE   I don't see why not.

MILLIE   You never hear Alan bragging that way.

MADGE   Alan never jumped out of a balloon.

MILLIE   Madge, I think he's girl crazy.

MADGE   You think every boy you see is something horrible.

MILLIE   Alan took us into the Hi Ho for Cokes and there was a gang of girls in the back booth—Juanita Badger and her gang. (MADGE *groans at hearing this name*) When they saw him, they started giggling and tee-heeing and saying all sorts of crazy things. Then Juanita Badger comes up to me and whispers, "He's the cutest thing I ever saw." Is he, Madge?

MADGE   (*Not willing to go overboard*)   I certainly wouldn't say he was "the cutest thing I ever *saw*."

MILLIE   Juanita Badger's an old floozy. She sits in the back row at the movie so the guys that come in will see her and sit with her. One time she and Rubberneck Krauss were asked by the management to leave—and they weren't just kissin', either!

MADGE   (*Proudly*)   I never even speak to Juanita Badger.

MILLIE   Madge, do you think he'll like me?

MADGE   Why ask me all these questions? You're supposed to be the smart one.

MILLIE   I don't really care. I just wonder.

FLO (*Coming out of kitchen*)   Now I tell myself I've got two beautiful daughters.

MILLIE (*Embarrassed*)   Be quiet, Mom!

FLO   Doesn't Millie look pretty, Madge?

MADGE   When she isn't picking her nose.

FLO   Madge! (*To* MILLIE) She doesn't want anyone to be pretty but her.

MILLIE   You're just saying I'm pretty because you're my mom. People we love are always pretty, but people who're pretty to begin with, everybody loves *them*.

FLO   Run over and show Helen Potts how nice you look.

MILLIE (*In a wild parody of herself*)   Here comes Millie Owens, the great beauty of all time! Be prepared to swoon when you see her!
(*She climbs up over the side of* MRS. POTTS' *porch and disappears*)

FLO (*Sits on chair on porch*)   Whatever possessed me to let Helen Potts ask that young hoodlum to take Millie on the picnic?

MADGE   Hal?

FLO   Yes, Hal, or whatever his name is. He left every towel in the bathroom black as dirt. He left the seat up, too.

MADGE   It's not going to hurt anyone just to be nice to him.

FLO   If there's any drinking tonight, you put a stop to it.

MADGE   I'm not going to be a wet blanket.

FLO   If the boys feel they have to have a few drinks, there's nothing you can do about it, but you can keep Millie from taking any.

MADGE   She wouldn't pay any attention to me.

FLO (*Changing the subject*)   You better be getting dressed. And don't spend the whole evening admiring yourself in the mirror.

MADGE   Mom, don't make fun of me.

FLO   You shouldn't object to being kidded if it's well meant.

MADGE   It seems like—when I'm looking in the mirror that's the only way I can prove to myself I'm alive.

FLO   Madge! You puzzle me.
(*The three schoolteachers come on, downstage right, making a rather tired return from their festivity. After their high-spirited exit in Act One, their present mood seems glum, as though they had expected from the homecoming some fulfillment that had not been realized*)

IRMA   We've brought home your wayward girl, Mrs. Owens!

FLO   (*Turning from* MADGE)   Hello, girls! Have a nice party?

IRMA   It wasn't a real party. Each girl paid for her own lunch. Then we played bridge all afternoon. (*Confidentially, to* ROSEMARY) I get tired playing bridge.

FLO   Food's good at the hotel, isn't it?

IRMA   Not very. But they serve it to you nice, with honest-to-goodness napkins. Lord, I hate paper napkins!

CHRISTINE   I had a French-fried pork chop and it was mostly fat. What'd you girls have?

ROSEMARY   I had the stuffed peppers.

IRMA   I had the Southern-fried chicken.

CHRISTINE   Linda Sue Breckenridge had pot roast of veal and there was only one little hunk of meat in it. All we girls at her table made her call the waiter and complain.

ROSEMARY   Well, I should hope so!

IRMA   Good for you! (*There is a pause*) I thought by this time someone might have noticed my new dress.

ROSEMARY   I was going to say something, kid, and then I . . . uh . . .

IRMA   Remember that satin-back crepe I had last year?

ROSEMARY   Don't tell me!

IRMA   Mama remodeled it for me while I was at Columbia. I feel like I had a brand-new outfit. (*Smarting*) But nobody said anything all afternoon!

CHRISTINE   It's—chic.

IRMA (*This soothes* IRMA *a bit and she beams. But now there is an awkward pause wherein no one can think of any more to say*)   Well—we better run along, Christine. Rosemary has a date. (*To* ROSEMARY) We'll come by for you in the morning. Don't be late.
(*She goes upstage and waits at the gate for* CHRISTINE)

CHRISTINE (*Crossing to* ROSEMARY)   Girl, I want to tell you, in one afternoon I feel I've known you my whole life.

ROSEMARY (*With assurance of devotion*)   I look upon you as an old friend already.

CHRISTINE (*Overjoyed*)   Aw . . .

ROSEMARY (*As* CHRISTINE *and* IRMA *go off*)   Good-bye, girls!

FLO (*To* ROSEMARY)   What time's Howard coming by?

ROSEMARY   Any minute now.

MADGE   Mom, is there any hot water?

FLO   You'll have to see.

MADGE (*Crosses to door, then turns to* ROSEMARY)   Miss Sydney, would you mind terribly if I used some of your Shalimar?

ROSEMARY   Help yourself!

MADGE   Thanks.
(*She goes inside*)

ROSEMARY   Madge thinks too much about the boys, Mrs. Owens.

FLO (*Disbelieving*)   Madge?
(*The conversation is stopped by the excited entrance of* MRS. POTTS *from her house. She is followed by* MILLIE, *who carries another cake*)

MRS. POTTS   It's a *miracle,* that's what it is! I never knew Millie could look so pretty. It's just like a movie I saw once with Betty Grable—or was it Lana Turner? Anyway, she played the part of a secretary to some very important businessman. She wore glasses and did her hair real plain and men didn't pay any attention to her at all. Then one day she took off her glasses and her boss wanted to marry her right away! Now all the boys are going to fall in love with Millie!

ROSEMARY   Millie have a date tonight?

FLO   Yes, I'm sorry to say.

MRS. POTTS   Why, Flo!

ROSEMARY   Who is he, Millie? Tell your Aunt Rosemary.

MILLIE   Hal.

ROSEMARY   Who?

FLO   The young man over at Helen's turned out to be a friend of Alan's.

ROSEMARY   Oh, *him!*
(MILLIE *exits into kitchen*)

FLO   Helen, have you gone to the trouble of baking another cake?

MRS. POTTS   An old lady like me, if she wants any attention from the young men on a picnic, all she can do is bake a cake!

FLO   (*Rather reproving*)   Helen Potts!

MRS. POTTS   I feel sort of excited, Flo. I think we plan picnics just to give ourselves an excuse—to let something thrilling happen in our lives.

FLO   Such as what?

MRS POTTS   I don't know.

MADGE   (*Bursting out the door*)   Mom, Millie makes me furious! Every time she takes a bath, she fills the whole tub. There isn't any hot water at all.

FLO   You should have thought of it earlier.

ROSEMARY   (*Hears* HOWARD'S *car drive up and stop*)   It's him! It's him!

MRS. POTTS   Who? Oh, it's Howard. Hello, Howard!

ROSEMARY   (*Sitting down again*)   If he's been drinking, I'm not going out with him.

HOWARD   (*As he comes on through gate*)   Howdy, ladies.
(HOWARD *is a small, thin man, rapidly approaching middle age. A small-town businessman, he wears a permanent smile of greeting which, most of the time, is pretty sincere*)

FLO   Hello, Howard.

HOWARD   You sure look nice, Rosemary.

ROSEMARY   (*Her tone of voice must tell a man she is inde-*

pendent of him)   Seems to me you might have left your
coat on.

HOWARD   Still too darn hot, even if it is September. Good
evening, Madge.

MADGE   Hi, Howard.

FLO   How are things over in Cherryvale, Howard?

HOWARD   Good business. Back to school and everybody buying.

FLO   When business is good, it's good for everyone.

MILLIE (*Comes out of kitchen, stands shyly behind* HOWARD)
Hi, Howard!

HOWARD (*Turning around, making a discovery*)   Hey, Millie's
a good-lookin' kid. I never realized it before.

MILLIE (*Crossing to* FLO, *apprehensive*)   Mom, what time
did the fellows say they'd be here?

FLO   At five-thirty. You've asked me a dozen times. (*There
is a sound of approaching automobiles, and* FLO *looks off
stage, right*) Alan's brought *both* cars!
(MILLIE *runs into the house*)

MRS. POTTS (*To* FLO)   Some day *you'll* be riding around in
that big Cadillac, ladybug.

ALAN (*Coming on from right*)   Everyone ready?

FLO   Come sit down, Alan.

ROSEMARY (*Like a champion hostess*)   The more the mer-
rier!

ALAN   I brought both cars. I thought we'd let Hal and Millie
bring the baskets out in the Ford. Hal's parking it now.
(*To* MADGE, *who is sitting up on* MRS. POTTS' *porch railing*) Hello, Beautiful!

MADGE   Hello, Alan!

ALAN (*Calling off stage*)   Come on, Hal.

FLO   Is he a careful driver, Alan?
(*This question does not get answered.* HAL *comes running
on, tugging uncomfortably at the shoulders of his jacket
and hollering in a voice that once filled the locker rooms*)

HAL   Hey, Seymour! Hey, I'm a big man, Seymour. I'm a
lot huskier than you are. I can't wear your jacket.

ALAN   Then take it off.

MRS. POTTS   Yes. I like to see a man comfortable.

HAL   (*With a broad smile of total confidence*)   I never could
wear another fellow's clothes. See, I'm pretty big through
the shoulders. (*He demonstrates the fact*) I should have all
my clothes tailor-made.
(*He now swings his arms in appreciation of their new freedom.* MRS. POTTS *is admiring, the other women speculative*)

ALAN   (*Wanting to get over the formalities*)   Hey—uh—
Hercules, you've met Mrs. Owens . . .

HAL   Sure!

(FLO *nods at him*)

ALAN   . . . and I believe you met Mrs. Potts this morning.

HAL   (*Throwing his arms around her*)   Oh, she's my best girl!

MRS. POTTS   (*Giggling like a girl*)   I baked a Lady Baltimore
cake!

HAL   (*Expansively, as though making an announcement of
public interest*)   This little lady, she took pity on me when
I was practically starving. I ran into some hard luck when I
was travelin'. Some characters robbed me of every cent I
had.

ALAN   (*Interrupting*)   And—er—this is Rosemary Sydney,
Hal. Miss Sydney teaches shorthand and typing in the
local high school.

ROSEMARY   (*Offering her hand*)   Yes, I'm an old-maid schoolteacher.

HAL   (*With unnecessary earnestness*)   I have every respect for
schoolteachers, ma'am. It's a lotta hard work and not much
pay.
(ROSEMARY *cannot decide whether or not this is a compliment*)

ALAN   And this is Howard Bevans, Hal. Mr. Bevans is a
friend of Miss Sydney.

HOWARD   (*As they shake hands*)   I run a little shop over in
Cherryvale. Notions, novelties and school supplies. You and
Alan drive over some time and get acquainted.
(MILLIE *enters and stands on the porch, pretending to be
nonchalant and at ease*)

HAL   (*To* HOWARD, *earnestly*)   Sir, we'll come over as soon as we can fit it into our schedule. (*He spies* MILLIE) Hey, kid! (*He does an elaborate imitation of a swan dive and lands beside her on the porch*) You got a little more tan today, didn't you? (*He turns to the others*) You folks shoulda seen Millie this morning. She did a fine jackknife off the high diving board!

MILLIE (*Breaking away, sitting on steps*)   Cut it out!

HAL   What'sa matter, kid? Think I'm snowin' you under? (*Back to the whole group*) I wouldn't admit this to many people, but she does a jackknife almost as good as me! (*Realizes that this sounds bragging so goes on to explain*) You see, I was diving champion on the West Coast, so I know what I'm talking about!
(*He laughs to reassure himself and sits beside* MILLIE *on doorstep*)

FLO (*After a moment*)   Madge, you should be getting dressed.

ALAN   Go on upstairs and get beautiful for us.

MADGE   Mom, can I wear my new dress?

FLO   No. I made you that dress to save for dances this fall.
(*The attention returns now to* HAL, *and* MADGE *continues to sit, unnoticed, watching him*)

ROSEMARY (*To* HAL)   Where'd you get those boots?

HAL   I guess maybe I should apologize for the way I look. But you see, those characters I told you about made off with all my clothes, too.

MRS. POTTS   What a pity!

HAL   You see, I didn't want you folks to think you were associatin' with a bum.
(*He laughs uncomfortably*)

MRS. POTTS (*Intuitively, she says what is needed to save his ego*)   Clothes don't make the man.

HAL   That's what I tell myself, ma'am.

FLO   Is your mother taken care of, Helen?

MRS. POTTS   Yes, Flo. I've got a baby sitter for her.
(*All laugh*)

FLO   Then let's start packing the baskets.
(*She goes into kitchen.* MRS. POTTS *starts after her, but* HAL'S *story holds her and she sits down again*)

HAL (*Continuing his explanation to Rosemary*)   See, ma'am, my old man left me these boots when he died.

ROSEMARY (*Impishly*)   That all he left you—just a pair of boots?

HAL   He said, "Son, the man of the house needs a pair of boots 'cause he's gotta do a lot of kickin'.

> "Your wages all are spent.
> The landlord wants his rent.
> You go to your woman for solace,
> And she fills you fulla torment."

(HAL *smiles and explains proudly*) That's a little poem he made up. He says, "Son, there'll be times when the only thing you got to be proud of is the fact you're a man. So wear your boots so people can hear you comin', and keep your fists doubled up so they'll know you mean business when you get there." (*He laughs*) My old man, he was a corker!

ALAN (*Laughing*)   Hal's always so shy of people before he meets them. Then you can't keep him still!
(*Suddenly* HAL'S *eye catches* MADGE, *perched on* MRS. POTTS' *porch*)

HAL   Hi!

MADGE   Hi!
(*Now they both look away from each other, a little guiltily*)

HOWARD   What line of business you in, son?

HAL (*He begins to expand with importance*)   I'm about to enter the oil business, sir.
(*He sits on the chair, center stage*)

HOWARD   Oh!

HAL   You see, while my old man was no aristocratic millionaire or anything, he had some very important friends who were very big men—in their own way. One of them wanted me to take a position with this oil company down in Texas, but . . .

ALAN (*Matter-of-factly*)   Dad and I have found a place for Hal on the pipeline.

HAL   Gee, Seymour, I think you oughta let *me* tell the story.

ALAN (*Knowing he might as well let* HAL *go on*)   Sorry, Hal.

HAL (*With devout earnestness to all*)   You see, I've decided

to start in from the very bottom, 'cause that way I'll learn
things lots better—even if I don't make much money for
a while.

MRS. POTTS (*Comes through again*)   Money isn't everything.

HAL   That's what I tell myself, ma'am. Money isn't everything. I've learned that much. And I sure do appreciate Alan
and his old . . . (*Thinks a moment and substitutes* father
for man) *father* . . . giving me this opportunity.

MRS. POTTS   I think that's wonderful.
(*She has every faith in him*)

HOWARD   It's a good business town. A young man can go far.

HAL   Sir! I intend to go *far*.

ROSEMARY (*Her two-bits' worth*)   A young man, coming to
town, he's gotta be a good mixer.

MRS. POTTS   Wouldn't it be nice if he could join the country
club and play golf?

ALAN   He won't be able to afford that.

ROSEMARY   The bowling team's a rowdy gang.

MRS. POTTS   And there's a young men's Bible class at the
Baptist Church.
(HAL'S *head has been spinning with these plans for his
future. Now he reassures them*)

HAL   Oh, I'm gonna join clubs and go to church and do all
those things.

FLO (*Coming out of the kitchen*)   Madge! Are you still here?

MADGE (*Running across to the front door of her own house*)
If everyone will pardon me, I'll get dressed.
(*She goes inside*)

FLO   It's about time.

ALAN (*Calling after* MADGE)   Hurry it up, will you, Delilah?

MILLIE   You oughta see the way Madge primps. She uses
about six kinds of face cream and dusts herself all over with
powder, and rubs perfume underneath her ears to make her
real mysterious. It takes her half an hour just to get her
lipstick on. She won't be ready for hours.

FLO   Come on, Helen. Alan, we'll need a man to help us chip
the ice and put the baskets in the car.
(MRS. POTTS *goes inside*)

HAL (*Generously*)   I'll help you, ma'am.

FLO (*She simply cannot accept him*)   No, thank you. Alan won't mind.

ALAN (*To* HAL *as he leaves*)   Mind your manners, Hal. (*He and* FLO *start in*)

MILLIE (*Uncertain how to proceed with* HAL *on her own, she runs to* FLO)   Mom!

FLO   Millie, show the young man your drawings.

MILLIE (*To* HAL)   Wanta see my art?

HAL   You mean to tell me you can draw pictures?

MILLIE (*Gets her sketch book and shows it to* HAL. FLO *and* ALAN *go inside*)   That's Mrs. Potts.

HAL (*Impressed*)   Looks just like her.

MILLIE   I just love Mrs. Potts. When I go to heaven, I expect everyone to be just like her.

HAL   Hey, kid, wanta draw me?

MILLIE   Well, I'll try.

HAL   I had a job as a model once. (*Strikes a pose*) How's this? (MILLIE *shakes her head*) Here's another. (*Sits on stump in another pose*) Okay?

MILLIE   Why don't you just try to look natural?

HAL   Gee, that's hard.
    (*But he shakes himself into a natural pose finally.* MILLIE *starts sketching him.* ROSEMARY *and* HOWARD *sit together on the doorstep. The sun now is beginning to set, filling the stage with an orange glow that seems almost aflame*)

ROSEMARY (*Grabs* HOWARD'S *arm*)   Look at that sunset, Howard!

HOWARD   Pretty, isn't it?

ROSEMARY   That's the most flaming sunset I ever did see.

HOWARD   If you painted it in a picture, no one'd believe you.

ROSEMARY   It's like the daytime didn't want to end, isn't it?

HOWARD (*Not fully aware of what she means*)   Oh—I don't know.

ROSEMARY   Like the daytime didn't wanta end, like it was

gonna put up a big scrap and maybe set the world on fire—
to keep the nighttime from creepin' on.

HOWARD   Rosemary . . . you're a poet.

HAL   (*As* MILLIE *sketches him he begins to relax and reflect
on his life*)   You know, there comes a time in every man's
life when he's gotta settle down. A little town like this, this
is the place to settle down in, where people are easygoin' and
sincere.

ROSEMARY   No, Howard, I don't think there ought to be any
drinking, while Millie's here.

HAL   (*Turns at the mention of drink*)   What's that?

ROSEMARY   We were just talkin'.

HAL   (*Back to* MILLIE)   What'd you do this afternoon, kid?

MILLIE   Read a book.

HAL   (*Impressed*)   You mean, you read a *whole* book in one
afternoon?

MILLIE   Sure. Hold still.

HAL   I'm a son of a gun. What was it about?

MILLIE   There wasn't much story. It's just the way you feel
when you read it—kind of warm inside and sad and amused
—all at the same time.

HAL   Yeah—sure. (*After a moment*) I wish I had more time
to read books. (*Proudly*) That's what I'm gonna do when I
settle down. I'm gonna read all the better books—and listen
to all the better music. A man owes it to himself. (MILLIE
continues sketching) I used to go with a girl who read books.
She joined the Book-of-the-Month Club and they had her
readin' books all the time! She wouldn't any more finish
one book than they'd send her another!

ROSEMARY   (*As* HOWARD *walks off*)   Howard, where you
goin'?

HOWARD   I'll be right back, honey.
(ROSEMARY *follows him to gate and watches him while he
is off stage*)

HAL   (*As* MILLIE *hands him the sketch*)   Is that *me*? (*Admiring it*) I sure do admire people who are artistic. Can I
keep it?

MILLIE   Sure. (*Shyly*) I write poetry, too. I've written poems
I've never shown to a living soul.

HAL   Kid, I think you must be some sort of a genius.

ROSEMARY (*Calling off to* HOWARD)   Howard, leave that bottle right where it is!

HAL (*Jumps at the word* bottle)   Did she say "bottle"?

ROSEMARY (*Coming down to* HAL)   He's been down to the hotel, buying bootleg whiskey off those good-for-nothing porters!

HOWARD (*Coming back, holding out a bottle*)   Young man, maybe you'd like a swig of this.

HAL   Hot damn!
  (*He takes a drink*)

ROSEMARY   Howard, put that away.

HOWARD   Millie's not gonna be shocked if she sees someone take a drink. Are you, Millie?

MILLIE   Gosh, no!

ROSEMARY   What if someone'd come by and tell the School Board? I'd lose my job quick as you can say Jack Robinson.

HOWARD   Who's gonna see you, honey? Everyone in town's at the park, havin' a picnic.

ROSEMARY   I don't care. Liquor's against the law in this state, and a person oughta abide by the law. (*To* HAL) Isn't that what you say, young fellow?

HAL (*Eager to agree*)   Oh, sure! A person oughta abide by the law.

HOWARD   Here, honey, have one.

ROSEMARY   No, Howard, I'm not gonna touch a drop.

HOWARD   Come on, honey, have one little drink just for *me*.

ROSEMARY (*Beginning to melt*)   Howard, you oughta be ashamed of yourself.

HOWARD (*Innocent*)   I don't see why.

ROSEMARY   I guess I know why you want me to take a drink.

HOWARD   Now, honey, that's not so. I just think you should have a good time like the rest of us. (*To* HAL) Schoolteachers gotta right to live. Isn't that what you say, young fella?

HAL   Sure, schoolteachers got a right to live.

ROSEMARY (*Taking the bottle*)   Now, Millie, don't you tell any of the kids at school.

MILLIE   What do you take me for?

ROSEMARY (*Looking around her*)   Anyone coming?

HOWARD   Coast is clear.

ROSEMARY (*Takes a hearty drink, and makes a lugubrious face*)   Whew! I want some water!

HOWARD   Millie, why don't you run in the house and get us some?

ROSEMARY   Mrs. Owens'd suspect something. I'll get a drink from the hydrant!
(*She runs off to* MRS. POTTS' *yard*)

HOWARD   Millie, my girl, I'd like to offer *you* one, but I s'pose your old lady'd raise Ned.

MILLIE   What Mom don't know won't hurt her!
(*She reaches for the bottle*)

HAL (*Grabs the bottle first*)   No, kid. You lay off the stuff!
(*He takes another drink*)

ROSEMARY (*Calling from offstage*)   Howard, come help me! I see a snake!

HOWARD   You go, Millie. She don't see no snake. (MILLIE *goes off. As* HAL *takes another drink, he sees a light go on in* MADGE'S *window.* HOWARD *follows* HAL'S *gaze*) Look at her there, powdering her arms. You know, every time I come over here I look forward just to seein' her. I tell myself, "Bevans, old boy, you can look at that all you want, but you couldn't touch it with a ten-foot pole."

HAL (*With some awe of her*)   She's the kind of girl a guy's gotta *respect*.

HOWARD   Look at her, putting lipstick on that cute kisser. Seems to me, when the good Lord made a girl as pretty as she is, he did it for a reason, and it's about time she found out what that reason is. (*He gets an idea*) Look, son, if you're agonizin', I know a couple of girls down at the hotel.

HAL   Thanks, but I've given up that sorta thing.

HOWARD   I think that's a very fine attitude.

HAL   Besides, I never had to pay for it.

ROSEMARY (*Entering, followed by* MILLIE)   Lord, I thought I was going to faint!

MILLIE (*Laughing at* ROSEMARY'S *excitability*)   It was just a piece of garden hose.

ROSEMARY (*Regarding the two men suspiciously*)   What're you two talking about?

HOWARD   Talkin' about the weather, honey. Talkin' about the weather.

ROSEMARY   I bet.

MILLIE (*Seeing* MADGE *in the window*)   Hey, Madge, why don't you charge admission?
(MADGE'S *curtains close*)

ROSEMARY   Shoot! When I was a girl I was just as good-looking as she is!

HOWARD   Of course you were, honey.

ROSEMARY (*Taking the bottle*)   I had boys callin' me all the time. But if my father had ever caught me showing off in front of the window he'd have tanned me with a razor strap. (*Takes a drink*) 'Cause I was brought up strict by a God-fearing man.
(*Takes another*)

MILLIE (*Music has started in the background*)   Hey, hit it, Ernie! (*Explaining to* HAL) It's Ernie Higgins and his Happiness Boys. They play at all the dances around here.

ROSEMARY (*Beginning to sway rapturously*)   Lord, I like that music! Come dance with me, Howard.

HOWARD   Honey, I'm no good at dancin'.

ROSEMARY   That's just what you menfolks tell yourselves to get out of it. (*Turns to* MILLIE) Come dance with me, Millie!
(*She pulls* MILLIE *up onto the porch and they push the chairs out of the way*)

MILLIE   I gotta lead! I gotta lead.
(ROSEMARY *and* MILLIE *dance together in a trim, automatic way that keeps time to the music but little else. Both women seem to show a little arrogance in dancing together, as though boasting to the men of their independence. Their rhythm is accurate but uninspired.* HOWARD *and* HAL *watch, laughing*)

HOWARD   S'posin' Hal and I did that.

ROSEMARY   Go ahead for all I care. (HOWARD *turns to* HAL

and, laughing, they start dancing together, HAL *giving his own version of a coy female.* ROSEMARY *is irritated by this)* Stop it!

HOWARD   I thought we were doin' very nicely.
(ROSEMARY *grabs* HOWARD *and pulls him up on the porch)*

HAL   Come and dance with me, Millie!

MILLIE   Well—I never danced with boys. I always have to lead.

HAL   Just relax and do the steps I do. Come on and try.
(*They dance together but* MILLIE *has an awkward feeling of uncertainty that shows in her dancing.* HOWARD, *dancing with* ROSEMARY, *has been cutting up)*

ROSEMARY   Quit clowning, Howard, and dance with me.

HOWARD   Honey, you don't get any fun out of dancing with *me.*

ROSEMARY   The band's playin'. You gotta dance with *some-*one.
(*They resume an uncertain toddle)*

MILLIE (*To* HAL)   Am I too bad?

HAL   Naw! You just need a little practice.

ROSEMARY (*While dancing)*   Lord, I love to dance. At school, kids all called me the Dancin' Fool. Went somewhere dancin' every night!

MRS. POTTS (*Coming out of kitchen, she sits and watches the dancers.* FLO *and* ALAN *appear and stand in doorway watching)*   I can't stay in the kitchen while there's dancing!

HAL (*Stops the dancing to deliver the needed instructions)*   Now look, kid, you gotta remember *I'm* the *man,* and you gotta do the steps *I* do.

MILLIE   I keep wantin' to do the steps I make up myself.

HAL   The man's gotta take the lead, kid, as long as he's able.
(*They resume dancing)*

MRS. POTTS   You're doing fine, Millie!

MILLIE (*As she is whirled around)*   I feel like Rita Hayworth!
(FLO *and* ALAN *go into the house)*

ROSEMARY (*Her youth returns in reverie)*   One night I went

dancin' at a big Valentine party. I danced so hard I swooned!
That's when they called me the Dancin' Fool.

HAL (*Stops dancing for a moment*)   I'll show you a new step,
kid. I learned this in L. A. Try it.
(*He nimbly executes a somewhat more intricate step*)

MRS. POTTS   Isn't he graceful?

MILLIE   Gee, that looks hard.

HAL   Takes a little time. Give it a try!
(MILLIE *tries to do it, but it is too much for her*)

MILLIE (*Giving up*)   I'm sorry, I just can't seem to get it.

HAL   Watch close, kid. If you learn this step you'll be the
sharpest kid in town. See?
(*He continues his demonstration*)

MILLIE (*Observing but baffled*)   Yah—but . . .

HAL   Real loose, see? You give it a little of this—and give it
a little of that.
(*He snaps his fingers, keeping a nimble, sensitive response
to the rhythm*)

MILLIE   Gee, I wish *I* could do that.
(*Now the music changes to a slower, more sensuous rhythm.*
HAL *and* MILLIE *stop dancing and listen*)

ROSEMARY (*Who has been watching* HAL *enviously*)   That's
the way to dance, Howard! That's the way.
(HAL *begins to dance to the slower rhythm and* MILLIE *tries
to follow him. Now* MADGE *comes out the front door, wearing her new dress. Although the dress is indeed "too fussy"
for a picnic, she is ravishing. She stands watching* HAL *and*
MILLIE)

HOWARD (*Drifting from* ROSEMARY)   You sure look pretty,
Madge.

MADGE   Thank you, Howard.

HOWARD   Would you like a little dance?
(*She accepts, and they dance together on the porch.* ROSE-
MARY *is dancing by herself on the porch, upstage, and does
not notice them*)

MRS. POTTS (*Seeing* MADGE *and* HOWARD *dancing*)   *More*
dancers! We've turned the backyard into a ballroom!

ROSEMARY (*Snatching* HOWARD *from* MADGE)   Thought you
couldn't dance.

(MADGE *goes down into the yard and watches* HAL *and* MILLIE)

MRS. POTTS (*To* MADGE)   The young man is teaching Millie a new step.

MADGE   Oh, that's fun. I've been trying to teach it to Alan.
(*She tries the step herself and does it as well as* HAL)

MRS. POTTS   Look, everyone! Madge does it, too!

HAL (*Turns around and sees* MADGE *dancing*)   Hey!
(*Some distance apart, snapping their fingers to the rhythm, their bodies respond without touching. Then they dance slowly toward each other and* HAL *takes her in his arms. The dance has something of the nature of a primitive rite that would mate the two young people. The others watch rather solemnly*)

MRS. POTTS (*Finally*)   It's like they were *made* to dance together, isn't it?
(*This remark breaks the spell.* MILLIE *moves to* MRS. POTTS' *steps and sits quietly in the background, beginning to inspect the bottle of whiskey*)

ROSEMARY (*Impatiently to* HOWARD)   Can't *you* dance that way?

HOWARD   Golly, honey, I'm a businessman.

ROSEMARY (*Dances by herself, kicking her legs in the air.* MILLIE *takes an occasional drink from the whiskey bottle during the following scene, unobserved by the others*)   I danced so hard one night, I swooned! Right in the center of the ballroom!

HOWARD (*Amused and observing*)   Rosemary's got pretty legs, hasn't she?

ROSEMARY (*This strikes her as hilarious*)   That's just like you men, can't talk about anything but women's legs.

HOWARD (*A little offended to be misinterpreted*)   I just noticed they had a nice shape.

ROSEMARY (*Laughing uproariously*)   How would you like it if we women went around talkin' 'bout *your* legs all the time?

HOWARD (*Ready to be a sport, stands and lifts his trousers to his knees*)   All right! There's *my* legs if you wanta talk about them.

ROSEMARY (*She explodes with laughter*)   Never saw anything
so ugly. Men's big hairy legs! (ROSEMARY *goes over to* HAL,
yanking him from MADGE *possessively*) Young man, let's
see your legs.

HAL (*Not knowing what to make of his seizure*)   Huh?

ROSEMARY   We passed a new rule here tonight. Every man
here's gotta show his legs.

HAL   Ma'am, I got on boots.

HOWARD   Let the young man alone, Rosemary. He's dancin'
with Madge.

ROSEMARY   Now it's his turn to dance with *me*. (*To* HAL) I
may be an old-maid schoolteacher, but *I* can keep up with
you. Ride 'em cowboy!
(*A little tight, stimulated by* HAL'S *physical presence, she
abandons convention and grabs* HAL *closely to her, plaster-
ing a cheek next to his and holding her hips fast against him.
One can sense that* HAL *is embarrassed and repelled*)

HAL (*Wanting to object*)   Ma'am, I . . .

ROSEMARY   I used to have a boy friend was a cowboy. Met
him in Colorado when I went out there to get over a case of
flu. He was in love with me, 'cause I was an older woman
and had some sense. Took me up in the mountains one night
and made love. Wanted me to marry him right there on the
mountain top. Said God'd be our preacher, the moon our
best man. Ever hear such talk?

HAL (*Trying to get away*)   Ma'am, I'd like another li'l drink
now.

ROSEMARY (*Jerking him closer to her*)   Dance with me,
young man. Dance with me. I can keep up with you. You
know what? You remind me of one of those ancient statues.
There was one in the school library until last year. He was a
Roman gladiator. All he had on was a shield. (*She gives a
bawdy laugh*) A shield over his arm. That was all he had
on. All we girls felt insulted, havin' to walk past that statue
every time we went to the library. We got up a petition and
made the principal do something about it. (*She laughs hilari-
ously during her narration*) You know what he did? He got
the school janitor to fix things right. He got a chisel and
made that statue decent. (*Another bawdy laugh*) Lord,
those ancient people were depraved.

HAL (*He seldom has been made so uncomfortable*)   Ma'am,
I guess I just don't feel like dancin'.

ROSEMARY (*Sobering from her story, grabs for* HAL, *catching
him by the shirt*)   Where you goin'?

HAL   Ma'am, I . . .

ROSEMARY (*Commanding him imploringly*)   Dance with me,
young man. Dance with me.

HAL   I . . . I . . .
(*He pulls loose from her grasp, but her hand, still clutching,
tears off a strip of his shirt as he gets away.* HOWARD *inter-
venes*)

HOWARD   He wants to dance with Madge, Rosemary. Let 'em
alone. They're young people.

ROSEMARY (*In a hollow voice*)   Young? What do you mean,
they're *young*?

MILLIE (*A sick groan from the background*)   Oh, I'm sick.

MRS. POTTS   Millie!

MILLIE   I wanna die.
(*All eyes are on* MILLIE *now as she runs over to the kitchen
door*)

MADGE   Millie!

HOWARD   What'd the little dickens do? Get herself tight?

HAL   Take it easy, kid.

ROSEMARY (*She has problems of her own. She gropes blindly
across the stage, suffering what has been a deep humiliation*)
I suppose that's something wonderful—they're *young*.

MADGE (*Going to* MILLIE)   Let's go inside, Millie.

MILLIE (*Turning on* MADGE *viciously*)   I *hate* you!

MADGE (*Hurt*)   Millie!

MILLIE (*Sobbing*)   Madge is the pretty one—Madge is the
pretty one.
(MILLIE *dashes inside the kitchen door,* MRS. POTTS *behind
her*)

MADGE (*To herself*)   What did she have to do that for?

HOWARD (*Examining the bottle*)   She must have had several
good snifters.

ROSEMARY (*Pointing a finger at* HAL. *She has found venge-ance*) It's all *his* fault, Howard.

HOWARD   Now, honey . . .

ROSEMARY (*To* HAL, *defiantly and accusingly*) Millie was your date. You shoulda been looking after her. But you were too busy making eyes at Madge.

HOWARD   Honey . . .

ROSEMARY   And you're no better than he is, Madge. You should be ashamed.

FLO (*Flies out on the porch in a fury*) Who fed whiskey to my Millie?

ROSEMARY (*Pointing fanatically at* HAL) He did, Mrs. Owens! It's all his fault!
(FLO *glares at* HAL)

HOWARD (*Trying to straighten things out*) Mrs. Owens, it was this way . . .

FLO   My Millie is too young to be drinking whiskey!

ROSEMARY   Oh, he'd have fed her whiskey and taken his pleasure with the child and then skedaddled!

HOWARD (*Trying to bring them to reason*) Now listen, every-one. Let's . . .

ROSEMARY   I know what I'm doing, Howard! And I don't need any advice from *you*. (*Back at* HAL) You been stomp-ing around here in those boots like you owned the place, thinking every woman you saw was gonna fall madly in love. But here's one woman didn't pay you any mind.

HOWARD   The boy hasn't done anything, Mrs. Owens!

ROSEMARY (*Facing* HAL, *drawing closer with each accusation*) Aristocratic millionaire, my foot! You wouldn't know an aristocratic millionaire if he spit on you. Braggin' about your father, and I bet he wasn't any better'n you are.
(HAL *is as though paralyzed*. HOWARD *still tries to reason with* FLO)

HOWARD   None of us saw Millie drink the whiskey.

ROSEMARY (*Closer to* HAL) You think just 'cause you're a man, you can walk in here and make off with whatever you like. You think just 'cause you're young you can push other people aside and not pay them any mind. You think just

'cause you're strong you can show your muscles and nobody'll know what a pitiful specimen you are. But you won't
stay young forever, didja ever thinka that? What'll become
of you then? You'll end your life in the gutter and it'll serve
you right, 'cause the gutter's where you came from and the
gutter's where you belong.
(*She has thrust her face into* HAL'S *and is spitting her final
words at him before* HOWARD *finally grabs her, almost as
though to protect her from herself, and holds her arms at
her sides, pulling her away*)

HOWARD   Rosemary, shut your damn mouth.
(HAL *withdraws to the far edge of the porch, no one paying
any attention to him now, his reaction to the attack still a
mystery*)

MRS. POTTS   (*Comes out of kitchen*)   Millie's going to be perfectly all right, Flo. Alan held her head and let her be sick.
She's going to be perfectly all right, now.

FLO   (*A general announcement, clear and firm*)   I want it understood by everyone that there's to be no more drinking
on this picnic.

HOWARD   It was all my fault, Mrs. Owens. My fault.
(ALAN *escorts a sober* MILLIE *out on the porch*)

MRS. POTTS   Here's Millie now, good as new. And we're all
going on the picnic and forget it.

ALAN   (*Quick to accuse* HAL)   Hal, what's happened?
(HAL *does not respond*)

FLO   (*To* ALAN)   Millie will come with *us*, Alan.

ALAN   Sure, Mrs. Owens. Hal, I told you not to drink!
(HAL *is still silent*)

FLO   Madge, why did you wear your new dress?

MADGE   (*As though mystified at herself*)   I don't know. I just
put it on.

FLO   Go upstairs and change, this minute. I mean it! You
come later with Rosemary and Howard!
(MADGE *runs inside*)

MRS. POTTS   Let's hurry. All the tables will be taken.

ALAN   Mr. Bevans, tell Madge I'll see her out there. Hal, the
baskets are all in the Ford. Get goin'.
(HAL *doesn't move.* ALAN *hurries off*)

FLO Millie, darling, are you feeling better?
(FLO *and* MILLIE *go off through alley, right*)

MRS. POTTS (*To* HAL) Young man, you can follow us and
find the way.
(MRS. POTTS *follows the others off. We hear the Cadillac
drive off.* HAL *is sitting silent and beaten on the edge of the
porch.* HOWARD *and* ROSEMARY *are on the lawn by* MRS.
POTTS' *house*)

HOWARD He's just a boy, Rosemary. You talked awful.

ROSEMARY What made me do it, Howard? What made me
act that way?

HOWARD You gotta remember, men have got feelings, too—
same as women. (*To* HAL) Don't pay any attention to her,
young man. She didn't mean a thing.

ROSEMARY (*Has gone up to the gate*) I don't want to go on
the picnic, Howard. This is my last night of vacation and I
want to have a good time.

HOWARD We'll go for a ride, honey.

ROSEMARY I want to drive into the sunset, Howard! I want to
drive into the sunset!
(*She runs off toward the car,* HOWARD *following.* HOWARD's
car drives away. HAL *sits on the porch, defeated.* MADGE
*soon comes out in another dress. She comes out very quietly
and he shows no recognition of her presence. She sits on
a bench on the porch and finally speaks in a soft voice*)

MADGE You're a wonderful dancer . . .

HAL (*Hardly audible*) Thanks.

MADGE . . . and I can tell a lot about a boy by dancing with
him. Some boys, even though they're very smart, or very
successful in some other way, when they take a girl in their
arms to dance, they're sort of awkward and a girl feels sort
of uncomfortable.

HAL (*He keeps his head down, his face in his hands*) Yah.

MADGE But when you took me in your arms—to dance—I
had the most relaxed feeling, that you knew what you were
doing, and I could follow every step of the way.

HAL Look, baby, I'm in a pretty bad mood.
(*He stands suddenly and walks away from her, his hands*

*thrust into his pockets. He is uncomfortable to be near her,
for he is trembling with insult and rage)*

MADGE   You mustn't pay any attention to Miss Sydney. (HAL
is silent) Women like her make mc mad at the whole female
sex.

HAL   Look, baby, why don't you beat it?

MADGE   *(She is aware of the depth of his feelings)*   What's
the matter?

HAL   *(Gives up and begins to shudder, his shoulders heaving as
he fights to keep from bawling)*   What's the use, baby? I'm
a bum. She saw through me like a goddamn X-ray machine.
There's just no place in the world for a guy like me.

MADGE   There's got to be.

HAL   *(With self-derision)*   Yah?

MADGE   Of course. You're young, and—you're very entertaining. I mean—you say all sorts of witty things, and I just
loved listening to you talk. And you're strong and—you're
very good-looking. I bet Miss Sydney thought so, too, or she
wouldn't have said those things.

HAL   Look, baby, lemme level with you. When I was fourteen,
I spent a year in the reform school. How ya like that?

MADGE   Honest?

HAL   Yah!

MADGE   What for?

HAL   For stealin' another guy's motorcycle. Yah! I *stole* it. I
stole it 'cause I wanted to get on the damn thing and go so
far away, so fast, that no one'd ever catch up with me.

MADGE   I think—lots of boys feel that way at times.

HAL   Then my old lady went to the authorities. *(He mimics
his "old lady")* "I've done everything I can with the boy. I
can't do anything more." So off I go to the goddamn reform
school.

MADGE   *(With all the feeling she has)*   Gee!

HAL   Finally some welfare league hauls me out and the old
lady's sorry to see me back. Yah! she's got herself a new
boy friend and I'm in the way.

MADGE   It's awful when parents don't get along.

HAL   I never told that to another soul, not even Seymour.

MADGE   (*At a loss*)   I—I wish there was something I could say—or *do*.

HAL   Well—that's the Hal Carter story, but no one's ever gonna make a movie of it.

MADGE   (*To herself*)   Most people would be awfully shocked.

HAL   (*Looking at her, then turning away cynically*)   There you are, baby. If you wanta faint—or get sick—or run in the house and lock the doors—go ahead. I ain't stoppin' you. (*There is a silence. Then* MADGE, *suddenly and impulsively, takes his face in her hands and kisses him. Then she returns her hands to her lap and feels embarrassed.* HAL *looks at her in amazement*) Baby! What'd you do?

MADGE   I . . . I'm proud you told me.

HAL   (*With humble appreciation*)   Baby!

MADGE   I . . . I get so tired of being told I'm pretty.

HAL   (*Folding her in his arms caressingly*)   Baby, baby, baby.

MADGE   (*Resisting him, jumping to her feet*)   Don't. We have to go. We have all the baskets in our car and they'll be waiting. (HAL *gets up and walks slowly to her, their eyes fastened and* MADGE *feeling a little thrill of excitement as he draws nearer*) Really—we have to be going. (HAL *takes her in his arms and kisses her passionately. Then* MADGE *utters his name in a voice of resignation*) Hal!

HAL   Just be quiet, baby.

MADGE   Really . . . We have to go. They'll be waiting.

HAL   (*Picking her up in his arms and starting off. His voice is deep and firm*)   We're not goin' on no goddamn picnic.

CURTAIN

SCENE: *It is after midnight. A great harvest moon shines in the sky, a deep, murky blue. The moon is swollen and full and casts a pale light on the scene below. Soon we hear* HOWARD'S *Chevrolet chugging to a stop by the house, then* HOWARD *and* ROSEMARY *come on,* ROSEMARY *first. Wearily, a groggy depression having set in, she makes her way to the doorstep and drops there, sitting limp. She seems preoccupied at first and her responses to* HOWARD *are mere grunts.*

HOWARD   Here we are, honey. Right back where we started from.

ROSEMARY (*Her mind elsewhere*) Uhh.

HOWARD   You were awful nice to me tonight, Rosemary.

ROSEMARY Uhh.

HOWARD   Do you think Mrs. Owens suspects anything?

ROSEMARY I don't care if she does.

HOWARD   A businessman's gotta be careful of talk. And after all, you're a schoolteacher. (*Fumbling to get away*) Well, I better be gettin' back to Cherryvale. I gotta open up the store in the morning. Good night, Rosemary.

ROSEMARY Uhh.

HOWARD (*He pecks at her cheek with a kiss*) Good night. Maybe I should say, good morning.
(*He starts off*)

ROSEMARY (*Just coming to*) Where you goin', Howard?

HOWARD   Honey, I gotta get home.

ROSEMARY You can't go off without me.

HOWARD   Honey, talk sense.

ROSEMARY You can't go off without me. Not after tonight. *That's* sense.

HOWARD (*A little nervous*) Honey, be reasonable.

ROSEMARY Take me with you.

128

HOWARD   What'd people say?

ROSEMARY   (*Almost vicious*)   To *hell* with what people'd say!

HOWARD   (*Shocked*)   Honey!

ROSEMARY   What'd people say if I thumbed my nose at them?
What'd people say if I walked down the street and showed
'em my pink panties? What do I care what people say?

HOWARD   Honey, you're not yourself tonight.

ROSEMARY   Yes, I am. I'm more myself than I ever was. Take
me with you, Howard. If you don't I don't know what I'll
do with myself. I mean it.

HOWARD   Now look, honey, you better go upstairs and get
some sleep. You gotta start school in the morning. We'll talk
all this over Saturday.

ROSEMARY   Maybe you won't be back Saturday. Maybe you
won't be back ever again.

HOWARD   Rosemary, you know better than that.

ROSEMARY   Then what's the next thing in store for me? To be
nice to the next man, then the next—till there's no one
left to care whether I'm nice to him or not. Till I'm ready
for the grave and don't have anyone to take me there.

HOWARD   (*In an attempt to be consoling*)   Now, Rosemary!

ROSEMARY   You can't let that happen to me, Howard. I won't
let you.

HOWARD   I don't understand. When we first started going together, you were the best sport I ever saw, always good for
a laugh.

ROSEMARY   (*In a hollow voice*)   I can't laugh any more.

HOWARD   We'll talk it over Saturday.

ROSEMARY   We'll talk it over *now*.

HOWARD   (*Squirming*)   Well—honey—I . . .

ROSEMARY   You said you were gonna marry me, Howard.
You said when I got back from my vacation, you'd be
waitin' with the preacher.

HOWARD   Honey, I've had an awful busy summer and . . .

ROSEMARY   Where's the preacher, Howard? Where is he?

HOWARD   (*Walking away from her*)   Honey, I'm forty-two

years old. A person forms certain ways of livin', then one day it's too late to change.

ROSEMARY (*Grabbing his arm and holding him*)   Come back here, Howard. I'm no spring chicken either. Maybe I'm a little older than you think *I* am. I've formed my ways too. But they can be changed. They *gotta* be changed. It's no good livin' like this, in rented rooms, meetin' a bunch of old maids for supper every night, then comin' back home alone.

HOWARD   *I* know how it is, Rosemary. My life's no bed of roses either.

ROSEMARY   Then why don't you do something about it?

HOWARD   I figure—there's some bad things about every life.

ROSEMARY   There's too much bad about mine. Each year, I keep tellin' myself, is the last. Something'll happen. Then nothing ever does—except I get a little crazier all the time.

HOWARD (*Hopelessly*)   Well . . .

ROSEMARY   A *well's* a hole in the ground, Howard. Be careful you don't fall in.

HOWARD   I wasn't tryin' to be funny.

ROSEMARY   . . . and all this time you just been leadin' me on.

HOWARD (*Defensive*)   Rosemary, that's not *so!* I've not been leading you *on*.

ROSEMARY   I'd like to know what else you call it.

HOWARD   Well—can't we talk about it Saturday? I'm dead tired and I got a busy week ahead, and . . .

ROSEMARY (*She grips him by the arm and looks straight into his eyes*)   You gotta marry me, Howard.

HOWARD (*Tortured*)   Well—honey, I can't marry you *now*.

ROSEMARY   You can be over here in the morning.

HOWARD   Sometimes you're unreasonable.

ROSEMARY   You gotta marry me.

HOWARD   What'll you do about your job?

ROSEMARY   Alvah Jackson can take my place till they get someone new from the agency.

HOWARD   I'll have to pay Fred Jenkins to take care of the store for a few days.

ROSEMARY   Then get him.

HOWARD   Well . . .

ROSEMARY   I'll be waitin' for you in the morning, Howard.

HOWARD   (*After a few moments' troubled thought*)   No.

ROSEMARY   (*A muffled cry*)   Howard!

HOWARD   I'm not gonna marry anyone that says, "You gotta marry me, Howard." I'm not gonna. (*He is silent.* ROSEMARY *weeps pathetic tears. Slowly* HOWARD *reconsiders*) If a woman wants me to marry her—she can at least say "please."

ROSEMARY   (*Beaten and humble*)   Please marry me, Howard.

HOWARD   Well—you got to give me time to think it over.

ROSEMARY   (*Desperate*)   Oh, God! Please marry me, Howard. Please . . . (*She sinks to her knees*) Please . . . please . . .

HOWARD   (*Embarrassed by her suffering humility*)   Rosemary . . . I . . . I gotta have some time to think it over. You go to bed now and get some rest. I'll drive over in the morning and maybe we can talk it over before you go to school. I . . .

ROSEMARY   You're not just tryin' to get out of it, Howard?

HOWARD   I'll be over in the morning, honey.

ROSEMARY   Honest?

HOWARD   Yah. I gotta go to the courthouse anyway. We'll talk it over then.

ROSEMARY   Oh, God, please marry me, Howard. Please.

HOWARD   (*Trying to get away*)   Go to bed, honey. I'll see you in the morning.

ROSEMARY   Please, Howard!

HOWARD   I'll see you in the morning. Good night, Rosemary. (*Starting off*)

ROSEMARY   (*In a meek voice*)   Please!

HOWARD   Good night, Rosemary.

ROSEMARY   (*After he is gone*)   Please.

(ROSEMARY *stands alone on the doorstep. We hear the sound of* HOWARD'S *car start up and drive off, chugging away in the distance.* ROSEMARY *is drained of energy. She pulls herself together and goes into the house. The stage is empty for several moments. Then* MADGE *runs on from the back, right. Her face is in her hands. She is sobbing.* HAL *follows fast behind. He reaches her just as she gets to the door, and grabs her by the wrist. She resists him furiously*)

HAL   Baby . . . you're not sorry, are you?
(*There is a silence.* MADGE *sobs*)

MADGE   Let me go.

HAL   Please, baby. If I thought I'd done anything to make you unhappy, I . . . I'd almost wanta die.

MADGE   I . . . I'm so ashamed.

HAL   Don't say that, baby.

MADGE   I didn't even know what was happening, and then . . . all of a sudden, it seems like my whole life was changed.

HAL   (*With bitter self-disparagement*)   I oughta be taken out and hung. I'm just a no-good bum. That schoolteacher was right. I oughta be in the gutter.

MADGE   Don't talk that way.

HAL   Times like this, I hate myself, baby.

MADGE   I guess . . . it's no more your fault than mine.

HAL   Sometimes I do pretty impulsive things. (MADGE *starts inside*) Will I see you tomorrow?

MADGE   I don't know.

HAL   Gee, I almost forgot. I start a new job tomorrow.

MADGE   I have to be at the dime store at nine.

HAL   What time you through?

MADGE   Five.

HAL   Maybe I could see you then, huh? Maybe I could come by and . . .

MADGE   I've got a date with Alan—if he'll still speak to me.

HAL   (*A new pain*)   Jesus, I'd forgot all about Seymour.

MADGE   So had I.

HAL   I can't go back to his house. What'll I do?

MADGE   Maybe Mrs. Potts could . . .

HAL   I'll take the car back to where we were, stretch out in the front seat and get a little sleep. (*He thinks a moment*) Baby, how you gonna handle your old lady?

MADGE   (*With a slight tremor*)   I . . . I don't know.

HAL   (*In a funk again*)   Jesus, I ought to be shot at sunrise.

MADGE   I . . . I'll think of something to tell her.

HAL   (*Awkward*)   Well—good night.

MADGE   Good night.
   (*She starts again*)

HAL   Baby—would you kiss me good night . . . maybe? Just one more time.

MADGE   I don't think I better.

HAL   Please!

MADGE   It . . . It'd just start things all over again. Things I better forget.

HAL   Pretty please!

MADGE   Promise not to hold me?

HAL   I'll keep my hands to my side. Swear to God!

MADGE   Well . . . (*Slowly she goes toward him, takes his face in her hands and kisses him. The kiss lasts.* HAL'S *hands become nervous and finally find their way around her. Their passion is revived. Then* MADGE *utters a little shriek, tears herself away from* HAL *and runs into the house, sobbing*) Don't. You *promised.* I never wanta see you again. I might as well be dead.
   (*She runs inside the front door, leaving* HAL *behind to despise himself. He beats his fists together, kicks the earth with his heel, and starts off, hating the day he was born*)

CURTAIN

SCENE: *It is very early the next morning.* MILLIE *sits on the doorstep smoking a cigarette. She wears a fresh wash dress in honor of the first day of school.* FLO *breaks out of the front door. She is a frantic woman.* MILLIE *puts out her cigarette quickly.* FLO *has not even taken the time to dress. She wears an old robe over her nightdress. She speaks to* MILLIE.

FLO   Were you awake when Madge got in?

MILLIE   No.

FLO   Did she say anything to you this morning?

MILLIE   No.

FLO   Dear God! I couldn't get two words out of her last night, she was crying so hard. Now she's got the door locked.

MILLIE   I bet I know what happened.

FLO (*Sharply*)   You don't know anything, Millie Owens. And if anyone says anything to you, you just . . . (*Now she sniffs the air*) Have you been smoking?

MRS. POTTS (*Coming down her back steps*)   Did Madge tell you what happened?

FLO   The next time you take in tramps, Helen Potts, I'll thank you to keep them on your own side of the yard.

MRS. POTTS   Is Madge all right?

FLO   Of course she's all right. She got out of the car and left that hoodlum alone. That's what she did.

MRS. POTTS   Have you heard from Alan?

FLO   He said he'd be over this morning.

MRS. POTTS   Where's the young man?

FLO   I know where he should be! He should be in the penitentiary, and that's where he's going if he shows up around here again!

134

ROSEMARY (*Sticking her head out front door*) Has anyone seen Howard?

FLO (*Surprised*) Howard? Why, no, Rosemary!

ROSEMARY (*Nervous and uncertain*) He said he might be over this morning. Mrs. Owens, I'm storing my summer clothes in the attic. Could someone help me?

FLO We're busy, Rosemary.

MRS. POTTS I'll help you, Rosemary.
(*She looks at* FLO, *then goes up on porch*)

ROSEMARY Thanks, Mrs. Potts.
(*Goes inside*)

FLO (*To* MRS. POTTS) She's been running around like a chicken with its head off all morning. Something's *up!* (MRS. POTTS *goes inside.* FLO *turns to* MILLIE) You keep watch for Alan.
(FLO *goes inside. Now we hear the morning voices of* IRMA *and* CHRISTINE, *coming by for* ROSEMARY)

IRMA Girl, I hope Rosemary is ready. I promised the principal that I'd be there early to help with registration.

CHRISTINE How do I look, Irma?

IRMA It's a cute dress. Let me fix it in the back.
(IRMA *adjusts the hang of the dress as* CHRISTINE *stands patiently*)

CHRISTINE I think a teacher should dress up first day of school, to give the students a good first impression.

IRMA (*Going up on the porch*) Good morning, Millie!

MILLIE Ili.

IRMA Is Rosemary ready?

MILLIE Go on up if you want to.

CHRISTINE (*To* MILLIE) We missed seeing Madge on the picnic last night.

MILLIE So did a lot of other people.

IRMA (*Gives* CHRISTINE *a significant look*) Come on, Christine. I bet we have to get that sleepy girl out of bed.
(*They go inside front door.* BOMBER *rides on, gets off his bicycle, throws a paper on* MRS. POTTS' *steps, then on* FLO'S *back porch. Then he climbs up on* MRS. POTTS' *porch so he can look across into* MADGE'S *room*)

BOMBER Hey, Madge! Wanta go dancin'? Let me be next, Madge!

MILLIE You shut up, crazy.

BOMBER My brother seen 'em parked under the bridge. Alan Seymour was lookin' for 'em all over town. She always put on a lot of airs, but I knew she liked guys.
(*He sees* ALAN *approaching from beyond the* OWENS' *house, and leaves quickly*)

MILLIE Some day I'm really gonna kill that ornery bastard. (*She turns and sees* ALAN)

ALAN Could I see Madge?

MILLIE I'll call her, Alan. (*Calls up to* MADGE'S *window*) Madge! Alan's here! (*Back to* ALAN) She prob'ly has to dress.

ALAN I'll wait.

MILLIE (*She sits on the stump and turns to him very shyly*) I . . . I always liked you, Alan. Didn't you know it?

ALAN (*With some surprise*) *Like* me?

MILLIE (*Nods her head*) It's awfully hard to show someone you like them, isn't it?

ALAN (*With just a little bitterness*) It's easy for *some* people.

MILLIE It makes you feel like such a sap. I don't know why.

ALAN (*Rather touched*) I . . . I'm glad you like me, Millie.

MILLIE (*One can sense her loneliness*) I don't expect you to do anything about it. I just wanted to tell you.
(HOWARD *comes bustling on through the gate, very upset. He addresses* MILLIE)

HOWARD Could I see Rosemary?

MILLIE My gosh, Howard, what are you doing here?

HOWARD I think she's expecting me.

MILLIE You better holler at the bottom of the stairs— (HOWARD *is about to go in the door, but turns back at this*) all the others are up there, too.

HOWARD (*He looks very grave*) The others?

MILLIE Mrs. Potts and Miss Kronkite and Miss Schoenwalder.

HOWARD   Golly, I gotta see her alone.

ROSEMARY (*Calling from inside*)   Howard! (*Inside, to all the women*) It's Howard! He's here!

HOWARD (*Knowing he is stuck*)   Golly!
(*We hear a joyful babble of women's voices from inside.* HOWARD *gives one last pitiful look at* MILLIE, *then goes in.* MILLIE *follows him in and* ALAN *is left alone in the yard. After a moment,* MADGE *comes out the kitchen door. She wears a simple dress, and her whole being appears chastened. She is inscrutable in her expression*)

MADGE   Hello, Alan.

ALAN (*Very moved by seeing her*)   Madge!

MADGE   I'm sorry about last night.

ALAN   Madge, whatever happened—it wasn't your fault. I know what Hal's like when he's drinking. But I've got Hal taken care of now! He won't be bothering you again!

MADGE   Honest?

ALAN   At school I spent half of my life getting him out of jams. I knew he'd had a few tough breaks, and I always tried to be sorry for the guy. But this is the thanks I get.

MADGE (*Still noncommittal*)   Where is he now?

ALAN   Don't worry about Hal! I'll take it on myself now to offer you his official good-bye!

MADGE (*One still cannot decipher her feelings*)   Is he gone?

FLO (*Running out kitchen door. She is dressed now*)   Alan, I didn't know you were here!
(*Now we hear shouts from inside the house.* MILLIE *comes out, throwing rice over her shoulder at all the others, who are laughing and shouting so that we only hear bits of the following*)

MRS. POTTS   Here comes the bride! Here comes the bride!

IRMA   May all your troubles be little ones!

CHRISTINE   You're getting a wonderful girl, Howard Bevans!

IRMA   Rosemary is getting a fine man!

CHRISTINE   They don't come any better'n Rosemary!

MRS. POTTS   Be happy!

IRMA   May all your troubles be little ones!

MRS. POTTS   Be happy forever and ever!
(*Now they are all out on the porch and we see that* HOWARD *carries two suitcases. His face has an expression of complete confusion.* ROSEMARY *wears a fussy going-away outfit*)

IRMA (*To* ROSEMARY)   Girl, are you wearing something old?

ROSEMARY   An old pair of nylons but they're as good as new.

CHRISTINE   And that's a brand-new outfit she's got on. Rosemary, are you wearing something blue? I don't see it!

ROSEMARY (*Daringly*)   And you're not gonna! (*They all laugh, and* ROSEMARY *begins a personal inventory*) Something borrowed! I don't have anything to borrow!
(*Now we see* HAL'S *head appear from the edge of the woodshed. He watches for a moment when he can be sure of not being observed, then darts into the shed*)

FLO   Madge, you give Rosemary something to borrow. It'll mean good luck for you. Go on, Madge! (*She takes* ALAN'S *arm and pulls him toward the steps with her*) Rosemary, Madge has something for you to borrow!

MADGE (*Crossing to the group by steps*)   You can borrow my handkerchief, Miss Sydney.

ROSEMARY   Thank you, Madge. (*She takes the handkerchief*) Isn't Madge pretty, girls?

IRMA *and* CHRISTINE   Oh, yes! Yes, indeed!
(MADGE *turns and leaves the group, going toward* MRS. POTTS' *house*)

ROSEMARY (*During the above*)   She's modest! A girl as pretty as Madge can sail through life without a care! (ALAN *turns from the group to join* MADGE. FLO *then turns and crosses toward* MADGE. ROSEMARY *follows* FLO) Mrs. Owens, I left my hot-water bottle in the closet and my curlers are in the bathroom. You and the girls can have them. I stored the rest of my things in the attic. Howard and I'll come and get 'em after we settle down. Cherryvale's not so far away. We can be good friends, same as before. (HAL *sticks his head through woodshed door and catches* MADGE'S *eye.* MADGE *is startled*)

FLO   I hate to mention it now, Rosemary, but you didn't give us much notice. Do you know anyone I could rent the room to?

IRMA (*To* ROSEMARY)   Didn't you tell her about Linda Sue Breckenridge?

ROSEMARY   Oh, yes! Linda Sue Breckenridge—she's the sewing teacher!

IRMA (*A positive affirmation to them all*)   And she's a darling girl!

ROSEMARY   She and Mrs. Bendix had a fight. Mrs. Bendix
wanted to charge her twenty cents for her orange juice in
the morning and none of us girls ever paid more'n fifteen.
Did we, girls?

IRMA *and* CHRISTINE (*In stanch support*)   No! Never! I certainly never did!

ROSEMARY   Irma, you tell Linda Sue to get in touch with Mrs.
Owens.

IRMA   I'll do that very thing.

FLO   Thank you, Rosemary.

HOWARD   Rosemary, we still got to pick up the license . . .

ROSEMARY (*To* IRMA *and* CHRISTINE, *all of them blubbering*)
Good-bye, girls! We've had some awfully jolly times to-
gether!
(IRMA, CHRISTINE *and* ROSEMARY *embrace*)

HOWARD (*A little restless*)   Come on, honey!
(ALAN *takes the suitcases from* HOWARD)

HOWARD (*To* ALAN)   A man's gotta settle down some time.

ALAN   Of course.

HOWARD   And folks'd rather do business with a married man!

ROSEMARY (*To* MADGE *and* ALAN)   I hope both of you are
going to be as happy as Howard and I will be. (*Turns to*
MRS. POTTS)   You've been a wonderful friend, Mrs. Potts!

MRS. POTTS   I wish you all sorts of happiness, Rosemary.

ROSEMARY   Good-bye, Millie. You're going to be a famous
author some day and I'll be proud I knew you.

MILLIE   Thanks, Miss Sydney.

HOWARD (*To* ROSEMARY)   All set?

ROSEMARY   All set and rarin' to go! (*A sudden thought*)
Where we goin'?

HOWARD (*After an awkward pause*)   Well . . . I got a
cousin who runs a tourist camp in the Ozarks. He and
his wife could put us up for free.

ROSEMARY   Oh, I love the Ozarks!

(*She grabs* HOWARD'S *arm and pulls him off stage.* ALAN *carries the suitcases off stage.* IRMA, CHRISTINE, MRS. POTTS *and* MILLIE *follow them, all throwing rice and calling after them*)

ALL   (*As they go off*)
           The Ozarks are lovely this time of year!
           Be happy!
           May all your troubles be little ones!
           You're getting a wonderful girl!
           You're getting a wonderful man!

FLO   (*Alone with* MADGE)   Madge, what happened last night? You haven't told me a word.

MADGE   Let me alone, Mom.

ROSEMARY   (*Offstage*)   Mrs. Owens, aren't you going to tell us good-bye?

FLO   (*Exasperated*)   Oh, dear! I've been saying good-bye to her all morning.

ALAN   (*Appearing in gateway*)   Mrs. Owens, Miss Sydney wants to give you her house keys.

MRS. POTTS   (*Behind* ALAN)   Come on, Flo!

FLO   (*Hurrying off*)   I'm coming. I'm coming.
(*She follows* ALAN *and* MRS. POTTS *to join the noisy shivaree in the background. Now* HAL *appears from the woodshed. His clothes are drenched and cling plastered to his body. He is barefoot and there is blood on his T-shirt. He stands before* MADGE)

HAL   Baby!

MADGE   (*Backing from him*)   You shouldn't have come here.

HAL   Look, baby, I'm in a jam.

MADGE   Serves you right.

HAL   Seymour's old man put the cops on my tail. Accused me of stealin' the car. I had to knock one of the bastards cold and swim the river to get away. If they ever catch up with me, it'll be too bad.

MADGE   (*Things are in a slightly different light now*)   You were born to get in trouble.

HAL   Baby, I just *had* to say good-bye.

MADGE (*Still not giving away her feelings*)   Where you going?

HAL   The freight train's by pretty soon. I'll hop a ride. I done it lotsa times before.

MADGE   What're you gonna do?

HAL   I got some friends in Tulsa. I can always get a job hoppin' bells at the Hotel Mayo. Jesus, I hate to say goodbye.

MADGE (*Not knowing what her precise feelings are*)   Well . . . I don't know what else there is to do.

HAL   Are you still mad, baby?

MADGE (*Evasively*)   I . . . I never knew a boy like you.
(*The shivaree is quieting down now, and* HOWARD *and* ROSEMARY *can be heard driving off as the others call.* FLO *returns, stopping in the gateway, seeing* HAL)

FLO   Madge!
(*Now* ALAN *comes running on*)

ALAN (*Incensed*)   Hal, what're you doing here?
(MRS. POTTS *and* MILLIE *come on, followed by* IRMA *and* CHRISTINE)

MRS. POTTS   It's the young man!

HAL   Look, Seymour, I didn't swipe your lousy car. Get that straight!

ALAN   You better get out of town if you know what's good for you.

HAL   I'll go when I'm ready.

MRS. POTTS   Go? I thought you were going to stay here and settle down.

HAL   No'm. I'm not gonna settle down.

ALAN (*Tearing into* HAL *savagely*)   You'll go *now*. What do you take me for?

HAL (*Holding* ALAN *off, not wanting a fight*)   Look, kid, I don't wanta fight with *you*. You're the only friend I ever had.

ALAN   We're not friends any more. I'm not scared of you.
(ALAN *plows into* HAL, *but* HAL *is far beyond him in strength and physical alertness. He fastens* ALAN'S *arms quickly behind him and brings him to the ground.* IRMA *and* CHRISTINE

watch excitedly from the gateway. MRS. POTTS *is apprehensive.* ALAN *cries out in pain*) Let me go, you goddamn tramp! Let me go!

FLO (*To* HAL)   Take your hands off him, this minute.
(*But* ALAN *has to admit he is mastered.* HAL *releases him and* ALAN *retires to* MRS. POTTS' *back doorstep, sitting there, holding his hands over his face, feeling the deepest humiliation. A train whistle is heard in the distance.* HAL *hurries to* MADGE's *side*)

HAL (*To* MADGE)   Baby, aren't you gonna say good-bye?

FLO (*To* IRMA *and* CHRISTINE)   You better run along, girls. This is no side show we're running.
(*They depart in a huff*)

MADGE (*Keeping her head down, not wanting to look at* HAL)
. . . Good-bye . . .

HAL   Please don't be mad, baby. You were sittin' there beside me lookin' so pretty, sayin' all those sweet things, and I . . . I thought you liked me, too, baby. Honest I did.

MADGE   It's all right. I'm not mad.

HAL   Thanks. Thanks a lot.

FLO (*Like a barking terrier*)   Young man, if you don't leave here this second, I'm going to call the police and have you put where you belong.
(MADGE *and* HAL *do not even hear*)

MADGE   *And I* . . . I *did* like you . . . the first time I saw you.

FLO (*Incensed*)   Madge!

HAL (*Beaming*)   Honest? (MADGE *nods*) I kinda thought you did.
(*All has been worth it now for* HAL. MILLIE *watches skeptically from doorstep.* MRS. POTTS *looks on lovingly from the back.* FLO *at times concerns herself with* ALAN, *then with trying to get rid of* HAL)

FLO   Madge, I want you inside the house this minute.
(MADGE *doesn't move*)

HAL   Look, baby, I never said it before. I never could. It made me feel like such a freak, but I . . .

MADGE   What?

HAL   I'm nuts about you, baby. I mean it.

MADGE   You make love to lots of girls . . .

HAL   A few.

MADGE   . . . just like you made love to me last night.

HAL   Not like last night, baby. Last night was . . . (*Gropes for the word*) *inspired.*

MADGE   Honest?

HAL   The way you sat there, knowin' just how I felt. The way you held my hand and talked.

MADGE   I couldn't stand to hear Miss Sydney treat you that way. After all, you're a man.

HAL   And you're a woman, baby, whether you know it or not. You're a real, live woman.
(*A police siren is heard stirring up the distance.* FLO, MRS. POTTS *and* MILLIE *are alarmed*)

MILLIE   Hey, it's the cops.

MRS. POTTS   I'll know how to take care of them.
(MRS. POTTS *hurries off, right,* MILLIE *watching.* HAL *and* MADGE *have not moved. They stand looking into each other's eyes. Then* HAL *speaks*)

HAL   Do—do you love me?

MADGE   (*Tears forming in her eyes*)   What good is it if I do?

HAL   I'm a poor bastard, baby. I've gotta claim the things in this life that're mine. Kiss me good-bye. (*He grabs her and kisses her*) Come with me, baby. They gimme a room in the basement of the hotel. It's kinda crummy but we could share it till we found something better.

FLO   (*Outraged*)   Madge! Are you out of your senses?

MADGE   I couldn't.
(*The train whistles in the distance*)

FLO   Young man, you'd better get on that train as fast as you can.

HAL   (*To* MADGE)   When you hear that train pull outa town and know I'm on it, your little heart's gonna be busted, 'cause you love me, God damn it! You love me, you love me, you love me.
(*He stamps one final kiss on her lips, then runs off to catch his train.* MADGE *falls in a heap when he releases her.* FLO *is quick to console* MADGE)

FLO   Get up, girl.

MADGE   Oh, Mom!

FLO   Why did this have to happen to you?

MADGE   I *do* love him! I *do!*

FLO   Hush, girl. Hush. The neighbors are on their porches,
watching.

MADGE   I never knew what the feeling was. Why didn't someone tell me?

MILLIE   (*Peering off at the back*)   He made it. He got on the
train.

MADGE   (*A cry of deep regret*)   Now I'll never see him again.

FLO   Madge, believe me, that's for the best.

MADGE   Why? Why?

FLO   At least you didn't marry him.

MADGE   (*A wail of anguish*)   Oh, Mom, what can you do
with the love you feel? Where is there you can take it?

FLO   (*Beaten and defeated*)   I . . . I never found out.
    (MADGE *goes into the house, crying.* MRS. POTTS *returns,
    carrying* HAL's *boots. She puts them on the porch*)

MRS. POTTS   The police found these on the river bank.

ALAN   (*On* MRS. POTTS' *steps, rises*)   Girls have always liked
Hal. Months after he'd left the fraternity, they still called.
"Is Hal there?" "Does anyone know where Hal's gone?"
Their voices always sounded so forlorn.

FLO   Alan, come to dinner tonight. I'm having sweet-potato
pie and all the things you like.

ALAN   I'll be gone, Mrs. Owens.

FLO   Gone?

ALAN   Dad's been wanting me to take him up to Michigan on
a fishing trip. I've been stalling him, but now I . . .

FLO   You'll be back before you go to school, won't you?

ALAN   I'll be back Christmas, Mrs. Owens.

FLO   Christmas! Alan, go inside and say good-bye to Madge!

ALAN   (*Recalling his past love*)   Madge is beautiful. It made
me feel so proud—just to *look* at her—and tell myself she's
mine.

FLO See her one more time, Alan!

ALAN (*His mind is made up*) No! I'll be home Christmas.
I'll run over then and—say hello.
(*He runs off*)

FLO (*A cry of loss*) Alan!

MRS. POTTS (*Consolingly*) He'll be back, Flo. He'll be back.

MILLIE (*Waving good-bye*) Good-bye, Alan!

FLO (*Getting life started again*) You better get ready for
school, Millie.

MILLIE (*Going to doorstep, rather sad*) Gee, I almost forgot.
(*She goes inside.* FLO *turns to* MRS. POTTS)

FLO You—you liked the young man, didn't you, Helen? Admit it.

MRS. POTTS Yes, I did.

FLO (*Belittlingly*) Hmm.

MRS. POTTS With just Mama and me in the house, I'd got so
used to things as they were, everything so prim, occasionally
a hairpin on the floor, the geranium in the window, the
smell of Mama's medicines . . .

FLO I'll keep things as they are in *my* house, thank you.

MRS. POTTS Not when a man is there, Flo. He walked
through the door and suddenly everything was different. He
clomped through the tiny rooms like he was still in the great
outdoors, he talked in a booming voice that shook the ceiling. Everything he did reminded me there was a man in the
house, and it seemed good.

FLO (*Skeptically*) Did it?

MRS. POTTS And that reminded *me* . . . I'm a woman, and
that seemed good, too.
(*Now* MILLIE *comes swaggering out the front door, carrying her schoolbooks*)

MILLIE (*Disparagingly*) Madge is in love with that crazy
guy. She's in there crying her eyes out.

FLO Mind your business and go to school.

MILLIE I'm never gonna fall in love. Not me.

MRS. POTTS Wait till you're a little older before you say that,
Millie-girl.

MILLIE I'm old enough already. Madge can *stay* in this jerk-water town and marry some ornery guy and raise a lot of dirty kids. When I graduate from college I'm going to New York, and write novels that'll shock people right out of their senses.

MRS. POTTS You're a talented girl, Millie.

MILLIE (*Victoriously*) I'll be so great and famous—I'll never have to fall in love.

A BOY'S VOICE (*From offstage, heckling* MILLIE) Hey, goon-girl!

MILLIE (*Spotting him in the distance*) It's Poopdeck McCullough. He thinks he's so smart.

BOY'S VOICE Hey, goongirl! Come kiss me. I wanna be sick.

MILLIE (*Her anger roused*) If he thinks he can get by with that, he's crazy.
(*She finds a stick with which to chastise her offender*)

FLO Millie! Millie! You're a grown girl now.
(MILLIE *thinks better of it, drops the stick and starts off*)

MILLIE. See you this evening.
(*She goes off*)

FLO (*Wanting reassurance*) Alan *will* be back, don't you think so, Helen?

MRS. POTTS Of course he'll be back, Flo. He'll be back at Christmas time and take her to the dance at the country club, and they'll get married and live happily ever after.

FLO I hope so.
(*Suddenly* MADGE *comes out the front door. She wears a hat and carries a small cardboard suitcase. There is a look of firm decision on her face. She walks straight to the gate-way*)

FLO (*Stunned*) Madge!

MADGE I'm going to Tulsa, Mom.

MRS. POTTS (*To herself*) For heaven's sake.

MADGE Please don't get mad. I'm not doing it to be spiteful.

FLO (*Holding her head*) As I live and breathe!

MADGE I know how you feel, but I don't know what else to do.

FLO (*Anxiously*)   Now look, Madge, Alan's coming back Christmas. He'll take you to the dance at the club. I'll make another new dress for you, and . . .

MADGE   I'm going, Mom.

FLO (*Frantic*)   Madge! Listen to what I've got to say . . .

MADGE   My bus leaves in a few minutes.

FLO   He's no good. He'll never be able to support you. When he does have a job, he'll spend all his money on booze. After a while, there'll be other women.

MADGE   I've thought of all those things.

MRS. POTTS   You don't love someone 'cause he's perfect, Flo.

FLO   Oh, God!

BOYS' VOICES (*In the distance*)   Hey, Madge! Hey, beautiful! You're the one for me!

MRS. POTTS   Who are those boys?

MADGE   Some of the gang, in their hot rod. (*Kisses* MRS. POTTS) Good-bye, Mrs. Potts. I'll miss you almost as much as Mom.

FLO (*Tugging at* MADGE, *trying to take the suitcase from her*)   Madge, now listen to me. I can't let you . . .

MADGE   It's no use, Mom. I'm going. Don't worry. I've got ten dollars I was saving for a pair of pumps, and I saw ads in the Tulsa *World*. There's lots of jobs as waitresses. Tell Millie good-bye for me, Mom. Tell her I never meant it all those times I said I hated her.

FLO (*Wailing*)   Madge . . . Madge . . .

MADGE   Tell her I've always been very proud to have such a smart sister.
(*She runs off now,* FLO *still tugging at her, then giving up and standing by the gatepost, watching* MADGE *in the distance*)

FLO   Helen, could I stop her?

MRS. POTTS   Could anyone have stopped you, Flo?
(FLO *gives* MRS. POTTS *a look of realization*)

BOYS' VOICES   Hey, Madge! You're the one for me!

FLO (*Still watching* MADGE *in the distance*)   She's so young.

There are so many things I meant to tell her, and never got around to it.

MRS. POTTS   Let her learn them for herself, Flo.

MRS. POTTS' MOTHER   Helen! Helen!

MRS. POTTS   Be patient, Mama.
(*Starts up the stairs to her back porch.* FLO *still stands in the gateway, watching in the distance*)

CURTAIN

☆

Bus Stop

★

Bus Stop *was first presented by Robert Whitehead and Roger L. Stevens at The Music Box, New York City, on March 2, 1955, with the following cast:*

ELMA DUCKWORTH	Phyllis Love
GRACE	Elaine Stritch
WILL MASTERS	Lou Polan
CHERIE	Kim Stanley
DR. GERALD LYMAN	Anthony Ross
CARL	Patrick McVey
VIRGIL BLESSING	Crahan Denton
BO DECKER	Albert Salmi

DIRECTED BY Harold Clurman
SETTING BY Boris Aronson
COSTUMES AND LIGHTING BY Paul Morrison

Scenes

The action of the play takes place in a street-corner restaurant in a small town about thirty miles west of Kansas City.

ACT ONE	A night in early March. 1:00 A.M.
ACT TWO	A few minutes later.
ACT THREE	Early morning. About 5:00 A.M.

ACT ONE

SCENE: *The entire play is set inside a street-corner restaurant in a small Kansas town about thirty miles west of Kansas City. The restaurant serves also as an occasional rest stop for the bus lines in the area. It is a dingy establishment with few modern improvements: scenic calendars and pretty-girl posters decorate the soiled walls, and illumination comes from two badly shaded light bulbs that hang on dangling cords from the ceiling; in the center are several quartet tables with chairs, for dining; at far left is the counter with six stools before it, running the depth of the setting; behind the counter are the usual restaurant equipment and paraphernalia (coffee percolator, dishes, glasses, electric refrigerator, etc.); on top of the counter are several large plates of doughnuts, sweet rolls, etc., under glass covers. At the far right, close to the outside entrance door, are a magazine stand and a rack of shelves piled with paperback novels and books. At back center is an old-fashioned Franklin stove. At the back right is a great window that provides a view of the local scenery. Against the wall, beneath the window, are two long benches meant for waiting passengers. At the back left is the rear door, close to the upper end of the counter. Above this door is a dim hand-painted sign, "Rest Rooms in the Rear."*

It is 1:00 A.M. on a night in early March and a near blizzard is raging outside. Through the windows we can see the sweeping wind and flying snow. Inside, by comparison, the scene is warm and cozy, the Franklin stove radiating all the heat of which it is capable. Two young women, in uniforms that have lost their starched freshness, are employed behind the counter. ELMA is a big-eyed girl still in high school. GRACE is a more seasoned character in her thirties or early forties. A bus is expected soon and they are checking, somewhat lackadaisically, the supplies. Outside, the powerful, reckless wind comes and goes, blasting against everything in its path, seeming to shake the very foundation of the little restaurant building; then subsiding, leaving a period of uncertain stillness.

When the curtain goes up, ELMA stands far right, looking out the large plate-glass window, awed by the fury of the elements. GRACE is at the telephone.

153

ELMA   Listen to that wind. March is coming in like a lion.
(GRACE *jiggles the receiver on the telephone with no results*)
Grace, you should come over here and look out, to see the
way the wind is blowing things all over town.

GRACE   Now I wonder why I can't get th' operator.

ELMA   I bet the bus'll be late.

GRACE   (*Finally hanging up*)   I bet it won't. The roads are
O.K. as far as here. It's *ahead* they're havin' trouble. I can't
even get the operator. She must have more calls than she
can handle.

ELMA   (*Still looking out the window*)   I bet the bus doesn't
have many passengers.

GRACE   Prob'ly not. But we gotta stay open even if there's
only *one*.

ELMA   I shouldn't think anyone would take a trip tonight
unless he absolutely *had* to.

GRACE   Are your folks gonna worry, Elma?

ELMA   No— Daddy said, before I left home, he bet this'd
happen.

GRACE   (*Going behind counter*)   Well, you better come back
here and help me. The bus'll be here any minute and we
gotta have things ready.

ELMA   (*Leaving the window, following* GRACE)   Nights like
this, I'm glad I have a home to go to.

GRACE   Well, I got a home to go to, but there ain't anyone
in it.

ELMA   Where's your husband now, Grace?

GRACE   How should I know?

ELMA   Don't you miss him?

GRACE   No!

ELMA   If he came walking in now, wouldn't you be glad to
see him?

GRACE   You ask more questions.

ELMA   I'm just curious about things, Grace.

GRACE   Well, kids your age *are*. I don't know. I'd be happy to
see him, I guess, if I knew he wasn't gonna stay very long.

ELMA   Don't you get lonesome, Grace, when you're not working down here?

GRACE   Sure I do. If I didn't have this restaurant to keep me busy, I'd prob'ly go nuts. Sometimes, at night, after I empty the garbage and lock the doors and turn out the lights, I get kind of a sick feelin', 'cause I sure don't look forward to walkin' up those stairs and lettin' myself into an empty apartment.

ELMA   Gee, if you feel that way, why don't you write your husband and tell him to come back?

GRACE   (*Thinks a moment*)   'Cause I got just as lonesome when he was here. He wasn't much company, 'cept when we were makin' love. But makin' love is *one* thing, and bein' lonesome is another. The resta the time, me and Barton was usually fightin'.

ELMA   I guess my folks get along pretty well. I mean . . . they really seem to like each other.

GRACE   Oh, I know *all* married people aren't like Barton and I. Not all! (*Goes to telephone again*) Now, maybe I can get the operator. (*Jiggles receiver*) Quiet as a tomb. (*Hangs up*)

ELMA   I *like* working here with you, Grace.

GRACE   Do you, honey? I'm glad, 'cause I sure don't know what I'd do without ya. Week ends especially.

ELMA   You know, I dreaded the job at first.

GRACE   (*Kidding her*)   Why? Thought you wouldn't have time for all your boy friends? (ELMA *looks a little sour*) Maybe you'd have more boy friends if you didn't make such good grades. Boys feel kind of embarrassed if they feel a girl is smarter than they are.

ELMA   What should I do? Flunk my courses?

GRACE   I should say not. You're a good kid and ya got good sense. I wish someone coulda reasoned with *me* when I was your age. But I was a headstrong brat, had to have my own way. I had my own way all right, and here I am now, a grass widow runnin' a restaurant, and I'll prob'ly die in this little town and they'll bury me out by the backhouse.
(WILL, *the sheriff, comes in the front door, wind and snow flying through the door with him. He is a huge, saturnine man, well over six feet, who has a thick black beard and a scar on his forehead. He wears a battered black hat, clumsy overshoes, and a heavy mackinaw. He looks somewhat forbidding*)

WILL (*On entering*) You girls been able to use your phone?

GRACE No, Will. The operator don't answer.

WILL That means *all* the lines are down. 'Bout time fer the Topeka bus, ain't it?

GRACE Due now.

WILL You're gonna have to hold 'em here, don't know how long. The highway's blocked 'tween here and Topeka. May be all night gettin' it cleared.

GRACE I was afraid a that.

WILL They got the highway gang workin' on it now and the telephone company's tryin' to get the lines back up. March is comin' in like a lion, all right.

GRACE Yah.

WILL (*Taking off his mackinaw, hanging it, going to the fire to warm his hands*) The station house's *cold*. Got any fresh coffee?

GRACE It just went through, Will. Fresh as ya could want it.

WILL (*Goes to counter*) A storm like this makes me mad. (GRACE *laughs at his remark and gives him a cup of coffee*) It *does*. It makes me mad. It's just like all the elements had lost their reason.

GRACE Nothin' you can do about a wind like *that*.

WILL Maybe it's just 'cause I'm a sheriff, but I like to see things in order.

GRACE Let the wind blow! I just pray to God to leave a roof over my head. That's about all a person *can* do.
(*The sound of the bus is heard outside, its great motor coming to a stop*)

WILL Here it is.

GRACE Better fill some water glasses, Elma. Remember, the doughnuts are left over from yesterday but it'll be all right to serve 'em. We got everything for sandwiches but *cheese*. We got no cheese.

WILL You *never* got cheese, Grace.

GRACE I guess I'm kinda self-centered, Will. I don't care for cheese m'self, so I never think t'order it for someone else.

ELMA Gee, I'm glad I'm not traveling on the bus tonight.

GRACE   I wonder who's drivin' tonight. This is Carl's night, isn't it?

ELMA   I think so.

GRACE   Yes it is. (*Obviously the idea of* CARL *pleases her. She nudges* ELMA *confidentially*) Remember, honey, *I* always serve Carl.

ELMA   Sure, Grace.

(*The door swings open, some of the snow flying inside, and* CHERIE, *a young blond girl of about twenty, enters as though driven. She wears no hat, and her hair, despite one brilliant bobby pin, blows wild about her face. She is pretty in a fragile, girlish way. She runs immediately to the counter to solicit the attention of* GRACE *and* ELMA. *She lugs along an enormous straw suitcase that is worn and battered. Her clothes, considering her situation, are absurd: a skimpy jacket of tarnished metal cloth edged with not luxuriant fur, a dress of sequins and net, and gilded sandals that expose brightly enameled toes. Also, her make-up has been applied under the influence of having seen too many movies. Her lipstick creates a voluptuous pair of lips that aren't her own, and her eyebrows also form a somewhat arbitrary line. But despite all these defects, her prettiness still is apparent, and she has the appeal of a tender little bird. Her origin is the Ozarks and her speech is Southern*)

CHERIE   (*Anxious, direct*)   Is there some place I kin hide?

GRACE   (*Taken aback*)   What?

CHERIE   There's a *man* on that bus . . . I wanta *hide.*

GRACE   (*Stumped*)   Well, gee . . . I dunno.

CHERIE   (*Seeing the sign above the rear door, starting for it*) I'll hide in the powder room. If a tall, lanky cowboy comes in here, you kin just tell him I disappeared.

GRACE   (*Her voice stopping* CHERIE *at the door*)   Hey, you can't hide out there. It's cold. You'll freeze your . . .

CHERIE   (*Having opened the door, seeing it is an outside toilet*) Oh! It's outside.

GRACE   This is just a country town.

CHERIE   (*Starting again*)   I kin stand anything fer twenty minutes.

GRACE   (*Stopping her again*)   I got news for ya. The bus may be here all night.

CHERIE (*Turning*) What?

GRACE The highway's blocked. You're gonna have to stay here till it's cleared.

CHERIE (*Shutting the door, coming to counter, lugging her suitcase. She is about to cry*) Criminey! What am I gonna do?

GRACE (*Coming from behind counter, going to front door*) I better go out and tell Carl 'bout the delay.

CHERIE (*Dropping to a stool at the counter*) What am I gonna do? What am I ever gonna do?

ELMA (*In a friendly way*) There's a little hotel down the street.

CHERIE What ya take me for? A millionaire?

WILL (*Coming to* CHERIE *with a professional interest*) What's the trouble, miss?

CHERIE (*Looking at* WILL *suspiciously*) You a p'liceman?

WILL I'm the local sheriff.

ELMA (*Feeling some endorsement is called for*) But everyone likes him. Really!

CHERIE Well . . . I ain't askin' t'have no one arrested.

WILL Who says I'm gonna arrest anyone? What's your trouble?

CHERIE I . . . I need protection.

WILL What from?

CHERIE There's a man after me. He's a cowboy.

WILL (*Looking around*) Where is he?

CHERIE He's on the bus, asleep, him and his buddy. I jumped off the bus the very second it stopped, to make my getaway. But there ain't no place to *get* away to. And he'll be in here purty soon. You just *gotta* make him lemme alone.

WILL Ya meet him on the bus?

CHERIE No. I met him in Kansas City. I work at the Blue Dragon night club there, down by the stockyards. *He* come there with the annual rodeo, and him and the resta the cowboys was at the night club ev'ry night. Ev'ry night there was a big fight. The boss says he ain't gonna let the cowboys in when they come back next year.

WILL   Then he followed ya on the bus?

CHERIE   He *put* me on the bus. I'm bein' abducted.

WILL   Abducted! But you took time to pack a suitcase!

CHERIE   I was goin' somewhere else, tryin' to get away from
him, but he picked me up and carried me to the bus and put
me on it. I din have nothin' to say about it at all.

WILL   Where's he plan on takin' ya?

CHERIE   Says he's got a ranch up in Montana. He says we're
gonna git married soon as we get there.

WILL   And yor against it?

CHERIE   I don't wanta go up to some God-forsaken ranch in
Montana.

WILL   Well, if this cowboy's really takin' ya against yor will,
I s'pose I'll have to stop him from it.

CHERIE   You just don't know this cowboy. He's mean.

WILL   I reckon I kin handle him. You relax now. I'll be
around mosta the night. If there's any trouble, I'll put a stop
to it.

ELMA   You're safe with Will here. Will is very respected
around here. He's never lost a fight.

WILL   What're ya talkin' about, Elma? Of course I've lost a
fight . . . once.

ELMA   Grace always said you were *invincible*.

WILL   There ain't no one that's . . . *invincible*. A man's
gotta learn that, the sooner the better. A good fighter has
gotta know what it is to *get* licked. Thass what makes the
diff'rence 'tween a fighter and a *bully*.

CHERIE   (*Shuddering*)   There's gonna be trouble. I kin feel it
in my bones.
(*Enter* DR. GERALD LYMAN, *a man of medium height, about
fifty, with a ruddy, boyish face that smilingly defies the
facts of his rather scholarly glasses and iron-gray hair. He
wears an old tweed suit of good quality underneath a worn
Burberry. His clothes are mussed, and he wears no hat,
probably having left it somewhere; for he has been drinking
and is, at present, very jubilant. He looks over the restaurant
approvingly*)

DR. LYMAN   Ah! "This castle hath a pleasant seat."

CHERIE (*To* ELMA) Could I hide my suitcase behind the counter, so's he won't see it when he comes in? I ain't gonna say anything to him at all 'bout not goin' on to Montana with him. I'm just gonna let 'im think I'm goin' till the bus pulls out and he finds I ain't on it. Thass th' only thing I know t' do.

ELMA (*Taking the suitcase and putting it behind counter*) Oh, you needn't worry with Will here.

CHERIE Think so? (*She studies* WILL) Looks kinda like Moses, don't he?

ELMA He *is* a very religious man. Would you believe it? He's a deacon in the Congregational Church.

CHERIE (*Just because she happens to think of it*) My folks was Holy Rollers. Will ya gimme a cup of coffee, please? Lotsa cream.
(ELMA *draws a cup of coffee for her. Then* CARL, *the bus driver, comes in, followed by* GRACE. CARL *is a hefty man, loud and hearty, who looks very natty in his uniform*)

WILL (*Calling to him from across the room*) Howdy, Carl! You bring this wind?

CARL (*Hollering back*) No! It brought *me!*
(*This greeting probably has passed between them a dozen times, but they still relish it as new*)

GRACE Aren't you the comedian?

CARL The wind is doin' ninety miles an hour. The bus is doin' twenty. What's *your* guess about the roads, Will?

WILL They got the highway gang out. It may take a few hours.

CARL Telephone lines down, too?

WILL Yah. But they're workin' on 'em.
(DR. LYMAN, *having got his extremities warmed at the fire, seeks* CARL *privately to make certain clarifications*)

DR. LYMAN Driver, it seems to me we are still in the state of Kansas. Is that right?

CARL What do ya mean, *still?* You been in the state of Kansas about a half-hour.

DR. LYMAN But I don't understand. I was told, when I left Kansas City, that I would be across the state line immediately. And now I find . . .

CARL (*Eying* DR. LYMAN *suspiciously*) You was kinda anxious to get across that state line, too, wasn't you, Jack?

DR. LYMAN (*Startled*) Why . . . what ever do you mean?

CARL Nothin'. Anyway, you're across the line now. In case you didn't know it, Kansas City is in *Missouri*.

DR. LYMAN Are you joking?

CARL There's a Kansas City, Kansas, too, but *you* got on in Kansas City, Missouri. That's the trouble with you easterners. You don't know anything about any of the country west of the Hudson River.

DR. LYMAN Come, come now. Don't scold.

GRACE (*As* CARL *gets out of his heavy coat*) Carl, let me hang up your coat fer ya, while you get warm at the stove. (DR. LYMAN'S *eyes brighten when he sees* ELMA, *and he bows before her like a cavalier*)

DR. LYMAN "Nymph, in thy orisons be all my sins remembered!"

ELMA (*Smiling*) I'm sorry your bus is held up.

DR. LYMAN Oohh! Is that a nice way to greet me?

ELMA (*Confused*) I mean . . .

DR. LYMAN After my loving greeting, all you can think of to say is, "I'm sorry your bus is held up." Well, I'm not. I would much rather sit here looking into the innocent blue of your eyes than continue riding on that monotonous bus.

ELMA Don't you have to get somewhere?

DR. LYMAN I have a ticket in my pocket to Denver, but I don't have to get there. I never have to get *any*where. I travel around from one town to another just to prove to myself that I'm *free*.

ELMA The bus probably won't get into Denver for another day.

DR. LYMAN Ah, well! What is our next stop?

ELMA Topeka.

DR. LYMAN Topeka? Oh, yes! that's where the famous hospital is, isn't it?

ELMA The Menninger Clinic? Yes, it's a very famous place. Lots of movie stars go there for nervous breakdowns and things.

DR. LYMAN (*Wryly*) Does the town offer anything else in the way of diversion?

ELMA It's the capital of Kansas. It's almost as big as Kansas City. They have a university and a museum, and sometimes symphony concerts and plays. I go over there every Sunday to visit my married sister.

DR. LYMAN Aren't there any Indian tribes around here that have war dances?

ELMA (*Laughing*) No, silly! We're very civilized.

DR. LYMAN I'll make my own judgment about that. Meanwhile, you may fix me a double shot of rye whiskey . . . on the rocks.

ELMA I'm sorry, sir. We don't sell drinks.

DR. LYMAN You don't sell drinks?

ELMA Not intoxicating drinks. No, sir.

DR. LYMAN Alas!

ELMA We have fresh coffee, homemade pies and cakes, all kinds of sandwiches . . .

DR. LYMAN No, my girl. You're not going to sober me up with your dainties. I am prepared for such emergencies. (*Draws a pint bottle of whiskey from his overcoat pocket*) You may give me a bottle of your finest lemon soda.

ELMA (*Whispering*) You'd better not let Will see you do that. You're not supposed to.

DR. LYMAN Who is *he*, the sheriff?

ELMA Yes. Lots of people do spike their drinks here and we never say anything, but Will would have to make you stop if *he* saw you.

DR. LYMAN I shall be *most* cautious. I promise.
(*She sets the bottle of soda before him as he smiles at her benignly. He pours some soda in a glass, then some whiskey, and ambles over to a table, far right, sitting down with his drink before him.* WILL *moves over to* CARL, *who's at the end of the counter, chiding* GRACE, *where the two of them have been standing, talking in very personal voices that can't be overheard*)

WILL I sure don't envy ya, Carl, drivin' in weather like this.

CARL (*Making it sound like a personal observation*) Yah! March is comin' in like a *lion*.

WILL   This all the passengers ya got?

CARL   There's a coupla crazy cowboys rolled up in the back seat, asleep. I thought I woke 'em, but I guess I didn't.

WILL   Shouldn't you go out and do it now?

CARL   I'd jest as soon they stayed where they're at. One of 'em's a real troublemaker. You know the kind, first time off a ranch and wild as a bronco. He's been on the make fer this li'l blonde down here . . .
(*Indicates* CHERIE)

WILL   She was tellin' me.

CARL   I've had a good mind to put him off the bus, the way he's been actin'. I say, there's a time and place for ev'rything.

WILL   That bus may get snowbound purty soon.

CARL   I'll go wake 'em in a minute, Will. Just lemme have a li'l *time* here. (WILL *sizes up the situation as* CARL *returns his attention to* GRACE, *then* WILL *picks up a copy of the* Kansas City Star, *sitting down close to the fire to read*) Ya know what, Grace? This is the first time you and I ever had more'n twenty minutes t'gether.

GRACE (*Coyly*)   So what?

CARL   Oh, I dunno. I'll prob'ly be here mosta the night. It'd sure be nice to have a nice li'l apartment to go to, some place to sit and listen to the radio, with a good-lookin' woman . . . somethin' like you . . . to talk with . . . maybe have a few beers.

GRACE   That wouldn't be a hint or anything, would it?

CARL (*Faking innocence*)   Why? Do you have an apartment like that, Grace?

GRACE   Yes, I do. But I never told *you* about it. Did that ornery Dobson fella tell you I had an apartment over the restaurant?

CARL (*In a query*)   Dobson? Dobson? I can't seem to remember anyone named Dobson.

GRACE   You know him better'n *I* do. He comes through twice a week with the Southwest Bus. He told me you and him meet in Topeka sometimes and paint the town.

CARL   Dobson? Oh, yah, I know Dobson. Vern Dobson. A prince of a fella.

GRACE   Well, if he's been gabbin' to you about my apartment,
I can tell ya he's oney been up there *once,* when he come in
here with his hand cut, and I took him up there to bandage
it. Now that's the oney time he was ever up there. On my
word of honor.

CARL   Oh, Vern Dobson speaks very highly of you, Grace.
Very highly.

GRACE   Well . . . he better. Now, what ya gonna have?

CARL   Make it a ham and cheese on rye.

GRACE   I'm sorry, Carl. We got no cheese.

CARL   What happened? Did the mice get it?

GRACE   None of your wise remarks.

CARL   O.K. Make it a ham on rye, then.

GRACE   (*At breadbox*)   I'm sorry, Carl, but we got no rye,
either.

DR. LYMAN   (*Chiming in, from his table*)   I can vouch for
that, sir. I just asked for rye, myself, and was refused.

CARL   Look, mister, don't ya think ya oughta lay off that stuff
till ya get home and meet the missus?

DR. LYMAN   The *missus,* did you say? (*He laughs*) I have no
missus, sir. I'm *free.* I can travel the universe, with no one
to await my arrival anywhere.

CARL   (*To* GRACE, *bidding for a little sympathy*)   That's all I
ever get on my bus, drunks and hoodlums.

GRACE   How's fer whole wheat, Carl?

CARL   O.K. Make it whole wheat.

DR. LYMAN   (*To* ELMA, *as she brings him more soda*)   Yes, I
am free. My third and last wife deserted me several years
ago . . . for a ballplayer.
(*He chuckles as though it were all a big absurdity*)

ELMA   (*A little astounded*)   Your *third?*

DR. LYMAN   Yes, my third! Getting married is a careless habit
I've fallen into. Sometime, really, I *must* give it all up. Oh,
but she was pretty! Blonde, like the young lady over there.
(*He indicates* CHERIE) And Southern, too, or pretended to
be. However, she was kinder than the others when we
parted. She didn't care about money. All she wanted was to
find new marital bliss with her ballplayer, so I never had to

pay her alimony . . . as if I could. (*He chuckles, sighs and recalls another*) My second wife was a different type entirely. But she was very pretty, too. I have always exercised the most excellent taste, if not the best judgment. She was a student of mine, when I was teaching at an eastern university. Alas! she sued me for divorce on the grounds that I was incontinent and always drunk. I didn't have a chance to resign from that position.
(*Still he manages to chuckle about it*)

CHERIE (*From the counter*) Hey! how much are them doughnuts?
(*She is counting the coins in her purse*)

ELMA (*Leaving* DR. LYMAN, *hurrying back to counter*) I'll make you a special price, two for a nickel.

CHERIE   O.K.

DR. LYMAN (*Musingly, he begins to recite as though for his own enjoyment*)
     "That time of year thou may'st in me behold
     When yellow leaves, or none, or few, do hang
     Upon those boughs—"

CHERIE (*Shivering, she goes to the stove*) I never was so cold in my life.

ELMA (*Setting the doughnuts before her*) Do you honestly work in a night club?

CHERIE (*Brightening with this recognition*) Sure! I'm a *chanteuse*. I call m'self *Cherie*.

ELMA   That's French, isn't it?

CHERIE   I dunno. I jest seen the name once and it kinda appealed t'me.

ELMA   It's French. It means "dear one." Is that all the name you use?

CHERIE   Sure. Thass all the name ya need. Like Hildegarde. She's a *chanteuse*, too.

ELMA   *Chanteuse* means singer.

CHERIE   How come *you* know so much?

ELMA   I'm taking French in high school.

CHERIE   Oh! (*A reflective pause*) I never got as far as high school. See, I was the oldest girl left in the fam'ly after my sister Violet ran away. I had two more sisters, both young-

er'n me, and five brothers, most of 'em older. Was they
mean! Anyway, I had to quit school when I was twelve, to
stay home and take care a the house and do the cookin'.
I'm a real good cook. Honest!

ELMA   Did you *study* singing?

CHERIE   (*Shaking her head*)   Huh-uh. Jest picked it up listenin' to the radio, seein' movies, tryin' to put over my songs
as good as them people did.

ELMA   How did you get started in the night club?

CHERIE   I won a amateur contest. Down in Joplin, Missouri.
I won the second prize there . . . a coupla boys won *first*
prize . . . they juggled milk bottles . . . I don't think
that's fair, do you? To make an artistic performer compete
with jugglers and knife-throwers and people like that?

ELMA   No, I don't.

CHERIE   Anyway, second prize was good enough to get me
to Kanz City t'enter the contest there. It was a real *big* contest and I didn't win any prize at all, but it got me the job
at the Blue Dragon.

ELMA   Is that where you're from, Joplin?

CHERIE   (*With an acceptance of nature's catastrophes*)   No.
Joplin's a *big* town. I lived 'bout a hundred miles from there,
in River Gulch, a li'l town in the Ozarks. I lived there till
the floods come, three years ago this spring, and washed us
all away.

ELMA   Gee, that's too bad.

CHERIE   I dunno where any a my folks are now, 'cept my
baby sister Nan. We all just separated when the floods come
and I took Nan into Joplin with me. She got a job as a
waitress and I went to work in Liggett's drug store, till the
amateur contest opened.

ELMA   It must be fun working in a night club.

CHERIE   (*A fleeting look of disillusionment comes over her
face*)   Well . . . it ain't all roses.

CARL   (*Leaving* GRACE *for the moment*)   You gonna be here
a while, Will?

WILL   I reckon.

CARL   I'm gonna send them cowboys in here now, and leave
you to look after 'em.

WILL   I'll do my best.

CARL   Tell ya somethin' else, Will.
(CARL *looks at* DR. LYMAN *cautiously, as though he didn't want to be overheard by him, then moves very closely to* WILL *and whispers something in his ear.* WILL *looks very surprised*)

WILL   I'll be jiggered.

CARL   So, ya better keep an eye on *him*, too.
(*Starts off*)

WILL   Ain't you comin' back, Carl?

CARL   (*Obviously he is faking, and a look between him and* GRACE *tells us something is up between them. He winks at her and stretches*)   To tell the truth, Will, I git so darn *stiff*, sittin' at the wheel all day, I thought I'd go out fer a long walk.

WILL   In this blizzard? You gone crazy?

CARL   No. That's just the kinda fclla I am, Will. I like to go fer long walks in the rain and snow. Freshens a fella up. Sometimes I walk fer hours.

WILL   Ya do?

CARL   Yah. Fer hours. That's just the kinda fella I am.
(*He saunters out now, whistling to show his nonchalance*)

WILL   (*To* GRACE)   Imagine! Goin' out fer a walk, a night like this.

GRACE   Well, it's really very good for one, Will. It really is.

CHERIE   (*Leaning over counter to talk to* ELMA *privately*)   He said he was gonna wake him up. Then he'll be in here pretty soon. You won't let on I said anything 'bout him, will ya?

ELMA   No. Cross my heart.
(DR. LYMAN *is suddenly reminded of another poem, which he begins to recite in full voice*)

DR. LYMAN

> "Shall I compare thee to a summer's day?
> Thou art more lovely and more temperate:
> Rough winds do shake the darling buds of May,
> And summer's lease hath all too short a date."

ELMA   (*Still behind counter, she hears* DR. LYMAN, *smiles fondly, and calls to him across room*)   Why, that's one of my favorite sonnets.

DR. LYMAN   It is? Do *you* read Shakespeare?

ELMA   I studied him at school, in English class. I loved the sonnets. I memorized some of them myself.

DR. LYMAN   (*Leaving table, returning to counter*)   I used to know them *all*, by heart. And many of the plays I could recite in their entirety. I often did, for the entertainment and the annoyance of my friends.
(*He and* ELMA *laugh together*)

ELMA   Last fall I memorized the Balcony Scene from *Romeo and Juliet*. A boy in class played Romeo and we presented it for convocation one day.

DR. LYMAN   Ah! I wish I had been there to see.
(CHERIE *feels called upon to explain her own position in regard to Shakespeare, as* ELMA *resumes work behind counter*)

CHERIE   Where I went to school, we din read no Shakespeare till the ninth grade. In the ninth grade everyone read *Julius Caesar*. I oney got as far as the eighth. I seen Marlon Brando in the movie, though. I sure do like that Marlon Brando.

DR. LYMAN   (*Now that* CHERIE *has called attention to herself*) Madam, where is thy Lochinvar?

CHERIE   (*Giggling*)   I don't understand anything you say, but I just love the way you say it.

DR. LYMAN   And *I* . . . understand *every*thing I say . . . but privately despise the way I say it.

CHERIE   (*Giggling*)   That's so cute. (*A memory returns*) I had a very nice friend once that recited poetry.

DR. LYMAN   (*With spoofing seriousness*)   Whatever could have happened to him?

CHERIE   I dunno. He left town. His name was Mr. Everett Brubaker. He sold second-hand cars at the corner of Eighth and Wyandotte. He had a lovely Pontiac car-with-the-top-down. He talked nice, but I guess he really wasn't any nicer'n any of the others.

DR. LYMAN   The others?

CHERIE   Well . . . ya meet quite a few men in the place I worked at, the Blue Dragon night club, out by the stock-yards. Ever hear of it?

DR. LYMAN   No, and I deeply regret the fact.

CHERIE   You're just sayin' that. An educated man like you, you wouldn't have no use fer the Blue Dragon.

DR. LYMAN   (*With a dubious look*)   I wouldn't?
(*The front door swings open again and the two cowboys,* BO DECKER *and* VIRGIL BLESSING, *enter. Their appearance now is rumpledly picturesque and they both could pass, at first glance, for outlaws.* BO *is in his early twenties, is tall and slim and good-looking in an outdoors way. Now he is very unkempt. He wears faded jeans that cling to his legs like shedding skin; his boots, worn under his jeans, are scuffed and dusty; and the Stetson on the back of his head is worn and tattered. Over a faded denim shirt he wears a shiny horsehide jacket, and around his neck is tied a bandanna.* VIRGIL *is a man in his forties who seems to regard* BO *in an almost parental way. A big man, corpulent and slow-moving, he seems almost an adjunct of* BO. *Dressed similarly to* BO, *perhaps a trifle more tidy, he carries a guitar in a case and keeps a bag of Bull Durham in his shirt pocket, out of which he rolls frequent cigarettes. Both men are still trying to wake up from their snooze, but* BO *is quick to recognize* CHERIE. *Neither cowboy has thought to shut the door behind them, and the others begin to shiver*)

BO   (*In a full voice, accustomed to speaking in an open field*)   Hey! Why din anyone wake us up? Virg'n I mighta froze out there.

GRACE   Hey! Shut the door.

BO   (*Calling across the room*)   Cherry! how come you get off the bus, 'thout lettin' me know? That any way to treat the man you're gonna marry?

WILL   (*Lifting his eyes from the paper*)   Shut the door, cowboy!
(BO *doesn't even hear* WILL, *but strides across the room to* CHERIE, *who is huddled over the counter as though hoping he might overlook her.* VIRGIL, *still rubbing sleep out of his eyes, lingers open-mouthed in the open doorway*)

BO   Thass no way to treat a fella, Cherry, to slip off the bus like ya wanted to get rid of him, maybe. And come in here and eat by yourself. I thought we'd have a li'l snack t'*gether*. Sometimes, I don't understand you, Cherry.

CHERIE   Fer the hunderth time, my name ain't *Cherry*.

BO   I cain't say it the way you do. What's wrong with Cherry?

CHERIE   It's kinda embarrassin'.

WILL (*In a firmer, louder voice*)   Cowboy, will you have the
decency to shut that door!
(VIRGIL *now responds immediately and quickly closes the
door as* BO *turns to* WILL)

BO (*There is nothing to call him for the moment but insolent*)
Why, what's the matter with you, mister? You afraid of a
little fresh air? (WILL *glowers but* BO *is not fazed*) Why,
man, ya oughta breathe real deep and git yor lungs full of it.
Thass the trouble with you city people. You git *soft*.

VIRGIL (*Whispering*)   He's the sheriff, Bo.

BO (*In full voice, for* WILL's *benefit*)   S'posin' he *is* the
sheriff! What's that matter t'*me*? That don't give him the
right t'insult my manners, does it? No man ever had to tell
me what t'do, did he, Virge? Did he?

VIRGIL   No. No. But there allus comes a time, Bo, when . . .

BO (*Ignoring* VIRGIL, *speaking out for the benefit of all*)   My
name's Bo Decker. I'm twenty-one years old and own me
m'own ranch up in Timber Hill, Montana, where I got a
herd a fine Hereford cattle and a dozen horses, and the
finest sheep and hogs and chickens anywhere in the country.
And I jest come back from a rodeo where I won 'bout ev'ry
prize there *was*, din I, Virge? (*Joshingly, he elbows* VIRGIL
in the ribs) Yap, I'm the prize bronco-buster, 'n steer-roper,
'n bulldogger, anywhere 'round. I won 'em all. And what's
more, had my picture taken by *Life* magazine. (*Confronting* WILL) So I'd appreciate your talkin' to me with a little
respect in yor voice, mister, and not go hollerin' orders to
me from across the room like I was some no-'count servant.
(WILL *is flabbergasted*)

CHERIE (*Privately to* ELMA)   Did ya ever see anybody like
him?

WILL (*Finally finds his voice and uses it, after a struggle with
himself to sound just and impartial*)   You was the last one
in, cowboy, and you left the door open. You shoulda closed
it, I don't care *who* y'are. That's all I'm saying.

BO   Door's closed now. What ya arguin' 'bout? (*Leaving a
hushed and somewhat awed audience,* BO *strides over to the
counter and drops to a stool*) Seems like we're gonna be
here a while, Virge. How's fer some grub?

VIRGIL (*Remaining by magazine counter*)   Not yet, Bo. I'm
chewin' t'backy.

BO (*Slapping a thigh*)   Thass ole Virge for ya. Allus happy
long's he's got a wad a t'backy in his mouth. Wall, I'm
gonna have me a li'l snack. (*To* ELMA) Miss, gimme 'bout
three hamburgers.

ELMA   Three? How do you want them?

BO   I want 'em *raw*.
(CHERIE *makes a sick face.* DR. LYMAN *quietly withdraws,
taking his drink over to the window*)

ELMA   Honest?

BO   It's the only way t'eat 'em, raw, with a thick slice a onion
and some piccalilli.

ELMA (*Hesitant*)   Well . . . if you're sure you're not joking.

BO (*His voice holding* ELMA *on her way to refrigerator*)   Jest
a minute, miss. That ain't all. I'd also like me some ham
and eggs . . . and some potaty salad . . . and a piece a
pie. I ain't so pertikler what *kinda* pie it is, so long as it's
got that murang on top of it.

ELMA   We have lemon and choc'late. They both have meringue.

BO (*Thinking it over*)   Lemon'n choc'late. I like 'em both. I
dunno which I'd ruther have. (*Ponders a moment*) I'll have
'em *both,* miss.
(CHERIE *makes another sick face*)

ELMA   Both?

BO   Yep! 'N set a quart a milk beside me. I'm still a growin'
boy. (ELMA *starts preparations as* BO *turns to* CHERIE) Travelin' allus picks up my appetite. That all you havin', jest
a measly doughnut?

CHERIE   I ain't hungry.

BO   Why not?

CHERIE   I jest ain't.

BO   Ya oughta be.

CHERIE   Well—I ain't!

BO   Wait till I get ya up to the Susie-Q. I'll fatten ya up. I
bet in two weeks time, ya won't recognize yorself. (*Now he
puts a bearlike arm around her, drawing her close to him
for a snuggle, kissing her on the cheek*) But doggone, I *love*
ya, Cherry, jest the way ya are. Yor about the cutest li'l

piece I ever did see. And, man! when I walked into that night club place and hear you singin' my favorite song, standin' before that orkester lookin' like a angel, I told myself then and there, she's fer *me*. I ain't gonna leave this place without her. And now I got ya, ain't I, Cherry?

CHERIE (*Trying to avoid his embrace*) Bo . . . there's people here . . . they're lookin' . . .
(*And she's right. They are*)

BO   What if they are? It's no crime to show a li'l affection, is it? 'Specially, when we're gonna git married. It's no crime I ever heard of.
(*He squeezes her harder now and forces a loud, smacking kiss on the lips.* CHERIE *twists loose of him and turns away*)

CHERIE   Bo! fer cryin' out loud, lemme *be!*

BO   Cherry, thass no way to talk to yor husband.

CHERIE   That's all ya done since we left Kanz City, is maul me.

BO   Oh, is zat so? (*This is a deep-cutting insult*) Wall, I certainly ain't one to *pester* any woman with my affections. I never had to *beg* no woman to make love to me. (*Calling over his shoulder to* VIRGIL) Did I, Virge? I never had to coax no woman to make love to me, *did* I?

VIRGIL (*In a voice that sounds more and more restrained*) No . . . no . . .

BO (*Still in full voice*)   No! Ev'rywhere I go, I got all the wimmin I want, don't I, Virge? I gotta fight 'em to keep 'em off me, don't I, Virge?
(VIRGIL *is saved from having to make a response as* ELMA *presents* BO *with his hamburgers*)

ELMA   Here are the hamburgers. The ham and eggs will take a little longer.

BO   O.K. These'll gimme a start.
(GRACE *rubs her forehead with a feigned expression of pain*)

GRACE   Elma, honey, I got the darndest headache.

ELMA   I'm sorry, Grace.

GRACE   Can you look after things awhile?

ELMA   Sure.

GRACE   'Cause the only thing for me to do is go upstairs and lie down awhile. That's the only thing gonna do me any good at all.

WILL (*From his chair*)   What's the matter, Grace?

GRACE (*At the rear door*)   I got a headache, Will, that's just drivin' me *wild*.

WILL   That so?
(GRACE *goes out*)

DR. LYMAN (*To* ELMA)   You are now the Mistress of the Inn.

ELMA   You haven't told me anything about your first wife.

DR. LYMAN   Now, how could I have omitted her?

ELMA   What was *she* like?

DR. LYMAN (*Still in the highest of spirits*)   Oh . . . she was the loveliest of them all. I do believe she was. We had such an idyllic honeymoon together, a golden month of sunshine and romance, in Bermuda. She sued me for divorce later, on the grounds of mental cruelty, and persuaded the judge that she should have my house and my motorcar, and an alimony that I still find it difficult to pay, for she never chose to marry again. She found that for all she wanted out of marriage, she didn't have to marry. (*He chuckles*) Ah, but perhaps I am being unkind.
(ELMA *is a little mystified by the humor with which he always tells of his difficulties.* BO *now leans over the counter and interrupts*)

BO   Miss, was you waitin' fer me to lay them eggs?

ELMA (*Hurrying to stove*)   Oh, I'm sorry. They're ready now.
(BO *jumps up, grabs a plate and glides over the counter for* ELMA *to serve him from the stove*)

BO   Them hamburgers was just a *horse d'oovrey*. (*He grins with appreciation of this word.* ELMA *fills his plate*) Thank ya, miss. (*He starts back for the stool but trips over* CHERIE'S *suitcase on the way*) Daggone! (*He looks down to see what has stopped him.* CHERIE *holds a rigid silence.* BO *brings his face slowly up, looking at* CHERIE *suspiciously*) Cherry! (*She says nothing*) Cherry, what'd ya wanta bring yor suitcase in here fer? (*She still says nothing*) Cherry, I'm askin' ya a civil question. What'd ya bring yor suitcase in fer? *Tell* me?

CHERIE (*Frightened*)   I . . . I . . . now don't you come near me, Bo.

BO (*Shaking* CHERIE *by the shoulders*)   Tell me! What's yor suitcase doin' there b'hind the counter? What were ya tryin' to do, *fool* me? Was you plannin' to git away from me? That what you been sittin' here plannin' t'do?

CHERIE (*Finding it hard to speak while he is shaking her*) Bo . . . lemme be . . . take your hands off me, Bo Decker.

BO   Tell me, Cherry. Tell me.
(*Now* WILL *intercedes, coming up to* BO, *laying a hand on his shoulder*)

WILL   Leave the little lady alone, cowboy.

BO (*Turning on* WILL *fiercely*)   Mister, ya got no right interferin' 'tween me and my feeancy.

WILL   Mebbe she's yor feeancy and maybe she ain't. Anyway, ya ain't gonna abuse her while *I'm* here. Unnerstand?

BO   *Abuse* her?

WILL (*To* CHERIE)   I think you better tell him now, miss, jest how you feel about things.
(BO *looks at* CHERIE *with puzzled wonder*)

CHERIE (*Finding it impossible to say*)   I . . . I . . .

BO   What's this critter tryin' to say, Cherry?

CHERIE   Well . . . I . . .

WILL   You better tell him, miss.

CHERIE   Now, Bo, don't git mad.

BO   I'll git mad if I feel like it. What you two got planned?

CHERIE   Bo, I don't wanta go up to Montana and marry ya.

BO   Ya do too.

CHERIE   I do not!

BO   Anyways, you'll come to like it in time. I *promised* ya would. Now we been through all that b'fore.

CHERIE   But, Bo . . . I ain't goin'.

BO (*A loud blast of protest*)   What?

CHERIE   I ain't goin'. The sheriff here said he'd help me. He ain't gonna let you take me any farther. I'm stayin' here and take the next bus back to Kanz City.

BO (*Grabbing her by the shoulders to reassure himself of her*)   You ain't gonna do nothin' of the kind.

CHERIE Yes, I am, Bo. You gotta b'lieve me. I ain't goin'
with ya. That's final.

BO (*In a most personal voice, baffled*) But, Cherry . . . we
was *familiar* with each other.

CHERIE That don't mean ya gotta *marry* me.

BO (*Shocked at her*) Why . . . I oughta take you across
my knee and blister yer li'l bottom.

CHERIE (*More frightened*) Don't you touch me.

BO (*To* WILL) You cain't pay no tension to what she says,
mister. Womenfolk don't know their own minds. Never
did.
(*Back to* CHERIE)

CHERIE Don't you come near me!

BO Yor gonna follow me back to Timber Hill and marry up.
You just think you wouldn't like it now 'cause ya never
been there and the whole idea's kinda strange. But you'll
get over them feelin's. In no time at all, yor gonna be
happy as a mudhen. I ain't takin' *no* fer an answer. By
God, yor comin' along.
(*He grabs her forcefully to him, as* WILL *interferes again,
pulling the two apart*)

WILL You're not takin' her with ya if she don't wanta go.
Can't you get that through your skull? Now leave her be.
(BO *stands looking at* WILL *with sullen hatred.* CHERIE
trembles. VIRGIL *stands far right, looking apprehensive*)

BO (*Confronts* WILL *threateningly*) This ain't no biznes of
yors.

WILL It's *my* business when the little lady comes t'me
wantin' protection.

BO Is that right, Cherry? Did you go to the sheriff askin' fer
pertection?

CHERIE (*Meekly*) . . . yes, I guess I did.

BO (*Bellowing out again*) *Why?* What'd ya need pertection
for . . . from a man that wants to *marry* ya?

CHERIE (*Shuddering*) . . . 'cause . . .

BO (*Bellowing angrily*) 'Cause *why?* I said I *loved* ya, din I?

CHERIE (*About to cry*) I know ya did.

BO (*Confronting* WILL *with a feeling of angry unjustness*)

See there? I told her I loved her and I wanta marry her.
And with a world fulla crazy people goin' 'round killin'
each other, *you* ain't got nothin' better t'do than stand here
tryin' to keep me from it.

WILL   Yor overlookin' jest one thing, cowboy.

BO (*With gruff impatience*)   Yor so smart. Tell me what I'm
overlookin'.

WILL   Yor overlookin' the simple but important fack that
the little lady don't love *you*.
(BO *now is trapped into silence. He can say nothing, and
one can tell that* WILL *has named a fact that* BO *did not intend to face.* VIRGIL *watches him alertly. He can tell that*
BO *is angry enough to attack* WILL *and is about to.* VIRGIL
hurries to BO'S *side, holding his arms as though to restrain
him*)

VIRGIL (*Pacifyingly*)   Now, Bo. Take it easy, Bo. Don't
blow your lid. He's the sheriff, Bo. Hold yor temper.

BO (*To* VIRGIL)   That polecat bastard! He said she din love
me.

VIRGIL (*Trying to draw him away from the scene*)   Pay no
'tention, Bo. Come on over here and sit down. Ya gotta
think things over, Bo.

BO (*Twisting loose from* VIRGIL'S *hold*)   Lemme be, Virge.

WILL   Ask the li'l lady, if ya don't b'lieve *me*. Ask her if
she loves ya.

BO   I won't ask her nothin' of the kind.

WILL   All right then, take my word for it.

BO   I wouldn't take yor word for a cloudy day. I'm tellin' ya,
she loves me. And *I* oughta know.
(CHERIE *flees to the counter, sobbing*)

WILL   Wall . . . she ain't gettin' back on the bus with ya.
We'll leave it at that. So you better take my advice and sit
down with yor friend there, and have a quiet game a pi-
nochle till the bus gets on its way and takes you with it.

VIRGIL   Do like he tells ya, Bo. I think mebbe ya got the
li'l lady all wrong, anyway.

BO (*A defender of womanhood*)   Don't you say nothin'
against her, Virge.

VIRGIL   I *ain't* sayin' nothin' *against* her. I jest see no reason why you should marry a gal that says she don't love ya. That's all. And I kinda doubt she's as good a gal as you think she is. Now come on over here and sit down.

BO (*Turns restlessly from* VIRGIL)   I don't feel like sittin'. (*Instead, he paces up to the big window, standing there looking out, his back to the audience*)

ELMA (*From behind counter, to* VIRGIL)   What shall I do with the ham and eggs?

VIRGIL   Just put 'em on the stove and keep 'em warm, miss. He'll have 'em a li'l later.

WILL (*To* CHERIE)   I don't think you'll be bothered any more, miss. If y'are, my station's right across the road. You kin holler.

CHERIE (*Dabbing at her eyes*)   Thank you very much, I'm sure.

WILL   Are you gonna be all right, Elma?

ELMA (*Surprised at the question*)   Why yes, Will! (WILL *just looks at* DR. LYMAN, *who, we can tell, is made to feel a little uncomfortable*)

WILL   I'll look in a little later.

ELMA   O.K., Will. (WILL *goes to the door, takes a final look at* BO, *then goes out*)

DR. LYMAN   I don't know why, but . . . I always seem to relax more easily . . . when a sheriff leaves the room. (*He chuckles bravely*)

ELMA   I think it's awfully unfair that people dislike Will just because he's a sheriff.

DR. LYMAN   But you see, my dear, he stands as a symbol of authority, the most dreaded figure of our time. Policemen, teachers, lawyers, judges, doctors, and I suppose, even tax collectors . . . we take it for granted that they are going to punish us for something we didn't do . . . or did do.

ELMA   But you said you were a teacher once.

DR. LYMAN   But not a successful one. I could never stay in one place very long at a time. And I hated having anyone *over* me, like deans and presidents and department heads. I never was a man who could take *orders* . . . from *any*one . . . without feeling resentment. Right or wrong, I have always insisted on having my own way.

(BO *walks slowly down from his corner retreat, seeking* VIRGIL, *who is taking his guitar out of its case.* BO *speaks hesitantly, in a low voice*)

BO   What am I gonna do, Virge?

VIRGIL   Bo, ya jest gotta quit dependin' on me so much. I don't know what to tell ya to do, except to sit down and be peaceful.

BO   I—I can't be peaceful.

VIRGIL   All right then, pace around like a panther and be miserable.

BO   (*To himself*)   I—I jest can't believe it!

VIRGIL   *What* can't ya believe?

BO   (*Now he becomes embarrassed*)   Oh . . . nothin'.

VIRGIL   If ya got anything on your chest, Bo, it's best to get it off.

BO   Well, I . . . I just never realized . . . a gal might not . . . love me.

                                                    CURTAIN

ACT TWO

SCENE: *Only a few minutes have elapsed since the close of* ACT ONE. *Our characters now are patiently trying to pass the time as best they can.* VIRGIL *has taken out his guitar and, after tuning it, begun to play a soft, melancholy cowboy ballad. He keeps his music an almost unnoticeable part of the background.* BO *lingers in the corner up right, a picture of troubled dejection.* CHERIE *has found a movie magazine, which she sets on one of the tables and reads.* DR. LYMAN *continues sitting at the bar, sipping his drink and courting* ELMA, *although* ELMA *does not realize she is being courted. She is immensely entertained by him.*

ELMA . . . And where else did you teach?

DR. LYMAN My last position was at one of those revolting little progressive colleges in the East, where they offer a curriculum of what they call *functional* education. Educators, I am sure, have despaired of ever teaching students *any*thing, so they have decided the second-best thing to do is to *understand* them. Every day there would be a meeting of everyone on the entire faculty, with whom the students ever came into any contact, from the President down to the chambermaids, and we would put our collective heads together to try to figure out why little Jane or little Mary was not getting out of her classes what she *should*. The suggestion that perhaps she wasn't studying was too simple, and if you implied that she simply did not have the brains for a college education, you were being undemocratic.

ELMA You must have disapproved of that college.

DR. LYMAN My dear girl, I have disapproved of my entire life.

ELMA Really?

DR. LYMAN Yes, but I suppose I couldn't resist living it over again.
(*There is a touch of sadness about him now*)

ELMA Did you resign from that position?

DR. LYMAN One day I decided I had had enough. I walked blithely into the Dean's office and said, "Sir! I graduated

179

magna cum laude from the University of Chicago, I studied at Oxford on a Rhodes Scholarship, and returned to take my Ph.D. at Harvard, receiving it with highest honors. I think I have the right to expect my students to try to understand *me*."

ELMA (*Very amused*)   What did he say?

DR. LYMAN   Oh, I didn't wait for a response. I walked out of the door and went to the railroad station, where I got a ticket for the farthest place I could think of, which happened to be Las Vegas. And I have been traveling ever since. It's a merry way to go to pot.
(*He chuckles*)

ELMA   I had thought *I* might teach one day, but you don't make it sound very attractive.

DR. LYMAN   Ah, suit yourself. Don't let me influence you one way or the other. (ELMA *smiles and* DR. LYMAN *gives in to the sudden compulsion of clasping her hand*) You're a lovely young girl.

ELMA (*Very surprised*)   Why . . . thank you, Dr. Lyman.

DR. LYMAN (*Clears his throat and makes a fresh approach*) Did you tell me you plan to go to Topeka tomorrow?

ELMA (*Looking at clock*)   You mean *today*. Yes. I have a ticket to hear the Kansas City Symphony. They come to Topeka every year to give a concert.

DR. LYMAN (*Feeling his way*)   You say . . . you stay with your sister there?

ELMA   Yes, then I take an early morning bus back here, in time for school Monday. Then after school, I come here to work for Grace.

DR. LYMAN (*Obviously he is angling for something*)   Didn't you say there was a university in Topeka?

ELMA   Yes. Washburn University.

DR. LYMAN   Washburn University—of course! You know, it just occurs to me that I should stop there to check some references on a piece of research I'm engaged on.

ELMA   Oh, I've been to Washburn library lots of times.

DR. LYMAN   You have? (*He shows some cunning, but obviously* ELMA *does not see it*)   Perhaps you would take me there!

ELMA (*Hesitant*) Well, I . . .

DR. LYMAN I'll arrive in Topeka before you do, then meet your bus . . .

ELMA If you really want me to.

DR. LYMAN You can take me to the library, then perhaps we could have dinner together, and perhaps you would permit me to take you to the symphony.

ELMA (*Overjoyed*) Are you serious?

DR. LYMAN Why, of course I'm serious. Why do you ask?

ELMA I don't know. Usually, older people are too busy to take notice of kids. I'd just love to.

DR. LYMAN Then I may depend on it that I have an engagement?

ELMA Yes. Oh, that'll be lots of fun. I can't wait.

DR. LYMAN But, my dear . . . let's not tell anyone of our plans, shall we?

ELMA Why not?

DR. LYMAN You see . . . I have been married, and I am somewhat older than you, though perhaps not quite as old as you might take me to be . . . anyway, people might not understand.

ELMA Oh!

DR. LYMAN So let's keep our plans to ourselves. Promise?

ELMA O.K. If you think best.

DR. LYMAN I think it best.
      (VIRGIL *has finished playing a ballad and* CHERIE *applauds*)

CHERIE That was real purty, Virgil.

VIRGIL Thank ya, miss.
      (*From his corner,* BO *has seen the moment's intimacy between them. He winces.* CHERIE *goes over to the counter and speaks to* ELMA)

CHERIE Isn't there some other way of me gettin' back to Kanz City?

ELMA I'm sorry. The bus comes through here from Topeka, and it can't get through, either, until the road's cleared.

CHERIE I was jest gettin' sorta restless.
      (*She sits at center table and lights a cigarette. Suddenly, the*

front door swings open and WILL *appears, carrying a thermos jug*)

WILL (*Crossing to counter*)   Elma, fill this up for me, like a good girl.

ELMA   Sure, Will.
(*Takes thermos from him and starts to fill it at urn*)

WILL   I'm goin' down the highway a bit to see how the men are gettin' on. Thought they'd enjoy some hot coffee.

ELMA   Good idea, Will.

WILL (*With a look around*)   Everyone behavin'?

ELMA   Of course.

WILL (*Puzzled*)   Grace not down yet?

ELMA   No.

WILL   I didn't see Carl any place outside. Suppose somethin' coulda happened to him?

ELMA   I wouldn't worry about him, Will.

WILL   I s'pose he can take care of himself. (ELMA *hands him thermos*) Thank you, Elma. (*He pays her, then starts back out, saying for the benefit primarily of* BO *and* DR. LYMAN) Oh, Elma. If anyone should be wantin' me, I won't be gone very long.
(*He looks around to make sure everyone has heard him, then goes out.* BO *has heard and seen him, and suddenly turns from his corner and comes angrily down to* VIRGIL)

BO   That dang sheriff! If it wasn't fer *him,* I'd git Cherry now and . . . I . . .

VIRGIL   Where would ya take her, Bo?

BO   There's a justice a the peace down the street. You can see his sign from the window.

VIRGIL   Bo, ya cain't *force* a gal to marry ya. Ya jest cain't do it. That sheriff's a stern man and he'd shoot ya in a minute if he saw it was his duty. Now, why don't ya go over to the counter and have yourself a drink . . . like the perfessor?

BO   I never did drink and I ain't gonna let no woman drive me to it.

VIRGIL   Ya don't drink. Ya don't smoke or chew. Ya oughta have *some* bad habits to rely on when things with women go wrong.

(BO *thinks for a moment then sits opposite* VIRGE)

BO   Virge. I hate to sound like some pitiable weaklin' of a man, but there's been times the last few months, I been so lonesome, I . . . I jest didn't know what t'do with m'self.

VIRGIL   It's no disgrace to feel that way, Bo.

BO   How 'bout you, Virge? Don't you ever git lonesome, too?

VIRGIL   A long time ago, I gave up romancin' and decided I was just gonna take bein' lonesome for granted.

BO   I wish I could do that, but I cain't.
(*They now sit in silence.* CHERIE, *at the counter, lifts her damp eyes to* ELMA, *seeking a confidante*)

CHERIE   Mebbe I'm a sap.

ELMA   Why do you say that?

CHERIE   I dunno why I *don't* go off to Montana and marry him. I might be a lot better off'n I am now.

ELMA   He says he *loves* you.

CHERIE   He dunno what love is.

ELMA   What makes you say that?

CHERIE   All he wants is a girl to throw his arms around and hug and kiss, that's all. The resta the time, he don't even know I exist.

ELMA   What made you decide to marry him in the first place?

CHERIE   (*Giving* ELMA *a wise look*) Ya ain't very experienced, are ya?

ELMA   I guess not.

CHERIE   I never *did* decide to marry him. Everything was goin' fine till he brought up *that* subjeck. Bo come in one night when I was singin' "That Ole Black Magic." It's one a my best numbers. And he liked it so much, he jumped up on a chair and yelled like a Indian, and put his fingers in his mouth and whistled like a steam engine. Natur'ly, it made me feel good. Most a the customers at the Blue Dragon was too drunk to pay any attention to my songs.

ELMA   And you liked him?

CHERIE   Well . . . I thought he was awful *cute*.
(*She shows a mischievous smile*)

ELMA   I think he looks a little like Burt Lancaster, don't you?

CHERIE   Mebbe. Anyway . . . I'd never seen a cowboy before. Oh, I'd seen 'em in movies, a course, but never in the
flesh . . . Anyway, he's so darn healthy-lookin', I don't
mind admittin', I was attracted, right from the start.

ELMA   You were?

CHERIE   But it was only what ya might call a *sexual* attraction.

ELMA   Oh!

CHERIE   The very next mornin', he wakes up and hollers,
"Yippee! We're gettin' married." I honestly thought he was
crazy. But when I tried to reason with him, he wouldn't
listen to a word. He stayed by my side all day long, like a
shadow. At night, a course, he had to go back to the rodeo,
but he was back to the Blue Dragon as soon as the rodeo
was over, in time fer the midnight show. If any other fella
claimed t'have a date with me, Bo'd beat him up.

ELMA   And you never told him you'd marry him?

CHERIE   No! He kep tellin' me all week, he and Virge'd be
by the night the rodeo ended, and they'd pick me up and
we'd all start back to Montana t'gether. I knew that if I was
around the Blue Dragon that night, that's what'd happen.
So I decided to beat it. One a the other girls at the Blue
Dragon lived on a farm 'cross the river in Kansas. She said
I could stay with her. So I went to the Blue Dragon last
night and just sang fer the first show. Then I told 'em I
was quittin' . . . I'd been wantin' to find another job anyway . . . and I picked up my share of the kitty . . . but
darn it, I had to go and tell 'em I was takin' the midnight
bus. They had to go and tell Bo, a course, when he come in
a li'l after eleven. He paid 'em five dollars to find out. So
I went down to the bus station and hadn't even got my
ticket, when here come Bo and Virge. He just steps up to
the ticket window and says, "Three tickets to Montana!"
I din know what to say. Then he dragged me onto the bus
and I been on it ever since. And somewhere deep down inside me, I gotta funny feelin' I'm gonna end up in Montana.
(*She sits now in troubled contemplation as* ELMA *resumes
her work. On the other side of the stage,* BO, *after a period
of gestation, begins to question* VIRGIL)

BO   Tell me somethin', Virge. We been t'gether since my
folks died, and I allus wondered if mebbe I din spoil yer
chances a settlin' down.

VIRGIL (*Laughs*) No, you never, Bo. I used to tell myself ya did, but I just wanted an excuse.

BO But you been lookin' after me since I was ten.

VIRGIL I coulda married up, too.

BO Was ya ever in love?

VIRGIL Oncet. B'fore I went to work on your daddy's ranch.

BO What happened?

VIRGIL Nuthin'.

BO Ya ask her to marry ya?

VIRGIL Nope.

BO Why not?

VIRGIL Well . . . there comes a time in every fella's life, Bo, when he's gotta give up his own ways . . .

BO How ya mean?

VIRGIL Well, I was allus kinda uncomfortable around this gal, 'cause she was sweet and kinda refined. I was allus scared I'd say or do somethin' wrong.

BO I know how ya mean.

VIRGIL It was cowardly of me, I s'pose, but ev'ry time I'd get back from courtin' her, and come back to the bunkhouse where my buddies was sittin' around talkin', or playin' cards, or listenin' to music, I'd jest relax and feel m'self so much at home, I din wanta give it up.

BO Yah! Gals can scare a fella.

VIRGIL Now I'm kinda ashamed.

BO Y'are?

VIRGIL Yes I am, Bo. A fella can't live his whole life de-pendin' on buddies.
(BO *takes another reflective pause, then asks directly*)

BO Why don't she like me, Virge?

VIRGIL (*Hesitant*) Well . . .

BO Tell me the truth.

VIRGIL Mebbe ya don't go about it right.

BO What do I do wrong?

VIRGIL Sometimes ya sound a li'l bullheaded and mean.

BO   I do?

VIRGIL   Yah.

BO   How's a fella s'posed to act?

VIRGIL   I'm no authority, Bo, but it seems t'me you should be a little more gallant.

BO   Gall——? Gallant? I'm as gallant as I know how to be. You hear the way Hank and Orville talk at the ranch, when they get back from sojournin' in town, 'bout their women.

VIRGIL   They like tó brag, Bo. Ya caint b'lieve ev'rything Hank and Orville say.

BO   Is there any reason a gal wouldn't go fer *me*, soon as she would fer Hank or Orville?

VIRGIL   They're a li'l older'n you. They learned a li'l more. They can be *gallant* with gals . . . when they *wanta* be.

BO   I ain't gonna *pertend*.

VIRGIL   I caint blame ya.

BO   But a gal *oughta* like me. I kin read and write, I'm kinda tidy, and I got good manners, don't I?

VIRGIL   I'm no judge, Bo. I'm used to ya.

BO   And I'm tall and strong. Ain't that what girls like? And if I do say so, m'self, I'm purty good-lookin'.

VIRGIL   Yah.

BO   When I get spruced up, I'm just as good-lookin' a fella as a gal might hope to see.

VIRGIL   I know ya are, Bo.

BO   (*Suddenly seized with anger at the injustice of it all*) Then hellfire and damnation! Why don't she go back to the ranch with me?
(*His hands in his hip pockets, he begins pacing, returning to his corner like a panther, where he stands with his back to the others, watching the snow fly outside the window*)

ELMA   (*Having observed* BO'S *disquiet*) —Gee, if you only loved him!

CHERIE   That'd solve ev'rything, wouldn't it? But I don't. So I jest can't see m'self goin' to some God-forsaken ranch in Montana where I'd never see no one but him and a lotta cows.

ELMA   No. If you don't love him, it'd be awfully lonely.

CHERIE   I dunno why I keep expectin' m'self to fall in love
with someone, but I do.

ELMA   I know *I* expect to, some day.

CHERIE   I'm beginnin' to seriously wonder if there *is* the
kinda love I have in mind.

ELMA   What's that?

CHERIE   Well . . . I dunno. I'm oney nineteen, but I been
goin' with guys since I was fourteen.

ELMA   (*Astounded*)   Honest?

CHERIE   Honey, I almost married a cousin a mine when I
was fourteen, but Pappy wouldn't have it.

ELMA   I never heard of anyone marrying so young.

CHERIE   Down in the Ozarks, we don't waste much time.
Anyway, I'm awful glad I never married my cousin Malcolm, 'cause he turned out real bad, like Pappy predicted.
But I sure was crazy 'bout him at the time. And I been
losin' my head 'bout some guy ever since. But Bo's the first
one wanted to marry me, since Cousin Malcolm. And
natur'ly, I'd like to get married and raise a fam'ly and all
them things, but . . .

ELMA   But you've *never* been in love?

CHERIE   Mebbe I have and din know it. Thass what I mean.
Mebbe I don't know what love is. Mebbe I'm expectin' it
t'be somethin' it ain't. I jest feel that, regardless how crazy
ya are 'bout some guy, ya gotta feel . . . and it's hard to
put into words, but . . . ya gotta feel he *respects* ya. Yah,
thass what I means.

ELMA   (*Not impudent*)   I should think so.

CHERIE   I want a guy I can look up to and respect, but I
don't want one that'll browbeat me. And I want a guy who
can be sweet to me but I don't wanta be treated like a baby.
I . . . I just gotta feel that . . . whoever I marry . . .
has some real regard for me, apart from all the lovin' and
sex. Know what I mean?

ELMA   (*Busily digesting all this*)   I think so. What are you
going to do when you get back to Kansas City?

CHERIE   I dunno— There's a hillbilly program on one a the
radio stations there. I might git a job on it. If I don't, I'll

prob'ly git me a job in Liggett's or Walgreen's. Then after a while, I'll prob'ly marry some guy, whether I think I love him or not. Who'm *I* to keep insistin' I should fall in love? You hear all about love when yor a kid and jest take it for granted that such a thing really exists. Maybe ya have to find out fer yorself it don't. Maybe everyone's afraid to tell ya.

ELMA (*Glum*)   Maybe you're right . . . but I hope not.

CHERIE (*After squirming a little on the stool*)   Gee, I hate to go out to that cold powder room, but I guess I better not put it off any longer.
(CHERIE *hurries out the rear door as* DR. LYMAN *sits again at the counter, having returned from the book shelves in time to overhear the last of* CHERIE'S *conversation. He muses for a few moments, gloomily, then speaks to* ELMA *out of his unconscious reflections*)

DR. LYMAN   How defiantly we pursue love, like it was an inheritance due, that we had to wrangle about with angry relatives in order to get our share.

ELMA   You shouldn't complain. You've had three wives.

DR. LYMAN   Don't shame me. I loved them all . . . with passion. (*An afterthought*) At least I *thought* I did . . . for a while.
(*He still chuckles about it as though it were a great irony*)

ELMA   I'm sorry if I sounded sarcastic, Dr. Lyman. I didn't mean to be.

DR. LYMAN   Don't apologize. I'm too egotistical ever to take offense at anything people *say*.

ELMA   You're not egotistical at all.

DR. LYMAN   Oh, believe me. The greatest egos are those which are too egotistical to show just how egotistical they are.

ELMA   I'm sort of idealistic about things. I like to think that people fall in love and stay that way, forever and ever.

DR. LYMAN   Maybe we have lost the ability. Maybe Man has passed the stage in his evolution wherein love is possible. Maybe life will continue to become so terrifyingly complex that man's anxiety about his mere survival will render him too miserly to give of himself in any true relation.

ELMA   You're talking over my head. *Any*one can fall in love, I always thought . . . and . . .

DR. LYMAN But two people, *really* in love, must give up
something of them*selves.*

ELMA (*Trying to follow*) Yes.

DR. LYMAN That is the gift that men are afraid to make.
Sometimes they keep it in their bosoms forever, where it
withers and dies. Then they never know love, only its fac-
similes, which they seek over and over again in meaningless repetition.

ELMA (*A little depressed*) Gee! How did we get onto this
subject?

DR. LYMAN (*Laughs heartily with sudden release, grabbing
ELMA'S hand*) Ah, my dear! Pay no attention to me, for
whether there is such a thing as love, we can always . . .
(*Lifts his drink*) . . . pretend there is. Let us talk instead
of our forthcoming trip to Topeka. Will you wear your
prettiest dress?

ELMA Of course. If it turns out to be a nice day, I'll wear a
new dress Mother got me for spring. It's a soft rose color
with a little lace collar.

DR. LYMAN Ah, you'll look lovely, *lovely*. I know you will. I
hope it doesn't embarrass you for me to speak these en-
dearments . . .

ELMA No . . . it doesn't embarrass me.

DR. LYMAN I'm glad. Just think of me as a fatherly old fool,
will you? And not be troubled if I take such rapturous delight in your sweetness, and youth, and innocence? For
these are qualities I seek to warm my heart as I seek a fire
to warm my hands.

ELMA Now I *am* kind of embarrassed. I don't know what to
say.

DR. LYMAN Then say nothing, or nudge *me* and I'll talk endlessly about the most trivial matters.
(*They laugh together as* CHERIE *comes back in, shivering*)

CHERIE Brrr, it's cold. Virgil, I wish you'd play us another
song. I think we all need somethin' to cheer us up.

VIRGIL I'll make a deal with ya. I'll play if you'll sing.

ELMA (*A bright idea comes to her*) Let's have a floor show!
(*Her suggestion comes as a surprise and there is silence
while all consider it*) Everyone here can do *some*thing!

DR. LYMAN A brilliant idea, straight from Chaucer. You must read Juliet for me.

ELMA (*Not hearing* DR. LYMAN, *running to* VIRGIL) Will you play for us, Virgil?

VIRGIL I don't play opery music or jitterbug.

ELMA Just play anything you want to play. (*To* BO) Will you take part? (*Stubbornly,* BO *just turns the other way*) Please! It won't be fun unless we all do something.

VIRGIL G'wan, Bo.

BO I never was no play-actor, miss.

VIRGIL Ya kin say the Gettysburg Address.

BO (*Gruffly*) I ain't gonna say it now.

VIRGIL Then why don't ya do your rope tricks? Yer rope's out on the bus. I could get it for ya easy enough.

ELMA Oh, please! Rope tricks would be lots of fun.

BO (*Emphatically*) No! I ain't gonna get up before a lotta strangers and make a fool a m'self.

VIRGIL (*To* ELMA) I guess he means it, miss.

ELMA Shucks!

VIRGIL (*Quietly to* BO) I don't see why ya couldn't a co-operated a little, Bo.

BO I got too much on my mind to worry about doin' stunts.

ELMA (*To* CHERIE) You'll sing a song for us, won't you, Cherie?

CHERIE I will fer a piece a pie and another cup a coffee.

ELMA Sure.
    (CHERIE *hurries to* VIRGIL)

CHERIE Virgil, kin you play "That Ole Black Magic"?

VIRGIL You start me out and I think I can pick out the chords.
    (CHERIE *sits by his side as they work out their number together.* ELMA *hurries to* DR. LYMAN)

ELMA And you'll read poetry for us, won't you?

DR. LYMAN (*Already assuming his character*) Why, I intend to play Romeo opposite your Juliet.

ELMA Gee, I don't know if I can remember the lines.

DR. LYMAN (*Handing her a volume he has taken off the shelves*) Sometimes one can find Shakespeare on these shelves among the many lurid novels of juvenile delinquents. Here it is, *Four Tragedies of Shakespeare,* with my compliments.
(*They begin to go over the scene together as* BO, *resentful of the closeness between* CHERIE *and* VIRGIL, *goes to them belligerently*)

BO (*To* CHERIE) Thass *my* seat.

ELMA (*Taking book from* DR. LYMAN) If I read it over a few times, it'll come back. Do you know the Balcony Scene?

CHERIE (*Jumping to her feet*) You kin have it.
(*Hurries to* ELMA, *at counter*)

DR. LYMAN My dear, I know the entire play by heart. I can recite it backwards.

CHERIE (*To* ELMA) I got a costume with me. Where can I change?

ELMA Behind the counter. There's a mirror over the sink.
(CHERIE *darts behind the counter, digging into her suitcase*)

BO (*To* VIRGIL) She shines up to *you* like a kitten to milk.

ELMA Gee, costumes and everything.
(*She resumes her study with* DR. LYMAN)

VIRGIL (*Trying to make a joke of it*) Kin *I* help it if I'm so darn attractive to women? (*Unfortunately* BO *cannot take this as a joke, as* VIRGIL *intended.* VIRGIL *perceives he is deeply hurt*) Shucks, Bo, it don't mean nothin'.

BO Maybe it don't mean nothin' to *you.*

VIRGIL She was bein' nice to me cause I was playin' my guitar, Bo. Guitar music's kinda tender and girls seem to like it.

BO Tender?

VIRGIL Yah, Bo! Girls like things t'be *tender.*

BO They do!

VIRGIL Sure they do, Bo.

BO A fella gets "tender," then someone comes along and makes a sap outa him.

VIRGIL Sometimes, Bo, but not always. You just gotta take a chance.

BO   Well . . . I allus tried t'be a *decent* sorta fella, but I don't know if I'm *tender*.

VIRGIL   I think ya are, Bo. You know how ya feel about deer huntin'. Ya never could do it. Ya couldn't any more *shoot* one a them sweet li'l deers with the sad eyes than ya could jump into boilin' oil.

BO   Are you makin' fun of me?

VIRGIL   (*Impatient with him*)   No, I'm not makin' fun of ya, Bo. I'm just tryin' to show ya that *you* got a tender side to your nature, same as anyone else.

BO   I s'pose I do.

VIRGIL   A course ya do.

BO   (*With a sudden feeling of injustice*)   Then how come Cherry don't come over and talk sweet to *me,* like she does to *you?*

VIRGIL   Ya *got* a tender side, Bo, but ya don't know how to *show* it.

BO   (*Weighing the verdict*)   I don't!

VIRGIL   No, ya just don't know how.

BO   How does a person go about showin' his tender side, Virge?

VIRGIL   Well . . . I dunno as I can tell ya.
(ELMA *comes over to them ready to start the show*)

ELMA   Will you go first, Virgil?

VIRGIL   It's all right by me.

ELMA   O.K. Then I'll act as Master of the Ceremonies. (*Centerstage, to her audience*) Ladies and Gentlemen! Grace's Diner tonight presents its gala floor show of celebrated artists from all over the world! (VIRGIL *plays an introductory chord*) The first number on our show tonight is that musical cowboy, Mr. Virgil—(*She pauses and* VIRGIL *supplies her with his last name*)—Virgil Blessing, who will entertain you with his guitar.
(*Applause.* ELMA *retires to the back of the room with* DR. LYMAN. VIRGIL *begins to play. During his playing,* BO *is drawn over to the counter, where he tries to further himself with* CHERIE, *who is behind the counter, dressing*)

BO   (*Innocently*)   I think you got me all wrong, Cherry.

CHERIE   Don't you come back here. I'm dressing.

BO Cherry . . . I think you misjudged me.

CHERIE Be quiet. The show's started.

BO Cherry, I'm really a very *tender* person. You jest don't know. I'm so tender-hearted I don't go deer huntin'. 'Cause I jest couldn't kill them "sweet li'l deers with the sad eyes." Ask Virge.

CHERIE I ain't int'rested.

BO Ya ain't?

CHERIE No. And furthermore I think you're a louse fer comin' over here and talkin' while yor friend is tryin' to play the guitar.

BO Ya talk like ya thought more a Virge than yo da a me.

CHERIE Would ya go away and lemme alone?

BO (*A final resort*) Cherry, did I tell ya 'bout my color-television set with the twenty-four-inch screen?

CHERIE One million times! Now go 'way.
(ELMA *begins to make a shushing noise to quiet* BO. *Finally* BO *dejectedly returns to the other side of the room, where* VIRGIL *is just finishing his number.* BO *sits down in the midst of* VIRGIL'S *applause*)

CHERIE That was wonderful, Virge!

DR. LYMAN Brilliant!   } (*Together*)

ELMA Swell! Play us another!

VIRGIL No more just now. I'm ready to see the rest of ya do somethin'.

BO (*To* VIRGIL) A lot *she* cares how tender I am!

ELMA (*Coming forth again as Master of Ceremonies*) That was swell, Virgil. (*Turns back to* DR. LYMAN) Are you ready?

DR. LYMAN (*Preening himself*) I consider myself so.

ELMA (*Taking the book to* VIRGIL) Will you be our prompter?

VIRGIL It's kinda funny writin', but I'll try.

ELMA (*Back to* DR. LYMAN) Gee, what'll we use for a balcony?

DR. LYMAN That offers a problem.
(*Together they consider whether to use the counter for* ELMA *to stand on or one of the tables*)

BO (*To* VIRGIL)   What is it these folks are gonna do, Virge?

VIRGIL   *Romeo and Juliet* . . . by Shakespeare!

BO   Shakespeare!

VIRGIL   This Romeo was a great lover, Bo. Watch him and pick up a few pointers.
(CHERIE *comes running out from behind the counter now, a dressing gown over her costume, and she sits at one of the tables*)

CHERIE   I'm ready.

BO (*Reading some of the lines from* VIRGIL's *book*)   "But, soft . . . what light through . . . yonder window breaks? It is the east . . . and Juliet is the sun . . . Arise, fair . . ."
(*He has got this far only with difficulty, stumbling over most of the words.* VIRGIL *takes the book away from him now*)

VIRGIL   Shh, Bo!
(ELMA *comes forth to introduce the act*)

ELMA   Ladies and gentlemen! you are about to witness a playing of the Balcony Scene from *Romeo and Juliet*. Dr. Gerald Lyman will portray the part of Romeo, and I'll play Juliet. My name is Elma Duckworth. The scene is the orchard of the Capulets' house in Verona, Italy. This table is supposed to be a balcony. (DR. LYMAN *helps her onto the table, where she stands, waiting for him to begin*) O.K.?
(DR. LYMAN *takes a quick reassuring drink from his bottle, then tucks it in his pocket, and comes forward in the great Romantic tradition. He is enjoying himself tremendously. The performance proves to be pure ham, but there is pathos in the fact that he does not seem to be aware of how bad he is. He is a thoroughly selfish performer, too, who reads all his speeches as though they were grand soliloquies, regarding his Juliet as a prop*)

DR. LYMAN
   "He jests at scars, that never felt a wound.
   But, soft! what light through yonder window breaks?
   It is the east, and Juliet is the sun!
(*He tries to continue, but* ELMA, *unmindful of cues and eager to begin her performance, reads her lines with compulsion*)
   Arise . . . fair sun, and . . . kill the envious. . . ."

ELMA (*At same time as* DR. LYMAN)
    "O Romeo, Romeo! wherefore art thou, Romeo?
    Deny thy father and refuse thy name:
    Or if thou wilt not, be but sworn my love,
    And I'll no longer be a Capulet."

DR. LYMAN
    "She speaks, yet she says nothing: what of that?
    Her eye discourses; I will answer it.
    I am too bold—"

BO (*To* VIRGIL)   Bold? He's drunk.

VIRGIL   Ssssh!

DR. LYMAN
    ". . . 'tis not to me she speaks:
    Two of the fairest stars in all the heaven,
    Having some business, do entreat her eyes
    To twinkle in their spheres till they return."

ELMA

                "Ay me!"

DR. LYMAN
    "O! speak again, bright angel; for thou art
    As glorious to this night, being o'er my head,
    As is a winged messenger of heaven
    Unto the white-upturned . . ."
(DR. LYMAN *continues with this speech, even though* BO
talks over him.)

BO   I don't understand all them words, Virge.

VIRGE   It's *Romeo and Juliet,* for God's sake. Now will you
shut up?

DR. LYMAN (*Continuing uninterrupted*)
    ". . . wondering eyes
    Of mortals, that fall back to gaze on him
    When he bestrides the lazy-pacing clouds,
    And sails upon the bosom of the air."
(*He is getting weary but he is not yet ready to give up*)

ELMA
    " 'Tis but thy name that is my enemy;
    Thou art thyself though, not a Montague.
    What's Montague? it is nor hand, nor foot,
    Nor arm, nor face, nor any other part
    Belonging to a man. O! be some other name:
    What's—"

DR. LYMAN (*Interrupts. Beginning to falter now*)
    "I take thee at thy word.
    Call me but love, and . . . I'll be new baptiz'd;
    Henceforth . . . I never . . . will be Romeo."
(*It is as though he were finding suddenly a personal meaning in the lines*)

ELMA
    "What man art thou, that, thus bescreen'd in night,
    So stumblest on my counsel?"

DR. LYMAN (*Beginning to feel that he cannot continue*)
                              "By a name
I know not how to tell thee . . . who I am:
My name, dear saint, is . . . is *hateful* to myself."
(*He stops here. For several moments there is a wondering silence.* ELMA *signals* VIRGIL)

VIRGIL (*Prompting*)
    "Because it is an enemy to thee."

DR. LYMAN (*Leaving the scene of action, repeating the line dumbly, making his way stumblingly back to the counter*)
    "My name . . . is hateful . . . to myself . . ."
(ELMA *hurries to* DR. LYMAN'S *side.* VIRGIL *grabs hold of* BO, *pulls him back to the floor and shames him*)

ELMA   Dr. Lyman, what's the matter?

DR. LYMAN   My dear . . . let us not continue this meaningless little act!

ELMA   Did I do something wrong?

DR. LYMAN   You couldn't possibly do anything wrong . . . if you tried.

ELMA   I can try to say the lines differently.

DR. LYMAN   Don't. Don't. Just tell your audience that Romeo suddenly is fraught with remorse.
(*He drops to a stool,* ELMA *remaining by him a few moments, uncertainly.* BO *turns to* VIRGIL)

BO   Virge, if thass the way to make love . . . I'm gonna give up.

ELMA (*To* VIRGIL)   I'm afraid he isn't feeling well.

VIRGIL (*To* ELMA)   I tried to prompt him.

ELMA (*To herself*)   Well, we've only got one more number.
(*To* CHERIE) Are you ready?

CHERIE   Sure.

ELMA   Ladies and gentlemen, our next number is Mademoi-
sell Cherie, the international *chanteuse,* direct from the Blue
Dragon night club in Kansas City, *Cherie!*
(*All applaud as* CHERIE *comes forth,* VIRGIL *playing an introduction for her.* BO *puts his fingers through his teeth and
whistles for her*)

CHERIE   (*Takes off her robe, whispering to* ELMA)   Remember, I don't allow no table service during my numbers.

ELMA   O.K.
(*In the background now, we can observe that* DR. LYMAN *is
drinking heavily from the bottle in his overcoat pocket.*
CHERIE *gets up on one of the tables and begins singing "That
Old Black Magic" with a chord accompaniment from* VIR-
GIL. *Her rendition of the song is a most dramatic one, that
would seem to have been created from* CHERIE'S *observa-
tions of numerous torch singers. But she has appeal, and if
she is funny, she doesn't seem to know it. Anyway, she re-
kindles* BO'S *most fervent love, which he cannot help ex-
pressing during her performance*)

BO   (*About the middle of the song*)   Ain't she beautiful,
Virge?

VIRGIL   (*Trying to keep his mind on his playing*)   Shh, Bo!

BO   I'm gonna git her, Virge.

VIRGIL   Ssshh!

BO   (*Pause. He pays no attention to anyone*)   I made up my
mind. I told myself I was gonna git me a gal. Thass the only
reason I entered that rodeo, and I ain't takin' no fer an
answer.

VIRGIL   Bo, will you hush up and lemme be!

BO   Anything I ever wanted in this life I went out and got,
and I ain't gonna stop now. I'm gonna git her.
(CHERIE *is enraged. She jumps down from her table and
slaps* BO *stingingly on the face*)

CHERIE   You ain't got the manners God gave a monkey.

BO   (*Stunned*)   Cherry!

CHERIE   . . . and if I was a man, I'd beat the livin' daylights
out of ya, and thass what some man's gonna do some day,
and when it happens, I hope I'm there to *see.*
(*She flounces back to her dressing room, as* BO *gapes. By*

this time DR. LYMAN *has drunk himself almost to insensibility, and we see him weaving back and forth on his stool, mumbling almost incoherently*)

DR. LYMAN   "Romeo . . . Romeo . . . wherefore art thou? Wherefore art thou . . . Romeo?"
(*He laughs like a loon, falls off the stool and collapses on the floor.* ELMA *and* VIRGIL *rush to him.* BO *remains rooted, glaring at* CHERIE *with puzzled hurt*)

ELMA (*Deeply concerned*)   Dr. Lyman! Dr. Lyman!

VIRGIL   The man's in a purty bad way. Let's get him on the bench.
(ELMA *and* VIRGIL *manage to get* DR. LYMAN *to his feet as* BO *glides across the room, scales the counter in a leap and takes* CHERIE *in his arms*)

BO   I was tellin' Virge I love ya. Ya got no right to come over and slap me.

CHERIE (*Twisting*)   Lemme be.

BO (*Picking her up*)   We're goin' down and wake up the justice of the peace and you're gonna marry me t'night.

CHERIE (*As he takes her in his arms and transports her to the door, just as* ELMA *and* VIRGIL *are helping* DR. LYMAN *onto the bench*)   Help! Virgil, help!

BO   Shut up! I'll make ya a good husband. Ya won't never have nothin' to be sorry about.

CHERIE (*As she is carried to the door*)   Help! Sheriff! Help me, someone! Help me!
(*The action is now like that of a two-ringed circus for* ELMA *and* VIRGIL, *whose attention suddenly is diverted from the plight of* DR. LYMAN *to the much noisier plight of* CHERIE. BO *gets her, kicking and protesting, as far as the front door when it suddenly opens and* BO *finds himself confronted by* WILL)

WILL   Put her down, cowboy!

BO (*Trying to forge ahead*)   Git outta my way.

WILL (*Shoving* BO *back as* CHERIE *manages to jump loose from his arms*)   Yor gonna do as I say.

BO   I ain't gonna have no one interferin' in my ways.
(*He makes an immediate lunge at* WILL, *which* WILL *is prepared for, coming up with a fist that sends* BO *back reeling*)

VIRGIL (*Hurrying to* BO's *side*) Bo, ya cain't do this, Bo. Ya cain't pick a fight with the sheriff.

BO (*Slowly getting back to his feet*) By God, mister, there ain't no man ever got the best a me, and there ain't no man ever gonna.

WILL I'm ready and willin' to try, cowboy. Come on.
(BO *lunges at him again.* WILL *steps aside and lets* BO *send his blow into the empty doorway as he propels himself through it, outside. Then* WILL *follows him out, where the fight continues.* VIRGIL *immediately follows them, as* ELMA *and* CHERIE *hurry to the window to watch*)

CHERIE I knowed this was gonna happen. I knowed it all along.

ELMA Gee! I'd better call Grace.
(*Starts for the rear door but* GRACE *comes through it before she gets there.* GRACE *happens to be wearing a dressing gown*)

GRACE Hey, what the hell's goin' on?

ELMA Oh, Grace, they're fighting. Honest! It all happened so suddenly, I . . .

GRACE (*Hurrying to window*) Let's see.

CHERIE (*Leaving the window, not wanting to see any more, going to a chair by one of the tables*) Gee, I never wanted to cause so much trouble t'anyone.

GRACE Wow! Looks like Will's gettin' the best of him.

ELMA (*At the window, frightened by what she sees*) Oh!

GRACE Yap, I'll put my money on Will Masters *any* time. Will's got it up here. (*Points to her head*) Lookit that cowboy. He's green. He just swings out wild.

ELMA (*Leaving the window*) I . . . I don't want to watch any more.

GRACE (*A real fight fan, she reports from the window*) God, I love a good fight. C'mon Will—c'mon, Will—give him the old uppercut. That'll do it every time. Oh, oh, what'd I tell you, the cowboy's down. Will's puttin' handcuffs on him now.
(CHERIE *sobs softly.* ELMA *goes to her*)

ELMA Will'll give him first aid. He always does.

CHERIE Well . . . you gotta admit. He had it comin'.

GRACE (*Leaving the window now*) I'm glad they got it
settled outside. (*Looks around to see if anything needs to be
straightened up*) Remember the last time there was a fight
in here, I had to put in a new window.
(*She goes back up to her apartment, and we become aware
once more of* DR. LYMAN, *who gets up from the bench and
weaves his way center*)

DR. LYMAN   It takes strong men and women to *love* . . .
(*About to fall, he grabs the back of a chair for support*)
People strong enough inside themselves to love . . . without humiliation. (*He sighs heavily and looks about him with
blurred eyes*) People big enough to *grow* with their love and
live inside a whole, wide new dimension. People brave
enough to bear the responsibility of *being* loved and not fear
it as a burden. (*He sighs again and looks about him wearily*)
I . . . I never had the generosity to love, to give my own
most private self to another, for I was *weak*. I thought the
gift would somehow lessen *me. Me!* (*He laughs wildly and
starts for the rear door*) Romeo! Romeo! I am disgusting!
(ELMA *hurries after him, stopping him at the door*)

ELMA   Dr. Lyman! Dr. Lyman!

DR. LYMAN   Don't bother, dear girl. Don't ever bother with a
foolish old man like me.

ELMA   You're not a foolish old man. I like you more than
anyone I've ever known.

DR. LYMAN   I'm flattered, my dear, and pleased, but you're
young. In a few years, you will turn . . . from a girl into
a woman; a kind, thoughtful, loving, intelligent woman
. . . who could only pity me. For I'm a child, a drunken,
unruly child, and I've nothing in my heart for a true woman.
(GRACE *returns in time to observe the rest of the scene. She
is dressed now*)

ELMA   Let me get you something to make you feel better.

DR. LYMAN   No . . . no . . . I shall seek the icy comfort of
the rest room.
(*He rushes out the rear door*)

GRACE (*Feeling concern for* ELMA) Elma, honey, what's the
matter? What was he sayin' to you, Elma?
(*Goes to her and they have a quiet talk between themselves
as the action continues.* GRACE *is quite motherly at these
times. Now* VIRGIL *comes hurrying through the front door,
going to* CHERIE.)

VIRGIL Miss, would ya help us? The sheriff says if you don't
hold charges against Bo, he'll let him out to get back on the
bus, if it ever goes.

CHERIE So he can come back here and start maulin' me
again?

VIRGIL He won't do that no more, miss. I promise.

CHERIE *You promise!* How 'bout him?

VIRGIL I think you can trust him now.

CHERIE Thass what I thought before. Nothin' doin'. He grabs
ahold of a woman and kisses her . . . like he was Na-
poleon.

VIRGIL (*Coming very close, to speak as intimately as possible*)
Miss . . . if he was to know I told ya this, he'd never forgive me, but . . . yor the first woman he ever made love
to at all.

CHERIE Hah! I sure don't b'lieve that.

VIRGIL It's true, miss. He's allus been as shy as a rabbit.

CHERIE (*In simple amazement*) My God!

GRACE (*To* ELMA) Just take my advice and don't meet him
in Topeka or anywhere else.

ELMA I won't, Grace, but honest! I don't think he meant any
harm. He just drinks a little too much. (DR. LYMAN *returns
now through the rear door.* ELMA *hurries to him*) Dr. Lyman, are you all right?

DR. LYMAN (*On his way to the bench*) I'm an old man, my
dear. I feel very weary.
(*He stretches out on the bench, lying on his stomach. He
goes almost immediately to sleep.* ELMA *finds an old jacket
and spreads it over his shoulders like a blanket. There is a
long silence.* ELMA *sits by* DR. LYMAN *attentively.* CHERIE *is
very preoccupied*)

GRACE Let him sleep it off. It's all you can do.
(*Now* CARL *comes in the rear door. There is a look of impatient disgust on his face, as though he had just witnessed
some revolting insult. He casts a suspicious look at* DR. LY-
MAN, *now oblivious to everything, and turns to* GRACE)

CARL Grace, fer Christ sake! who puked all over the backhouse?

GRACE Oh, God!

(DR. LYMAN *snores serenely*)

CHERIE (*Jumps up suddenly and grabs* VIRGIL'S *jacket off hook*) Come on, Virge. Let's go.

VIRGIL (*Enthused*) I'm awful glad you're gonna help him, miss.

CHERIE But if you're tellin' me a fib just to get him out of jail, I'll never forgive ya.

VIRGIL It's no fib, miss. You're the first gal he ever made love to at all.

CHERIE Well, I sure ain't never had that honor before.
(*They hurry out together*)

                                                    CURTAIN

ACT THREE

SCENE: *By this time, it is early morning, about five o'clock. The storm has cleared, and outside the window we see the slow dawning, creeping above the distant hills, revealing a landscape all in peaceful white.*

BO, CHERIE *and* VIRGIL *are back now from the sheriff's office.* BO *has returned to his corner, where he sits as before, with his back to the others, his head low. We can detect, if we study him, that one eye is blackened and one of his hands is bandaged.* VIRGIL *sits close to him like an attendant.* DR. LYMAN *is still asleep on one of the benches, snoring loudly.* CHERIE *tries to sleep at one of the tables.* ELMA *is clearing the tables and sweeping. The only animated people right now are* CARL *and* GRACE. CARL *is at the telephone, trying to get the operator, and* GRACE *is behind the counter.*

CARL (*After jiggling the receiver*) Still dead.
(*He hangs up*)

GRACE (*Yawns*) I'll be glad when you all get out and I can go to bed. I'm tired.

CARL (*Returning to counter, he sounds a trifle insinuating*) Had enough a me, baby? (GRACE *gives him a look, warning him not to let* ELMA *overhear*) I'm kinda glad the highway was blocked tonight.

GRACE (*Coquettishly*) Y'are?

CARL Gave us a chance to become kinda acquainted, din it?

GRACE Kinda!

CARL Just pullin' in here three times a week, then pullin' out again in twenty minutes, I . . . I allus left . . . just wonderin' what you was like, Grace.

GRACE I always wondered about *you,* too, Carl!

CARL Ya did?

GRACE Yah. But ya needn't go blabbing anything to the other drivers.

CARL (*His honor offended*) Why, what makes ya think I'd . . . ?

GRACE Shoot! I know how you men talk when ya get t'gether. Worse'n women.

203

CARL Well, not *me*, Grace.

GRACE I certainly don't want the other drivers on this route, some of 'em especially, gettin' the idea I'm gonna serve 'em any more'n what they order over the counter.

CARL Sure. I get ya. (*It occurs to him to feel flattered*) But ya . . . ya kinda *liked* me . . . din ya, Grace?

GRACE (*Coquettish again*)   Maybe I did.

CARL (*Trying to get more of a commitment out of her*) Yah? Yah?

GRACE Know what I first liked about ya, Carl? It was your hands. (*She takes one of his hands and plays with it*) I like a man with big hands.

CARL You got *everything*, baby.
(*For just a moment, one senses the animal heat in their fleeting attraction. Now* WILL *comes stalking in through the front door, a man who is completely relaxed with the authority he possesses. He speaks to* GRACE)

WILL One of the highway trucks just stopped by. They say it won't be very long now.

GRACE I hope so.

WILL (*With a look around*)   Everything peaceful?

GRACE Yes, Will.

WILL (*He studies* BO *for a moment, then goes to him*)   Cowboy, if yor holdin' any grudges against me, I think ya oughta ask yourself what you'd'a done in my *place*. I couldn't let ya carry off the li'l lady when she din wanta go, could I? (BO *has no answer. He just avoids* WILL'S *eyes. But* WILL *is determined to get an answer*) *Could* I?

BO I don't feel like talkin', mister.

WILL Well, I couldn't. And I think you might also remember that this li'l lady . . . (CHERIE *begins to stir*) if she wanted to . . . could press charges and get you sent to the penitentiary for violation of the Mann Act.

BO The *what* act?

WILL The Mann Act. You took a woman over the state line against her will.

VIRGIL That'd be a serious charge, Bo.

BO (*Stands facing* WILL)   I loved her.

WILL   That don't make any difference.

BO   A man's gotta right to the things he loves.

WILL   Not unless he deserves 'em, cowboy.

BO   I'm a hard-workin' man, I own me my own ranch, I got
six thousand dollars in the bank.

WILL   A man don't deserve the things he loves, unless he kin
be a little humble about gettin' em.

BO   I ain't gonna get down on my knees and *beg*.

WILL   Bein' humble ain't the same thing as bein' *wretched*.
(BO *doesn't understand*) I had to learn that once, too, cowboy. I wasn't quite as old as you. I stole horses instead of
women because you could *sell* horses. One day, I stole a
horse off the wrong man, the Rev. Hezekiah Pearson. I
never thought I'd get mine from any preacher, but he was
very fair. Gave me every chance to put myself clear. But I
wouldn't admit the horse was his. Finally, he did what he
had to do. He thrashed me to within a inch of my life. I
never forgot. 'Cause it was the first time in my life, I had
to admit I was wrong. I was miserable. Finally, after a few
days, I decided the only thing to do was to admit to the man
how I felt. Then I felt different about the whole thing. I
joined his church, and we was bosom pals till he died a few
years ago. (*He turns to* VIRGIL) Has he done what I asked
him to?

VIRGIL   Not yet, sheriff.

WILL   (*To* BO)   Why should ya be so scared?

BO   Who says I'm scared?

WILL   Ya gimme yor word, didn't ya?

BO   (*Somewhat resentful*)   I'm gonna do it, if ya'll jest gimme
time.

WILL   But I warn ya, it ain't gonna do no good unless you
really mean it.

BO   I'll mean it.

WILL   All right then. Go ahead.
(*Slowly, reluctantly,* BO *gets to his feet and awkwardly, like
a guilty boy, makes his way over to the counter to* GRACE)

BO   Miss, I . . . I wanna apologize.

GRACE   What for?

BO   Fer causin' such a commotion.

GRACE Ya needn't apologize to *me,* cowboy. I like a good fight. You're welcome at Grace's Diner *any* time. I mean *any* time.

BO (*With an appreciative grin*) Thanks. (*Now he goes to* ELMA) I musta acted like a hoodlum. I apologize.

ELMA Oh, that's all right.

BO Thank ya, miss.

ELMA I'm awfully sorry we never got to see your rope tricks.

BO They ain't much. (*Pointing to the sleeping* DR. LYMAN) Have I gotta wake up the perfessor t'apologize t'him?

WILL You can overlook the perfessor.
(*He nods toward* CHERIE, *whom* BO *dreads to confront, most of all. He starts toward her but doesn't get very far*)

BO I cain't do it.

VIRGIL (*Disappointed*) Aw, Bo!

BO I jest cain't do it.

WILL Why not?

BO She'd have no respeck for me now. She saw me beat.

WILL You gave me your promise. You owe that girl an apology, whether you got beat or not, and you're going to say it to her or I'm not lettin' you back on the bus.
(BO *is in a dilemma. He wipes his brow*)

VIRGIL G'wan, Bo. G'wan.

BO Well . . . I . . . I'll try. (*He makes his way to her tortuously and finally gets out her name*) Cherry!

CHERIE Yah?

BO Cherry . . . it wasn't right a me to treat ya the way I did, draggin' ya onto the bus, tryin' to make ya marry me whether ya wanted to or not. Ya think ya could ever forgive me?

CHERIE (*After some consideration*) I guess I been treated worse in my life.

BO (*Taking out his wallet*) Cherry . . . I *got* ya here and I think I oughta get ya back in good style. So . . . take this.
(*He hands her a bill*)

CHERIE Did the sheriff make you do this?

BO (*Angrily*)   No, by God! He din say nothin' bout my givin' ya money.

WILL   That's *his* idea, miss. But I think it's a good one.

CHERIE   Ya don't have to gimme this much, Bo.

BO   I want ya to have it.

CHERIE   Thanks. I can sure use it.

BO   And I . . . I wish ya good luck, Cherry . . . Honest I do.

CHERIE   I wish you the same, Bo.

BO   Well . . . I guess I said ev'rything that's to be said, so . . . so long.

CHERIE (*In a tiny voice*)   So long.
(*Awkward and embarrassed now,* BO *returns to his corner, and* CHERIE *sits back down at the table, full of wistful wonder*)

WILL   Now, that wasn't so bad, was it, son?

BO   I'd ruther break in wild horses than have to do it again.
(WILL *laughs heartily, then strolls over to the counter in a seemingly casual way*)

WILL   How's your headache, Grace?

GRACE   Huh?

WILL   A while back, you said you had a headache.

GRACE   Oh, I feel fine now, Will.

WILL (*He looks at* CARL)   You have a nice walk, Carl?

CARL   Yah. Sure.

WILL   Well, I think ya better go upstairs 'cause someone took your overshoes and left 'em outside the door to Grace's apartment.
(WILL *laughs long and heartily, and* ELMA *cannot suppress a grin.* CARL *looks at his feet and realizes his oversight.* GRACE *is indignant*)

GRACE   Nosy old snoop!

WILL   I'll have me a cup of coffee, Grace, and one a these sweet rolls.
(*He selects a roll from the glass dish on counter*)

VIRGIL   Come on over to the counter now, Bo, and have a bite a breakfast.

BO   I ain't hungry, Virge.

VIRGIL   Maybe a cup a coffee?

BO   I couldn't get it down.

VIRGIL   Now what's the matter, Bo? Ya oughta feel purty good. The sheriff let ya go and . . .

BO   I might as well a stayed in the jail.

VIRGIL   Now, what kinda talk is that? The bus'll be leavin' purty soon and we'll be back at the ranch in a coupla days.

BO   I don't care if I never see that dang ranch again.

VIRGIL   Why, Bo, you worked half yor life earnin' the money to build it up.

BO   It's the lonesomest damn place I ever did see.

VIRGIL   Well . . . I never thought so.

BO   It'll be like goin' back to a graveyard.

VIRGIL   Bo . . . I heard Hank and Orville talkin' 'bout the new schoolmarm, lives over to the Stebbins'. They say she's a looker.

BO   I ain't int'rested in no schoolmarm.

VIRGIL   Give yourself time, Bo. Yor young. You'll find lotsa gals, gals that'll love *you*, too.

BO   I want Cherry.
      (*And for the first time we observe he is capable of tears*)

VIRGIL   (*With a futile shrug of his shoulders*)   Aw—Bo—

BO   (*Dismissing him*)   Go git yorself somethin' t'eat, Virge.
      (BO *remains in isolated gloom as* VIRGIL *makes his slow way to the counter. Suddenly the telephone rings.* GRACE *jumps to answer it*)

GRACE   My God! the lines are up. (*Into the telephone*) Grace's Diner! (*Pause*) It is? (*Pause*) O.K. I'll tell him. (*Hangs up and turns to* CARL) Road's cleared now but you're gonna have to put on your chains 'cause the road's awful slick.

CARL   God damn! (*Gets up and hustles into his overcoat, going center to make his announcement*) Road's clear, folks! Bus'll be ready to leave as soon as I get the chains on. That'll take about twenty minutes . . . (*Stops and looks back at them*) . . . unless someone wants to help me.
      (*Exits.* WILL *gets up from the counter*)

WILL I'll help ya, Carl.
(*Exits.* CHERIE *makes her way over to* BO)

CHERIE Bo?

BO Yah?

CHERIE I just wanted to tell ya somethin', Bo. It's kinda personal and kinda embarrassin', too, but . . . I ain't the kinda gal you thought I was.

BO What ya mean, Cherry?

CHERIE Well, I guess some people'd say I led a real wicked life. I guess I have.

BO What you tryin' to tell me?

CHERIE Well . . . I figgered since ya found me at the Blue Dragon, ya just took it fer granted I'd had other boy friends 'fore you.

BO Ya had?

CHERIE Yes, Bo. Quite a few.

BO Virge'd told me that, but I wouldn't b'lieve him.

CHERIE Well, it's true. So ya see . . . I ain't the kinda gal ya want at all.
(BO *is noncommittal.* CHERIE *slips back to her table.* ELMA *makes her way to the bench to rouse* DR. LYMAN)

ELMA Dr. Lyman! Dr. Lyman!
(*He comes to with a jump, staring out wildly about him*)

DR. LYMAN Where am I? (*Recognizing* ELMA) Oh, it's *you*. (*A great smile appears*) Dear girl. What a sweet awakening!

ELMA How do you feel?

DR. LYMAN That's not a polite question. How long have I been asleep here?

ELMA Oh—a couple of hours.

DR. LYMAN Sometimes Nature blesses me with a total blackout. I seem to remember absolutely nothing after we started our performance. How were we?

ELMA Marvelous.

DR. LYMAN Oh, I'm glad. Now I'll have a cup of that coffee you were trying to force on me last night.

ELMA All right. Can I fix you something to eat?

DR. LYMAN No. Nothing to eat.

(*He makes a face of repugnance*)

ELMA   Oh, Dr. Lyman, you *must* eat something. Really.

DR. LYMAN   *Must* I?

ELMA   Oh, yes! Please!

DR. LYMAN   Very well, for your sweet sake, I'll have a couple
of three-minute eggs, and some toast and orange juice. But
I'm doing this for *you,* mind you. Just for you.
(ELMA *slips behind the counter to begin his breakfast, as*
VIRGIL *gets up from the counter and goes to* BO)

VIRGIL   I'll go help the driver with his chains, Bo. You stay
here and take care a that hand.
(*He goes out.* BO *finds his way again to* CHERIE)

BO   Cherry . . . would I be molestin' ya if I said somethin'?

CHERIE   No . . .

BO   Well . . . since you brought the subject up, you *are* the
first gal I ever had anything to do with. (*There is a silence*)
By God! I never thought I'd hear m'self sayin' that, but I
said it.

CHERIE   I never woulda guessed it, Bo.

BO   Ya see . . . I'd lived all my life on a ranch . . . and I
guess I din know much about women . . . 'cause they're
diff'rent from men.

CHERIE   Well, natur'ly.

BO   Every time I got around one . . . I began to feel kinda
scared . . . and I din know how t'act. It was aggravatin'.

CHERIE   Ya wasn't scared with *me,* Bo.

BO   When I come into that night club place, you was singin'
. . . and you smiled at me while you was singin', and
winked at me a coupla times. Remember?

CHERIE   Yah. I remember.

BO   Well, I guess I'm kinda green, but . . . no gal ever done
that to me before, so I thought you was singin' yor songs
just fer *me.*

CHERIE   Ya did kinda attrack me, Bo . . .

BO   Anyway, you was so purty, and ya seemed so kinda
warm-hearted and sweet. I . . . I felt like I *could* love ya
. . . and I did.

CHERIE   Bo—ya think you really did love me?

BO   Why, Cherry! I couldn't be *familiar* . . . with a gal I din love.
   (CHERIE *is brought almost to tears. Neither she nor* BO *can find any more words for the moment, and drift away from each other back to their respective places.* CARL *comes back in, followed by* VIRGIL *and* WILL. CARL *has got his overshoes on now. He comes center again to make an announcement*)

CARL   Bus headed west! All aboard! Next stop, Topeka!
   (*He rejoins* GRACE *at the counter and, taking a pencil from his pocket, begins making out his report.* WILL *speaks to* BO)

WILL   How ya feelin' now, cowboy?

BO   I ain't the happiest critter that was ever born.

WILL   Just 'cause ya ain't happy now don't mean ya ain't gonna be happy t'morrow. Feel like shakin' hands now, cowboy?

BO   (*Hesitant*)   Well . . .

VIRGIL   Go on, Bo. He's only trying to be friends.

BO   (*Offering his hand, still somewhat reluctantly*)   I don't mind.
   (*They shake*)

WILL   I just want you to remember there's no hard feelin's. So long.

BO   S'long.

WILL   I'm goin' home now, Grace. See you Monday.

GRACE   S'long, Will.

CARL   Thanks for helpin' me, Will. I'll be pullin' out, soon as I make out the reports.

WILL   (*Stops at the door and gives a final word to* CHERIE)
   Montana's not a bad place, miss.
   (*He goes out*)

VIRGIL   Nice fella, Bo.

BO   (*Concentrating on* CHERIE)   Maybe I'll think so some day.

VIRGIL   Well, maybe we better be boardin' the bus, Bo.
   (*Without even hearing* VIRGIL, BO *makes his way suddenly over to* CHERIE)

BO   Cherry!

CHERIE   Hi, Bo!

BO   Cherry, I promised not to molest ya, but if you was to give yor permission, it'd be all right. I . . . I'd like to kiss ya g'bye.

CHERIE   Ya would? (BO *nods*) I'd like ya to kiss me, Bo. I really would. (*A wide grin cracks open his face and he becomes all hoodlum boy again, about to take her in his arms roughly as he did before, but she stops him*) Bo! I think this time when ya kiss me, it oughta be diff'rent.

BO   (*Not sure what she means*)   Oh!
(*He looks around at* VIRGIL, *who turns quickly away, as though admitting his inability to advise his buddy.* BO *then takes her in his arms cautiously, as though holding a precious object that was still a little strange to him*)

BO   Golly! When ya kiss someone fer serious, it's kinda scary, ain't it?

CHERIE   Yah! It is.
(*Anyway, he kisses her, long and tenderly*)

GRACE   (*At the counter*)   It don't look like he was molestin' her now.
(BO, *after the kiss is ended, is dazed. Uncertain of his feelings, he stampedes across the room to* VIRGIL, *drawing him to a bench where the two men can confer. The action continues with* DR. LYMAN, *at the counter, having his breakfast*)

DR. LYMAN   I could tell you with all honesty that this was the most delicious breakfast I've ever eaten, but it wouldn't be much of a compliment because I have eaten very few breakfasts.
(*They laugh together*)

ELMA   It's my favorite meal.
(*Turns to the refrigerator as he brings bottle out secretly and spikes his coffee*)

DR. LYMAN   (*When* ELMA *returns*)   Dear girl, let us give up our little spree, shall we? You don't want to go traipsing over the streets of the state's capital with an old reprobate like me.

ELMA   Whatever you say.

DR. LYMAN   I shall continue my way to Denver. I'm sure it's best.

ELMA   Anyway, I've certainly enjoyed knowing you.

DR. LYMAN   Thank you. Ah! sometimes it is so gratifying to feel that one is doing the "right" thing, I wonder that I don't choose to always.

ELMA   What do you mean?

DR. LYMAN   Oh, I was just rambling. You know, perhaps while I am in the vicinity of Topeka, I should drop in at that hospital and seek some advice.

ELMA   Sometimes their patients come in here. They look perfectly all right to me.

DR. LYMAN   (*To himself*)   Friends have been hinting for quite a while that I should get psychoanalyzed. (*He chuckles*) I don't know if they had my best interests at heart or their own.

ELMA   Golly. I don't see anything the matter with you.

DR. LYMAN   (*A little sadly*)   No. Young people never do. (*Now with a return of high spirits*) However, I don't think I care to be psychoanalyzed. I rather cherish myself as I am (*The cavalier again, he takes her hand*) Good-bye, my dear! You were the loveliest Juliet since Miss Jane Cowl. (*Kisses her hand gallantly, then goes for his coat.* ELMA *comes from behind counter and follows him*)

ELMA   Thank you, Dr. Lyman. I feel it's been an honor to know you. You're the smartest man I've ever met.

DR. LYMAN   The smartest?

ELMA   Really you are.

DR. LYMAN   Oh, yes. I'm terribly smart. Wouldn't it have been nice . . . to be intelligent? (*He chuckles, blows a kiss to her, then hurries out the door.* ELMA *lingers behind, watching him get on the bus*)

CARL   (*To* GRACE)   Hey, know what I heard about the perfessor? The detective at the bus terminal in Kanz City is a buddy of mine. He pointed out the perfessor to me before he got on the bus. Know what he said? He said the p'lice in Kanz City picked the perfessor up for *loiterin'* round the schools.

GRACE   (*Appalled*)   Honest?

CARL   Then they checked his record and found he'd been in trouble several times, for gettin' involved with young girls.

GRACE   My God! Did you tell Will?

CARL   Sure, I told him. They ain't *got* anything on the perfessor now, so there's nothin' Will could do. (ELMA *makes
her way back to the counter now and hears the rest of what*
CARL *has to say*) What gets *me* is why does he call hisself a
doctor? Is he some kinda phony?

ELMA   No, Carl. He's a Doctor of Philosophy.

CARL   What's that?

ELMA   It's the very highest degree there is, for scholarship.

GRACE   Ya'd think he'd have philosophy enough to keep outa
trouble.
(ELMA *resumes her work behind the counter now*)

CARL   (*To* GRACE)   Sorry to see me go, baby?

GRACE   No . . . I told ya, I'm tired.

CARL   (*Good-naturedly*)   Ya know, sometimes I get to
thinkin', what the hell good is marriage, where ya have to
put up with the same broad every day, and lookit her in the
morning, and try to get along with her when she's got a bad
disposition. This way suits me fine.

GRACE   I got no complaints, either. Incidentally, are you
married, Carl?

CARL   Now, who said I was married, Grace? Who said it?
You just tell me and I'll fix him.

GRACE   Relax! Relax! See ya day after tomorrow.
(*She winks at him*)

CARL   (*Winks back*)   You might get surprised . . . what
can happen in twenty minutes. (*Slaps* GRACE *on the but-
tocks as a gesture of farewell*) All aboard!
(*He hustles out the front door as* BO *hurries to* CHERIE)

GRACE   (*To herself*)   He still never said whether he was married.

BO   Cherry?

CHERIE   (*A little expectantly*)   Yah?

BO   I been talkin' with my buddy, and he thinks I'm virgin
enough fer the two of us.

CHERIE   (*Snickers, very amused*)   Honest? Did Virgil say
that?

BO   Yah . . . and I like ya like ya are, Cherry. So I don't
care how ya got that way.

CHERIE (*Deeply touched*)   Oh God, thass the sweetest, tend-
   erest thing that was ever said to me.

BO (*Feeling awkward*)   Cherry . . . it's awful· hard for a
   fella, after he's been turned down once, to git up enough
   guts to try again . . .

CHERIE   Ya don't need guts, Bo.

BO (*Not quite sure what she means*)   I don't?

CHERIE   It's the last thing in the world ya need.

BO   Well . . . anyway, I jest don't have none now, so I'll
   . . . just have to say what I feel in my heart.

CHERIE   Yah?

BO   I still wish you was goin' back to the ranch with me,
   more'n anything I know.

CHERIE   Ya do?

BO   Yah. I do.

CHERIE   Why, I'd go anywhere in the world with ya now, Bo.
   Anywhere at all.

BO   Ya would? Ya would?
   (*They have a fast embrace. All look*)

GRACE (*Nudging* ELMA)   I knew this was gonna happen all
   the time.

ELMA   Gee, I didn't.
   (*Now* BO *and* CHERIE *break apart, both running to opposite
   sides of the room,* BO *to tell* VIRGIL; CHERIE, ELMA)

BO   Hear that, Virge? Yahoo! We're gettin' married after all.
   Cherry's goin' back with me.

CHERIE (*At counter*)   Ain't it wonderful when someone so
   awful turns out t'be so nice? We're gettin' married. I'm
   goin' to Montana.
   (CARL *sticks his head through the door and calls impatiently*)

CARL   Hey! All aboard, fer Christ's sake!
   (*Exits.* BO *grabs* VIRGIL *now by the arm*)

BO   C'mon, Virge, y'old raccoon!

VIRGIL (*Demurring*)   Now look, Bo . . . listen t'me for a
   second.

BO (*Who can't listen to anything in his high revelry. One arm*

is around CHERIE, *the other tugs at* VIRGIL)   C'mon! Doggone it, we wasted enough time. Let's git goin'.

VIRGIL   Listen, Bo. Now be quiet jest a minute. You gotta
hear me, Bo. You don't need me no more. I ain't goin'.

BO (*Not believing his ears*)   You ain't *what?*

VIRGIL   I . . . I ain't goin' with ya, Bo.

BO (*Flabbergasted*)   Well, what ya know about that?

VIRGIL   It's best I don't, Bo.

BO   Jest one blame catastrophe after another.

VIRGIL   I . . . I got another job in mind, Bo. Where the
feed's mighty good, and I'll be lookin' after the cattle. I
meant to tell ya 'bout it 'fore this.

BO   Virge, I can't b'lieve you'd leave yor old sidekick. Yor
jokin', man.

VIRGIL   No . . . I ain't jokin', Bo. I ain't.

BO   Well, I'll be a . . .

CHERIE   Virgil—I wish you'd come. I liked *you* . . . 'fore I
ever liked Bo.

BO   Ya *know* Cherry likes ya, Virge. It jest don't make sense,
yor not comin'.

VIRGIL   Well . . . I'm doin' the right thing. I know I am.

BO   Who's gonna look after the cattle?

VIRGIL   Hank. Every bit as good as *I* ever was.

BO (*Very disheartened*)   Aw, Virge, I dunno why ya have to
pull a stunt like this.

VIRGIL   You better hurry, Bo. That driver's not gonna wait all
day.

BO (*Starting to pull* VIRGIL, *to drag him away just as he tried
once with* CHERIE)   Daggone it, yor my buddy, and I ain't
gonna let ya go. Yor goin' *with* Cherry and me cause we
want ya . . .

VIRGIL (*It's getting very hard for him to control his feelings*)
No . . . No . . . lemme be, Bo . . .

CHERIE (*Holding* BO *back*)   Bo . . . ya can't do it that way
. . . ya jest can't . . . if he don't wanta go, ya can't make
him . . .

BO   But, Cherry, there ain't a reason in the world he shouldn't go. It's plum crazy.

CHERIE   Well, sometimes people have their *own* reasons, Bo.

BO   Oh? (*He reconsiders*) Well, I just hate to think of gettin' along without old Virge.

VIRGIL   (*Laughing*)   In a couple weeks . . . ya'll never miss me.

BO   (*Disheartened*)   Aw, Virge!

VIRGIL   Get along with ya now.

CHERIE   Virgil—(*Brightly*)   Will ya come and visit us, Virgil?

VIRGIL   I'll be up in the summer.

BO   Where ya gonna be, Virge?

VIRGIL   I'll write ya th' address. Don't have time to give it to ya now. Nice place. Mighty nice. Now hurry and get on your bus.
(CARL *honks the horn*)

BO   (*Managing a quick embrace*)   So long, old boy. So long!

VIRGIL   'Bye, Bo! G'bye!
(*Now, to stave off any tears,* BO *grabs* CHERIE'S *hand*)

BO   C'mon, Cherry. Let's make it fast.
(*Before they are out the door, a thought occurs to* BO. *He stops, takes off his leather jacket and helps* CHERIE *into it. He has been gallant. Then he picks up her suitcase and they go out, calling their farewells behind them*)

CHERIE   'Bye—'bye—'bye, everyone! 'Bye!
(VIRGIL *stands at the door, waving good-bye. His eyes look a little moist. In a moment, the bus's motor is heard to start up. Then the bus leaves*)

GRACE   (*From behind counter*)   Mister, we gotta close this place up now, if Elma and me're gonna get any rest. We won't be open again till eight o'clock, when the day girl comes on. The next bus through is to Albuquerque, at eight forty-five.

VIRGIL   Albuquerque? I guess that's as good a place as any.
(*He remains by the front entrance, looking out on the frosty morning.* ELMA *and* GRACE *continue their work behind the counter*)

ELMA   Poor Dr. Lyman!

GRACE   Say, did you hear what Carl told me about that guy?

ELMA   No. What was it, Grace?

GRACE   Well, according to Carl, they run him outa Kanz City.

ELMA   I don't believe it.

GRACE   Honey, Carl got it straight from the detective at the bus terminal.

ELMA   (*Afraid to ask*)   What . . . did Dr. Lyman do?

GRACE   Well, lots of old fogies like him just can't let young girls alone. (*A wondering look comes over* ELMA's *face*) So, it's a good thing you didn't meet him in Topeka.

ELMA   Do you think . . . he wanted to make *love*, to *me?*

GRACE   I don't think he meant to play hopscotch.

ELMA   (*Very moved*)   Gee!

GRACE   Next time any guy comes in here and starts gettin' fresh, you come tell your Aunt Grace.

ELMA   I guess I'm kinda stupid.

GRACE   Everyone has gotta learn. (*Looking into refrigerator*) Now Monday, for sure, I gotta order some cheese.

ELMA   I'll remind you.

GRACE   (*Coming to* ELMA, *apologetically*)   Elma, honey?

ELMA   Yes?

GRACE   I could kill Will Masters for sayin' anything about me and Carl. I didn't want you to know.

ELMA   I don't see why I shouldn't know, Grace. I don't wanta be a baby forever.

GRACE   Of course you don't. But still, you're a kid, and I don't wanta set no examples or anything. Do you think you can overlook it and not think bad of me?

ELMA   Sure, Grace.

GRACE   'Cause I'm a restless sort of woman, and every once in a while, I gotta have me a man, just to keep m'self from gettin' grouchy.

ELMA   It's not my business, Grace. (*She stops a moment to consider herself in the mirror, rather pleased*) Just think, he wanted to make love to *me.*

GRACE   Now don't start gettin' *stuck* on yourself.

ELMA   I'm not, Grace. But it's nice to know that someone *can* feel that way.

GRACE   You're not gonna have any trouble. Just wait'll you get to college and start meeting all those cute *boys*.
(GRACE *seems to savor this*)

ELMA   All right. I'll wait.

GRACE   You can run along now, honey. All I gotta do is empty the garbage.

ELMA   (*Getting her coat from closet behind counter*)   O.K.

GRACE   G'night!

ELMA   (*Coming from behind counter, slipping into her coat*) Good night, Grace. See you Monday. (*Passing* VIRGIL) It was very nice knowing you, Virgil, and I just loved your music.

VIRGIL   Thank you, miss. G'night.
(ELMA *goes out*)

GRACE   We're closing now, mister.

VIRGIL   (*Coming center*)   Any place warm I could stay till eight o'clock?

GRACE   Now that the p'lice station's closed, I don't know where you could go, unless ya wanted to take a chance of wakin' up the man that runs the hotel.

VIRGIL   No—I wouldn't wanta be any trouble.

GRACE   There'll be a bus to Kanz City in a few minutes. I'll put the sign out and they'll stop.

VIRGIL   No, thanks. No point a goin' back there.

GRACE   Then I'm sorry, mister, but you're just left out in the cold. (*She carries a can of garbage out the rear door, leaving* VIRGIL *for the moment alone*)

VIRGIL   (*To himself*)   Well . . . that's what happens to some people.
(*Quietly, he picks up his guitar and goes out.* GRACE *comes back in, locks the back door, snaps the wall switch, then yawns and stretches, then sees that the front door is locked. The sun outside is just high enough now to bring a dim light into the restaurant.* GRACE *stops at the rear door and casts her eyes tiredly over the establishment. One senses her aloneness. She sighs, then goes out the door. The curtain comes down on an empty stage*)

The Dark at the Top of the Stairs

The Dark at the Top of the Stairs

was first presented by Saint Subber and Elia Kazan at The Music Box, New York City, on December 5, 1957, with the following cast:

(IN ORDER OF APPEARANCE)

CORA FLOOD, *a young housewife*	Theresa Wright
RUBIN FLOOD, *her husband*	Pat Hingle
SONNY FLOOD, *the ten-year-old son*	Charles Saari
BOY OUTSIDE	Jonathan Shawn
REENIE FLOOD, *the sixteen-year-old daughter*	Judith Robinson
FLIRT CONROY, *a flapper friend of Reenie's*	Evans Evans
MORRIS LACEY, *Cora's brother-in-law*	Frank Overton
LOTTIE LACEY, *Cora's older sister*	Eileen Heckart
PUNKY GIVENS, *Flirt's boy friend*	Carl Reindel
SAMMY GOLDENBAUM, *Punky's friend*	Timmy Everett
CHAUFFEUR	Anthony Ray

DIRECTED BY Elia Kazan
SETTING BY Ben Edwards
COSTUMES BY Lucinda Ballard
LIGHTING BY Jean Rosenthal

Scenes

The home of Rubin Flood, his wife and two children, in a small Oklahoma town close to Oklahoma City. The time is the early 1920's.

ACT ONE	A Monday afternoon in early spring.
ACT TWO	After dinner, the following Friday.
ACT THREE	The next day, late afternoon.

ACT ONE

SCENE: *The setting for the entire play is the home of* RUBIN
FLOOD *and his wife and two children, in a small Oklahoma
town close to Oklahoma City. The time is the early 1920's,
during an oil boom in the area. The house is comfortable
and commodious, with probably eight or nine rooms. It is
one of those square, frame houses built earlier in the century, that stand secure as blocks, symbols of respectability
and material comfort.*

All we see of the FLOODS' *house is the living room, where
the action of the play takes place. There is a flight of stairs
at the far left. At the top of them is the upstairs hallway,
which is not accessible to windows and sunlight. During the
daytime scenes, this small area is in semidarkness, and at
night it is black. When the hallway is lighted, we can see the
feet of the characters who happen to be there. We are conscious of this area throughout the play, as though it holds
some possible threat to the characters.*

*On the far right, downstairs, is the outside entrance, with
a small hallway one must go through before coming into the
living room.*

*In the middle of the living room is a wicker table and two
comfortable wicker chairs, placed one on each side. Upstage
center are sliding doors leading into the parlor, where we see
a player piano. To the left of these doors and under the
stairway, is a swinging door leading into the dining room.
Extreme downstage left is a fireplace and a large comfortable leather chair. This area is considered* RUBIN'S. *In the
rest of the room are book shelves, a desk, a few small tables
and portraits of* CORA FLOOD'S *mother and father. Through a
large window at the back, we see part of the front porch to
the house, and can see characters coming and going.*

*As for the atmosphere of the room, despite the moodiness
of shadowy corners and Victorian (more or less) furnish-
ings, there is an implied comfort and hospitality.*

*When the curtain goes up, it is a late Monday afternoon
in the early spring, about five o'clock. Outside, the sun is
setting, but the room is still filled with soft, warm light.*

The stage is empty when the curtain rises. CORA *and* RU-
BIN *are both upstairs, he preparing to leave on a business
trip.*

225

CORA (*Off*)   Rubin!

RUBIN (*Off*)   Yah!

CORA (*Off*)   How many times do I have to tell you to rinse your hands before you dry them on a towel? You leave the bathroom looking like a wild horse had been using it. (RU-BIN *laughs*) I can smell the bay rum clear over here. My! You're certainly getting spruced up!

RUBIN (*Starting downstairs, carrying a suitcase. He is quite a good-looking man of thirty-six, still robust, dressed in Western clothes—a big Stetson, boots, narrow trousers, colorful shirt and string tie*)   I gotta look good for my customers.

CORA (*Calling down to him*)   How long will you be gone this time?

RUBIN   I oughta be home end of the week. Saturday.

CORA (*Calling down*)   That's better than you usually do. Where will you be?

RUBIN (*Goes to his corner, where he keeps his business para-phernalia*)   I've made out my route for ya. I've left it on the mantel.

NEWSBOY (*Calling into house from outside*)   Hey, Mr. Flood. Jonsey says your tire's ready at the garage.

RUBIN   O.K., Ed, I'll be down to get it.

CORA (*Coming downstairs*)   Rubin, you've waited this long to go, why don't you wait now until morning? Here it is al-most suppertime. You won't be able to see any customers tonight, no matter where you go. Wait until morning. I'll get up early and fix you breakfast. I'll fix you biscuits, Rubin.

RUBIN   I shoulda been out first thing this mornin'. Monday, and I'm just gettin' away. I can make it to Muskogee to-night and be there first thing in the mornin'. I can finish up by noon and then get on to Chickasha.

CORA   I wish you were home more, Rubin.

RUBIN   I gotta make a livin'.

CORA   Other men make a living without traveling all over the country selling harness.

RUBIN   The way other men make a livin' is *their* business. I gotta make mine the best way I know how. I can't be no schoolmaster like your old man was when he brung you all out here from Pennsylvania. I can't be no dentist like your brother-in-law Morris. I was raised on a ranch and thought I'd spend my life on it. Sellin' harness is about all I'm prepared for . . . as long as there's any harness to sell.

CORA (*With a trace of self-pity*)   I envy women who have their husbands with them all the time. I never have anyone to take me any place. I live like a widow.

RUBIN   What do you want me to do? Give up my job and stay home here to pleasure you every day?

CORA (*She is often disturbed by his language*)   Rubin! Don't say that.

RUBIN   Jesus Christ, ya talk like a man had nothin' else to do but stay home and entertain you.

CORA   Rubin! It's not just myself I'm thinking of. It's the children. We have a daughter sixteen years old now. Do you realize that? Yes. Reenie's sixteen. And Sonny's ten. Sometimes they act like they didn't have a father.

RUBIN (*Sits at table to sharpen his knife*)   You're always tellin' me how good they do at school. The girl plays the piano, don't she? And the boy does somethin', too. Gets up and speaks pieces, or somethin' like that?
(*In* CORA'S *sewing basket he finds a sock on which to wipe his knife*)

CORA (*Again she is shocked*)   Rubin! Not on a clean sock!

RUBIN   Seems to me you all get along all right without me.

CORA   Rubin, I worry about them. Reenie's so shy of people her own age, I don't know what to make of her. She's got no confidence at all. And I don't know how to give her any, but you could. Her eyes light up like candles every time you go near her.

RUBIN (*A little embarrassed*)   Come on now, Cora.

CORA   It's true . . . and the boy. Other boys tease him and call him names, Rubin. He doesn't know how to get along with them.

RUBIN   He oughta beat the tar outa the other boys.

CORA   He's not like you, Rubin. He's not like anyone I ever knew. He needs a father, Rubin. So does Reenie. Kids need a father when they're growing up, same as they need a mother.

RUBIN   You din allus talk like that. God almighty, when those kids was born, you hugged 'em so close to ya, ya made me think they was your own personal property, and I din have nothin' to do with 'em at all.

CORA   Rubin, that's not so.

RUBIN   The hell it ain't. Ya pampered 'em so much and coddled 'em, they thought I was just bein' mean if I tried to drill some sense into their heads.

CORA   Rubin. Don't say that.

RUBIN   You're always kissin' and makin' over the boy until I sometimes wonder who's top man around here.

CORA   Rubin!

RUBIN   I just said I wonder.

CORA   If I kept the kids too close to me, it's only because you weren't there, and I had to have *someone* close to me. I had to have *some*one.

RUBIN   You're like an old mare Pa used to have on the ranch. Never wanted to give up her colts. By God, she'd keep 'em locked inside her and make all us men dig inside her with our hands to get 'em out. She never wanted to let 'em go.

CORA   (*A little repelled by the comparison*)   Rubin, I don't like what you just said.

RUBIN   Well, she was a good mare in every other way.

CORA   You talk shamefully at times.

RUBIN   Well . . . I got my own way of sayin' things and it's pretty hard to change.

CORA   (*Watching him primp before the mirror*)   You like being out on the road, don't you? You like to pretend you're still a young cowboy.

RUBIN   It wasn't a bad life.

CORA   Rubin, there are ever so many things you could do in town. Mr. Binny down here on the corner makes a very good living just selling groceries to the neighborhood people. We could find a store like that, Rubin, and the kids and I could help you, too. You'd be happier doing something like that, Rubin. I know you would.

RUBIN Don't tell me how t'be happy. I told you over and over, I ain't gonna spend my life cooped up in no store.

CORA Or a filling station, Rubin. You could run a filling station or a garage . . .

RUBIN God damn it, Cora. I don't mean to have that kinda life. I just wasn't cut out for it. Now, quit pickin' at me. We been married seventeen years now. It seems t'me, you'd be ready t'accept me the way I am, or start lookin' for a new man.

CORA I don't want a new man. You know that.

RUBIN Then start tryin' to put up with the one you got.

CORA I do try.

RUBIN 'Cause he ain't gonna change. Kiss me g'bye. (*Playfully rough with her*) You come here and kiss me.
(*He grabs her in a fast embrace, and they kiss*)

CORA (*Cautiously*) Rubin, you've got to leave me some money.

RUBIN How much you gonna need?

CORA Uh . . . could you let me have maybe twenty-five dollars?

RUBIN (*Hitting the ceiling*) Twenty-five dollars? I'm only gonna be gone till Saturday.

CORA I have a lot of expenses this week, and . . .

RUBIN *I* pay the bills.

CORA I take care of the utilities, Rubin. And we have a big gas bill this month, last month was so cold. And Reenie's invited to a big birthday party out at the country club. The Ralston girl, and Reenie has to take her a present.

RUBIN Me? Buy presents for Harry Ralston's girl when he owns half this town?

CORA I don't often ask for this much.

RUBIN (*Taking a bill from his wallet*) Twenty's the best I can do.

CORA Thank you, Rubin. The Ralstons are giving Mary Jane a big dance. (*Finding a button loose on his coat*) Here, let me fix that.

RUBIN Cora, that'll be all right.

CORA It'll only take a minute, sit down. (*They sit, and* CORA *takes needle and thread from her sewing basket*) They're having a dance orchestra from Oklahoma City.

RUBIN Harry and Peg Ralston puttin' on the dog now, are they?

CORA Oh, yes. I hardly ever see Peg any more.

RUBIN I guess they don't have time for any of their old friends, now that they've got so much money.

CORA Anyway, they've asked Reenie to the party, I'm thankful for that.

RUBIN The country club, huh? By God, I'd die in the poorhouse 'fore I'd ever do what Harry Ralston done.

CORA Now, Rubin . . .

RUBIN I mean it. He shot hisself in the foot to collect enough insurance money to make his first investment in oil.

CORA Do you believe all those stories?

RUBIN Hell, yes, I believe it. I know it for a fact. He shot hisself in the foot. He oughta be in jail now. Instead, he's a social leader, givin' parties out at the country club. And I'm supposed to feel real proud he invited my daughter. Hurry up.

CORA I ran into Peg downtown during the winter. My, she was wearing a beautiful fur coat. Gray squirrel. And she was wearing a lot of lovely jewelry, too.

RUBIN She's spendin' his money as fast as old Harry makes it.

CORA Why shouldn't she have a few nice things?

RUBIN They tell me they both started drinkin' now. They go out to those country club parties and get drunk as lords.

CORA Peg didn't used to be like that.

RUBIN They're all like that now. The town's gone oil-boom crazy. Chamber of Commerce says we're the wealthiest town per capita in all the Southwest. I guess they're not exaggeratin' much, either, with all this oil money, those damned Indians ridin' around in their limousines, gettin' all that money from the government, millions of dollars. Millions of dollars, and nobody knows what to do with it. Come on, hurry up now . . .

CORA (*Finishing with the button*)   Rubin, if you want to make an investment, if you should hear of something absolutely sure, you can take that money Mama left me when she died. Two thousand dollars, Rubin. You can make an investment with that.

RUBIN   There ain't no such thing as a *sure thing* in the oil business.

CORA   Isn't there?

RUBIN   No. Ya can make a million dollars or lose your ass overnight.

CORA   Rubin, you don't have to use words like that.

RUBIN   I do a good job supportin' ya, don't I?

CORA   Of course.

RUBIN   Then let's let well enough alone.

CORA   I was only thinking, it makes you feel kind of left out to be poor these days.
(*Suddenly, from outside, we hear the sounds of young boys' jeering voices*)

BOYS' VOICES
Sonny Flood! His name is mud!
Sonny runs home to Mama!
Sonny plays with paper dolls!
Sonny Flood, his name is mud!

CORA   See, there! (*She jumps up nervously and runs outside to face her son's accosters*) You boys run along. My Sonny hasn't done anything to hurt you. You go home now or I'll call your mothers, every last one of you. You should be ashamed of yourselves, picking on a boy who's smaller than you are.
(SONNY *comes running into the house now. It is hard to discern his feelings*)

RUBIN (*Follows* CORA *out to the porch*)   Cora, cut it out.

CORA   I can't stand quietly by while they're picking on my boy!

RUBIN   It's *his* battle. He's gotta fight it out for hisself.

CORA   If they touch one hair of that boy's head I'll destroy them.

VOICE (*One last heckler*)   Sonny Flood, his name is mud!

CORA I'll destroy them.
(CORA *re-enters the house*)

VOICE Sonny Flood, his name is mud.

RUBIN (*Still on the porch*) Hey, come here, you fat butterball.

BOY Hi, Mr. Flood.

RUBIN How you doin', Jonathan? Let me see how you're growin'. (*He lifts the boy up*) Gettin' fat as a pig. Say hello to your pa for me.
(*The boy runs off and* RUBIN *comes back inside*)

CORA Sonny, did they hurt you?

SONNY No.

CORA What started it this time?

SONNY I don't know.

CORA Did you say anything to make them mad?

SONNY No.

CORA They're just jealous because you make better grades than they do. They're just jealous, the little beasts.

RUBIN Son!

SONNY Huh?

RUBIN Want me to teach you how to put up a good fight?

SONNY (*Turning away from his father*) I don't think so.

RUBIN (*To* CORA) What else can I do? Buy him a shotgun?

CORA There should be *something* we can do. *Something.*

RUBIN Everybody's gotta figure out his own way of handlin' things, Cora. Whether he fights or whether he runs.

CORA I hate for anything to make me feel so helpless.

RUBIN I gotta be goin'.

CORA Say good-bye to your father, Sonny.

RUBIN (*Making a point of being friendly*) Good-bye, son.

SONNY (*Diffidently*) G'bye.

RUBIN (*Giving up*) Oh, hell.

CORA Isn't there anything you can say to him?

RUBIN Cora, if that boy wants me to help him, he's gotta

come to me and tell me how. I never know what's on his mind.

CORA   You're just not interested.

RUBIN   Oh, hell, I give up. I plain give up.
(*Exasperated,* RUBIN *bolts outside,* CORA *anxiously following him to the door*)

CORA   Rubin . . . Rubin . . . (*We hear* RUBIN'S *car drive off.* CORA *comes back inside*) Why don't you listen to your father, Sonny? Why don't you let him help you?

SONNY   Where's Reenie?

CORA   She's downtown. Your father isn't here very often. Why don't you try and get along with him when he is?

SONNY   (*Wanting to evade the issue*)   I don't know.

CORA   Most boys your age *worship* their fathers.

SONNY   I like him, all right. Where are my movie stars?

CORA   Forget your movie stars for a minute. You have a father to be proud of, Sonny. He and his family were pioneers. They fought Indians and buffalo, and they settled this country when it was just a wilderness. Why, if there was a movie about them, you couldn't wait to see it.

SONNY   Mom, it just makes it worse when you come out and tell those boys you're going to call their mothers.

CORA   You just won't listen to me, will you? You just won't listen to anyone. You're so set in your ways.

SONNY   I want my movie stars.

CORA   I put them in the book shelves when I was straightening up this morning. The only pastime you have is coming home here and playing with those pictures of movie stars. (SONNY *gets out his scrapbook and spreads it on the floor*)

SONNY   I like them.

CORA   That's all the friends you have. Not real friends at all. Just *pictures* of all the lovely friends you'd *like* to have. There's a mighty big difference between pictures of people and the way people really are.

SONNY   I like pictures.

CORA   Maybe you should get out and play with the other boys more often, Sonny.

SONNY   They play stupid games.

CORA   People distrust you if you don't play the same games they do, Sonny. It's the same after you grow up.

SONNY   I'm not going to play games just to make them like me.

CORA   (*Suddenly warm and affectionate*) Come to me, Sonny. I wish I understood you better, boy.

SONNY   I don't see why.

CORA   (*Caressing him*) No, I don't suppose you do. You're a speckled egg, and the old hen that laid you can't help wondering how you got in the nest. But I love you, Sonny. More than anything else in the world.

SONNY   Mom, can I go to a movie tonight?

CORA   You know the rules. One movie a week, on Friday night.

SONNY   Please, Mom. It's a real special movie tonight. Honest, I just *got* to see it.

CORA   Oh, I bet. It's always something special and you've just got to see it like your very life depended on it. No. You're supposed to study on week nights. Now, stay home and study.

SONNY   I've already got all my lessons.

CORA   You have to speak at Mrs. Stanford's tea party next Saturday. Why don't you memorize a new recitation?

SONNY   I can't find anything I like.

CORA   Oh! I found a cute little poem in the Oklahoma City paper this morning. It's about a little boy who hates to take castor oil. It starts off:
"Of all the nasty things, gee whiz!
I think the very worst there is . . ."

SONNY   (*Obviously bored*) I want to do something serious.

CORA   Serious! Like what?

SONNY   I dunno.

CORA   Goodness, it seems to me we've got enough serious things in the world without you getting up to recite sad pieces.
(*Outside the window, we see* FLIRT *and* REENIE *come onto the porch, giggling*)

SONNY   I'm tired of all those stupid pieces you cut out of the papers.

CORA   My goodness! Aren't we getting superior! Oh, here's your sister, Sonny. Be a little gentleman and open the door for her.

REENIE   (*Sticking her head in through the door, asking cautiously*)   Is Daddy gone, Mom?

CORA   Yes, he's gone. The coast is clear.

REENIE   (*Runs to* CORA *excitedly. She is a plain girl with no conscious desire to be anything else*)   Oh, Mom, it's the prettiest dress I ever had.

CORA   Bring it in.

REENIE   Come on in, Flirt.

FLIRT   (*Enters carrying a large dress box. She is a vivacious young flapper of the era*)   Hello, Mrs. Flood.

CORA   Hello, Flirt.
(FLIRT *opens the box*)

REENIE   And they took up the hem and took in the waist so that it fits me just perfectly now.

FLIRT   I think it's simply scrumptious, Mrs. Flood.

CORA   Thank you, Flirt. Hold it up, Reenie.

FLIRT   Yes, hold it up.

REENIE   (*Holding the dress before her*)   Is Dad going to be awfully mad, Mom?

CORA   I told you, he's not going to know anything about it for a while, Reenie. He gave me some money before he left, enough for me to make a small down payment. My, I bet Flirt thinks we're terrible, plotting this way.

FLIRT   Shucks, no. Mama and I do the same thing.

REENIE   Oh, Mom. You should see the dress Flirt got.

FLIRT   It's all red, with spangles on it, and a real short skirt. It's just darling. Daddy says he feels like disowning me in it.

CORA   Did you buy your dress at Delman's, too, Flirt?

FLIRT   (*She can't help boasting an advantage*)   No. Mama takes me into Oklahoma City to buy all my clothes.

CORA   Oh!

SONNY (*Feeling the dress*) Look, it's got stars.

REENIE (*Snapping angrily*) Sonny, take your dirty hands off my new dress.

SONNY (*Ready to start a fight any time* REENIE *is*) My hands are *not* dirty! So there.

REENIE You make me mad. Why don't you go outdoors and play ball instead of staying in the house all the time, spying on everything I do. Mother, why don't you make him go out and play?

SONNY It's my house as much as it's yours, and I've got as much right to be here as you do. So there!

CORA (*Always distressed by their fighting*) Reenie. He only wanted to touch the dress. He likes pretty things, too.

FLIRT Gee whiz, he hasn't done anything, Reenie.

CORA Of course he hasn't. You kids are just antagonistic to each other. You scrap all the time.

SONNY I hate you.

REENIE I hate you, too.

CORA Now stop that. Is that any way for a brother and sister to talk? I'm not going to have any more of it. Flirt, are you taking the Ralston girl a birthday present?

FLIRT Mama got me a compact to give her. It's the only thing we could think of. She already has everything under the sun.

CORA Yes, I suppose so. Her parents are so wealthy now. Well, I'll have to shop for something for Reenie to take her.

FLIRT You know, my folks knew the Ralstons before he made all his money. Mama says Mrs. Ralston used to clerk in a millinery store downtown.

CORA Yes, I knew her then.

FLIRT And my daddy says that Mr. Ralston was so crazy to make money in oil that he shot himself in the foot. Isn't that awful?

SONNY Why did he do that?
(REENIE *goes into the parlor to try on her dress.* SONNY *sits at the table.* FLIRT *fascinates him*)

FLIRT So he could collect enough insurance money to

make his first investment in oil. Did you hear that story, too, Mrs. Flood?

CORA Oh, yes . . . you hear all kinds of stories about the Ralstons now.

FLIRT And you know, some of the women out at the country club didn't want to give Mr. Ralston a membership because they disapproved of *her*.

CORA Is that so?

FLIRT But when you've got as much money as the Ralstons do, I guess you can be a member of *anything*. I just hate Mary Jane Ralston. Some of the boys at school think she's pretty but I think she's a *cow*. I'm not being jealous, either. I guess if I had as much money to spend on clothes as she does, I'd have been voted the prettiest girl in school, too. Anyway, I'm absolutely positive she peroxides her hair.

CORA Really?

REENIE (*Poking her head out between the sliding doors*) Are you sure?

FLIRT Yes. Because she and I play on the same volley ball team in gym class, and her locker is right next to mine, and . . .

CORA (*Reminding her of* SONNY'S *presence*)   Flirt!

FLIRT Isn't it terrible for me to say all these things, when I'm going to her birthday party? But I don't care. She just invited me because she had to. Because my daddy's her daddy's lawyer.

SONNY (*As* REENIE *comes out of parlor wearing her new dress, he makes a grotesque face and props his feet on the table*) Ugh . . .

CORA Oh, Reenie! it's lovely. Sonny, take your feet down. Let me see! Oh, Reenie. He did a fine job. Flirt! tell me more about the young man who's taking Reenie to the party.

FLIRT He's a Jew, Mrs. Flood.

CORA Oh, he is?

REENIE Do you think it's all right for me to go out with a Jew, Mom?

CORA Why, of course, dear, if he's a nice boy.

FLIRT   His name is Sammy Goldenbaum, and he comes from Hollywood, California, and his mother's a moving-picture actress.

CORA   Really?

REENIE   Flirt just found that out, Mom. I didn't know it before.

SONNY   (*All ears*)   A moving-picture actress!

FLIRT   Yes, but she just plays itsy-bitsy parts in pictures. I saw her once. She played a real stuck-up society woman, and she was Gloria Swanson's rival. You see, they were in love with the same man, Thomas Meighan, and she told all these lies about Gloria Swanson to make people think Gloria Swanson wasn't nice, so she could marry Thomas Meighan herself. But Thomas Meighan found out all about it, finally, and . . .

REENIE   Mom, what's a Jewish person like?

CORA   Well, I never knew many Jewish people, Reenie, but . . .

FLIRT   I've heard that some of them can be awful fast with girls.

CORA   I'm sure they're just like any other people.

FLIRT   (*Dancing coquettishly about room*)   They don't believe in Christianity.

CORA   Most of them don't.

REENIE   But do they act different?

CORA   (*Not really knowing*)   Well . . .

FLIRT   My daddy says they always try to get the best of you in business.

CORA   There are lots of very nice Jewish people, Reenie.

FLIRT   Oh, sure! Gee whiz, of course.

REENIE   I don't know what to expect.

FLIRT   Kid, he's a *boy*. That's all you have to know.

CORA   There are Jewish families over in Oklahoma City, but I guess there aren't any here in town.

FLIRT   Oh, yes there are, Mrs. Flood. The Lewises are Jewish, only they changed their name from Levin so no one would know.

CORA   I guess I did hear that some place.

REENIE   Mom, I feel sort of scared to go out with someone so different.

FLIRT   (*She never seems aware of her casual offensiveness*) Oh, you're crazy, Reenie. Gee whiz, I'd never go steady with a Jewish boy, but I'd sure take a date with one—if I didn't have any other way of going.

CORA   Now, Reenie, I'm sure that any friend of the Givens boy is nice, whether he's Jewish or not. And besides, his mother's a movie actress. Think of that.

FLIRT   Yes, but not a famous one.

CORA   (*To* REENIE)   Now, you have a nice date to the party, and a lovely new dress to wear. You can be sure you'll have a good time.

FLIRT   Gosh, yes! After all, a party's a party. And it's out at the country club, and they're having a swell dance orchestra from Oklahoma City, and they're giving favors. I can't wait. Fix your hair real cute and you'll look all right. (*Looks at her wrist watch*) Oh, heck! I've got to go home.

CORA   Do you want to stay here for supper, Flirt?

FLIRT   No. It's my night to fix supper for the folks. My mother makes me fix supper once a week, cook's night out. She says it's good for me to learn something about home-making. Isn't that crazy? The only thing I know how to cook is salmon loaf. I learned how to make it in domestic science class. I've made salmon loaf every Monday night now for the whole year. Kid, can you help me study for that stupid old civics test we're having next week?

REENIE   I guess so.

FLIRT   Civics! Why can't they teach us something in that old school that'd do us some good?

CORA   Good-bye, Flirt.

FLIRT   Good-bye, Mrs. Flood, good-bye, Reenie. Oh, Sonny, you come over to *my* house and play sometime. I know how to be nice to little boys.

CORA   Good-bye! (FLIRT *exits*) Sonny, you've got to go to the store now if we're going to have anything for supper tonight.

SONNY Mom! Can I get a candy bar?

CORA Wouldn't you rather have the nickel to put in your piggy bank?

SONNY No—I want a candy bar.

CORA All right. If you promise not to eat it before supper.

REENIE I want one, too. I want a nut Hershey.

CORA Bring one for Reenie, too.

SONNY She can get her own candy bar.

REENIE He's mean, Mom.

SONNY I don't care. She makes me mad, and I don't like her.

CORA Sonny, she's your sister.

SONNY I don't care. I don't like her.
(*He exits*)

CORA Oh, God, some day you kids are going to be sorry. When you can't even get along with people in your own family, how can you expect to get along with people out in the world? (*Goes to the window and looks out, protectively*) Poor Sonny, every time he leaves the house, those neighborhood bullies pick on him. I guess they've all gone home now.
(REENIE *takes off her new dress and throws it on a chair*)

REENIE I don't know if I like Flirt or not.

CORA (*Comes away from the window*) Why, what's the matter?

REENIE The only reason she likes me is because I help her with her studies.
(REENIE *goes into the parlor, gets her daytime clothes, and comes back into the living room to put them on*)

CORA Why do you say that?

REENIE I just do.

CORA You don't think *anyone* likes you, do you?

REENIE Mom, maybe we shouldn't have bought the dress.

CORA What?

REENIE I mean it, Mom. Dad'd be awful mad if he knew.

CORA I told you, he's not going to know.

REENIE Won't he be here the night of the party?

CORA   No. And even if he were, he wouldn't notice the dress was new unless you told him about it.

REENIE   Just the same, Mom, I don't feel right about it.

CORA   Why don't you feel right?

REENIE   Because . . . the dress cost so much, and what good is it going to do me? I never have a good time at those dances, anyway. No one ever dances with me.

CORA   This time it's going to be different. You've got a new dress, and you've got a nice young man coming here all the way from California to be your escort. Think of it. Why, most young girls would be too excited to breathe.

REENIE   It's just a *blind* date.

CORA   What are you talking about?

REENIE   They give blind dates to all the girls in town that nobody else wants to take.

CORA   Daughter, I'm sure that's not so.

REENIE   Oh, Mom, you just don't know.

CORA   I do too.

REENIE   Besides, he's Jewish. I never knew a Jewish boy before. I'm scared.

CORA   Daughter, you're just looking for excuses. You just don't want to go, do you? Reenie, don't you want to have friends?

REENIE   Yes, but . . .

CORA   You're not going to make friends just staying home playing the piano, or going to the library studying your lessons. I'm glad you're studious and talented, but those things aren't enough just in themselves.

REENIE   I don't want to talk about it any more.

CORA   You're going to have to talk about these things someday. Where are you going?

REENIE   To practice the piano.
   (*She goes into the parlor and starts playing scales*)

CORA   (*Angrily impatient*)   That's where you spend half your life, *practicing* at the piano. (REENIE *bangs on piano exasperatedly and exits to dining room*) But will you get up and play for people so they'll know how talented you are?

No. You hide your light under a bushel. You stay home and play behind closed doors, where no one can hear you except your own family. All you do is *pity* yourself at the piano. That's all. You go in there and pity yourself, playing all those sad pieces.

(REENIE *comes out of dining room, and calms herself by watering her plants*)

REENIE Mom, I just couldn't get up before an audience and play. I just couldn't.

CORA Why couldn't you? What good is it for your father to have bought the piano? What use is it? (REENIE *begins to sob*) Now, don't cry, Reenie. I'm sorry. (REENIE *goes into parlor and resumes her monotonous scales.* CORA *goes to telephone*) Long distance? Give me three-six-oh-seven-J in Oklahoma City, please. (*There is a wait of several moments*) Hello, Lottie. . . . Lottie, can you and Morris come over to dinner Friday night? I haven't seen you for so long, I want to talk with you, Lottie. I've just got to see some of my own flesh and blood. (*We hear* RUBIN'S *car slam to a stop outside; the car door slams and then he comes stomping up to the front porch*) Reenie's going to a big party out at the country club, and I thought I'd have a nice dinner first. . . . Rubin won't be here and I'll want company. Please come. Oh, I'm so glad. I'll be looking forward to seeing you.

RUBIN (*Bursting into the house*) What the hell's been goin' on behind my back? (*Sees the innocent dress lying on a chair*) There it is!

CORA (*Her phone call over*) Rubin!

RUBIN (*Displaying the dress as evidence*) So this is what ya wanted the extra money for. Fine feathers! Fine feathers! And ya buy 'em when my back is turned.

CORA Rubin, we were going to tell you. . . .

RUBIN A man has t'go downtown and talk with some of his pals before he knows what's goin' on in his own family.

CORA Who told you?

RUBIN That's all right who told me. I got my own ways a findin' out what goes on when my back is turned.

CORA You didn't leave town at all. You've been down to that dirty old pool hall.

RUBIN   I got a right to go to the pool hall whenever I damn please.

CORA   I thought you were in such a hurry to get out of town. Oh, yes, you had to get to Muskogee tonight.

RUBIN   I can still make it to Muskogee. (*Finds the price tag on the dress*) Nineteen seventy-five! Lord have mercy! Nineteen seventy-five.

CORA   Did Loren Delman come into the pool hall while you were there? Did he? Did he tell you? If he did I'll never buy anything in that store again.

RUBIN   That'd suit me just fine.

CORA   Oh, why couldn't he have kept his mouth shut? I was going to pay for the dress a little at a time, and . . .

RUBIN   "The finest dress I had in the store," he says, walkin' into the Arcade with a big cigar stuck in his mouth, wearin' a suit of fine tailored clothes. "I just sold your wife the finest dress I had in the store."

CORA   Oh, that makes me furious.

RUBIN   Jesus Christ, woman, whatta you take me for, one a those millionaire oil men? Is that what you think you're married to?

REENIE   (*Pokes her head in through parlor door, speaking with tears and anxiety*)   I told you he'd be mad, Mom. Let's take the dress back, Mom. I don't want to go to the party anyhow.

CORA   (*Angrily impatient*)   Get back in that parlor, Reenie, and don't come in here until I tell you to.
(CORA *slams the parlor doors shut*)

RUBIN   See there! That girl don't even want the dress. It's *you*, puttin' all these high-fallutin' ideas in her head about parties, and dresses and nonsense.

CORA   Rubin, of course Reenie doesn't want to go to the party. She never wants to go any place. All she wants to do is lock herself in the parlor and practice at the piano, or go to the library and hide her nose in a book. After all, she's going to want to get married one of these days, isn't she? And where's she going to look for a husband? In the public library?
(RUBIN *goes to his corner, sits in his big leather chair, and draws a pint of whiskey out of his desk drawer*)

RUBIN   I bought her a fine dress . . . just a little while back.

CORA   Oh, you did?

RUBIN   Yes, I did.

CORA   That's news to me. When?

RUBIN   Just a few months ago. Sure I did.

CORA   I certainly never saw it. What'd it look like?

RUBIN   It was white.

CORA   Rubin Flood, that was the dress you bought her three years ago when she graduated from the eighth grade. And she hasn't had a new dress since then, except for a few school clothes.

RUBIN   Why couldn't she wear the white dress to the party?

CORA   Because she's grown three inches since you got her that dress, and besides I cut it up two years ago and dyed it black and made her a skirt out of it to wear with a middy.

RUBIN   Just the same, I ain't got money to throw away on no party togs. I just ain't got it.

CORA   Oh, no. You don't have money when we need something here at home, do you?

RUBIN   I'm tellin' ya, right now I don't.

CORA   But you always have money for a bottle of bootleg whiskey when you want it, don't you? And I daresay you've got money for a few other things, too, that I needn't mention just at present.

RUBIN   What're ya talkin' about?

CORA   *You* know what I'm talking about.

RUBIN   The hell I do.

CORA   I know what goes on when you go out on the road. You may tell me you spruce up for your customers, but I happen to know better. Do you think I'm a fool?

RUBIN   I don't know what you're talkin' about.

CORA   I happen to have friends, decent, self-respecting people, who tell me a few things that happen when you visit Ponca City.

RUBIN   You mean the Werpel sisters!

CORA   It's all right, who I mean. I have friends over there. That's all I need to say.

RUBIN   Those nosy old maids, the Werpel sisters! God damn! Have they been runnin' to you with stories?

CORA   Maybe you don't have money to buy your daughter a new dress, but it seems you have money to take Mavis Pruitt to dinner whenever you're over there, and to a movie afterwards, and give her presents.

RUBIN   I've known Mavis . . . Pruitt ever since I was a boy! What harm is there if I take her to a movie?

CORA   You're always too tired to take *me* to a movie when you come home.

RUBIN   Life's different out on the road.

CORA   I bet it is.

RUBIN   Besides, I din ask her. She come into the Gibson House one night when I was havin' my dinner. What could I do but let her join me?

CORA   She went to the Gibson House because she knew *you* were there. I know what kind of woman she is.

RUBIN   She's not as bad as she's painted. That poor woman's had a hard time of it, too.

CORA   Oh, she has!

RUBIN   Yes, she has. I feel sorry for her.

CORA   Oh, you do!

RUBIN   Yes, I do. Is there any law that says I can't feel sorry for Mavis Pruitt?

CORA   She's had her eye on you ever since I can remember.

RUBIN   Oh, shoot!

CORA   What happened to the man she left town with after we were married?

RUBIN   He run off and left her.

CORA   For good reason, too, I bet. I also heard that she was seen sporting a pair of black-bottom hose shortly after you left town, and that you were seen buying such a pair of hose at the Globe Dry Goods Store.

RUBIN   By God, you got yourself a real detective service goin', haven't you?

CORA I don't ask people to tell me these things. I wish to God they didn't.

RUBIN All right. I bought her a pair of hose. I admit it. It was her birthday. The hose cost me sixty-eight cents. They made that poor woman happy. After all, I've known her ever since I was a boy. Besides, I was a li'l more flush then.

CORA How do you think it makes me feel when people tell me things like that?

RUBIN Ya oughtn'ta listen.

CORA How can I help it?

RUBIN (*He has to stop to remember to call Mavis Pruitt by her full name, to keep* CORA *from suspecting too much familiarity between them*) There's nothin' 'tween me and Mavis . . . Pruitt . . . Mavis Pruitt, nothin' for you to worry about.

CORA There's probably a woman like her in every town you visit. That's why you want to get out of town, to go frisking over the country like a young stallion.

RUBIN You just hush your mouth. The daughter'll hear you.

CORA (*Indulging in a little self-pity*) A lot you care about your daughter. A lot you care about any of us.

RUBIN You don't think I care for ya unless I set ya on my knee and nuzzle ya.

CORA What you need for a wife is a squaw. Why didn't you marry one of those Indian women out on the reservation? Yes. She'd make you rich now, too, wouldn't she? And you wouldn't have to pay any attention to her at all.
(SONNY *is seen coming onto porch*)

RUBIN All right. Maybe that's what I *shoulda* done.

CORA Oh. So you want to throw it up to me!

RUBIN Throw what?
(SONNY *quietly enters the room, carrying a sack of groceries.* CORA *and* RUBIN *are too far into battle to notice him*)

CORA You know what, Rubin Flood.

RUBIN I don't know nothin'.

CORA You never *wanted* to marry me.

RUBIN   I never said that.

CORA   It's true, isn't it?

RUBIN   I'm tellin' ya, it ain't.

CORA   It is. I've felt it all these years.
(SONNY *crosses and goes through the parlor into the dining room, still unobserved by* RUBIN *and* CORA)

RUBIN   All right. If you're so determined to think it, then go ahead. I admit, in some ways I din wanna marry nobody. Can't ya understand how a man feels, givin' up his freedom?

CORA   And how does a woman feel, knowing her husband married her only because . . . because he . . . (CORA *now spots* REENIE *spying between the parlor doors. She screams at her*) Reenie, get away from there!

RUBIN   None of this is what we was arguin' about in the first place. We was arguin' about the dress. Ya gotta take it back.

CORA   *I won't.*

RUBIN   *Ya will.*

CORA   Reenie's going to wear her new dress to the party, or you'll have to bury me.

RUBIN   You'll take that dress back to Loren Delman, or I'm leavin' this house for good and never comin' back.

CORA   Go on. You're only home half the time as it is. We can get along without you the rest of the time.

RUBIN   Then that's what you're gonna do. There'll be ice-cream parlors in hell before I come back to this place and listen to your jaw.
(*He bolts into the hallway*)

CORA   Get out! Get out and go to Ponca City. Mavis Pruitt is waiting. She's probably getting lonesome without you.
(SONNY *quietly enters from the dining room, and watches*)

RUBIN   By God, Cora, it's all I can do to keep from hittin' you when you talk like that.

CORA   (*Following him into hallway, taunting him. Here they are both unseen by audience*)   Go on and hit me! You wouldn't dare! (*But he does dare. We hear the sound of his blow, which sends* CORA *reeling back into parlor*) Rubin!

(REENIE *watches from the parlor.* SONNY *is still in the living room*)

RUBIN   I'll go to Ponca City, and drink booze and take Mavis to the movies, and raise every kind of hell I can think of. T'hell with you!
(*He bolts outside*)

CORA   (*Running to the door*)   Don't you ever set foot in this house again, Rubin Flood. I'll never forget what you've said. Never! Don't you ever come back inside this house again!
(*We hear* RUBIN'S *car drive off now.* CORA *returns to the living room, still too dazed to be sure what has happened*)

SONNY   Gee, Mom. That was the worst fight you ever had, wasn't it?

CORA   How long have you been standing there, Sonny?

SONNY   Since he hit you.

REENIE   (*Coming forth*)   Did he mean it about not coming back? Oh, Mom, why did you have to say all those things? I love Daddy. Why do you say those things to him?

CORA   Oh, God, I hate for you kids to see us fight this way.

SONNY   What did he mean, he didn't want to marry you?

CORA   You're not old enough to understand these things, Sonny.

SONNY   Did he hurt you, Mom. Did he?

CORA   I'm still too mad to know whether he did or not.

REENIE   I don't think he'll ever come back. What'll we do, Mom?

CORA   Now, don't worry, Reenie.

REENIE   Will we have to go to the poorhouse?

CORA   No, of course not. Now, quit worrying.

REENIE   But if Daddy doesn't come back?

CORA   I still have the money my mother left me, haven't I? And if worst comes to worst we can always go to Oklahoma City and move in with your Aunt Lottie and Uncle Morris.

SONNY   (*Jumping up and down in glee*)   Goody, goody, goody. I wanta move to Oklahoma City.

REENIE   Listen to him, Mom. He's *glad* Daddy's gone. He's *glad*.

SONNY   I don't care. I wanta move to Oklahoma City.

REENIE   I don't. *This* is home. *This* is. And I don't want to move,

CORA   Now, children!

REENIE   I hate you.

SONNY   I hate you, too. So there! Oklahoma City! Oklahoma City! I wanta move to Oklahoma City!

CORA   Stop it! There's been enough fighting in this house for one night. Reenie, take your dress upstairs and hang it in the closet.

REENIE   I hate the old dress now. It's the cause of all the trouble. I hate it.

CORA   You do what I tell you. You take that dress upstairs and hang it in the closet. You're going to go to that party if I have to take you there myself. (REENIE *starts upstairs*) The next time you're invited to a party, I'll let you go in a hand-me-down.

SONNY   (*With the joy of discovering a new continent*)   Oklahoma City.

CORA   (*Wearily*)   I'll go out and fix supper, although I don't imagine any of us will feel like eating.

SONNY   I do. I'm hungry.

CORA   (*A little amused*)   Are you? Good. Come to me, Sonny! (*With a sudden need for affection*) Do you love me, boy? Do you love your old mom?

SONNY   More than all the world with a fence around it.

CORA   (*Clasping him to her*)   Oh, God, what would I do without you kids? I hope you'll always love me, Sonny. I hope you always will. (REENIE *comes downstairs*) Where are you going, daughter?
(REENIE *looks disdainfully at them, and marches into the parlor, where, in a moment, we hear her playing a lovely Chopin nocturne*)

SONNY   Mom, I'm going to sell my autographed photograph of Fatty Arbuckle. Millicent Dalrymple said she'd give me fifteen cents for it. And Fatty Arbuckle isn't one of my favorites any more. If I sold the photograph, I'd have enough to go to the movie tonight and buy a sack of popcorn, besides.

CORA (*Lying on the floor beside him*) If the world was falling to pieces all about you, you'd still want to go to the movies, wouldn't you?

SONNY I don't see why not.

CORA Your mother's unhappy, Sonny. Doesn't that mean anything to you?

SONNY Well . . . I'm sorry.

CORA I want you kids near me tonight. Can't you understand? Oh, God, wouldn't it be nice if life were as sweet as music! (*For a moment, mother and son lie together in each other's arms. Then* CORA *stands, as though fearing her own indulgence, and takes* SONNY *by the hand*) Come! Help me set the table, Sonny.

CURTAIN

SCENE: *At rise of curtain, we hear a banging rendition of "Smiles" coming from the parlor, where* LOTTIE *is at the piano,* SONNY *by her side, both singing in hearty voices.* REENIE *stands listlessly watching, drying a dish.* MORRIS *sits in* RUBIN'S *chair, working one of those baffling little hand puzzles, which has got the best of him.* LOTTIE *proves to be a big, fleshy woman, a few years older than* CORA. *She wears a gaudy dress and lots of costume jewelry.* MORRIS *is a big defeated-looking man of wrecked virility.*

LOTTIE *and* SONNY (*Singing*)   "There are smiles that make us happy . . ."

CORA (*Coming into living room from kitchen*)   I won't need you to help me with the dishes, Reenie. I want you to go upstairs now and get ready for your party. (*Calls into parlor*) Sonny! Sonny!

MORRIS   Sure was a good dinner, Cora.

CORA   What, Morris?

MORRIS (*Trying to make himself heard above the piano*) I said, it sure was a good dinner.

CORA   Thank you, Morris. Now go and get dressed, Reenie. (REENIE *reluctantly goes upstairs*) Sonny! Sonny! Lottie, will you please stop that racket. A body can't hear himself think.
(LOTTIE *and* SONNY *finish the chorus*)

CORA   Sonny, I said you've got to help me in the kitchen.

SONNY   Why can't Reenie?

CORA   She cleared the table for me, and now she has to bathe and get ready for her party.

SONNY   I have to do everything around here.

LOTTIE (*In the voice one uses to indulge a child*)   I think it's a shame. (SONNY *and* CORA *exit into the dining room.* LOTTIE *comes into the living room. To* MORRIS) Cora always was jealous because I could play the piano and she couldn't. (*Looks to see if* CORA *is out of hearing distance*) Do I

251

have something to tell you! Do you know why she asked us over here?

(*She hurries over to* MORRIS)

MORRIS   For dinner.

LOTTIE   No! She and Rubin have had another fight. She told me all about it while I was in the kitchen helping her get dinner on the table.

MORRIS   What about, this time?

LOTTIE   About a new dress she bought for Reenie. But what difference does that make? They could fight about anything. Only this time he hit her.

MORRIS   He did?

LOTTIE   Don't tell her I told you. Poor Cora. I guess maybe she has a hard time with Rubin.

MORRIS   Has Rubin walked out again?

LOTTIE   You guessed it. Do you know what she wants to do now, honey? She wants to bring the kids over to Oklahoma City to live *with us?* She says I suggested they do that some time ago. I guess maybe I did, but my God, I never thought they'd do it. We'd be perfectly miserable with her and the two kids living with us, wouldn't we, Morris? With only one extra bedroom, one of 'em would have to sleep on the davenport in the living room, and then what would happen when your patients started coming in the morning?

MORRIS   Yah. It wouldn't work out very well.

LOTTIE   No. Oh, my! The way she pampers those kids, Morris. If she had her way, she'd spoil 'em rotten.

MORRIS   What did you tell her, honey?

LOTTIE   Well, I haven't told her anything yet. I was so flabbergasted when she asked me, I just hemmed . . . (SONNY *enters the parlor to put away a big vase that* CORA *has just washed.* LOTTIE *sees him*) Hi! Honey.

SONNY   They got me working again.

LOTTIE   I think it's terrible.

(SONNY *exits into the dining room*)

LOTTIE   . . . and hawed until I could think of something to say. Oh, Morris, put away that puzzle and listen to me. She's going to come to you sometime this evening and ask you about it, and all you need to say is, "I'm leaving all that in Lottie's hands, Cora." Can you remember that? Just say it real nice, like it was none of your business.

MORRIS   I'll remember.

LOTTIE   You say you will, but will you?

MORRIS   Yes, honey.

LOTTIE   I don't know. You're so afraid of hurting people's feelings.

MORRIS   That's not so.

LOTTIE   Oh, it is too. Don't I know! You had to go to see some psychologist over in Oklahoma City because you were so afraid of hurting your patients when you drilled their teeth. Now, confess it. It was actually making you sick, that you had to drill your patients' teeth and hurt them.

MORRIS   Honey, I wasn't really *sick* about it.

LOTTIE   You were too. Now remember what I say. Don't get *soft-hearted* at the last minute and tell Cora to bring the kids and come on over. My God, Morris, we'd be in the loony bin in less than two days with them in the house. Cora may be my own flesh and blood but I couldn't live with her to save my life. And I love those kids of hers. I do, Morris. But I couldn't live with them. They'd drive me crazy. You, too. You know they would.

CORA (*Enters the parlor to put napkins in the sideboard*) Almost finished.

LOTTIE   You shoulda let me help you. (*But* CORA *has returned to the kitchen*) Cora said something to me about her getting a job at one of the big department stores over in Oklahoma City. Can you see her doin' a thing like that? I can't. "Cora," I said, "you wouldn't last two days at that kind of work, on your feet all day, taking people's sass." Well, I don't know if I convinced her or not, but I gave her something to think about. (*Sneaks back to parlor door to see if* CORA *is within earshot, then comes back to* MORRIS, *speaking in a very confidential voice*) Morris? Do you think Rubin still plays around with Mavis Pruitt over in Ponca City?

MORRIS (*Clamming up*)   I don't know, honey.

LOTTIE   You do too.

MORRIS   I'm telling you, I don't.

LOTTIE   You men, you tell each other everything, but you all want to protect each other. And wild horses and screaming ravens couldn't get you to talk.

MORRIS   Well, whatever Rubin does . . . like that . . . is *his* business.

LOTTIE   My! Don't we sound righteous all of a sudden! Well, I bet anything he still sees her.

MORRIS   Well, don't you let on to Cora.

LOTTIE   I won't. Did I ever tell you about the first time she met Rubin?

MORRIS   Yes, honey.

LOTTIE   I did not! Cora and I were coming out of the five-and-ten. She'd wanted to buy a little lace to put on a dress. And here comes Rubin, like a picture of Sin, riding down the street on a shiny black horse. My God, he was handsome. Neither of us knew who he was. But he looked at Cora and smiled, and Cora began to get all nervous and fluttery. And do you know what? He came by the house that very night and wanted to see her. Mama and Papa didn't know what to do. They stood around like they were afraid of Rubin. But Cora went out riding with him. He'd brought a buggy with him. And six weeks later they were married. Mama and Papa were worried sick. Rubin's people were all right, but they were ranchers. Kind of wild. And Cora only seventeen, not out of high school. I think that's the reason Papa had his stroke, don't you, Morris?

MORRIS   Maybe . . .

LOTTIE   I do. They just felt like Cora might as well be dead as married to a man like Rubin. But Cora was always a determined creature. Mama and Papa were no match for her when she wanted her own way.

MORRIS   Well, I like Rubin.

LOTTIE   I do, too, honey. I'm not saying anything against him. And he's made a lot better husband than I ever thought he would. But I'm glad *I'm* not married to him. I'd be worried to death all the time. I'm glad I'm married to a nice man I can trust.

(MORRIS *does not know how to respond to this endearment. He crosses the room troubledly*)

MORRIS   What'll Cora do if Rubin doesn't come back?

LOTTIE   Well, that's not our problem, honey.

MORRIS   Yes, but just the same, I . . .

LOTTIE   Listen, she's got a nice big house here, hasn't she? She can take in roomers if she has to. And Mama left her two thousand dollars when she died, didn't she? Yes, Cora was the baby, so Mama left the money to her. I'm not going to worry.

REENIE   (*Upstairs*)   Aunt Lottie!

MORRIS   All right. I was just wondering.

LOTTIE   Now, remember. All you've got to say is, "I'm leaving all that to Lottie, Cora."

MORRIS   Yes, honey.
(REENIE *comes downstairs looking somewhat wan and frightened*)

LOTTIE   Shhhh! (*Now she turns to* REENIE *with a prepared smile*) Well, honey, aren't you getting ready for your party? Morris and I are dying to see your new dress.

REENIE   I don't feel well. I wish I didn't have to go.

LOTTIE   (*Alarmed*)   You don't feel well? Did you tell your mother?

REENIE   Yes. But she won't believe me. I wish you'd tell her, Aunt Lottie.

LOTTIE   (*Rushes excitedly into dining room, where we hear her speaking to* CORA)   Cora! Reenie says she isn't feeling well. Cora, I think maybe she shouldn't go to the party. She says she doesn't want to go. Cora, what do you think is wrong?

CORA   (*Enters living room from dining room—followed by* LOTTIE)   There's nothing wrong with the child, Lottie.

LOTTIE   But she says she isn't feeling well, Cora. (*Turns to* REENIE) Come here, honey, let me see if you've got a temperature. No. Not a sign of temperature. Stick out your tongue. Are you sick at your stomach?

REENIE   Kind of.

LOTTIE   My God, Cora. Her little hands are like ice.

CORA   (*Quite calm and wise*)   There's nothing wrong with the child, Lottie. She gets to feeling like this every time she goes to a party.

LOTTIE She's not going to have a very good time if she doesn't feel well.

CORA It's something she's got to get over, Lottie. Plans are already made now. I got her the dress and she's got a date with a boy who's come here all the way from California. Now, I'm not going to let her play sick and not go. The Ralston girl would never invite Reenie to another party as long as she lived if she backed out now.

(*Her strategy defeated,* REENIE *goes back up the stairs*)

LOTTIE It's awful funny when a young girl doesn't want to go to a party, don't you think so, Morris? (*She watches* REENIE'S *departure, puzzledly*) I just thought of something. I've got a bottle of perfume I'm going to give her. It's Coty's L'Origan. Finest perfume made. One of the big drugstores in Oklahoma City was having an anniversary sale. With each box of Coty's face powder, they gave you a little bottle of perfume, stuck right on top of the box. Morris, run out to the car and get me that package. It's on the back seat. I'll take it upstairs to Reenie. It'll make her feel good, don't you think?

CORA That's very thoughtful of you, Lottie.

MORRIS (*On his way to door*) You'll have her smelling like a fancy woman.

LOTTIE (*With a sudden bite*) How do *you* know what a fancy woman smells like?

MORRIS I can make a joke, can't I?

(MORRIS *exits.* CORA *and* LOTTIE *sit on either side of the table*)

LOTTIE It was a wonderful dinner, Cora.

CORA I'm glad you thought so. It all tasted like ashes to me.

LOTTIE Oh, now, Cora, quit taking on.

CORA Seventeen years we've been married, Lottie, and we still can't get along.

LOTTIE What are you talking about? Why, I've known times when you got along just fine . . . for months at a time.

CORA When Rubin was gone.

LOTTIE Cora, that's not so.

CORA Lottie, it's not good for kids to see their parents fighting.

LOTTIE   Cora, you've got the two nicest kids in the whole world. Why, they're wonderful children, Cora.

CORA   I worry about them, Lottie . . . You saw Reenie just now. Here she is, sick because she's going to a party, when most girls her age would be tickled to death. And the other boys tease Sonny so.

LOTTIE   Oh, Reenie'll get over that. So will Sonny.

CORA   Kids don't just "get over" these things, in some magic way. These troubles stay with kids sometimes, and affect their lives when they grow up.

MORRIS (*Returns with a small package*)   This what you want?

LOTTIE   Yes. Reenie—I've got something for you, Reenie. I've got something here to make you smell good. Real French perfume. Morris says it'll make you smell like a fancy woman.
(*She goes running upstairs, exuding her own brand of warmth and affection*)

CORA   Lottie's awful good-hearted, Morris.

MORRIS   She thinks an awful lot of your kids, Cora.

CORA   I know she does. Morris, I've been thinking, wouldn't it be nice if Sonny and Reenie could go to those big schools you have in Oklahoma City? I mean . . .

LOTTIE (*Hurrying back downstairs*)   Cora, I wish you'd let me curl Reenie's hair for her. I could have her looking like a real baby doll. I'm an artist at it. Last week, Morris took me to a party at the Shrine, and everybody told me I had the prettiest head of hair at the whole party.

CORA   Go on and do it.

LOTTIE   I can't right now. She's in the bathtub. When are you going to get your hair bobbed, Cora?

CORA   Rubin doesn't like bobbed hair.

LOTTIE   Oh, he doesn't! You like my bobbed hair, don't you, Morris?

MORRIS   It's all right, honey.

LOTTIE   I'll be darned if I'd let any man tell me whether I could bob my hair or not. Why, I wouldn't go back to long hair now for anything. Morris says maybe I should take up smoking cigarettes now. Would you believe it,

Cora? Women all over Oklahoma City are smoking cigarettes now. Isn't that disgraceful? What in God's name are we all coming to?

CORA (*There is too much on her mind for her to partake now of* LOTTIE's *small talk*) I . . . I'd better finish up in the kitchen.
(*She exits through the dining-room door*)

LOTTIE Morris, I don't know what to do. I just can't bear to see little Cora so unhappy.

MORRIS After all, it's not your worry, honey.

LOTTIE Oh, I know, but in a way it *is* my worry. I mean, I've always looked after Cora, ever since we were girls. I took her to her teacher the first day of school. I gave up the wishbone for her every time we had fried chicken. She was the baby of the family, and I guess we all felt we had to pamper her.

MORRIS Honey, if you want to take in her and the kids, it's up to you. We'd manage somehow.

LOTTIE Oh, God, Morris! Life'd be miserable.

SONNY (*Enters through parlor*) Wanta see my movie stars, Aunt Lottie?

LOTTIE I guess so, honey. (SONNY *goes into parlor to get scrapbooks as* LOTTIE *turns to* MORRIS *with a private voice*) Every time we come over here we've got to look at his movie stars.

MORRIS Got any of Norma Talmadge?

SONNY (*Spreading the scrapbook on the floor before them*) Sure.

LOTTIE Norma Talmadge, Norma Talmadge! That's all you ever think about is Norma Talmadge. I don't know what you see in her. Besides, she's a Catholic.

MORRIS Honey, you've just got a bug about the Catholics.

LOTTIE Oh I do, do I! Maybe you'd like to marry Norma Talmadge someday and then let the Pope tell you what to do the rest of your life, making you swear to leave all your money to the church, and bring up all your children Catholic, and then join the Knights of Columbus and take an oath to go out and kill all the nice Protestant women when the day comes for the Catholics to take over the world.

(CORA *enters the parlor on her way to the sideboard, then wanders into the living room*)

MORRIS   Honey, where do you pick up these stories?

LOTTIE   Well, it's the truth. Marietta Flagmeyer told me. Cora, Marietta has this very close friend who used to be a Catholic but isn't any more. She even joined a convent, but she ran away because she found out all those things and wouldn't stand for them. This friend told Marietta that the Catholics keep the basements of their churches filled with guns and all kinds of ammunition . . .

CORA   (*She has heard* LOTTIE's *rantings before*)   Lottie! (*She shakes her head hopelessly and returns to the parlor, on her way to the kitchen*)

LOTTIE   . . . because some day they plan to rise and take over the world, and kill off all the rest of us who don't want to be Catholics. I believe every word of it, too.

MORRIS   Well . . . I still like Norma Talmadge. Got any of Bebe Daniels?

SONNY   Yes. (*He hands* MORRIS *a picture, which* LOTTIE *snaps up first for an approving look*)

LOTTIE   I don't know what you see in her. (*She now passes the picture on to* MORRIS)

MORRIS   You don't like any of the women stars, honey.

LOTTIE   I guess I don't. I hear they're all a bunch of trollops. (*To* SONNY) Honey, when is your daddy coming home?

SONNY   Oh, he's not coming back at all. He and Mom had a fight. Here's one of your favorites, Aunt Lottie. (*He hands her a picture*)

LOTTIE   Who? Rudolph Valentino. He's not one of my favorites at all.

MORRIS   You saw *The Sheik* four times.

LOTTIE   That's just because Marietta Flagmeyer wanted me to keep her company.

MORRIS   Rudolph Valentino must be a Catholic, too. He's an Eyetalian.

LOTTIE   But he's not a Catholic. Marietta's friend has a book that lists all the people in Hollywood who are Catholics. (*She studies the picture very intently*) You know, it scares me a little to look at him. Those eyes, that seem to be laughing at you, and all those white teeth. I think it's a sin for a man to be as pretty as he is. Why, I'd be scared to death to let a man like him touch me. (CORA *returns now, without her apron; she is carrying a paper bag*) But you know, they say he's really a very nice man. Cora, do you know there's this woman over in Oklahoma City who worships Rudolph Valentino? That's the truth. Marietta knows her. She's made a little shrine to him down in her basement, and she keeps the room filled with candles and she goes down there every day and says a little prayer for him.

CORA   I thought you were going to fix Reenie's hair.

LOTTIE   Oh, yes. I guess she's out of the bathtub now.

CORA (*Puts the bag on the table*)   There's a lot of fried chicken left, Lottie. I brought you some to take home with you.

LOTTIE   Won't you and the kids want it?

CORA   They won't eat anything but the breast.

LOTTIE   Thanks, Cora.

CORA   Sonny, I don't want your pictures all over the floor when the young people come by for Reenie.

SONNY   All right.

MORRIS (*As* LOTTIE *takes a drumstick out of the bag*) Honey, you just ate.

LOTTIE   Don't scold me, Daddy. (*She whispers boldly to him before starting upstairs*) Remember what I told you, Morris. (*Now she goes hurrying up the stairs*) Reenie! I'm coming up to fix your hair. I'm going to turn you into a real baby doll.

REENIE (*Upstairs*)   I'm in here, Aunt Lottie.
(MORRIS *draws over to the door, as though hoping to evade* CORA)

CORA   Morris . . . Morris! I suppose Lottie told you what's happened.

MORRIS   Well, uh . . . yes, Cora . . . she said something about it.

CORA   I guess now that maybe my folks were right, Morris. I shouldn't have married Rubin.

MORRIS You're going to forget all this squabble after a while, Cora. So's Rubin.

CORA I don't think we *should* forget it. I don't think we should *try* to come back together. I think I've failed.

MORRIS Now, Cora, I think you're exaggerating things in your own mind.

CORA Morris, I'm only thirty-four. That's still young. I thought I'd like to take the kids to Oklahoma City and put them in school there, and get myself a job in one of the department stores. I know I've never done work like that, but I think I'd like it, and . . . it seems to me that I've got to, Morris. I've got to.

MORRIS Well, Cora . . . maybe . . .

LOTTIE (*Upstairs we see her feet treading the hallway*) Let's go into the bathroom, Reenie, where the light's better.

MORRIS It's awful hard, Cora, being on your feet all day.

CORA But I'd get used to it.

MORRIS Well . . . it's hard for me to advise you, Cora.

CORA Morris, I was wondering if maybe the kids and I could come and live with you and Lottie for a while. Just for a while. Until we got used to the city. Until I got myself a job and we felt more or less at home.

MORRIS Well, I . . . uh . . .

CORA I promise we wouldn't be any bother. I mean, I'd keep things straightened up after the kids, and do as much of the cooking as Lottie wanted me to do.

MORRIS Well, I . . . uh . . .

CORA I just don't know what else the kids and I can do, Morris.

MORRIS Yes. Well . . . Cora, I don't know just what to say.

CORA Would we be too much in the way, Morris?

MORRIS Oh, no. Of course not, Cora. *But* . . .

CORA (*Hopefully*) I think we could manage. And I'd pay our share of the bills. I'd insist on that.
  (FLIRT, PUNKY and SAMMY *are seen through the window, coming onto the porch*)

MORRIS Well, Cora, I . . .

LOTTIE (*Comes hurtling halfway down the stairs, full of anxiety*) Cora, Reenie's sick. She's vomiting all over the bathroom.
(*She bustles back upstairs as* CORA *starts to follow*)

CORA Oh, my God! (*The doorbell rings, catching* CORA *for a moment*) Oh, dear! It's the young people after Reenie. Sonny, put on your manners and answer the door. (SONNY *runs to the door, stopping to turn on the porch light before opening it. We see the three young people on the porch outside—*FLIRT *in dazzling party dress, and the two boys in uniforms from a nearby military academy. One boy,* PUNKY GIVENS, *is seen drinking from a flask, preparing himself to meet people. Inside,* CORA *starts upstairs in worried concern*) Oh, dear! What could be wrong with the child? Morris, try to entertain the young people until I get back.
(CORA *goes off.* SONNY *swings open the door*)

SONNY Won't you come in?

FLIRT (*Comes dancing into the hallway, bringing the atmosphere of a chilly spring night with her*) Hi, Sonny! Is your sister ready?

SONNY Not yet.

FLIRT Oh, shucks! (*Sticks her head out the door*) Come on in, fellows. We're going to have to wait. (PUNKY GIVENS *and* SAMMY GOLDENBAUM *make a colorful entrance. Both are dressed in uniforms of lustrous blue, which fit them like smooth upholstery.* FLIRT *begins the introductions*) Sammy, this is Sonny Flood, Reenie's little brother.
(SAMMY GOLDENBAUM *steps forth correctly, his plumed headgear in his hand. He is a darkly beautiful young man of seventeen, with lustrous black hair, black eyes and a captivating smile. Yet, something about him seems a little foreign, at least in comparison with the Midwestern company in which he now finds himself. He could be a Persian prince, strayed from his native kingdom. But he has become adept over the years in adapting himself, and he shows an eagerness to make friends and to be liked*)

SAMMY Hi, Sonny!

SONNY (*Shaking hands*) Hi!

FLIRT (*Bringing* PUNKY *up from the rear*) And this is Punky Givens. (*She all but drags him from the dark corner of*

the hallway to face the lighted room full of people. For
PUNKY *is a disappointment as a human being. The military
academy has done nothing as yet for his posture, and he
wears his uniform as though embarrassed by its splendor.
He offers a limp hand when being introduced, mumbles
some incoherent greeting, and then retires in hopes that no
one will notice him. These introductions made,* FLIRT *now
notices* MORRIS) Oh, hello! I'm Flirt Conroy. How're you?

MORRIS   How d'ya do? I'm Morris Lacey. Reenie's uncle.
From Oklahoma City.

FLIRT   Oh, yes, I've heard her speak about you. Fellows, this
is Dr. Lacey. He's Reenie's uncle. From Oklahoma City.

SAMMY (*Crossing the room to present himself to* MORRIS, *he
is brisk and alert, even though his speech betrays a slight
stammer*)   How do you do, sir? My name is G-Golden-
baum. Sammy, they call me.

MORRIS   Glad to know you, Sammy.

FLIRT   And this is Punky Givens. (*Nudging him*) Stand up
straight, Punky.

MORRIS   Glad to know you, Punky. (PUNKY *mumbles.*
MORRIS *now feels the burden of his responsibility as temporary host*) Uh . . . anyone care for a Life Saver?
(*He offers a pack from his pocket, but no one is interested.*
LOTTIE *comes bustling down the stairs, eager to take over
the situation, exuberantly babbling inconsequentials all the
way down*)

LOTTIE   Hello, everyone! I'm Lottie Lacey, Reenie's aunt. I'm
Cora Flood's sister. From Oklahoma City. Oklahoma City's
a great big town now. People say in another ten years it's
going to be the biggest city in the whole United States, bigger even than New York or Chicago. You're the little Conroy girl, aren't you? I've heard my sister speak of you. My!
What a pretty red dress. Have you all met my husband?
Dr. Lacey. He's a dentist. Come over to Oklahoma City and
he'll pull all your teeth. (*She laughs heartily, and then her
eyes slowly widen at the magnificent uniforms*) My goodness! Aren't those handsome getups?

SAMMY (*Stepping forth*) How do you do, ma'am? I'm
Sammy Goldenbaum. From California.

LOTTIE   Oh, yes. Cora told me about the young man from

California. He's from Hollywood, Morris. His mother's in the movies. Has she played in anything I might have seen?

SAMMY   She was in T-Thomas Meighan's last picture. Her name is Gertrude Vanderhof. It was a very small part. She isn't a star or anything.

LOTTIE   Gertrude Vanderhof! Did we see Thomas Meighan's last picture, Morris? I don't believe so. I like Thomas Meighan, but we don't have time to see *all* the movies. Do you think you ever saw Gertrude Vanderhof in anything, Morris?
(LOTTIE *seems to refer to her husband on every topic without waiting for his judgment. Nevertheless,* MORRIS *mulls over this last query as* FLIRT *interrupts*)

FLIRT   Mrs. Lacey, have you met Punky Givens?

LOTTIE   How do you do? I've heard my sister speak of you. Your people are very prominent in town, aren't they? Yes, I've heard Cora speak of them. (PUNKY *offers a hand and mumbles*) What did you say? (*He repeats his mumble.* LOTTIE *is still at sea but makes the best of things*) Thank you very much.
(*At the top of the stairs, we see* REENIE'S *feet trying to get up the courage to bring her down, and we hear* CORA *coaxing her*)

CORA (*Off*)   Go on, Reenie.
(*But* REENIE *can't make it yet. The feet go scurrying back to safety*)

LOTTIE (*Trying to avoid embarrassment*)   Well, I'm afraid you're all going to have to wait a few minutes. Reenie isn't quite ready.

CORA (*Upstairs*)   Reenie, not another word.

LOTTIE   Cora's upstairs now, helping her. I guess you'll have to entertain yourselves awhile. Do any of you play mah-jong?
(*She notices the bag of fried chicken, and hides it under the table*)

FLIRT   I want to play some music. Got any new piano rolls, Sonny?

SONNY   A few.
(*They run into the parlor, to the piano*)

FLIRT   Gee, I wish you had a Victrola like we do.

LOTTIE (*Sitting, turning her attention to* SAMMY) My, you're a long way from home, aren't you?

SAMMY   Yes, ma'am.

LOTTIE   Morris and I went to California once. A Shriners' convention. Oh, we thought it was perfectly wonderful, all those oranges and things. Didn't we, Morris? I should think you'd want to go home on your spring vacation.

SAMMY   Well, I . . . I guess I don't really have a home . . . Mrs. Lacey.
(SONNY *wanders back from the parlor.* SAMMY *fills him with curiosity and fascination*)

LOTTIE   Did you tell me your mother lived out there?

SAMMY   Yes, but, you see, she's pretty busy in moving pictures, and . . . Oh, she feels awfully bad that she doesn't have more time for me. Really she does. But she doesn't have a place where I could stay right now . . . and . . . But, it's not *her* fault.

LOTTIE   Where's your father?

SAMMY   Oh, I never knew him.

LOTTIE   You never knew your father?

SAMMY   No. You see, he died before I was born. My mother has been married . . . a few times since then. But I never met any of her husbands . . . although they were all very fine gentlemen.

LOTTIE   Well—I just never knew anyone who didn't have a home. Do you spend your whole life in military academies?

SAMMY   Just about. I bet I've been in almost every military academy in the whole country. Well, I take that back. There's some I didn't go to. I mean . . . there's some that wouldn't take me.

SONNY (*Out of the innocent blue*) My mother says you're a Jew.

LOTTIE (*Aghast*) Sonny!

SAMMY   Well . . . yes, Sonny. I guess I am.

LOTTIE (*Consolingly*) That's perfectly all right. Why, we don't think a thing about a person's being Jewish, do we, Morris?

MORRIS   No. Of course not.

SAMMY   My father was Jewish. Mother told me. Mother isn't Jewish at all. Oh, my mother has the most beautiful blond hair. I guess I take after my father . . . in looks, anyhow. He was an actor, too, but he got killed in an automobile accident.

LOTTIE   That's too bad. Sonny, I think you should apologize.

SONNY   Did I say something bad?

SAMMY   Oh, that's all right. It doesn't bother me that I'm Jewish. Not any more. I guess it used to a little . . . Yes, it did used to a little.

LOTTIE   (*Who must find a remedy for everything*) You know what you ought to do? You ought to join the Christian Science church. Now, I'm not a member myself, but I know this Jewish woman over in Oklahoma City, and she was very, very unhappy, wasn't she, Morris? But she joined the Christian Science church and has been perfectly happy ever since.

SONNY   I didn't mean to say anything wrong.

SAMMY   You didn't say anything wrong, Sonny.
(*The piano begins playing "The Sheik of Araby" with precise, automatic rhythm.* FLIRT *dances in from the parlor*)

FLIRT   Come on, Punky, let's dance. (*She sings*) The Sheik of Araby—boom—boom—boom—his heart belongs to me. Come *on*, Punky.

SAMMY   (*Always courteous, to* LOTTIE) Would you care to dance, ma'am?

LOTTIE   Me? Good heavens, no. I haven't danced since I was a girl. But I certainly appreciate your asking. Isn't he respectful, Morris?
(LOTTIE *exits to dining room*)

SAMMY   Wanta wild West ride, Sonny?
(*He kneels on the floor, permitting* SONNY *to straddle his back. Then* SAMMY *kicks his feet in the air like a wild colt, as* SONNY *holds to him tight*)

FLIRT   (*At the back of the room, instructs* PUNKY *in the intricacies of a new step*) No, Punky. That's not it. You take one step to the left and then *dip*. See? Oh, it's a wonderful step, and all the kids are doing it.

LOTTIE   (*Enters from kitchen with a plate of cookies, which she offers to* SAMMY *and* SONNY) Would you like a cookie?

SAMMY (*Getting to his feet, the ride over*) Gee, that gets to be pretty strenuous.
(FLIRT *and* PUNKY *now retire to the parlor where they indulge in a little private lovemaking*)

SONNY Where did you get those clothes?

SAMMY They gave them to me at the academy, Sonny.

FLIRT (*Protesting* PUNKY'S *advances*) Punky, *don't*.
(LOTTIE *observes this little intimacy, having just started into the parlor with the plate of cookies. It rouses some of her righteousness*)

SAMMY No. I take that back. They didn't *give* them to me. They never give you anything at that place. I paid for them. Plenty!

SONNY Why do you wear a sword?

SAMMY (*Pulls the sword from its sheath, like a buccaneer, and goes charging about the room in search of imagined villains*) I wear a sword to protect myself! See! To kill off all the villains in the world. (*He frightens* LOTTIE) Oh, don't worry, ma'am. It's not sharp. I couldn't hurt anyone with it, even if I wanted to. We just wear them for show.

SONNY (*Jumping up and down*) Can I have a sword? I want a sword.

SAMMY Do you, Sonny? Do you want a sword? Here, Sonny, I'll give you *my* sword, for all the good it'll do you.

LOTTIE (*To* MORRIS) Cora will probably buy Sonny a sword now. (*Now* SONNY *takes the sword and imitates the actions of* SAMMY. LOTTIE *is apprehensive*) Now, you be careful, Sonny.

SAMMY What do you want a sword for, Sonny?

SONNY (*With a lunge*) To *show* people.

LOTTIE Sonny! Be careful with that thing.

SAMMY And what do you want to show people, Sonny?

SONNY I just want to *show* 'em.
(*He places the sword between his arm and his chest, then drops to the floor, the sword rising far above his body, giving the appearance that he is impaled.* LOTTIE *is horrified*)

LOTTIE   Oh, darling—put it down. Sonny, please don't play with that nasty thing any more.
(SONNY *rises now and laughs with* SAMMY. LOTTIE *puts the sword away in the parlor, where she again comes upon* FLIRT *and* PUNKY, *now engaged in more serious necking. Morally outraged, she runs up the stairs to inform* CORA)

SAMMY (*Kneeling beside* SONNY, *as though to make himself a physical equal*)   What'll we do now, Sonny? Are there any games you want to play? Do you want to fight Indians? or set bear traps? or go flying over volcanoes? or climb the Alps?

SONNY (*Eagerly*)   Yes . . . yes.

SAMMY   Gee, so do I, Sonny. But we can't. Not tonight anyway. What else can we do?

SONNY   I can show you my movie stars.

SAMMY   I've had enough of movie stars. What else?

SONNY   I can speak a piece.

SAMMY   You can? (*Jumps to his feet*) Hey, everyone! Stop the music. Sonny's going to speak a piece.
(SAMMY *stops the piano, which* FLIRT *finds quite annoying*)

LOTTIE (*Hurrying downstairs*)   Did you hear that, Morris? Sonny's going to speak a piece.

FLIRT (*To* SAMMY)   Hey, what are you doing?

SAMMY (*To* SONNY)   Where do you want to stand, sir?

LOTTIE   He's got a little platform in the parlor where he practices.

SAMMY (*Having taken over as impresario*)   Into the parlor, everyone. Into the parlor to hear Sonny speak his piece.

FLIRT (*Pulling* PUNKY's *arm*)   Come on, Punky. Come on. We *have* to listen, don't we?

SAMMY   Quiet, everyone. Quiet!
(*All enter the parlor, except* MORRIS, *who crosses toward the door, as though he hoped to escape, as* SONNY *begins the famous soliloquy with boyish fervor.* MORRIS *looks as though he might share some of Hamlet's woes. After* SONNY *begins,* CORA *starts down the stairs with* REENIE.)

SONNY

    "To be, or not to be: that is the question:
    Whether 'tis nobler in the mind to suffer
    The slings and arrows of outrageous fortune,
    Or to take arms against a sea of troubles,
    And by opposing end them? To die: to sleep;
    No more; and, by a sleep to say we end
    The heart-ache and the thousand natural shocks
    That flesh is heir to, 'tis a consummation
    Devoutly to be wish'd. To die, to sleep;
    To sleep: perchance to dream: ay, there's the rub,
    For in that sleep of death what dreams may come
    When we have shuffled off this mortal coil,
    Must give us pause. . . ."

CORA (*While* SONNY *is reciting*) Oh, Sonny's reciting. Why, he's reciting Shakespeare. He must have gotten out that dusty volume of Shakespeare over in the bookcase, and memorized that speech all on his own. (*Points to* SAMMY *in the parlor*) Reenie, there's your young man. Isn't he handsome? Now you're going to have a good time. I can feel it in my bones.

(SONNY *and* CORA *finish speaking at the same time. There is immediate loud acclaim for* SONNY)

SAMMY That was *wonderful*, Sonny.

(*All come into the living room now,* SAMMY *carrying* SONNY *on his shoulders like a triumphant hero*)

LOTTIE He's a second Jackie Coogan.

FLIRT That was just wonderful, Sonny.

LOTTIE Cora, you should have been here. Sonny recited Shakespeare. It was just wonderful.

CORA Yes. I heard him.

SAMMY Sonny's a genius. I'm going to take you to Hollywood, Sonny, and put you in the movies. You'll be the greatest actor out there, Sonny.

FLIRT Oh, I think Shakespeare's just wonderful. I'm going to read him sometime, really I am.

CORA (*Going to* SAMMY) Good evening, young man. I'm Mrs. Flood.

SAMMY (*Putting* SONNY *down*) Beg your pardon, ma'am. I'm Sammy Goldenbaum.

CORA   Welcome. I see my son's been entertaining you.

SAMMY   He sure has, ma'am.

CORA   He started speaking pieces about a year ago. Just picked it up. Some people think he's talented.

SAMMY   I think so, too, ma'am. Very.

CORA   (*Brings* REENIE *forth*)   Reenie! Sammy, this is my daughter Reenie.

SAMMY   Good evening, Reenie.

REENIE   (*Reluctantly*)   Good evening.

SAMMY   You certainly look nice. That's a very beautiful dress.

FLIRT   Isn't it cute! I helped her pick it out. (CORA *quietly grabs* FLIRT'S *arm and prevents her from taking over*) Ouch!

SAMMY   Gee! I didn't expect you to be . . . like you are. I mean . . . well, Punky told me you were a friend of Flirt's, so I just naturally thought you'd be . . . well, kind of like Flirt is. Although Flirt is a very nice girl. I didn't mean to imply anything against her. But . . . *you're* very nice, too, in a different way.

REENIE   (*Still a little distrustful*)   Thank you . . .

SAMMY   Would you call me *Sammy?*

REENIE   Sammy.

SAMMY   And may I call you Reenie?

REENIE   I guess so.

SAMMY   It's awfully nice of you to let me take you to the party. I know just how a girl feels, going out with some crazy guy she doesn't even know.

REENIE   Oh . . . that's all right. After all, you don't know anything about me, either.

SAMMY   You know, I've never been to many parties, have you?

REENIE   Not many.

SAMMY   I always worry that maybe people aren't going to like me, when I go to a party. Isn't that crazy? Do you ever get kind of a sick feeling in the pit of your stomach when you dread things? Gee, I wouldn't want to miss a party for anything. But every time I go to one, I have to reason with myself to keep from feeling that the whole world's against me. See, I've spent almost my whole life in military academies. My mother doesn't have a place for me, where she lives. She . . . she just doesn't know what else to do with me. But you mustn't misunderstand about my mother. She's really a very lovely person. I guess every boy thinks his mother is very beautiful, but my mother really is. She tells me in every letter she writes how sorry she is that we can't be together more, but she has to think of her work. One time we were together, though. She met me in San Francisco once, and we were together for two whole days. She let me take her to dinner and to a show and to dance. Just like we were sweethearts. It was the most wonderful time I ever had. And then I had to go back to the old military academy. Every time I walk into the barracks, I get kind of a depressed feeling. It's got hard stone walls. Pictures of generals hanging all over . . . oh, they're very fine gentlemen, but they all look so kind of hard-boiled and stern . . . you know what I mean. (CORA *and* LOTTIE *stand together, listening to* SAMMY's *speech with motherly expressions.* FLIRT *is bored.* PUNKY *is half asleep, and now he gives a sudden, audible yawn that startles everyone*) Well, gee! I guess I've bored you enough, telling you about myself.

CORA *and* LOTTIE   Oh, no. You haven't either.

FLIRT (*Impatient to get to the party*)   Come on, kids. Let's hurry.

SAMMY (*Tenderly, to* REENIE)   Are you ready?

CORA (*As though fearing* REENIE *might bolt and run*) Reenie?

REENIE   Yes.

SAMMY   May I help you into your wrap?
(*The word "wrap" is a false glorification of her Sunday coat, which he offers her, helping her into it*)

REENIE   Thank you.

CORA (*Whispering to* LOTTIE)   I wish I could have bought her one of those little fur jackets like Flirt is wearing.

FLIRT   Stand up straight, Punky, and say good night to everyone.
(PUNKY *tries again, but remains inarticulate*)

CORA (*Assuming that* PUNKY *said good night*)   Good night, Punky. Tell your mother hello for me.

FLIRT   Very pleased to have met you, Mr. and Mrs. Lacey. Good night, Mrs. Flood.

CORA   Good night, Flirt.

LOTTIE *and* MORRIS   Good night.

SONNY (*Pulling at* SAMMY'S *coat tails*)   Do you have to go?

SAMMY   I'm afraid I do, Sonny.

SONNY   Can I go, too? Please? Can I go, too?

SAMMY   Gee, I don't know. (*He thinks a moment and then consults* FLIRT *and* PUNKY)   Hey, is there any reason Sonny can't come along? I promise to look after him. Think what a great time he'd have.
(FLIRT *and* PUNKY *look dubious*)

SONNY (*Takes his welcome immediately for granted and dances about the room joyously*)   Goody, goody! I'm going to the party. I'm going to the party.

REENIE (*Running to* CORA'S *side*)   Mother, I'm not going if Sonny goes too. Other girls don't have to be bothered by their little brothers.

CORA   I agree with you, daughter.

FLIRT (*She loves to lash out when she has a victim*)   No. It's not a kids' party, Sammy. That was a stupid idea. I think you should mind your own business.

CORA (*Trying to cool* FLIRT'S *temper*)   Now, Flirt.

FLIRT (*To* REENIE)   He's always trying to boss everyone.

CORA (*To* SAMMY)   I guess Sonny'd better not go.

SONNY (*Crying, jumping in protest*)   I want to go to the party. I want to go to the party.

SAMMY (*Trying to be consoling*)   I guess it was a pretty dumb idea, Sonny.

SONNY   I WANT TO GO TO THE PARTY! I WANT TO GO TO THE PARTY!
(SONNY *flies into a real tantrum now, throws himself on the floor, pounding the floor with his fists and kicking it with his toes, his face red with rage.* CORA *and* LOTTIE *flutter about him like nervous hens*)

CORA Sonny! Sonny! Stop it this instant. Sonny, I'll not let you go to another movie for a whole month if you don't stop.

LOTTIE Oh, what'll I do? Oh, here, Sonny, do you want a little cookie, sweetheart?

FLIRT Now we'll never get there.

CORA I never can do a thing with him when he throws one of these tantrums.

SAMMY (*Quietly goes to* SONNY'S *side and speaks in a voice that is firm with authority, yet still thoughtful and considerate*) Sonny, that's no way to behave.

SONNY (*Suddenly quiet*) Isn't it?

SAMMY No, Sonny. You mustn't ever act like that.

SONNY (*More reasonable now*) But I want to go to the party.

SAMMY But if you act that way, no one's *ever* going to ask you to a party.

SONNY Aren't they?

SAMMY No, Sonny. You have to be a good boy before people ask you to parties. Even then, they don't always ask you.

SONNY I love parties more than anything else in the world.

SAMMY So do I, Sonny. I love parties, too. But there's lots of parties I can't go to.

SONNY Honest?

SAMMY Honest. It was wrong of me to suggest that you go to the party tonight. You're not old enough yet. You'll be old enough someday though, and then you can go to all the parties you like.

SONNY Can I?

SAMMY Sure. Now, I tell you what I'll do. I'll gather up all the favors I can find at the party. Want me to? And I'll give them to your sister to bring home to you. And then you can have a party here all by yourself. Would you like that? You can throw a big party in Sammy's honor, without any old grownups around to interfere. Will that make you happy?

SONNY Yes, yes.

SAMMY   O.K. Are we still buddies?

SONNY   Yes.

SAMMY   Forever and ever?

SONNY   Forever and ever.
  (SONNY *impulsively hugs him*)

SAMMY   Gee! I love kids.

CORA (*Awed as though by a miracle*)   You're the first person in the entire world who's ever been able to do a thing with the boy when he goes into one of his tantrums.

SAMMY   You know, it's funny, but . . . I always seem to know just how kids feel.

FLIRT (*Still impatient*)   Come on, Sammy.
  (FLIRT *and* PUNKY *exit*)

CORA   Good night, Sammy. I hope you'll be able to come back sometime.

SAMMY   Thank you, ma'am. It's very nice to feel welcome.

LOTTIE *and* MORRIS   Good night. Come over to see us sometime in Oklahoma City. It's a big town. You can stay in the extra bedroom. I hope you like cats.

CORA (*While* LOTTIE *and* MORRIS *are speaking*)   Oh, Reenie, don't forget your present. You're feeling better now, aren't you?

REENIE   Yes, Mom.

SAMMY (*Breaking away from* LOTTIE *and* MORRIS)   Excuse me.
  (SAMMY *offers* REENIE *his arm now, and together they walk proudly out*)

CORA (*After they exit*)   Why, that's the nicest young man I ever met.

LOTTIE   I thought so, too, Cora. And my goodness, he was handsome. Morris says he felt sorry for him, though.

CORA   Sorry? Oh, Morris.

LOTTIE   He seemed like a perfectly happy boy to me. But Morris says he looked like a very unhappy boy to him. What makes you think that, Morris?

MORRIS   Oh . . . I don't know.

CORA   Unhappy? Why, he made himself right at home, didn't he?

LOTTIE   I should say he did. He was laughing and enjoying himself. But Morris says sometimes the people who act the happiest are really the saddest.

CORA   Oh, Morris.

LOTTIE   Morris, I think you make these things up. Ever since you went to that psychologist, you've gone around imagining everyone's unhappy. (MORRIS *quietly gets up and walks to the door, leaving* LOTTIE *to wonder if she has said anything wrong*) Where are you going, Morris?

MORRIS   Thought I'd go out for a little walk, honey.
(MORRIS *exits*)

LOTTIE   (*Following him to the door*) Oh. Well, don't be gone long. We've got to get started back soon.

CORA   Oh, please don't talk about going.

LOTTIE   My God, Cora, we can't stay here all night. (*She peers out the window now, wondering about* MORRIS) Morris is funny, Cora. Sometimes he just gets up like that and walks away. I never know why. Sometimes he's gone for hours at a time. He says the walk helps his digestion, but I think it's because he just wants to get away from me at times. Did you ever notice how he is with people? Like tonight. He sat there when all the young people were here, and he didn't say hardly a word. His mind was a thousand miles away. Like he was thinking about something. He seems to be always thinking about something.

CORA   Morris is nice to you. You've got no right to complain.

LOTTIE   He's nice to me . . . in *some* ways.

CORA   Good heavens, Lottie! He gave you those red patent-leather slippers, and that fox neckpiece . . . you should be grateful.

LOTTIE   I know, but . . . there's *some* things he hasn't given me.

CORA   Lottie! That's not his fault. You've got no right to hold that against him!

LOTTIE   Oh, it's just fine for you to talk. You've got two nice kids to keep you company. What have I got but a house full of cats?

CORA   Lottie, you always claimed you never wanted children.

LOTTIE   Well . . . what else can I say to people?

CORA   (*This is something of a revelation to her*)   I just never knew.

LOTTIE   (*Having suddenly decided to say it*)   Cora . . . I can't let you and the kids come over and live with us.

CORA   (*This is a blow to her*)   Oh . . . Lottie.

LOTTIE   I'm sorry, Cora. I just can't do it.

CORA   Lottie, I was depending on you . . .

LOTTIE   Maybe you've depended on me too much. Ever since you were a baby, you've run to me with your problems, and now I've got problems of my own.

CORA   What am I going to do, Lottie?

LOTTIE   Call up Rubin and ask him to come back. Beg him to come back, if you have to get down on your knees.

CORA   I mustn't do that, Lottie.

LOTTIE   Why not?

CORA   Because we just can't keep from fighting, Lottie. You know that. I just don't think it's right, our still going on that way.

LOTTIE   Do you still love him?

CORA   Oh . . . don't ask me, Lottie.

LOTTIE   Do you?

CORA   Oh . . . yes.

LOTTIE   Cora, I don't think you should listen to the stories those old Werpel sisters tell you.

CORA   He's as good as admitted it, Lottie.

LOTTIE   Well, Cora, I don't think it means he likes you any the less, because he's seen Mavis Pruitt a few times.

CORA   No . . . I know he loves me.

LOTTIE   (*Asking very cautiously*)   Does he still want to be intimate?

CORA   That's only animal, Lottie. I couldn't indulge myself that way if I didn't feel he was being honorable.

LOTTIE   (*Breaks into a sudden raucous laugh*)   My God, a big handsome buck like Rubin! Who cares if he's honorable?

CORA (*A little shocked*) Lottie!

LOTTIE (*We see now a sudden lewdness in* LOTTIE *that has not been discernible before*) Cora, did you hear what the old maid said to the burglar? You see, the burglar came walking into her bedroom with this big, long billy club and . . .

CORA Lottie!

LOTTIE (*Laughing so hard she can hardly finish the story*) And the old maid . . . she was so green she didn't know what was happening to her, she said . . .

CORA Lottie! That's enough. That's enough.

LOTTIE (*Shamed now*) Shucks, Cora. I don't see what's wrong in having a little fun just telling stories.

CORA Sometimes you talk shamefully, Lottie, and when I think of the way Mama and Papa brought us up . . .

LOTTIE Oh, Mama and Papa, Mama and Papa! Maybe they didn't know as much as we gave them credit for.

CORA You're changed since you were a girl, Lottie.

LOTTIE What if I am!

CORA I never heard such talk.

LOTTIE Well, that's all it is. It's only talk. Talk, talk, talk.

CORA Lottie, are you sure you can't take us in?

LOTTIE It'd mean the end of my marriage too, Cora. You don't understand Morris. He's always nice and quiet around people, so afraid of hurting people's feelings. But he's the most nervous man around the house you ever saw. He'd try to make the best of it if you and the kids came over, but he'd go to pieces. I know he would.

CORA Honest?

LOTTIE I'm not joking, Cora. My God, you're not the only one who has problems. Don't think that for a minute.

CORA A few moments ago, you said *you* had problems, Lottie . . .

LOTTIE Problems enough.

CORA Tell me, Lottie.

LOTTIE Oh, why should I?

CORA Doesn't Morris ever make love to you any more?

LOTTIE (*It takes her several moments to admit it*) . . . No. It's been over three years since he even touched me . . . that way.

CORA (*Another revelation*) Lottie!

LOTTIE It's the God's truth, Cora.

CORA Lottie! What's wrong?

LOTTIE How do I know what's wrong? How does anyone ever know what's wrong with anyone else?

CORA I mean . . . is there another woman?

LOTTIE Not unless she visits him from the spirit world. (*This releases her humor again and she is diverted by another story*) Oh, say, Cora, did I tell you about this woman over in Oklahoma City who's been holding séances? Well, Marietta went to her and . . . (*But suddenly, again, she loses her humor and makes another sad admission*) Oh, no, there isn't another woman. Sometimes I wish there was.

CORA Lottie, you don't mean that.

LOTTIE How the hell do *you* know what I mean? He's around the house all day long, now that he's got his dental office in the dining room. Day and night, day and night. Sometimes I get tired of looking at him.

CORA Oh, Lottie . . . I'd always felt you and Morris were so devoted to each other. I've always felt you had an almost perfect marriage.

LOTTIE Oh, we're still devoted, still call each other "honey," just like we did on our honeymoon.

CORA But what happened? Something must have happened to . . .

LOTTIE Did you notice the way Morris got up out of his chair suddenly and just walked away, with no explanation at all? Well, something inside Morris did the same thing several years ago. Something inside him just got up and went for a walk, and never came back.

CORA I . . . just don't understand.

LOTTIE Sometimes I wonder if maybe I've been too bossy. Could be. But then, I always supposed that Morris *liked* me because I was bossy.

CORA I always envied you, having a husband you could boss.

LOTTIE   Yes, I can boss Morris because he just isn't there any more to fight back. He doesn't care any more if I boss him or not.

CORA   Just the same, he never hit you.

LOTTIE   I wish he would.

CORA   Lottie!

LOTTIE   I do. I wish to God someone *loved* me enough to hit me. You and Rubin fight. Oh, God I'd like a good fight. Anything'd be better than this *nothing*. Morris and I go around always being so sweet to each other, but sometimes I wonder maybe he'd like to kill me.

CORA   Lottie, you don't mean it.

LOTTIE   Do you remember how Mama and Papa used to caution us about men, Cora?

CORA   Yes, I remember.

LOTTIE   My God, they had me so afraid of ever giving in to a man, I was petrified.

CORA   So was I.

LOTTIE   Yes, you were until Rubin came along and practically raped you.

CORA   Lottie! I don't want Sonny to hear talk like that.

LOTTIE   Why not? Let him hear!

CORA   (*Newly aghast at her sister's boldness*)   Lottie!

LOTTIE   Why do we feel we always have to protect kids?

CORA   Keep your voice down. Rubin never did anything like that.

LOTTIE   Didn't he?

CORA   Of course not!

LOTTIE   My God, Cora, he had you pregnant inside of two weeks after he started seeing you.

CORA   Sssh.

LOTTIE   I never told. I never even told Morris. My God, do you remember how Mama and Papa carried on when they found out?

CORA   I remember.

LOTTIE   And Papa had his stroke just a month after you were married. Oh, I just thought Rubin was the wickedest man alive.

CORA I never blamed Rubin for that. I was crazy in love with him. He just swept me off my feet and made all my objections seem kinda silly. He even made Mama and Papa seem silly.

LOTTIE Maybe I shoulda married a man like that. I don't know. Maybe it was as much my fault as Morris'. Maybe I didn't . . . respond right . . . from the very first.

CORA What do you mean, Lottie?

LOTTIE Cora, I'll tell you something. Something I've never told another living soul. I never did enjoy it the way some women . . . say they do.

CORA Lottie! You?

LOTTIE Why do you say *me* like that? Because I talk kinda dirty at times? But that's all it is, is talk. I talk all the time just to convince myself that I'm alive. And I stuff myself with victuals just to feel I've got something inside me. And I'm full of all kinds of crazy curiosity about . . . all the things in life I seem to have missed out on. Now I'm telling you the truth, Cora. Nothing ever really happened to me while it was going on.

CORA Lottie . . .

LOTTIE That first night Morris and I were together, right after we were married, when we were in bed together for the first time, after it was all over, and he had fallen asleep, I lay there in bed wondering what in the world all the cautioning had been about. Nothing had happened to me at all, and I thought Mama and Papa musta been makin' things up.

CORA Oh, Lottie!

LOTTIE So, don't come to me for sympathy, Cora. I'm not the person to give it to you.
(*Outside there is a low rumble of thunder.* SONNY *enters from the dining room with a cup of flour paste and his scrapbook.* MORRIS *returns from his walk, his face mysterious and grave*)

MORRIS We'd better be starting back now, honey. It looks like rain.

CORA Oh, don't talk about leaving. Can't you and Lottie

stay all night? I'd get up early and fix you breakfast. I'll fix you biscuits.

MORRIS   I can't, Cora. I got patients coming first thing in the morning.

LOTTIE   And I have to go home to let out the cats.

MORRIS   It was a wonderful dinner, Cora.

CORA   Thank you, Morris.

LOTTIE   (*On a sudden impulse, she springs to her feet, hoists her skirt to her waist, and begins wrestling with her corset*) My God, I'm gonna take off this corset and ride back home in comfort.

CORA   (*Runs protectively to* SONNY, *and stands between him and* LOTTIE, *to prevent his seeing this display*) Sonny! Turn your head.

LOTTIE   My God! That feels good. (*She rolls the corset under her arm and rubs the flesh on her stomach in appreciation of its new freedom. Then she reaches for the bag of fried chicken*) Thanks for the fried chicken, Cora. Oh, good! A gizzard. (*She brings out a gizzard to gnaw on*) It was a wonderful dinner. You're a better cook than I am.

CORA   That's not so.

LOTTIE   Kiss me good-bye, Sonny.

SONNY   Good-bye, Aunt Lottie.

LOTTIE   (*Hugging him close*)   Good night, darling.

MORRIS   That was a fine recitation, Edwin Booth.

SONNY   Thank you, Uncle Morris.

LOTTIE   (*Facing her husband with a bright smile, as though nothing but happiness had ever passed between them*)   I'm ready, Daddy.

MORRIS   All right, Mama. Good of you to have us, Cora.

CORA   Glad you could come, Morris.

LOTTIE   (*At the door, thinks of one last piece of news she must impart to her sister before leaving*) Oh, Cora! I forgot to tell you. Mamie Keeler's in the hospital.

MORRIS   (*Goes out on the porch now*)   Looks like it's gonna rain any minute now.

CORA   What's wrong?

LOTTIE   Some kind of female trouble.

CORA   Oh . . . that's too bad.
(*But* LOTTIE *can tell by the sound of* CORA'S *voice that she is too preoccupied now with her own worries to care about Mamie Keeler*)

LOTTIE   Oh, God, Cora . . . I just can't go off and leave you this way.

CORA   I'll be all right, Lottie.

LOTTIE   Look, Cora . . . if you and the kids wanta come over and stay with us . . . we'll manage somehow . . .

CORA   Oh, thank you, Lottie. (*They embrace as though recognizing the bond of their blood*) But I'm going to work this out for myself, Lottie.

LOTTIE   Good-bye, Cora.

MORRIS   (*From outside*)   It's beginning to rain, honey.

LOTTIE   (*Hurrying out the door*)   Hold your horses, Morris. I'm coming. Don't be impatient now. (*They exit. Now* CORA *returns to the center of the room, feeling somehow deserted*)

SONNY   It's always so quiet after company leaves, isn't it?

CORA   Hush, Sonny. I'm trying to think.
(*From outside, we hear the sound of* MORRIS' *car driving off, and then the sound of the rain and the wind*)

SONNY   Let's move to California, Mom. Please, let's move to California.
(*But* CORA *has made a sudden decision. She rushes to the telephone*)

CORA   Long distance. (*A moment's wait*) This is Mrs. Flood, three-two-one. I want to talk to Mr. Rubin Flood at the Hotel Boomerang in Blackwell . . . Yes, I'll wait.

SONNY   (*In an innocent voice*)   I bet he isn't there. I bet anything.

CORA   Hello? He isn't? Would you ask them if he's been there this week? (*A moment's wait*) He hasn't! Oh . . . Well, please tell him, if he does come, to call his family immediately. It's very important.
(*A fallen expression on her face, she sits for a moment, wondering what next move to make. Then she hears a car*

approaching from the distance. She jumps up and runs to the window)

SONNY   It isn't Dad. I can always tell the sound of his car.
(CORA *comes back to the middle of the room*)

CORA   Run along to bed now, Sonny. It's late. I have to go out and empty the pan under the icebox.
(CORA *goes out through the dining-room door.* SONNY *walks slowly, hesitantly, to the foot of the stairs and stands there, looking up at the blackness at the top. He stands there several moments, unable to force himself to go further. From the kitchen we hear* CORA'S *muffled sobs.* SONNY *cries out in fear*)

SONNY   Mom!
(CORA *returns now, not wanting* SONNY *to know she has been crying*)

CORA   Sonny, I thought I told you to go upstairs. (*She looks at him now and sees his embarrassed fear*) Sonny, why are you so afraid of the dark?

SONNY   'Cause . . . you can't see what's in front of you. And it might be something awful.

CORA   You're the man of the house now, Sonny. You mustn't be afraid.

SONNY   I'm not afraid . . . if someone's with me.
(CORA *walks over to him and takes his hand*)

CORA   Come, boy. We'll go up together.
(*They start up the stairs to face the darkness hovering there like an omen*)

                                                        CURTAIN

ACT THREE

SCENE: *It is the next day, late afternoon. Outside, there is a drizzling rain that has continued through the day.* REENIE *has not dressed all day. She sits by the fire in her robe, rubbing her freshly shampooed hair with a towel.* CORA *enters from the dining room, wearing a comfortable old kimono. She looks at the tray by* REENIE'S *side.*

CORA   Reenie! Is that all you feel like eating?

REENIE   Yes.

CORA   But that's all you've had all day, Reenie. You don't eat enough to keep a bird alive.

REENIE   I . . . I'm not hungry, Mom.

CORA   Now quit feeling sorry for yourself, just because you didn't have a good time last night.

REENIE   Mom, is Dad coming back?

CORA   I don't know. I tried to call him last night but couldn't get him.

REENIE   Aren't you mad at him any more?

CORA   No . . . I'm not mad.

REENIE   Even though he hit you?

CORA   Even though he hit me. I was defying him to do it . . . and he did. I can't blame him now.

REENIE   Do you think he *will* be back, Mom?

CORA   This is the day he was supposed to come back. It's almost suppertime and he still isn't here.

REENIE   But it's been raining, Mom. I'll bet the roads are bad.

CORA   You love your father, don't you?

REENIE   Yes.

CORA   Well, I'm glad. The people we love aren't always perfect, are they? But if we love them, we have to take them as they are. After all, I guess I'm not perfect, either.

REENIE   You are too, Mom. You're absolutely perfect, in every way.

284

CORA No, I'm not, Reenie. I . . . I have my own score to settle for. I've always accused your father of neglecting you kids, but maybe I've hurt you more with pampering. You . . . and Sonny, too.

REENIE What do you mean, Mom?

CORA Oh, nothing. I can't say anything more about it right now. Forget it. (*For some reason we don't yet know, she tries to change the subject*) Are you feeling a little better now?

REENIE I guess so.

CORA Well, the world isn't going to end just because your young man went off and left you.

REENIE Oh, Mom. It was the most humiliating thing that ever happened to me.

CORA Where do you think Sammy went?

REENIE He went out to the cars at intermission time with some other girl.

CORA To spoon?

REENIE They call it *necking*.

CORA Are you sure of this?

REENIE Mom, that's what all the boys do at intermission time. They take girls and go out to the cars. Some of them don't even come back for the rest of the dance.

CORA But are you sure Sammy did that? Did you see him?

REENIE No, Mom. I just know that's what he did.

CORA Wouldn't *you* have gone out to one of the cars with him?

REENIE (*With self-disparagement*) Oh, Mom.

CORA What makes you say "Oh, Mom" that way?

REENIE He wouldn't have liked *me* that way.

CORA But why? Why not?

REENIE I'm just not *hot stuff* like the other girls.

CORA Reenie, what an expression! You're pretty. You're every bit as pretty as Flirt or Mary Jane. Half a woman's beauty is in her confidence.

REENIE Oh, Mom.

CORA   Reenie, I've tried to raise you proper, but . . . you're sixteen now. It's perfectly natural if a boy wants to kiss you, and you let him. It's all right if you *like* the boy.

REENIE   (*A hesitant admission*)   Oh . . . Sammy kissed me.

CORA   (*Quite surprised*)   He did?

REENIE   On the way out to the party, in Punky's car. Flirt and Punky were in the front seat, Sammy and I in the back. Punky had a flask . . .

CORA   The little devil!

REENIE   Mom, most of those wealthy boys who go away to school are kind of wild.

CORA   Go on.

REENIE   Well, Punky and Flirt started necking, very first thing. Flirt, I don't mean to be tattling, but she *is* kind of fast.

CORA   I guessed as much. You aren't tattling.

REENIE   Well, Sammy and I felt kind of embarrassed, with no one else to talk to, and so he took my hand. Oh, he was very nice about it, Mom. And then he put an arm around me, and said . . . "May I kiss you, Reenie?" And I was so surprised, I said yes before I knew *what* I was saying. And he kissed me. Was it all right, Mom?

CORA   Did you like the young man? That's the important thing.

REENIE   Yes, I . . . I liked him . . . very much. (*She sobs helplessly*) Oh, Mom.

CORA   There, there, Reenie dear. If he's the kind of young man who goes around kissing all the girls, you don't want to worry about him any more. You did right to leave the party!

REENIE   Did I, Mom?

CORA   Of course you did. I'm very disappointed in Sammy. I thought he was such a nice boy. But I guess appearances can be deceiving.

REENIE   Oh, Mom!

CORA   There, there, dear. There are plenty of other young men in the world. You're young. You're not going to have to worry.

REENIE (*Struggling to her feet*)   Mom, I don't think I ever want to get married.

CORA   Reenie!

REENIE   I mean it, Mom.

CORA   You're too young to make a decision like that.

REENIE   I'm serious.

CORA   What makes you say such a thing? Tell me.

REENIE   I don't want to fight with anyone, like you and Daddy.

CORA   Oh, God.

REENIE   Every time you and Daddy fight, I just feel that the whole house is going to cave in all around me.

CORA   Then I *am* to blame.

REENIE   And I think I'd be lots happier, just by myself, teaching school, or working in an office building.

CORA   No, daughter. You need someone after you grow up. You need someone.

REENIE   But I don't want to. I don't *want* to need anyone, ever in my life. It's a horrible feeling to need someone.

CORA (*Disturbed*)   Daughter!

REENIE   Anyway, the only times I'm really happy are when I'm alone, practicing at the piano or studying in the library.

CORA   Weren't you happy last night when Sammy kissed you?

REENIE   I guess you can't count on happiness like that.

CORA   Daughter, when you start getting older, you'll find yourself getting lonely and you'll want someone; someone who'll hear you if you get sick and cry out in the night; and someone to give you love and let you give your love back to him in return. Oh, I'd hate to see any child of mine miss that in life. (*There is a moment of quiet realization between them. Then we hear the sound of a car drawing up to the house.* CORA, *running to the window, is as excited as a girl*) That must be your father! No, it's Sonny. In a big limousine. He's getting out of the car as if he owned it. Mrs. Stanford must have sent him home with her chauffeur. (*She gives "chauffeur" its American pronunciation.* SONNY, *in his Sunday suit, bursts into the house waving a five-dollar bill in his mother's face*)

SONNY Mom. Look, Mom! Mrs. Stanford gave me five dollars for speaking my piece. See? Five whole dollars. She said I was the most talented little boy she ever saw. See, Mom? Then she got out her pocketbook and gave me five whole dollars. See?

CORA I declare. Why, Sonny, I'm proud of you, boy. That's the very first money you ever earned, and I'm very proud.

SONNY And Mrs. Stanford sent me home with her chauffeur, too, Mom. (*He gives the word its French pronunciation*) That's the way you're supposed to pronounce it, chauf*feur*. It's French.

CORA If you spend any more time at Mrs. Stanford's, you'll be getting too high-hat to come home. (*She notices* REENIE *starting upstairs*) We'll talk later, Reenie. (REENIE *exits.* CORA *again turns her attention to* SONNY) Did you have anything to eat?

SONNY Oh, Mom, it was just delicious. She had all kinds of little sandwiches. Gee, they were good. And cocoa, too, Mom, with lots of whipped cream on top, in little white cups with gold edges. Gee, they were pretty. And lots of little cakes, too, with pink frosting and green. And ice cream, too. I just ate and ate and ate.

CORA Good. That means I won't have to get you any supper.

SONNY No. I don't want any supper. I'm going to the movies tonight. And to the Royal Candy Kitchen afterwards, to buy myself a great big sundae with chocolate and marshmallow and cherries and . . .

CORA Now, wait a minute, Sonny. This is the first money you've ever earned in your life, and I think you should save it.

SONNY Oh, Mom!

CORA I mean it. Five dollars is a lot of money, and I'm not going to let you squander it on movies and sundaes. You'll thank me for this some day.
(*She takes his piggy bank from the bookcase*)

SONNY I will not. I will not thank you!

CORA Sonny.
(*She takes the bill from him and drops it into the bank.* SONNY *is wild at the injustice*)

SONNY Look what you've done. I hate you! I wanta see the

movie. I've just gotta see the movie. If I can't see the movie, I'll kill myself.

CORA   Such foolish talk!

SONNY   I mean it. I'll kill myself.

CORA   Now, be quiet, Sonny. I want to have a little talk.

SONNY   Can I sell the milk bottles for money?

CORA   No! Now quit pestering me about the movies. You've already talked me into letting you see one movie this week. I have scarcely any money now, and I can't spare a cent. (SONNY *is badly frustrated. He finds the favors that* SAMMY *promised him, displayed on the settee. He throws a handful of confetti recklessly into the air, then dons a paper hat, and blows violently on a paper horn*) Sonny! Stop that racket! You're going to have to clean up that mess.

SONNY   You won't let me have any fun at all.

CORA   The young man was very thoughtful to have sent you the favors. I wish he had been as thoughtful in other ways.

SONNY   Didn't Reenie have a good time at the party last night?

CORA   No.

SONNY   Serves her right. Serves her right.

CORA   Sonny! I'm not going to have any more talk like that. If you and your sister can't get along, you can at least have a little respect for one another. Now, come here, Sonny, I want to talk serious for a little while. (SONNY *taunts her with the horn*) Will you go sit down?

SONNY   What's the matter?
(*He sits opposite her at the table*)

CORA   Nothing. I just want to talk awhile.

SONNY   (*Suddenly solemn and apprehensive*)   Have I done something bad?

CORA   Well, I don't know if you have or if I have. Anyway, we've got to talk about it. Sonny, you mustn't come crawling into my bed any more. I let you do it last night, but I shouldn't have. It was wrong.

SONNY   I was scared.

CORA   Just the same, that's not to happen again, Sonny. It's not the same when a boy your age comes crawling into bed with his mother. You can't expect me to mean as much to you as when you were a baby. Can you understand, Sonny? (*He looks away from her with unconscious guilt. She studies him*) I think you're older in your feelings than I ever realized. You're a funny mixture, Sonny. In some ways, shy as your sister. In other ways, bold as a pirate.

SONNY   I don't like you any more at all.

CORA   Sonny!

SONNY   I don't care. You make me mad.

CORA (*Going to him*)   Oh, God, I've kept you too close to me, Sonny. Too close. I'll take the blame, boy. But don't be mad. Your mother still loves you, Sonny. (*But she sees that they are at an impasse*) Well, we won't talk about it any more. Run along to the store now, before it closes. (*We see* FLIRT'S *face in the door window. She is knocking on the door and calling for* REENIE. CORA *hurries to let her in*) Flirt!

FLIRT (*Rushing inside*)   Where's Reenie? Reenie . . . Reenie. Oh, Mrs. Flood, I have the most awful news.

CORA   What is it, Flirt?

FLIRT (FLIRT'S *face, her whole body are contorted by shock and confused grief*)   Oh, it's so awful.

CORA   Tell me.

FLIRT   Is Reenie here? I've got to tell her, too.

CORA (*Calls upstairs*)   Reenie, can you come down? Flirt is here.

REENIE (*Off*)   I'm coming.

FLIRT   Oh, Mrs. Flood, it's the most awful thing that ever happened in this town. It's the most awful thing I ever heard of happening anywhere.

CORA   Did something happen to you, or your family? . . .

FLIRT   No, it's Sammy.

CORA   Sammy? . . .

REENIE (*Coming downstairs*)   What is it, Flirt?

FLIRT   Kid! Sammy Goldenbaum . . . killed himself. (*There is a long silence*)

CORA   Where did you hear this, Flirt?

FLIRT   Mrs. Givens told me. The hotel people over in Oklahoma City called her about it just a little while ago. They found a letter in Sammy's suitcase Mrs. Givens had written him, inviting him to come home with Punky.

CORA   Oklahoma City?

FLIRT   He went over there last night after he left the party. He took the midnight train. That's what they figured out, because he registered at the hotel this morning at two o'clock.

CORA   How . . . did he do it, Flirt?

FLIRT   (*Hides her face in her hands as though hiding from the hideous reality of it*)   He . . . Oh, I just can't.

CORA   There, there, honey.

FLIRT   Oh, I'm such a silly about things. He . . . he jumped out of the window . . . on the fourteenth floor . . . and landed on the pavement below.

CORA   Oh, my God.

FLIRT   Oh . . . it's really the most terrible thing that ever happened to me. I never did know anyone who killed himself before.

CORA   Does anyone have any idea what made him do it?

FLIRT   No! Punky says that he used to get kind of moody at times, but Punky never expected him to do anything like *this*.

CORA   Why did he go to Oklahoma City in the middle of the night?

FLIRT   No one knows that either . . . for sure. But one thing did happen at the party. He was dancing with Mary Jane Ralston . . . that cow . . . just before intermission . . . and Mrs. Ralston . . . she'd had too much to drink . . . comes out in the middle of the floor and stops them.

CORA   What for?

FLIRT   Well, you know how Mrs. Ralston is. No one takes her very serious even if she does have money. Anyway, she came right out in the middle of the floor and gave Sammy a bawling out . . .

CORA   A bawling out? Why?

FLIRT   She said she wasn't giving this party for Jews, and she didn't intend for her daughter to dance with a Jew, and besides, Jews weren't allowed in the country club anyway. And that's not so. They are too allowed in the country club. Maybe they're not permitted to be members, but they're certainly allowed as guests. Everyone knows that. (*She turns now to* REENIE, *who has sat numb in a chair since* FLIRT'S *shocking announcement*) Where were you when it all happened?

REENIE I . . . I . . .
(*But she is inarticulate*)

CORA Reenie wasn't feeling well. She left the party and came home.

FLIRT The other kids told me Sammy was looking for you everywhere. He was going around asking everyone, Where's Reenie?

CORA That . . . that's too bad.

FLIRT (*Turning to* CORA) . . . But a thing like that isn't serious enough to make a boy kill himself, is it?

CORA Well . . . he did.

FLIRT An old blabbermouth like Mrs. Ralston?

CORA She was a stranger to Sammy. She probably sounded like the voice of the world.

FLIRT Gee . . . I just don't understand things like that. Do you know something else, Mrs. Flood? They called Sammy's mother way out in California, and told her, and I guess she was terribly sorry and everything, but she told them to go on and have the funeral in Oklahoma City, that she'd pay all the expenses, but she wouldn't be able to come for it because she was working. And she cried over the telephone and asked them please to try and keep her name out of the papers, because she said it wasn't generally known that she had a son.

CORA There won't be anyone Sammy knows at the funeral, will there?

FLIRT Mrs. Givens said Punky and his daddy could drive us over for it. Will you come, Reenie? (REENIE *nods*) Do you wanta come, too, Sonny? (SONNY *nods*) Well . . . it'll be day after tomorrow, in the afternoon. We'll all have to get excused from school. Oh, gee, it all makes me feel so kind of *strange*. Doesn't it *you*, kid? I think I'll go to Sunday

School tomorrow. Do you wanta go with me, Reenie?
(REENIE *nods yes*) Oh, I feel just terrible.
(FLIRT *bolts out the front door, as though wanting to run
away from all that is tragic or sorrowful in life.* CORA *keeps
silent for several moments, her eyes on* REENIE)

CORA   Where were you when Sammy went off?

REENIE   (*Twisting with grief*)   Stop it, Mom!

CORA   Tell me. Where were you?

REENIE   Don't, Mom!

CORA   (*Commanding*)   *Tell* me.

REENIE   I . . . was up in . . . the girls' room.

CORA   Where did you leave Sammy?

REENIE   As soon as we got to the party, Sammy and I started
dancing. He danced three straight dances with me, Mom.
Nobody cut in. I didn't think anybody was ever going to cut
in, Mom. I got to feeling so humiliated I didn't know what
to do. I just couldn't bear for Sammy to think that no one
liked me.

CORA   Dear God!

REENIE   So I told Sammy there was someone at the party
I had to talk to. Then I took him over to Mary Jane Ralston
and . . . introduced him to her . . . and told him to
dance with her.

CORA   Reenie!

REENIE   I . . . I thought he'd like her.

CORA   But you said that *you* liked Sammy. You told me
you did.

REENIE   But, Mom, I just couldn't *bear* for him to think I
was such a wallflower.

CORA   You ran off and *hid*, when an ounce of thoughtfulness,
one or two kind words, might have saved him.

REENIE   I didn't *know*. I didn't *know*.

CORA   A nice young man like that, bright and pleasant,
handsome as a prince, caught out here in this sandy soil
without a friend to his name and no one to turn to when
some thoughtless fool attacks him and he takes it to heart.
(REENIE *sobs uncontrollably*) Tears aren't going to do any
good now, Reenie. Now, you listen to me. I've heard all I

294 THE DARK AT THE TOP OF THE STAIRS

intend to listen to about being so shy and sensitive and afraid of people. I can't respect those feelings any more. They're nothing but selfishness. (REENIE *starts to bolt from the room, just as* FLIRT *did, but* CORA'S *voice holds her*) Reenie! It's a fine thing when we have so little confidence in ourselves, we can't stop to think of the other person.

SONNY (*Who has been a silent listener until now*) I *hate* people.

CORA Sonny!

SONNY I *do*.

CORA Then you're just as bad as Peg Ralston.

SONNY How can you keep from hating?

CORA There are all kinds of people in the world. And you have to live with them all. God never promised us any different. The bad people, you don't hate. You're only sorry they have to be. Now, run along to the store before it closes.

(SONNY *goes out, and finds himself again confronted by the jeers of the neighborhood boys, which sound like the voices that have plagued humanity from the beginning of time*)

BOYS' VOICES
Sissy Sonny!
Sonny Flood! His name is mud!
Sonny plays with dolls!
Sonny loves his mama!
(*Hearing the voices,* CORA *runs to the door, but stops herself from going further*)

CORA I guess I can't go through life protecting him from bullies. (*She goes to* REENIE) I'm sorry I spoke so harshly to you, Reenie.

REENIE He asked for *me* . . . for *me*. The only time anyone ever *wanted* me, or *needed* me, in my entire life. And I wasn't there. I didn't stop once to think of . . . Sammy. I've always thought I was the only person in the world who had any feelings at all.

CORA Well . . . you're not, if that's any comfort. Where are you going, dear?

REENIE (*Resignedly*) I haven't done anything to my room all day. I . . . I still have to make my bed.

(REENIE *exits upstairs*)

CORA (*Calling after her*)   It's Saturday. Change the linens. I
put them in the attic to dry. (CORA *goes into the parlor to
pull down the shades*. RUBIN *enters from the dining room.
He is in his stocking feet, and is carrying several bags,
which he drops onto the floor with a clatter.* CORA *comes
running from the parlor*) My God!

RUBIN   I scare ya?

CORA   Rubin! I hate to be frightened so.

RUBIN   I din *mean* to frighten ya.

CORA   I didn't hear you drive in.

RUBIN   I didn't.

CORA · Where's the car?

RUBIN   It ain't runnin' right. Left it downtown at the
garage. I walked home.

CORA   Why did you come in the back way?

RUBIN   Cora, what difference does it make if I come in the
back way or the front way, or down the chimney? My
boots was covered with mud. So I left 'em out on the back
porch. I din wanta track up your nice, clean house. Now,
wasn't that thoughtful of me?

CORA   Did you get my message?

RUBIN   What message?

CORA (*A little haughty*)   Oh . . . nothing.

RUBIN   What message you talkin' about?

CORA   The route you left me said you'd be in Blackwell last
night. I called you there, but . . . Well, I suppose you
had better places to be.

RUBIN.   That's right. I did. What'd ya call me for?

CORA (*Hurt*)   I don't know now. You'll be wanting a hot
bath. I'll go turn on the water tank. (CORA *exits through
dining-room door*. RUBIN *sits in his big chair and drops his
face into his hands with a look of sad discouragement. Then
he begins to unpack one of the bags, taking out small pieces
of harness and tossing them on the floor. In a few moments,* CORA *returns*) What made you decide to come back?

RUBIN   I lost my job.

CORA What?

RUBIN I said I lost my job.

CORA Rubin! You've always sold more harness for the company than any of the other salesmen.

RUBIN Yah. The on'y trouble is, *no* one's selling much harness today because no one's buyin' it. People are buyin' automobiles. Harness salesmen are . . . things of the past.

CORA Do you mean . . . your company's going out of business?

RUBIN That's it! You won the kewpie doll.

CORA Oh, Rubin!

RUBIN So that's why ya couldn't get me in Blackwell last night. I went somewhere else, regardless of what you were thinkin', lookin' for a job.

CORA (*A little embarrassed with regret*) Oh . . . I apologize, Rubin.

RUBIN Oh, that's all right. You have to get in your li'l digs ev'ry once in a while. I'm used to 'em.

CORA I'm really awfully sorry. Believe me.

RUBIN I was in Tulsa, talkin' to some men at the Southwest Supply Company. They're hirin' lotsa new men to go out in the fields and sell their equipment.

CORA (*Seizing her opportunity*) Rubin Flood, now that you've lost one traveling job, I'm not going to let you take another. You go downtown the first thing Monday morning and talk to John Fraser. He's bought out all the Curley Cue markets in town, and he needs men to manage them. He'd give you a job in a minute. Now, you do what I say, Rubin.

RUBIN (*He looks at her for several moments before getting to his feet*) God damn! I come home here t'apologize to you for hittin' ya. I been feelin' all week like the meanest critter alive, because I took a sock at a woman. My wife, at that. I walked in here ready to *beg* ya to forgive me. Now I feel like doin' it all over again. Don't you realize you can't talk to a man like that? Don't you realize that every time you talk that way, I just gotta go out and raise more hell, just to prove to myself I'm a free man? Don't

you know that when you talk to a man like that, you're
not givin' him credit for havin' any brains, or any guts, or
a spine, or . . . or a few other body parts that are pretty
important, too? All these years we been married, you
never once really admitted to yourself what kinda man I
am. No, ya keep talkin' to me like I was the kinda man
you think I *oughta* be. (*He grabs her by the shoulders*)
Look at me. Don't you know who I am? Don't you know
who I am?

CORA Rubin, you're hurting me.

RUBIN I'm takin' the job if I can get it. It's a damn good
job, pays good money.

CORA I don't care about money.

RUBIN No, you don't! Not until you see Peg Ralston come
waltzin' down the street in a new fur coat, and then you
start wonderin' why old Rubin don't shoot hisself in the
foot to make a lot of money.

CORA Rubin, I promise you I'll never envy Peg Ralston
another thing, as long as I live.

RUBIN Did it ever occur to you that maybe I feel like a
cheapskate because I can't buy you no fur coat? Did you
ever stop to think maybe I'd like to be able to send my
kids away to a fine college?

CORA All I'm asking is for you to give them something of
yourself.

RUBIN God damn it! What have *I* got to give 'em? In this day
and age, what's a man like me got to give? With the
whole world so all-fired crazy about makin' money, how
can *any* man, unless he's got a million dollars stuck in his
pocket, feel he's got anything else to give that's very important?

CORA Rubin!

RUBIN I mean it, Cora.

CORA I never realized you had such doubts.

RUBIN The new job is work I've never done. Work I never
even thought of doin'. Learnin' about all that goddamn
machinery, and how to get out there and demonstrate it.
Working with different kinds of men, that's smarter than I
am, that think fast and talk sharp and mean all business.
Men I can't sit around and chew tobacco with and joke

with like I did m'old customers. I . . . I don't like 'em. I don't know if I'm *gonna* like them.

CORA   But you just said you wanted the job.

RUBIN   I don't like them, but I'm gonna join them. A fellow's gotta get into the swim. There's nothing else to do. But I'm scared. I don't know how I'll make out. I . . . I'm scared.

CORA   I never supposed you had it *in* you to fear.

RUBIN   I s'pose all this time you been thinkin' you was married to one a them movin'-pitcher fellas that jump off bridges and hold up trains and shoot Indians, and are never scared a nothin'. Times are changin', Cora, and I dunno where they're goin'. When I was a boy, there wasn't much more to this town than a post office. I on'y had six years a schoolin' cause that's all the Old Man thought I'd ever need. Now look at things. School buildin's, churches, fine stores, movie theatres, a country club. Men becomin' millionaires overnight, drivin' down the street in big limousines, goin' out to the country club and gettin' drunk, acting like they was the lords of creation. I dunno what to think of things now, Cora. I'm a stranger in the very land I was born in.

CORA   (*Trying to restore his pride*)   Your folks pioneered this country.

RUBIN   Sometimes I wonder if it's not a lot easier to pioneer a country than it is to settle down in it. I look at the town now and don't recognize anything in it. I come home here, and I still have to get used to the piano, and the telephone, and the gas stove, and the lace curtains at the windows, the carpets on the floor. All these things are still *new* to me. I dunno what to make of 'em. How can *I* feel I've got anything to give to my children when the world's as strange to me as it is to them?

CORA   (*With a new awareness of him*)   Rubin!

RUBIN   I'm doin' the best I can, Cora. Can't ya understand that? I'm doin' the best I can.

CORA   Yes, Rubin. I know you are.

RUBIN   Now, there's a few more things I gotta say . . . I wanna apologize. I'm sorry I hit ya, Cora. I'm awful sorry.

CORA   I know I provoked you, Rubin.

RUBIN You provoked me, but . . . I still shouldn'ta hit ya.
It wasn't manly.

CORA I'm not holding it against you, Rubin.

RUBIN And I'm sorry I made such a fuss about you
gettin' the girl a new dress. But I was awful worried about
losin' my job then, and I din have much money left in
the bank.

CORA Rubin, if I'd known that, I wouldn't have *thought* of
buying the dress. You should have told me, Rubin.

RUBIN I din wanta make you worry, too.

CORA But that's what I'm for.

RUBIN That's all I gotta say, Cora, except that . . . I love
ya. You're a good woman and I couldn't git along without
you.

CORA I love you, too, Rubin. And I couldn't get along without you another day.

RUBIN You're clean, and dainty. Give a man a feeling of
decency . . . and order . . . and respect.

CORA Thank you, Rubin.

RUBIN Just don't get the idea you can rearrange *me* like
ya do the house, whenever ya wanta put it in order.

CORA I'll remember. (*There is a short silence between them
now, filled with new understanding*) When you have fears
about things, please tell me, Rubin.

RUBIN It's hard for a man t'admit his fears, even to hisself.

CORA Why? Why?

RUBIN He's always afraid of endin' up like . . . like your
brother-in-law Morris.

CORA Oh!
(CORA *has a new appreciation of him. She runs to him,
throwing her arms about him in a fast embrace. A glow of
satisfaction radiates from* RUBIN, *to have his woman back
in his arms*)

RUBIN Oh, my goodness. (RUBIN *carries* CORA *center,
where they sit like honeymooners, she on his lap; and he
kisses her.* SONNY *returns now with a sack of groceries,
and stands staring at his parents until they become aware
of him*) H'lo, son.

SONNY Hi!

CORA Take the groceries to the kitchen, Sonny. (*Obediently,* SONNY *starts for the dining-room door*) Rubin, Mrs. Stanford paid Sonny five dollars this afternoon for speaking a piece at her tea party.

RUBIN I'll be damned. He'll be makin' more money than his Old Man.
(SONNY *exits now through dining-room door*)

CORA Be nice to him, Rubin. Show him you want to be his friend.

RUBIN I'm nice to that boy, ain't I?

CORA Sometimes you do talk awfully rough and bad-natured.

RUBIN Well . . . *life's* rough. *Life's* bad-natured.

CORA I know. And I keep trying to pretend it isn't.

RUBIN I'll remind ya.

CORA Every time I see the kids go out of the house, I worry . . . like I was watching them go out into life, and they seem so young and helpless.

RUBIN But ya gotta let 'em go, Cora. Ya can't hold 'em.

CORA I've always felt I could give them life like a present, all wrapped in white, with every promise of happiness inside.

RUBIN That ain't the way it works.

CORA No. All I can promise them is life itself. (*With this realization, she gets off* RUBIN'S *lap*) I'd better go to the kitchen and put the groceries away.

RUBIN (*Grabs her to him, not willing to let her go*) T'hell with the groceries!

CORA (*A maidenly protest*) Rubin!

RUBIN (*Caressing her*) Is there any chance of us bein' alone t'night?

CORA (*Secretively*) I think Reenie plans to go to the library. If you give Sonny a dime, I'm sure he'll go to the movies.

RUBIN It's a deal.
(*He tries again to re-engage her in lovemaking*)

CORA Now, Rubin, be patient.

(*She exits through the dining-room door as* REENIE *comes running downstairs*)

REENIE   Did I hear Daddy?

RUBIN   Hello, daughter.

REENIE   (*She runs into his arms and he lifts her high in the air*)   Oh, Daddy!

RUBIN   Well, how's my girl?

REENIE   I feel better now that you're home, Daddy.

RUBIN   Thank ya, daughter.

REENIE   I've been practicing a new piece, Daddy. It's Chopin. Do you want me to play it for you?

RUBIN   Sure. I like sweet music same as anyone.

REENIE   I can't play it quite perfect yet, but almost.
(REENIE *goes into parlor and in a moment we hear another wistful piece by Chopin*)

RUBIN   That's all right. (SONNY *now returns and stands far right.* RUBIN, *center, faces him. They look at each other with wonder and just a little resentment. But* RUBIN *goes to* SONNY, *making the effort to offer himself*) Son, your mom tells me you do real well, goin' around speaking pieces, gettin' to be a reg'lar Jackie Coogan. I got a customer has a daughter does real well at that kinda thing. Gets up before people and whistles.

SONNY   Whistles?

RUBIN   Yah! Like birds. Every kinda bird ya ever heard of. Maybe you'd like to meet her sometime.

SONNY   Oh, maybe.
(RUBIN *feels himself on uncertain ground with his son*)

RUBIN   Your mom said maybe you'd like to go to the movie tonight. I guess I could spare you the money.
(*He digs into his pocket*)

SONNY   I've changed my mind. I don't want to now.
(SONNY *turns from his father*)

RUBIN   (*Looks at his son as though realizing sadly the breach between them. With a feeling of failure, he puts a warm hand on* SONNY'S *shoulder*) Oh! Well, I ain't gonna argue. (*He walks out, and as he passes the parlor, he speaks to* REENIE) That's real purty, daughter.

REENIE   Thank you, Daddy.

RUBIN (*Opens dining-room door and speaks to* CORA)   Cora, those kids ain't goin' to the movies. Come on now.

CORA (*Off*)   I'll be up in a minute, Rubin.

RUBIN (*Closing the door behind him, speaking to* REENIE *and* SONNY)   I'm goin' upstairs now, and have my bath.
(REENIE *and* SONNY *watch him all the way as he goes upstairs*)

SONNY   They always want to be alone.

REENIE   All married people do, crazy.
(SONNY *impulsively sticks out his tongue at her. But she ignores him, picking up one of the favors, a reminder of* SAMMY, *and fondling it tenderly.* SONNY *begins to feel regret*)

SONNY   I'm sorry I made a face at you, Reenie.

REENIE (*Sobbing softly*)   Go on and make as many faces as you like. I'm not going to fight with you any more.

SONNY   Don't cry, Reenie.

REENIE   I didn't know Sammy had even remembered the favors until I started to go. Then I went to find my coat, and there they were, sticking out of my pocket. At the very moment he was putting them there . . . he must have had in mind doing what he did.

SONNY (*With a burst of new generosity*)   *You! You* keep the favors, Reenie.

REENIE   He promised them to *you.*

SONNY   Just the same . . . *you* keep them, Reenie.

REENIE   Do you mean it?

SONNY   Yes.

REENIE   You never were thoughtful like this . . . before.
(CORA *comes through the dining-room door now, hears the children's plans, and stands unobserved, listening*)

SONNY   Reenie, do you want to go to the movie tonight? It's Mae Murray in *Fascination,* and there's an *Our Gang Comedy* first.

REENIE   I don't feel I should.

SONNY   When I feel bad, I just *have* to go to the movies. I just *have* to.

REENIE   I was supposed to go to the library tonight.

SONNY   Please go with me, Reenie. Please.

REENIE   Do you really want me?

SONNY   Yes, Reenie. Yes.

REENIE   Where would you get the money to take *me*, Sonny? I have to pay adult admission. It's thirty-five cents.

SONNY   I've got all the money we'll need.
(*He runs for his piggy bank as* CORA *makes a quick return to the dining room.*)

REENIE   Sonny! Mother told you you had to save that money.

SONNY   I don't care. She's not going to boss me for the rest of my life. It's *my* money, and I've got a right to spend it.
(*With a heroic gesture of defiance, he throws the piggy bank smashing against the fireplace, its pieces scattering on the floor*)

REENIE   Sonny!

SONNY   (*Finding his five-dollar bill in the rubble*)   And we'll have enough for popcorn, too, and for ice cream afterwards at the Royal Candy Kitchen.
(*Now we see* CORA *in the parlor again, a silent witness*)

REENIE   I feel very proud to be treated by my little brother.

SONNY   Let's hurry. The comedy starts at seven o'clock and I don't want to miss it.

REENIE   We can stay for the second show if we miss the comedy.

SONNY   Oh, I want to stay for the second show, anyway. I always see the comedy twice.

CORA   (*Coming forth now*)   Are you children going some place?

REENIE   We're going to the movie, Mom.

CORA   Together?

REENIE   Yes.

CORA   Well . . . that's nice.

REENIE   Darn it. I left my rubbers out on the porch.
(*She exits*)

RUBIN   (*From upstairs*)   Cora!

CORA   I'll be up in a minute, Rubin. (*She turns thoughtfully to her son*) Have you forgiven your mother, Sonny?

SONNY   (*Inscrutable*)   Oh . . . maybe.

CORA   Your mother still loves you, Sonny.
(*She puts an arm around him but he avoids her embrace*)

SONNY   Don't, Mom.

CORA   All right. I understand.

RUBIN   (*Upstairs, growing more impatient*)   Cora! Come on, honey!

CORA   (*Calling back to him*)   I'll be up in a minute, Rubin. (SONNY *looks at her with accusing eyes*) Good-bye, Sonny! (REENIE *sticks her head in the door from outside*)

REENIE   Hurry up, Sonny!

RUBIN   Come on, Cora!
(CORA *starts up the stairs to her husband, stopping for one final look at her departing son. And* SONNY, *just before going out the door, stops for one final look at his mother, his face full of confused understanding. Then he hurries out to* REENIE, *and* CORA, *like a shy maiden, starts up the stairs, where we see* RUBIN'S *naked feet standing in the warm light at the top*)

CORA   I'm coming, Rubin. I'm coming.

CURTAIN